ALSO FROM JOE BOOKS

Disney Frozen Cinestory Comic

Disney Cinderella Cinestory Comic

Disney 101 Dalmations Cinestory Comic

Disney Princess Comics Treasury

Disney • Pixar Comics Treasury

Disney's Darkwing Duck: The Definitively Dangerous Edition

Disney's Frozen: The Story of the Movie in Comics

Disney Big Hero 6 Cinestory Comic

Disney • Pixar Inside Out Cinestory Comic

Disney • Pixar Inside Out Fun Book

Disney Gravity Falls Cinestory Comic Volume One

Disney • Pixar The Good Dinosaur Cinestory Comic

Disney • Pixar The Good Dinosaur Fun Book

Published in the United States and Canada by Joe Books, Ltd.
567 Queen St W, Toronto, ON M5V 2B6
www.joebooks.com

Library and Archives Canada Cataloguing in Publication
information is available upon request.
ISBN 978-1-98803-281-8 (Mass edition)
ISBN 978-1-77275-271-7 (ebook edition)

First Joe Books, Ltd. edition: March 2016

Disney DESCENDANTS

Wicked World

Cinestory Comic

ADAPTED BY
Alberto Garrido

LETTERING AND LAYOUT
Salvador Navarro, Ester Salguero, Ernesto Lovera,
Rocío Salguero, and Eduardo Alpuente

DESIGNER
Heidi Roux

EDITOR
Aaron Sparrow

SENIOR EDITOR
Carolynn Prior

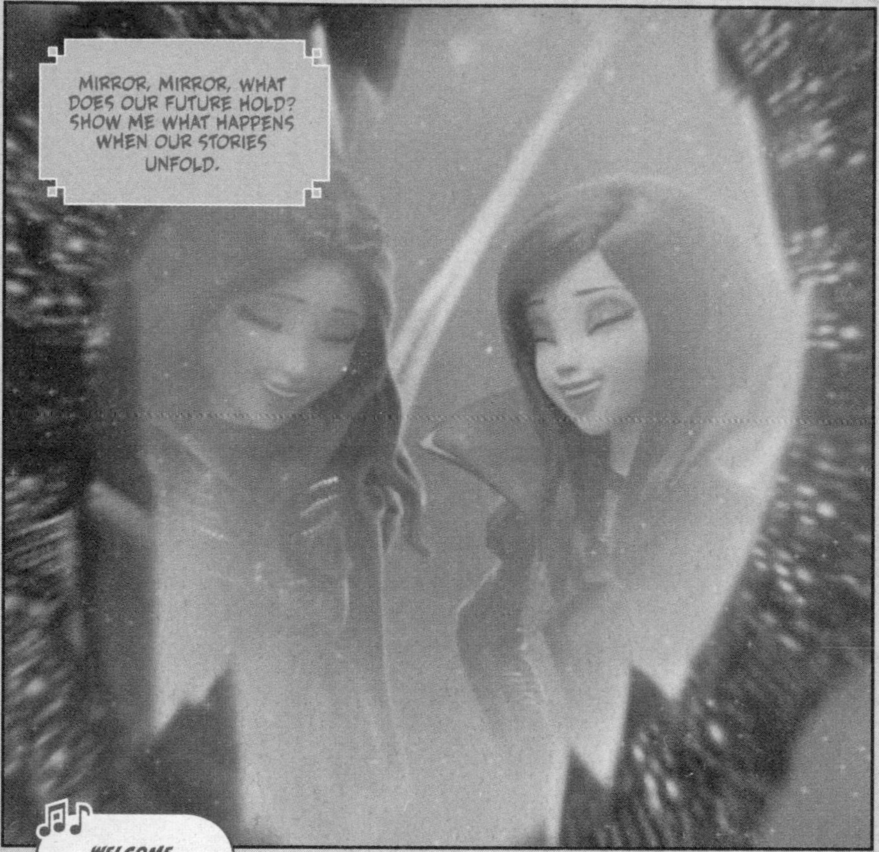
MIRROR, MIRROR, WHAT DOES OUR FUTURE HOLD? SHOW ME WHAT HAPPENS WHEN OUR STORIES UNFOLD.

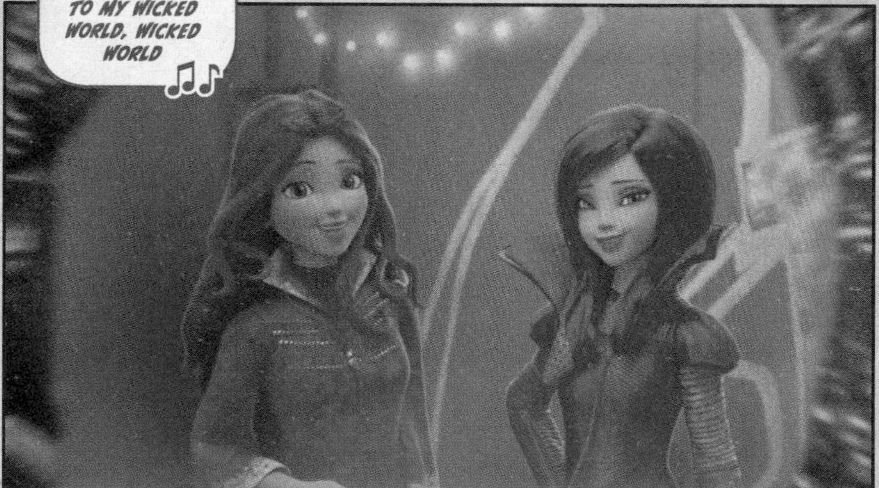
WELCOME TO MY WICKED WORLD, WICKED WORLD

Disney

Descendants

Wicked World

Wish Granted

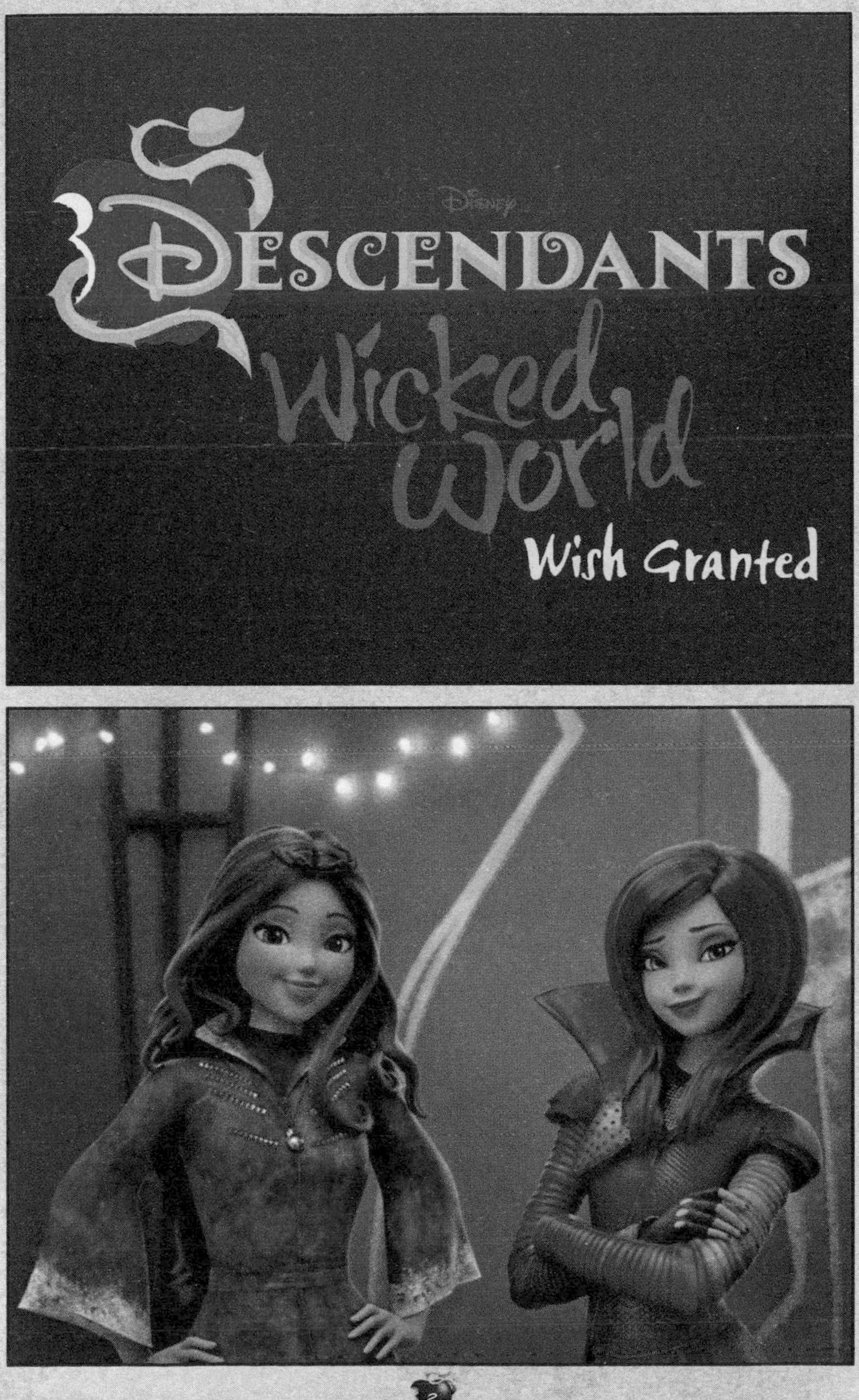

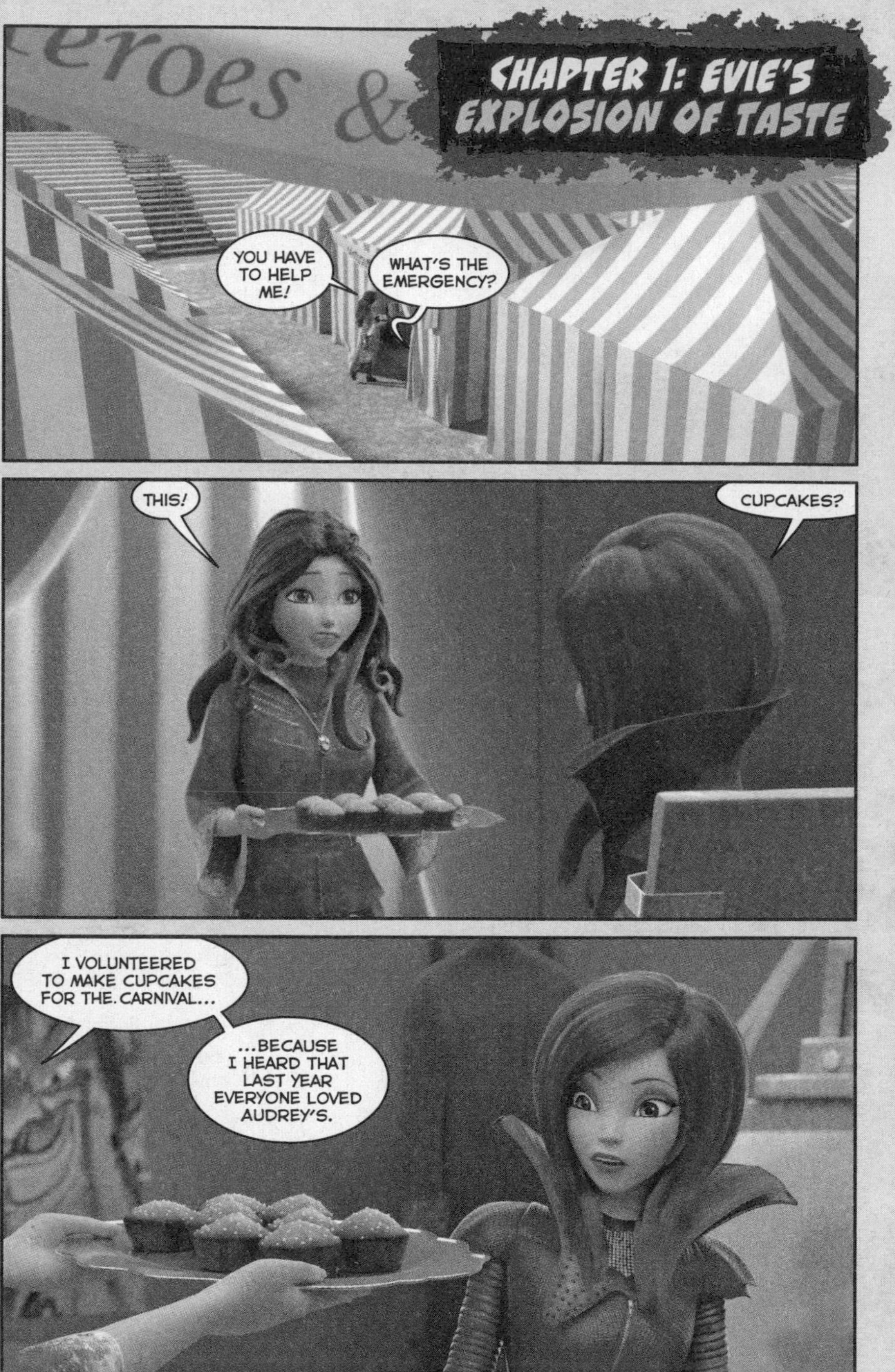
CHAPTER 1: EVIE'S EXPLOSION OF TASTE
YOU HAVE TO HELP ME!
WHAT'S THE EMERGENCY?
THIS!
CUPCAKES?
I VOLUNTEERED TO MAKE CUPCAKES FOR THE. CARNIVAL...
...BECAUSE I HEARD THAT LAST YEAR EVERYONE LOVED AUDREY'S.

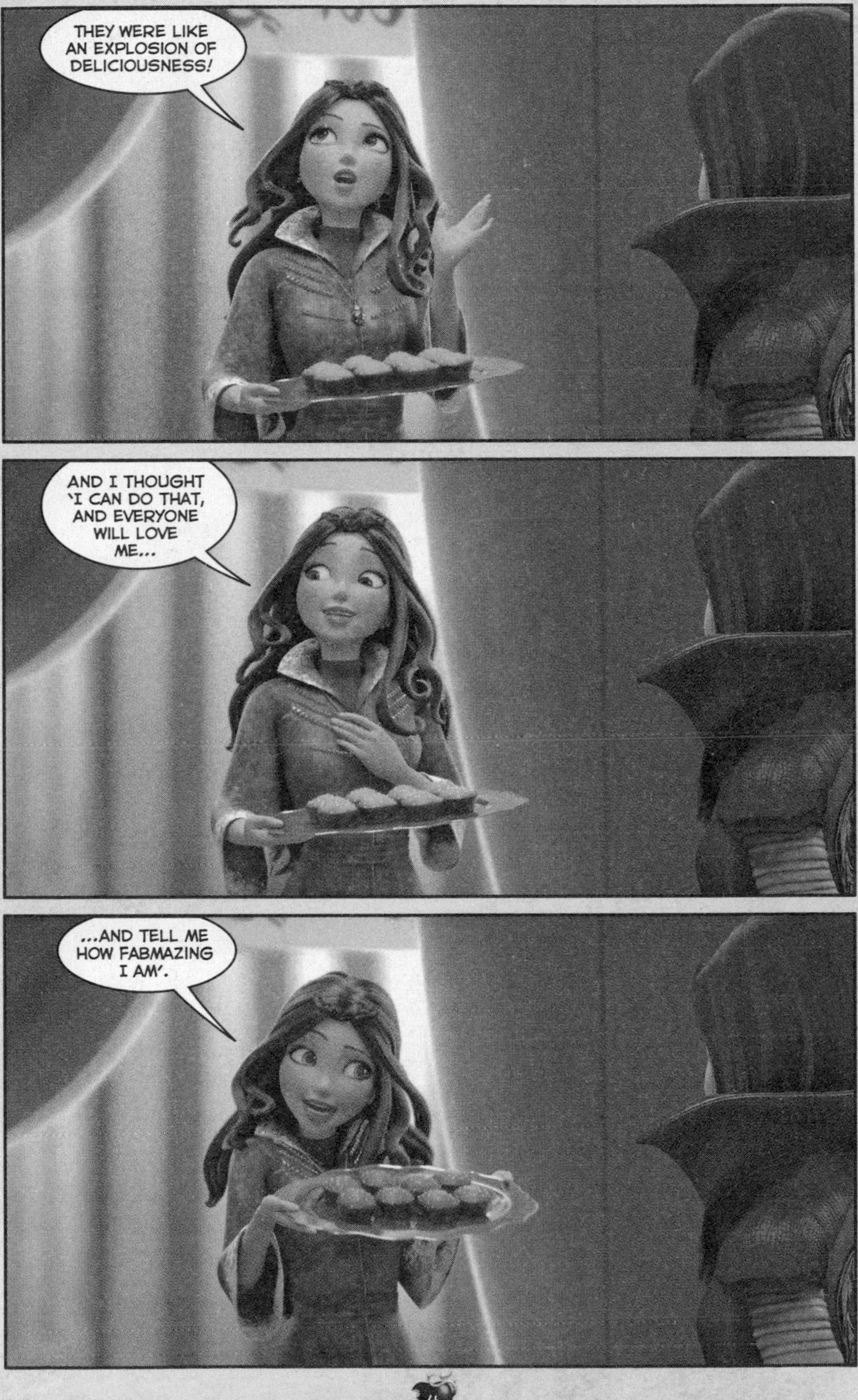
THEY WERE LIKE AN EXPLOSION OF DELICIOUSNESS!
AND I THOUGHT 'I CAN DO THAT, AND EVERYONE WILL LOVE ME...
...AND TELL ME HOW FABMAZING I AM'.

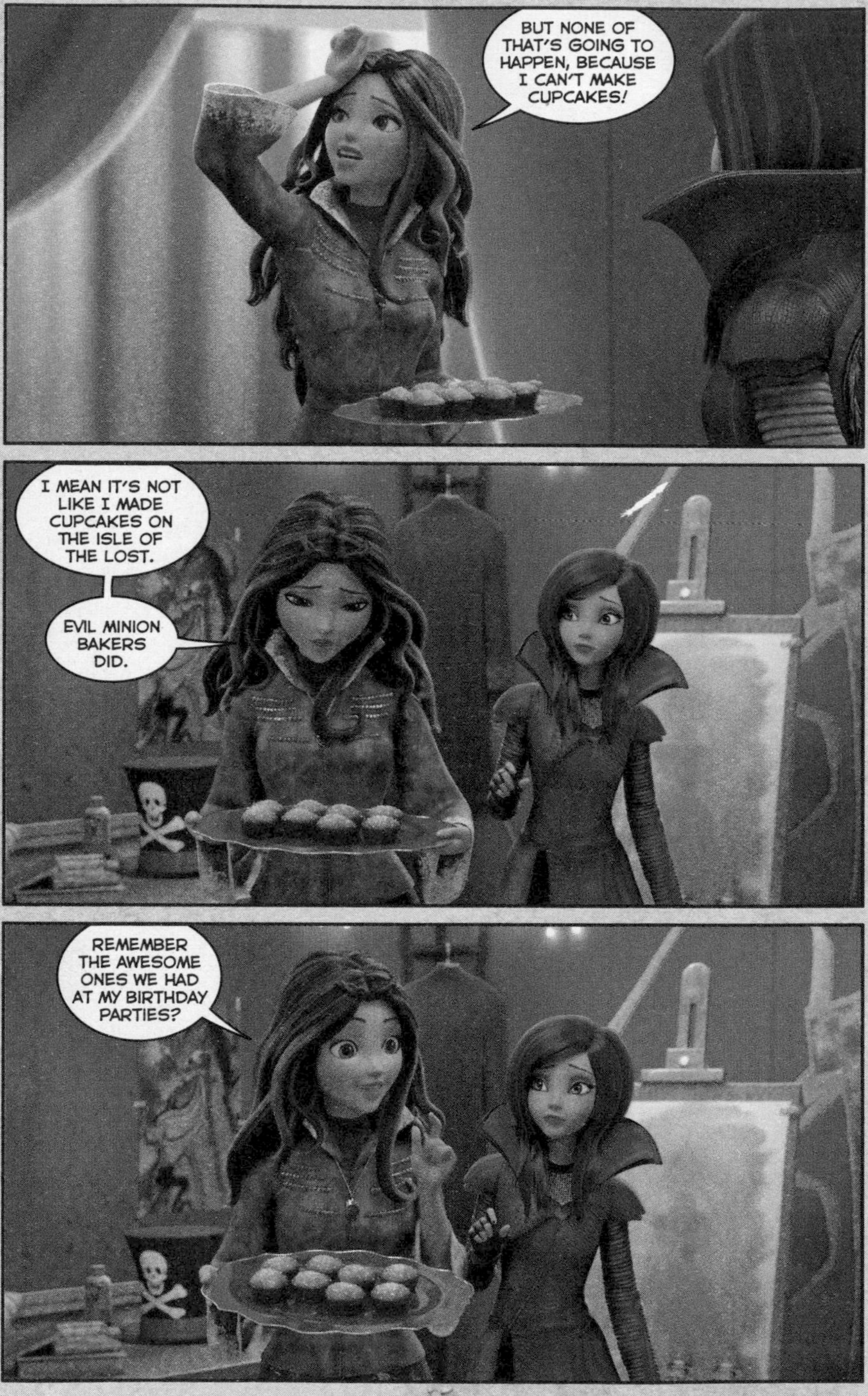
BUT NONE OF THAT'S GOING TO HAPPEN, BECAUSE I CAN'T MAKE CUPCAKES!
I MEAN IT'S NOT LIKE I MADE CUPCAKES ON THE ISLE OF THE LOST.
EVIL MINION BAKERS DID.
REMEMBER THE AWESOME ONES WE HAD AT MY BIRTHDAY PARTIES?

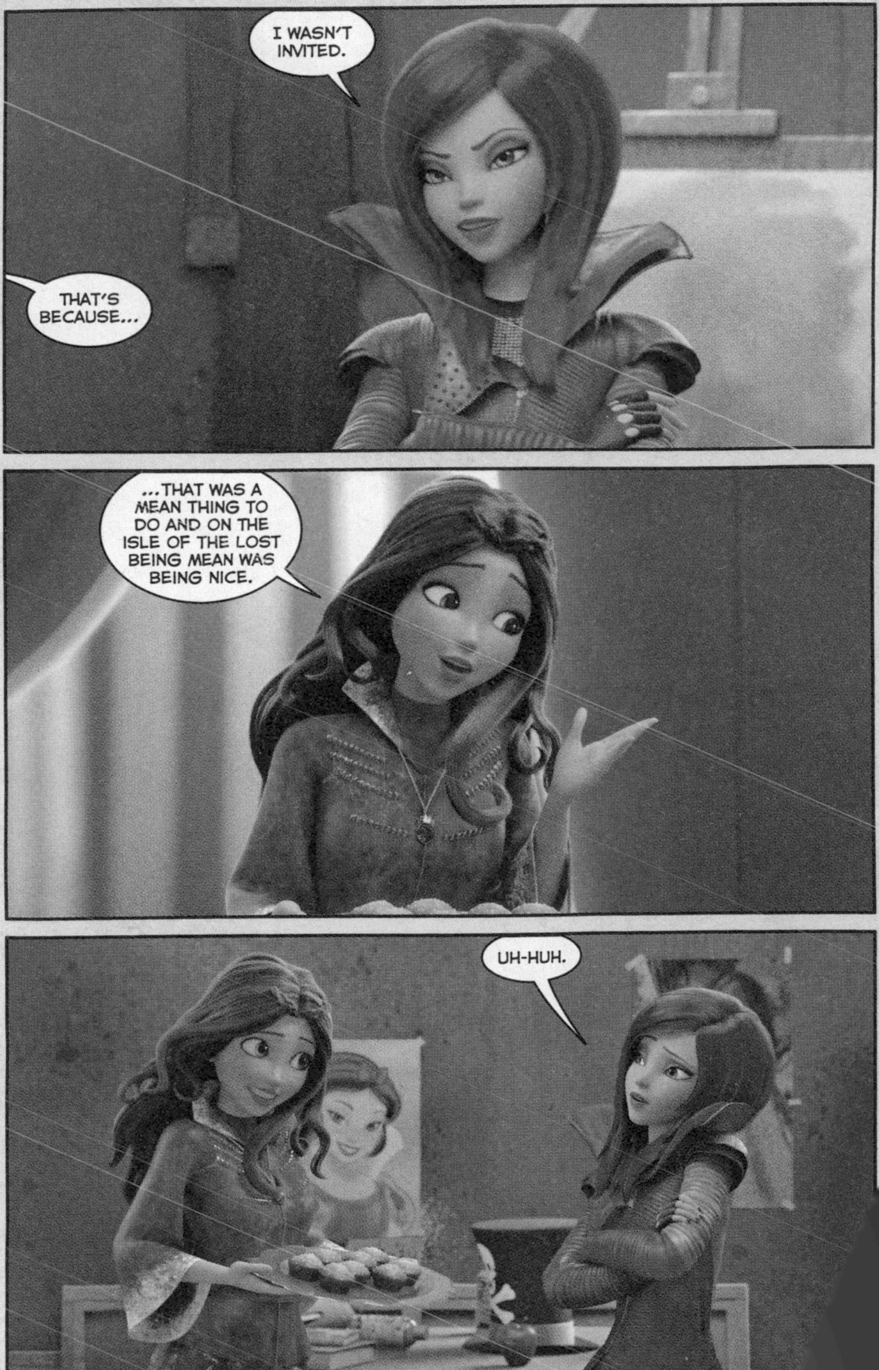
I WASN'T INVITED.
THAT'S BECAUSE...
...THAT WAS A MEAN THING TO DO AND ON THE ISLE OF THE LOST BEING MEAN WAS BEING NICE.
UH-HUH.

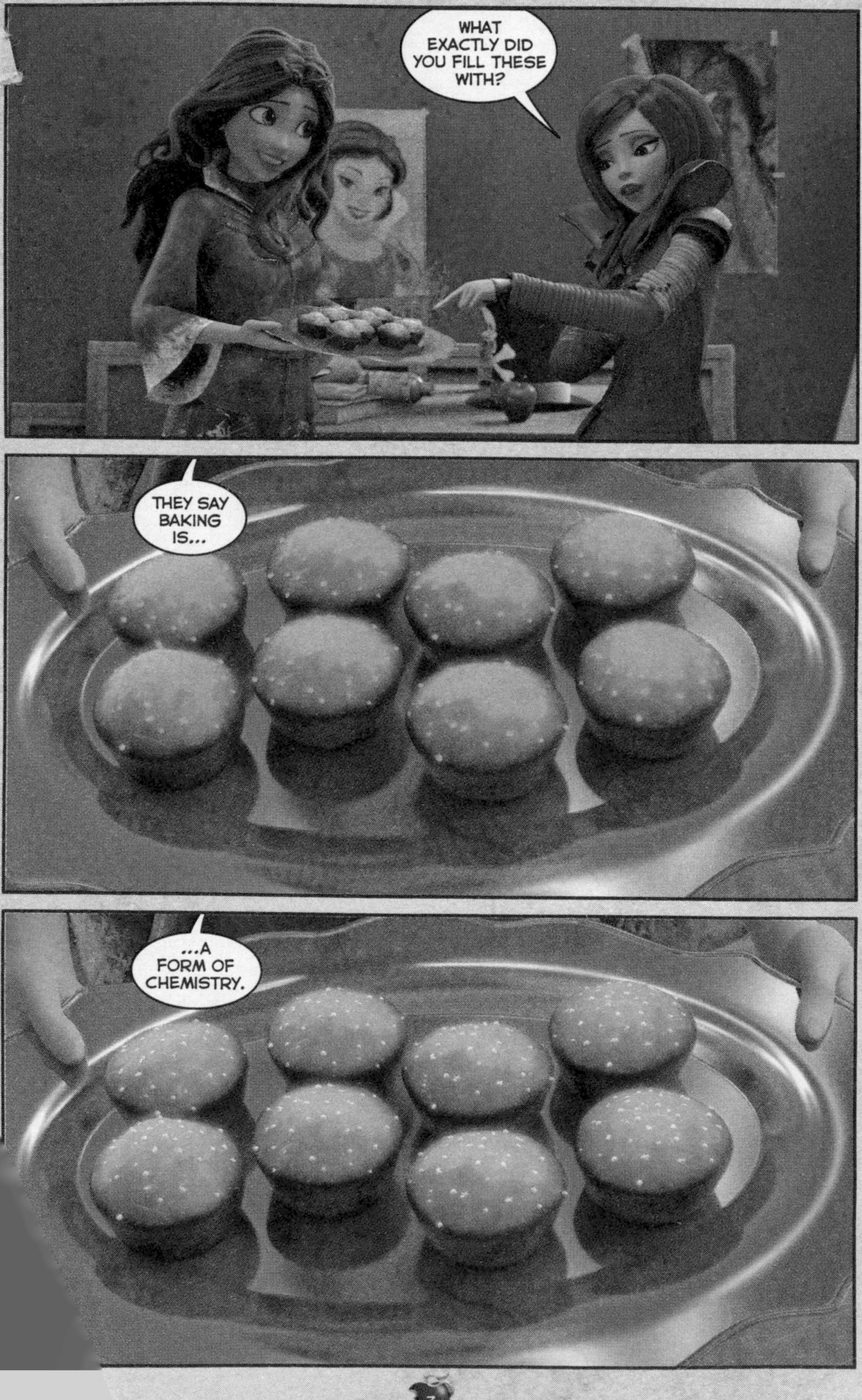
WHAT EXACTLY DID YOU FILL THESE WITH?
THEY SAY BAKING IS...
...A FORM OF CHEMISTRY.

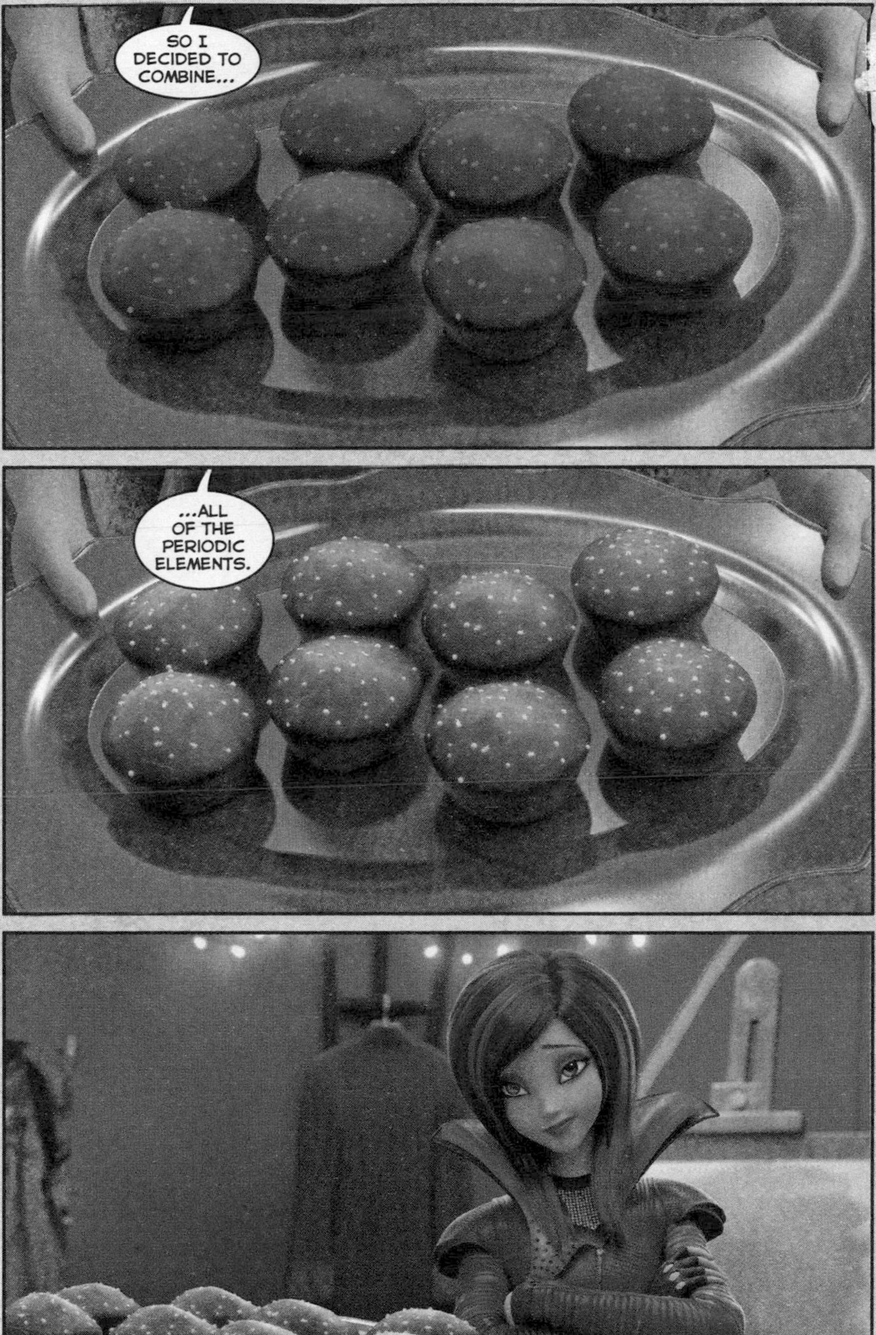
SO I DECIDED TO COMBINE...
...ALL OF THE PERIODIC ELEMENTS.

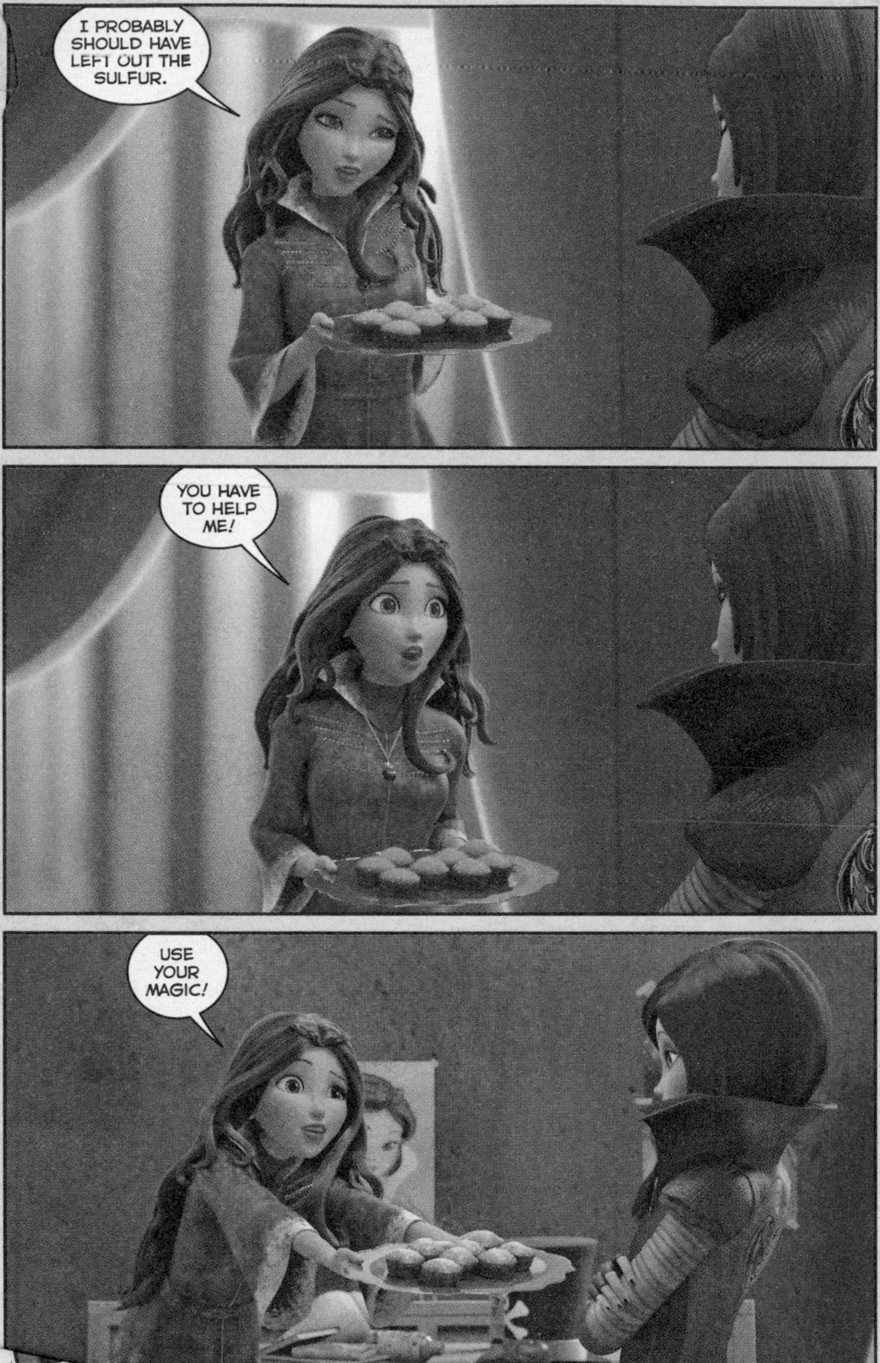
I PROBABLY SHOULD HAVE LEFT OUT THE SULFUR.
YOU HAVE TO HELP ME!
USE YOUR MAGIC!

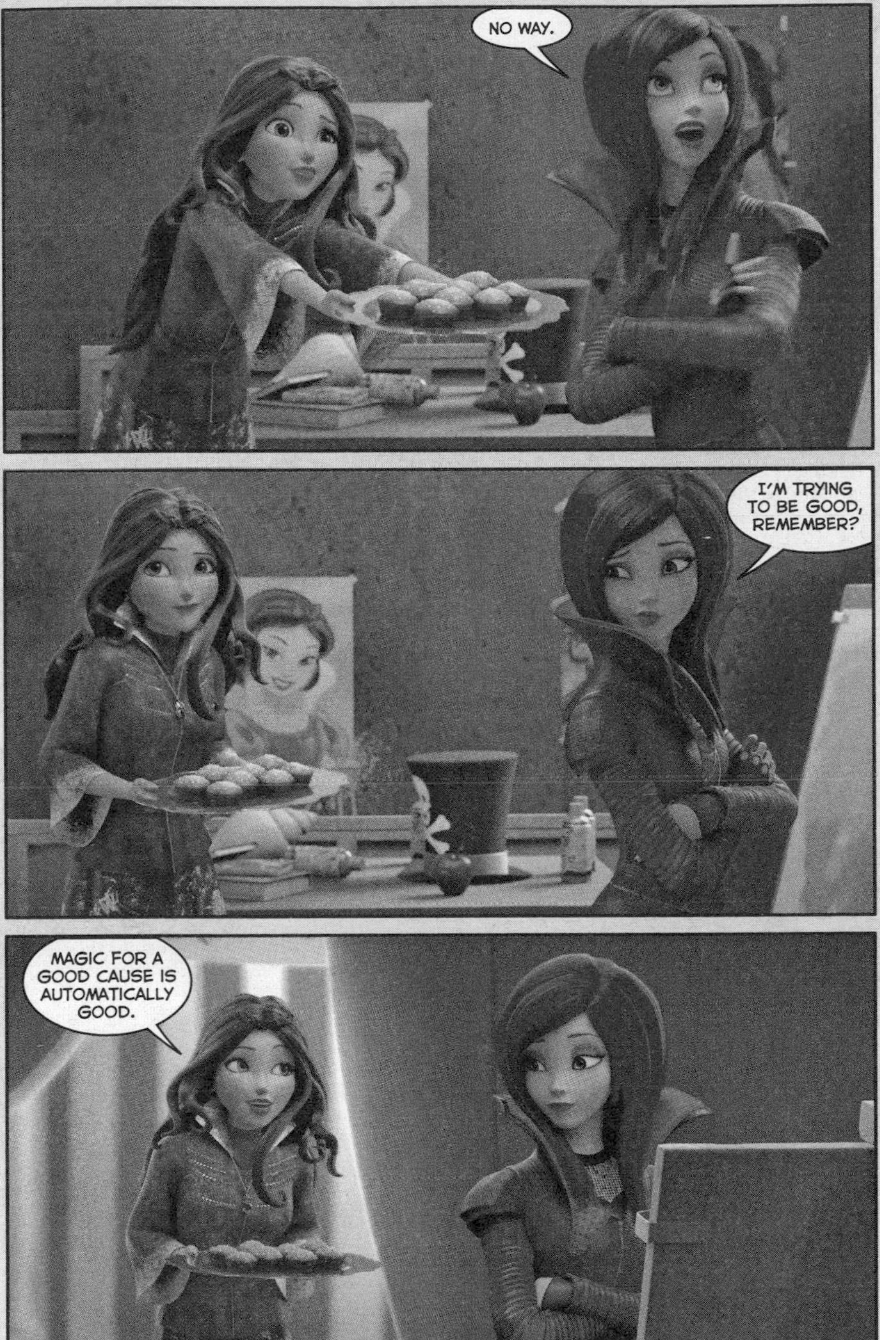
NO WAY.
I'M TRYING TO BE GOOD, REMEMBER?
MAGIC FOR A GOOD CAUSE IS AUTOMATICALLY GOOD.

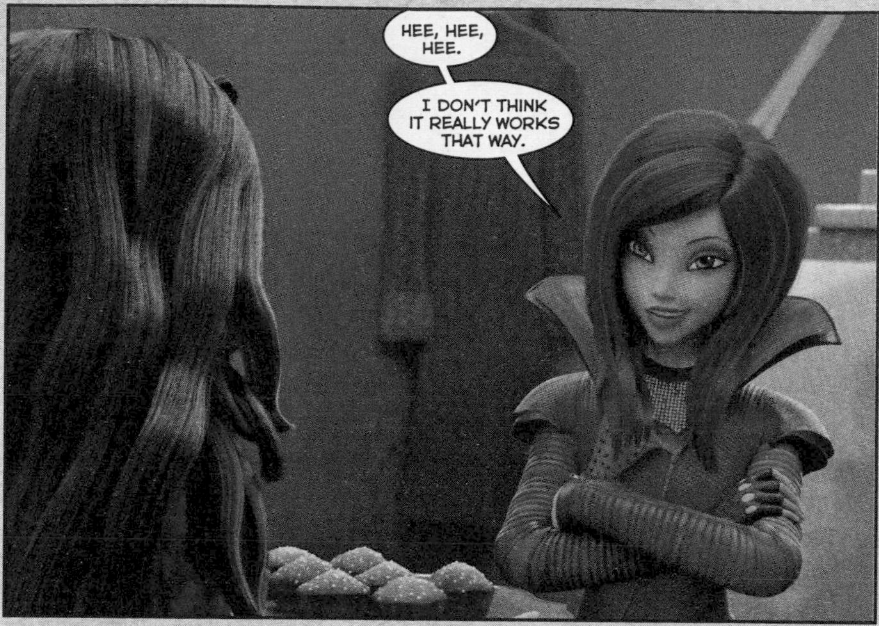
HEE, HEE, HEE.
I DON'T THINK IT REALLY WORKS THAT WAY.

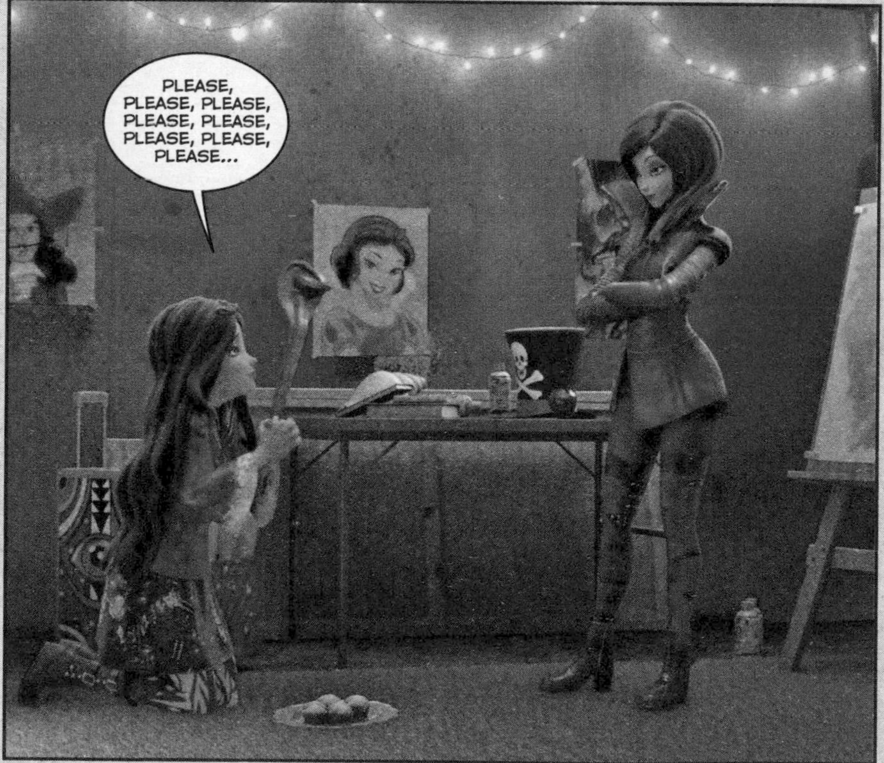
PLEASE, PLEASE, PLEASE, PLEASE, PLEASE, PLEASE, PLEASE, PLEASE...

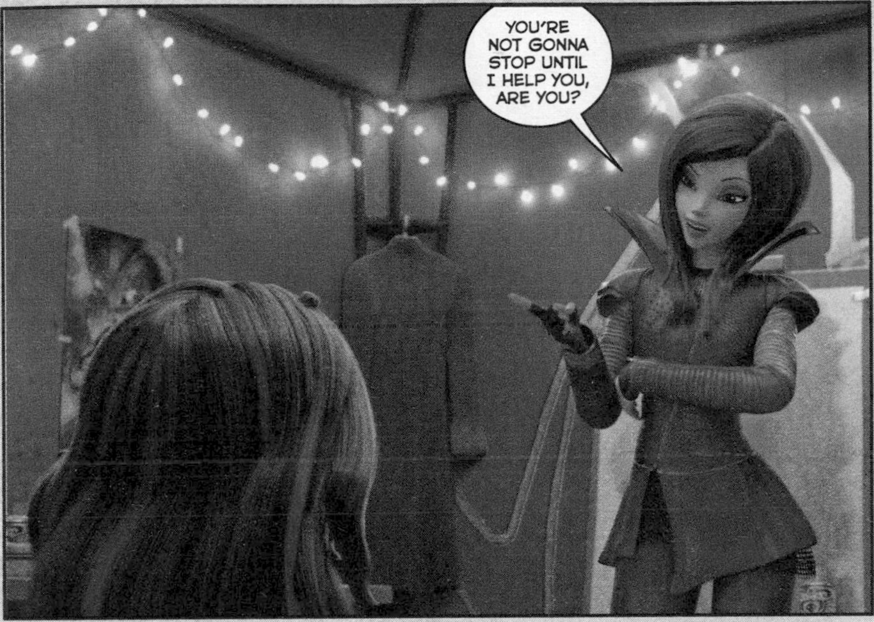
YOU'RE NOT GONNA STOP UNTIL I HELP YOU, ARE YOU?

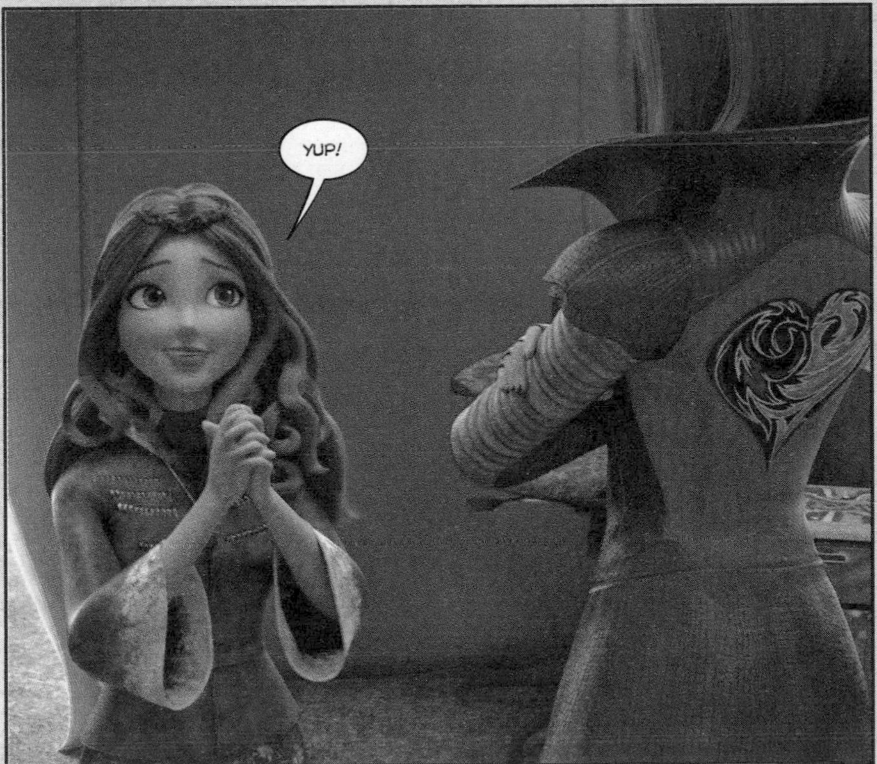
YUP!

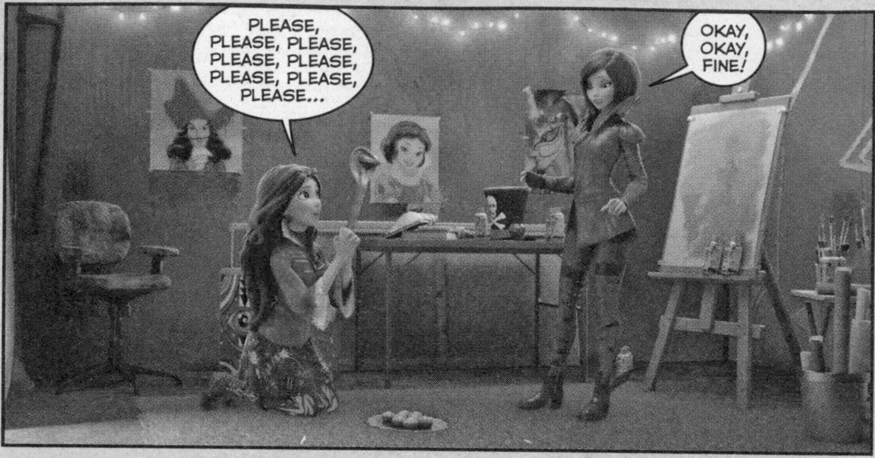
PLEASE, PLEASE, PLEASE, PLEASE, PLEASE, PLEASE, PLEASE, PLEASE...
OKAY, OKAY, FINE!

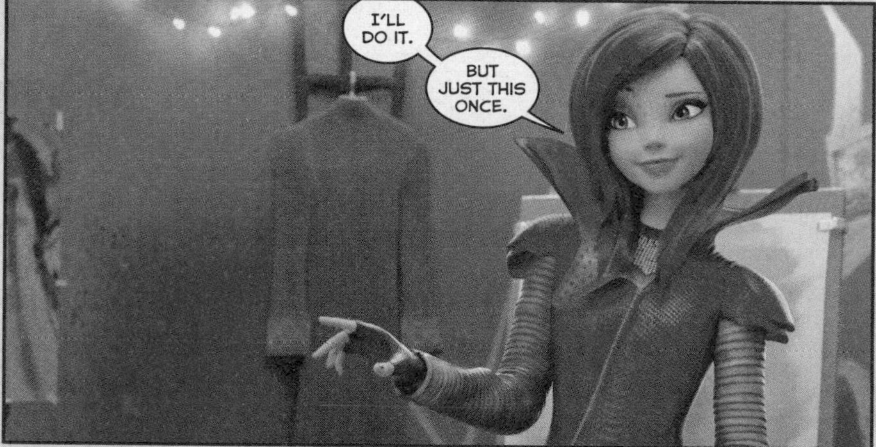
I'LL DO IT.
BUT JUST THIS ONCE.

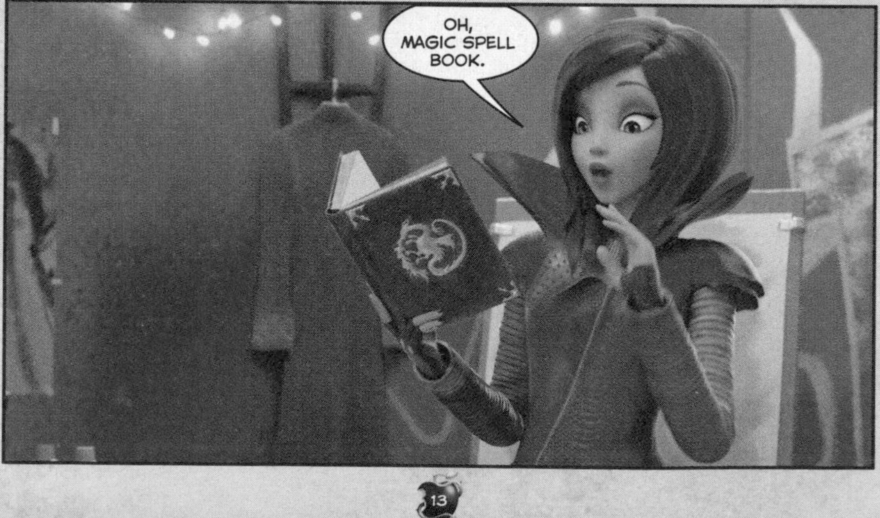
OH, MAGIC SPELL BOOK.

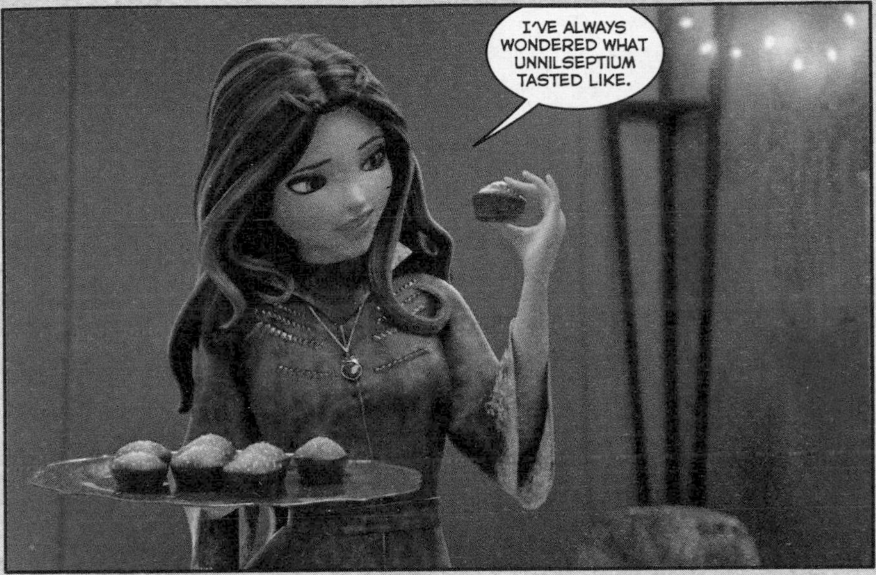
I'VE ALWAYS WONDERED WHAT UNNILSEPTIUM TASTED LIKE.

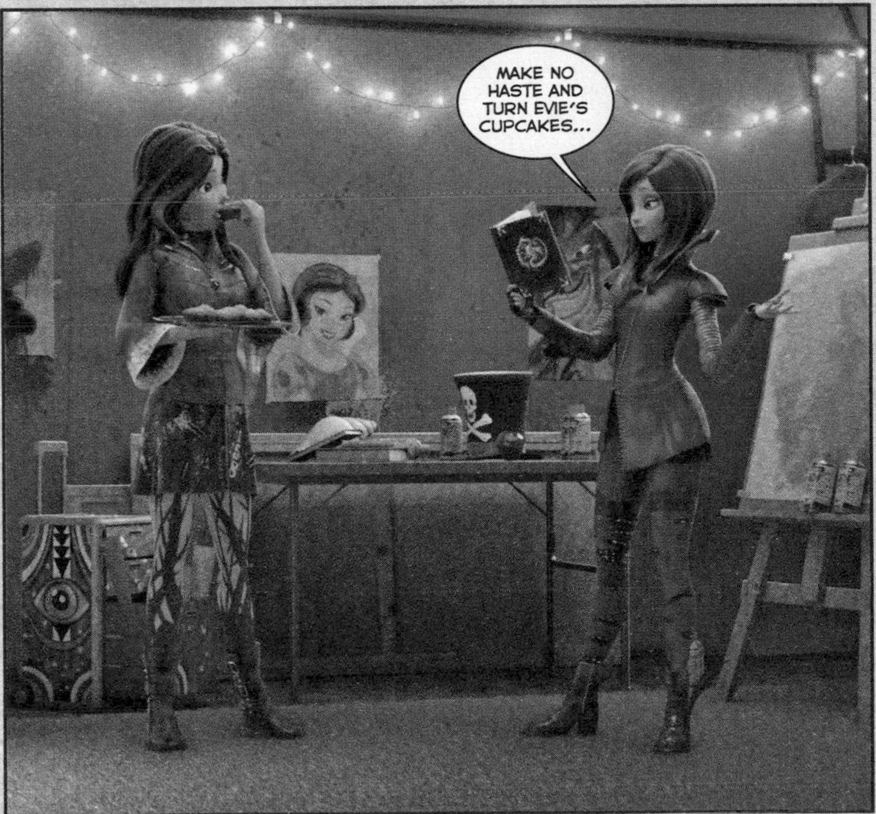
MAKE NO HASTE AND TURN EVIE'S CUPCAKES...

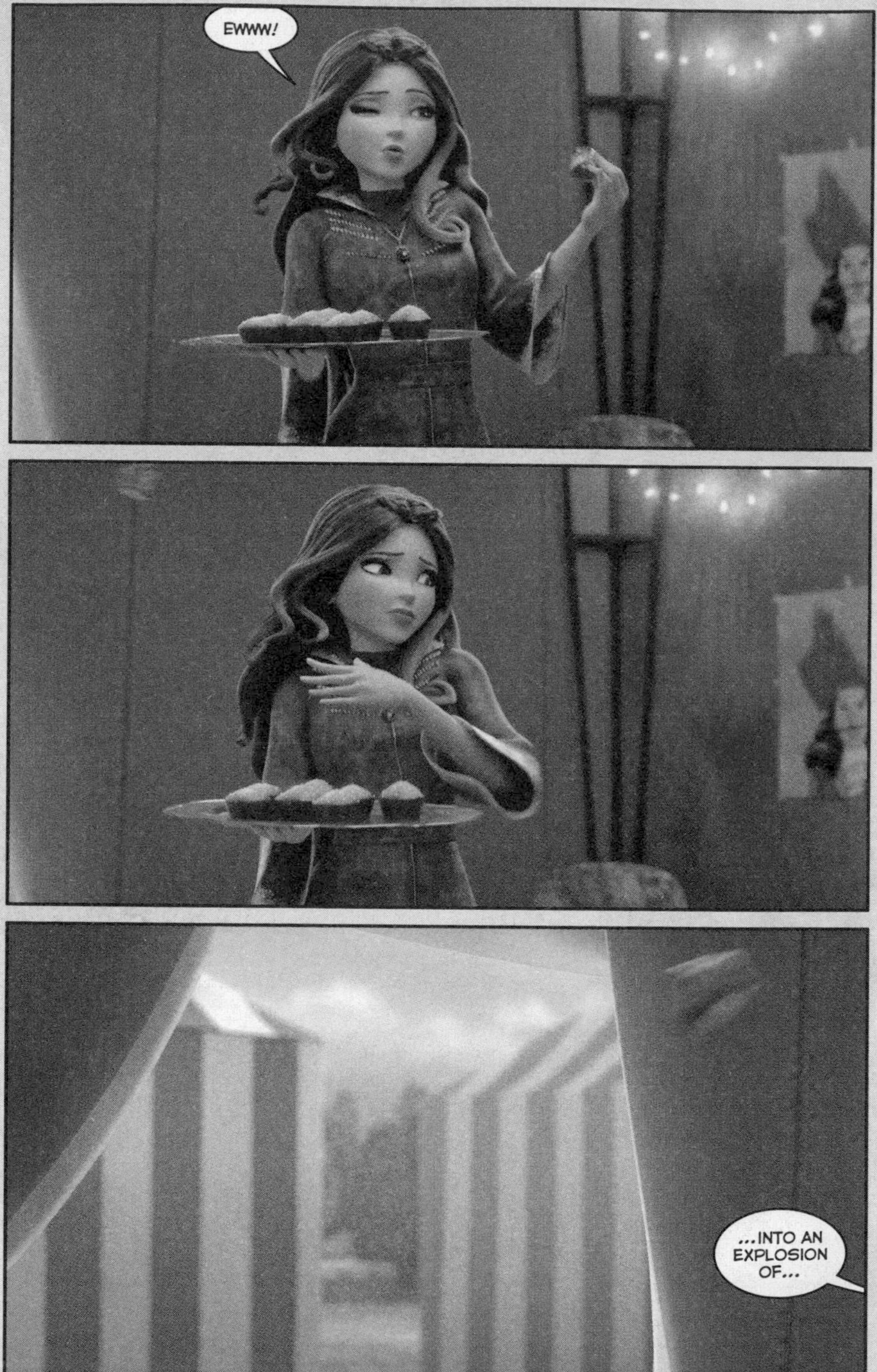
EWWW!
...INTO AN EXPLOSION OF...

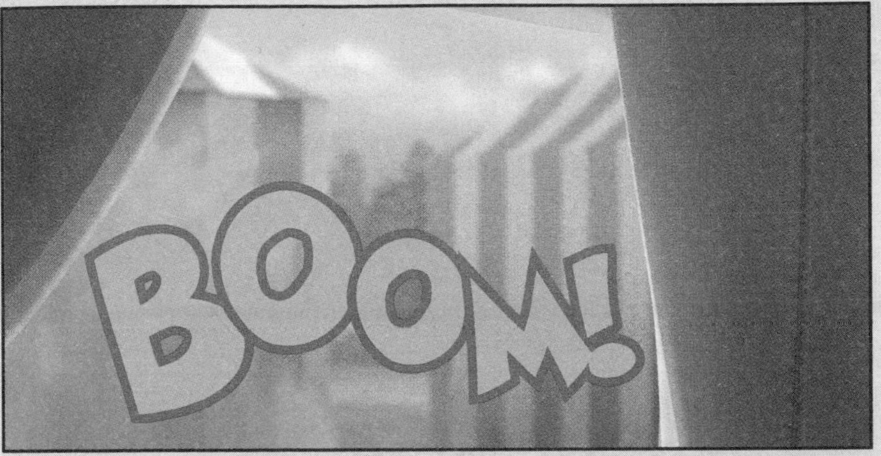
BOOM!

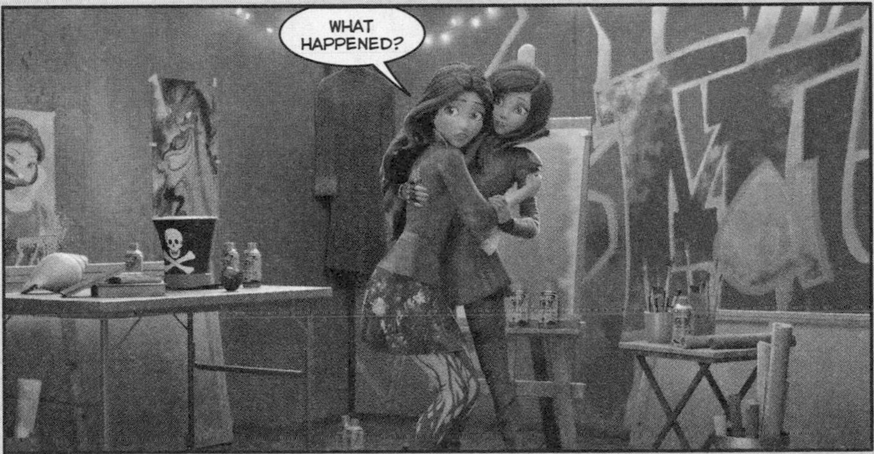
WHAT HAPPENED?

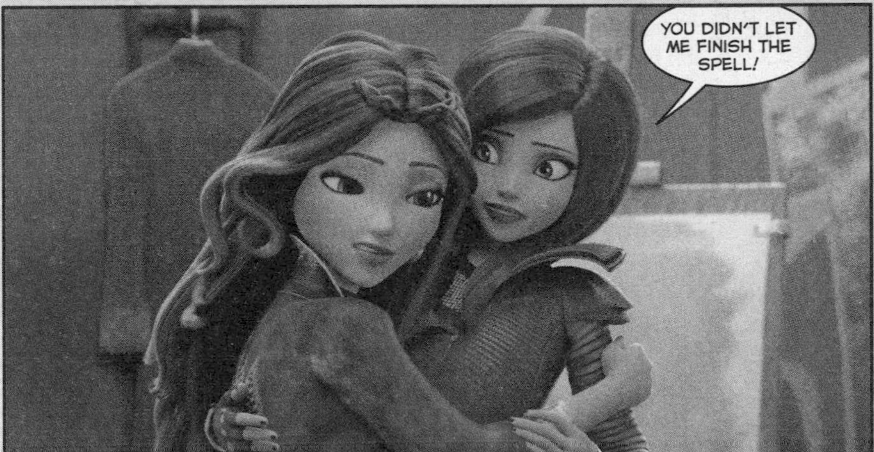
YOU DIDN'T LET ME FINISH THE SPELL!

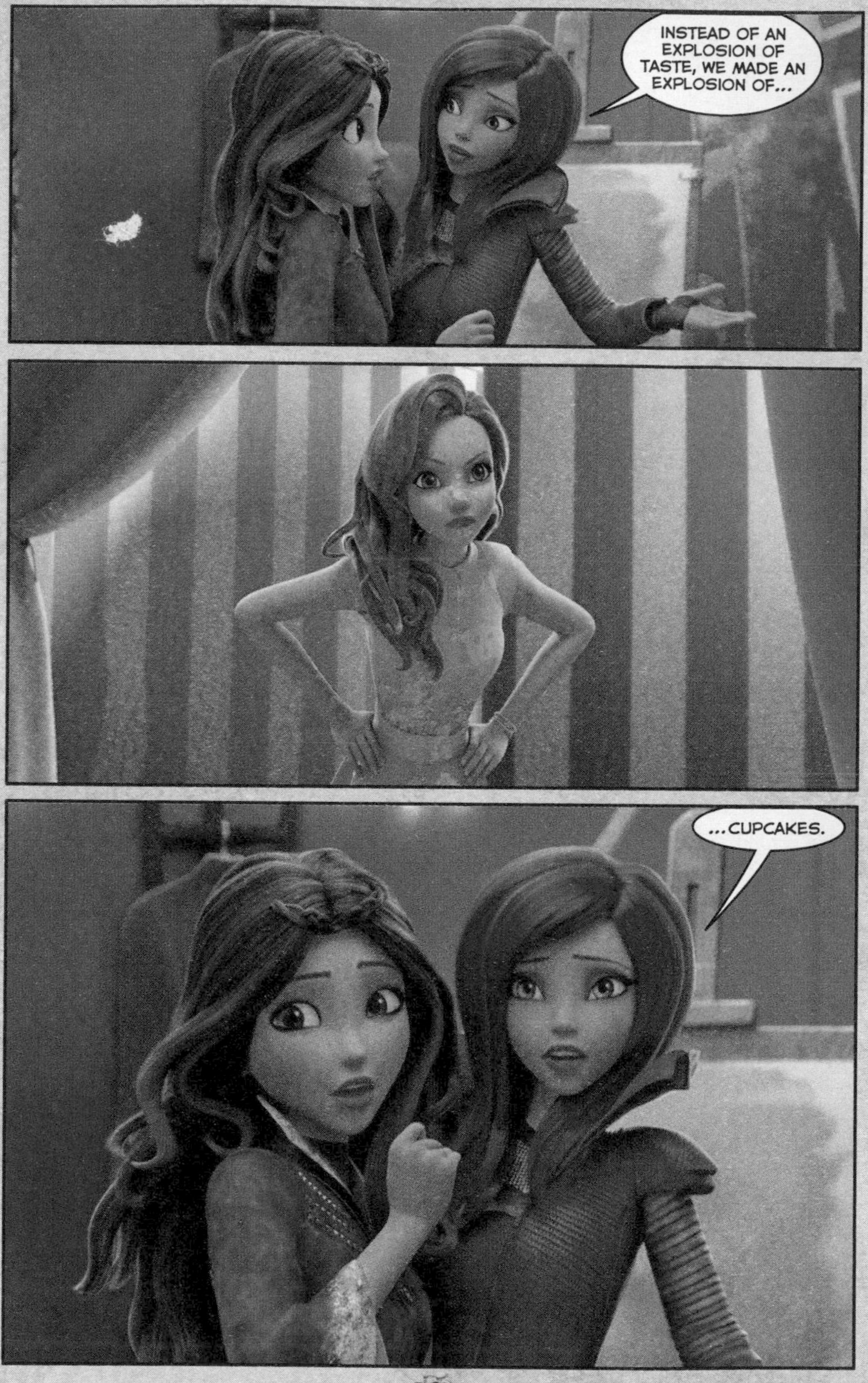
INSTEAD OF AN EXPLOSION OF TASTE, WE MADE AN EXPLOSION OF...
...CUPCAKES.

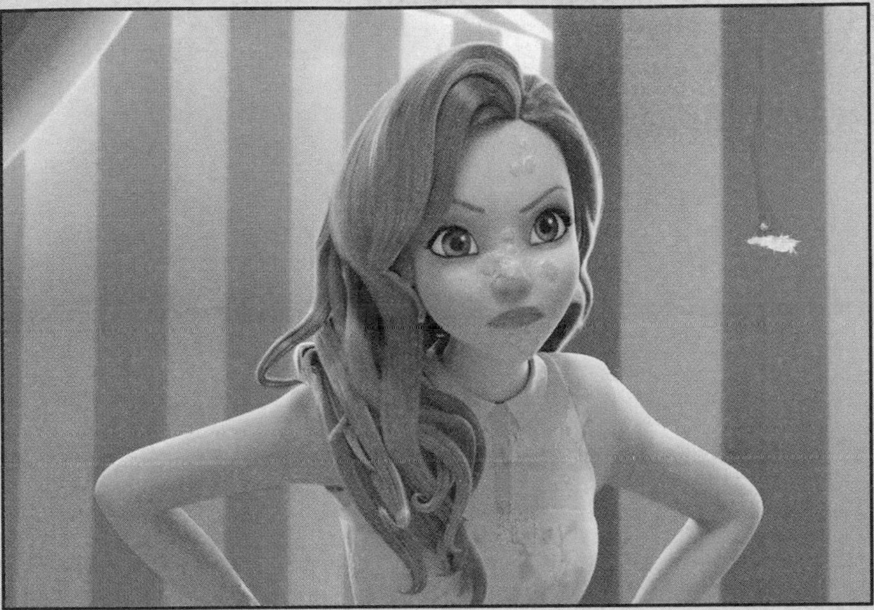

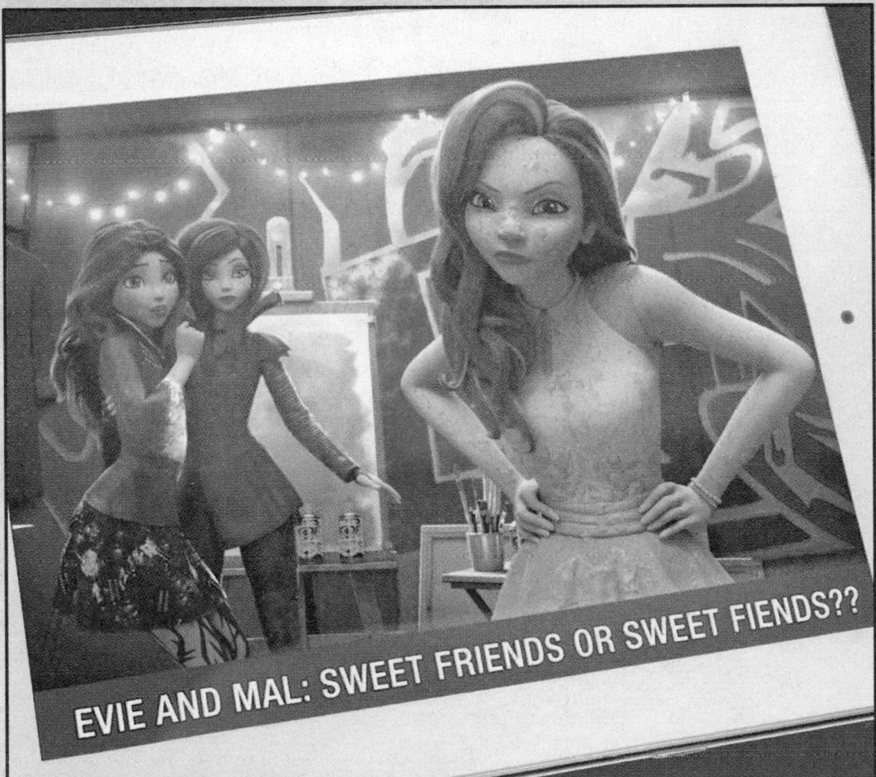
EVIE AND MAL: SWEET FRIENDS OR SWEET FIENDS??

CHAPTER 2: MAL'S DIGI-IMAGE PROBLEM

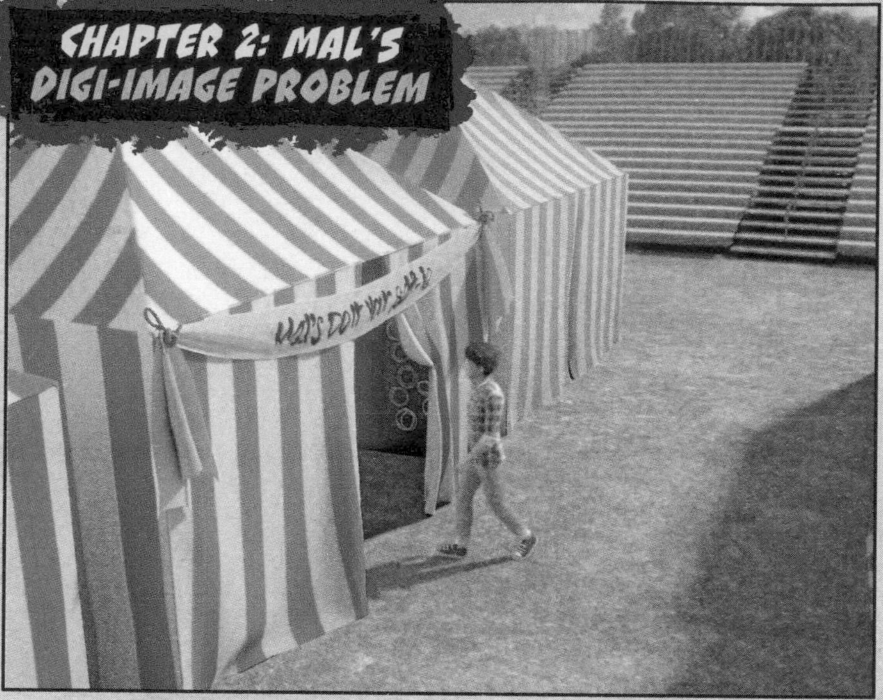

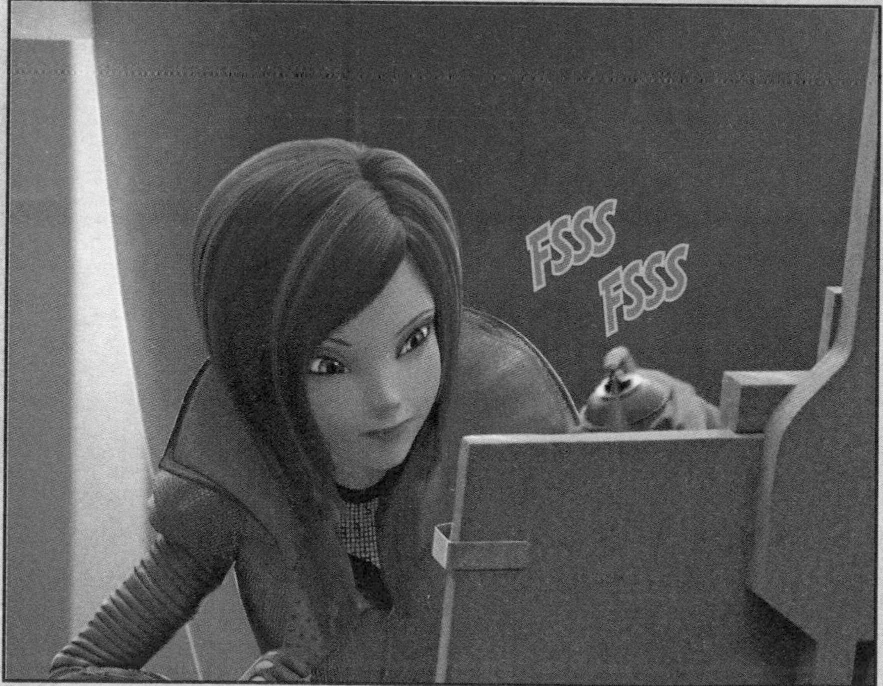
FSSS
FSSS

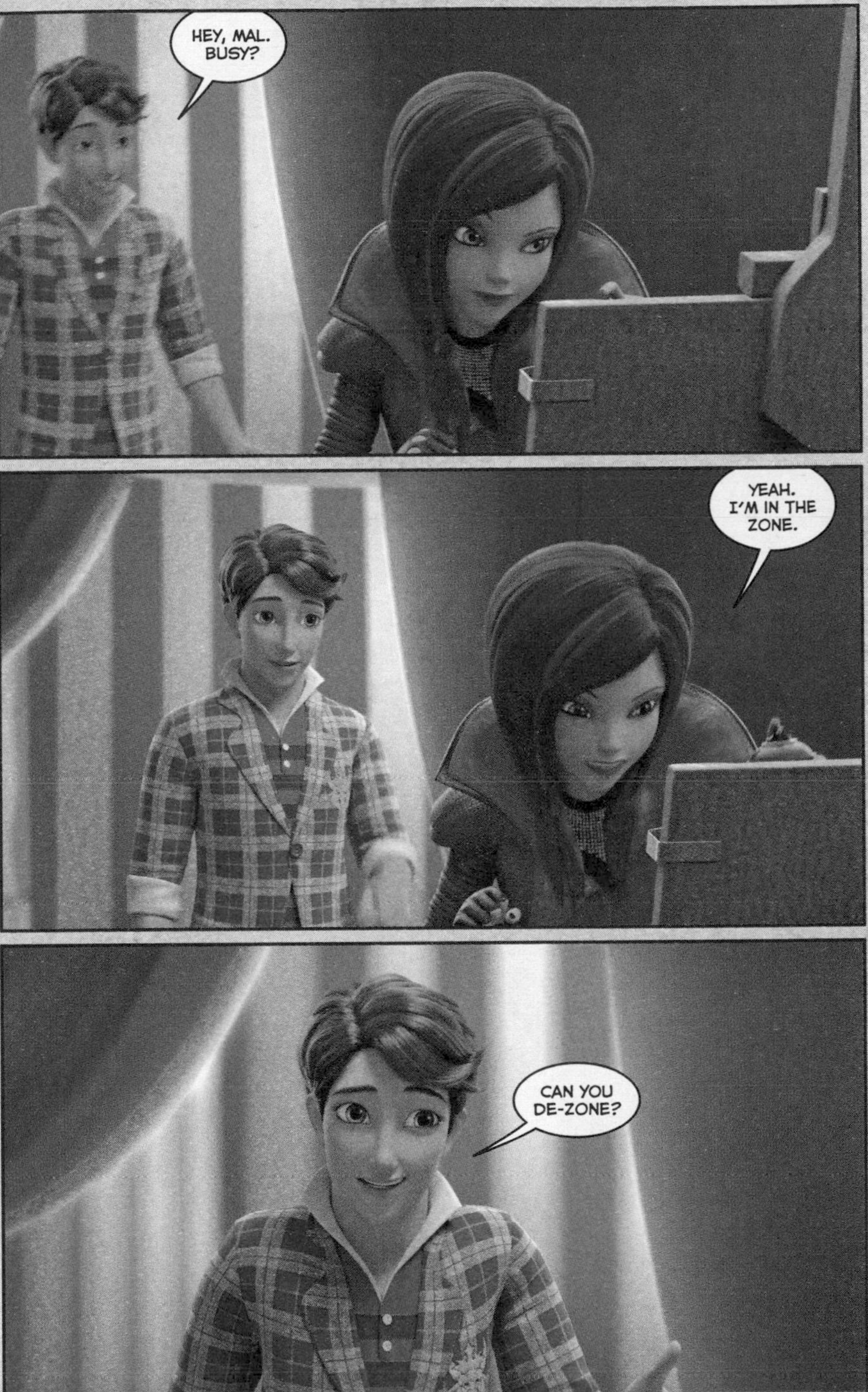
HEY, MAL. BUSY?
YEAH. I'M IN THE ZONE.
CAN YOU DE-ZONE?

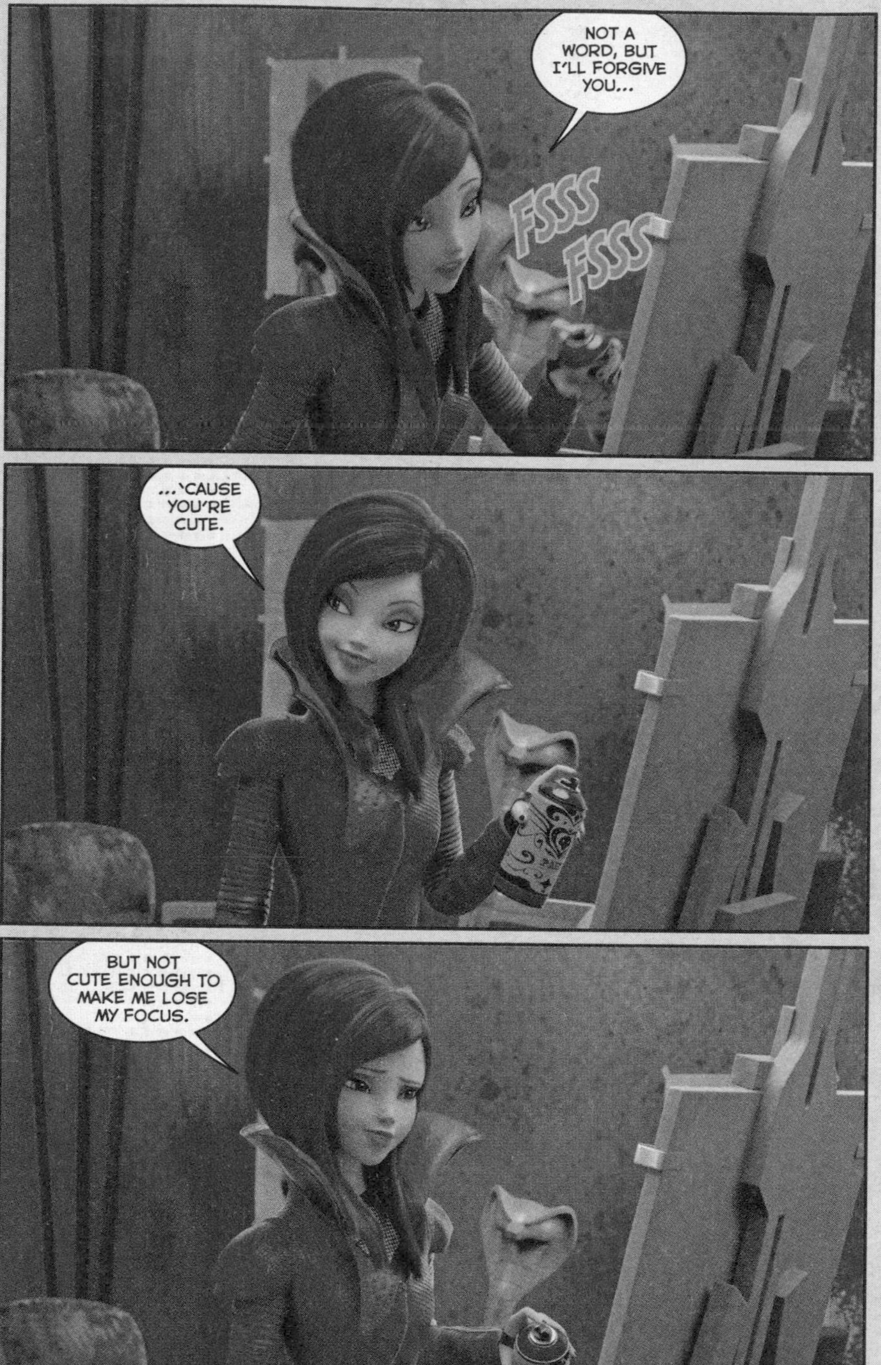
NOT A WORD, BUT I'LL FORGIVE YOU...
FSSS FSSS
...'CAUSE YOU'RE CUTE.
BUT NOT CUTE ENOUGH TO MAKE ME LOSE MY FOCUS.

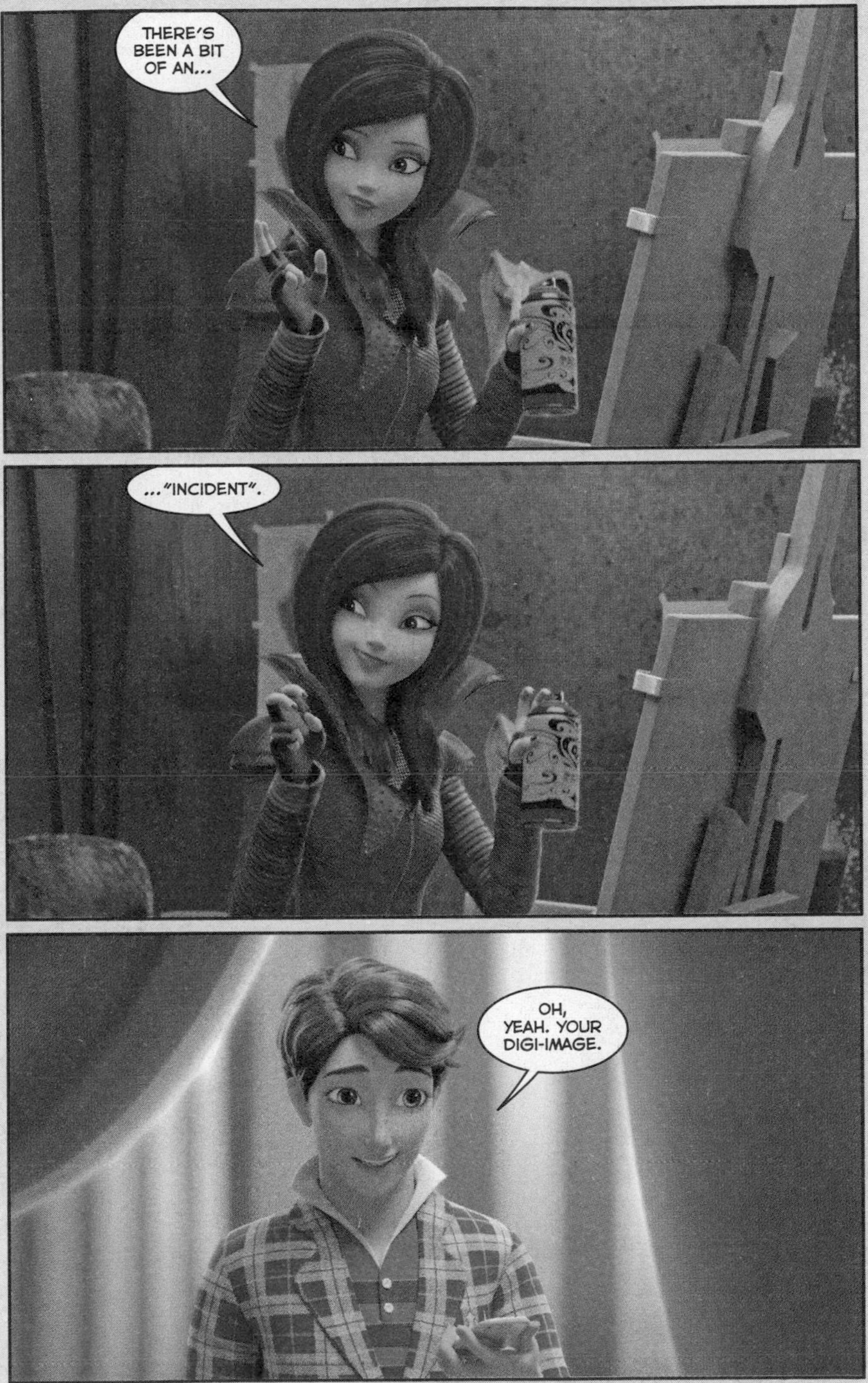
THERE'S BEEN A BIT OF AN...
..."INCIDENT".
OH, YEAH. YOUR DIGI-IMAGE.

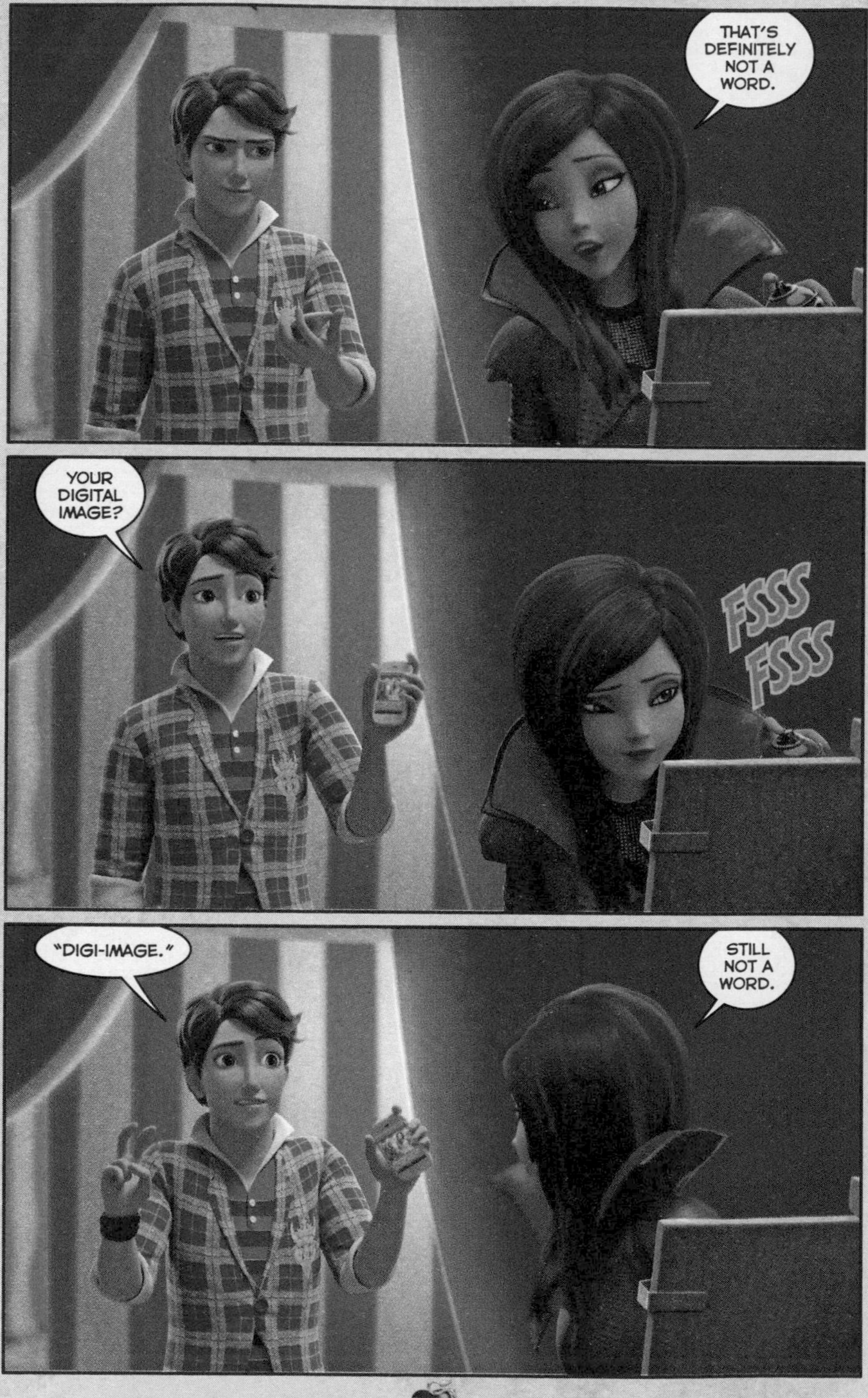
THAT'S DEFINITELY NOT A WORD.
YOUR DIGITAL IMAGE?
FSSS
FSSS
"DIGI-IMAGE."
STILL NOT A WORD.

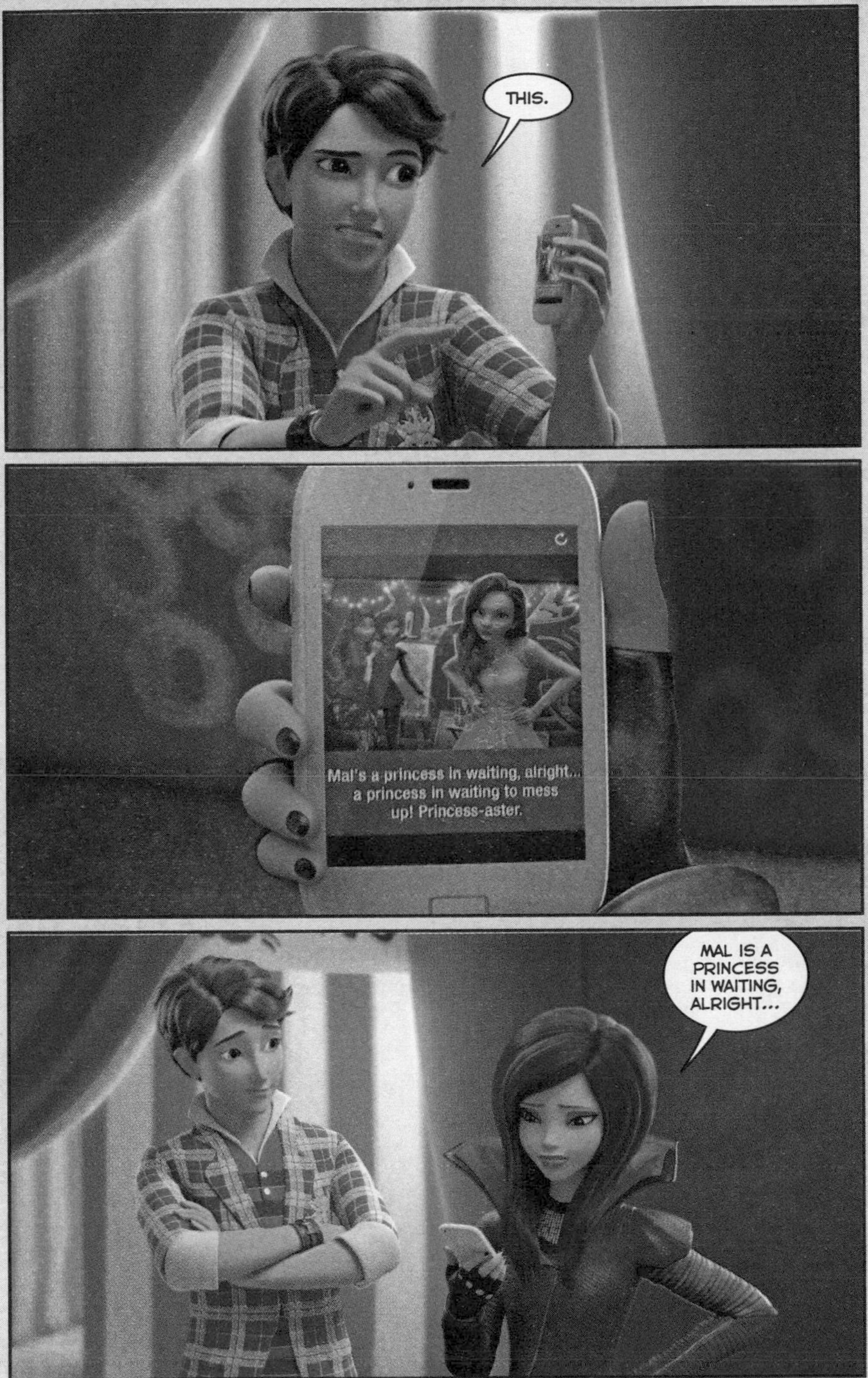
THIS.
Mal's a princess in waiting, alright... a princess in waiting to mess up! Princess-aster.
MAL IS A PRINCESS IN WAITING, ALRIGHT...

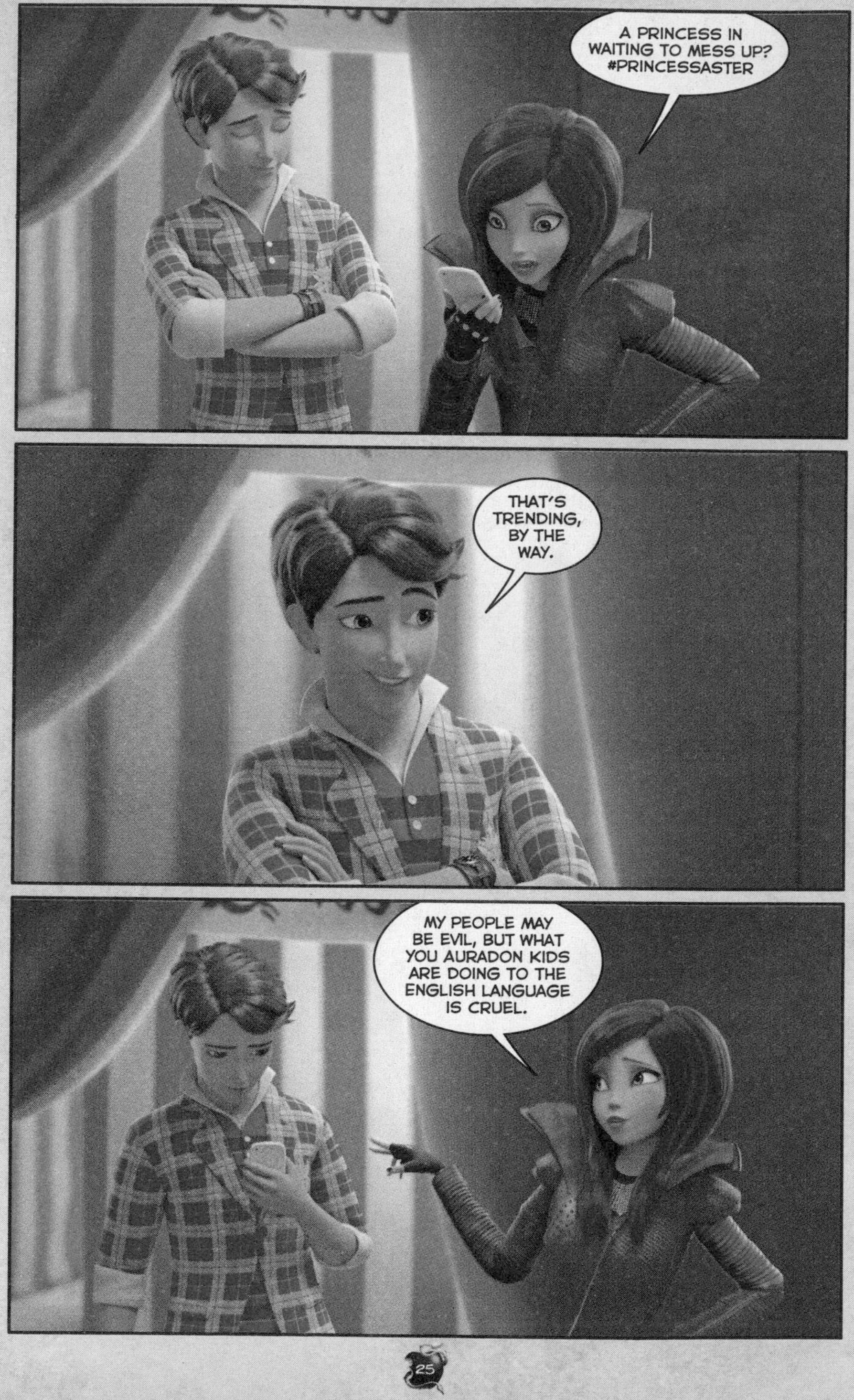
A PRINCESS IN WAITING TO MESS UP? #PRINCESSASTER
THAT'S TRENDING, BY THE WAY.
MY PEOPLE MAY BE EVIL, BUT WHAT YOU AURADON KIDS ARE DOING TO THE ENGLISH LANGUAGE IS CRUEL.

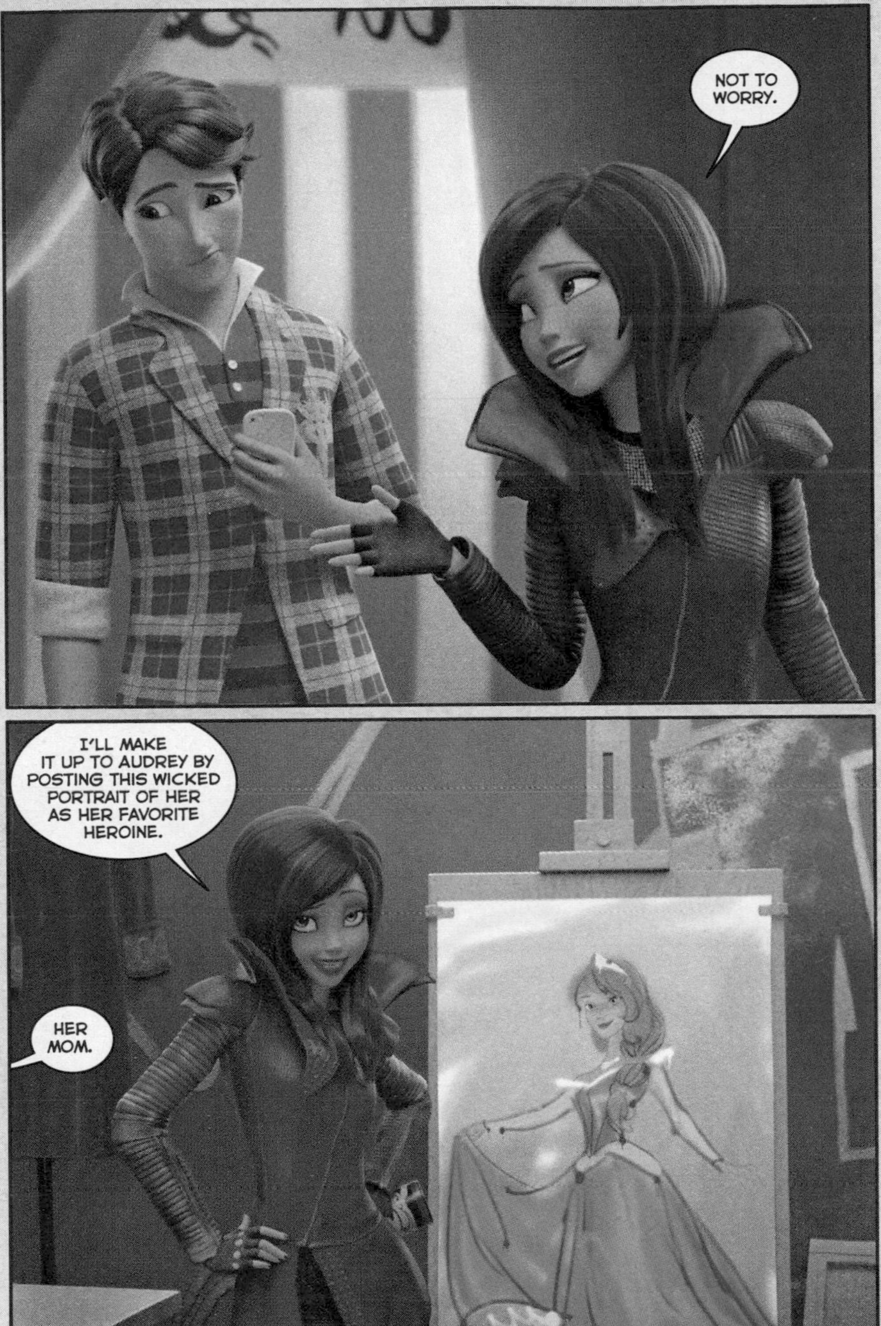
NOT TO WORRY.
I'LL MAKE IT UP TO AUDREY BY POSTING THIS WICKED PORTRAIT OF HER AS HER FAVORITE HEROINE.
HER MOM.

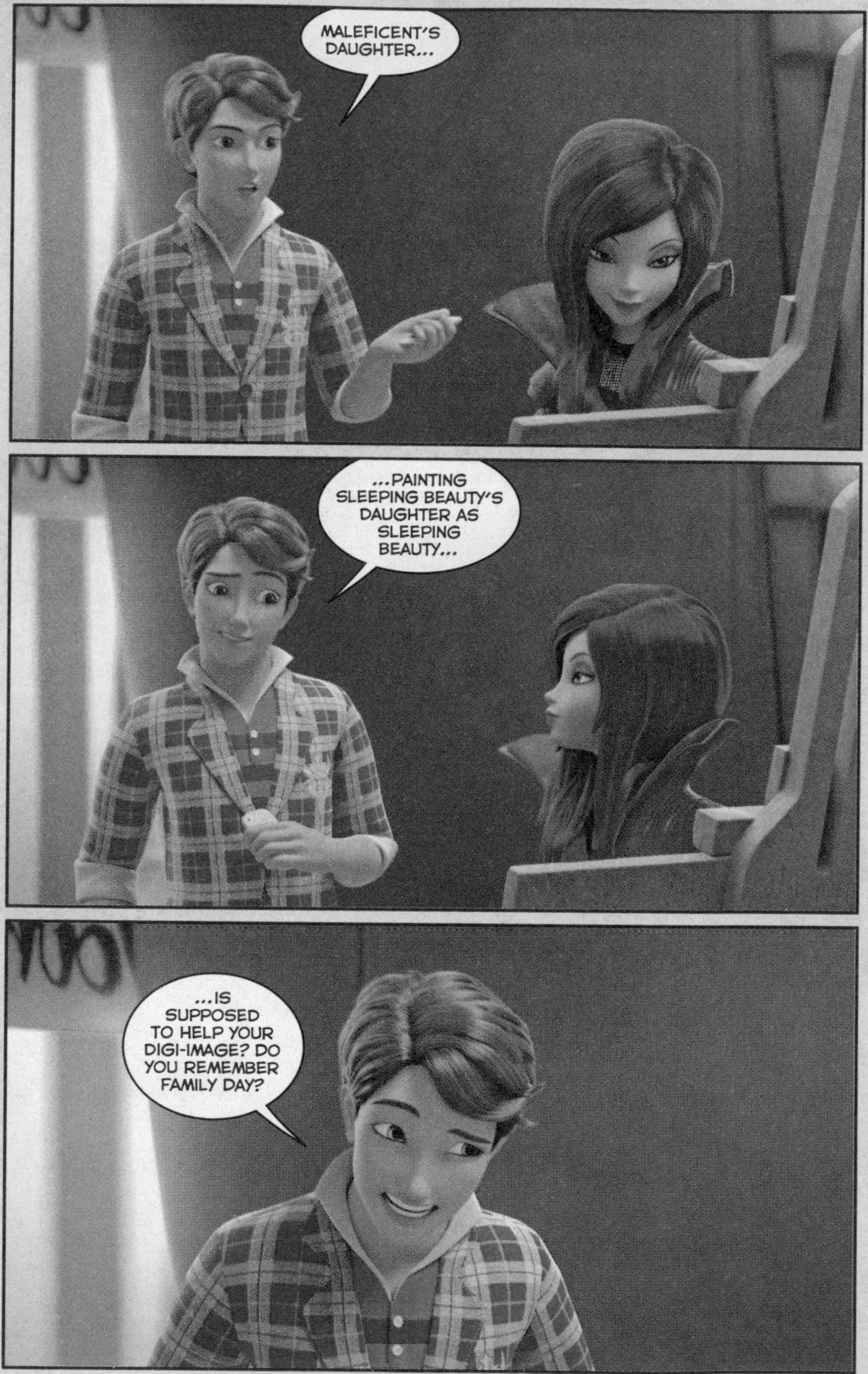
MALEFICENT'S DAUGHTER...
...PAINTING SLEEPING BEAUTY'S DAUGHTER AS SLEEPING BEAUTY...
...IS SUPPOSED TO HELP YOUR DIGI-IMAGE? DO YOU REMEMBER FAMILY DAY?

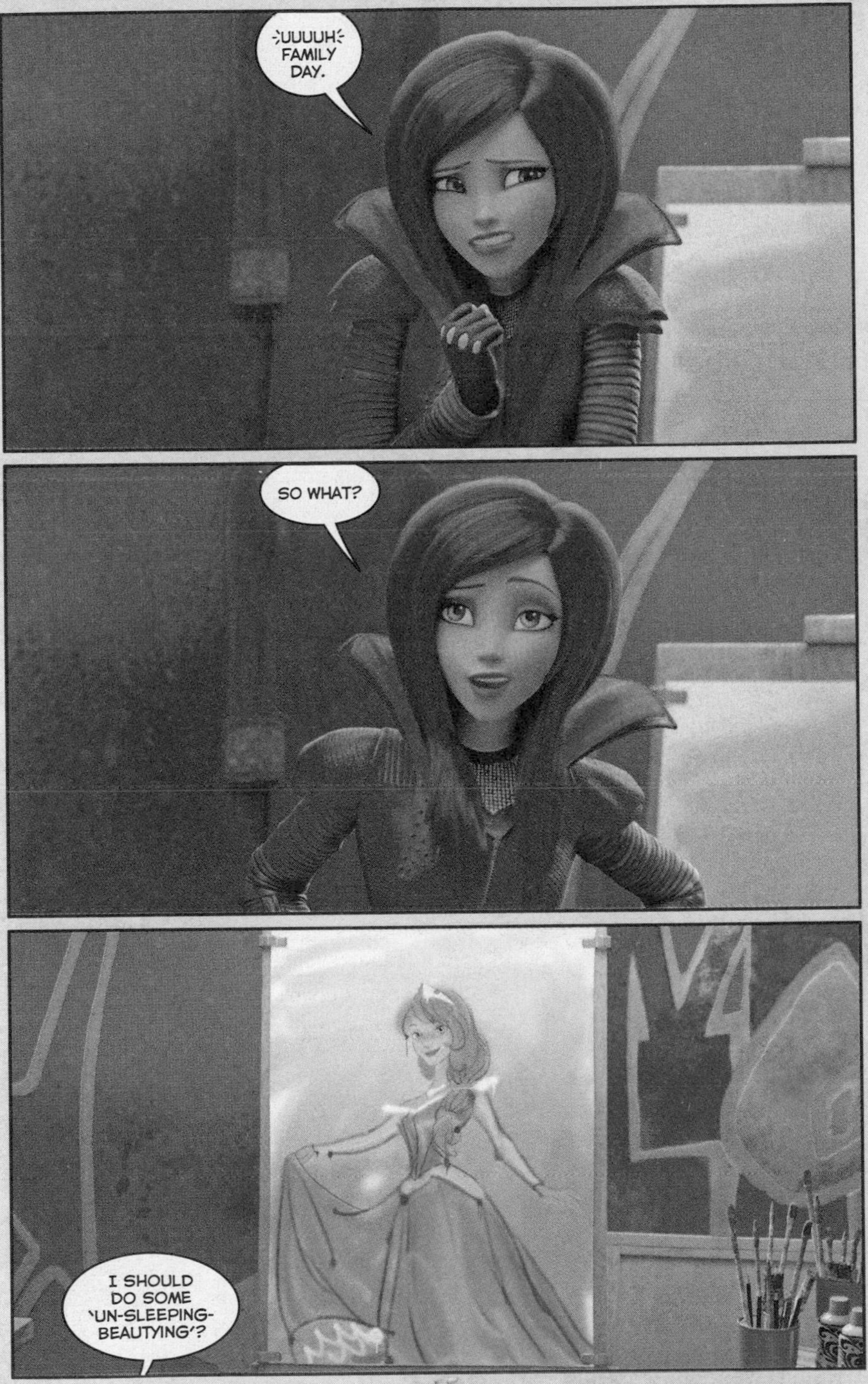
UUUUH FAMILY DAY.
SO WHAT?
I SHOULD DO SOME 'UN-SLEEPING-BEAUTYING'?

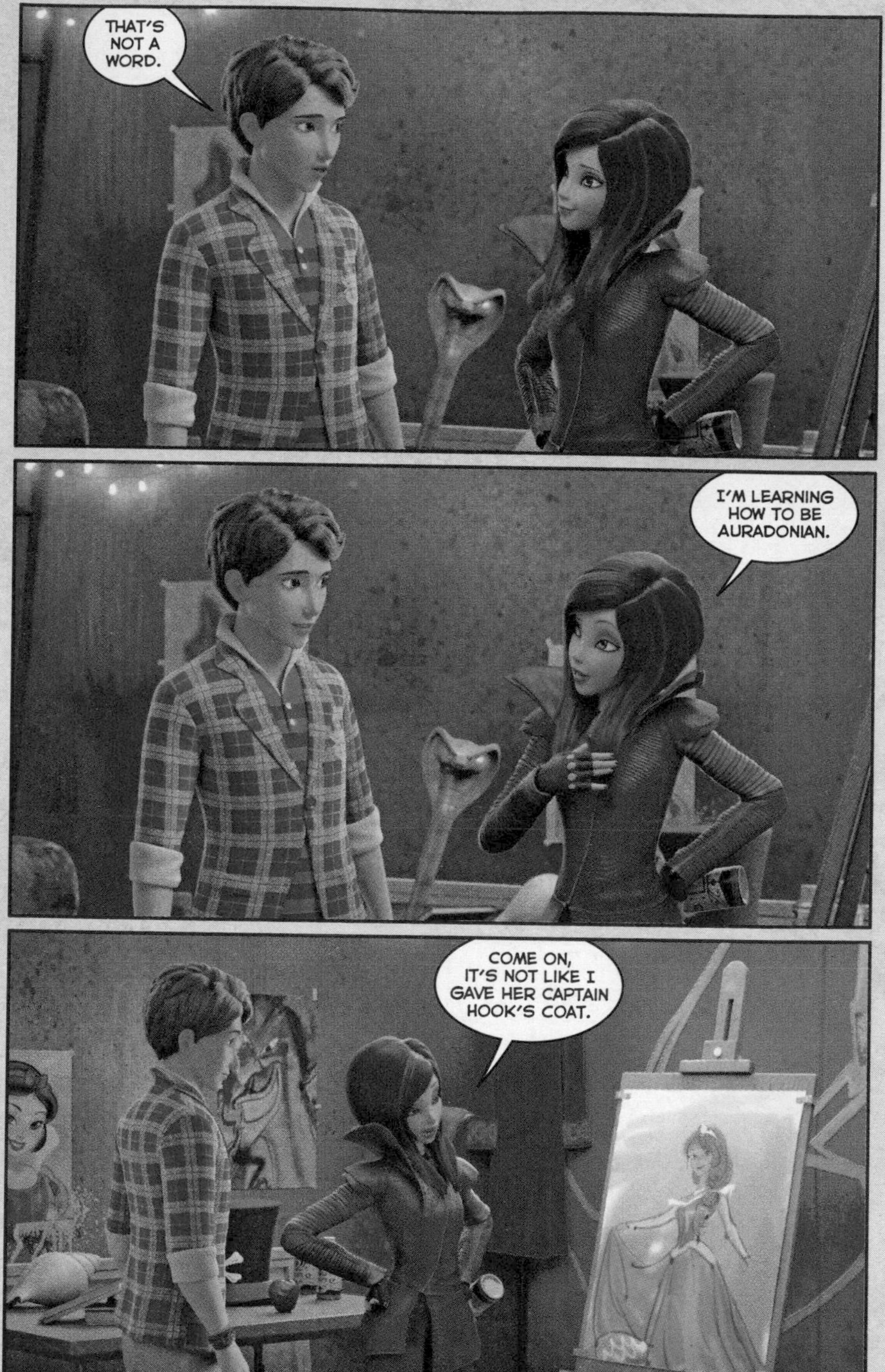
THAT'S NOT A WORD.
I'M LEARNING HOW TO BE AURADONIAN.
COME ON, IT'S NOT LIKE I GAVE HER CAPTAIN HOOK'S COAT.

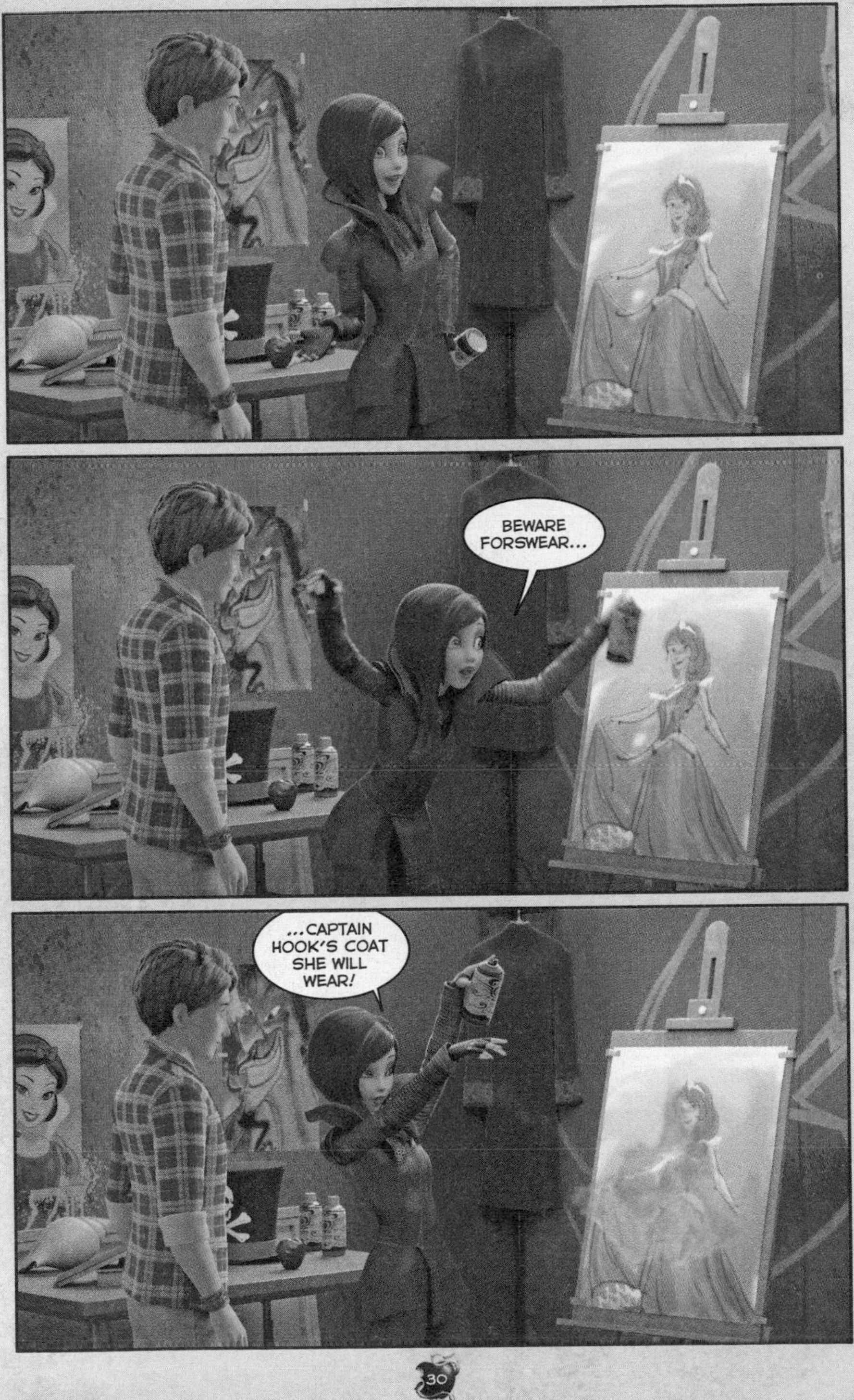
BEWARE FORSWEAR...
...CAPTAIN HOOK'S COAT SHE WILL WEAR!

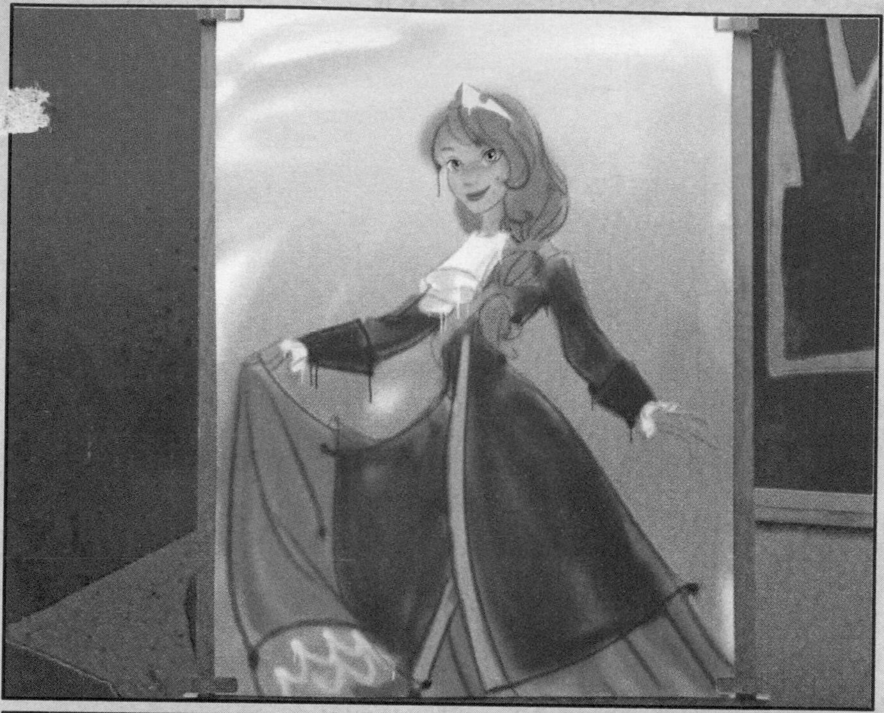

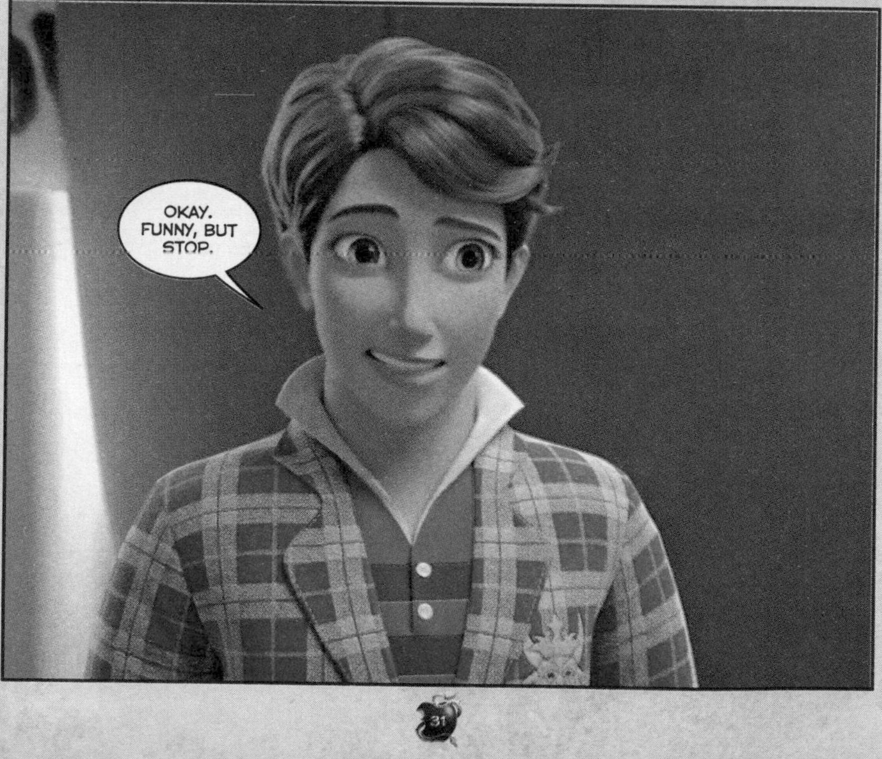
OKAY. FUNNY, BUT STOP.

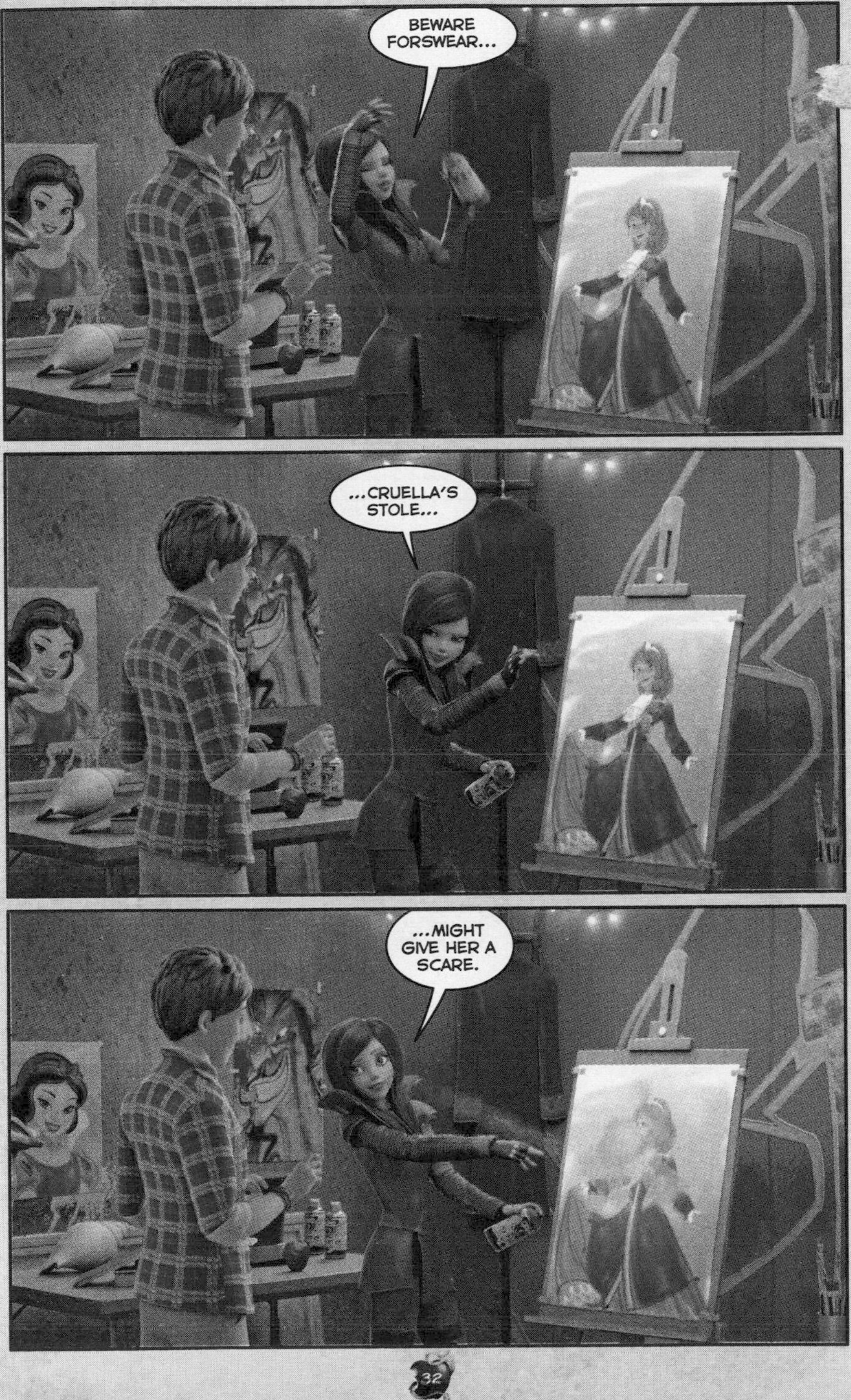
BEWARE FORSWEAR...
...CRUELLA'S STOLE...
...MIGHT GIVE HER A SCARE.

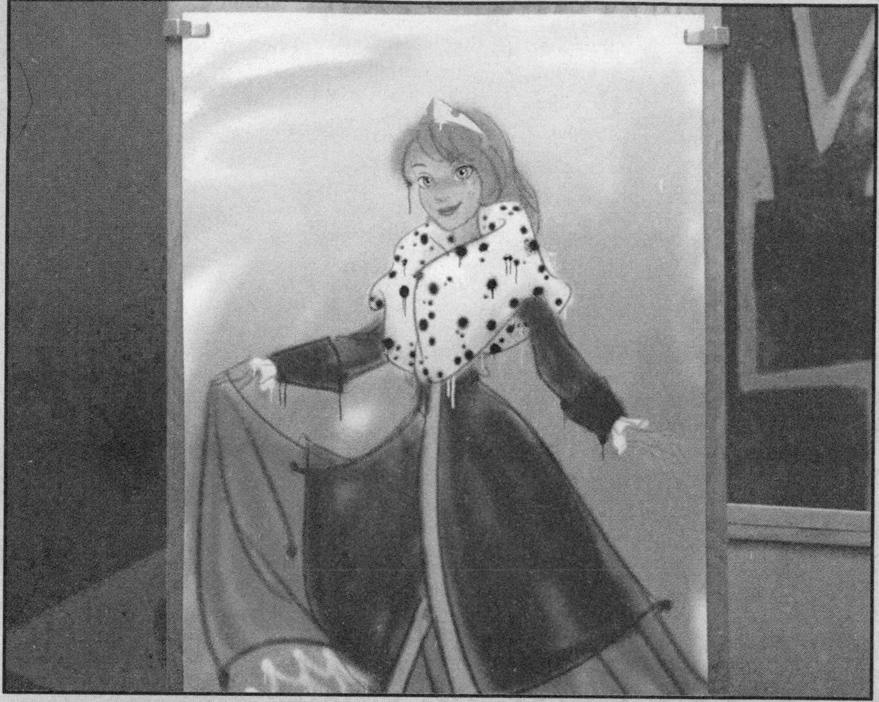

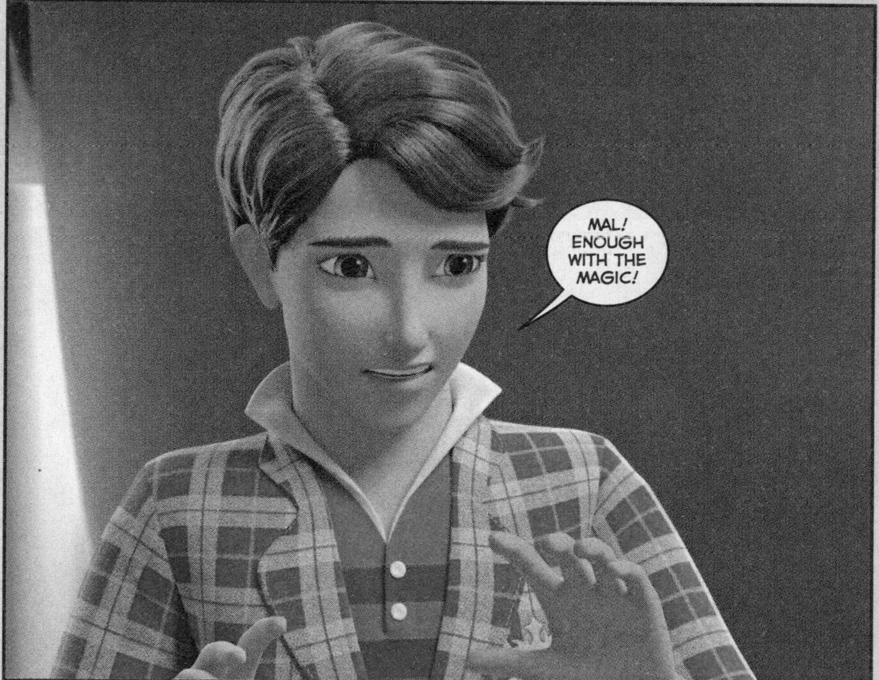
MAL! ENOUGH WITH THE MAGIC!

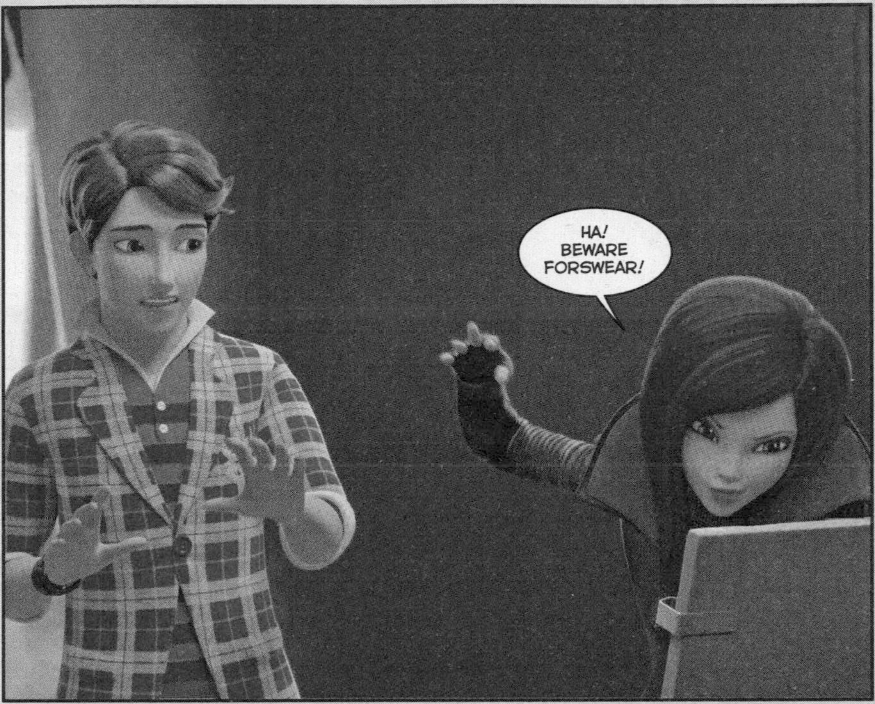
HA! BEWARE FORSWEAR!
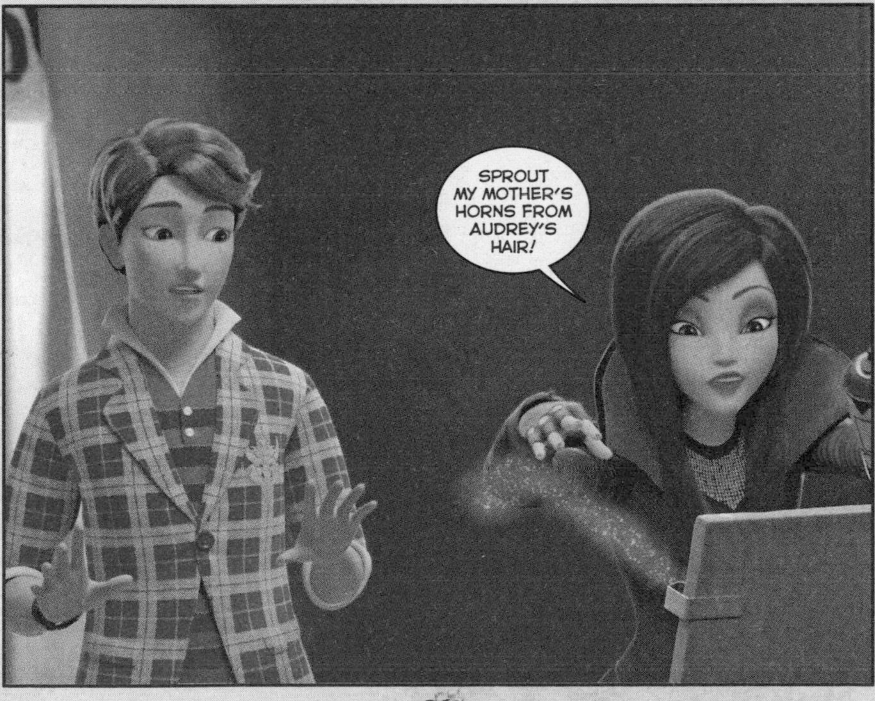
SPROUT MY MOTHER'S HORNS FROM AUDREY'S HAIR!

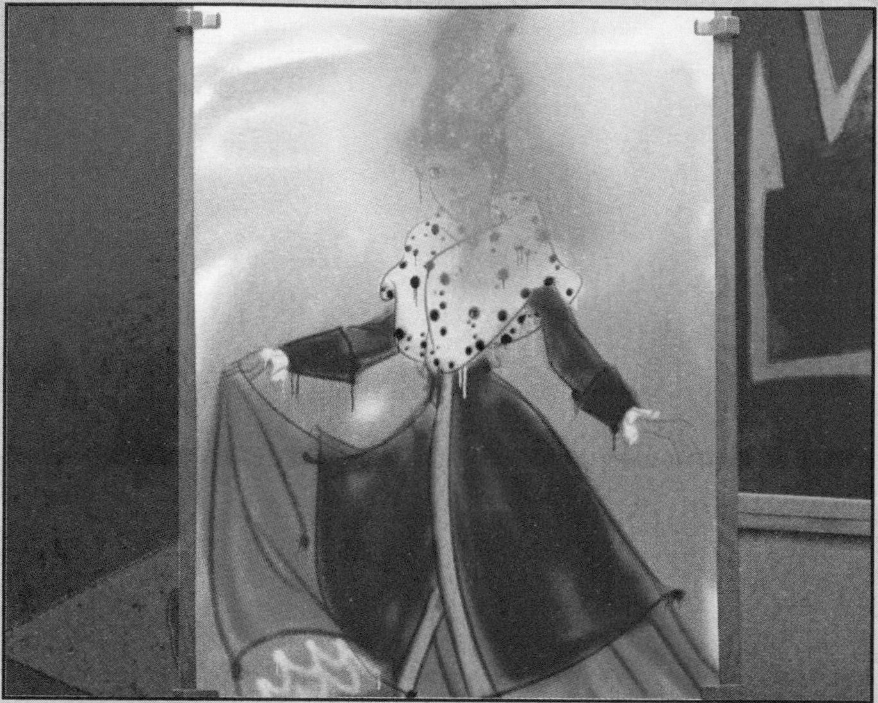

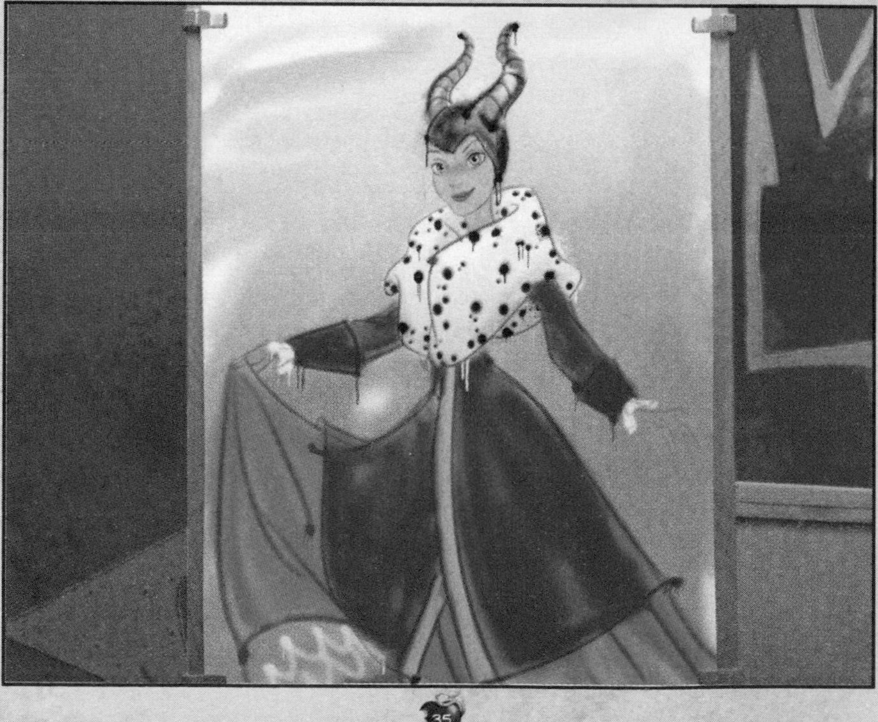

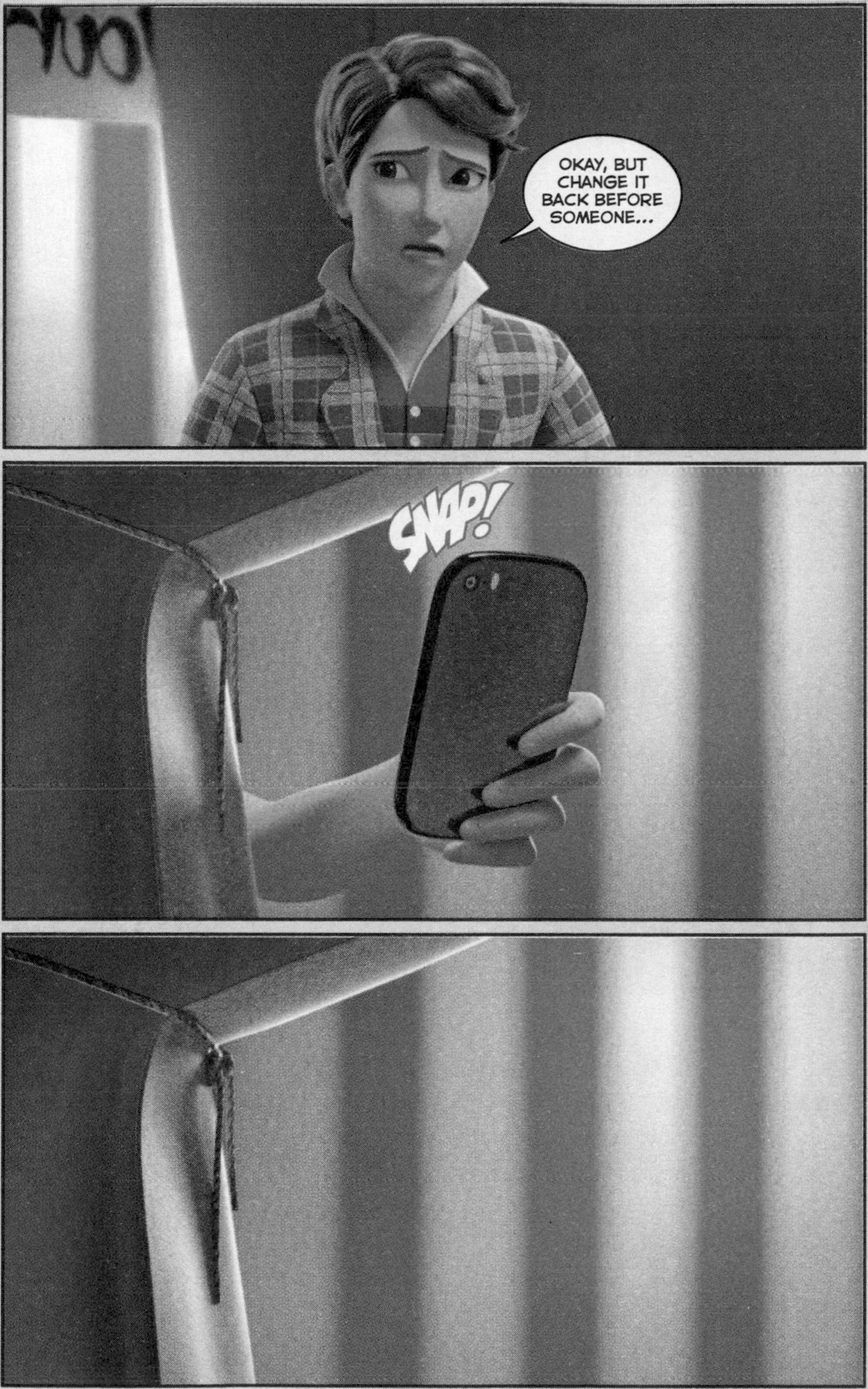
OKAY, BUT CHANGE IT BACK BEFORE SOMEONE...
SNAP!

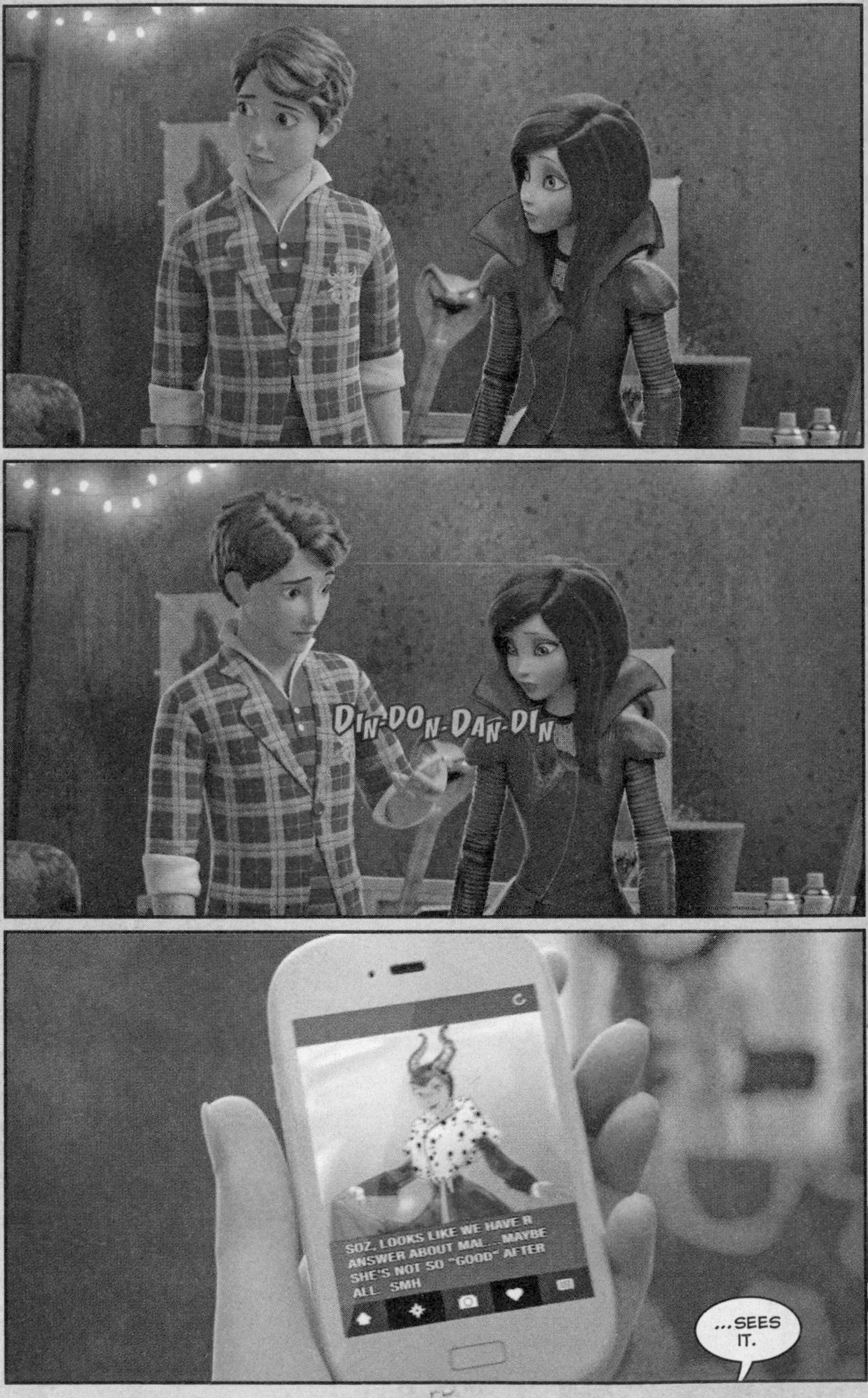
DIN-DON-DAN-DIN
SOZ, LOOKS LIKE WE HAVE R ANSWER ABOUT MAL... MAYBE SHE'S NOT SO "GOOD" AFTER ALL. SMH
...SEES IT.

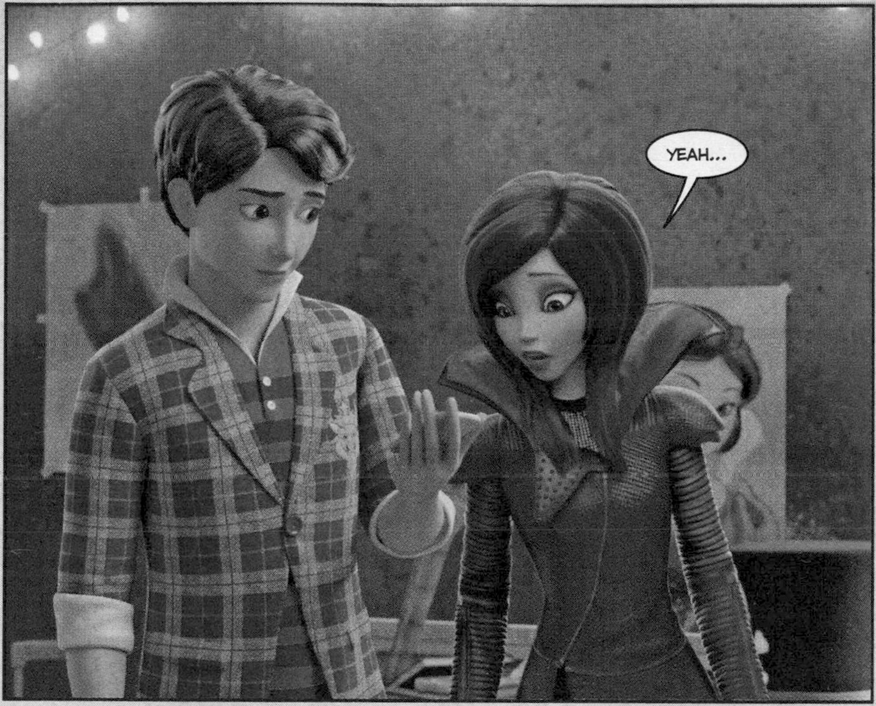
YEAH...

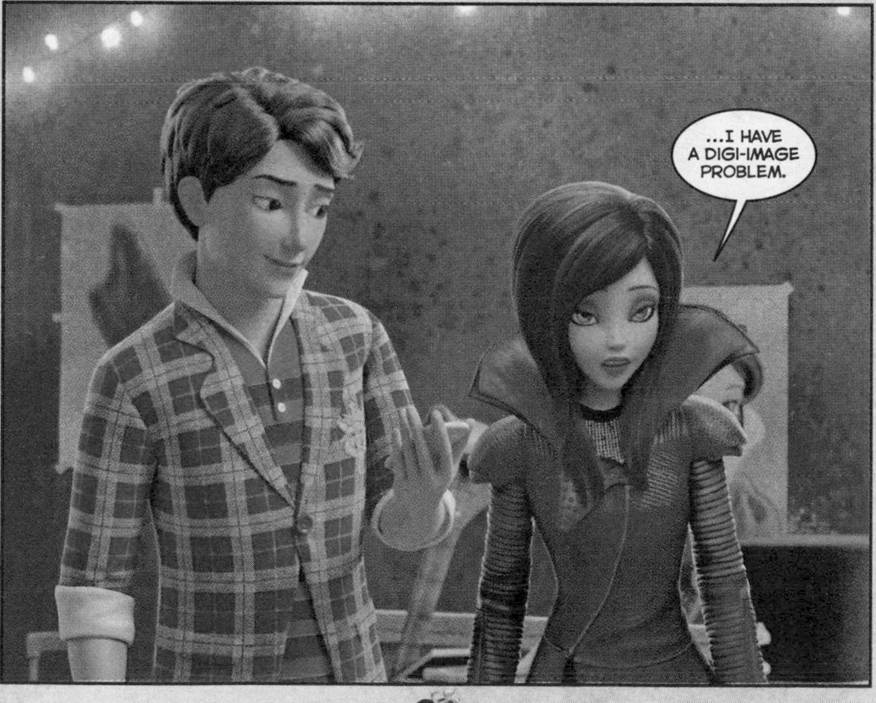
...I HAVE A DIGI-IMAGE PROBLEM.

CHAPTER 3: AUDREY'S NEW DO? NEW DON'T!

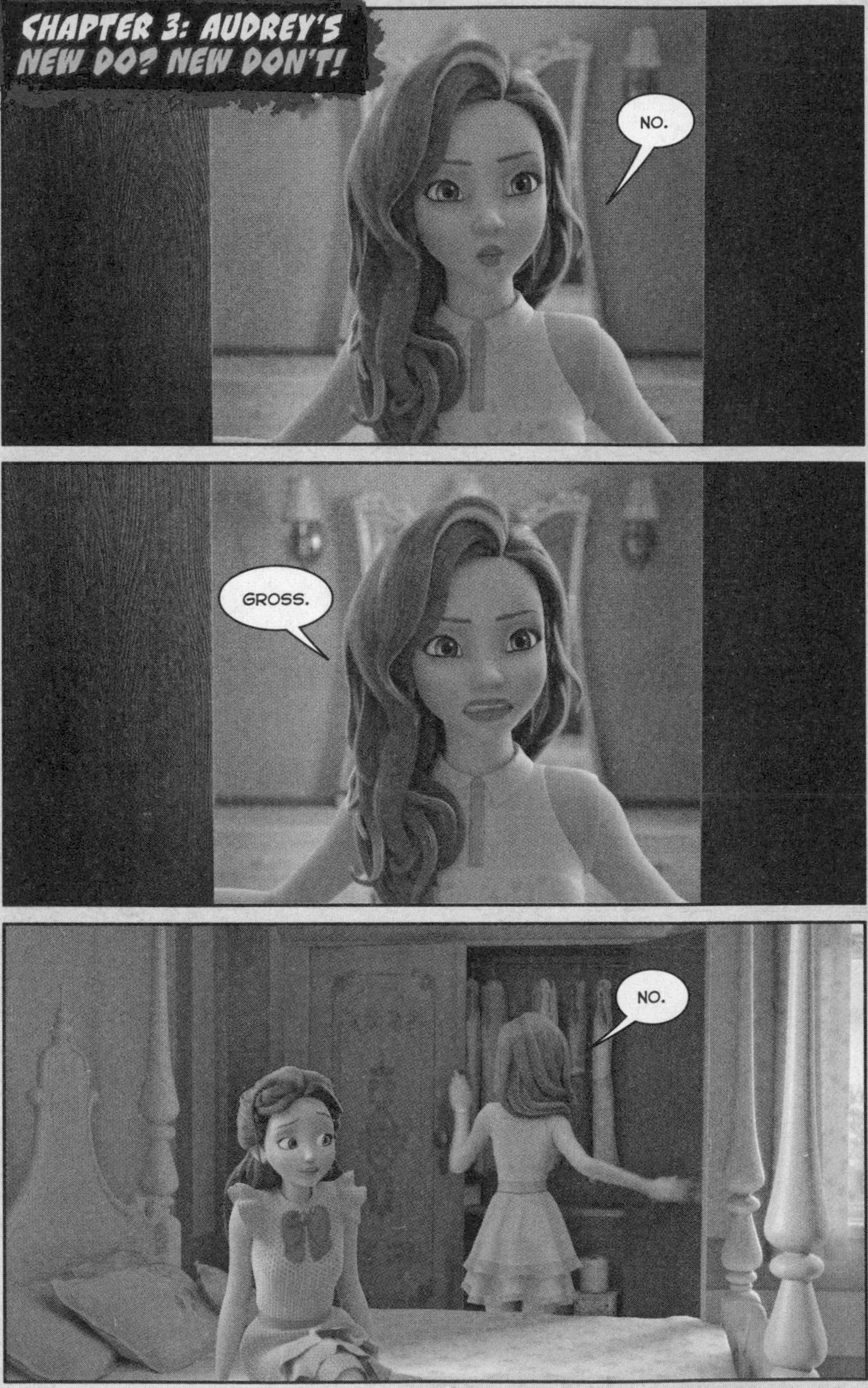
NO.
GROSS.
NO.

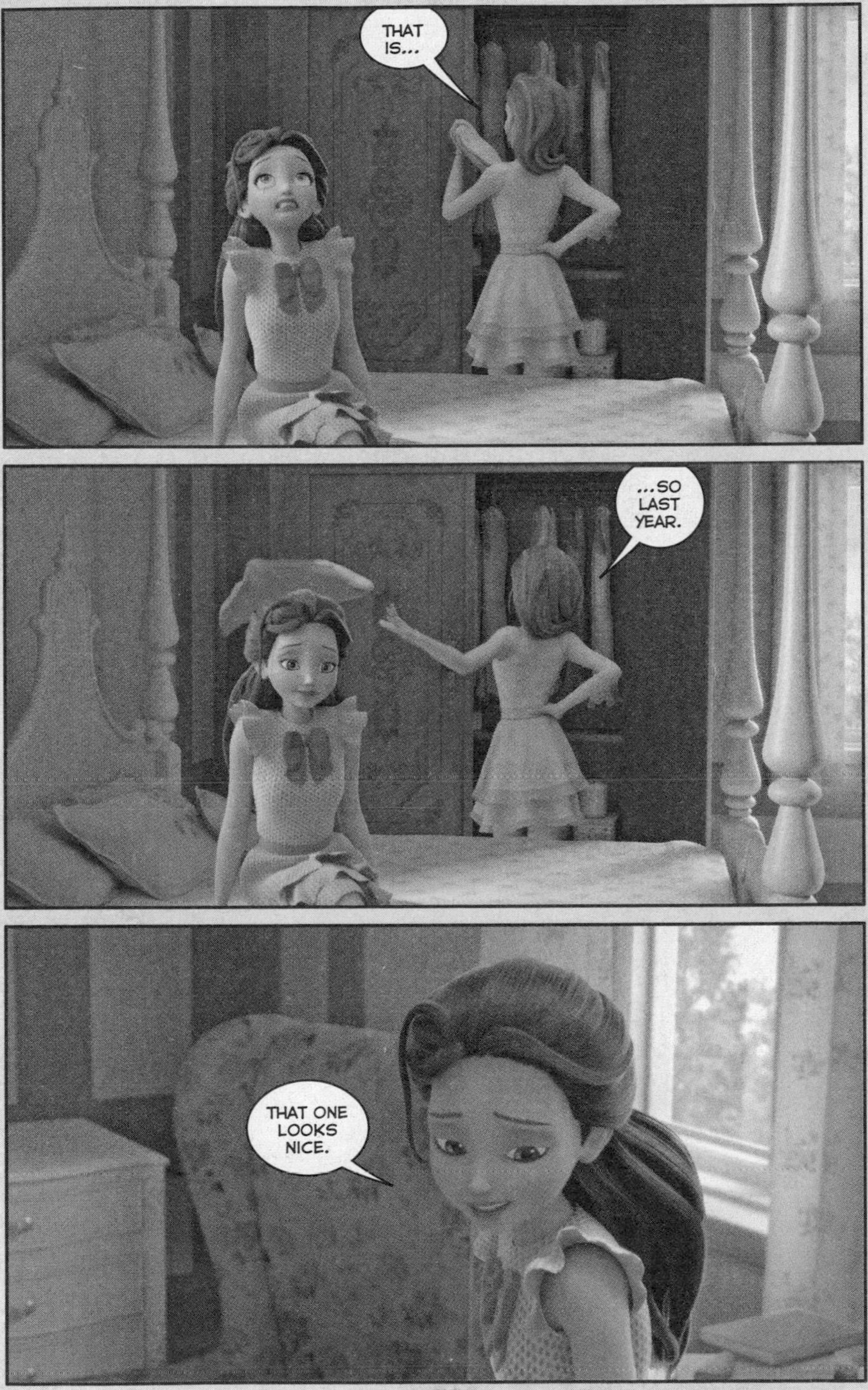
THAT IS...
...SO LAST YEAR.
THAT ONE LOOKS NICE.

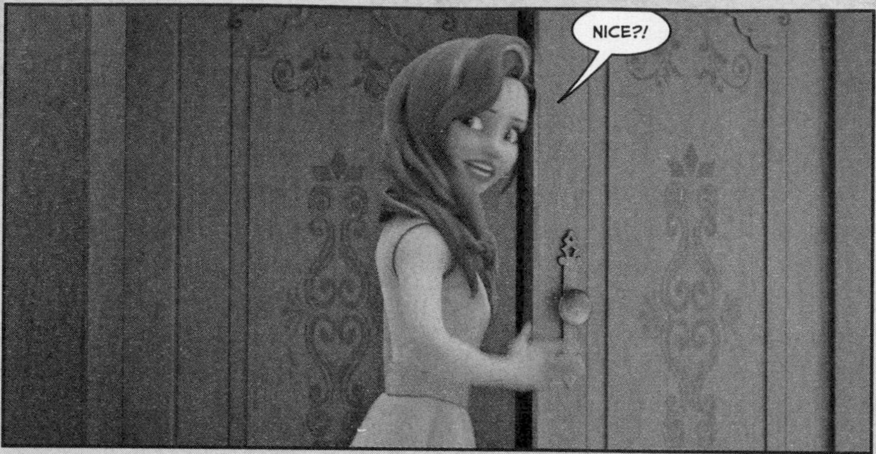
NICE?!

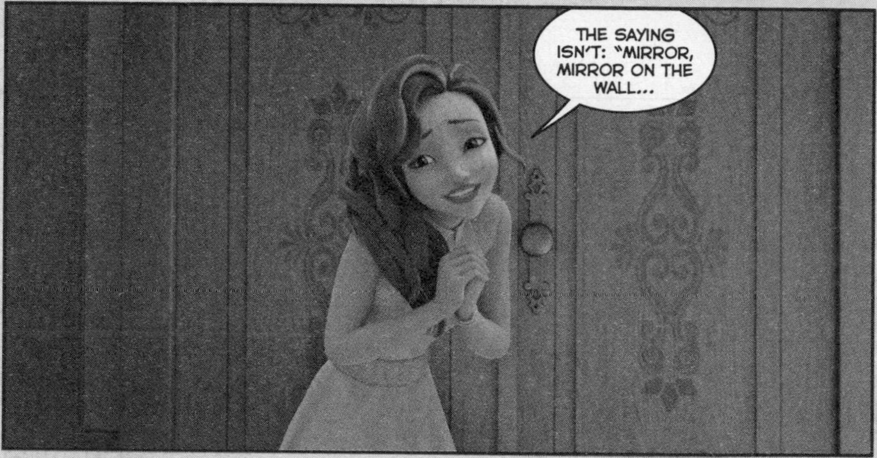
THE SAYING ISN'T: "MIRROR, MIRROR ON THE WALL...

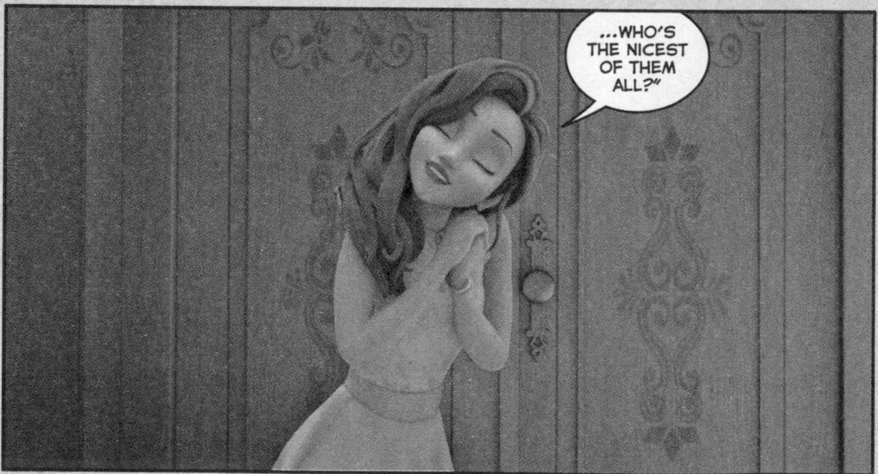
...WHO'S THE NICEST OF THEM ALL?"

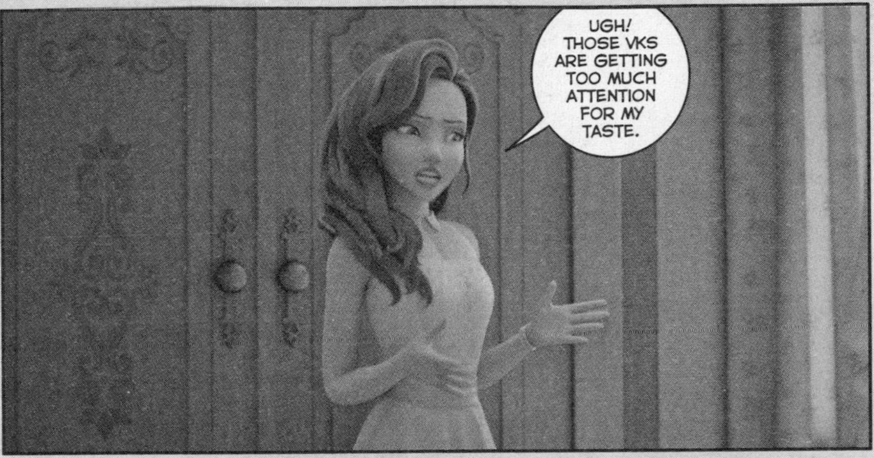
UGH! THOSE VKS ARE GETTING TOO MUCH ATTENTION FOR MY TASTE.

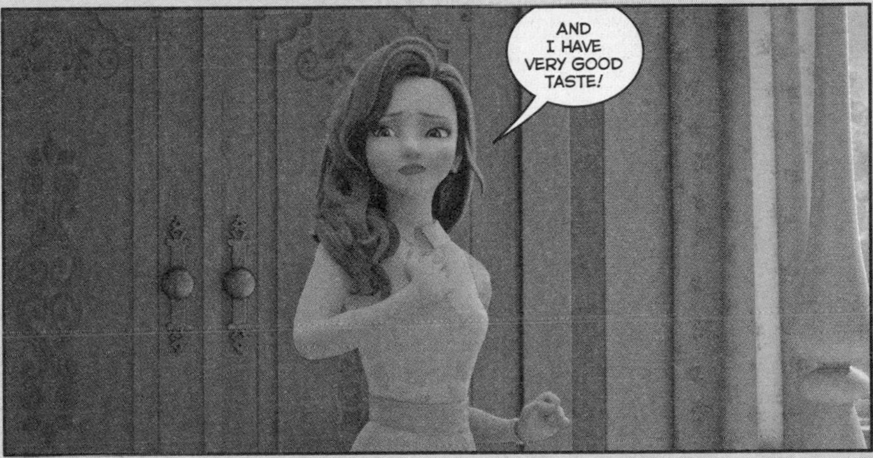
AND I HAVE VERY GOOD TASTE!

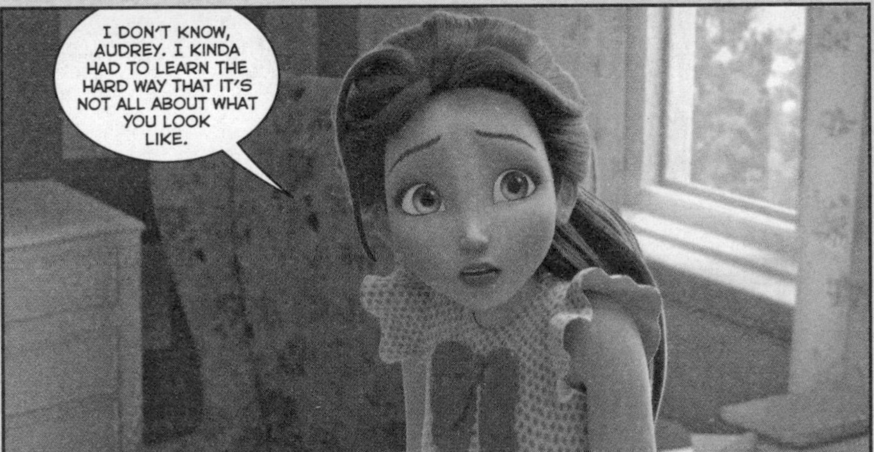
I DON'T KNOW, AUDREY. I KINDA HAD TO LEARN THE HARD WAY THAT IT'S NOT ALL ABOUT WHAT YOU LOOK LIKE.

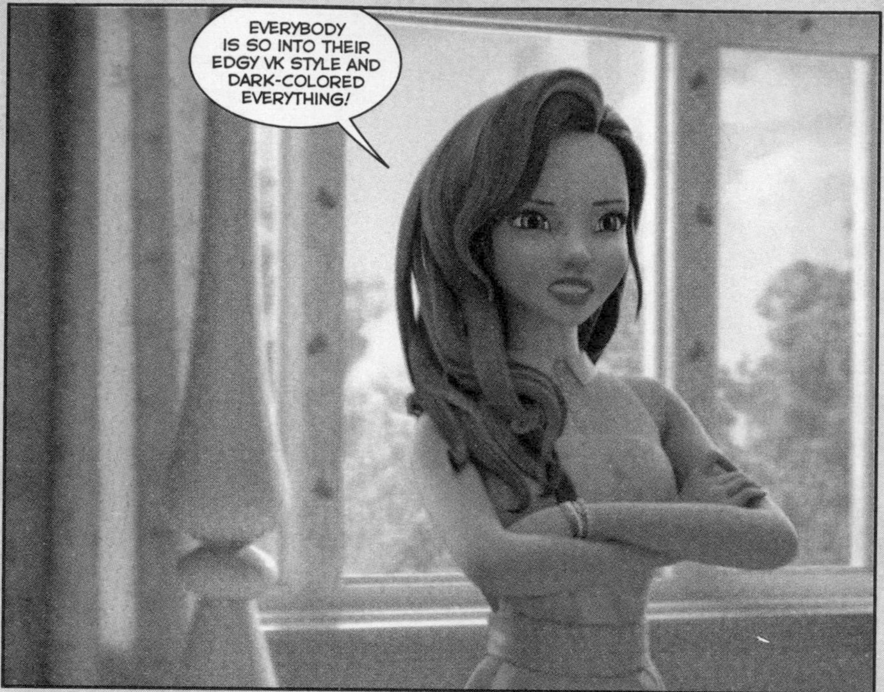
EVERYBODY IS SO INTO THEIR EDGY VK STYLE AND DARK-COLORED EVERYTHING!

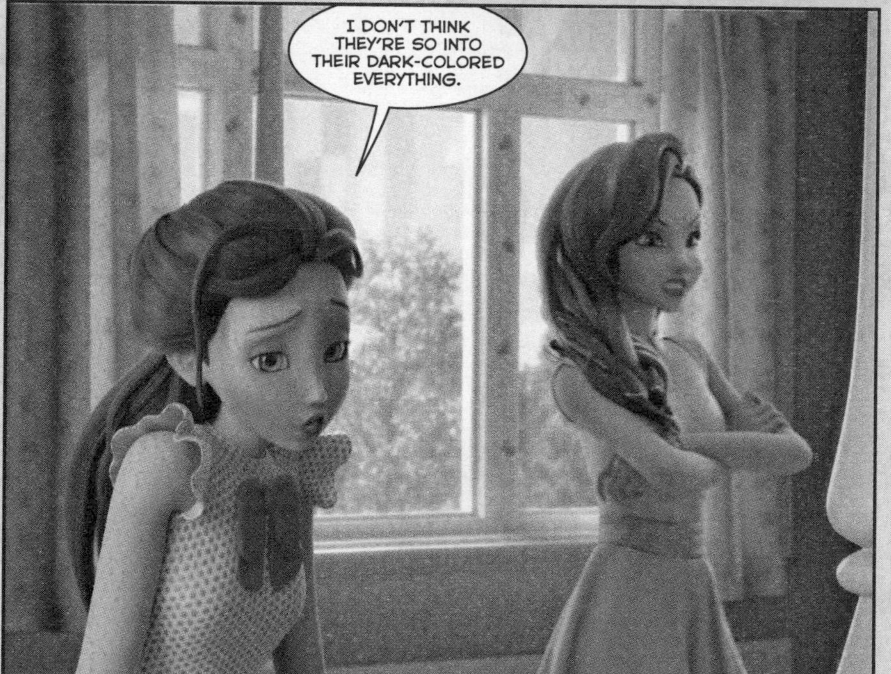
I DON'T THINK THEY'RE SO INTO THEIR DARK-COLORED EVERYTHING.

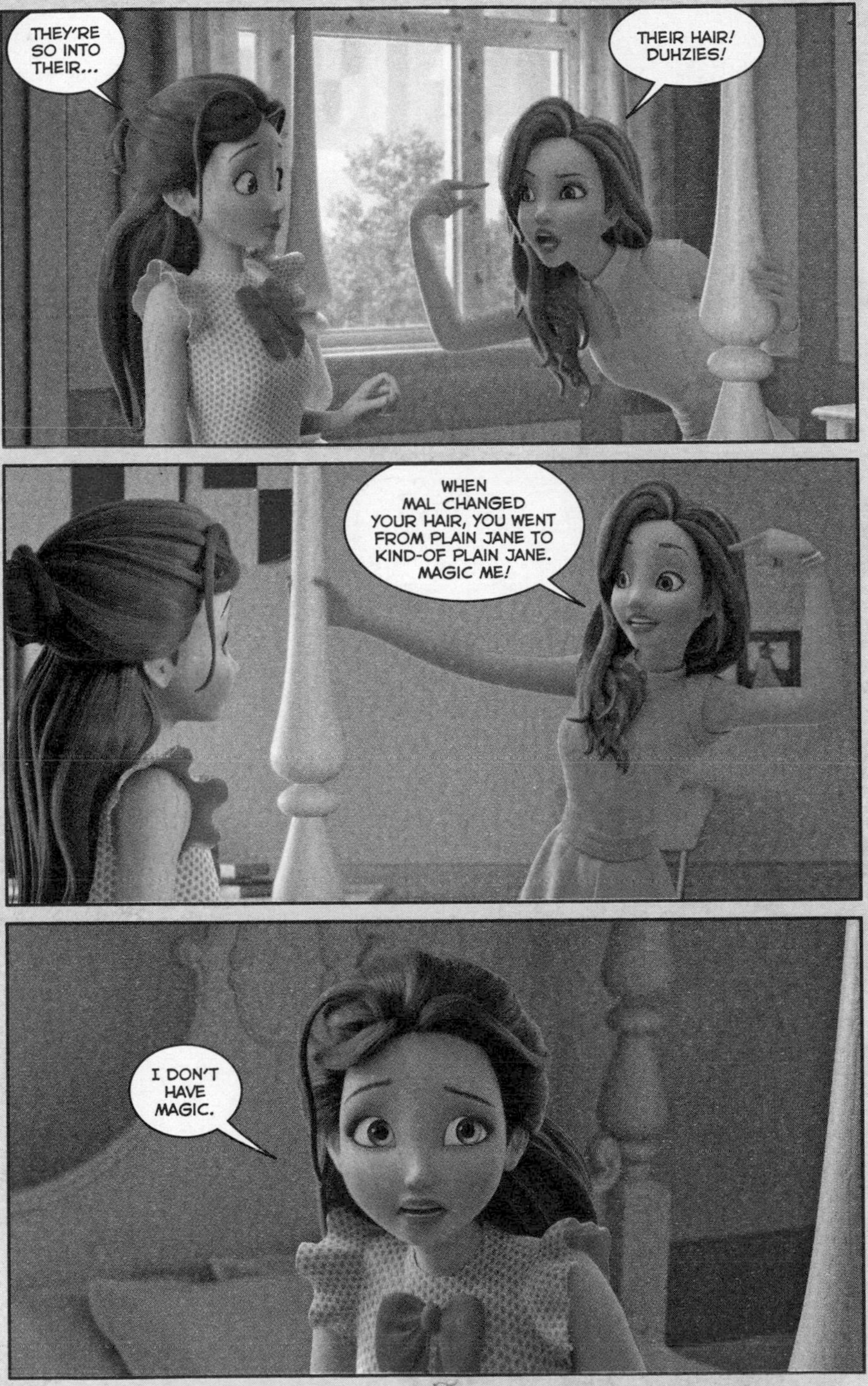
THEY'RE SO INTO THEIR...
THEIR HAIR! DUHZIES!
WHEN MAL CHANGED YOUR HAIR, YOU WENT FROM PLAIN JANE TO KIND-OF PLAIN JANE. MAGIC ME!
I DON'T HAVE MAGIC.

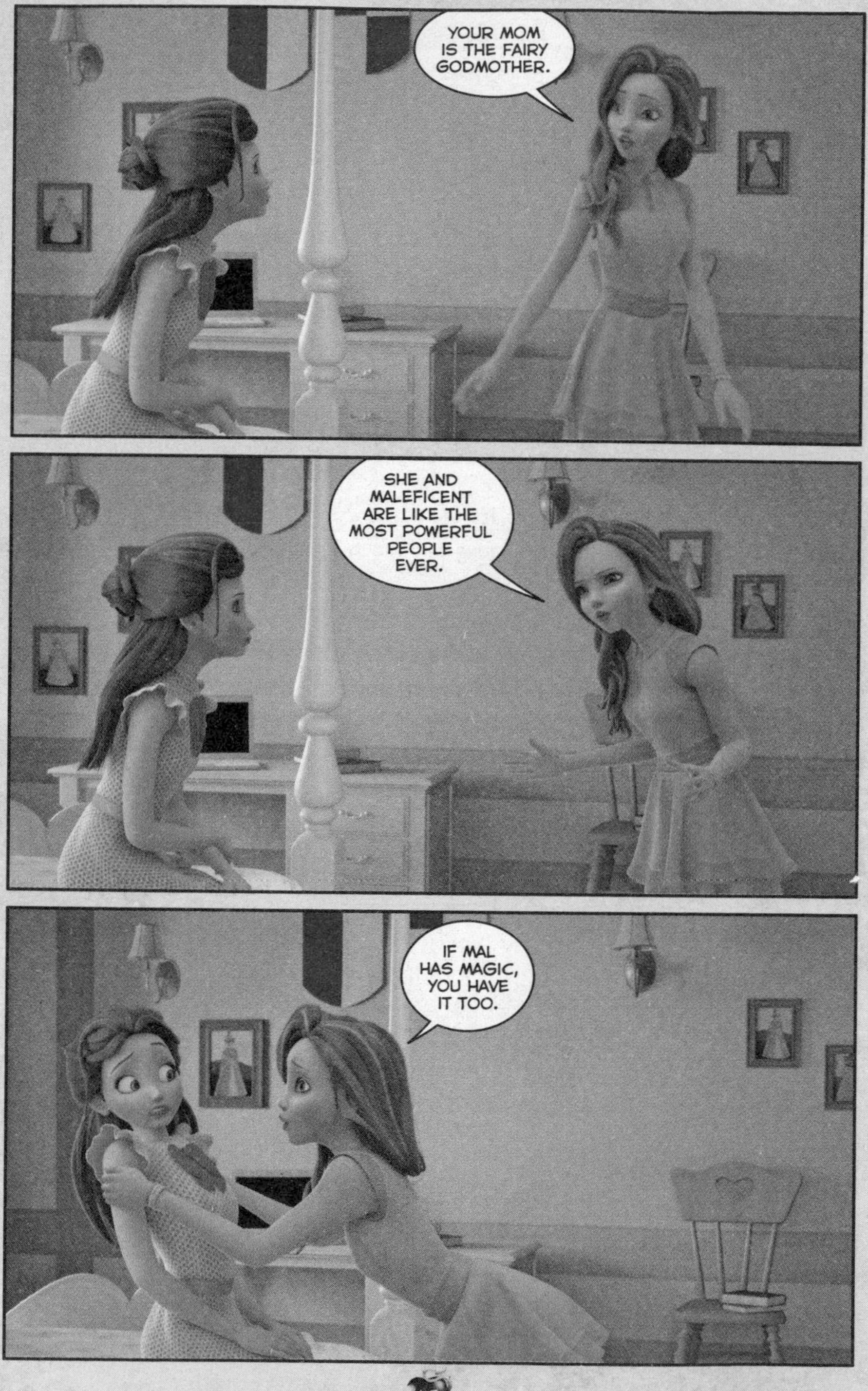
YOUR MOM IS THE FAIRY GODMOTHER.
SHE AND MALEFICENT ARE LIKE THE MOST POWERFUL PEOPLE EVER.
IF MAL HAS MAGIC, YOU HAVE IT TOO.

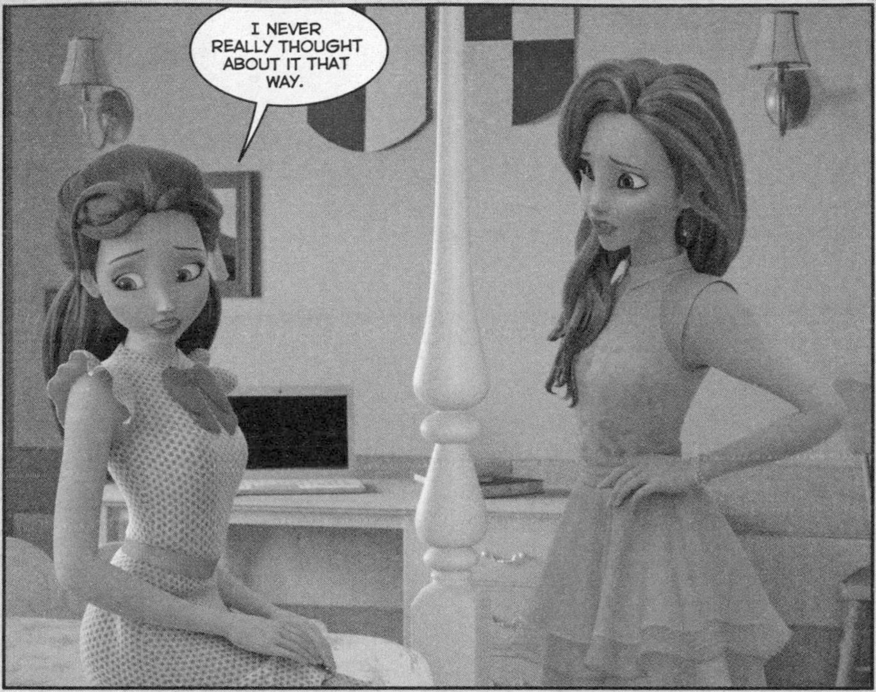
I NEVER REALLY THOUGHT ABOUT IT THAT WAY.

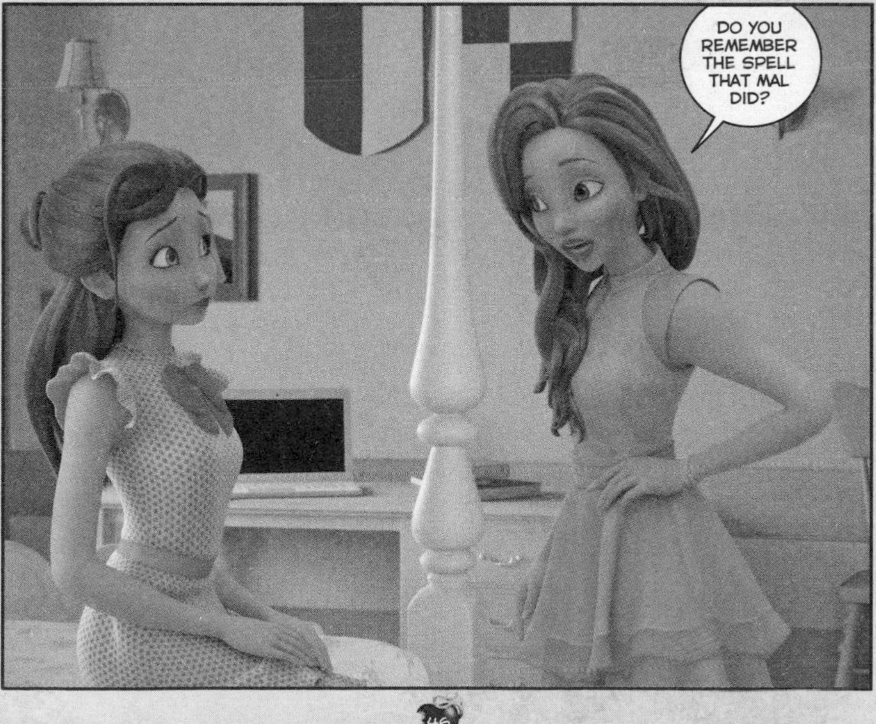
DO YOU REMEMBER THE SPELL THAT MAL DID?

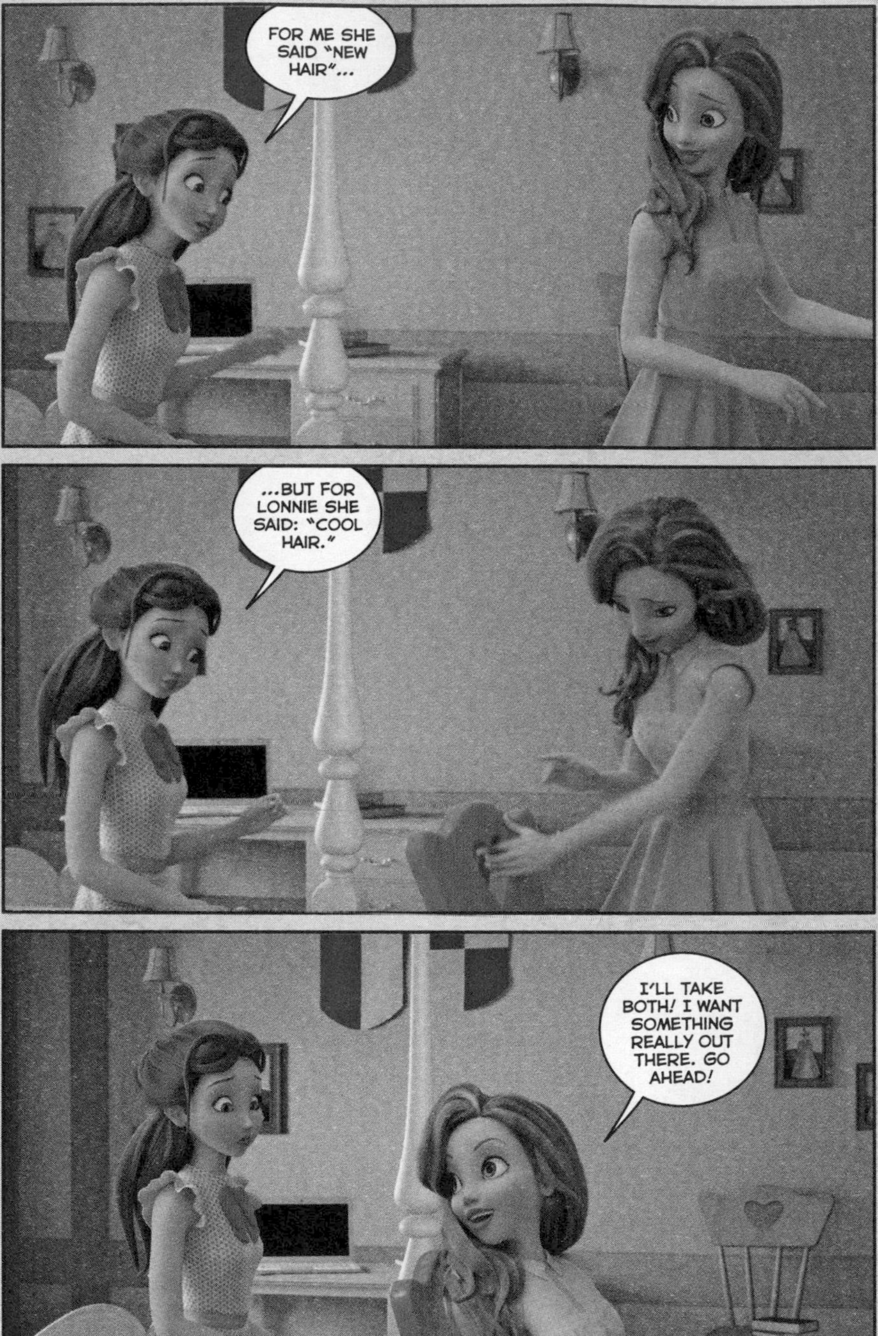
FOR ME SHE SAID "NEW HAIR"...
...BUT FOR LONNIE SHE SAID: "COOL HAIR."
I'LL TAKE BOTH! I WANT SOMETHING REALLY OUT THERE. GO AHEAD!

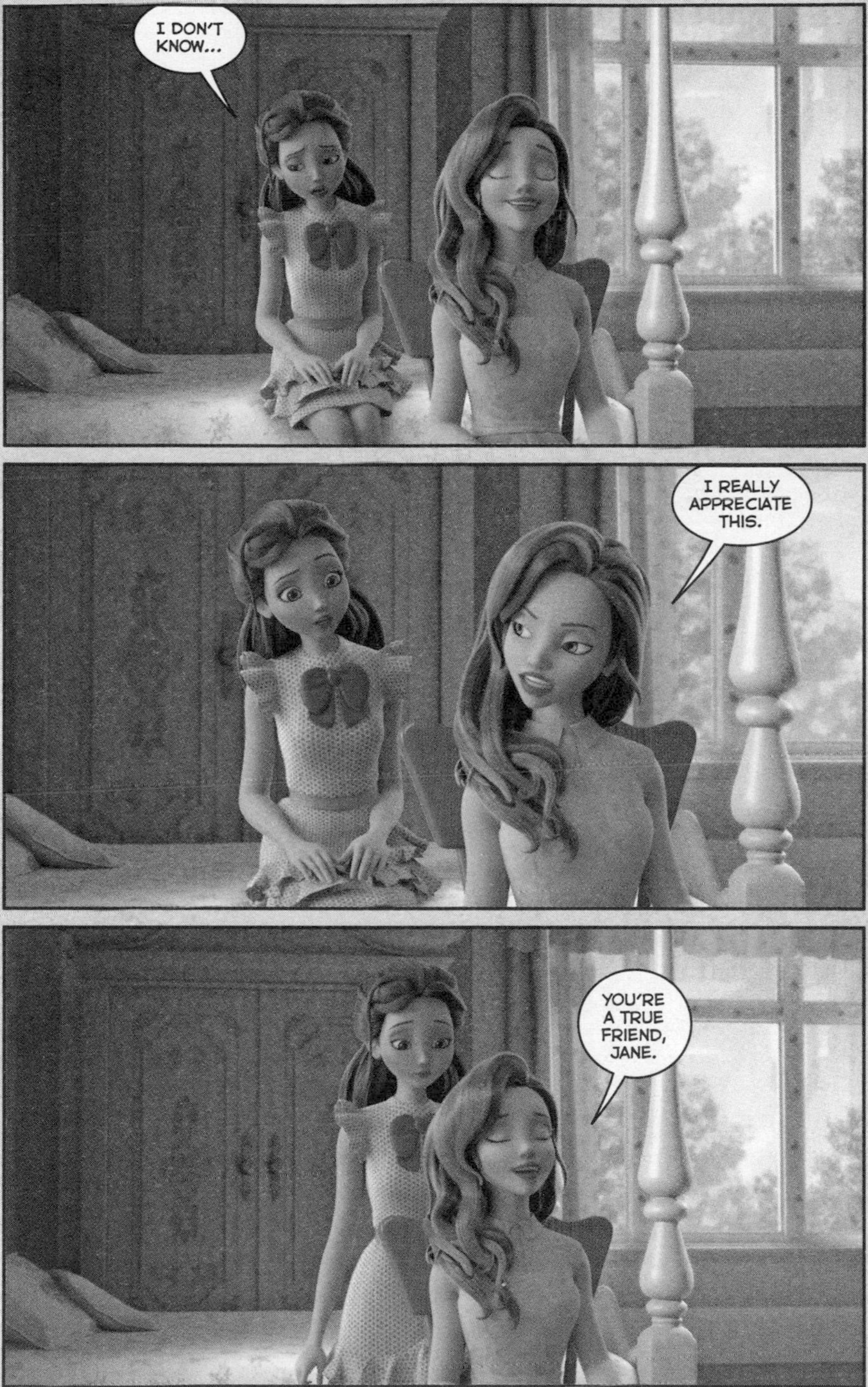
I DON'T KNOW...
I REALLY APPRECIATE THIS.
YOU'RE A TRUE FRIEND, JANE.

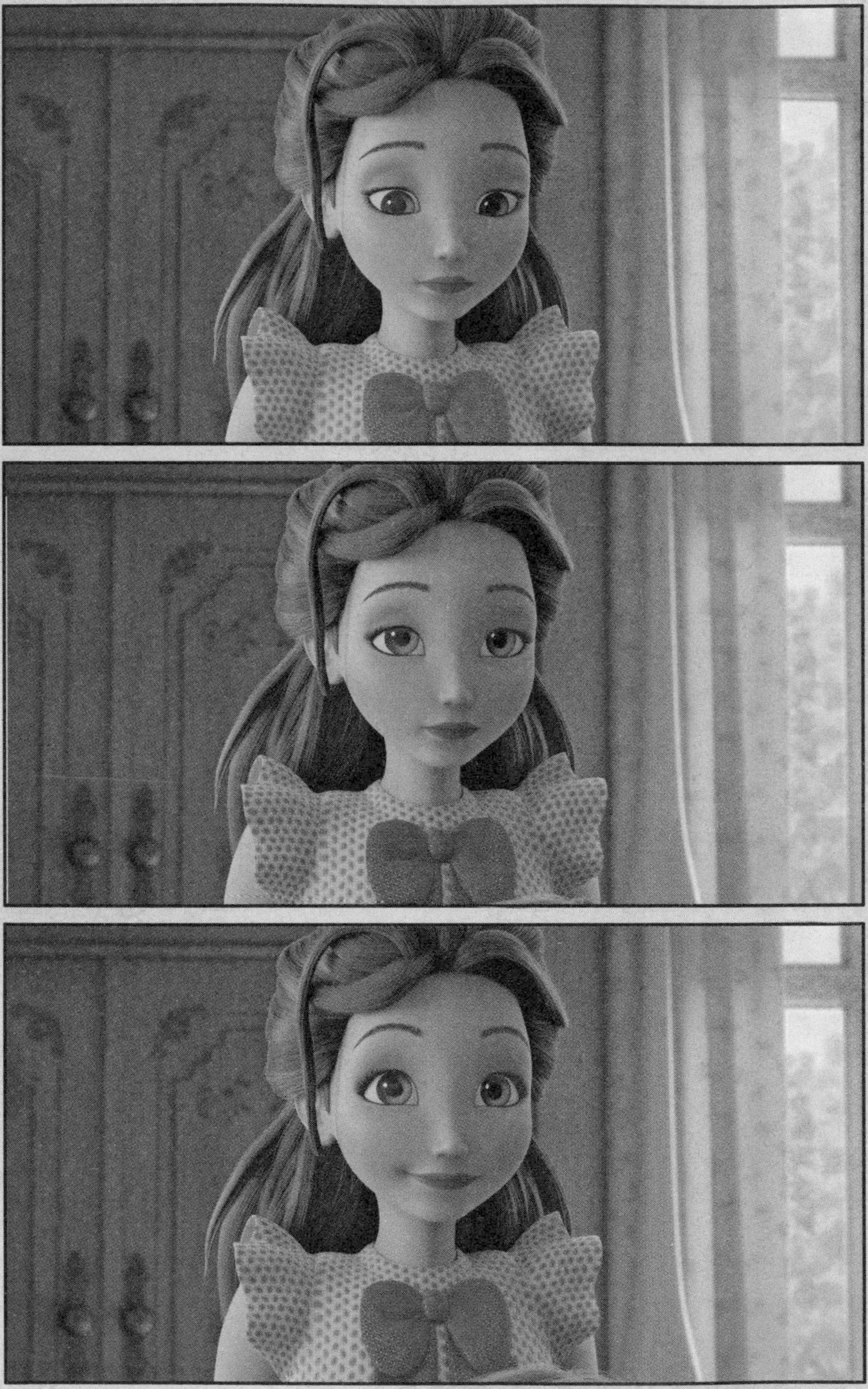

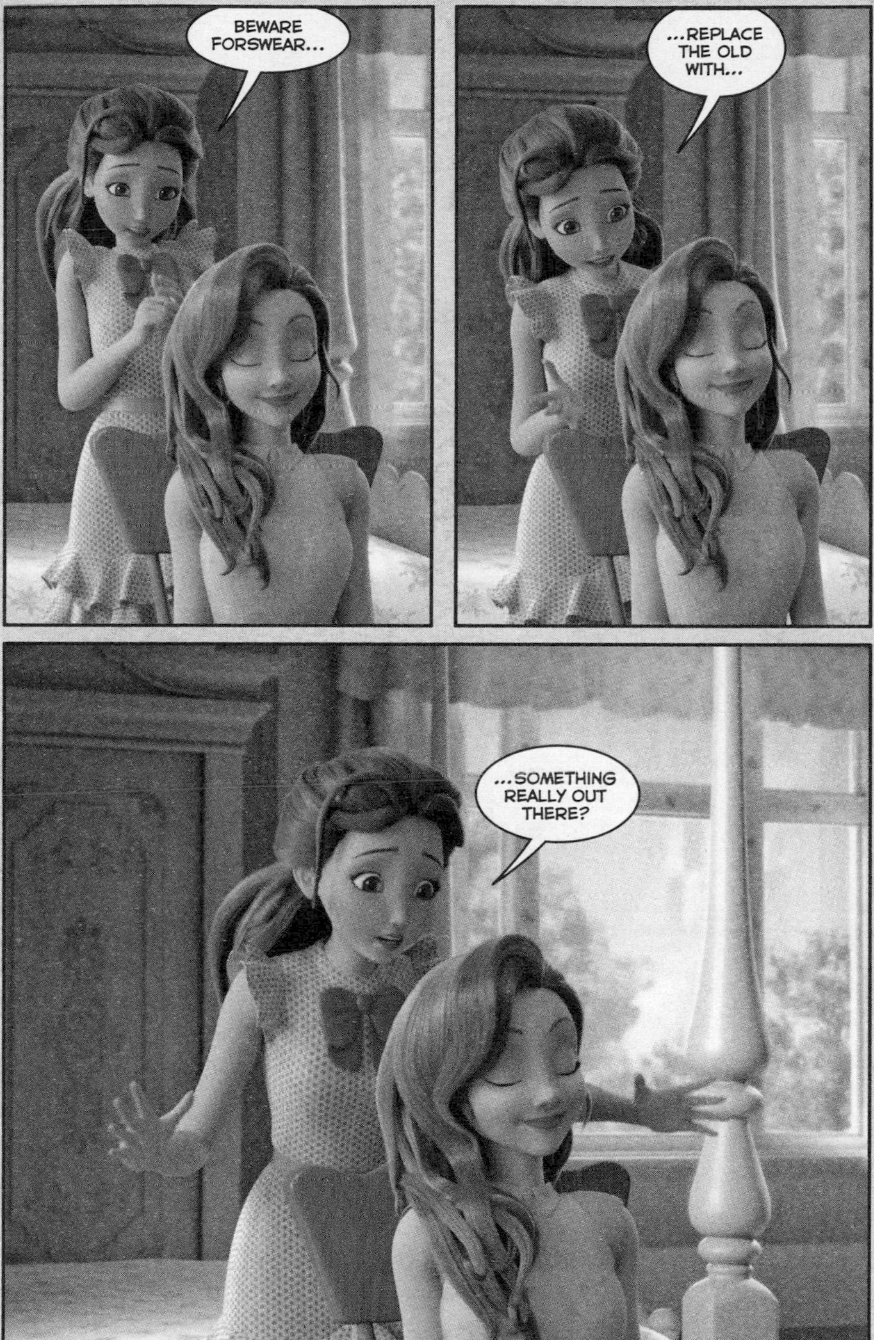
BEWARE FORSWEAR...
...REPLACE THE OLD WITH...
...SOMETHING REALLY OUT THERE?

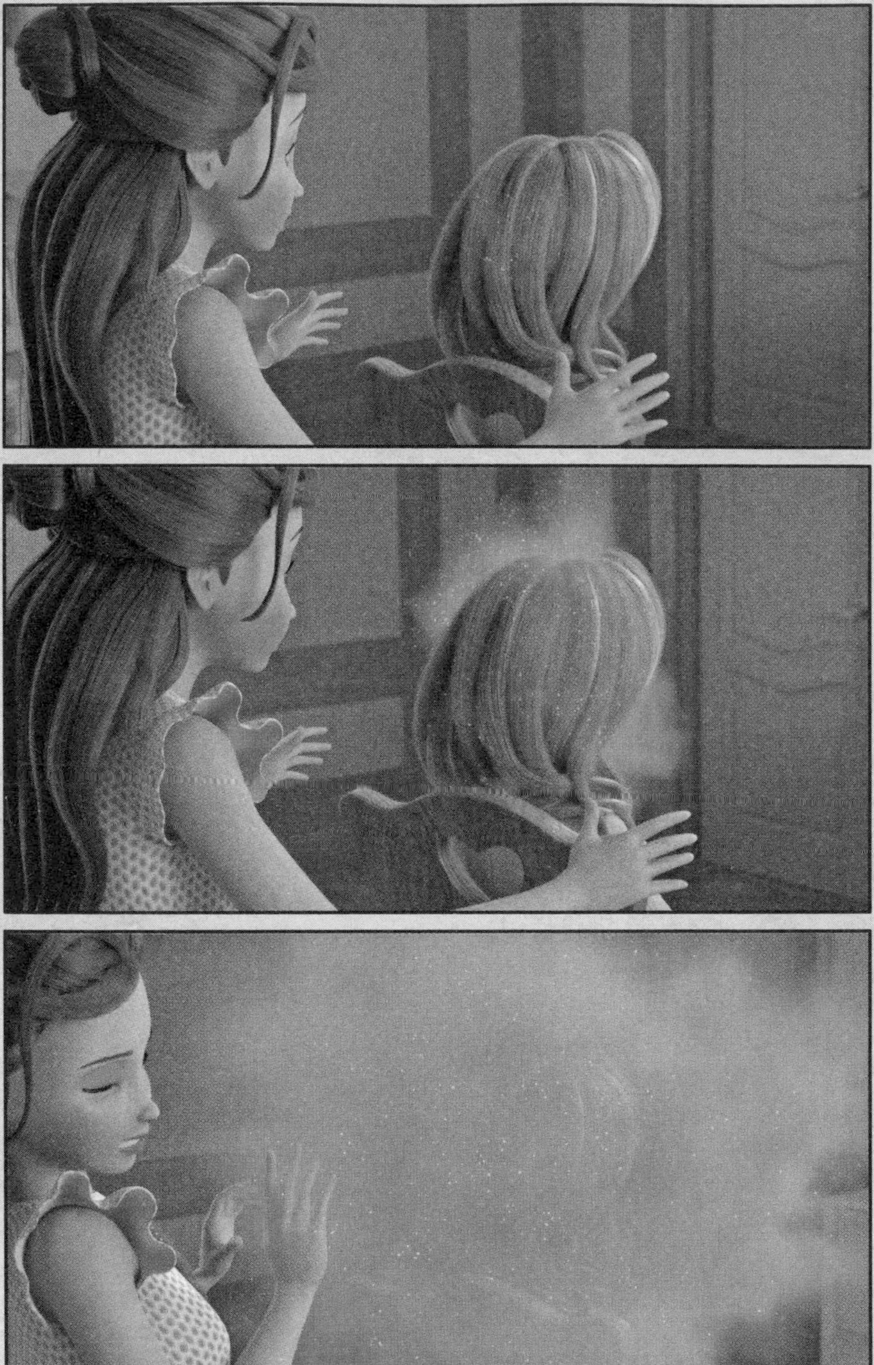

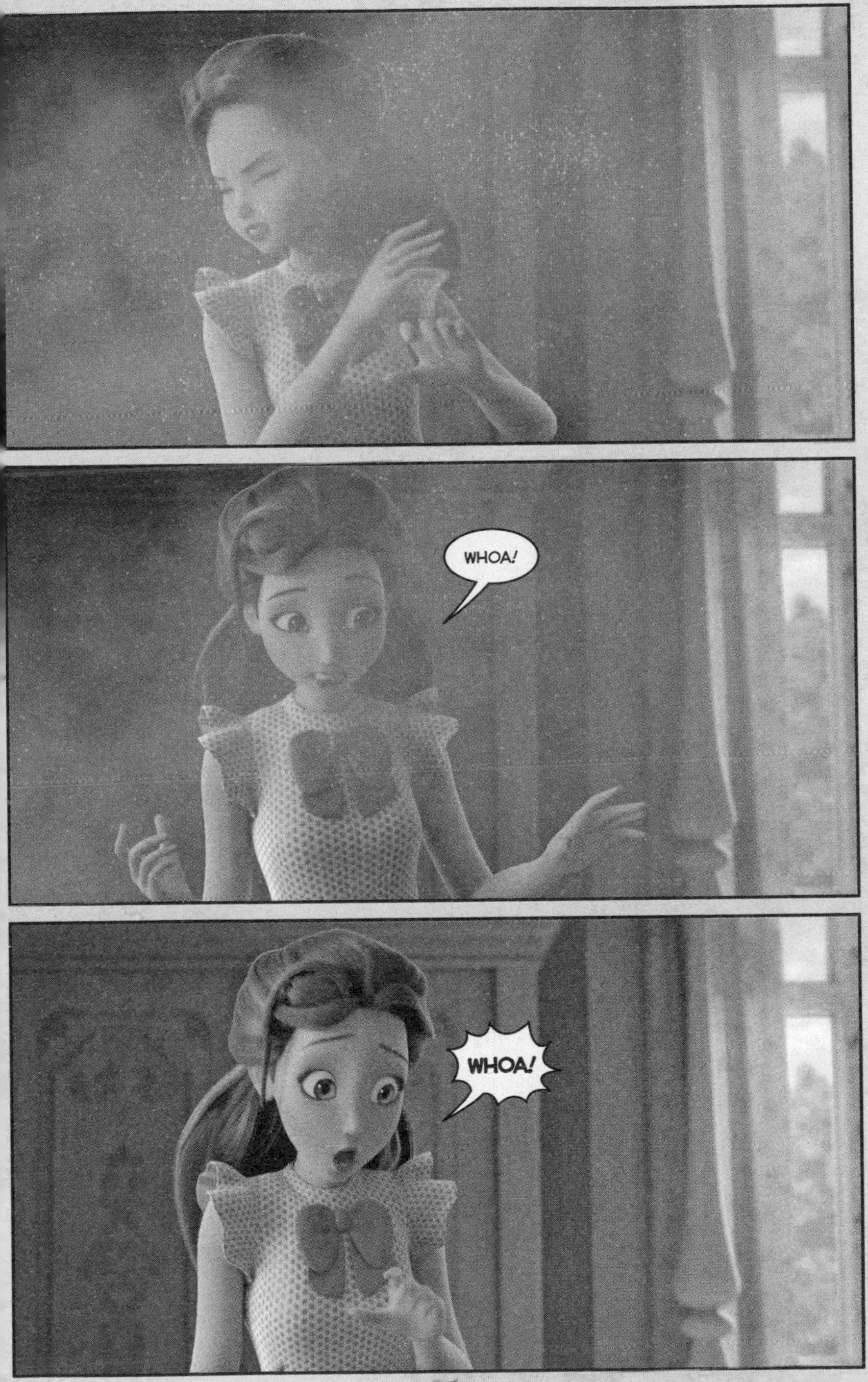
WHOA!
WHOA!

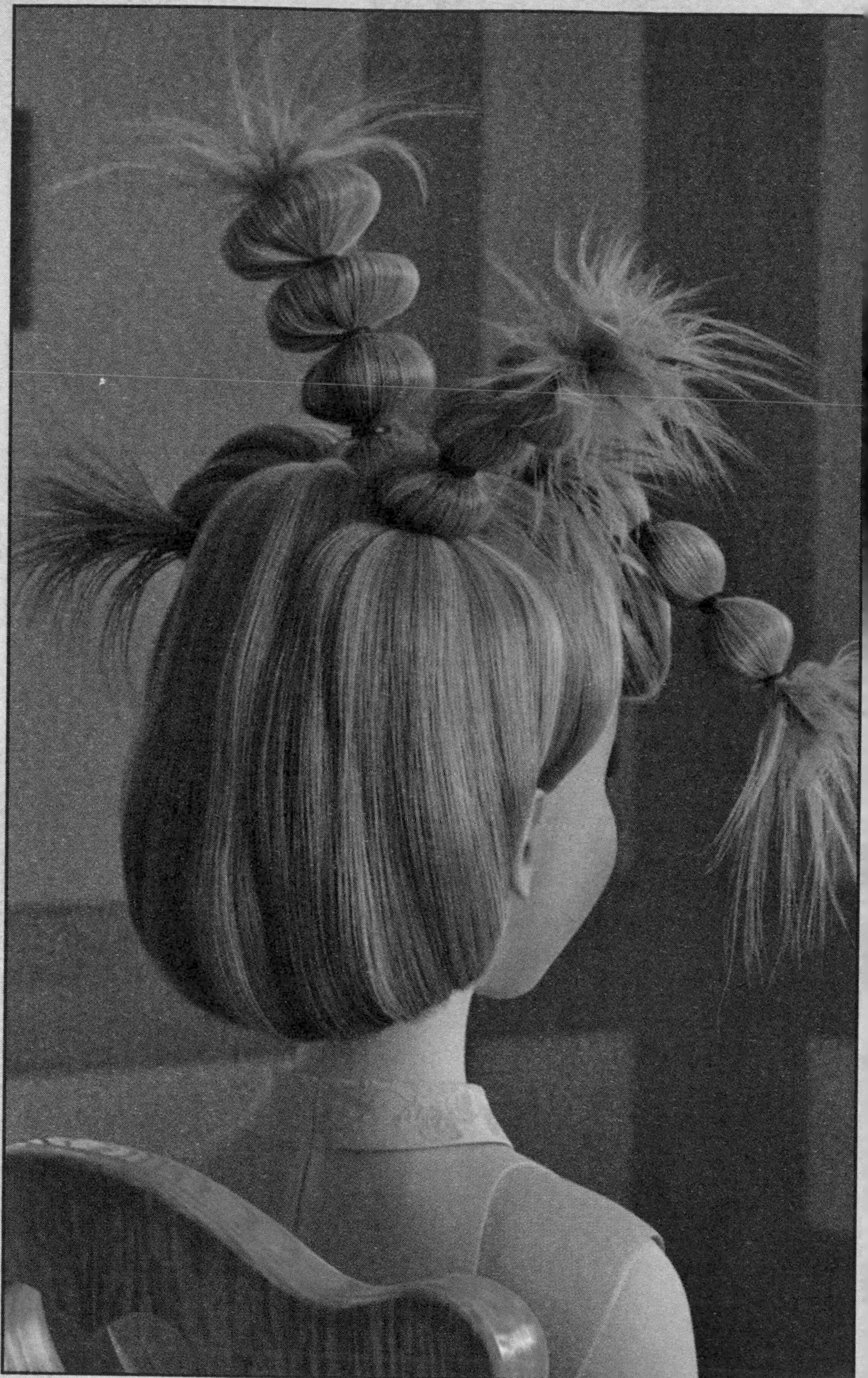

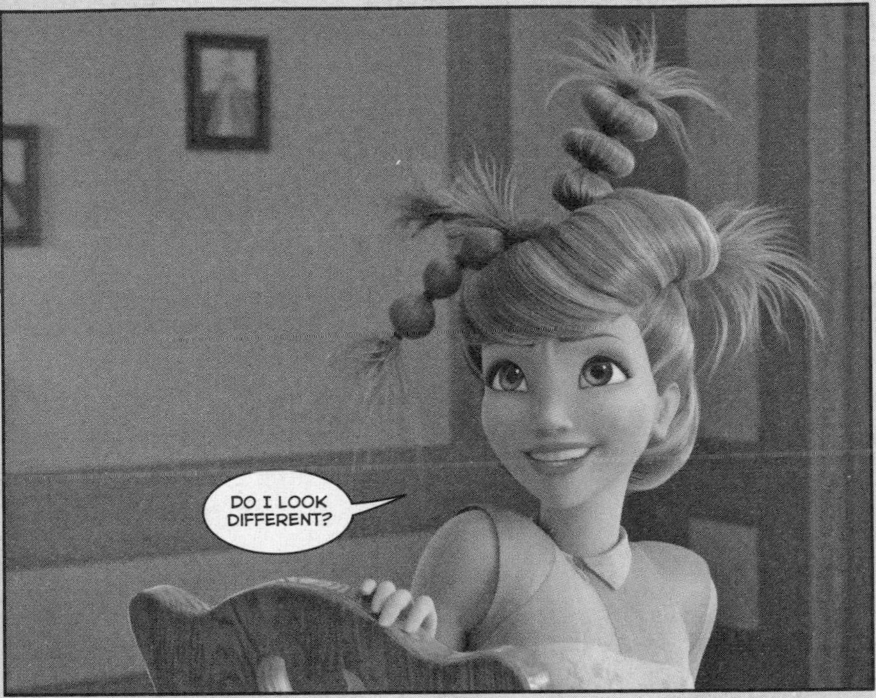
DO I LOOK DIFFERENT?

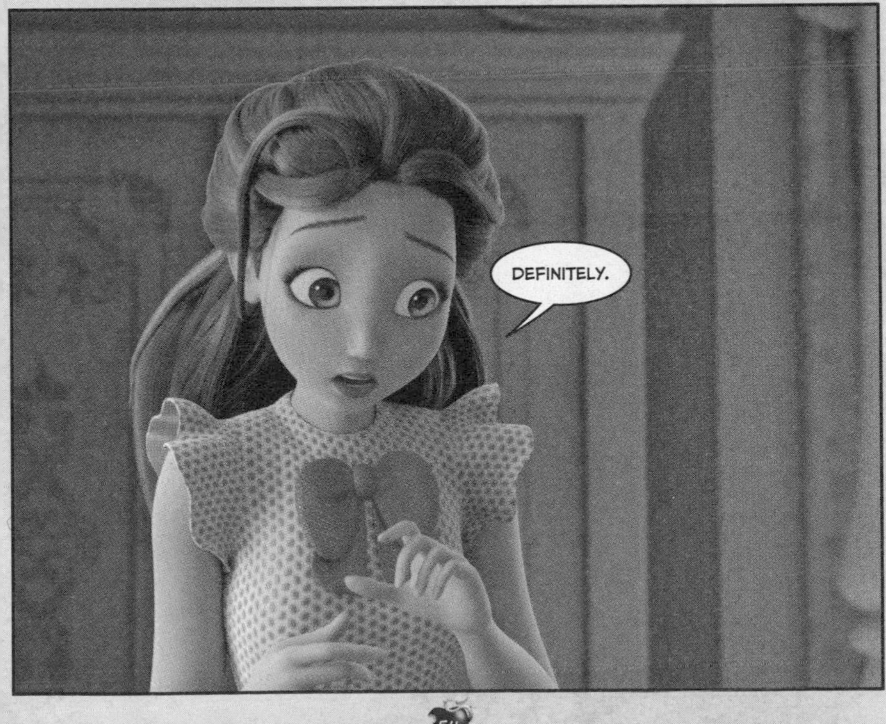
DEFINITELY.

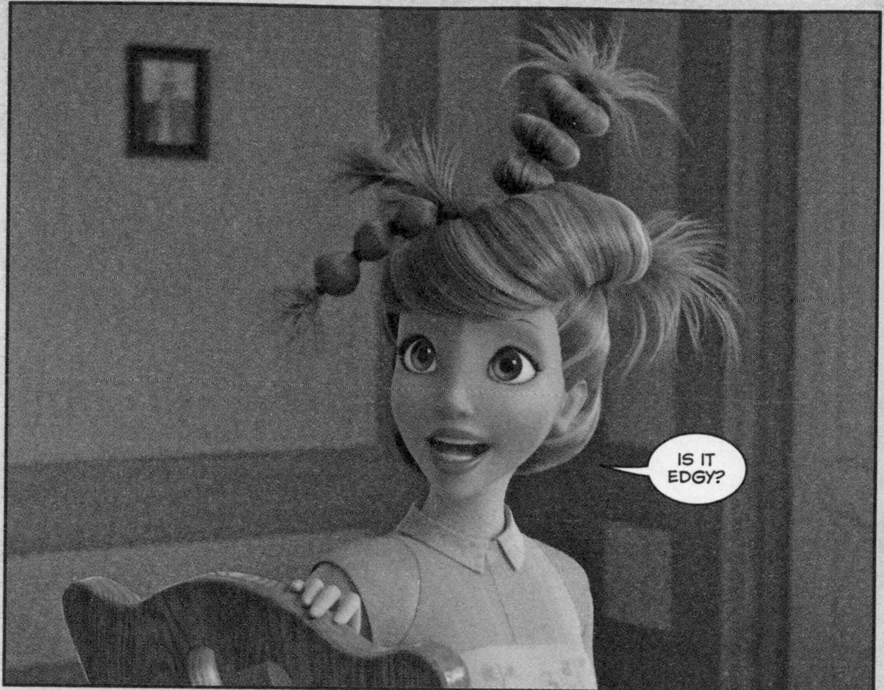
IS IT
EDGY?

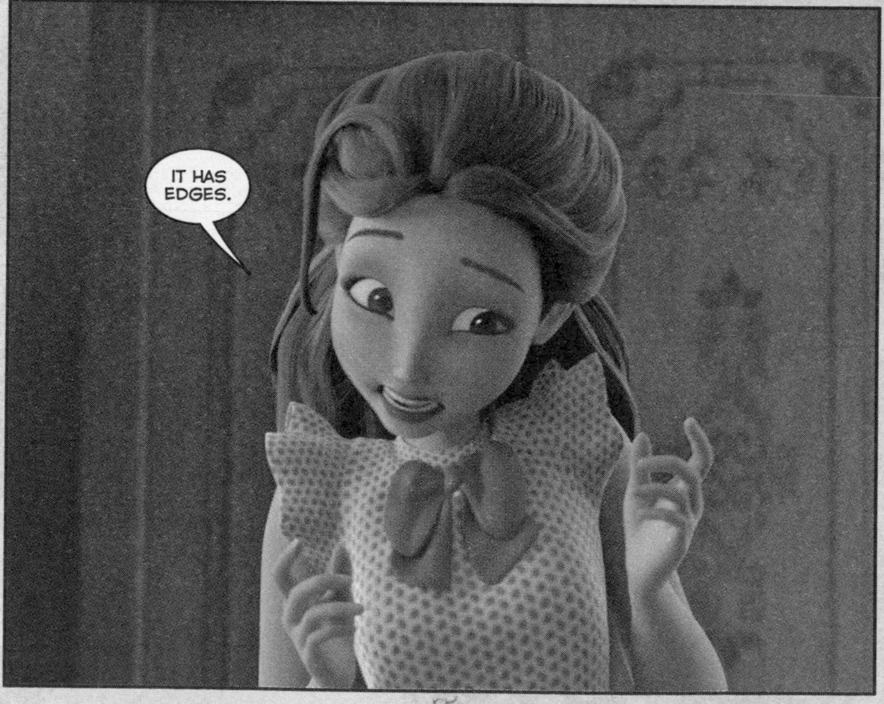
IT HAS
EDGES.

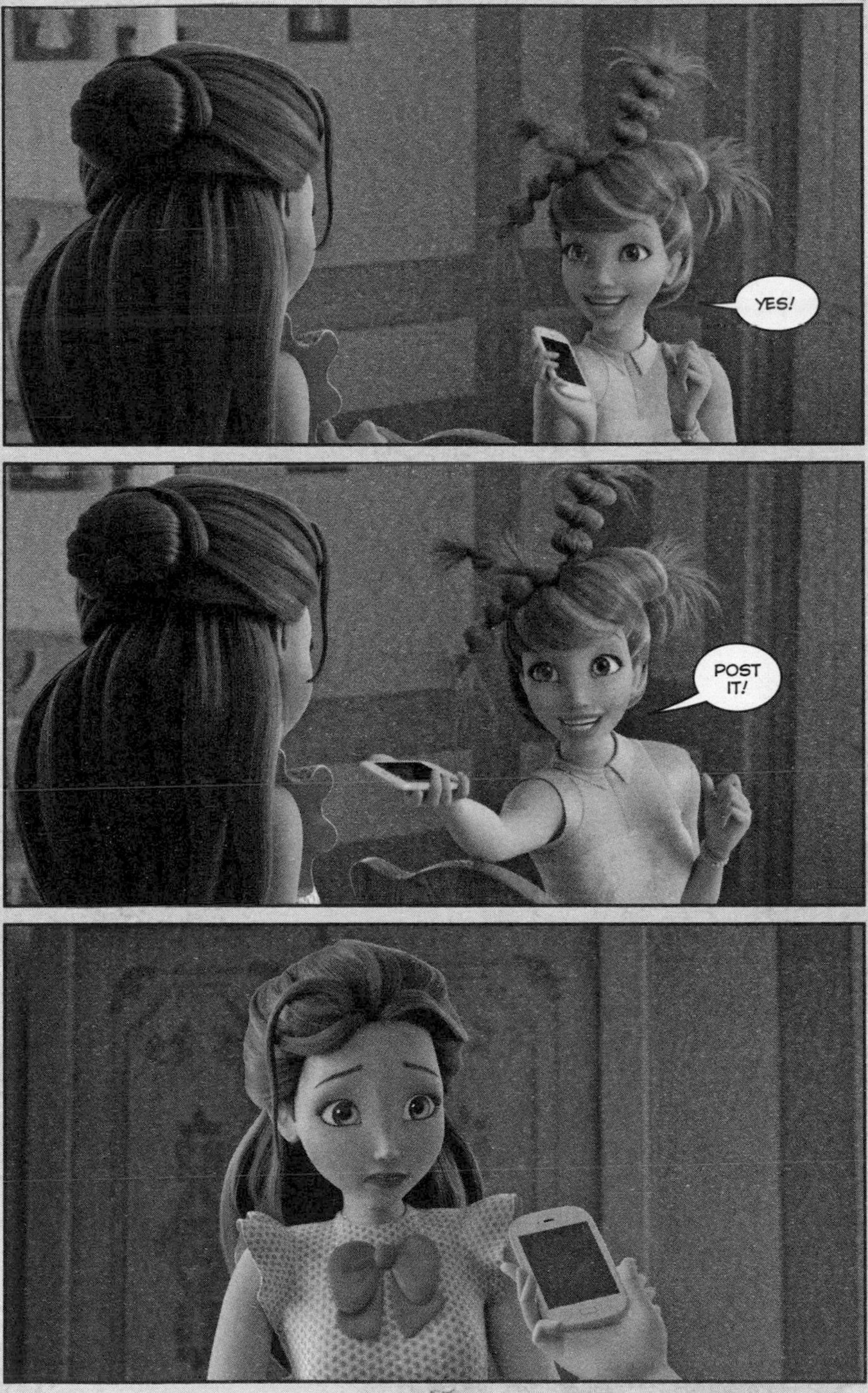
YES!
POST IT!

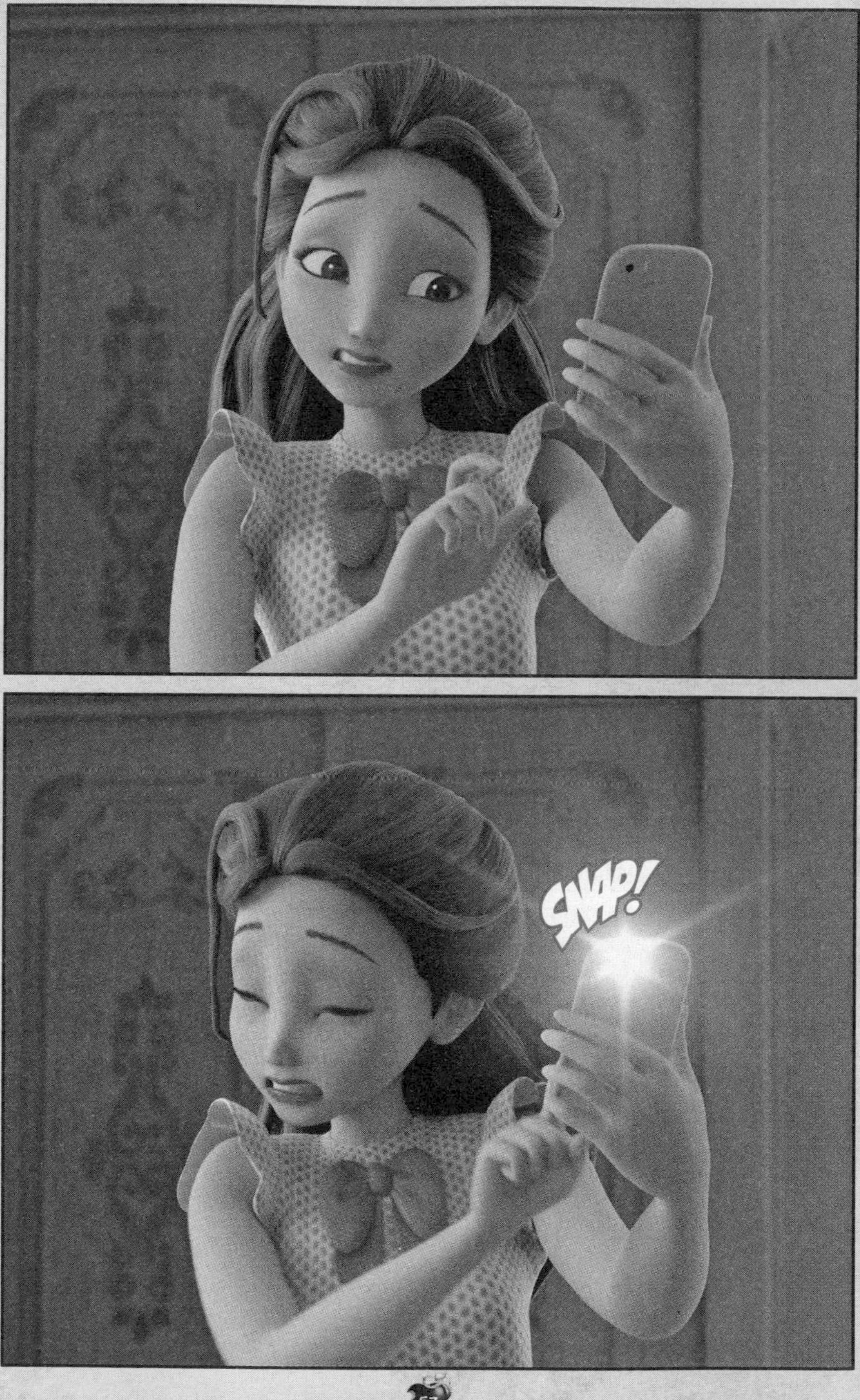
SNAP!

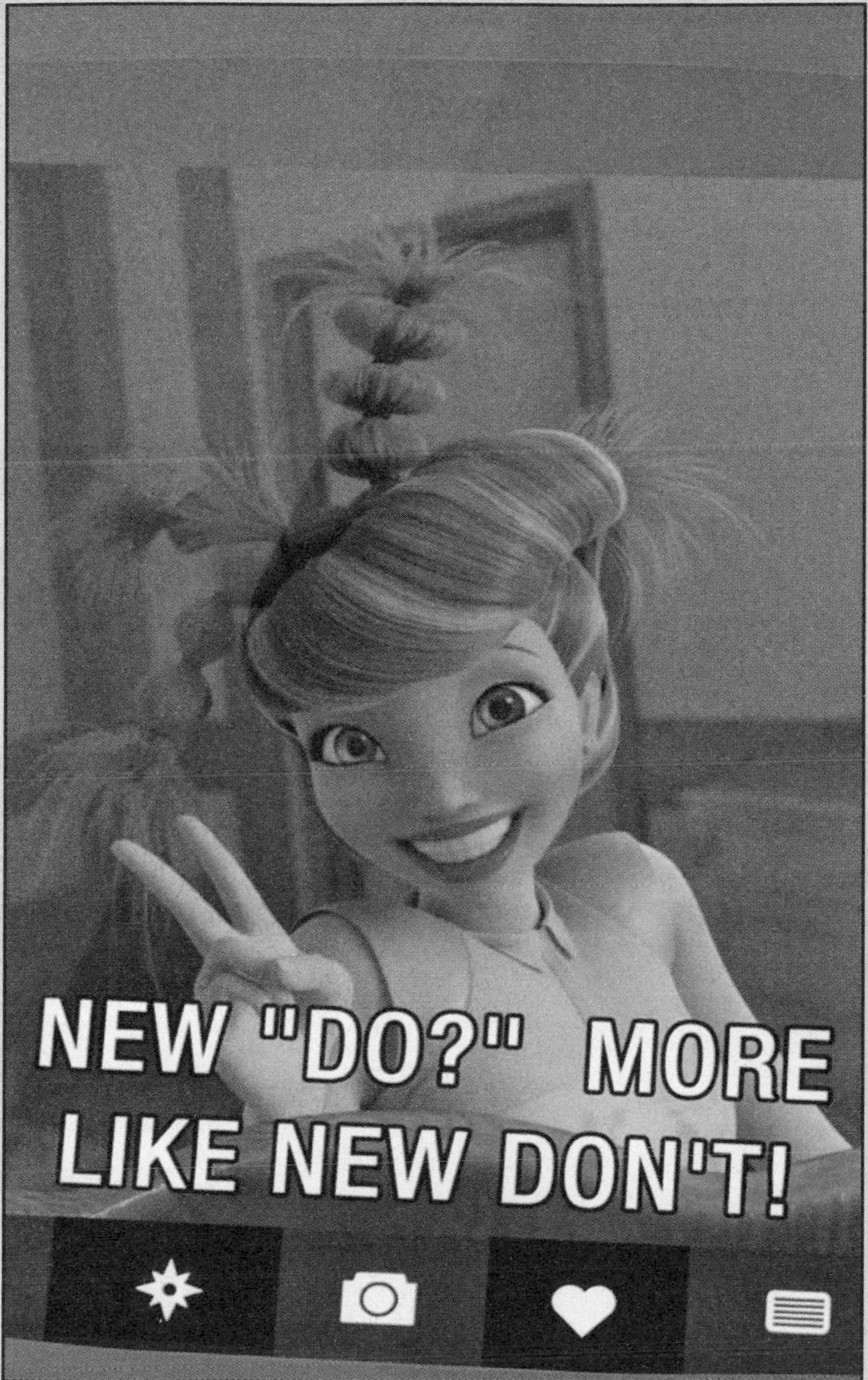
NEW "DO?" MORE
LIKE NEW DON'T!

CHAPTER 4: CAREFUL WHAT YOU WISH FOR

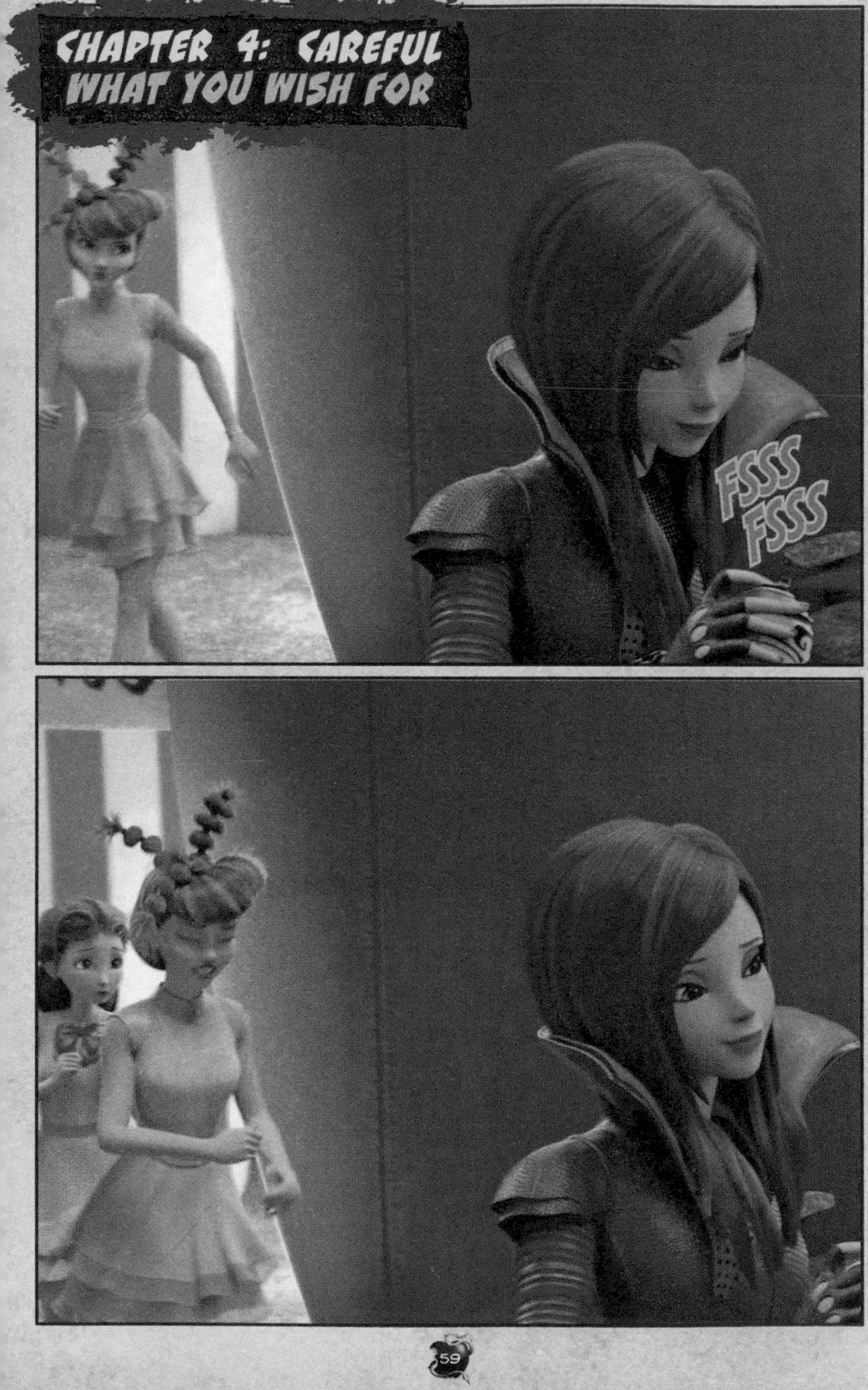
FSSS
FSSS

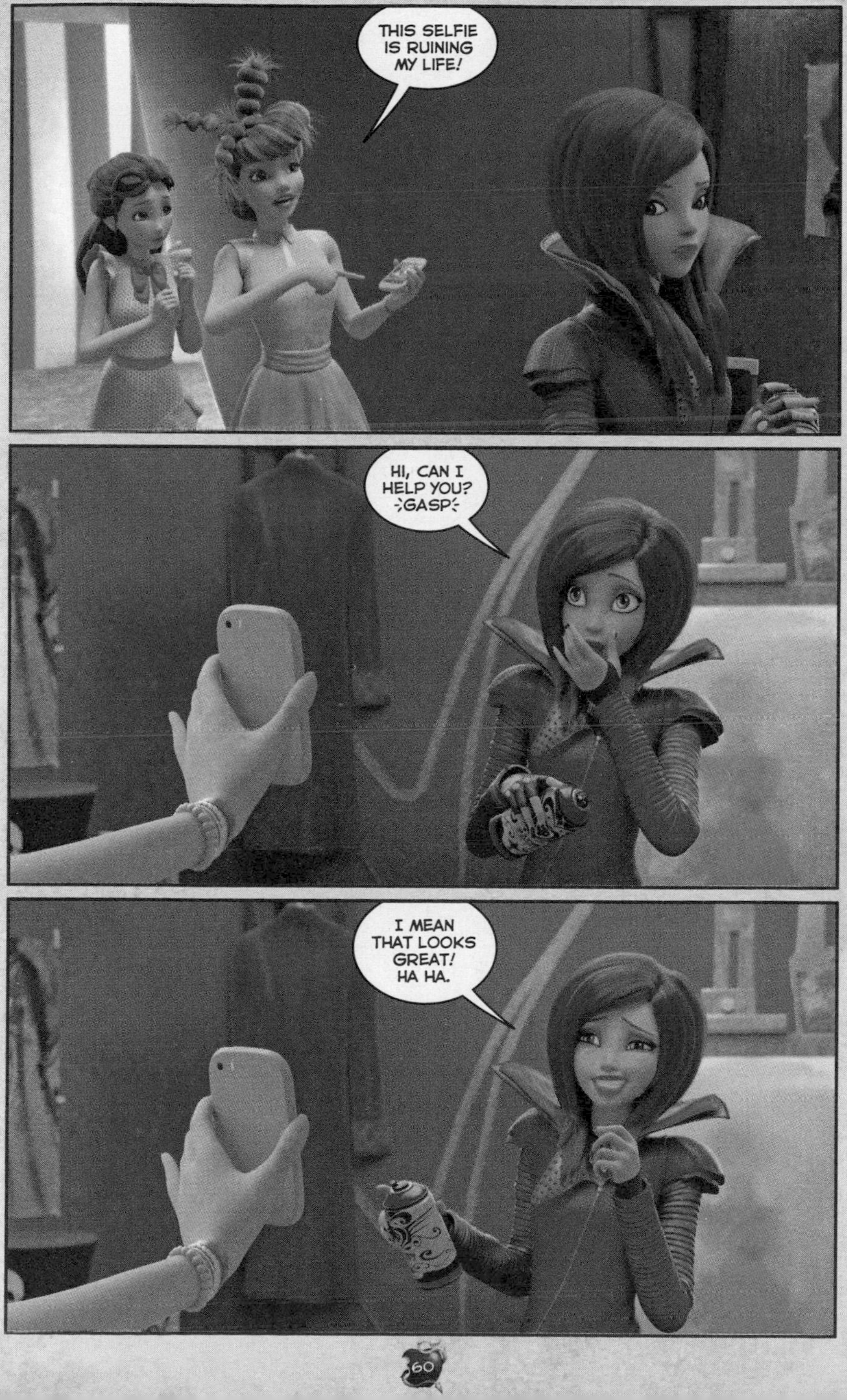
THIS SELFIE IS RUINING MY LIFE!
HI, CAN I HELP YOU? GASP
I MEAN THAT LOOKS GREAT! HA HA.

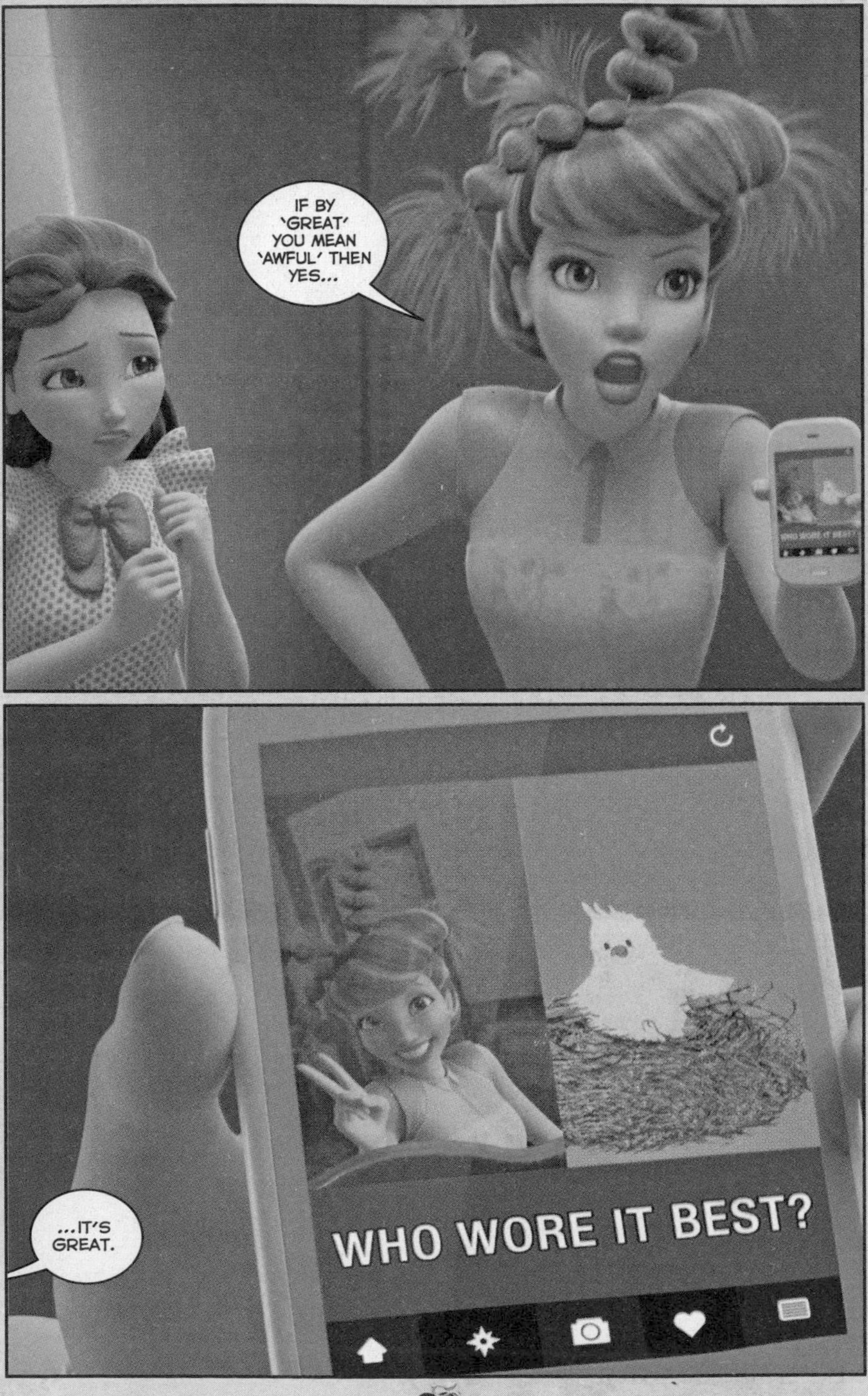
IF BY 'GREAT' YOU MEAN 'AWFUL' THEN YES...
WHO WORE IT BEST?
...IT'S GREAT.

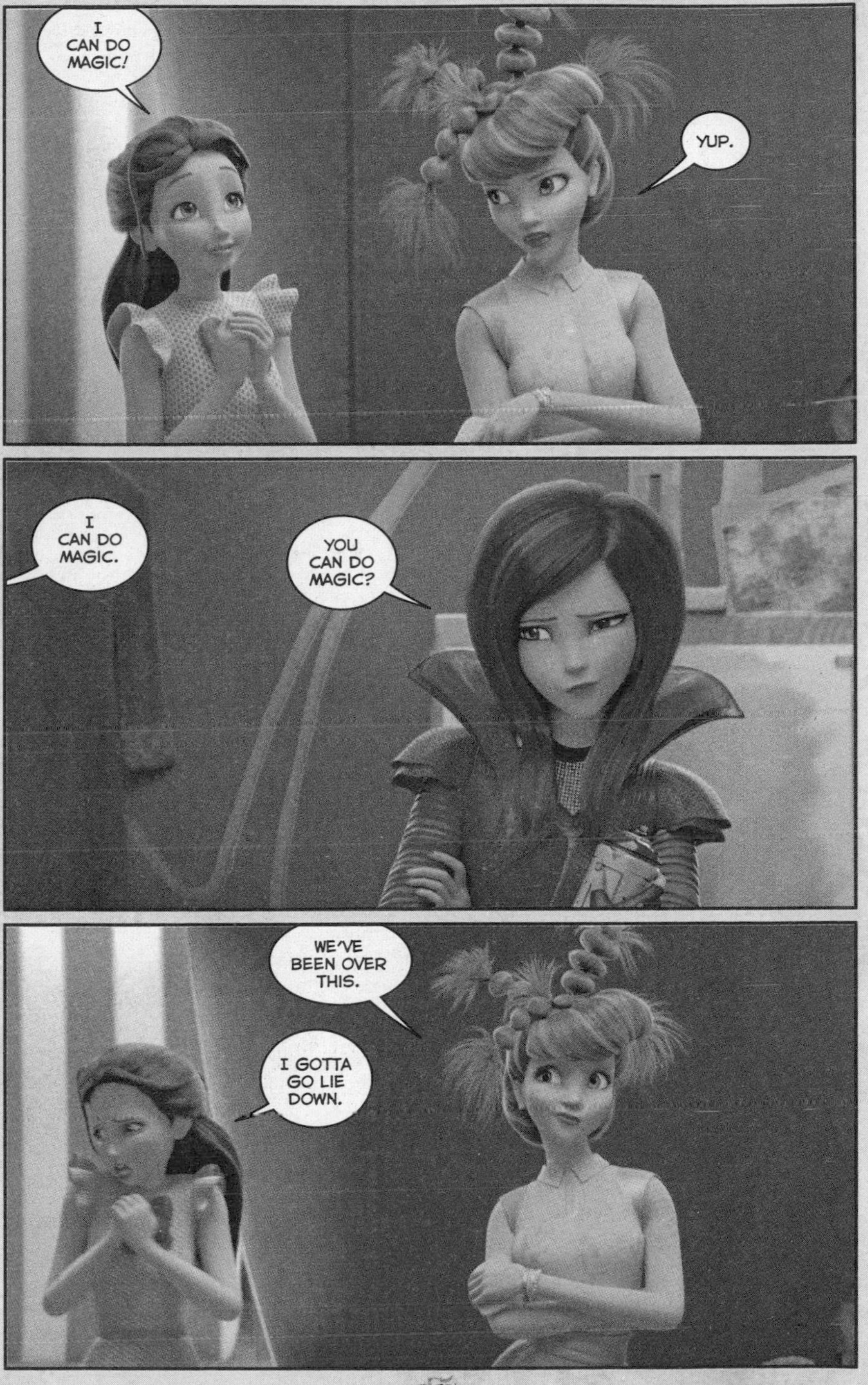
I CAN DO MAGIC!
YUP.
I CAN DO MAGIC.
YOU CAN DO MAGIC?
WE'VE BEEN OVER THIS.
I GOTTA GO LIE DOWN.

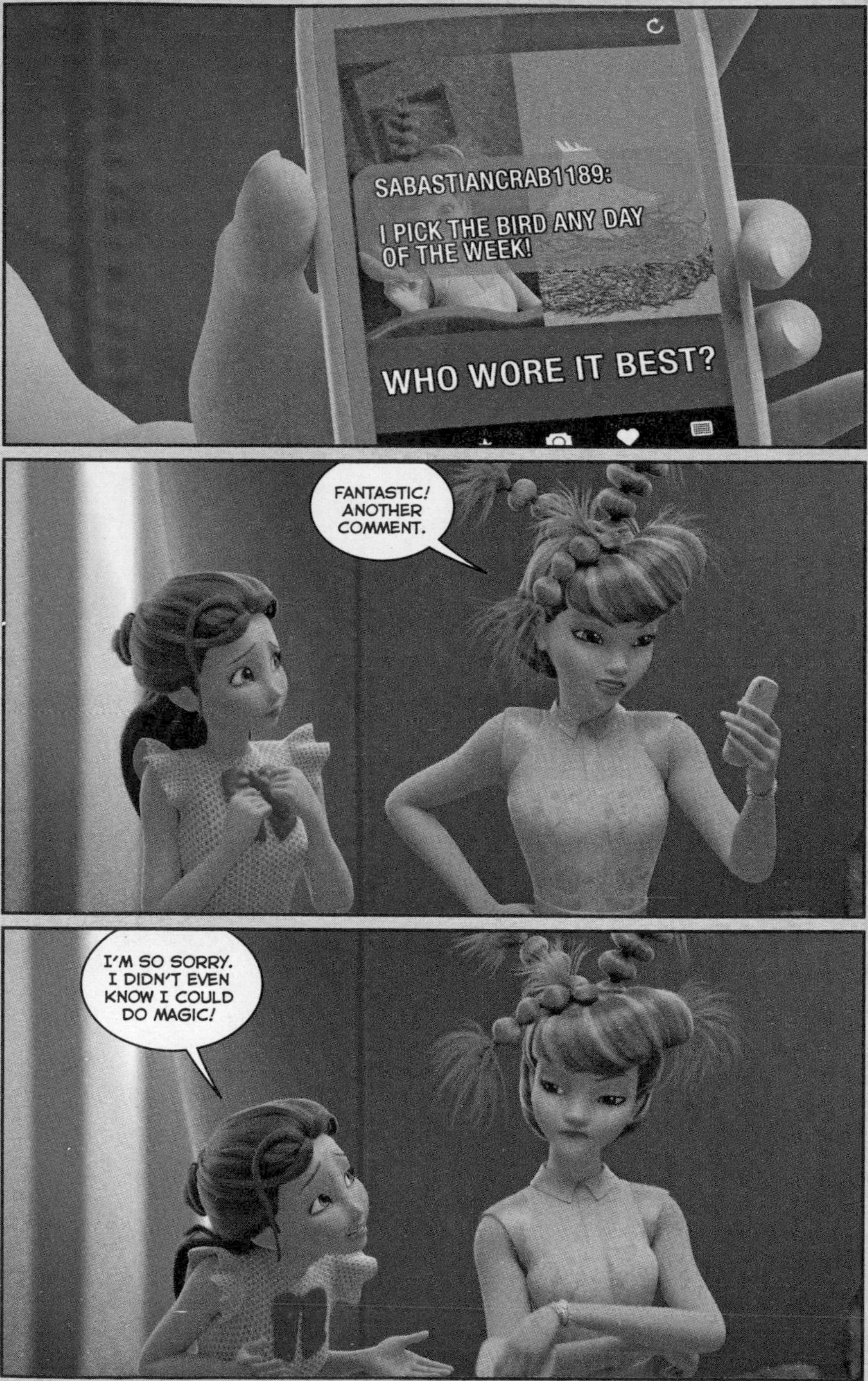
SABASTIANCRAB1189:
I PICK THE BIRD ANY DAY OF THE WEEK!
WHO WORE IT BEST?
FANTASTIC! ANOTHER COMMENT.
I'M SO SORRY. I DIDN'T EVEN KNOW I COULD DO MAGIC!

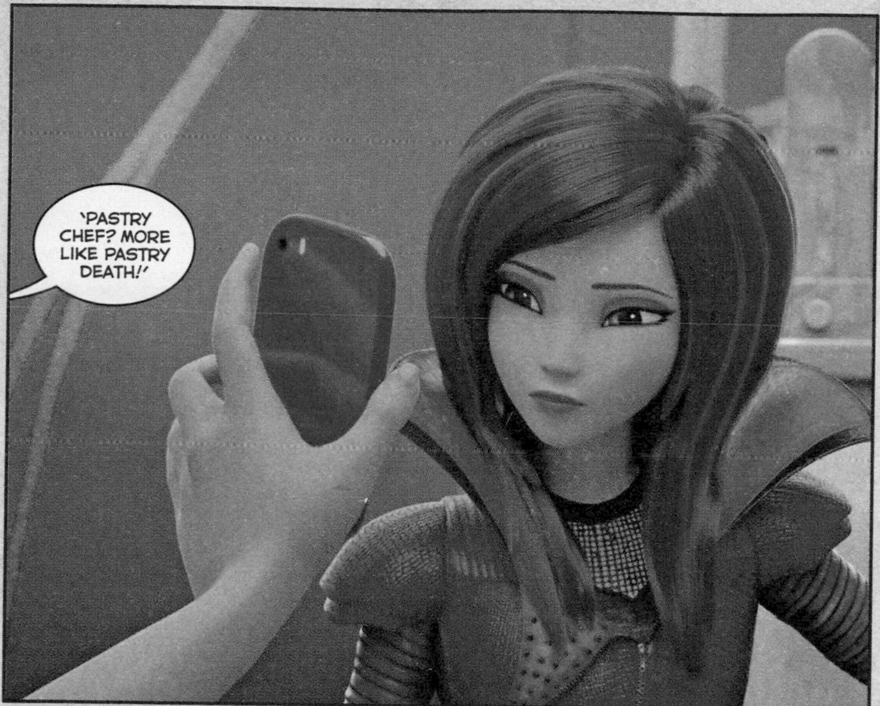
'PASTRY CHEF? MORE LIKE PASTRY DEATH!'

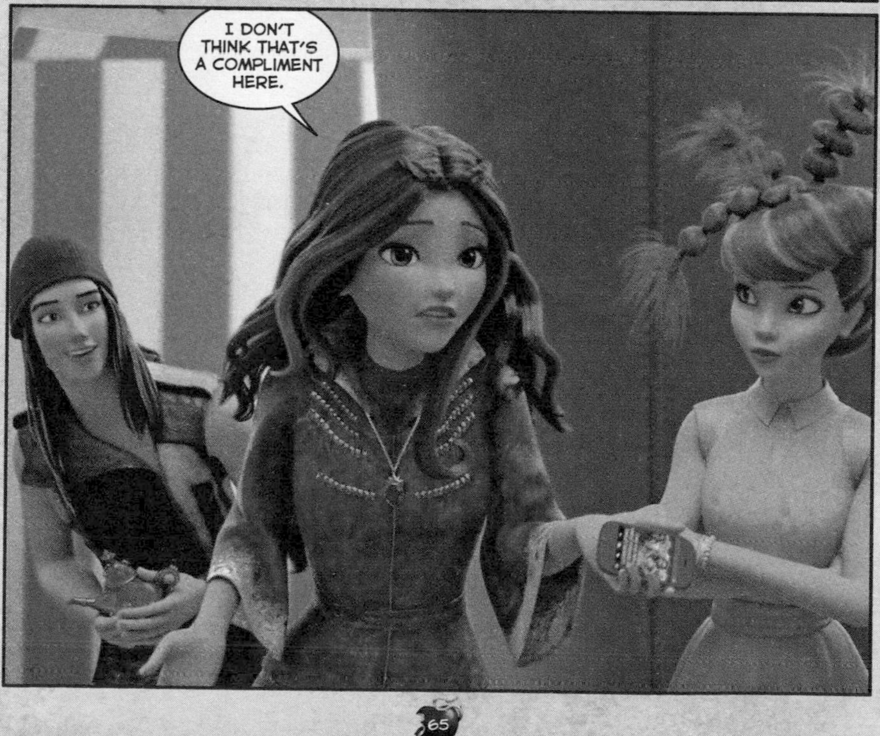
I DON'T THINK THAT'S A COMPLIMENT HERE.

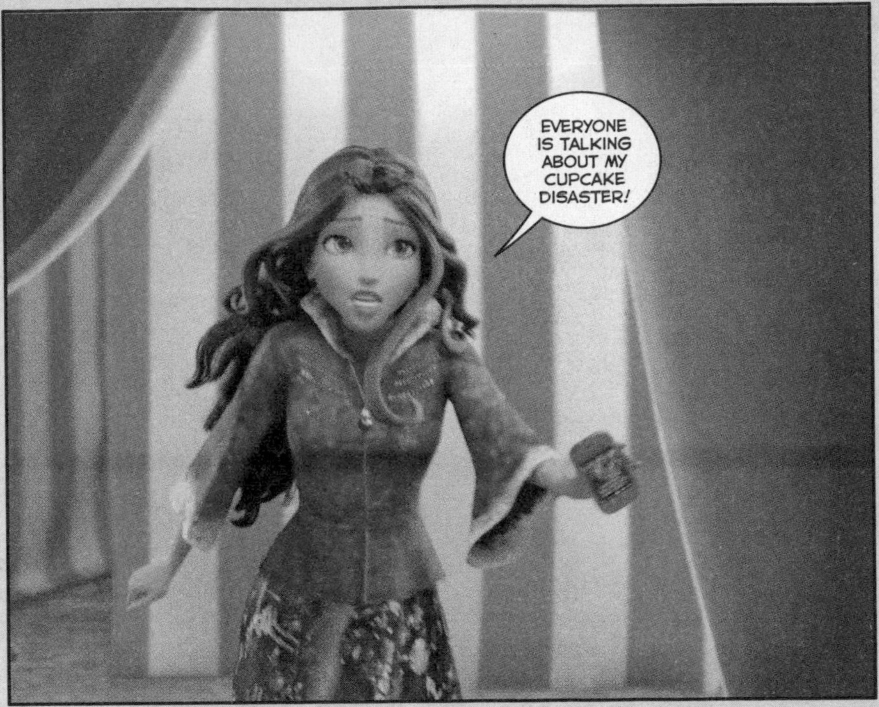
EVERYONE IS TALKING ABOUT MY CUPCAKE DISASTER!

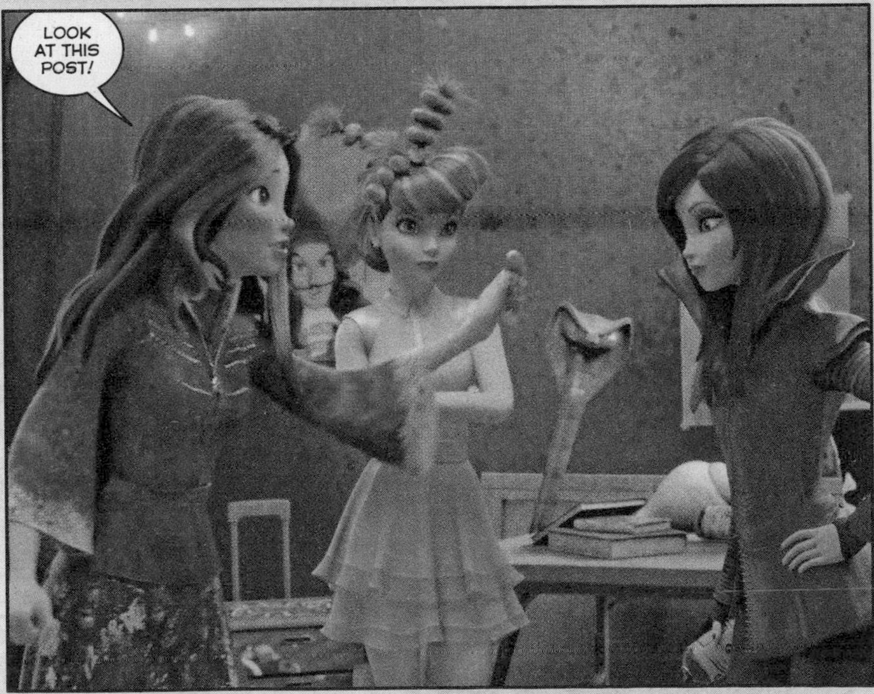
LOOK AT THIS POST!

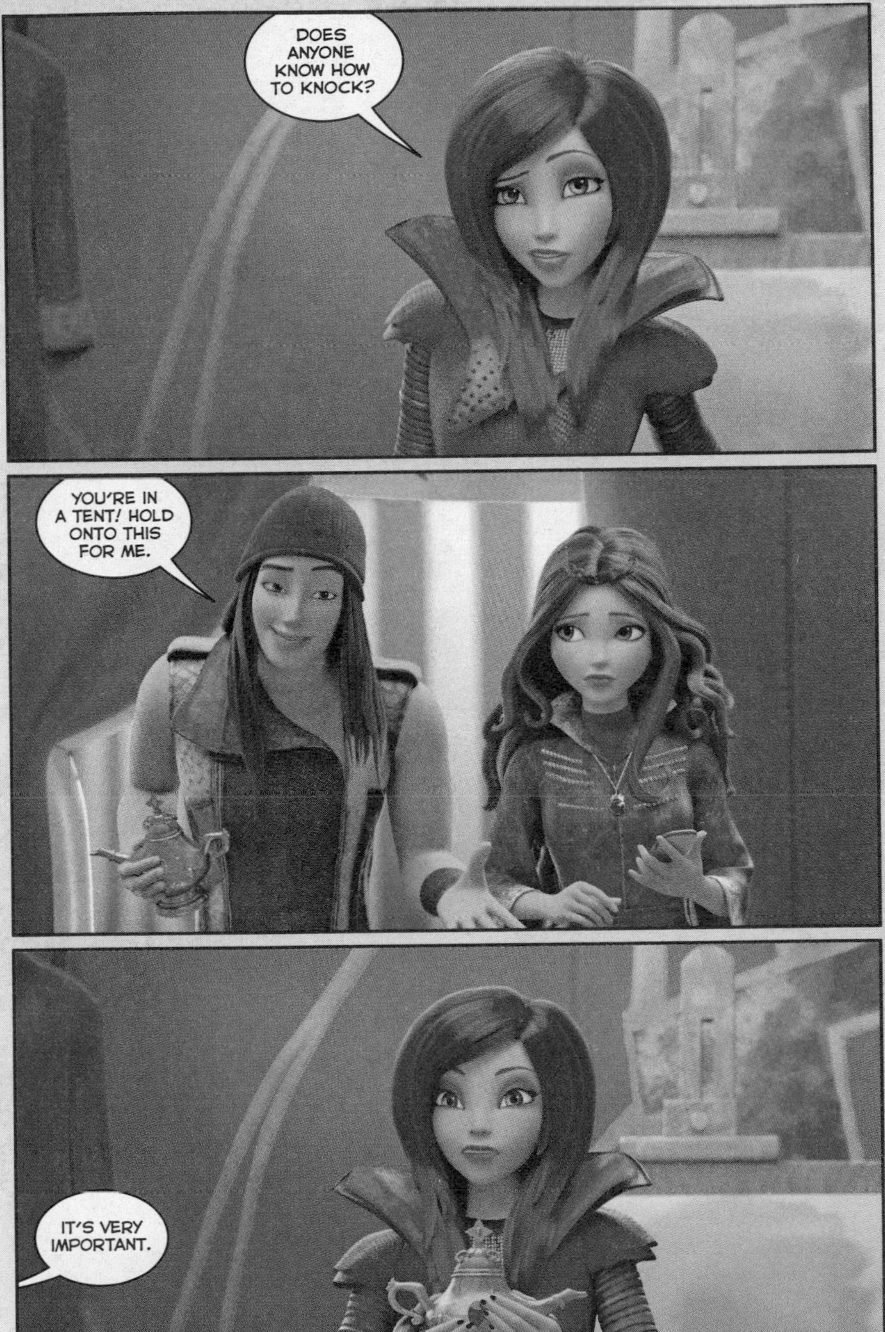
DOES ANYONE KNOW HOW TO KNOCK?
YOU'RE IN A TENT! HOLD ONTO THIS FOR ME.
IT'S VERY IMPORTANT.

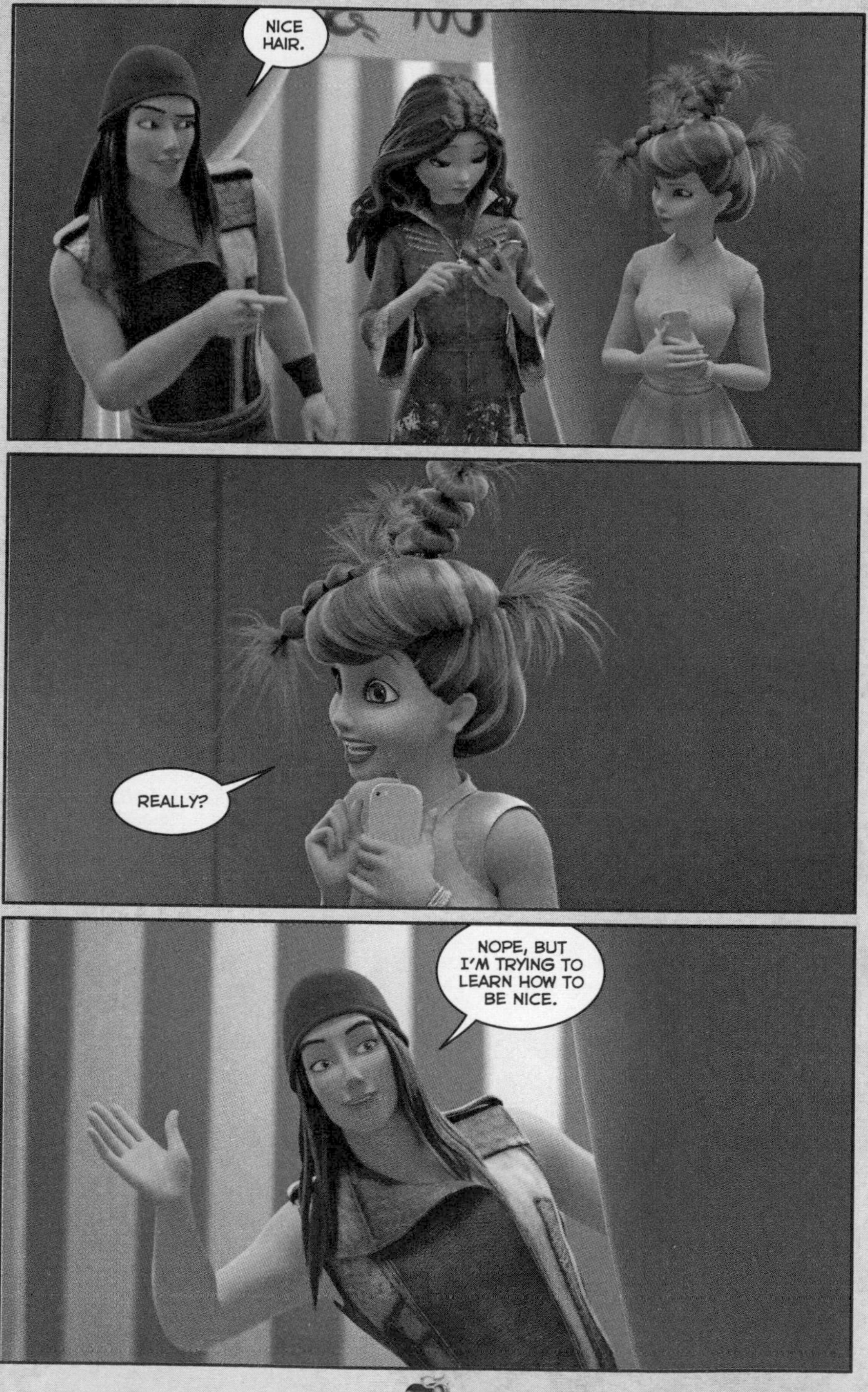
NICE HAIR.
REALLY?
NOPE, BUT I'M TRYING TO LEARN HOW TO BE NICE.

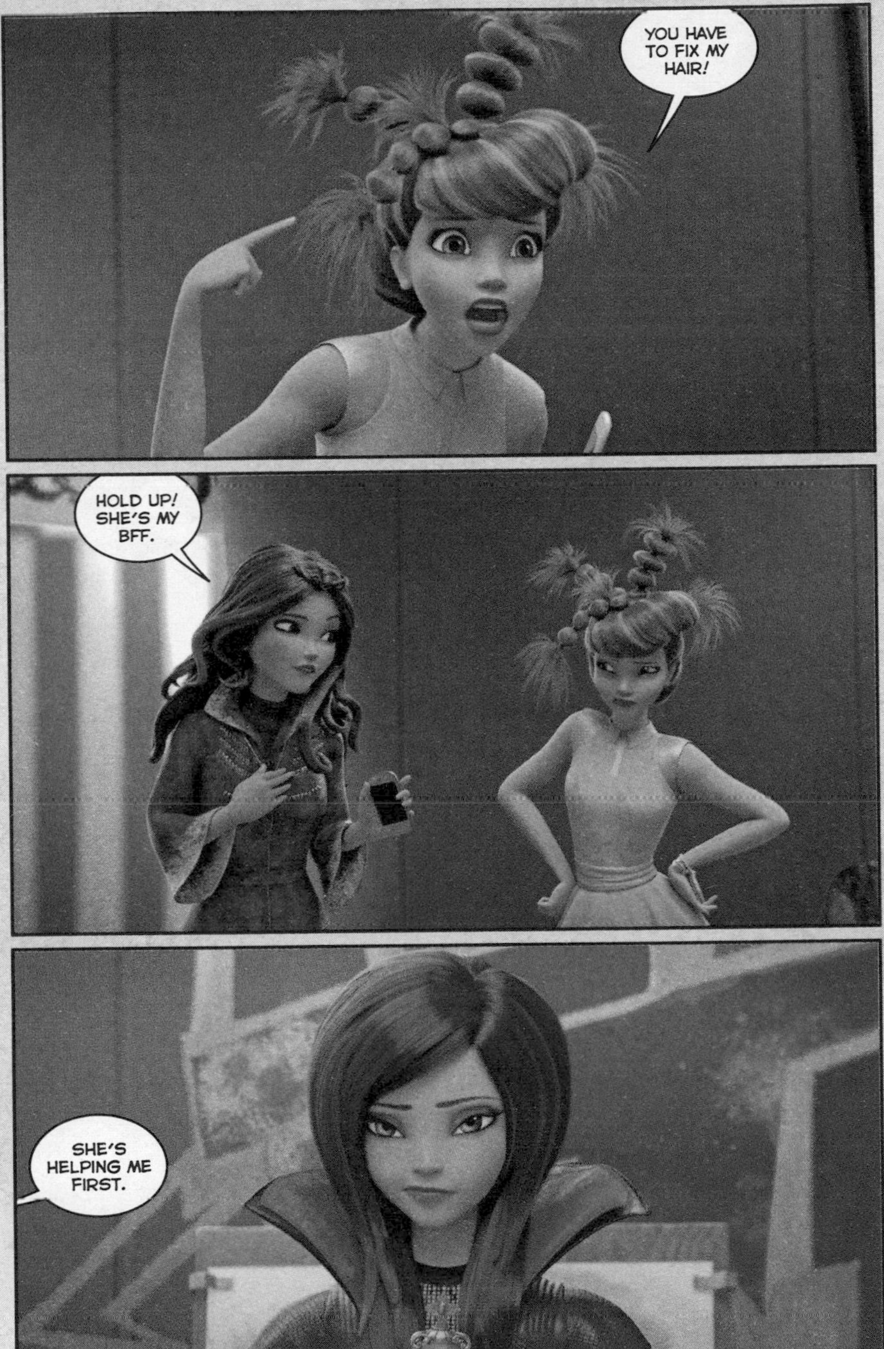
YOU HAVE TO FIX MY HAIR!
HOLD UP! SHE'S MY BFF.
SHE'S HELPING ME FIRST.

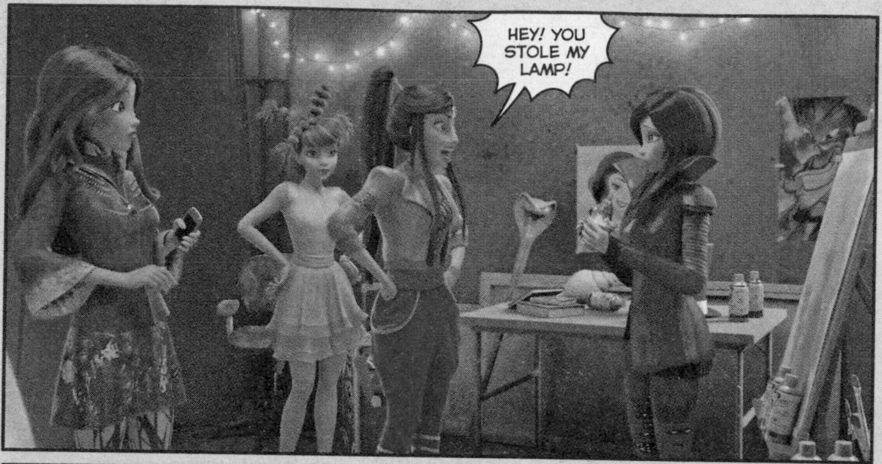
HEY! YOU STOLE MY LAMP!

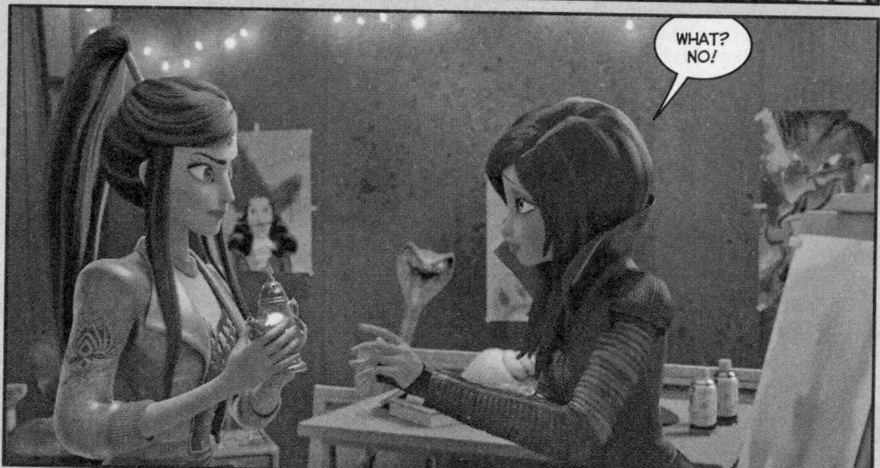
WHAT? NO!

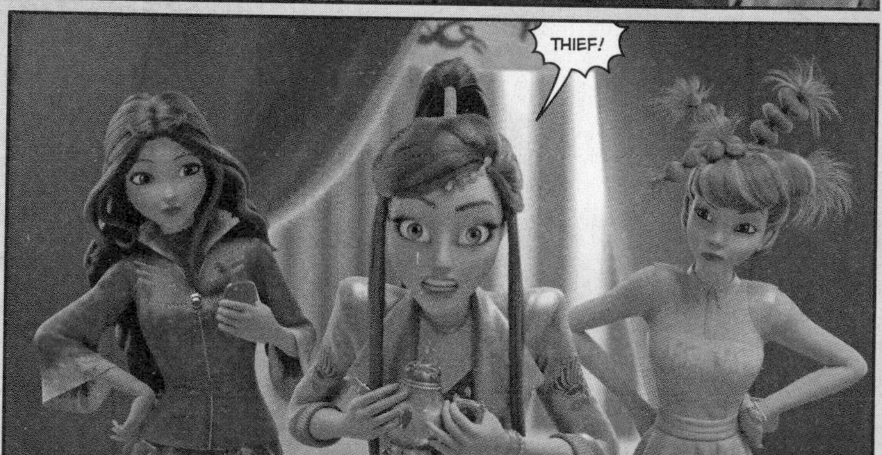
THIEF!

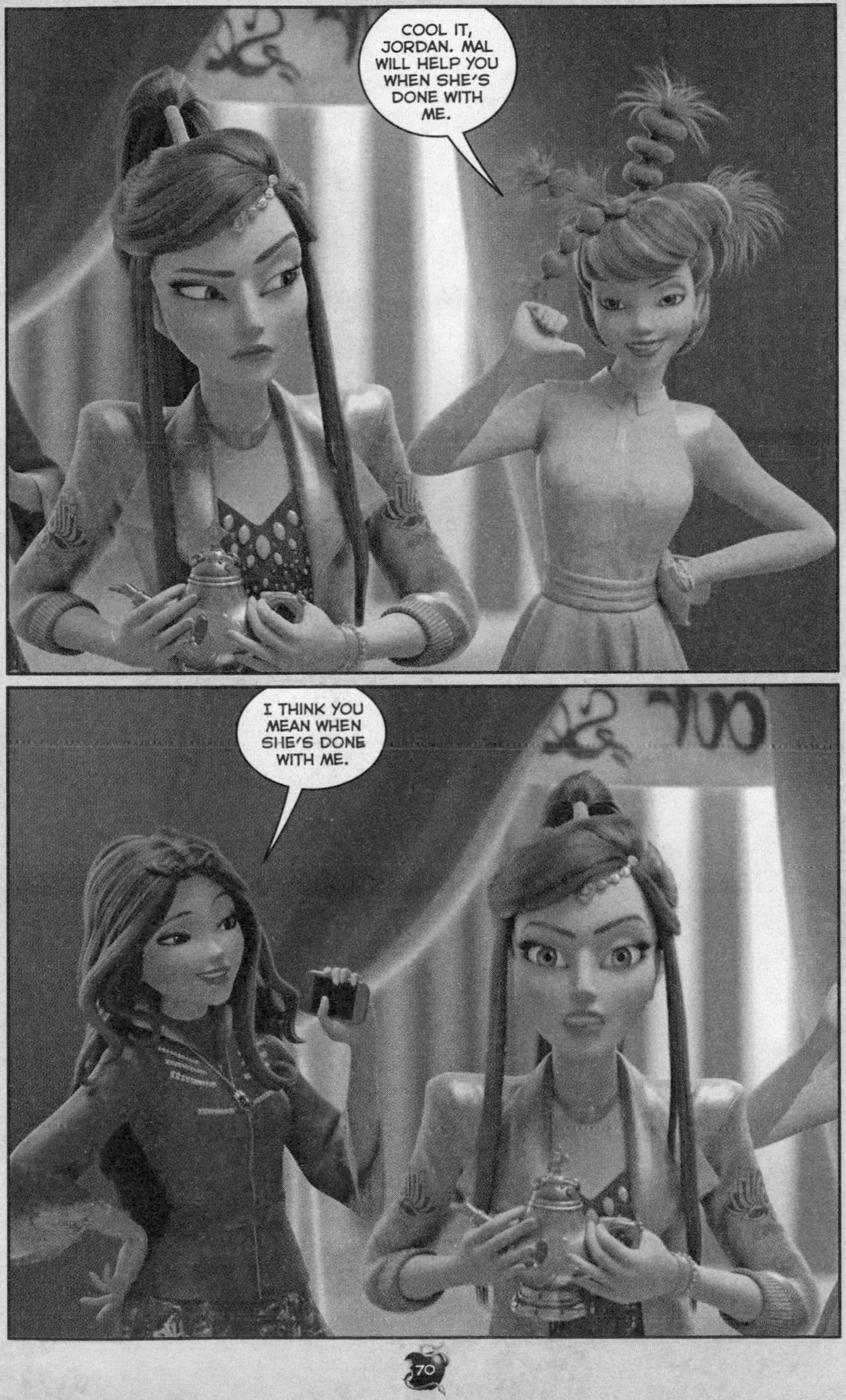
COOL IT, JORDAN. MAL WILL HELP YOU WHEN SHE'S DONE WITH ME.
I THINK YOU MEAN WHEN SHE'S DONE WITH ME.

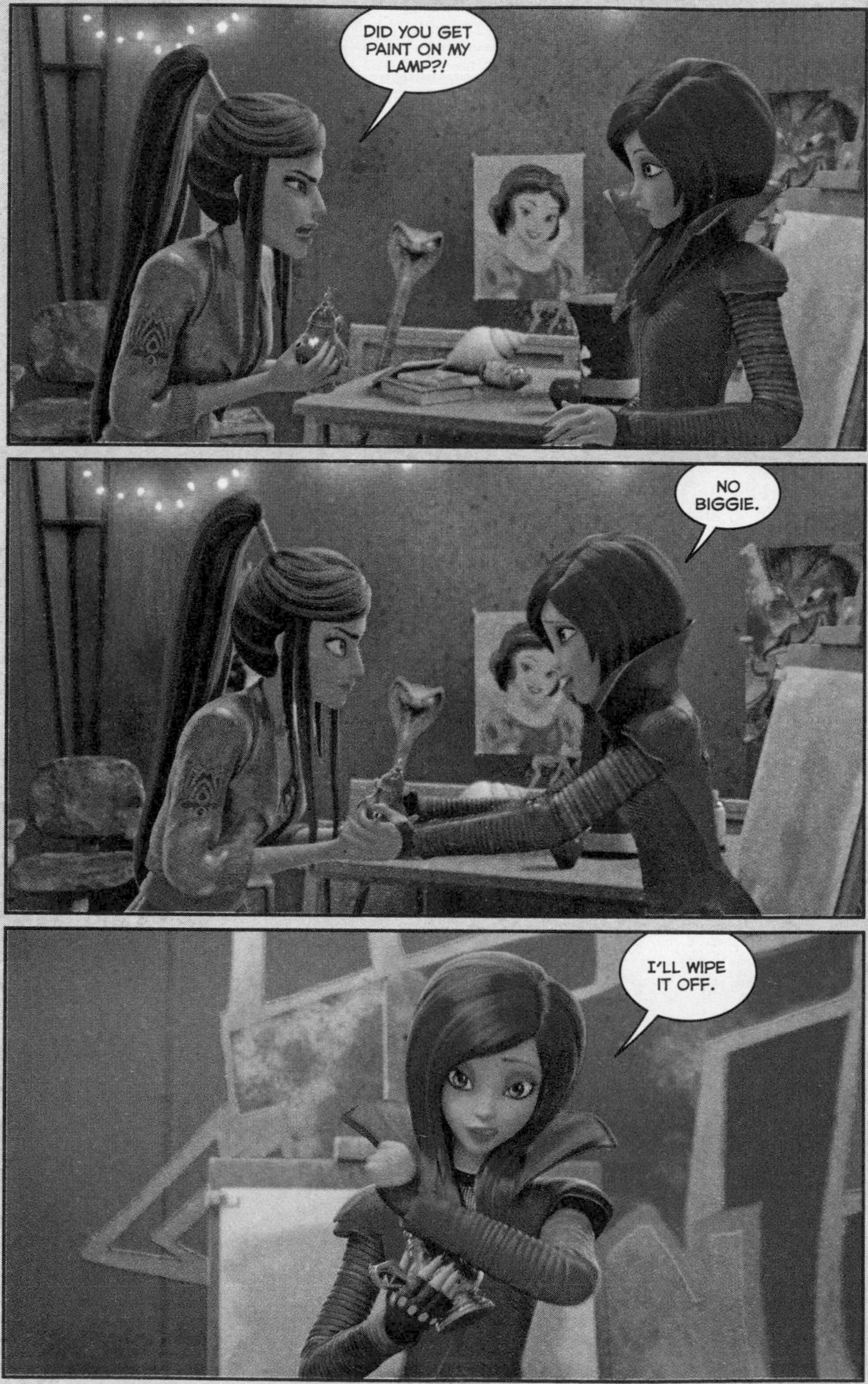
DID YOU GET PAINT ON MY LAMP?!
NO BIGGIE.
I'LL WIPE IT OFF.

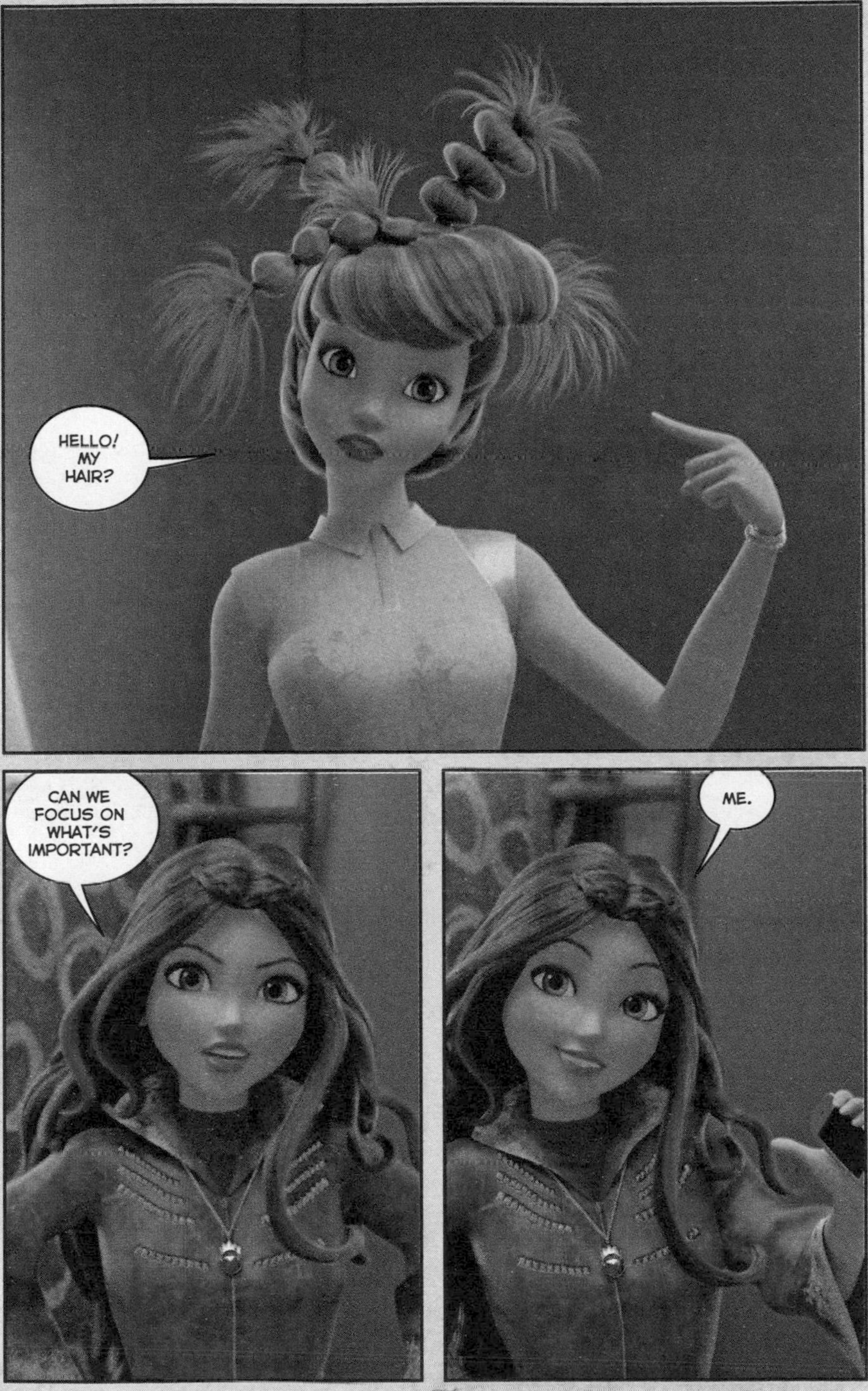
HELLO! MY HAIR?
CAN WE FOCUS ON WHAT'S IMPORTANT?
ME.

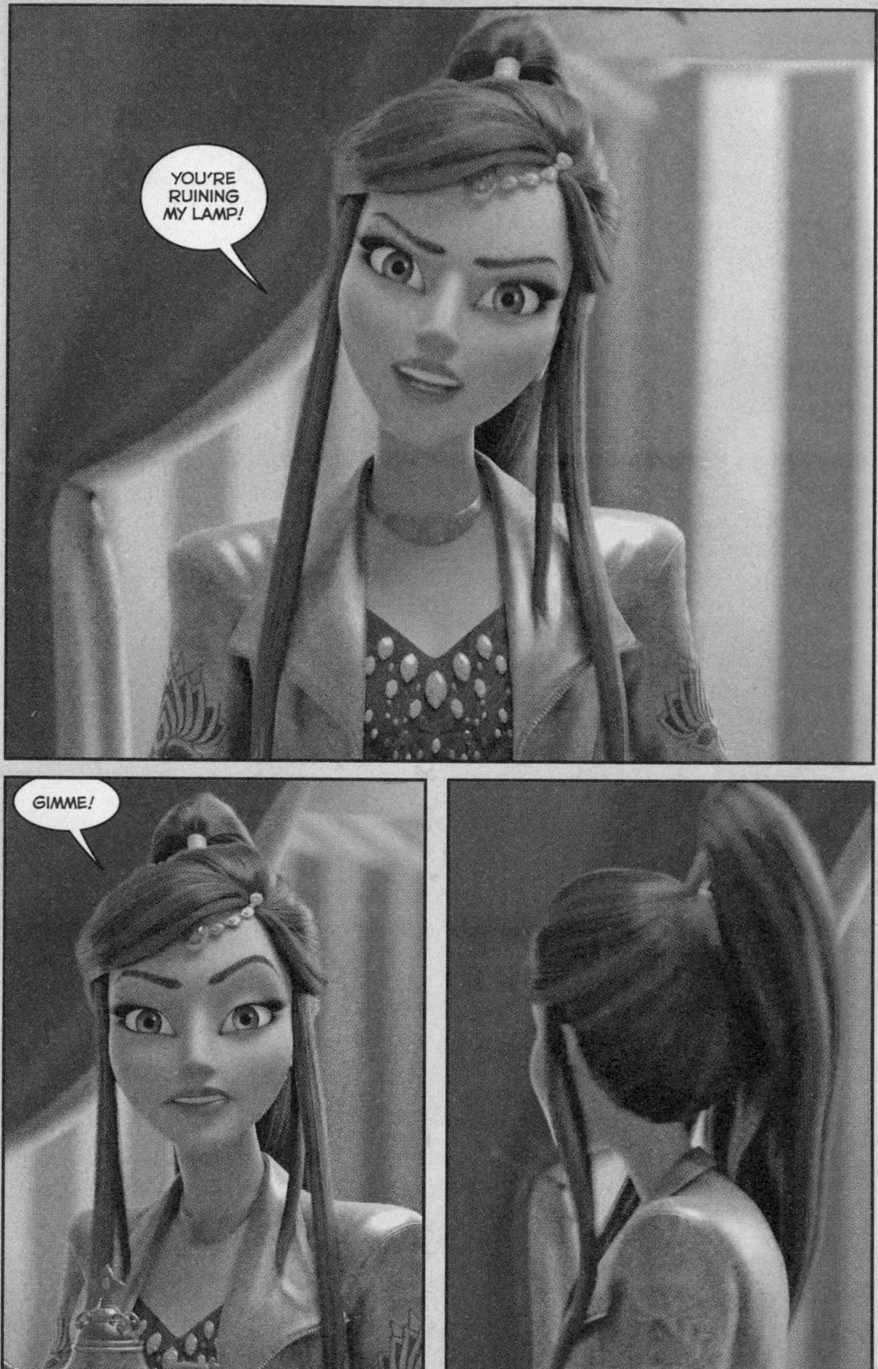
YOU'RE RUINING MY LAMP!
GIMME!

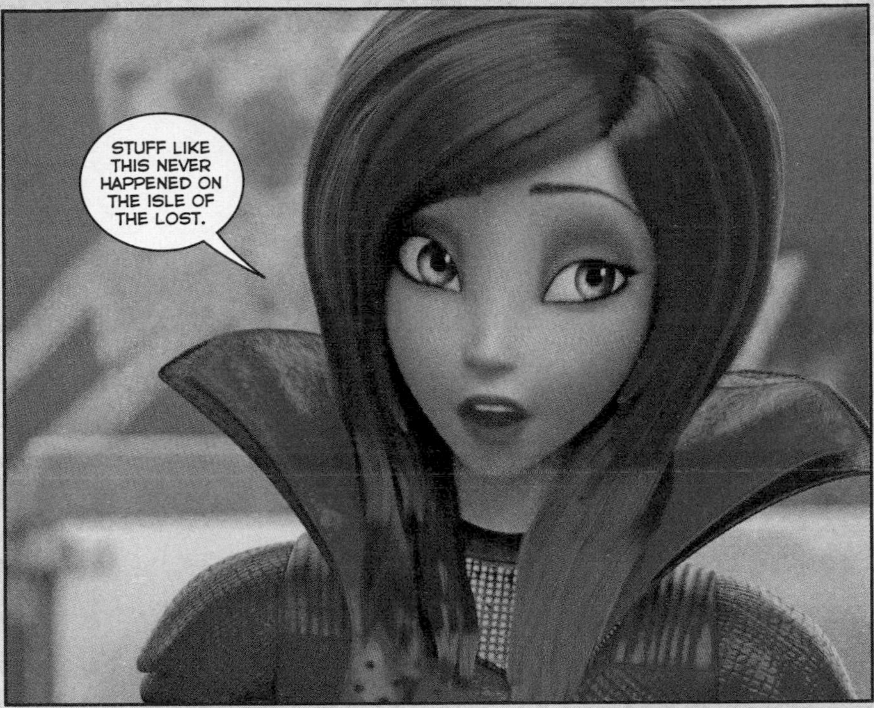
STUFF LIKE THIS NEVER HAPPENED ON THE ISLE OF THE LOST.

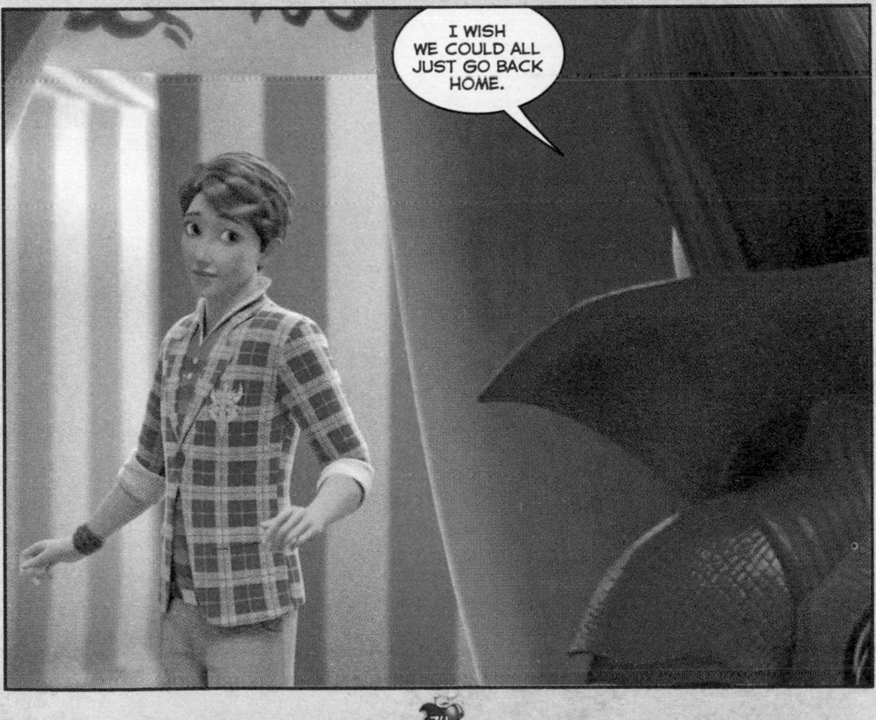
I WISH WE COULD ALL JUST GO BACK HOME.

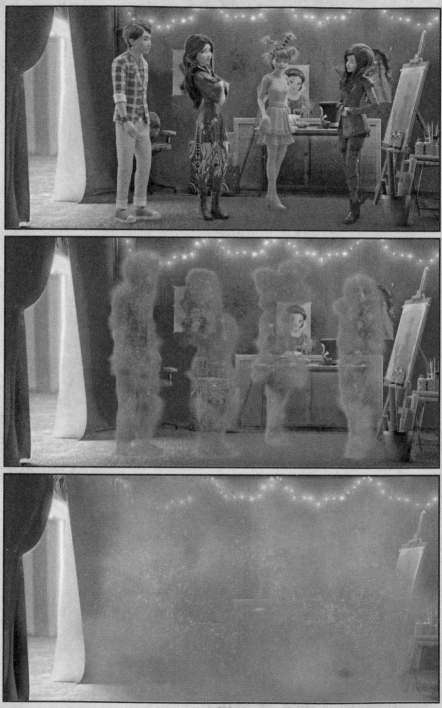

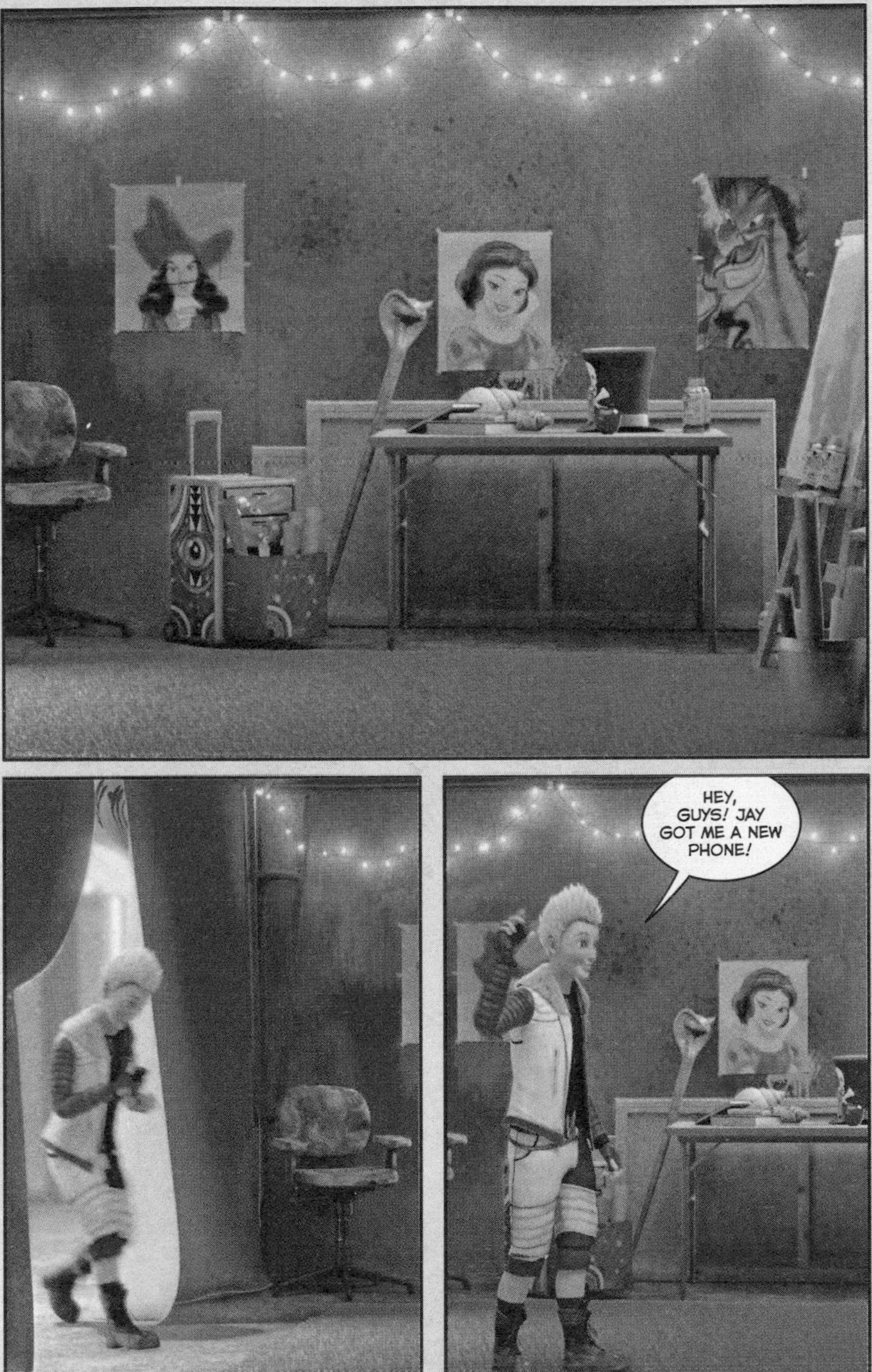
HEY, GUYS! JAY GOT ME A NEW PHONE!

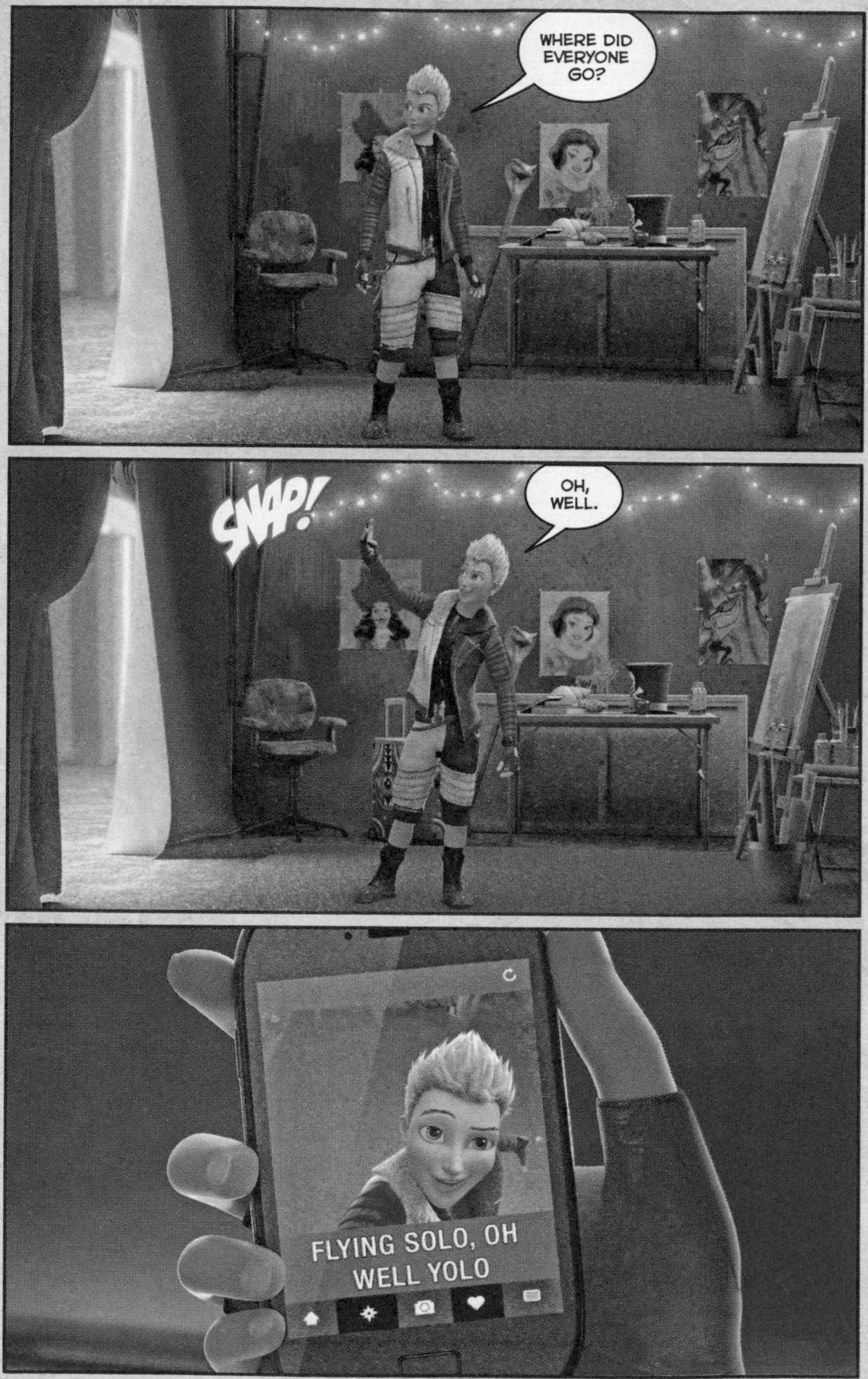
WHERE DID EVERYONE GO?
SNAP!
OH, WELL.
FLYING SOLO, OH WELL YOLO

CHAPTER 5: VOODOO? YOU DO

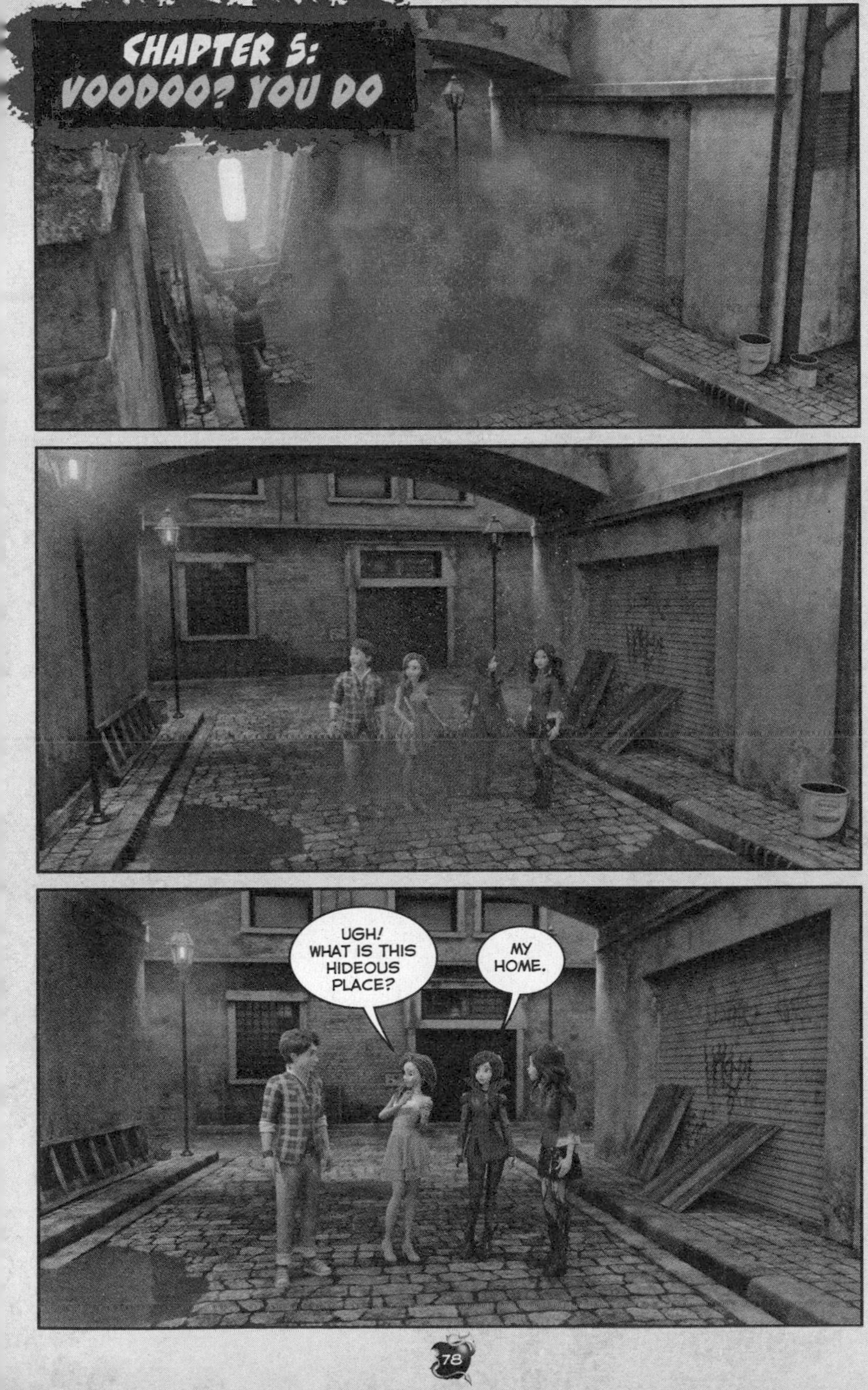
UGH! WHAT IS THIS HIDEOUS PLACE?
MY HOME.

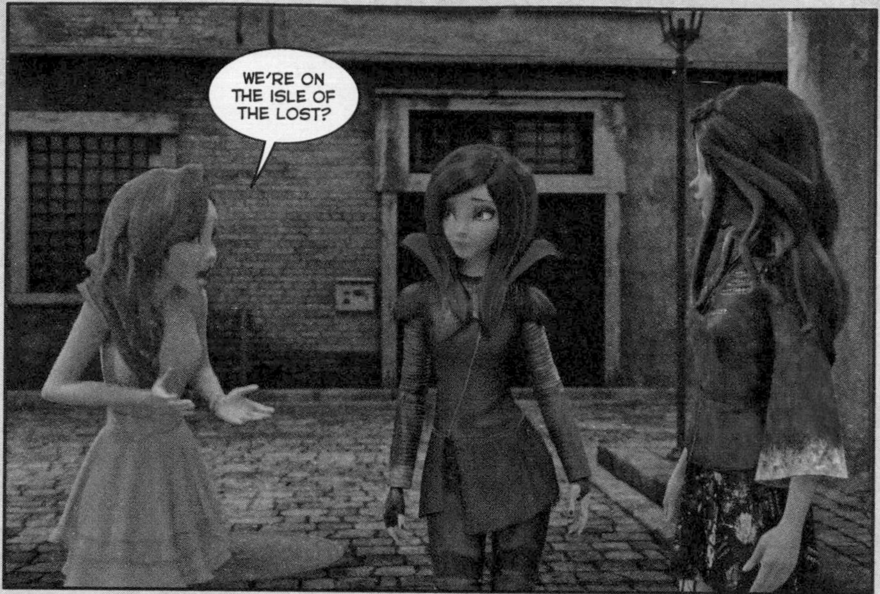
WE'RE ON THE ISLE OF THE LOST?

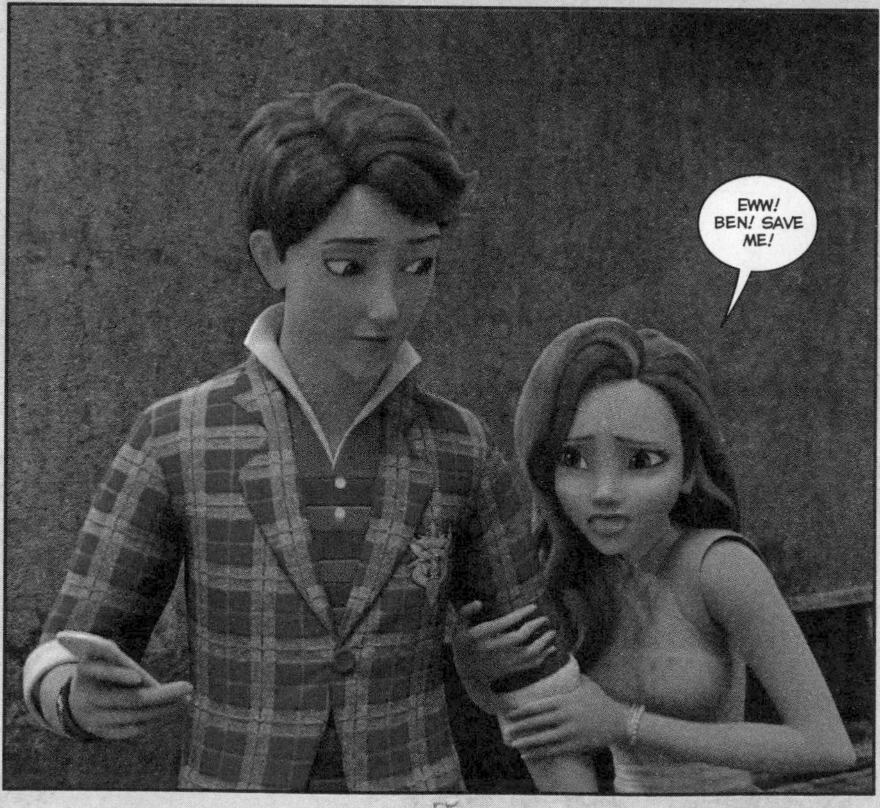
EWW! BEN! SAVE ME!

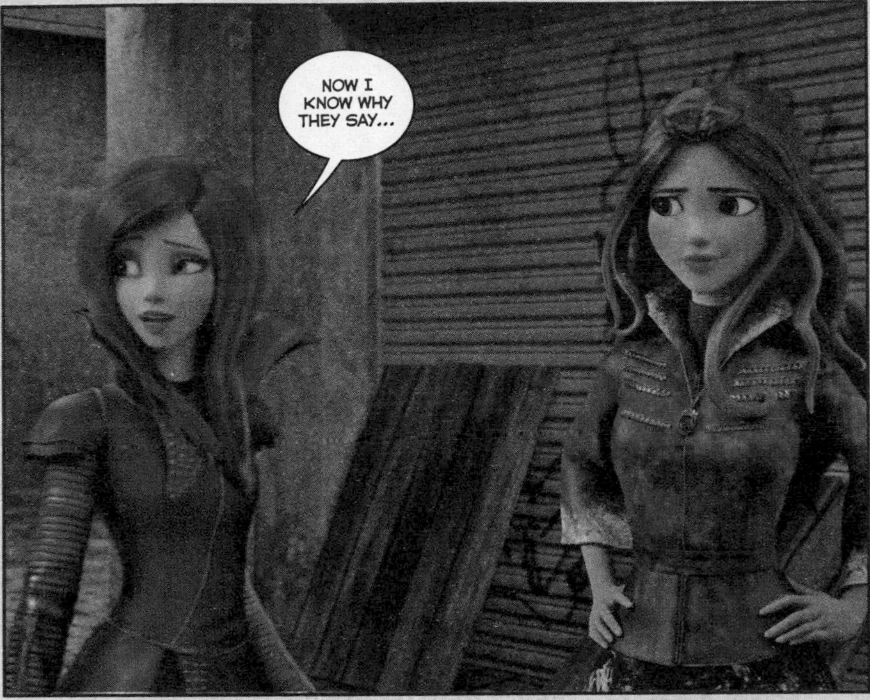
NOW I KNOW WHY THEY SAY...

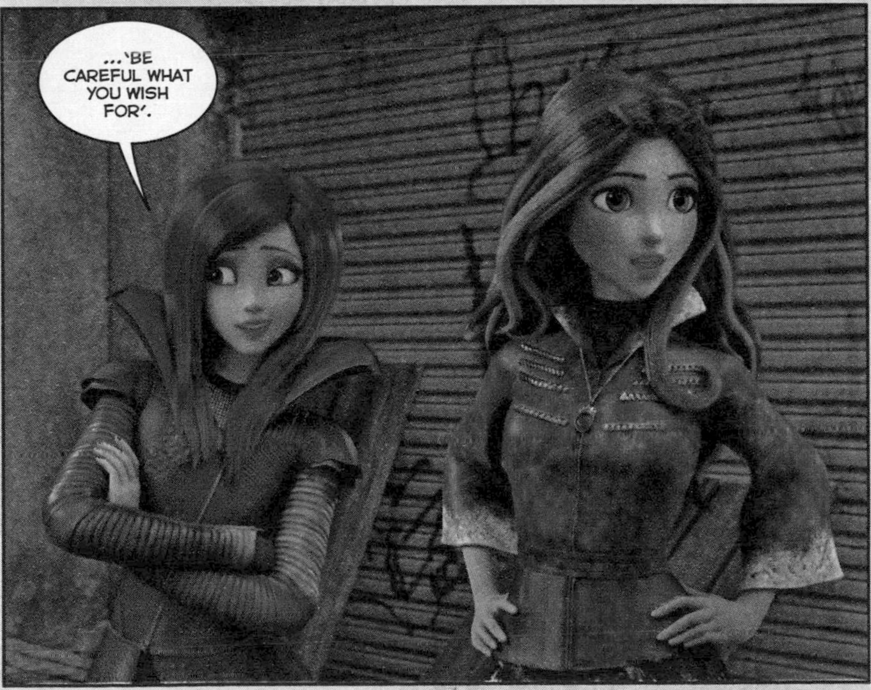
...'BE CAREFUL WHAT YOU WISH FOR'.

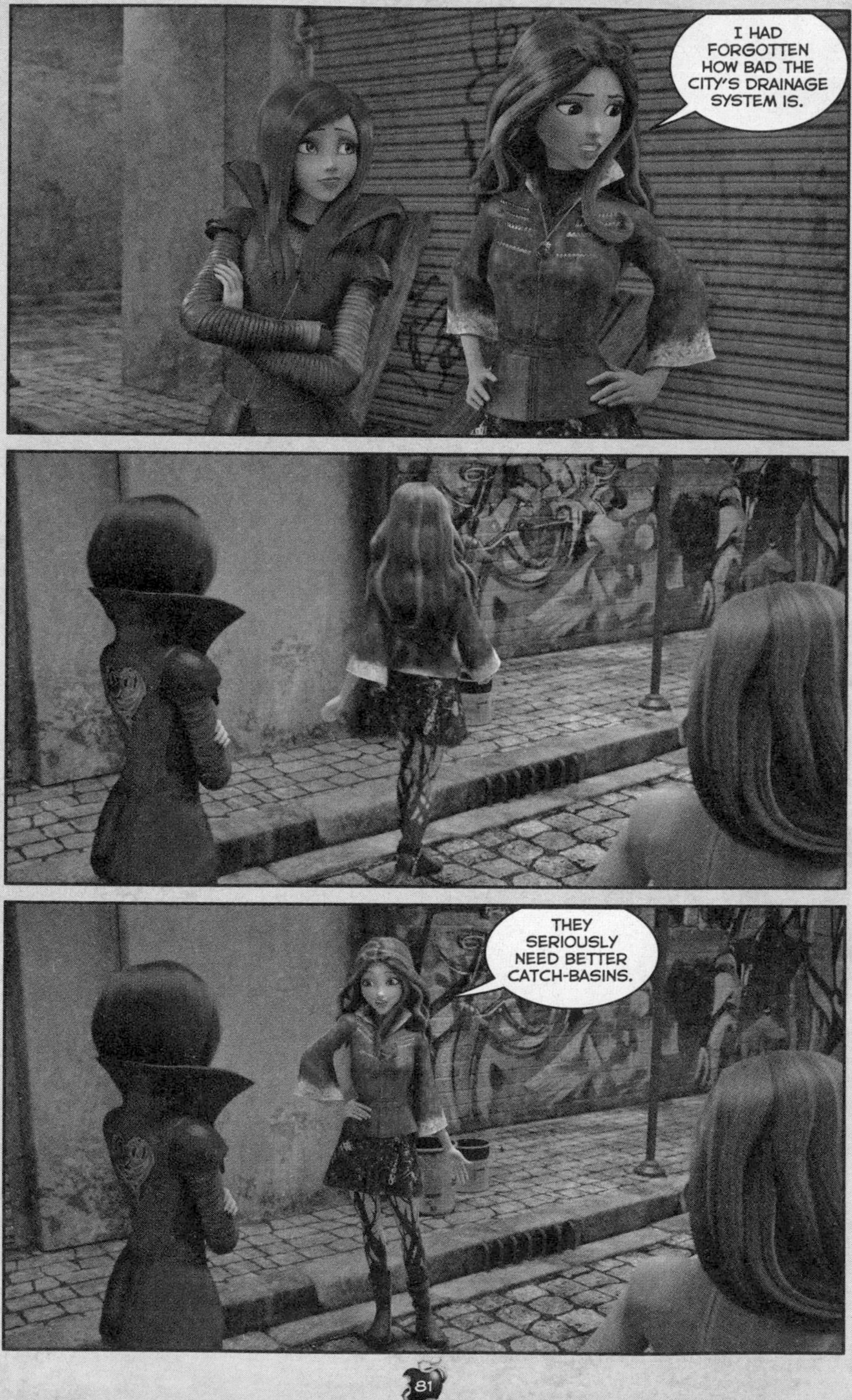
I HAD FORGOTTEN HOW BAD THE CITY'S DRAINAGE SYSTEM IS.
THEY SERIOUSLY NEED BETTER CATCH-BASINS.

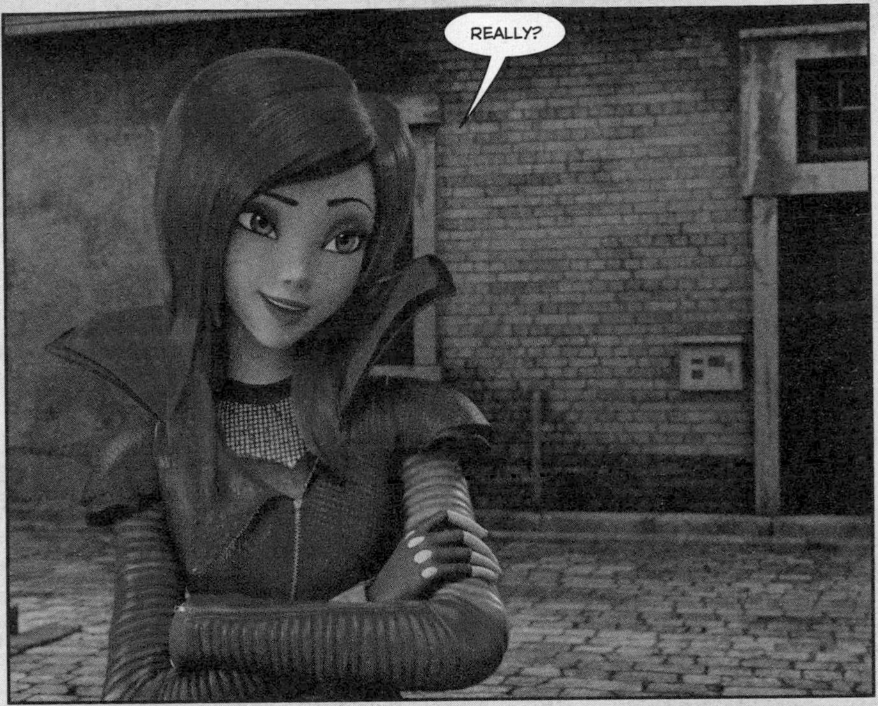
REALLY?

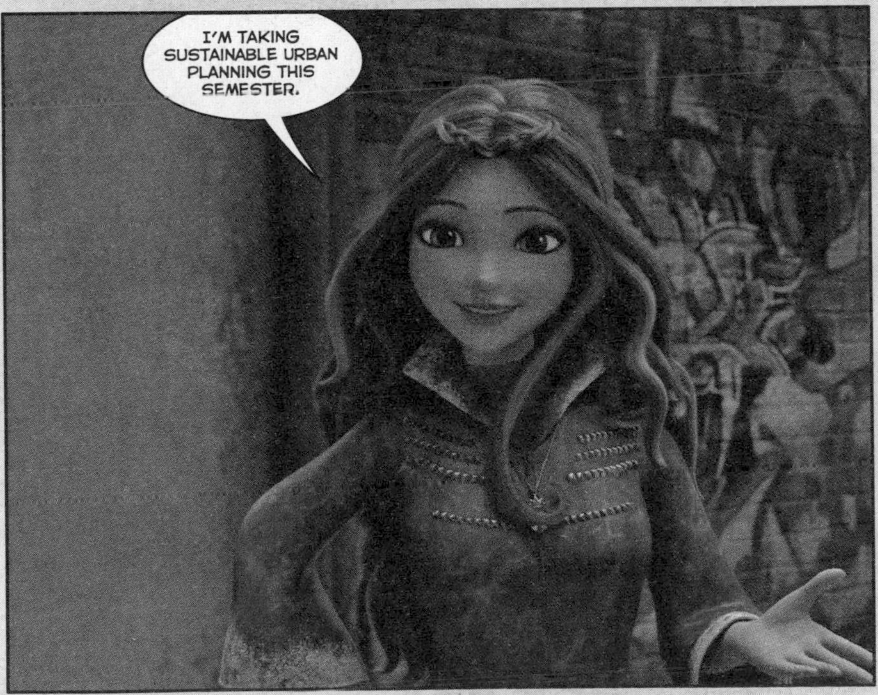
I'M TAKING SUSTAINABLE URBAN PLANNING THIS SEMESTER.

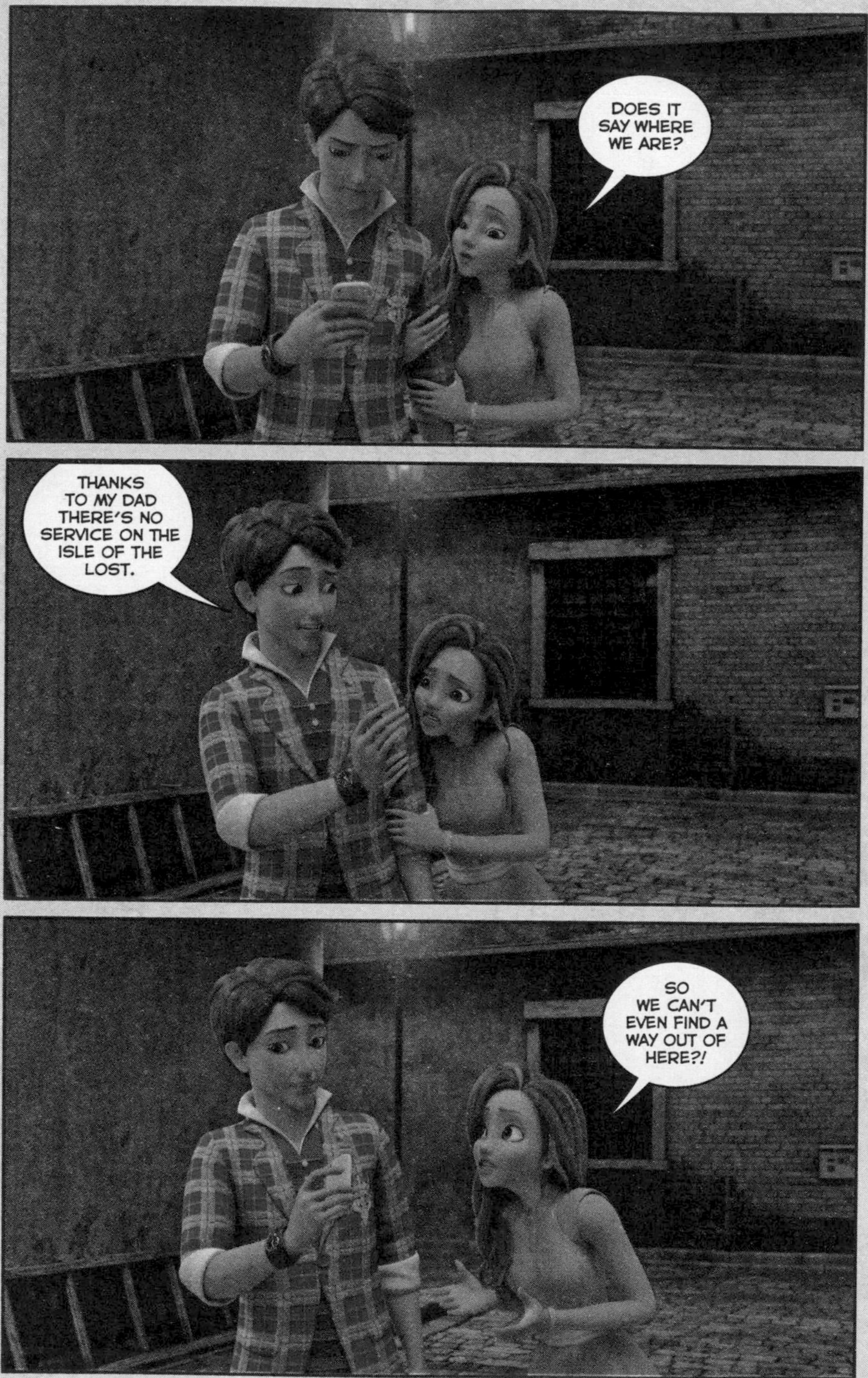
DOES IT SAY WHERE WE ARE?
THANKS TO MY DAD THERE'S NO SERVICE ON THE ISLE OF THE LOST.
SO WE CAN'T EVEN FIND A WAY OUT OF HERE?!

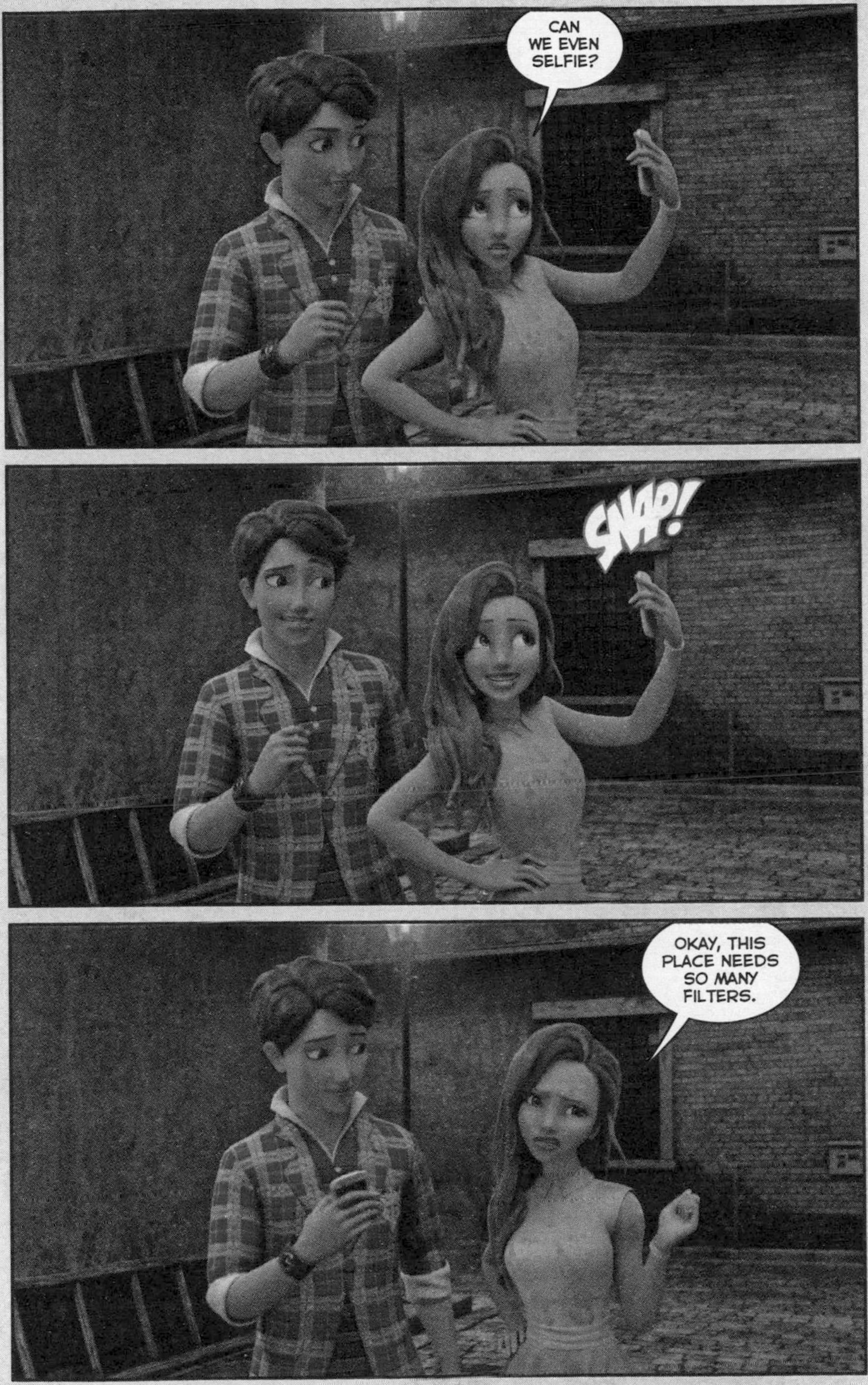
CAN WE EVEN SELFIE?
SNAP!
OKAY, THIS PLACE NEEDS SO MANY FILTERS.

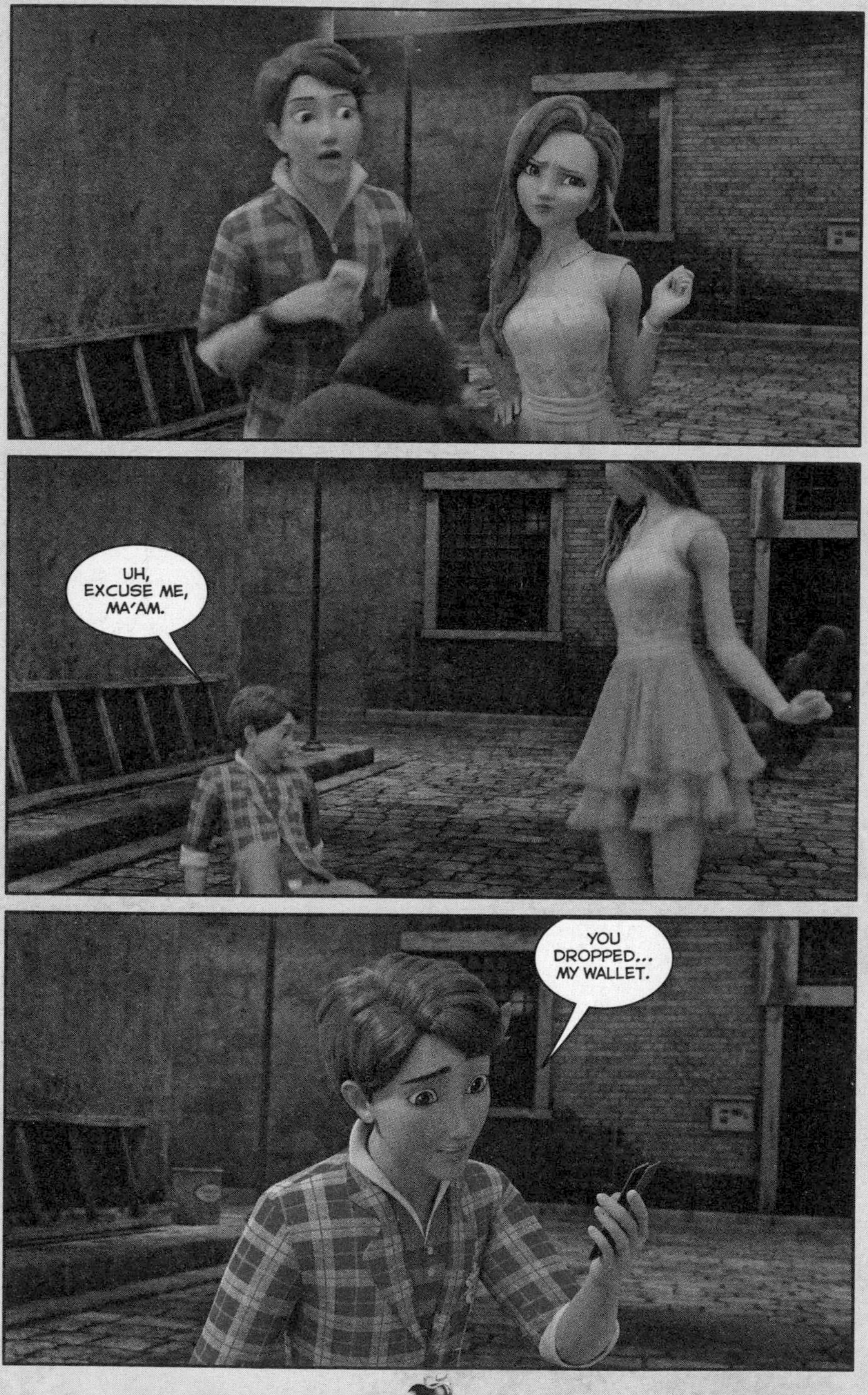
UH, EXCUSE ME, MA'AM.
YOU DROPPED... MY WALLET.

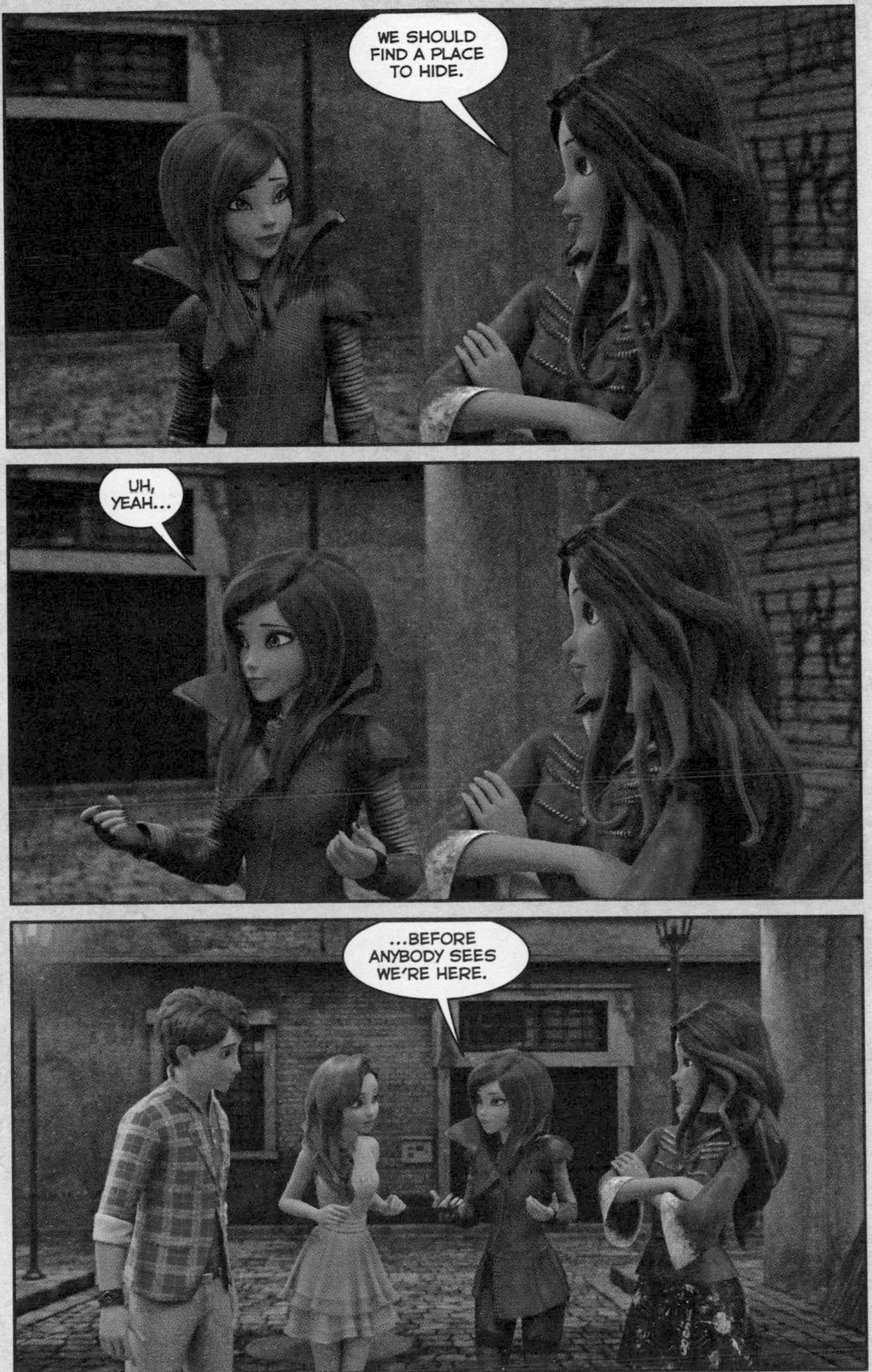
WE SHOULD FIND A PLACE TO HIDE.
UH, YEAH...
...BEFORE ANYBODY SEES WE'RE HERE.

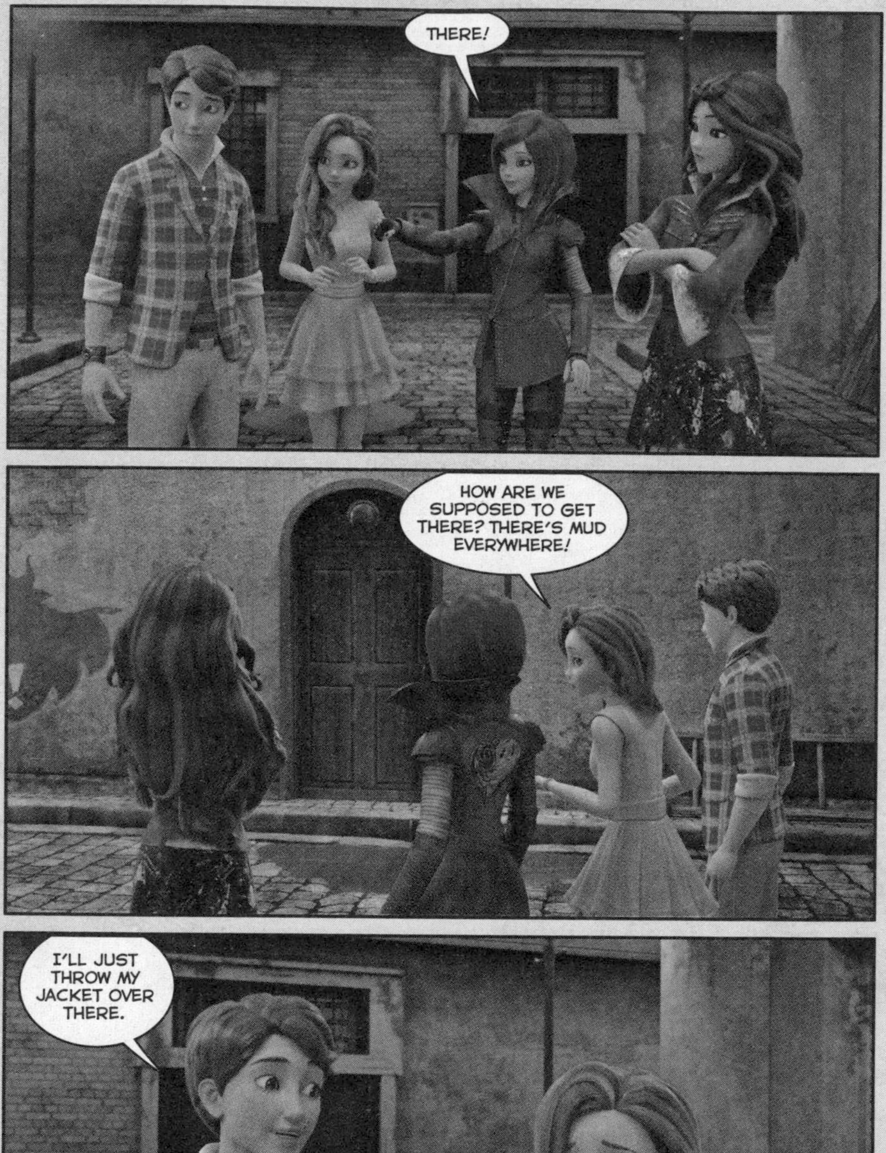
THERE!
HOW ARE WE SUPPOSED TO GET THERE? THERE'S MUD EVERYWHERE!
I'LL JUST THROW MY JACKET OVER THERE.

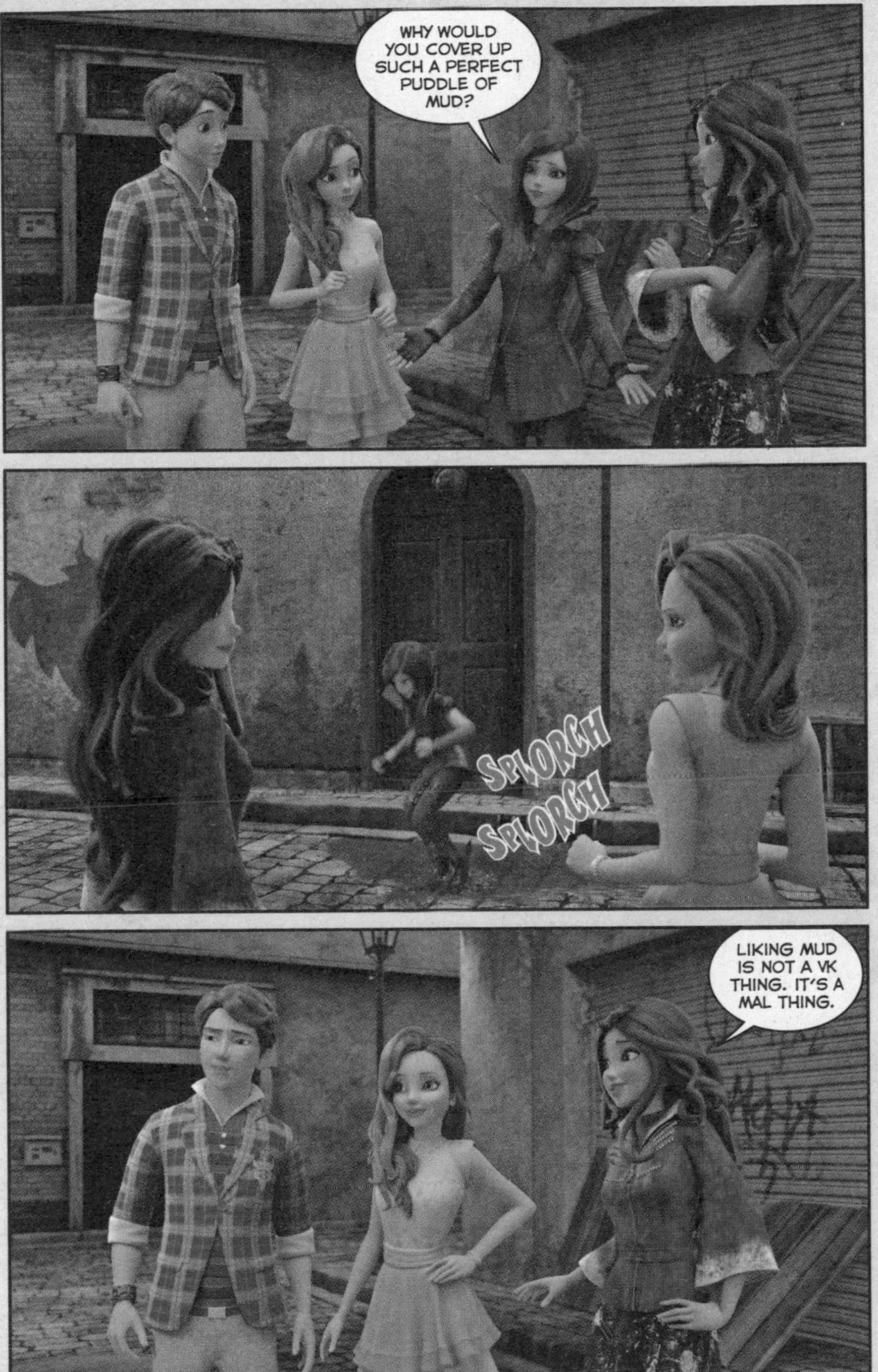
WHY WOULD YOU COVER UP SUCH A PERFECT PUDDLE OF MUD?
SPLORCH
SPLORCH
LIKING MUD IS NOT A VK THING. IT'S A MAL THING.

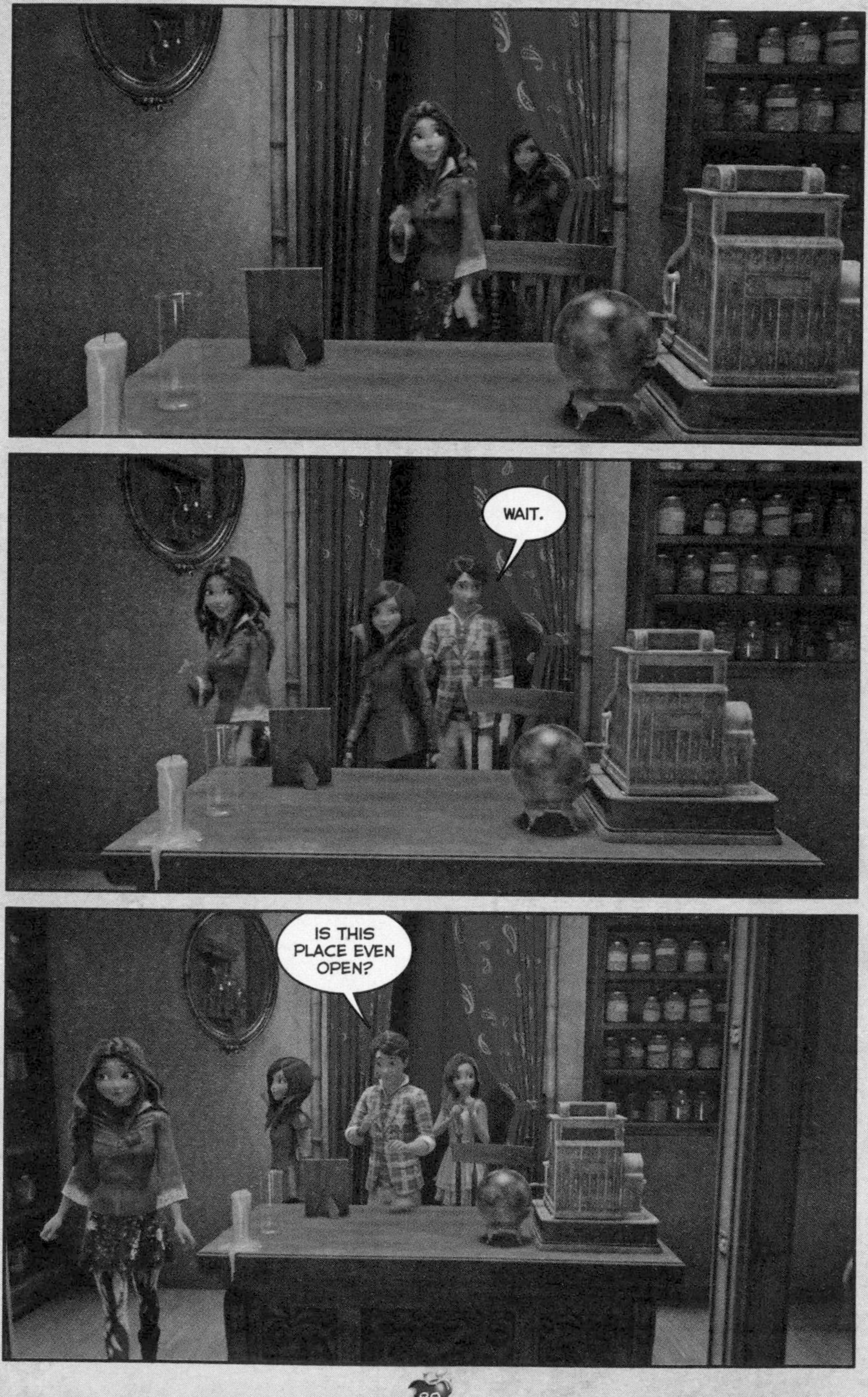
WAIT.
IS THIS PLACE EVEN OPEN?

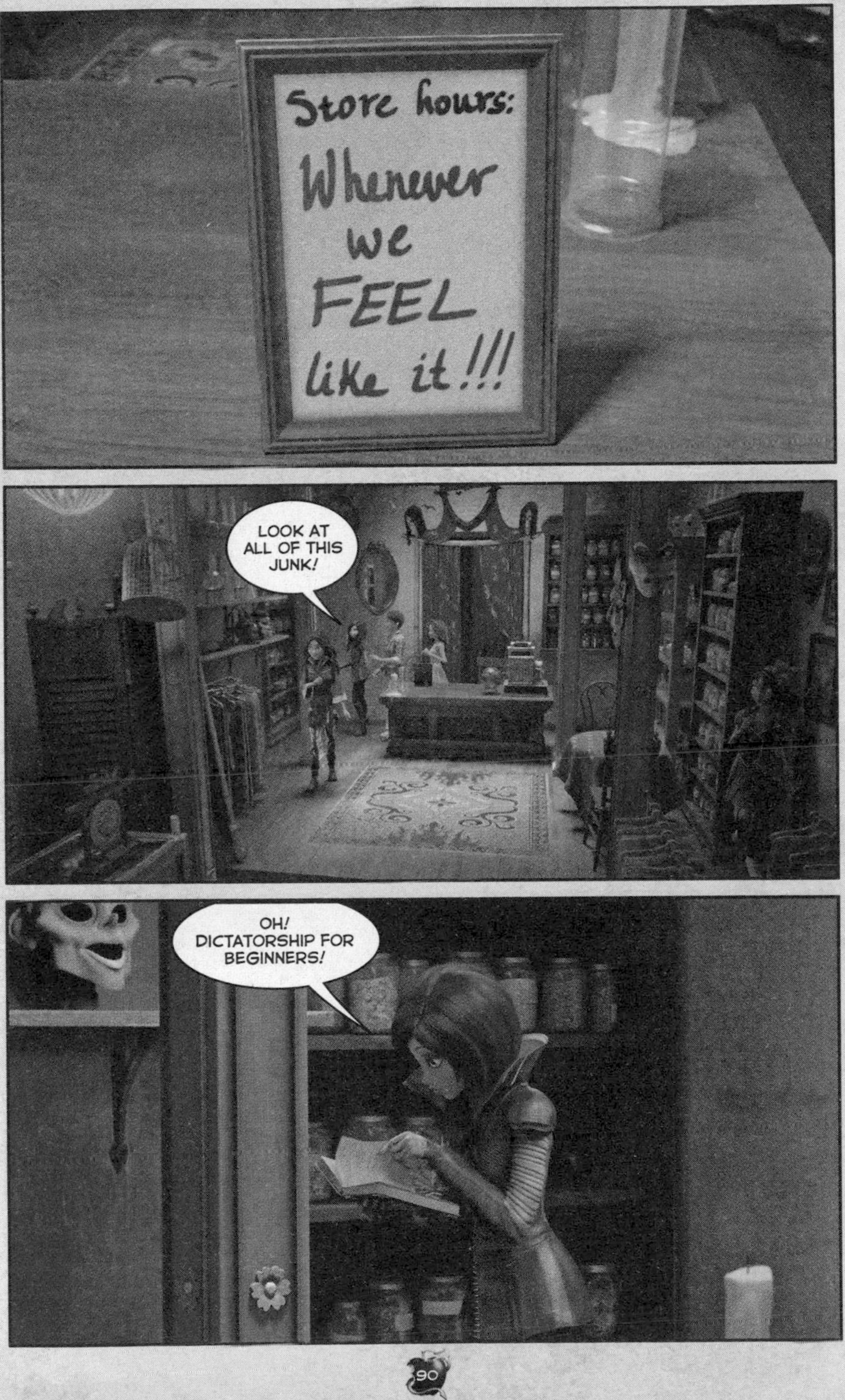
Store hours: Whenever we FEEL like it!!!
LOOK AT ALL OF THIS JUNK!
OH! DICTATORSHIP FOR BEGINNERS!

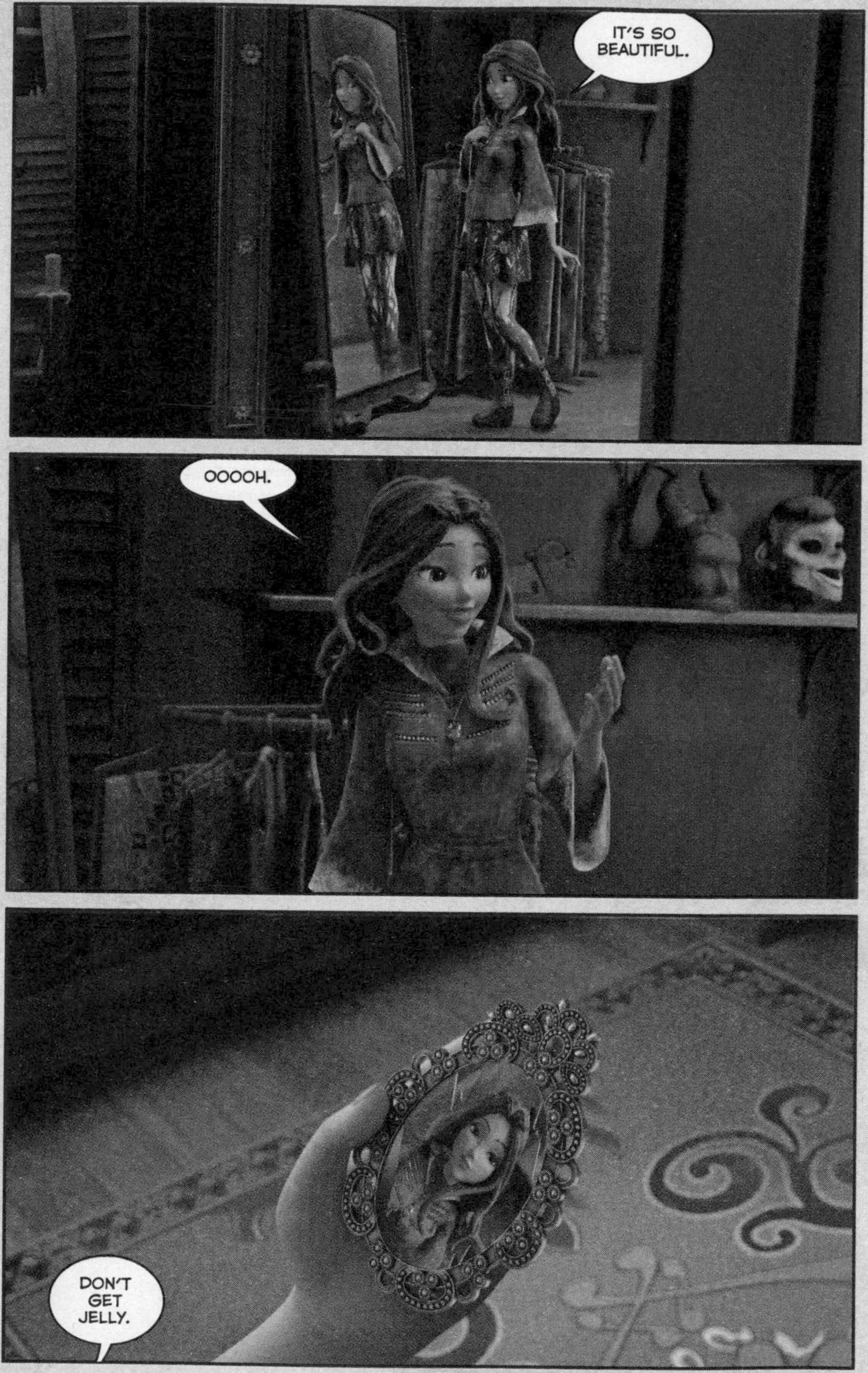
IT'S SO BEAUTIFUL.
OOOOH.
DON'T GET JELLY.

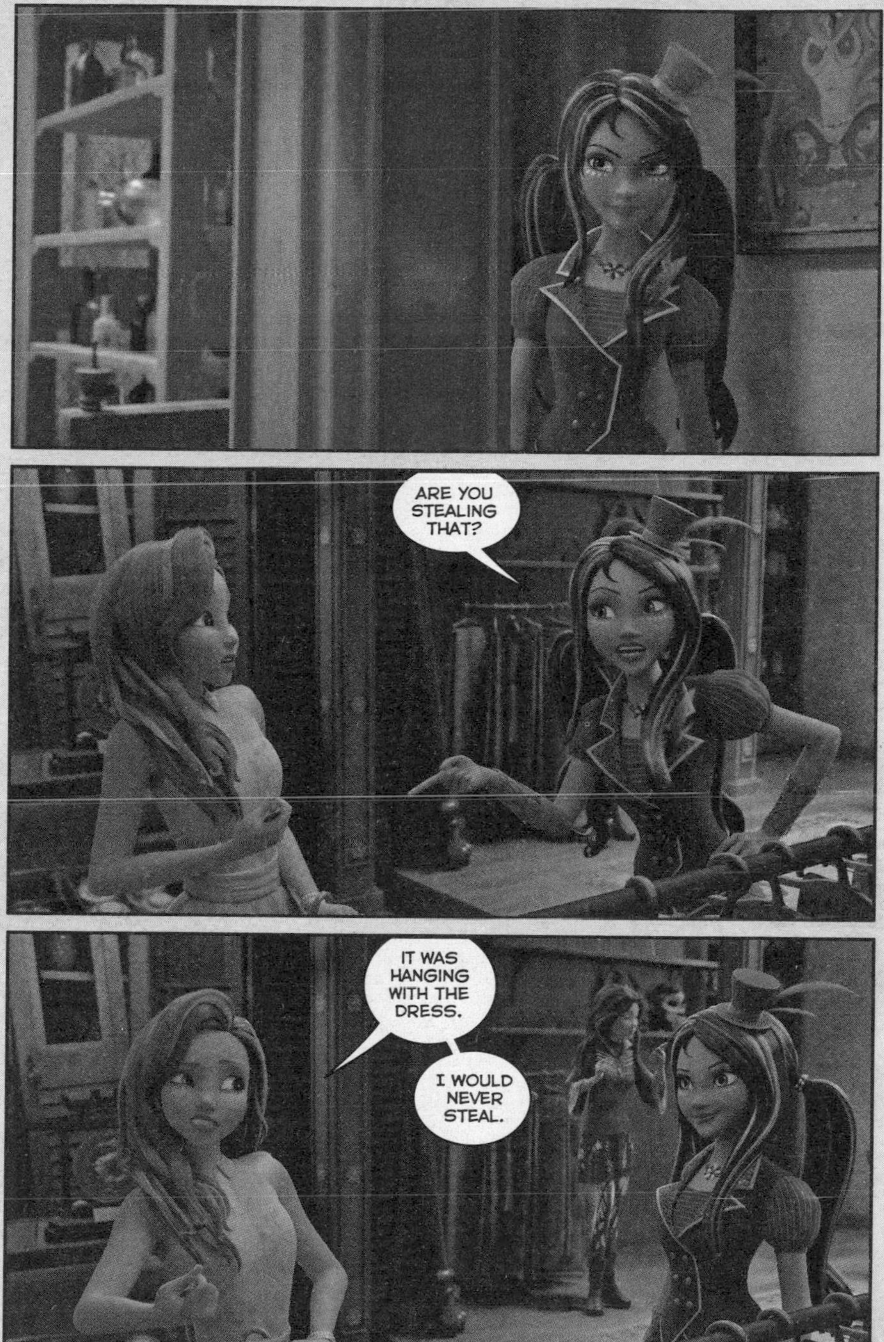
ARE YOU STEALING THAT?
IT WAS HANGING WITH THE DRESS.
I WOULD NEVER STEAL.

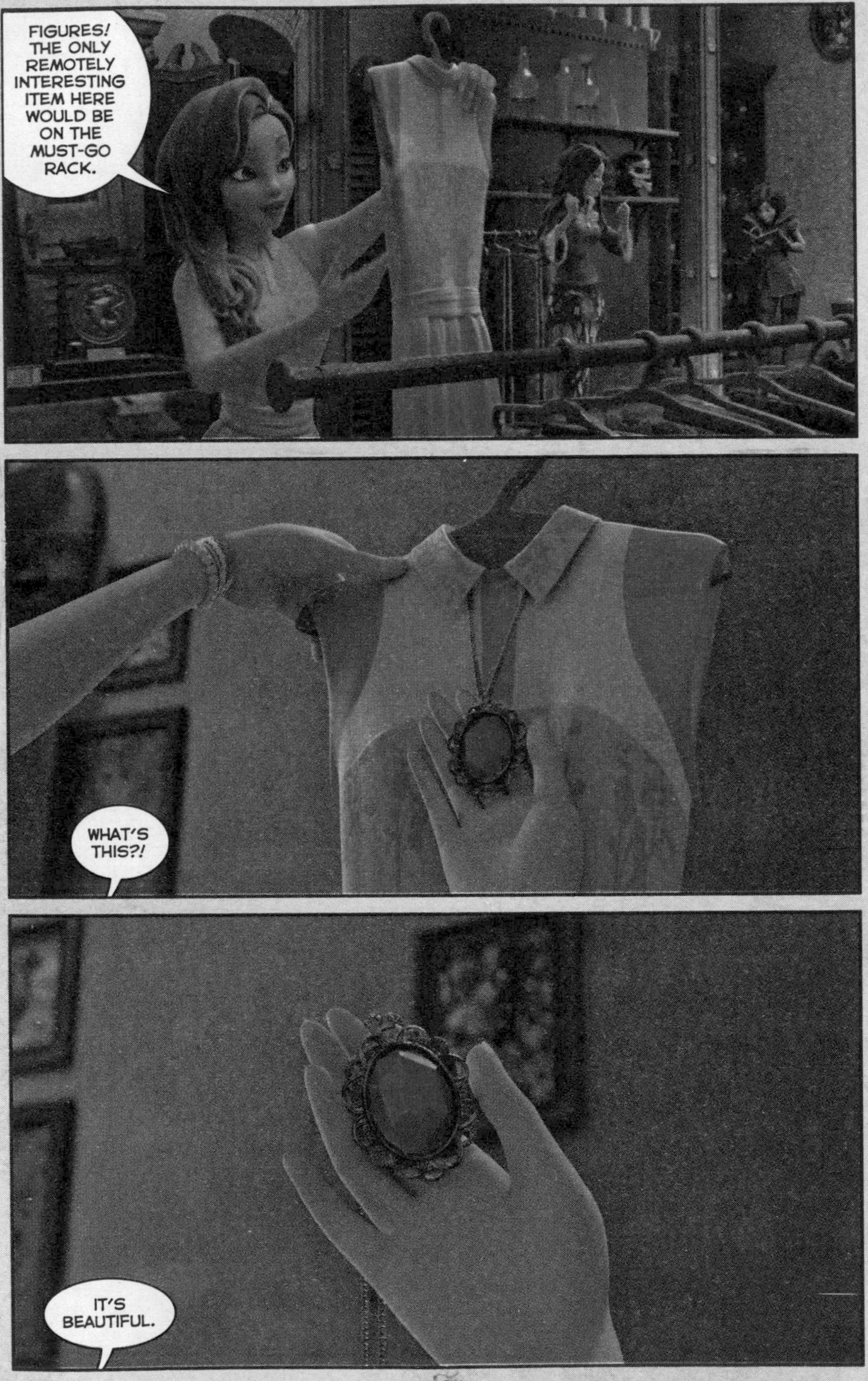
FIGURES! THE ONLY REMOTELY INTERESTING ITEM HERE WOULD BE ON THE MUST-GO RACK.
WHAT'S THIS?!
IT'S BEAUTIFUL.

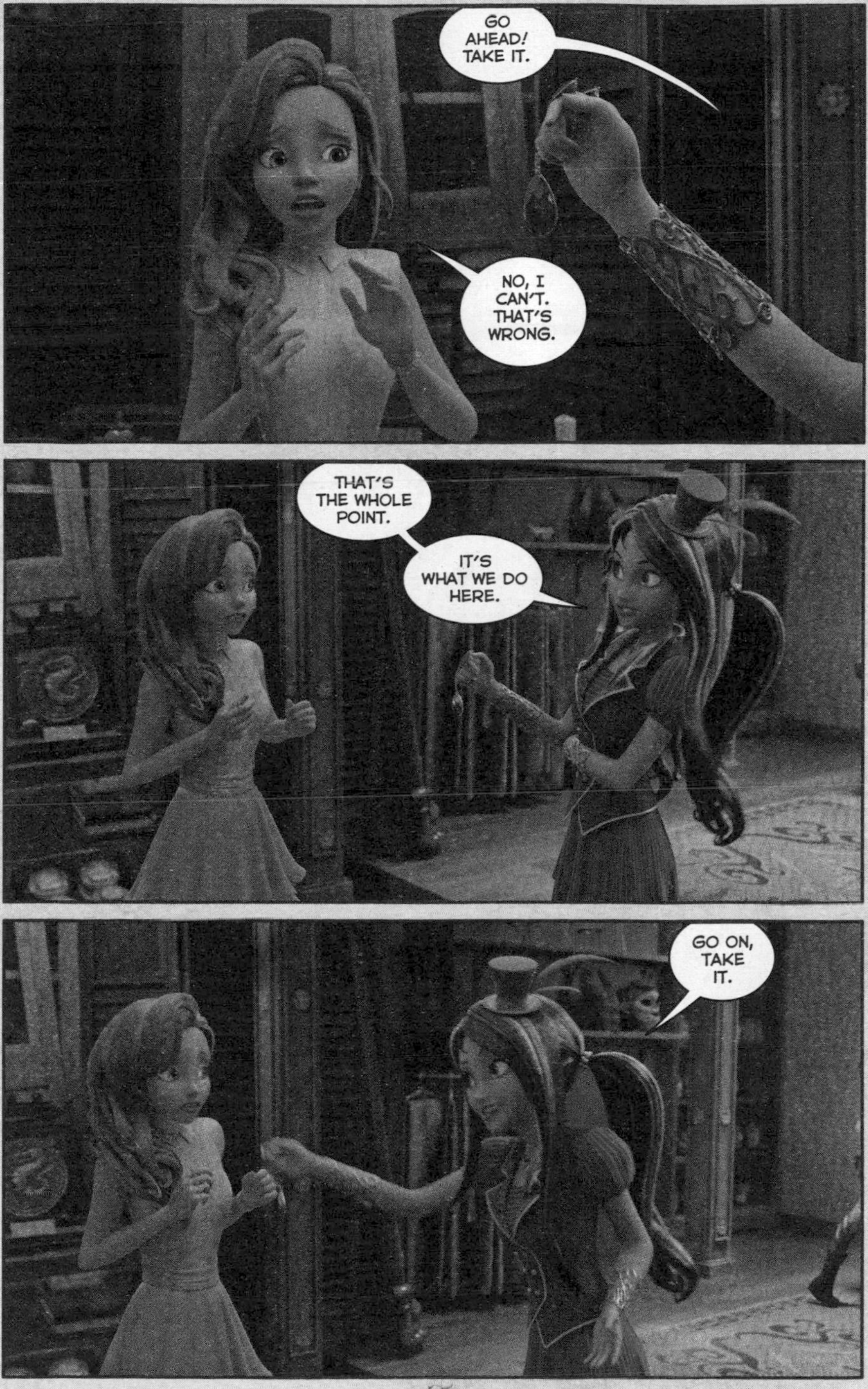
GO AHEAD! TAKE IT.
NO, I CAN'T. THAT'S WRONG.
THAT'S THE WHOLE POINT.
IT'S WHAT WE DO HERE.
GO ON, TAKE IT.

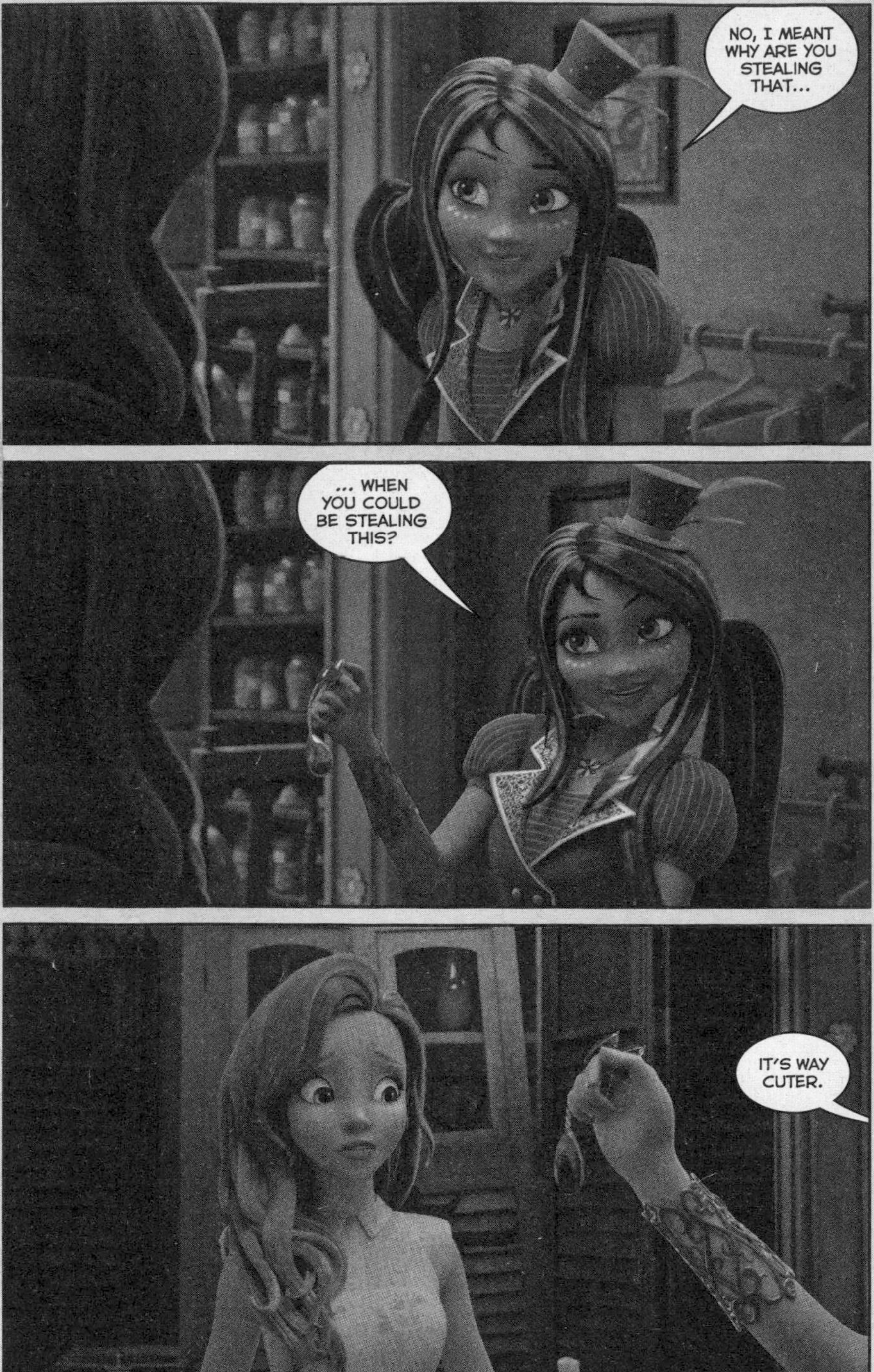
NO, I MEANT WHY ARE YOU STEALING THAT...
... WHEN YOU COULD BE STEALING THIS?
IT'S WAY CUTER.

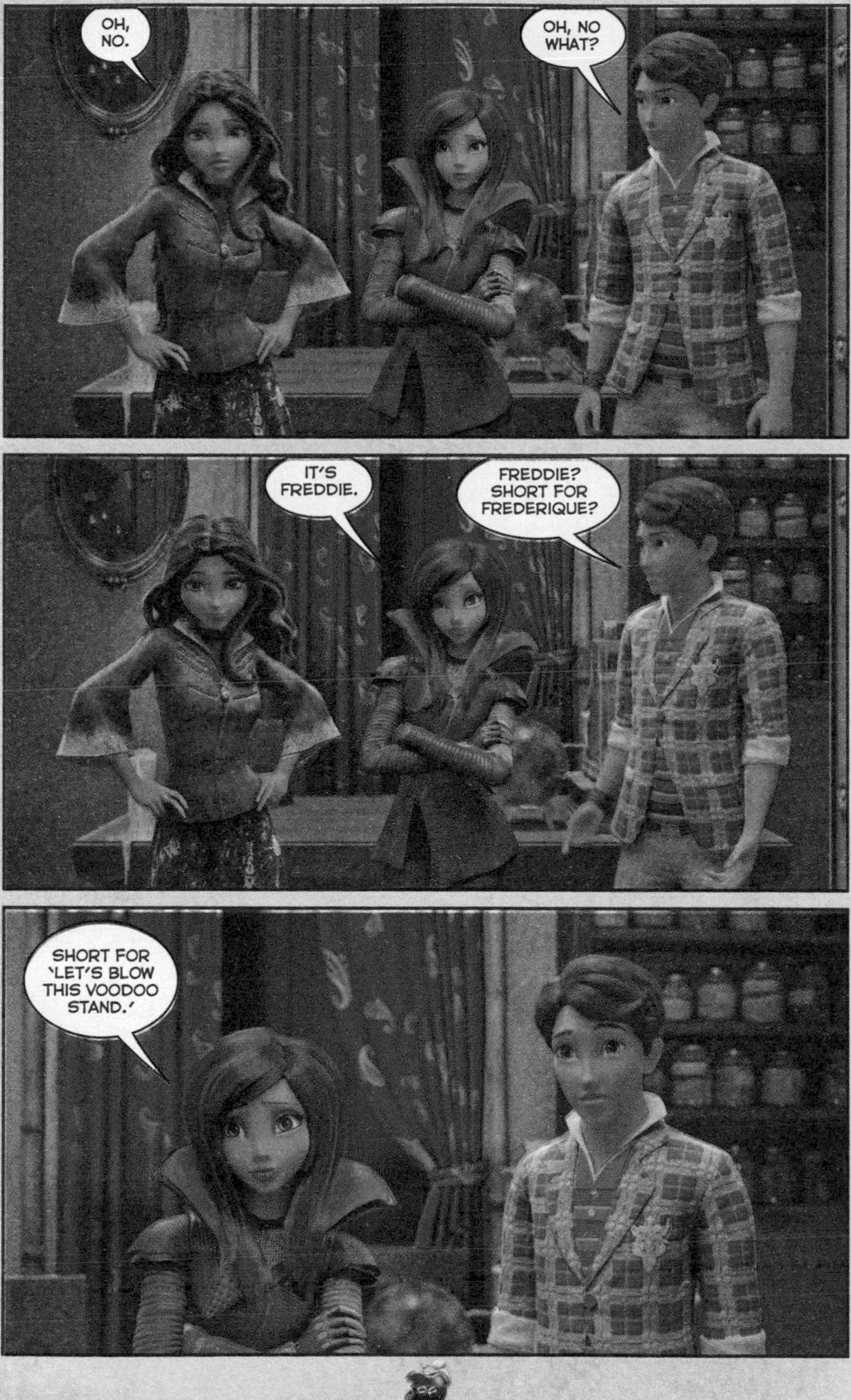
OH, NO.
OH, NO WHAT?
IT'S FREDDIE.
FREDDIE? SHORT FOR FREDERIQUE?
SHORT FOR 'LET'S BLOW THIS VOODOO STAND.'

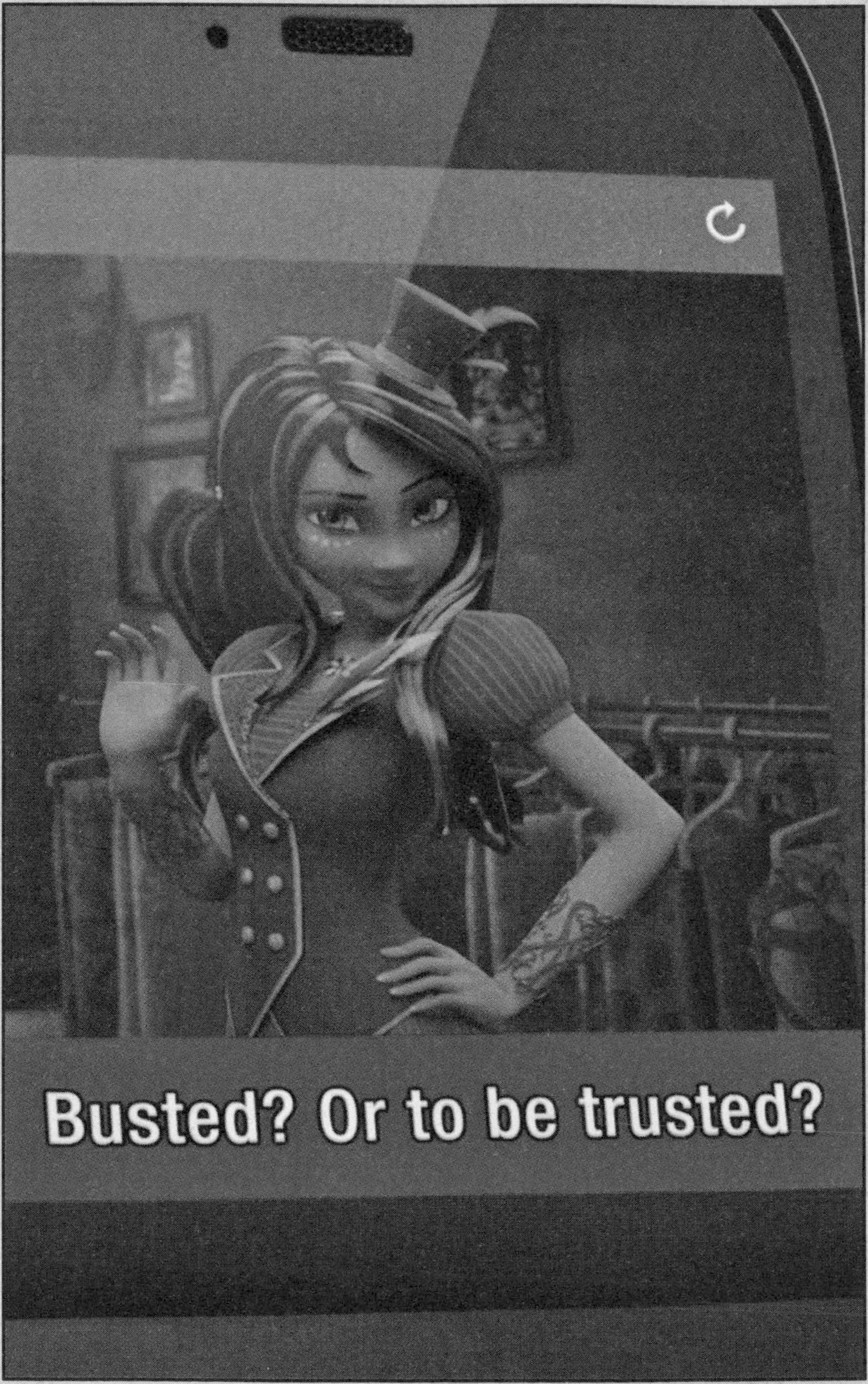
Busted? Or to be trusted?

CHAPTER 6: LAMP SWEET LAMP

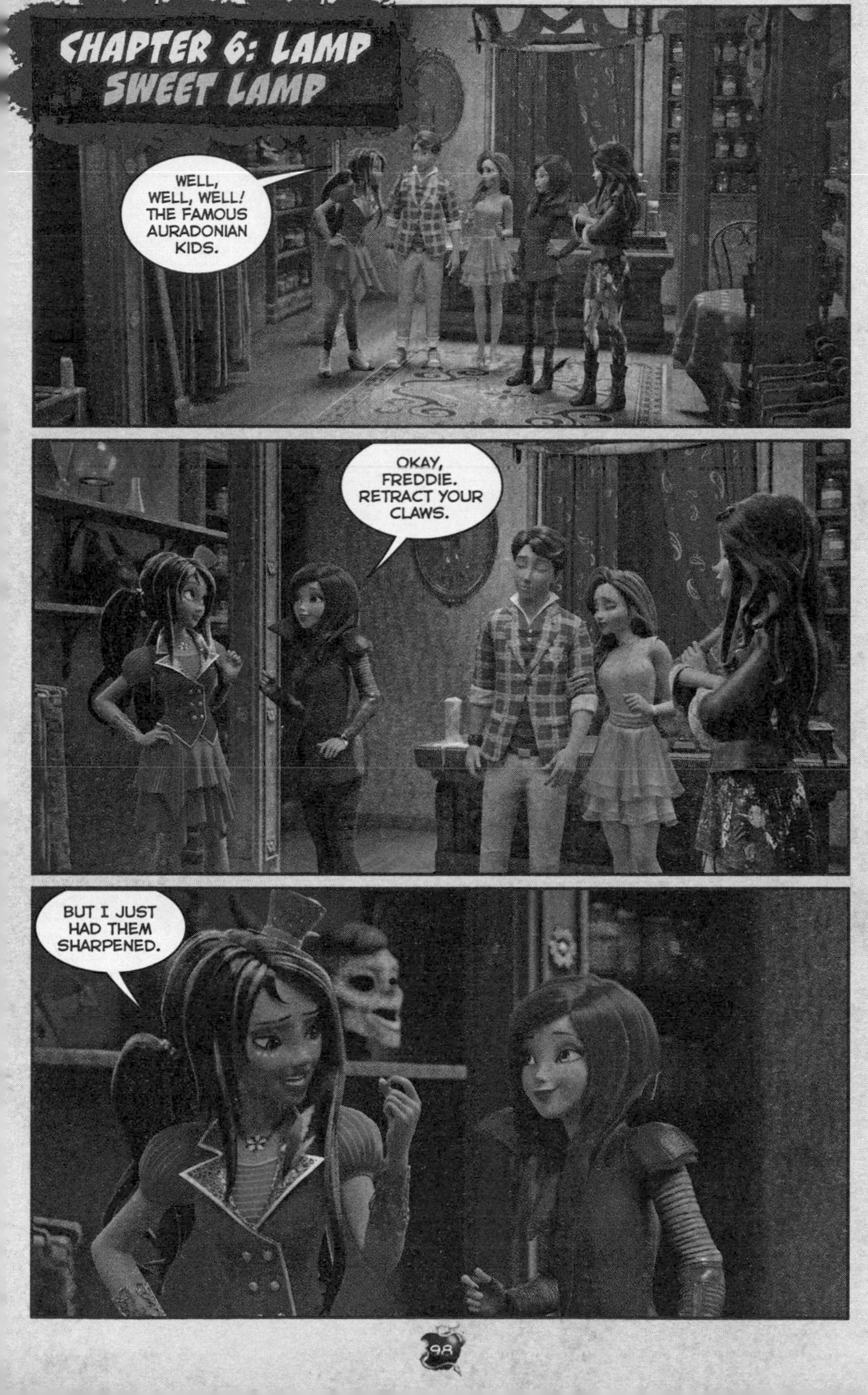
WELL, WELL, WELL! THE FAMOUS AURADONIAN KIDS.
OKAY, FREDDIE. RETRACT YOUR CLAWS.
BUT I JUST HAD THEM SHARPENED.

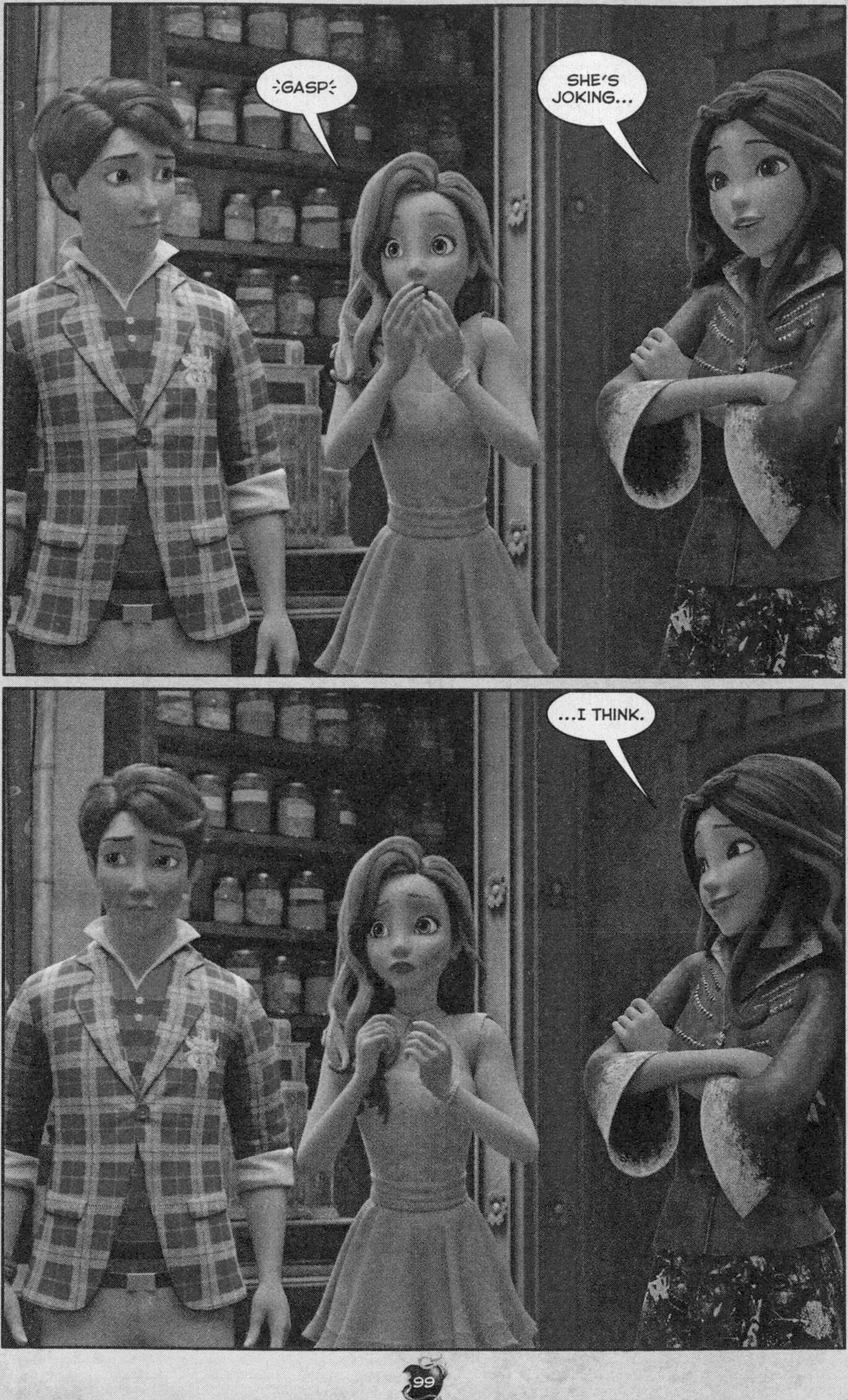
GASP
SHE'S JOKING...
...I THINK.

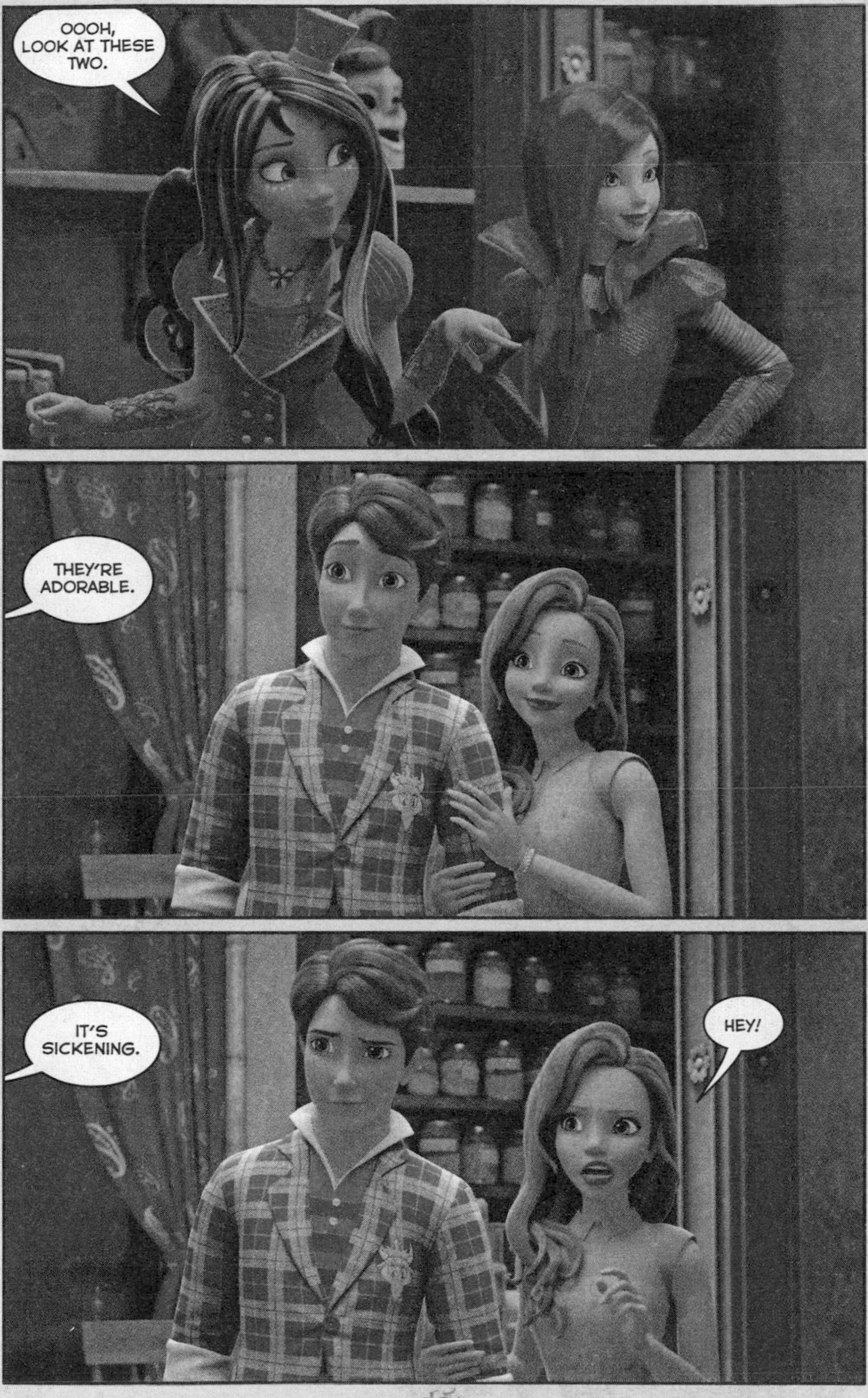
OOOH, LOOK AT THESE TWO.
THEY'RE ADORABLE.
IT'S SICKENING.
HEY!

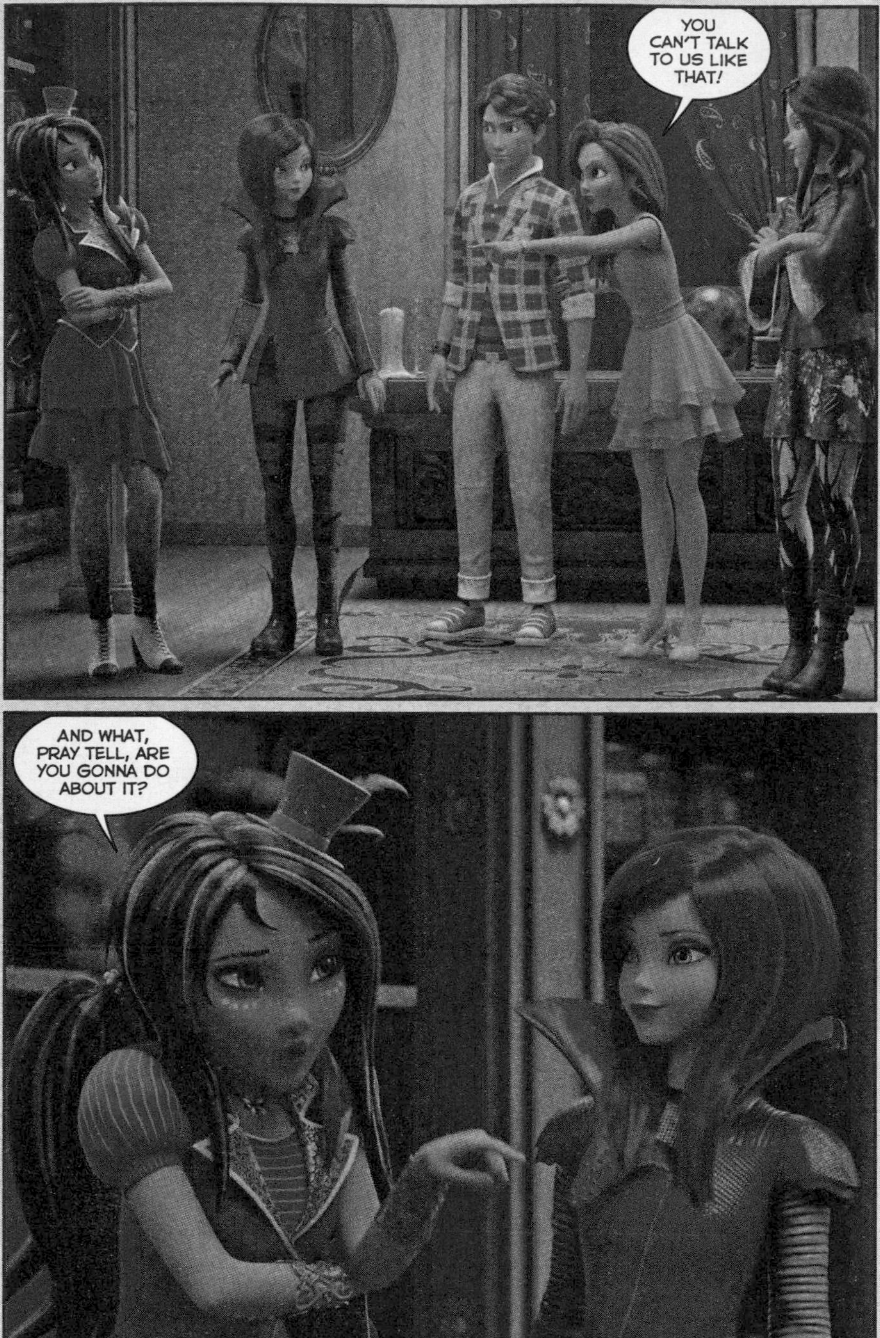
YOU CAN'T TALK TO US LIKE THAT!
AND WHAT, PRAY TELL, ARE YOU GONNA DO ABOUT IT?

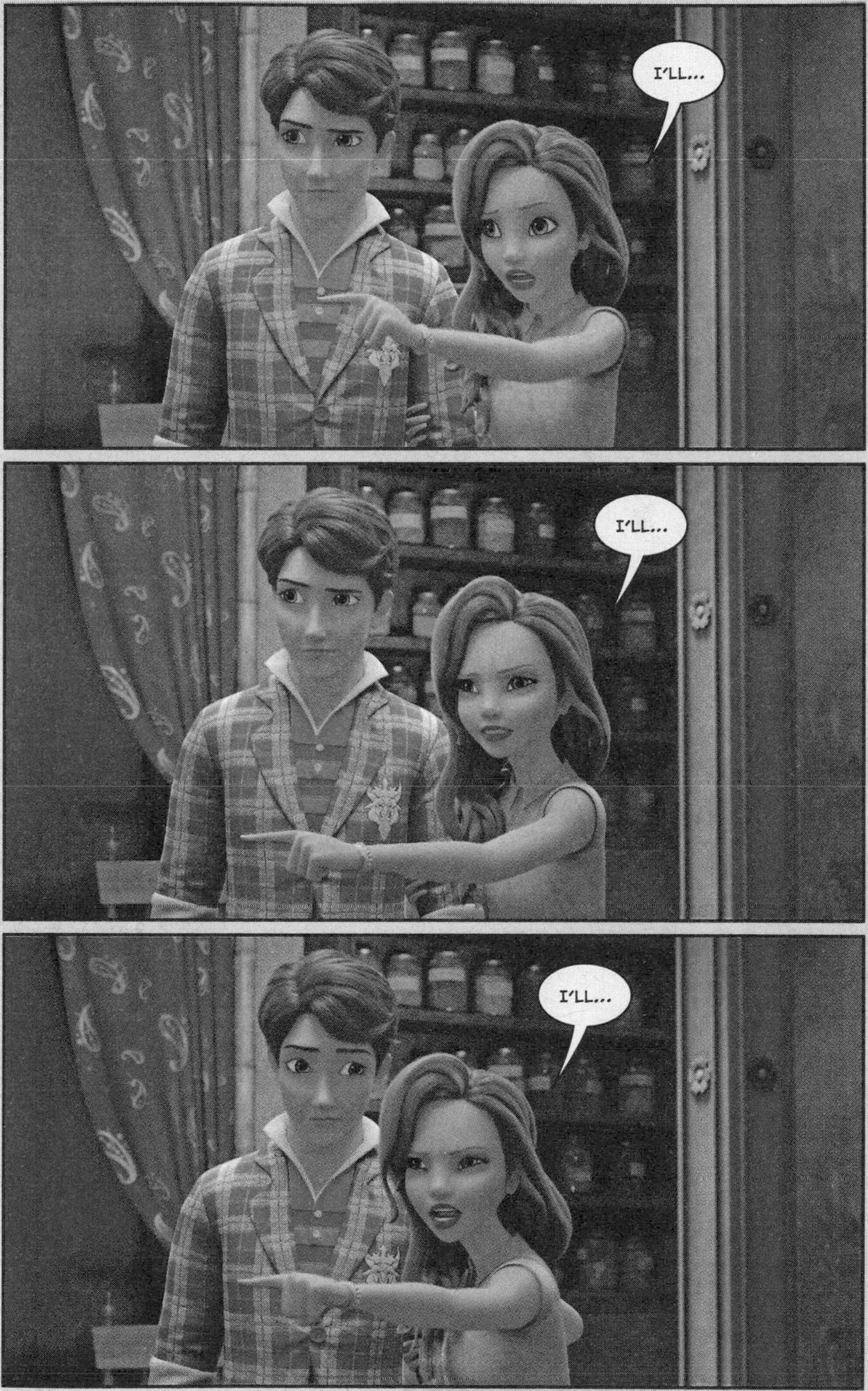
I'LL...
I'LL...
I'LL...

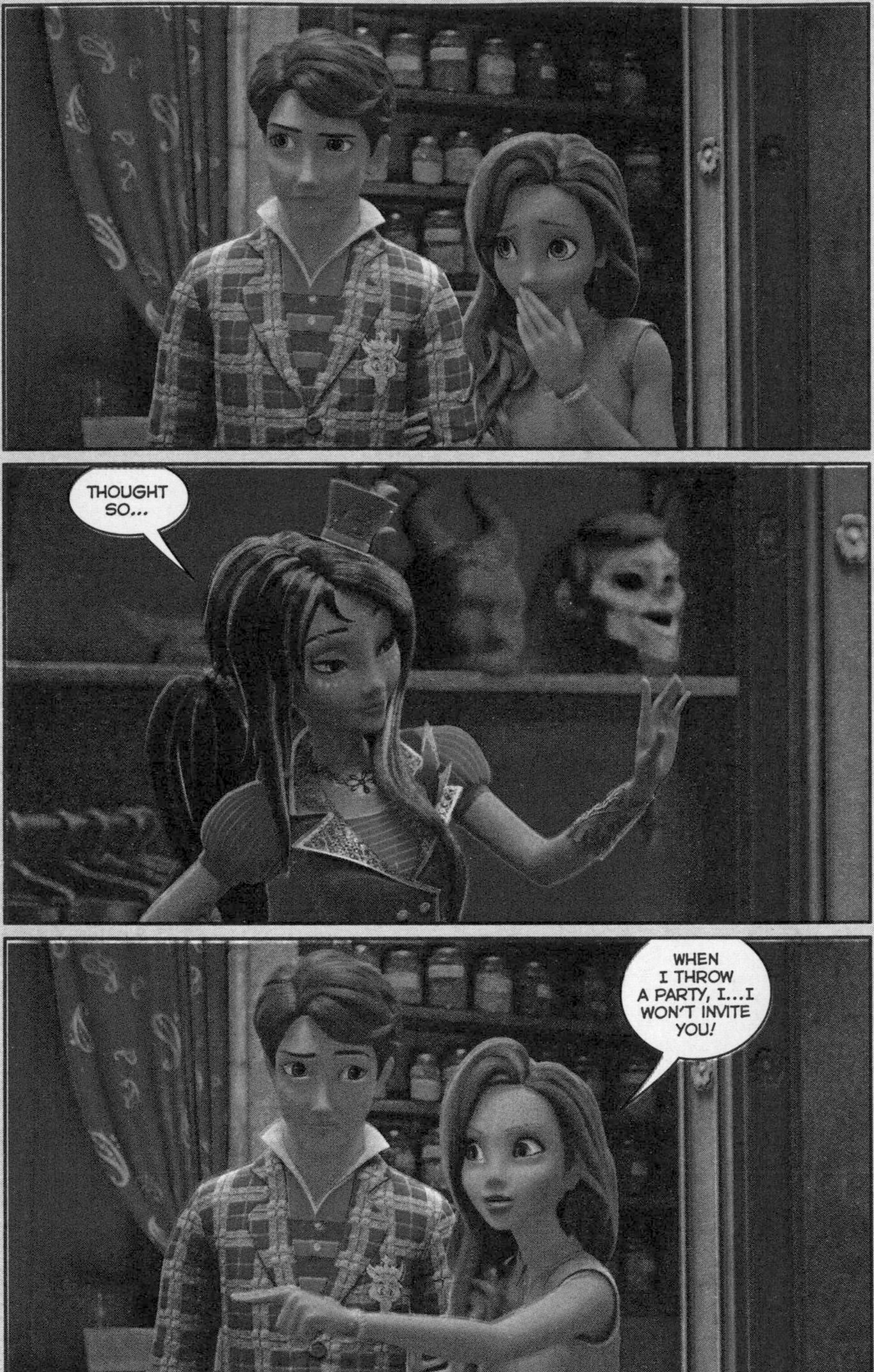
THOUGHT SO...
WHEN I THROW A PARTY, I...I WON'T INVITE YOU!

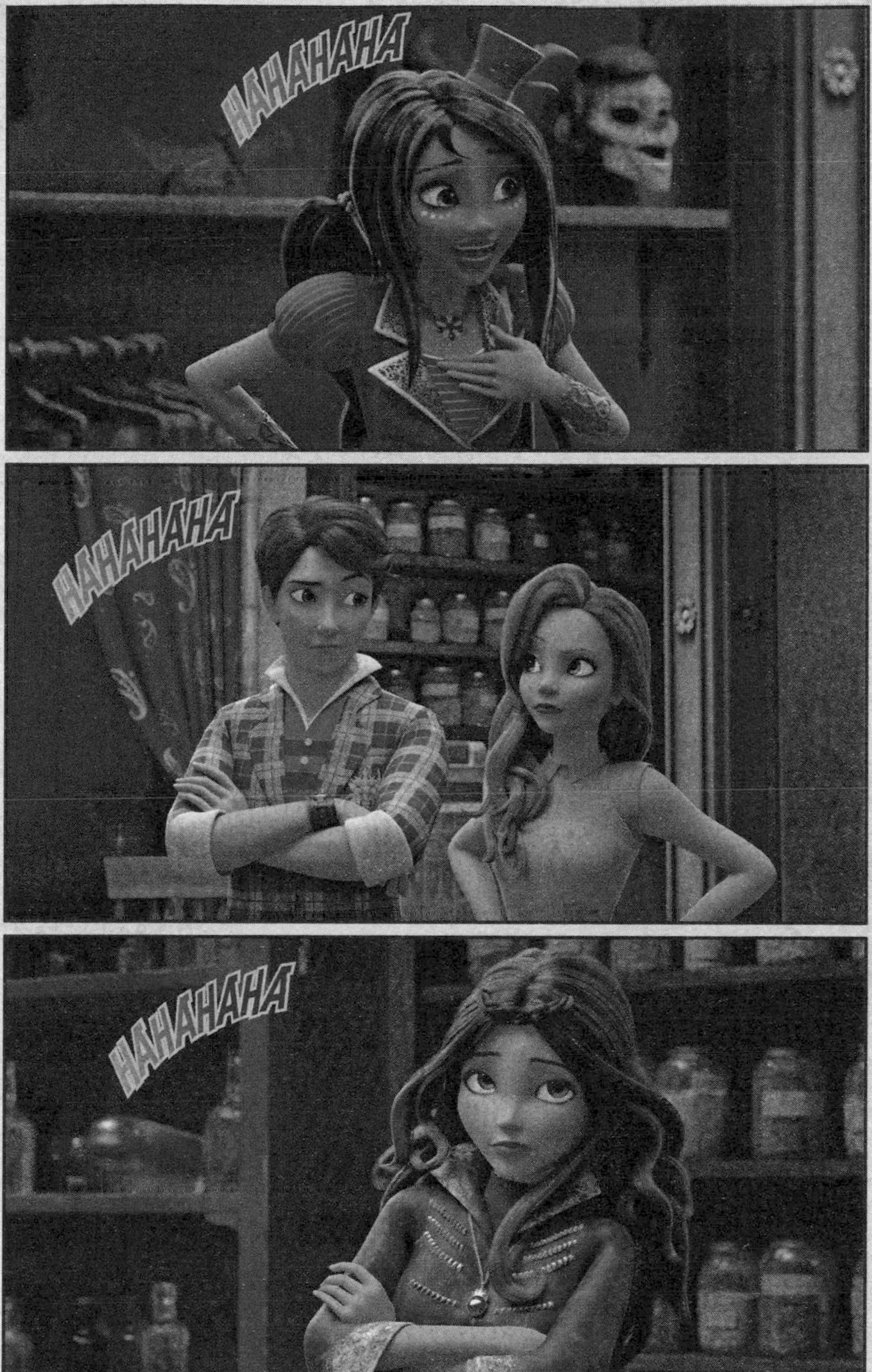
HAHAHAHA
HAHAHAHA
HAHAHAHA

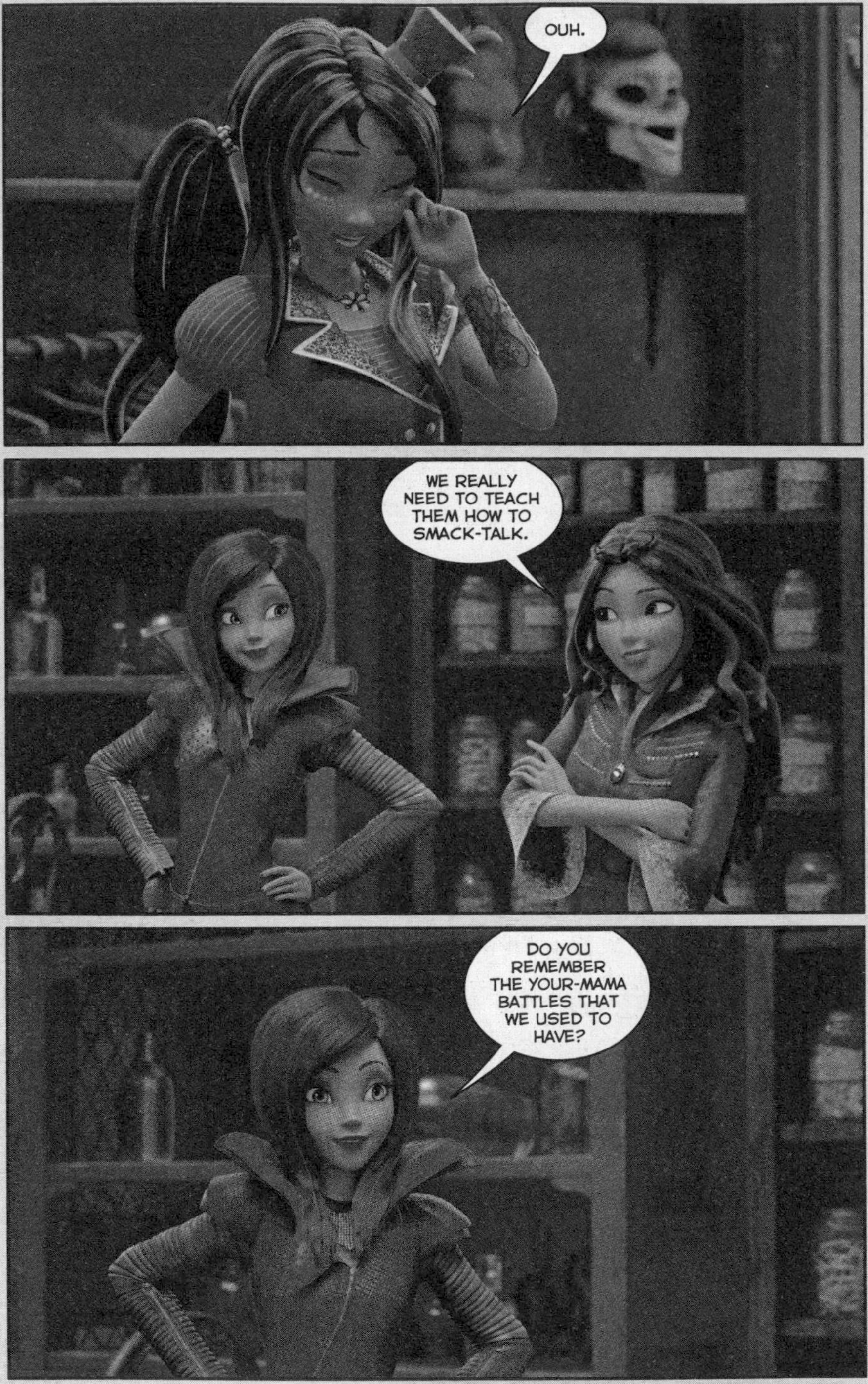
OUH.
WE REALLY NEED TO TEACH THEM HOW TO SMACK-TALK.
DO YOU REMEMBER THE YOUR-MAMA BATTLES THAT WE USED TO HAVE?

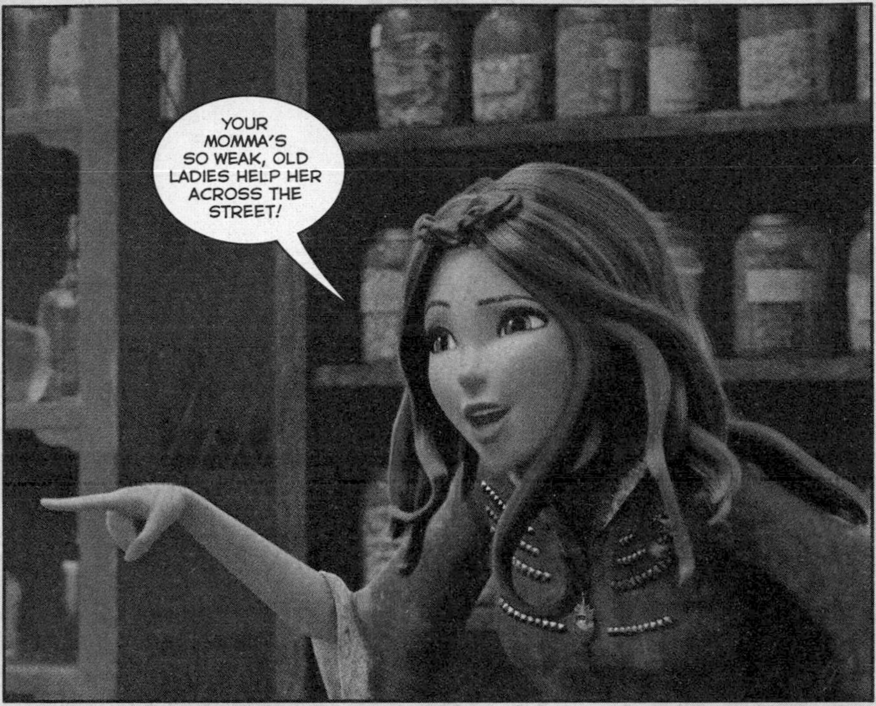
YOUR MOMMA'S SO WEAK, OLD LADIES HELP HER ACROSS THE STREET!

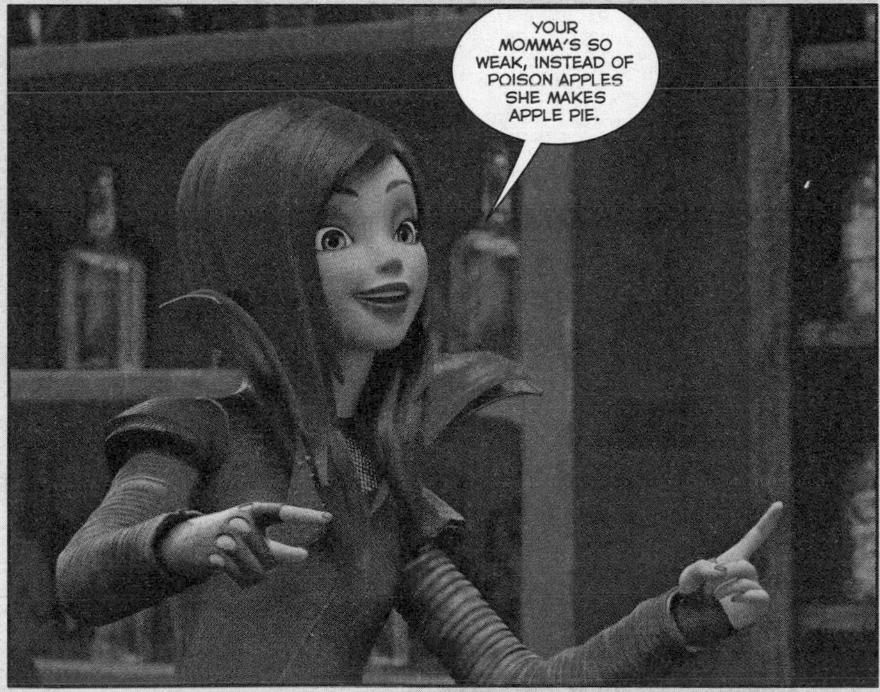
YOUR MOMMA'S SO WEAK, INSTEAD OF POISON APPLES SHE MAKES APPLE PIE.

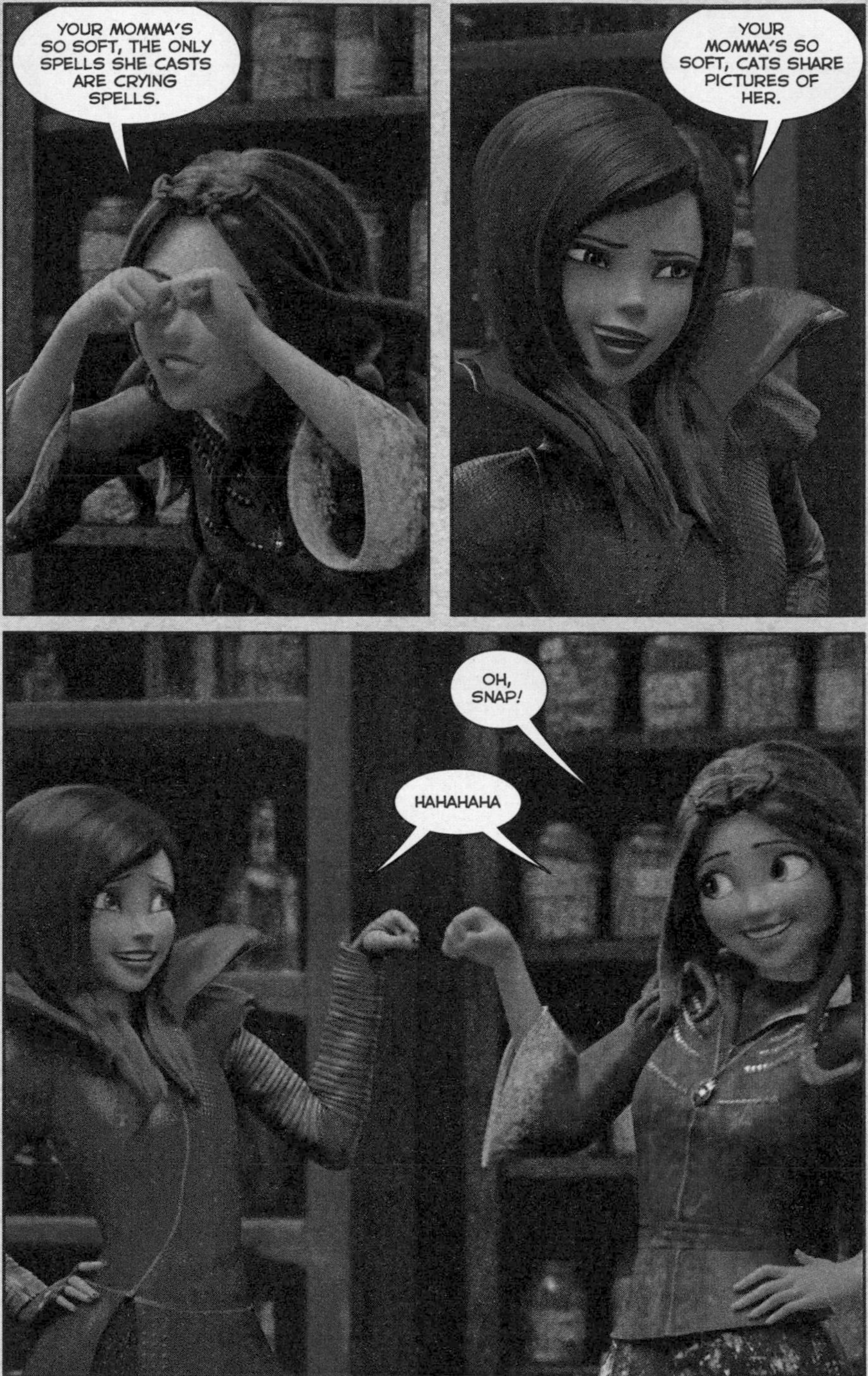
YOUR MOMMA'S SO SOFT, THE ONLY SPELLS SHE CASTS ARE CRYING SPELLS.
YOUR MOMMA'S SO SOFT, CATS SHARE PICTURES OF HER.
OH, SNAP!
HAHAHAHA

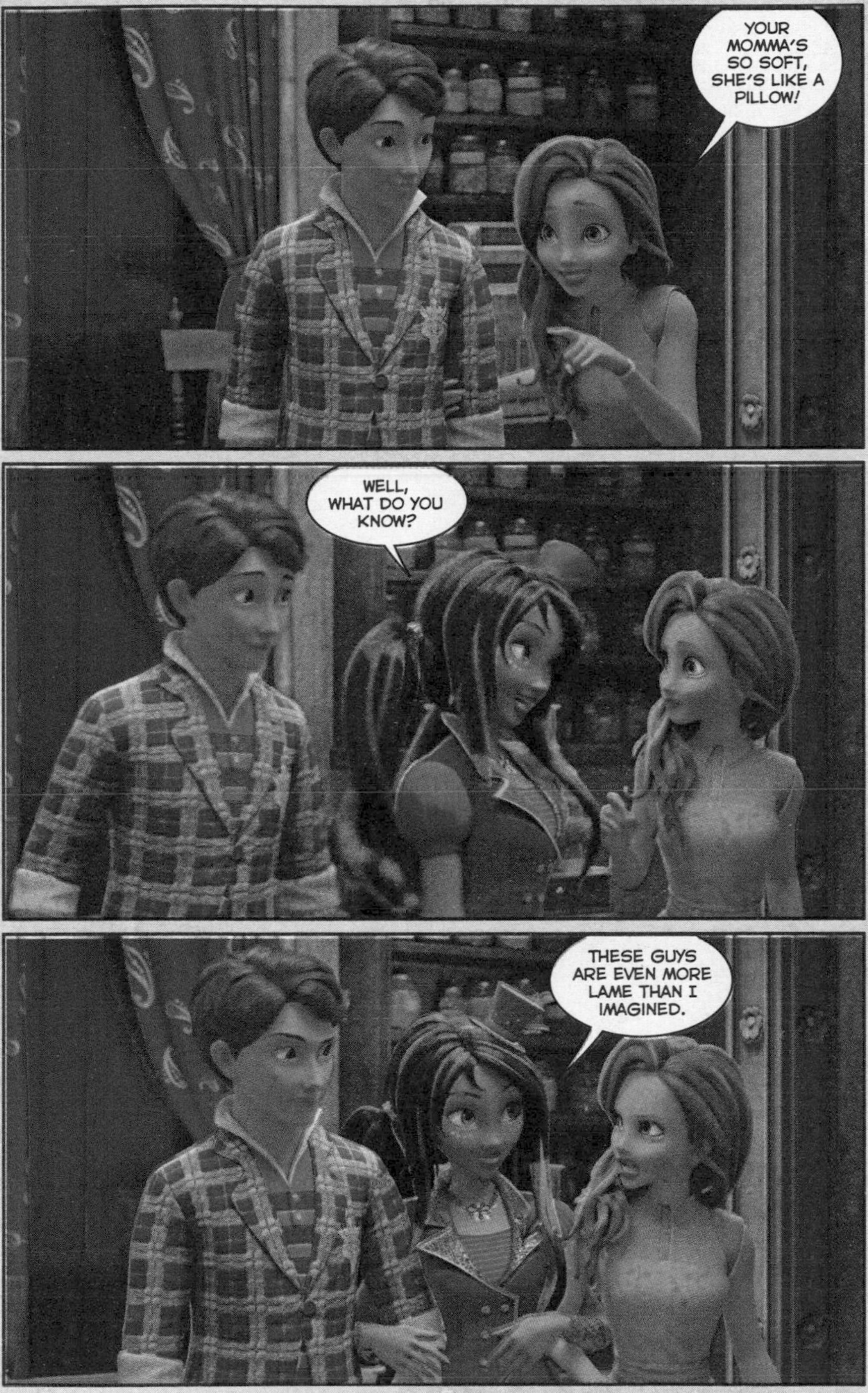
YOUR MOMMA'S SO SOFT, SHE'S LIKE A PILLOW!
WELL, WHAT DO YOU KNOW?
THESE GUYS ARE EVEN MORE LAME THAN I IMAGINED.

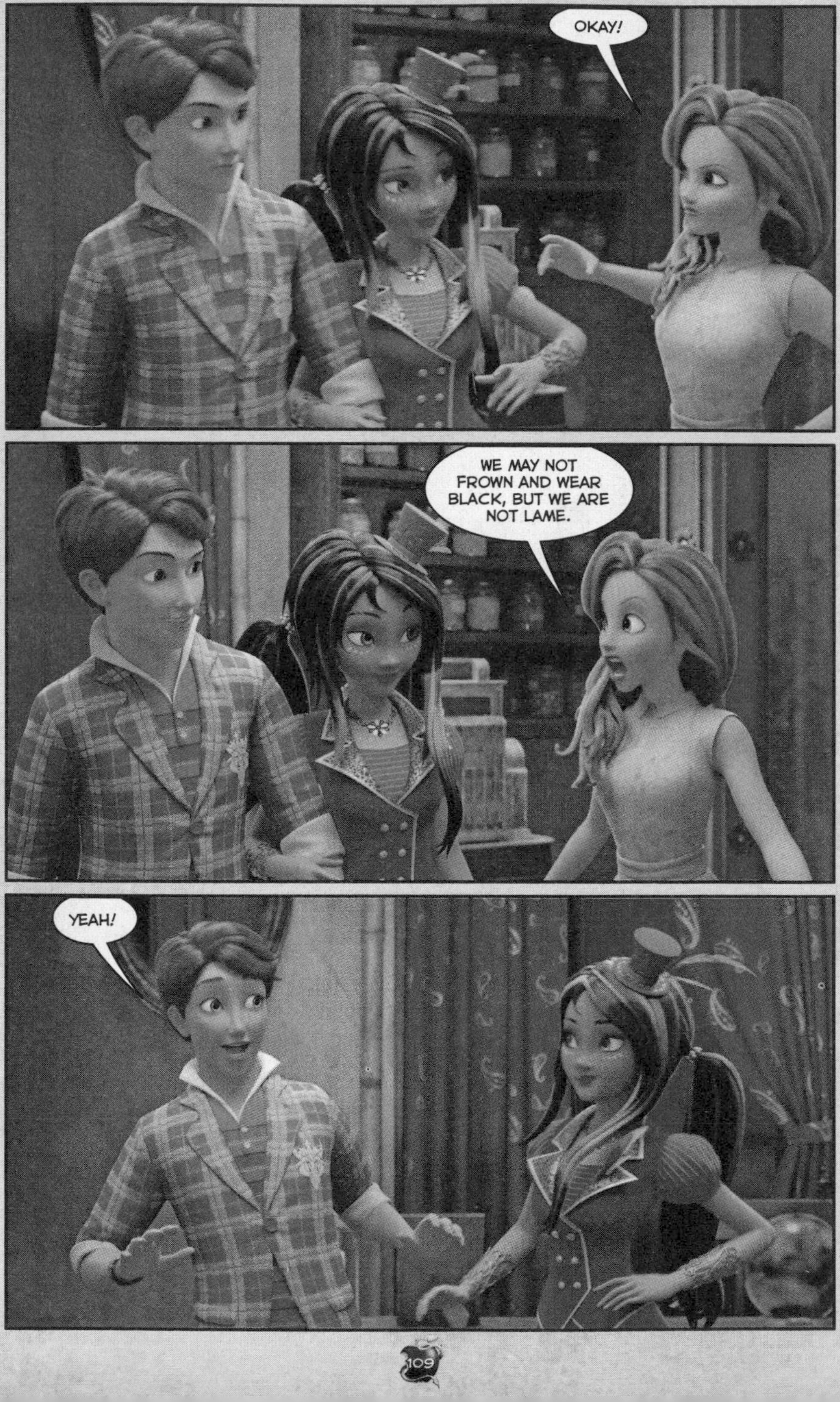
OKAY!
WE MAY NOT FROWN AND WEAR BLACK, BUT WE ARE NOT LAME.
YEAH!

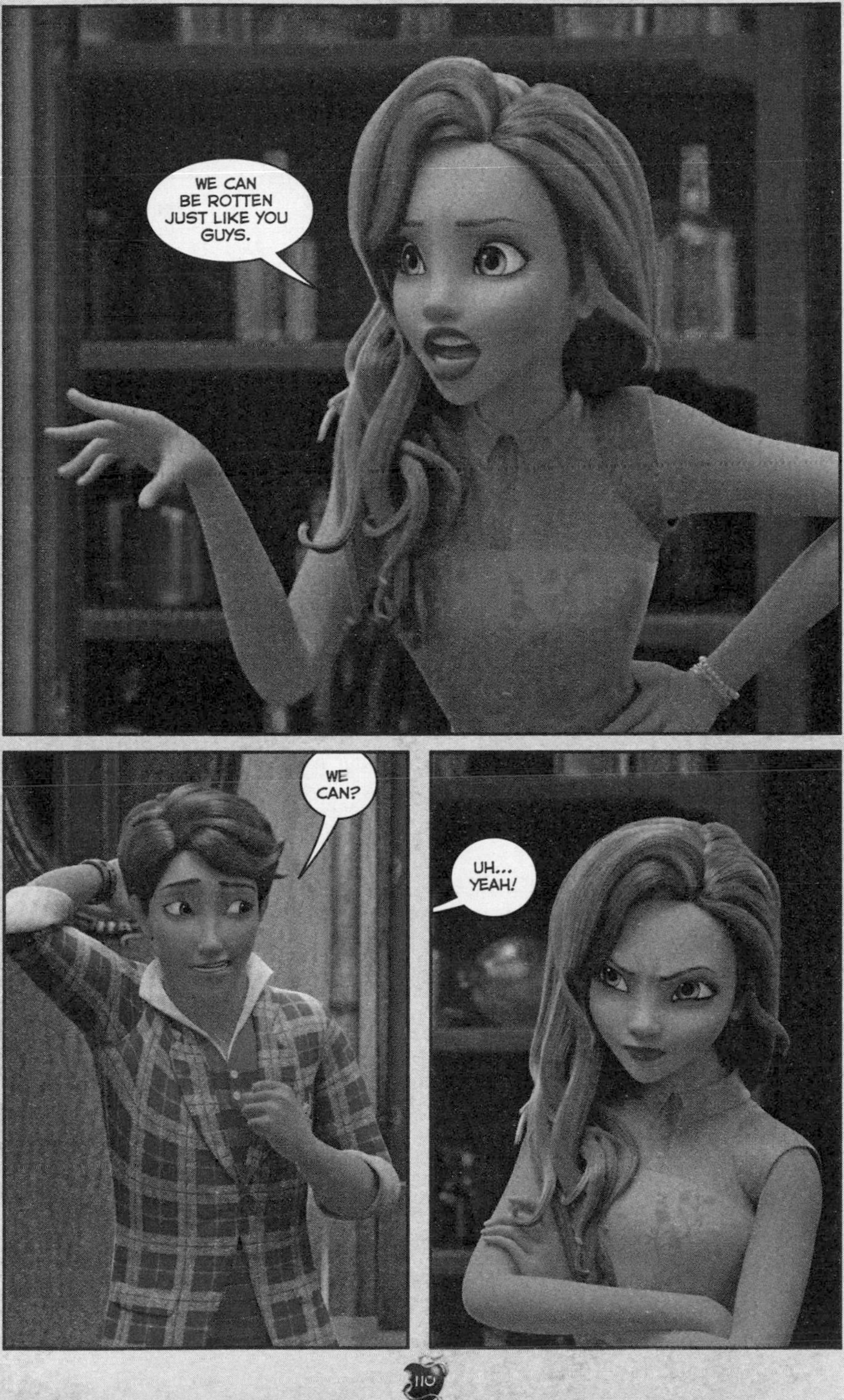
WE CAN BE ROTTEN JUST LIKE YOU GUYS.
WE CAN?
UH... YEAH!

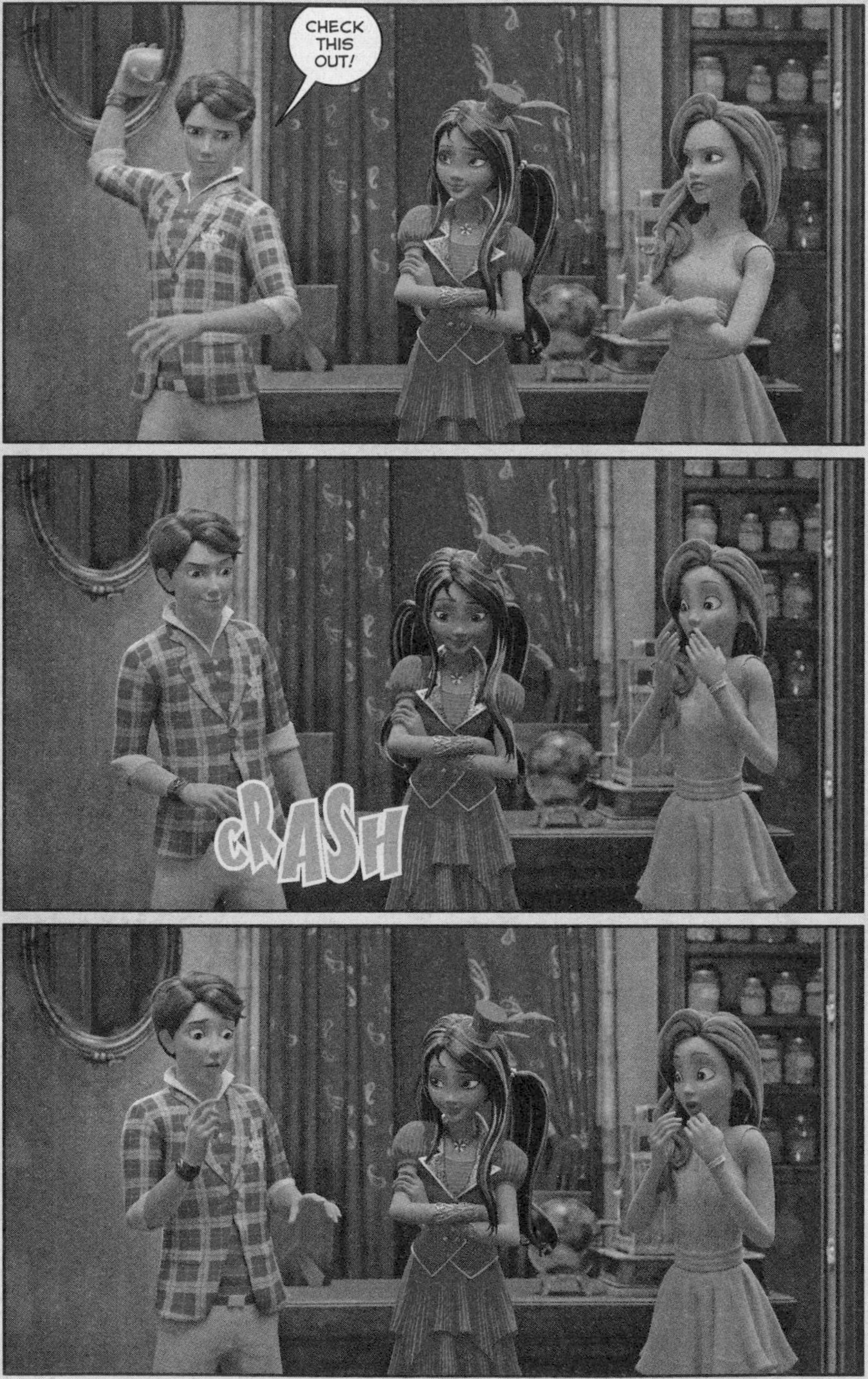
CHECK THIS OUT!
CRASH

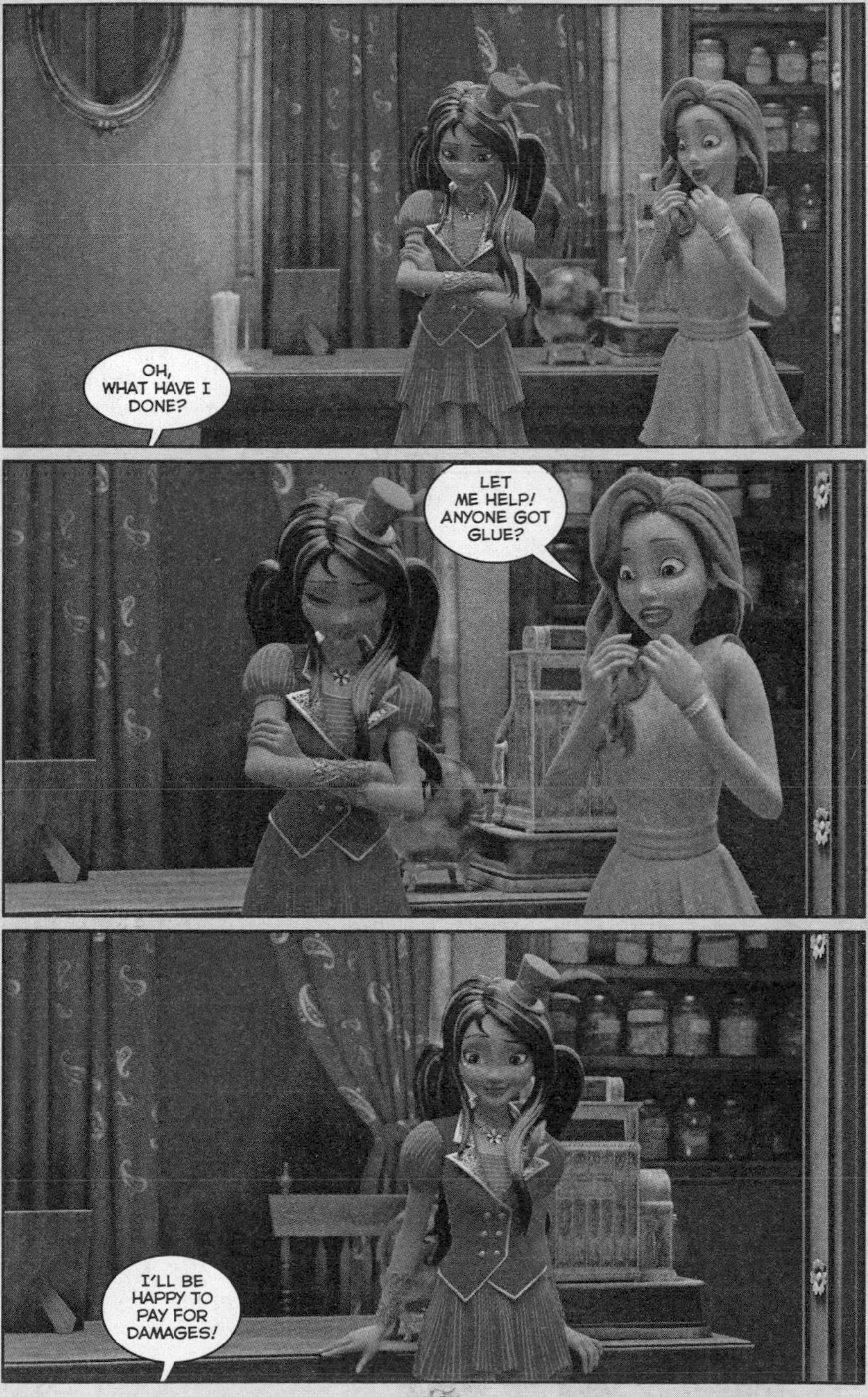
OH, WHAT HAVE I DONE?
LET ME HELP! ANYONE GOT GLUE?
I'LL BE HAPPY TO PAY FOR DAMAGES!

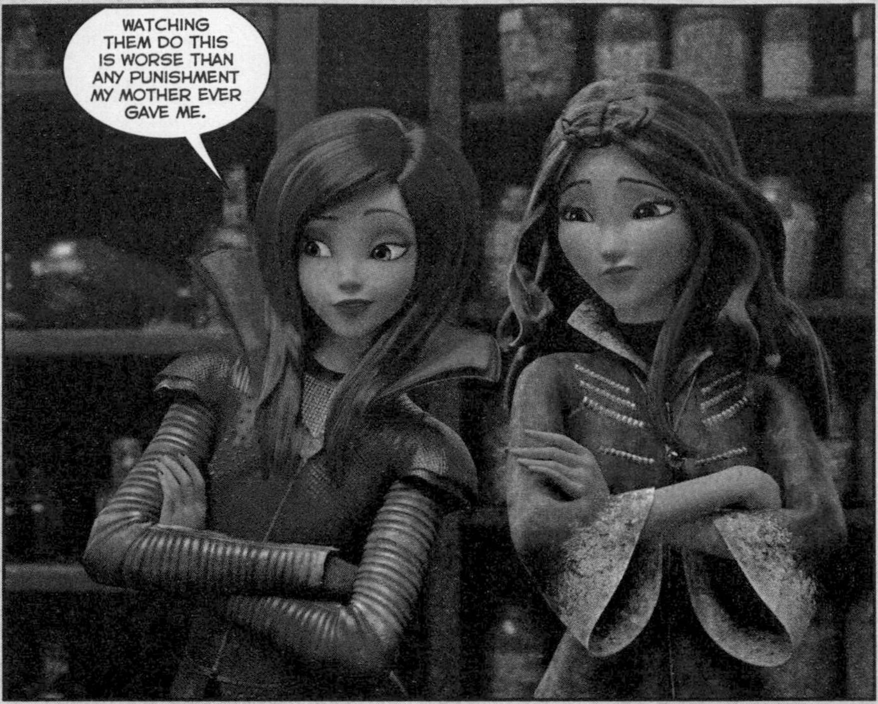
WATCHING THEM DO THIS IS WORSE THAN ANY PUNISHMENT MY MOTHER EVER GAVE ME.

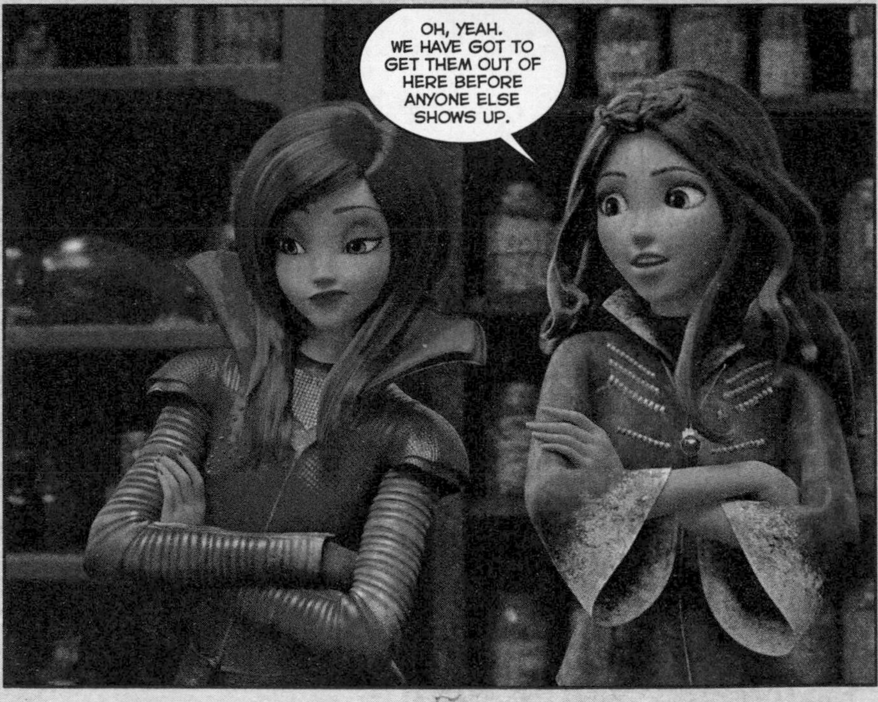
OH, YEAH. WE HAVE GOT TO GET THEM OUT OF HERE BEFORE ANYONE ELSE SHOWS UP.

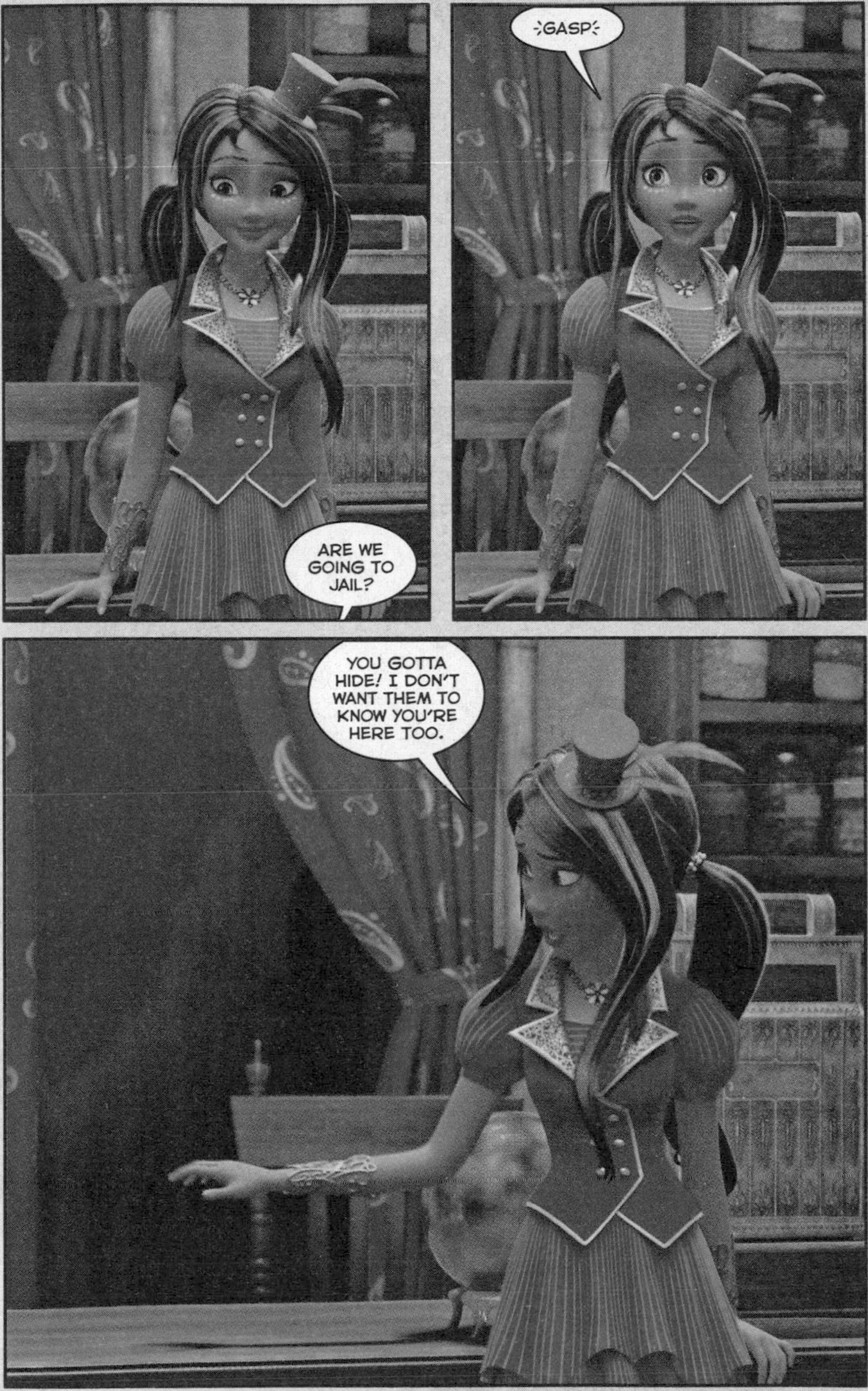
ARE WE GOING TO JAIL?
-GASP-
YOU GOTTA HIDE! I DON'T WANT THEM TO KNOW YOU'RE HERE TOO.

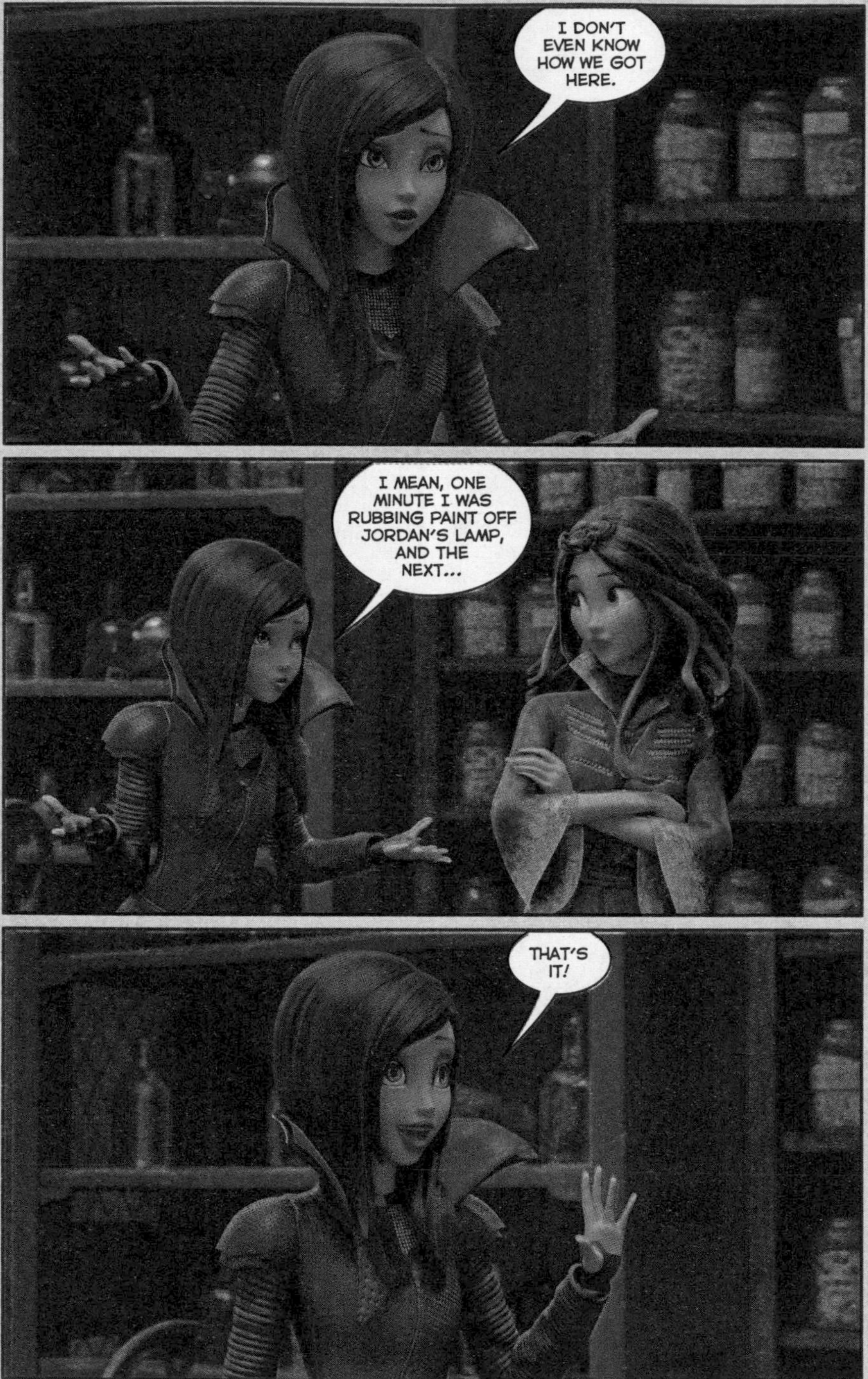
I DON'T EVEN KNOW HOW WE GOT HERE.
I MEAN, ONE MINUTE I WAS RUBBING PAINT OFF JORDAN'S LAMP, AND THE NEXT...
THAT'S IT!

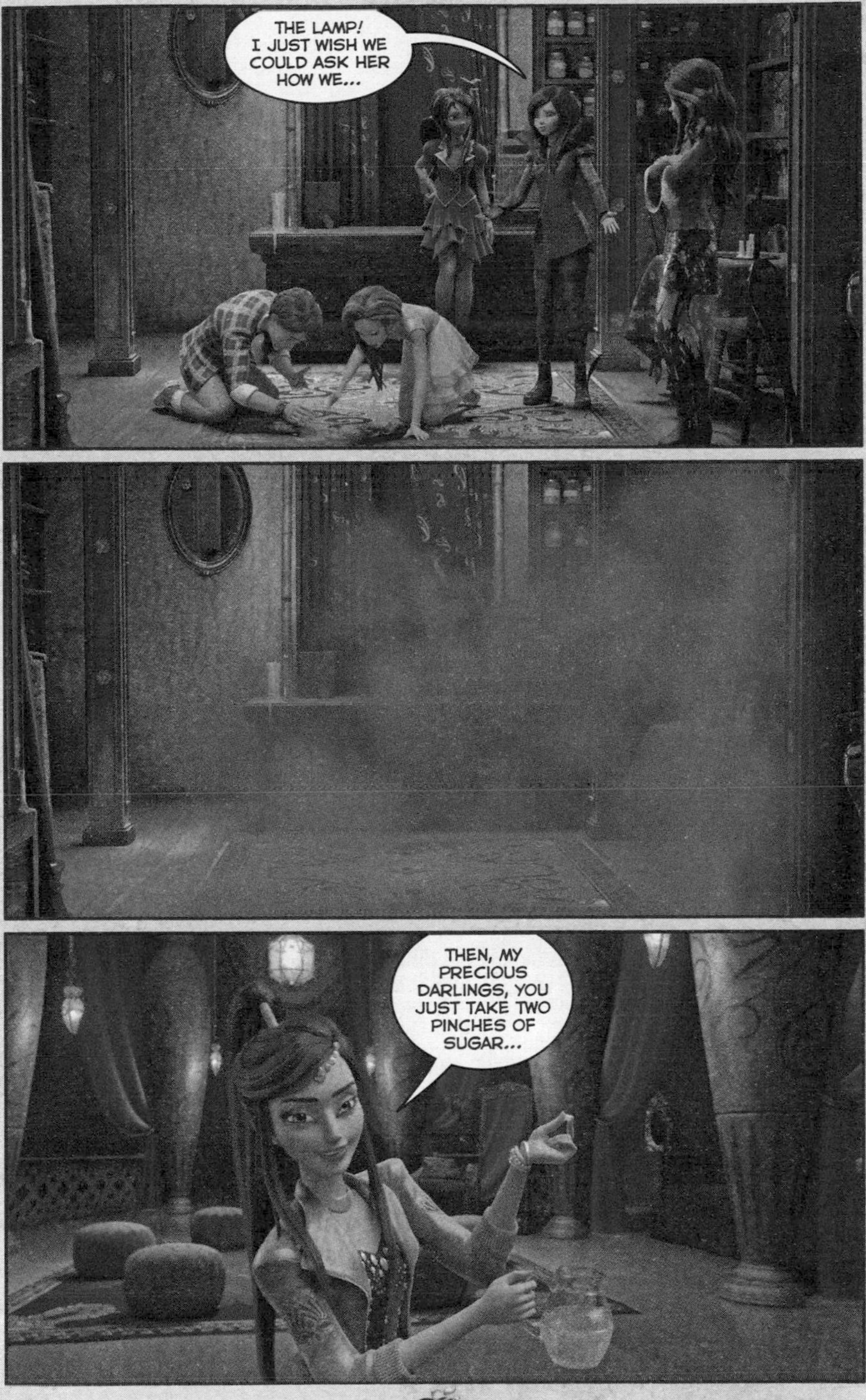
THE LAMP! I JUST WISH WE COULD ASK HER HOW WE...
THEN, MY PRECIOUS DARLINGS, YOU JUST TAKE TWO PINCHES OF SUGAR...

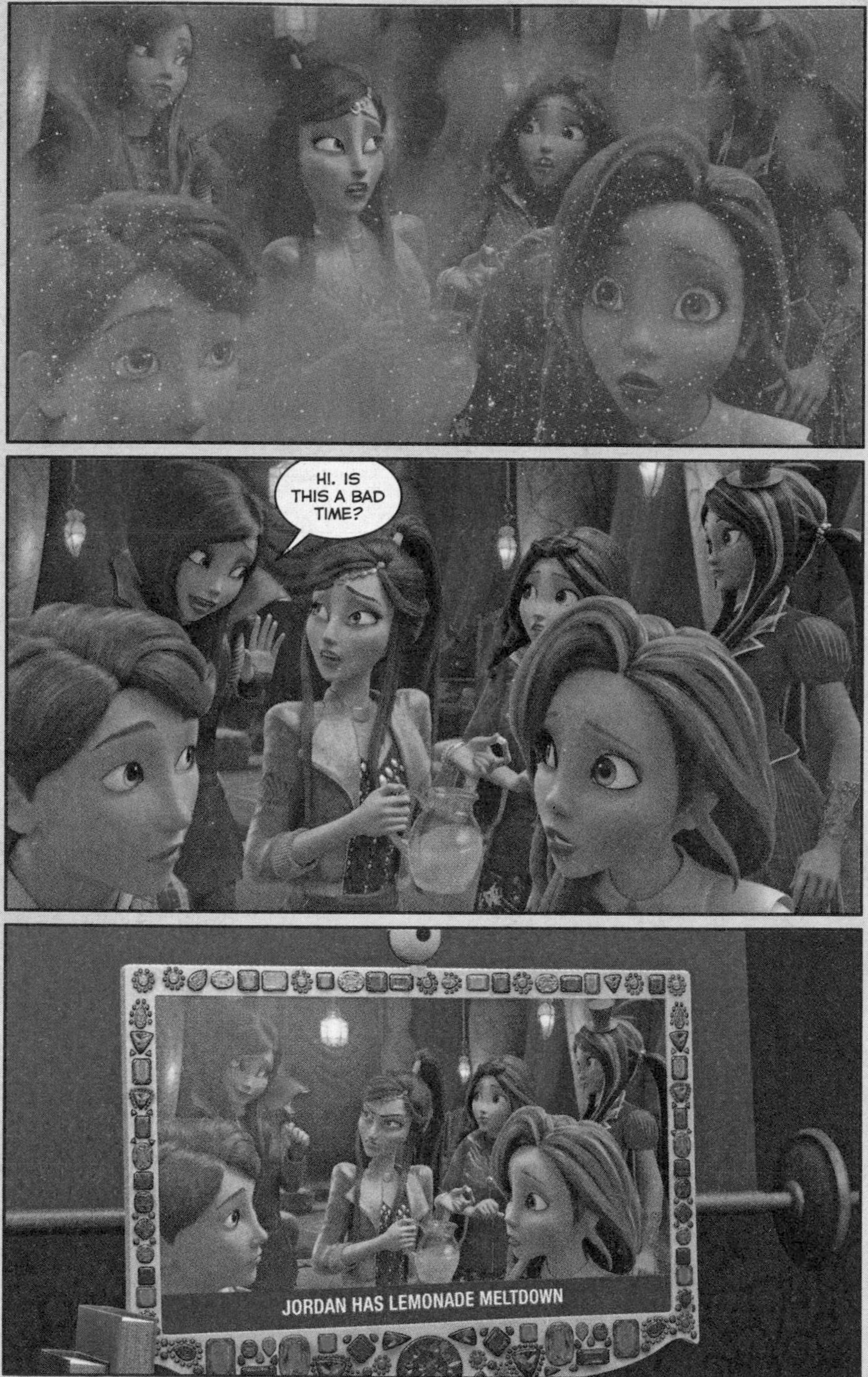
HI. IS THIS A BAD TIME?
JORDAN HAS LEMONADE MELTDOWN

CHAPTER 7: GENIE CHIC

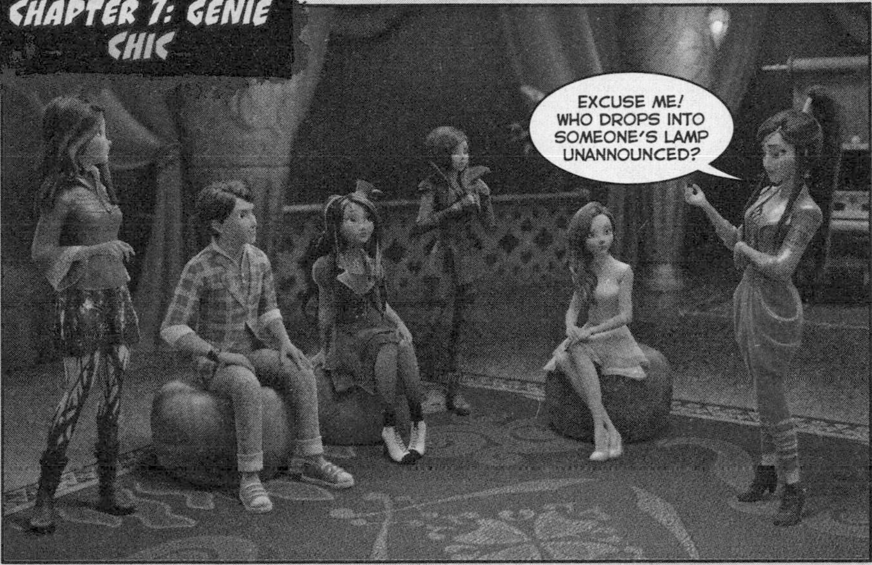
EXCUSE ME! WHO DROPS INTO SOMEONE'S LAMP UNANNOUNCED?

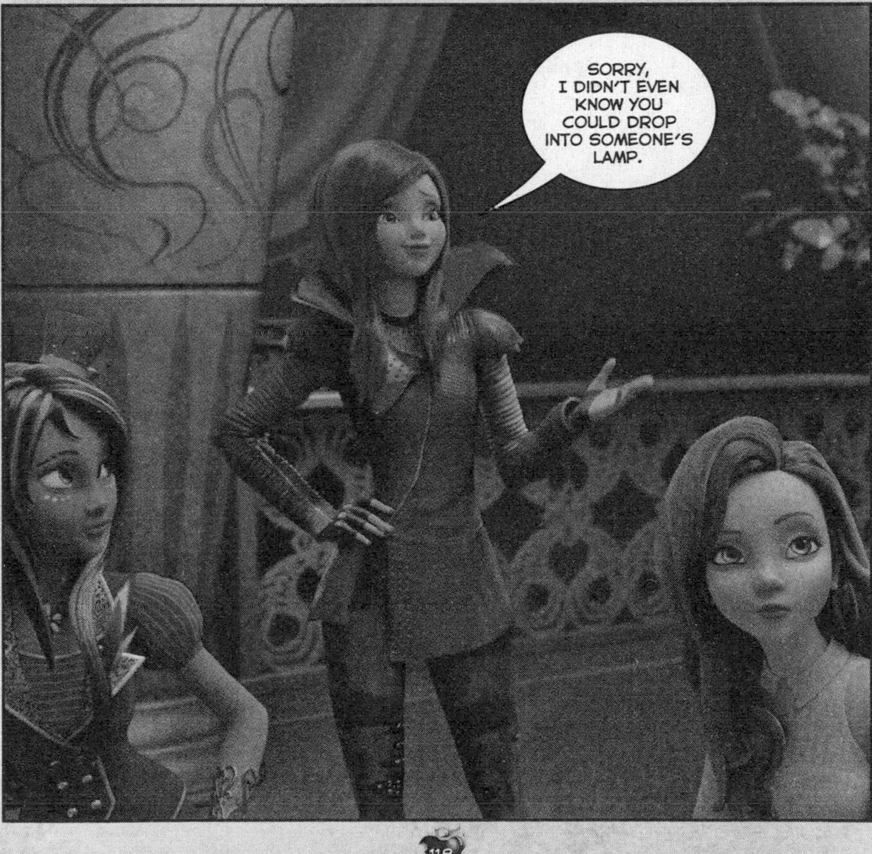
SORRY, I DIDN'T EVEN KNOW YOU COULD DROP INTO SOMEONE'S LAMP.

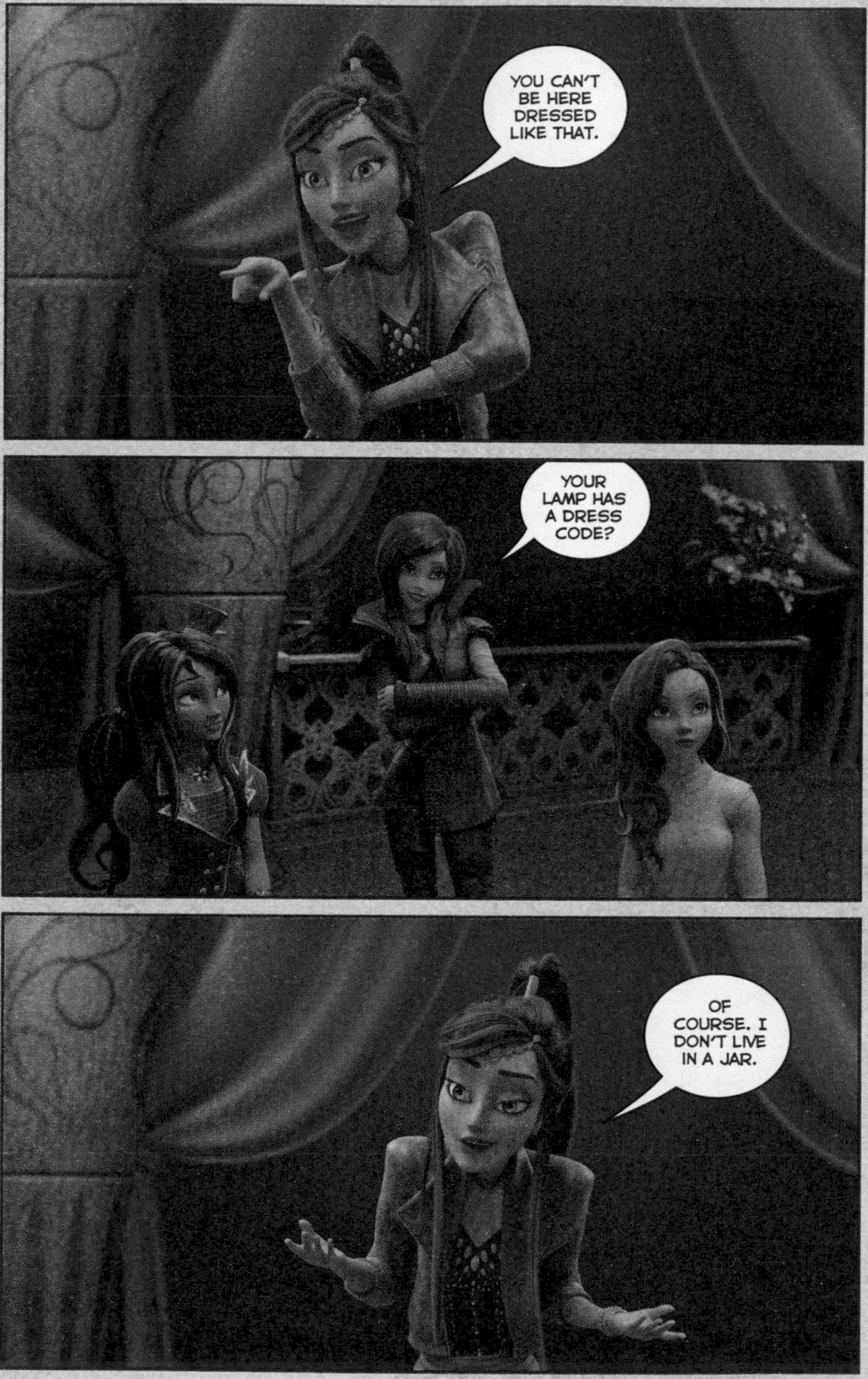
YOU CAN'T BE HERE DRESSED LIKE THAT.
YOUR LAMP HAS A DRESS CODE?
OF COURSE. I DON'T LIVE IN A JAR.

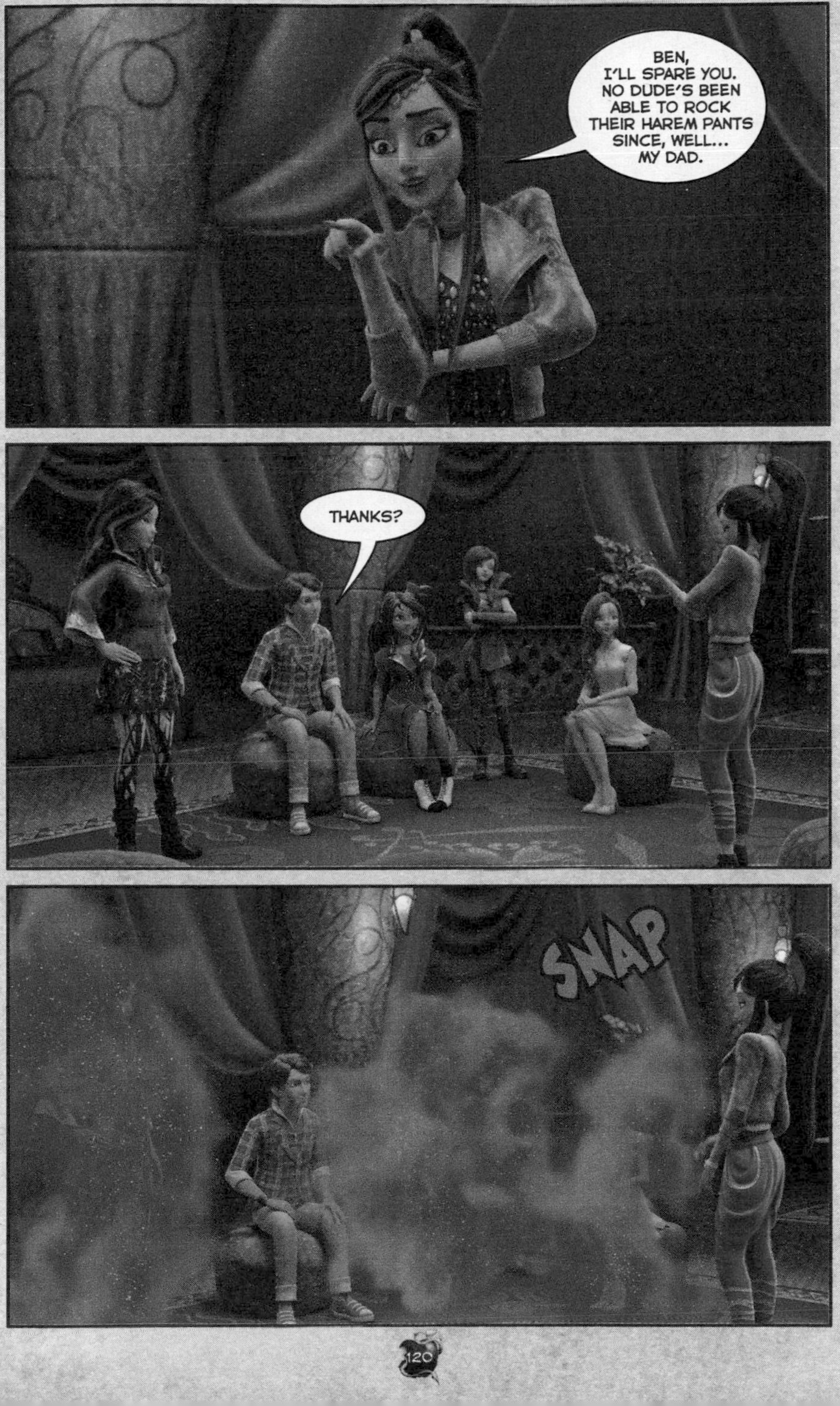
BEN, I'LL SPARE YOU. NO DUDE'S BEEN ABLE TO ROCK THEIR HAREM PANTS SINCE, WELL... MY DAD.
THANKS?
SNAP

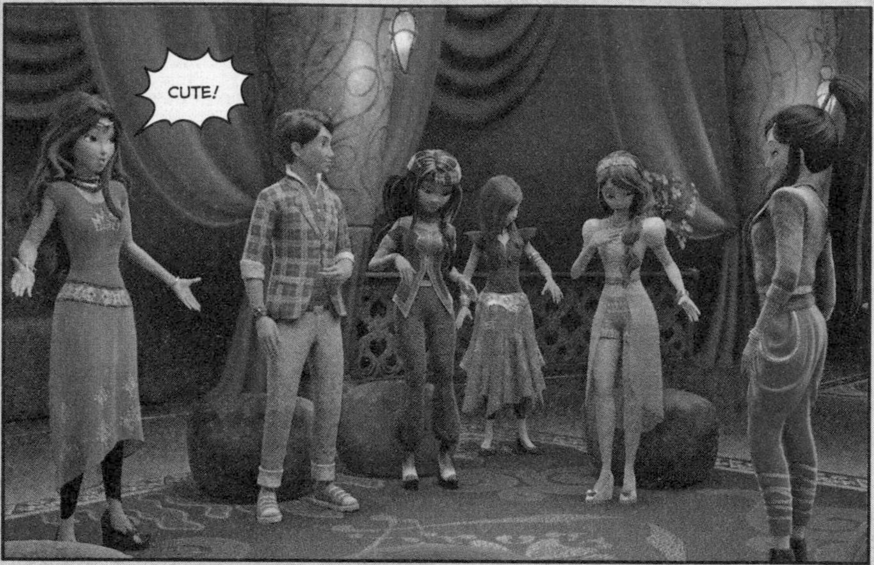
CUTE!

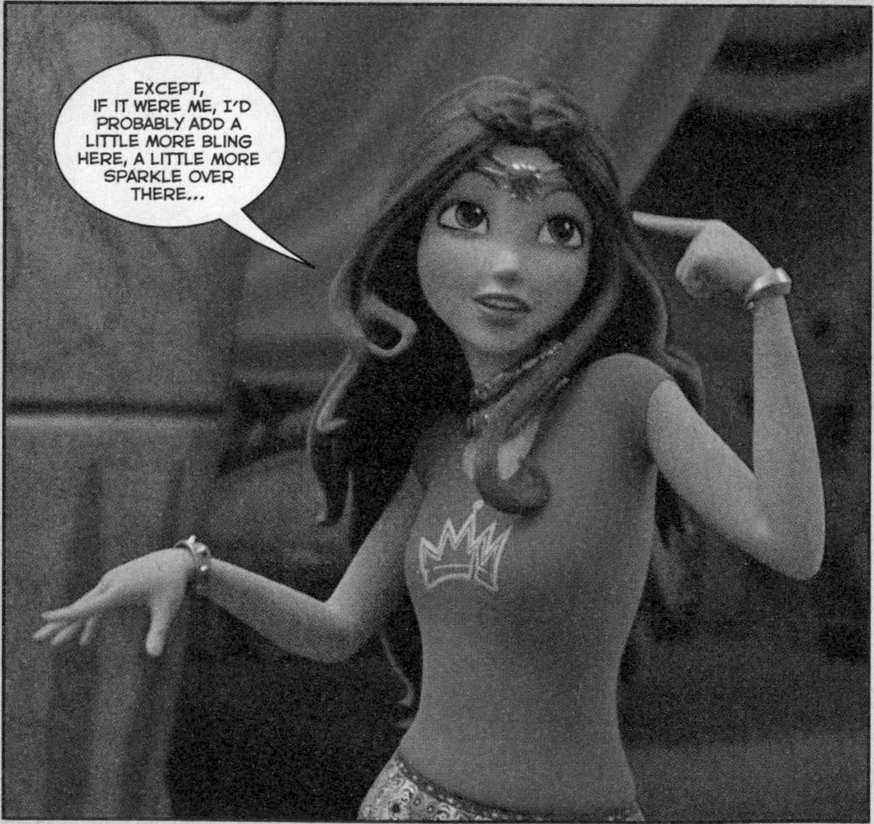
EXCEPT, IF IT WERE ME, I'D PROBABLY ADD A LITTLE MORE BLING HERE, A LITTLE MORE SPARKLE OVER THERE...

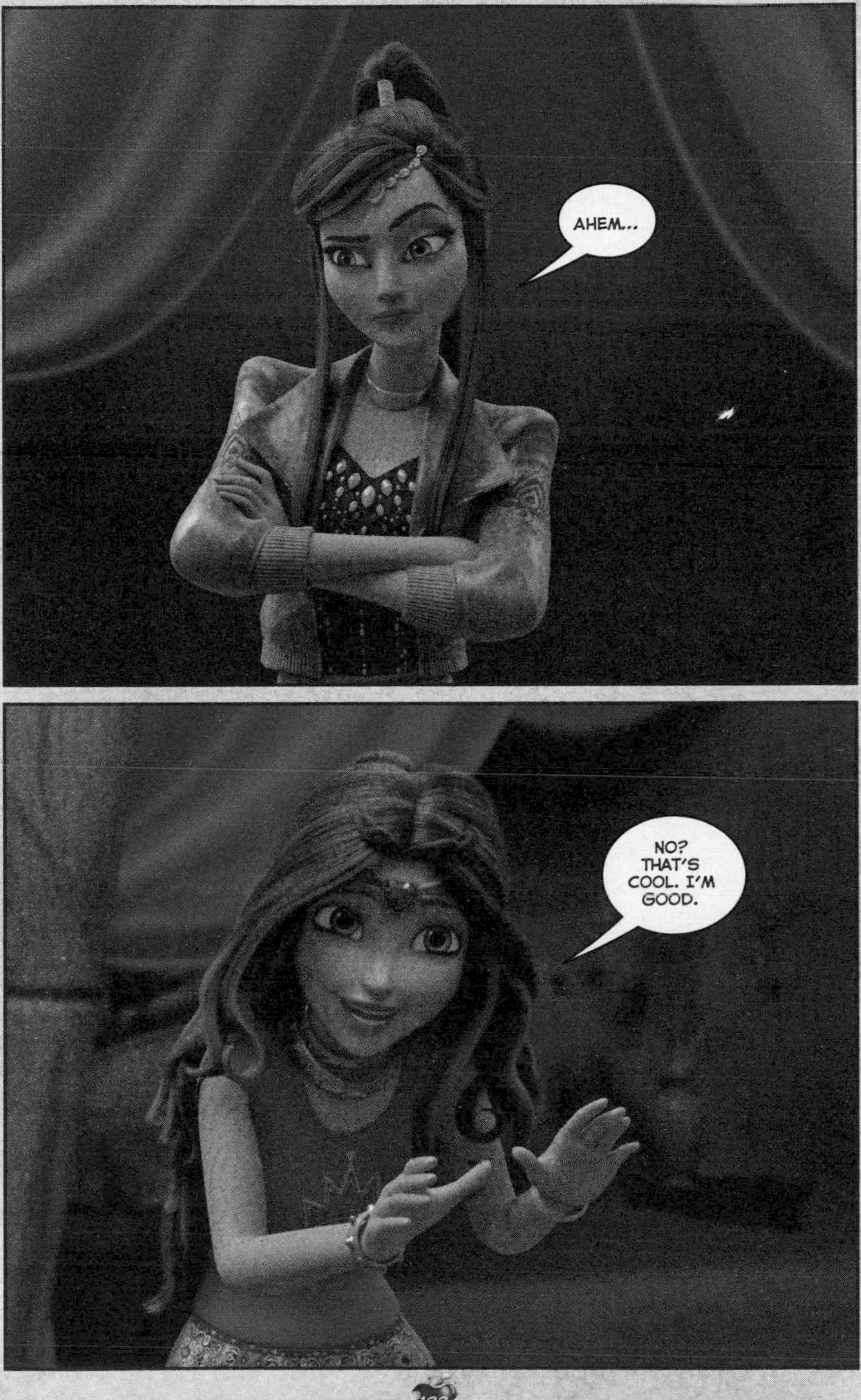
AHEM...
NO? THAT'S COOL. I'M GOOD.

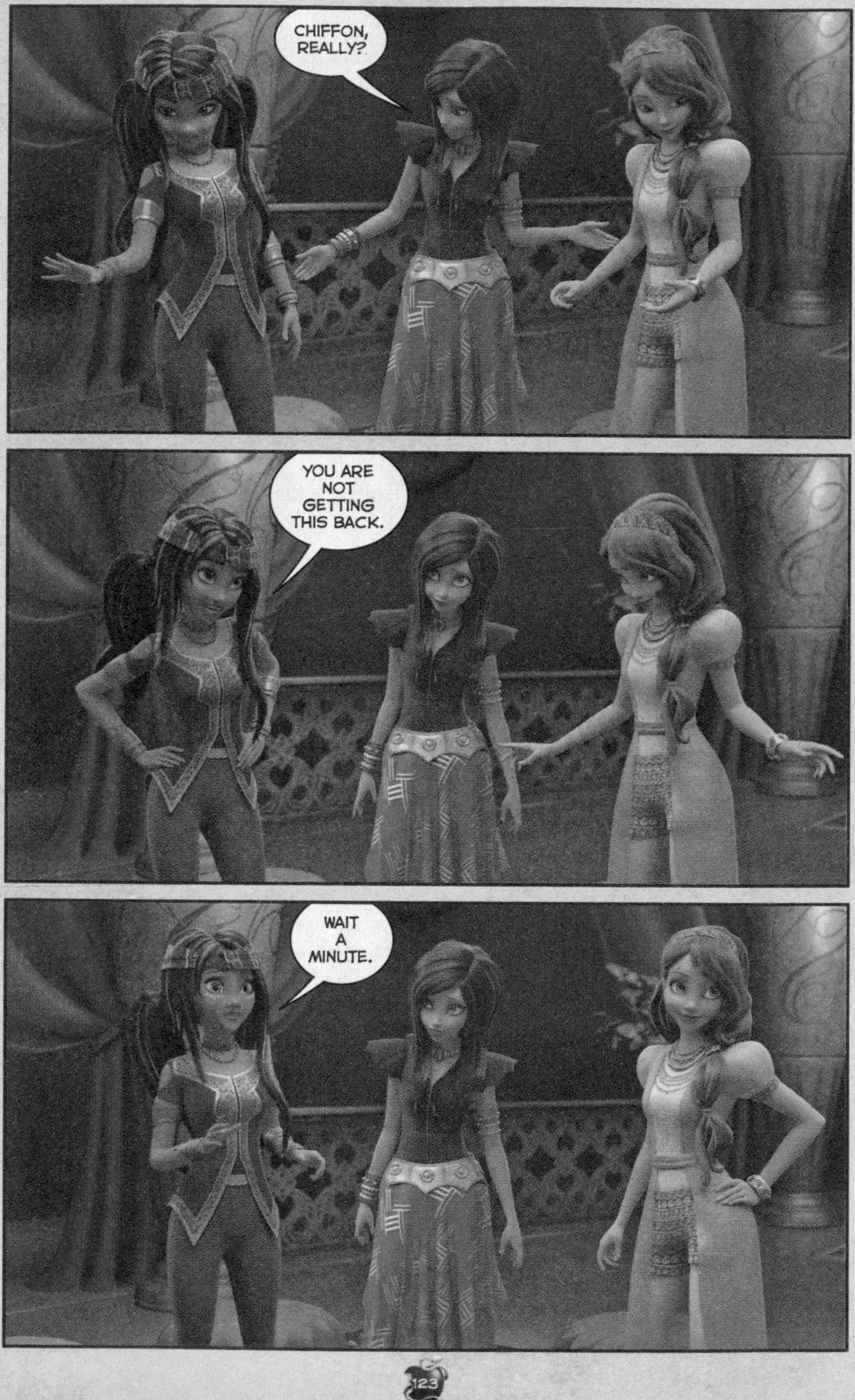
CHIFFON, REALLY?
YOU ARE NOT GETTING THIS BACK.
WAIT A MINUTE.

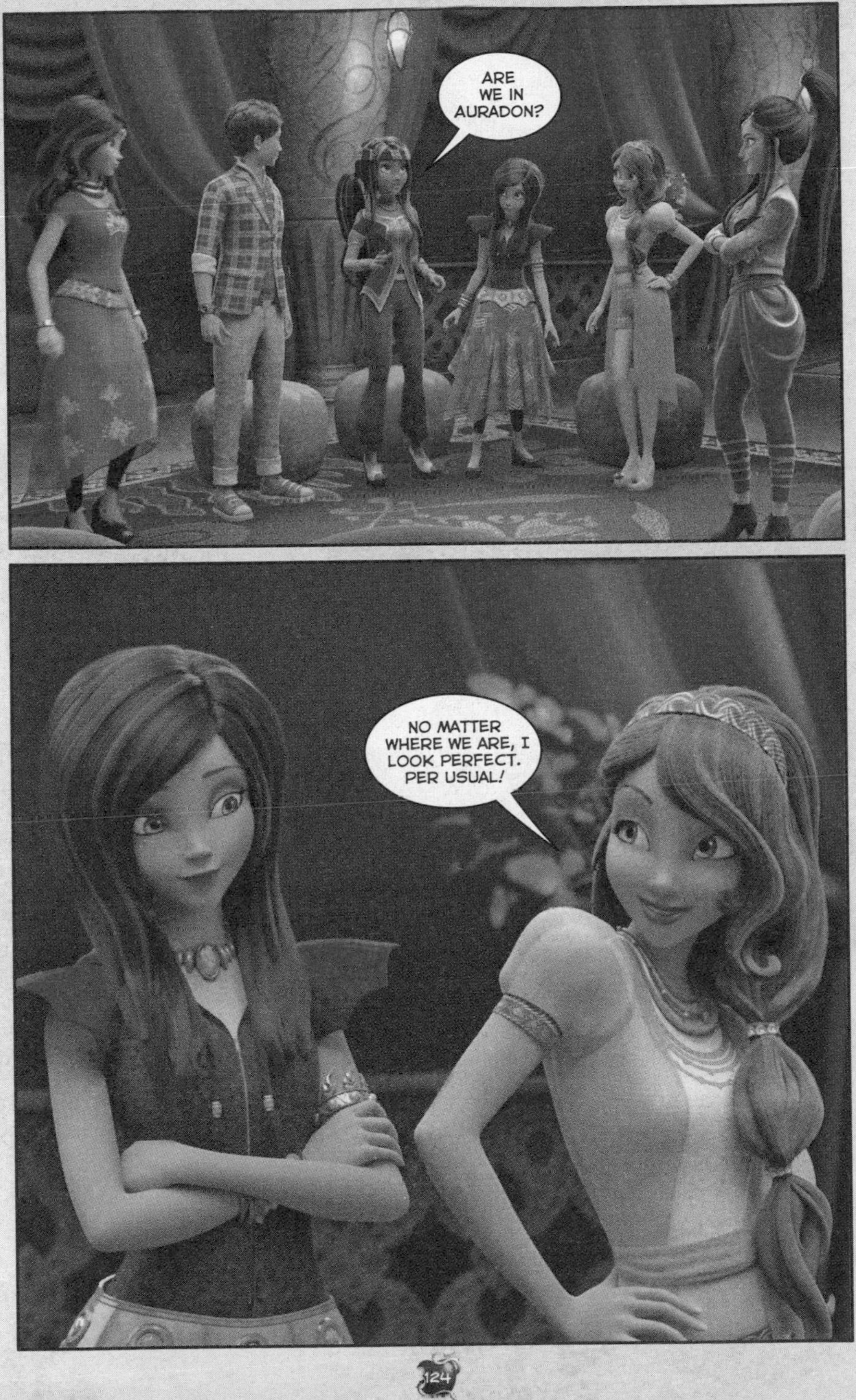
ARE WE IN AURADON?
NO MATTER WHERE WE ARE, I LOOK PERFECT. PER USUAL!

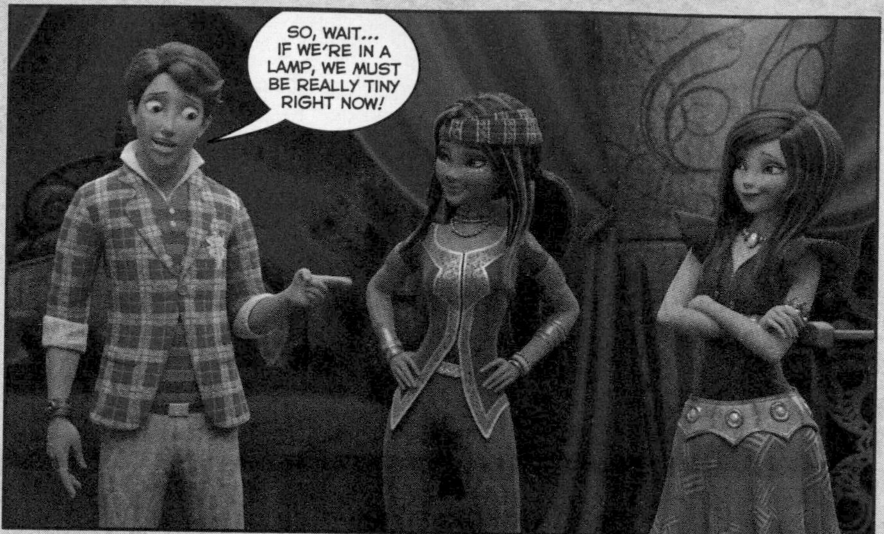
SO, WAIT... IF WE'RE IN A LAMP, WE MUST BE REALLY TINY RIGHT NOW!

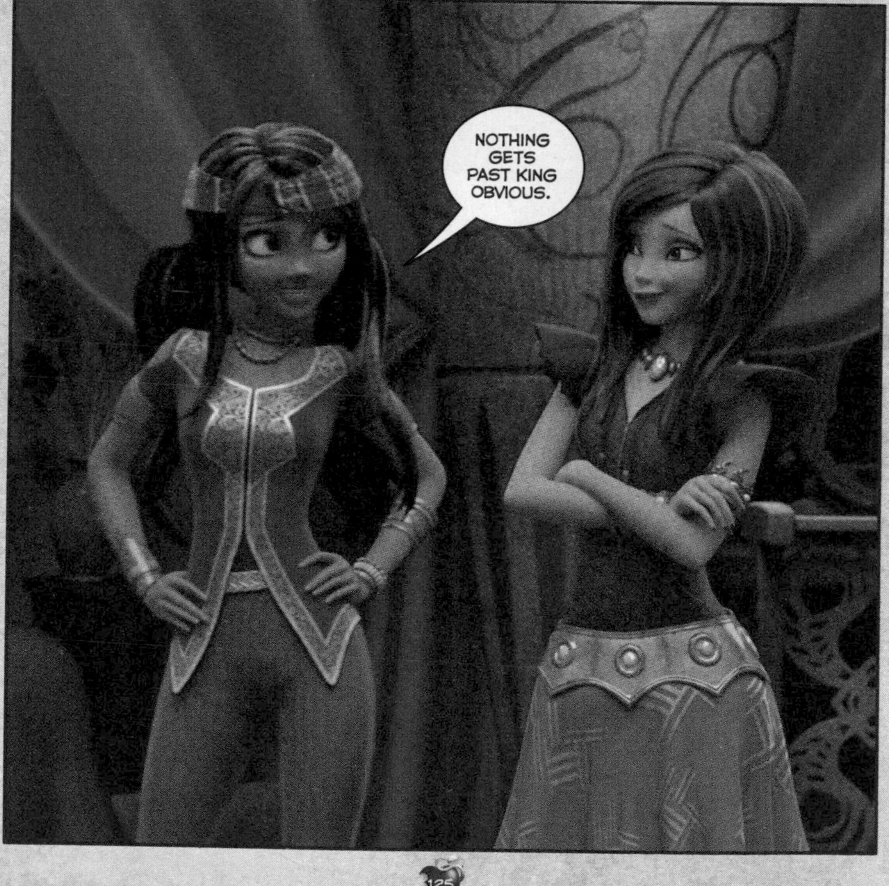
NOTHING GETS PAST KING OBVIOUS.

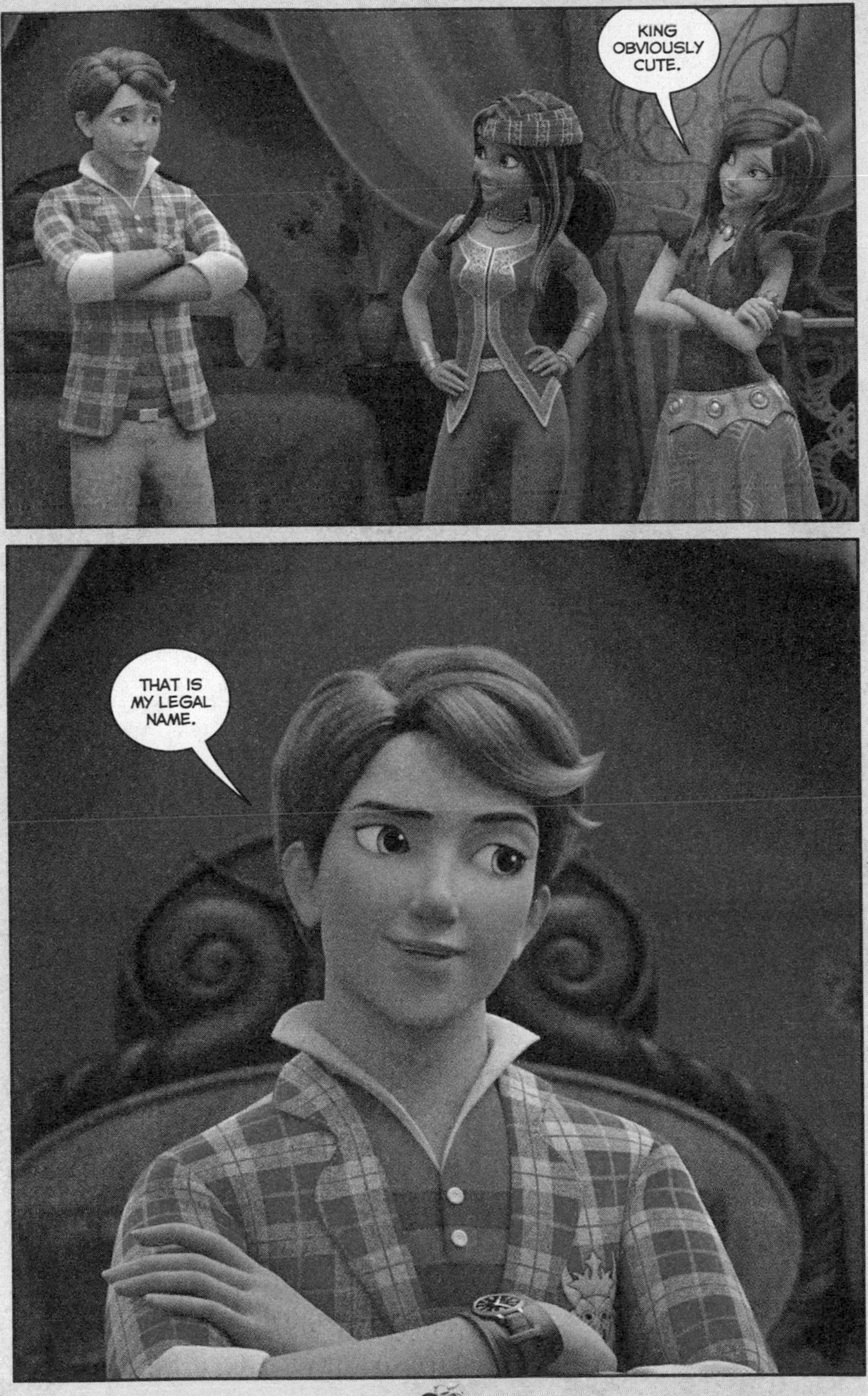
KING OBVIOUSLY CUTE.
THAT IS MY LEGAL NAME.

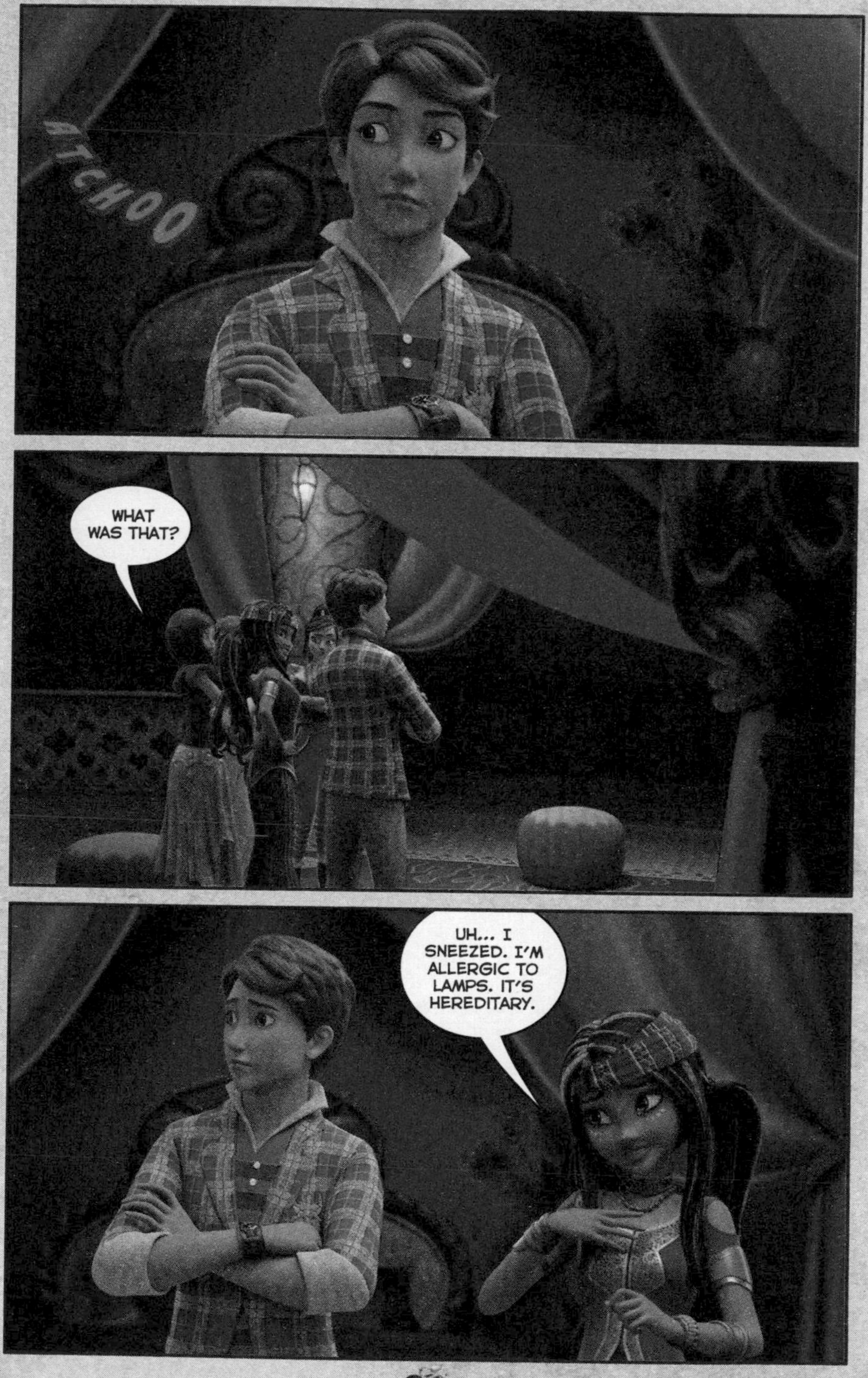
ATCHOO
WHAT WAS THAT?
UH... I SNEEZED. I'M ALLERGIC TO LAMPS. IT'S HEREDITARY.

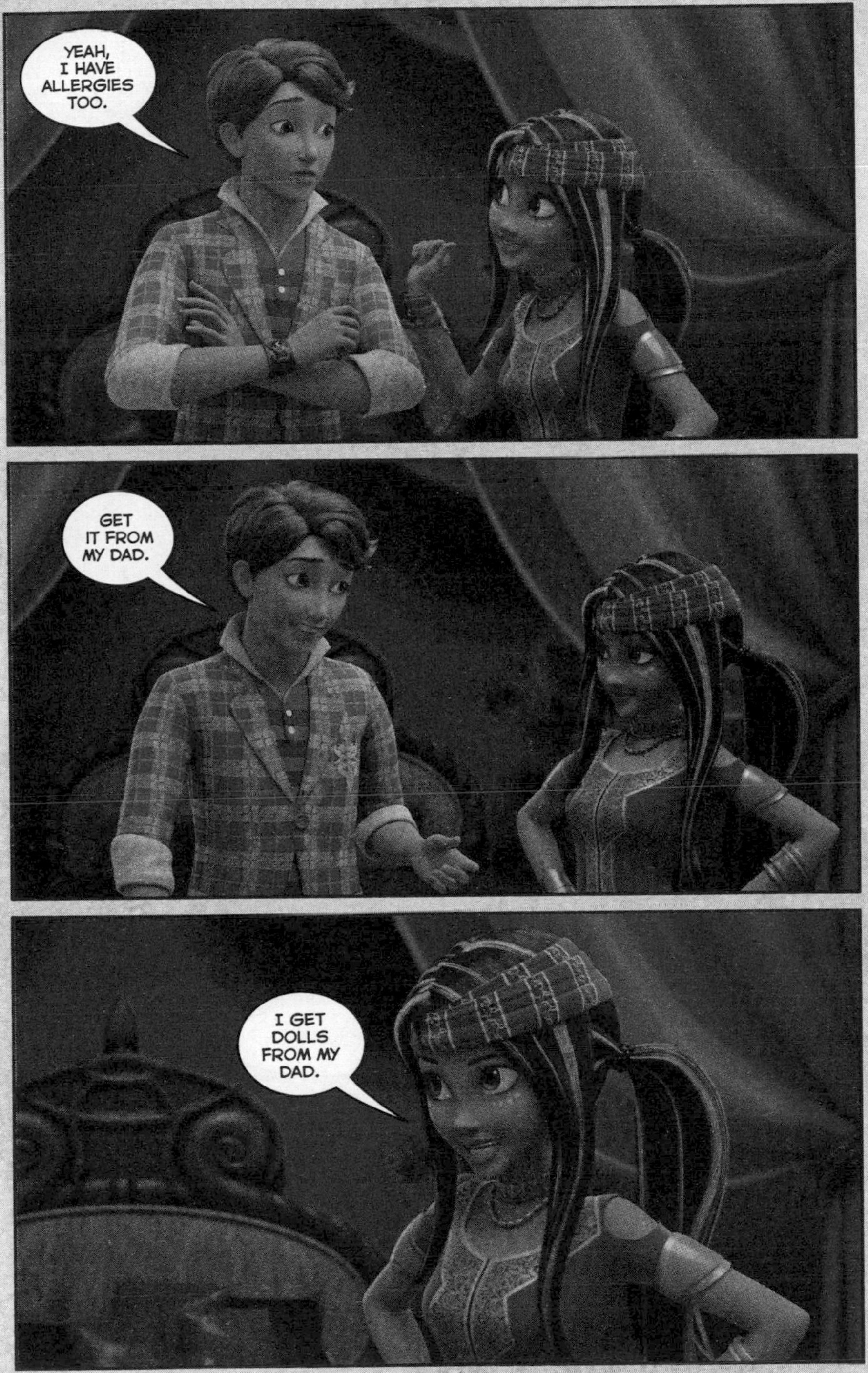
YEAH, I HAVE ALLERGIES TOO.
GET IT FROM MY DAD.
I GET DOLLS FROM MY DAD.

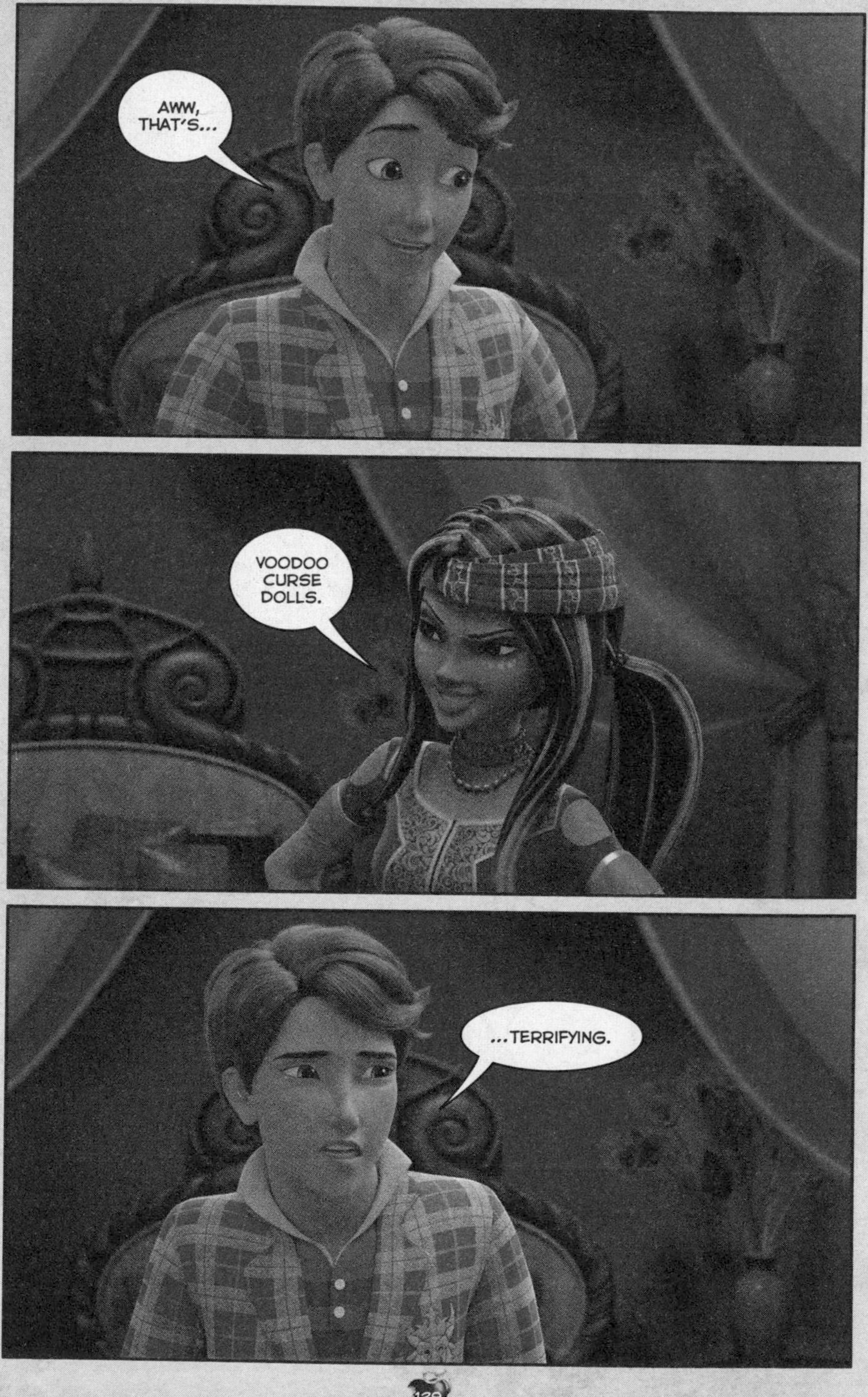
AWW, THAT'S...
VOODOO CURSE DOLLS.
...TERRIFYING.

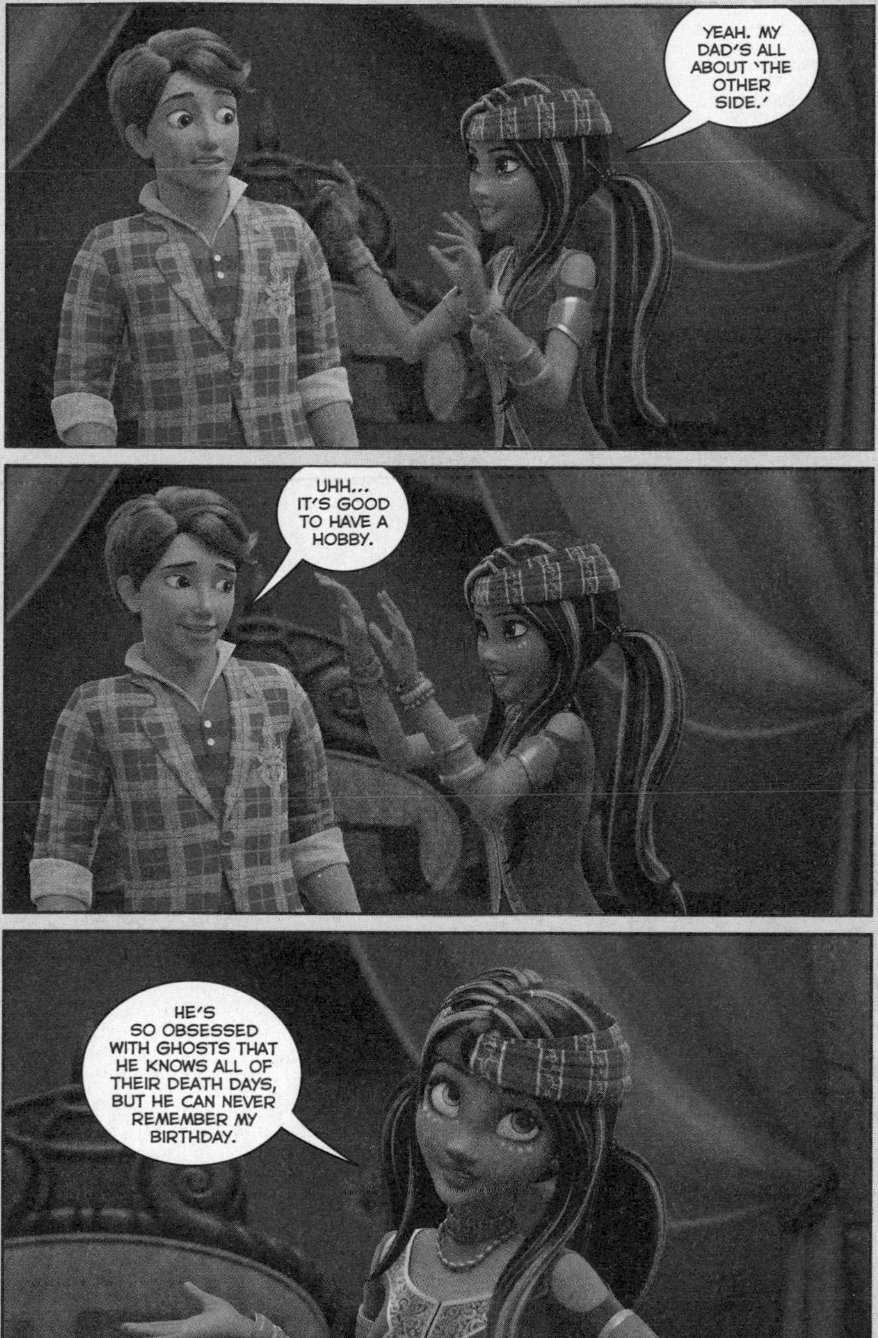
YEAH. MY DAD'S ALL ABOUT 'THE OTHER SIDE.'
UHH... IT'S GOOD TO HAVE A HOBBY.
HE'S SO OBSESSED WITH GHOSTS THAT HE KNOWS ALL OF THEIR DEATH DAYS, BUT HE CAN NEVER REMEMBER MY BIRTHDAY.

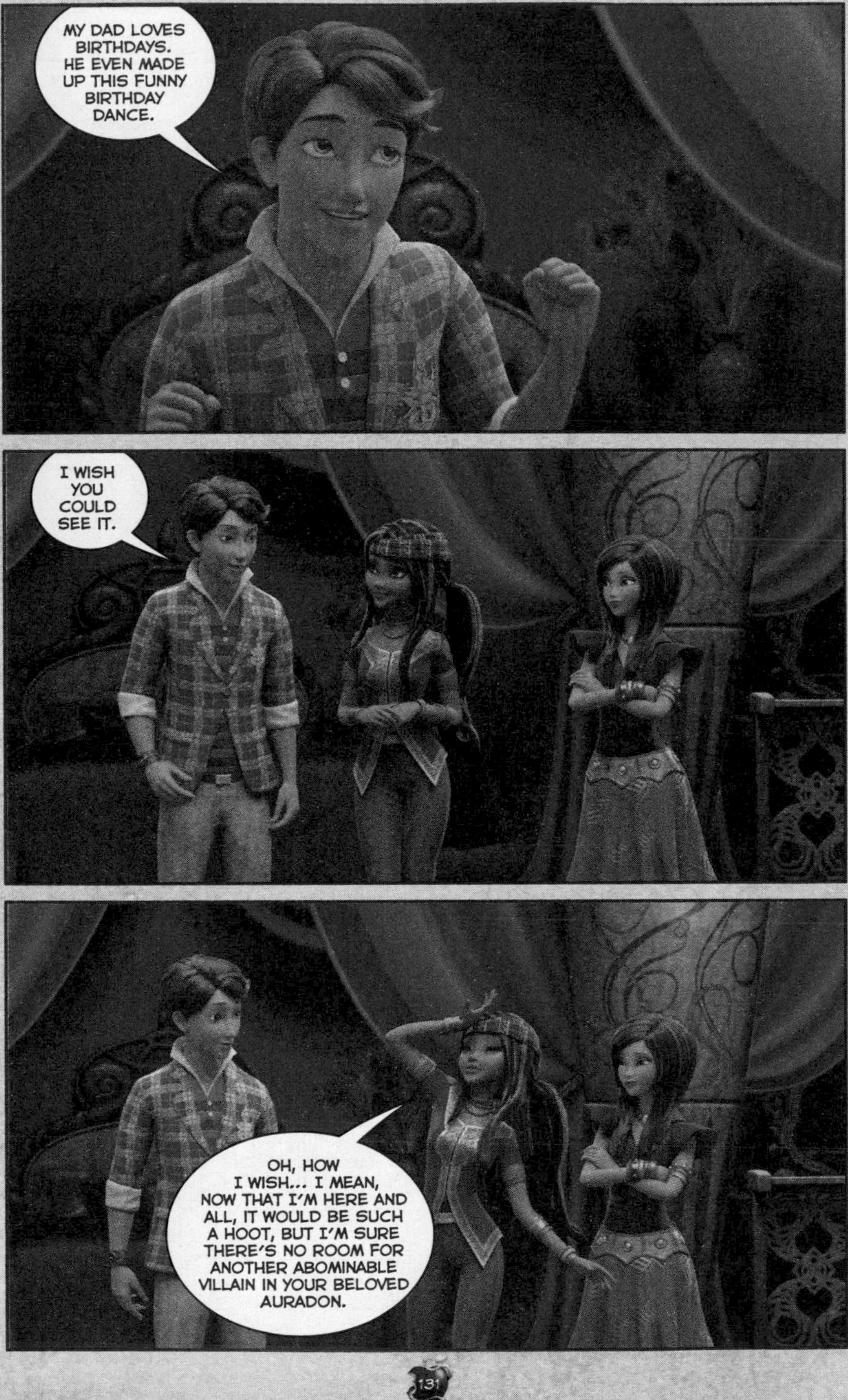
MY DAD LOVES BIRTHDAYS. HE EVEN MADE UP THIS FUNNY BIRTHDAY DANCE.
I WISH YOU COULD SEE IT.
OH, HOW I WISH... I MEAN, NOW THAT I'M HERE AND ALL, IT WOULD BE SUCH A HOOT, BUT I'M SURE THERE'S NO ROOM FOR ANOTHER ABOMINABLE VILLAIN IN YOUR BELOVED AURADON.

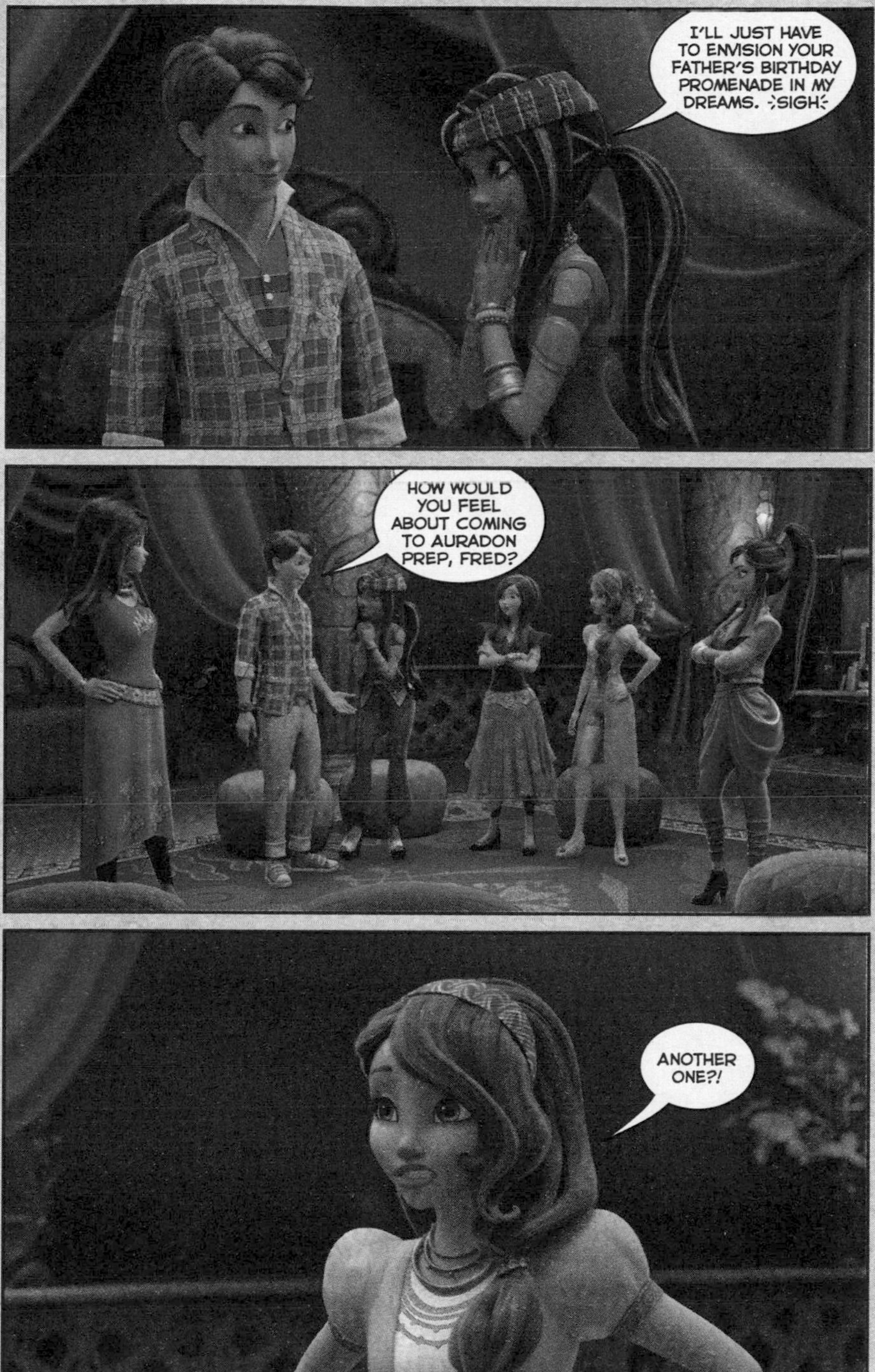
I'LL JUST HAVE TO ENVISION YOUR FATHER'S BIRTHDAY PROMENADE IN MY DREAMS. ⁂SIGH⁂
HOW WOULD YOU FEEL ABOUT COMING TO AURADON PREP, FRED?
ANOTHER ONE?!

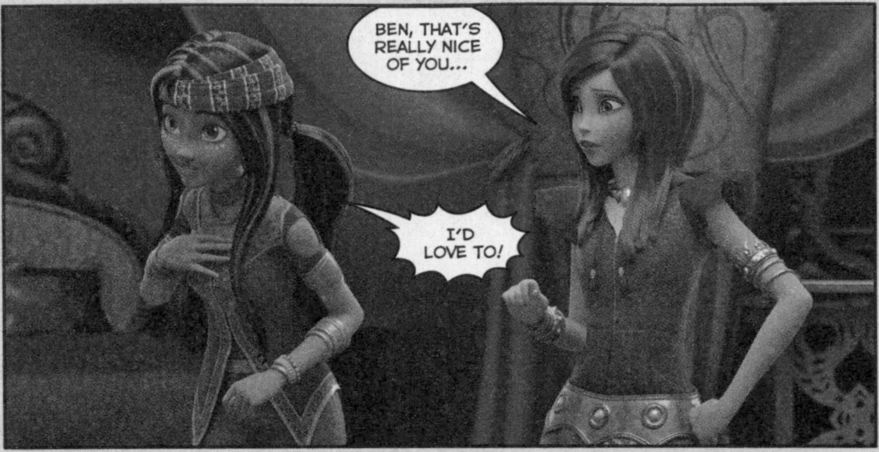
BEN, THAT'S REALLY NICE OF YOU...
I'D LOVE TO!
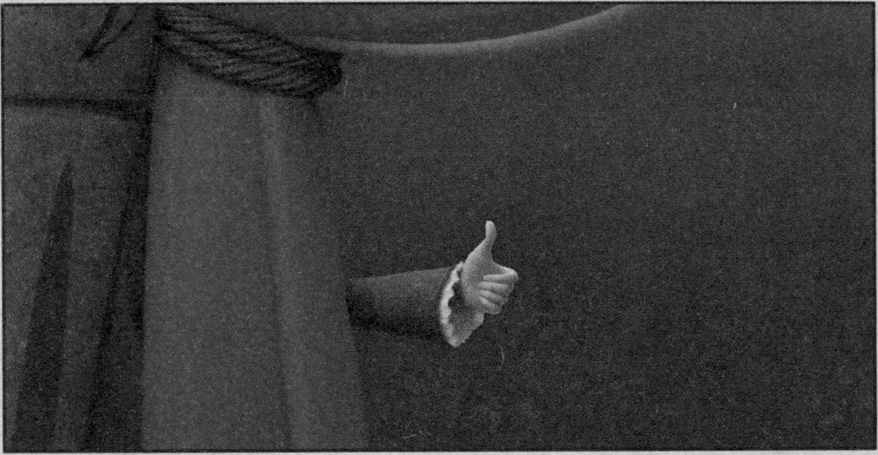
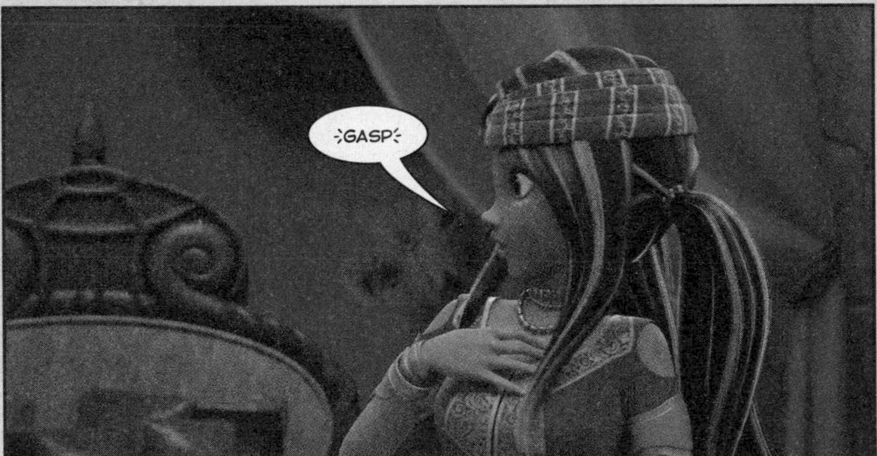
GASP

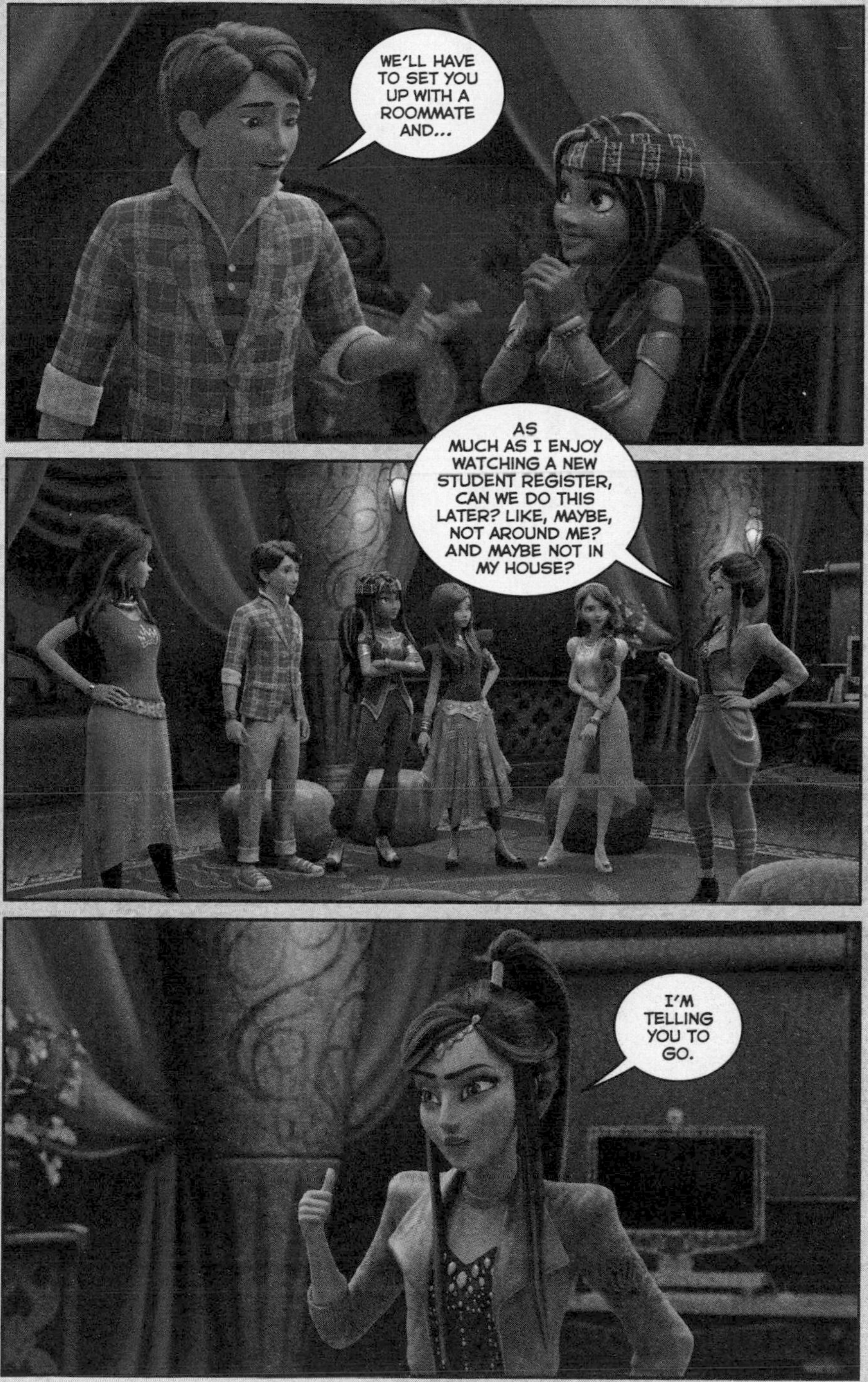
WE'LL HAVE TO SET YOU UP WITH A ROOMMATE AND...
AS MUCH AS I ENJOY WATCHING A NEW STUDENT REGISTER, CAN WE DO THIS LATER? LIKE, MAYBE, NOT AROUND ME? AND MAYBE NOT IN MY HOUSE?
I'M TELLING YOU TO GO.

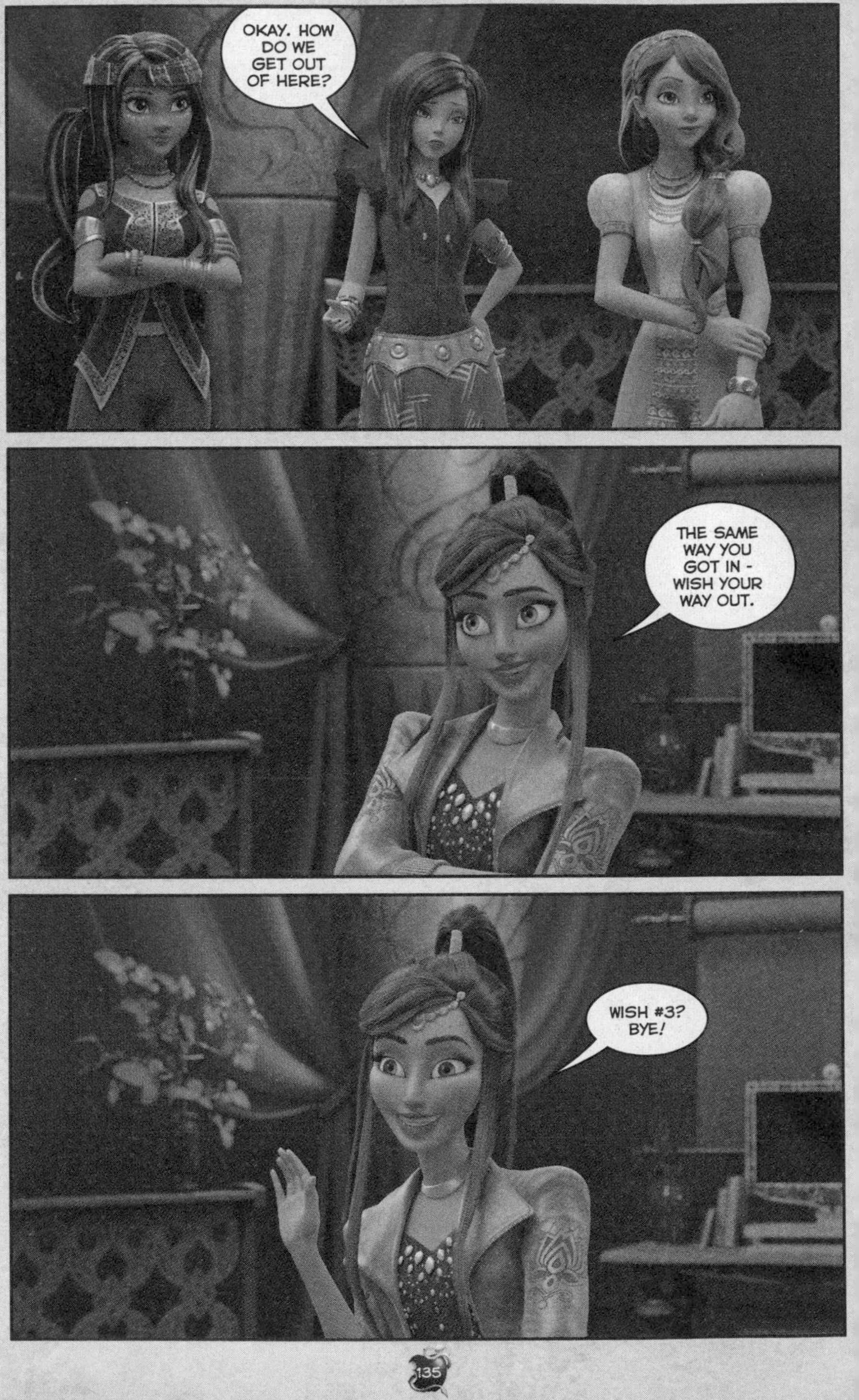
OKAY. HOW DO WE GET OUT OF HERE?
THE SAME WAY YOU GOT IN - WISH YOUR WAY OUT.
WISH #3? BYE!

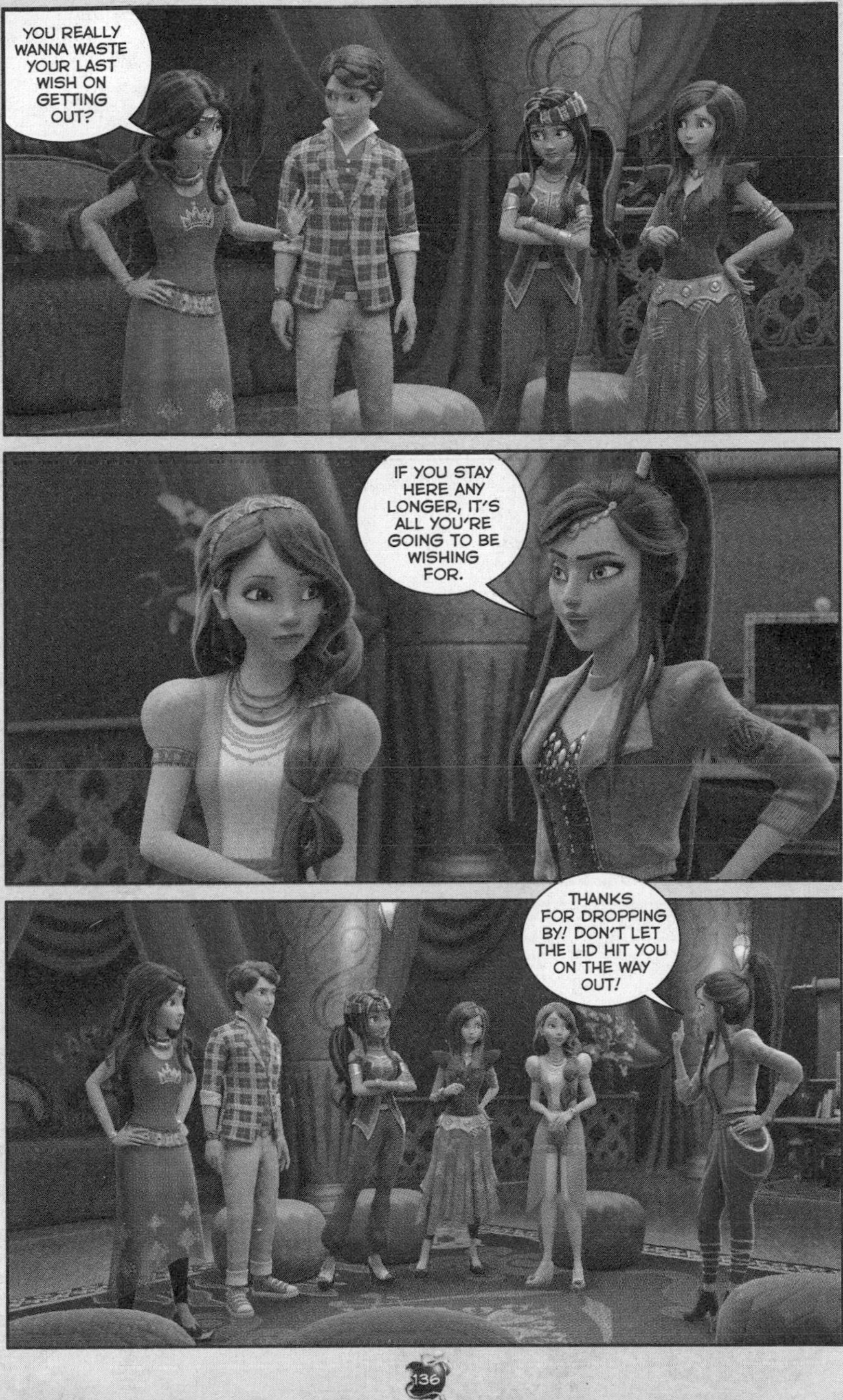
YOU REALLY WANNA WASTE YOUR LAST WISH ON GETTING OUT?
IF YOU STAY HERE ANY LONGER, IT'S ALL YOU'RE GOING TO BE WISHING FOR.
THANKS FOR DROPPING BY! DON'T LET THE LID HIT YOU ON THE WAY OUT!

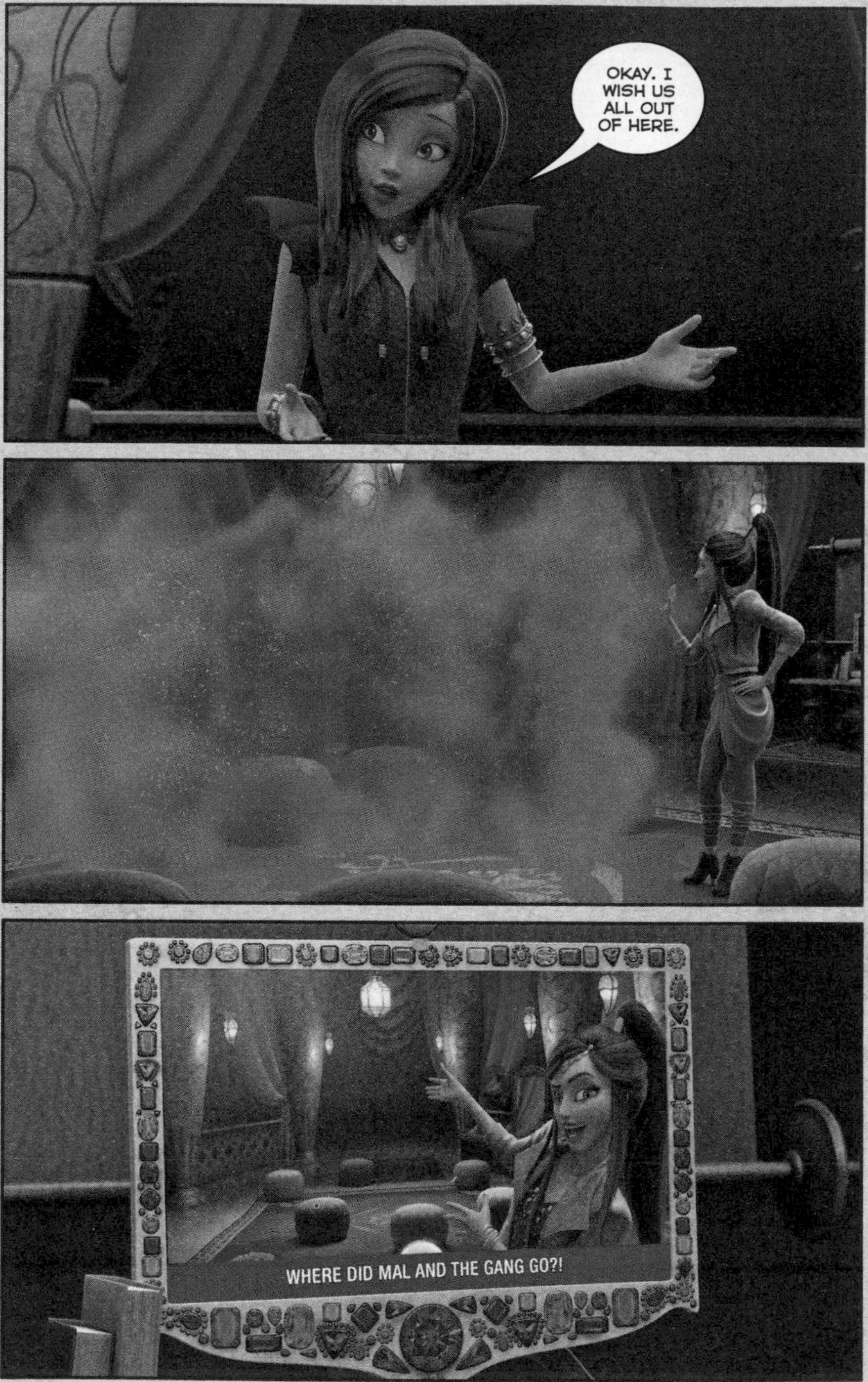
OKAY. I WISH US ALL OUT OF HERE.
WHERE DID MAL AND THE GANG GO?!

CHAPTER 8: PUFFED DELICIOUSNESS

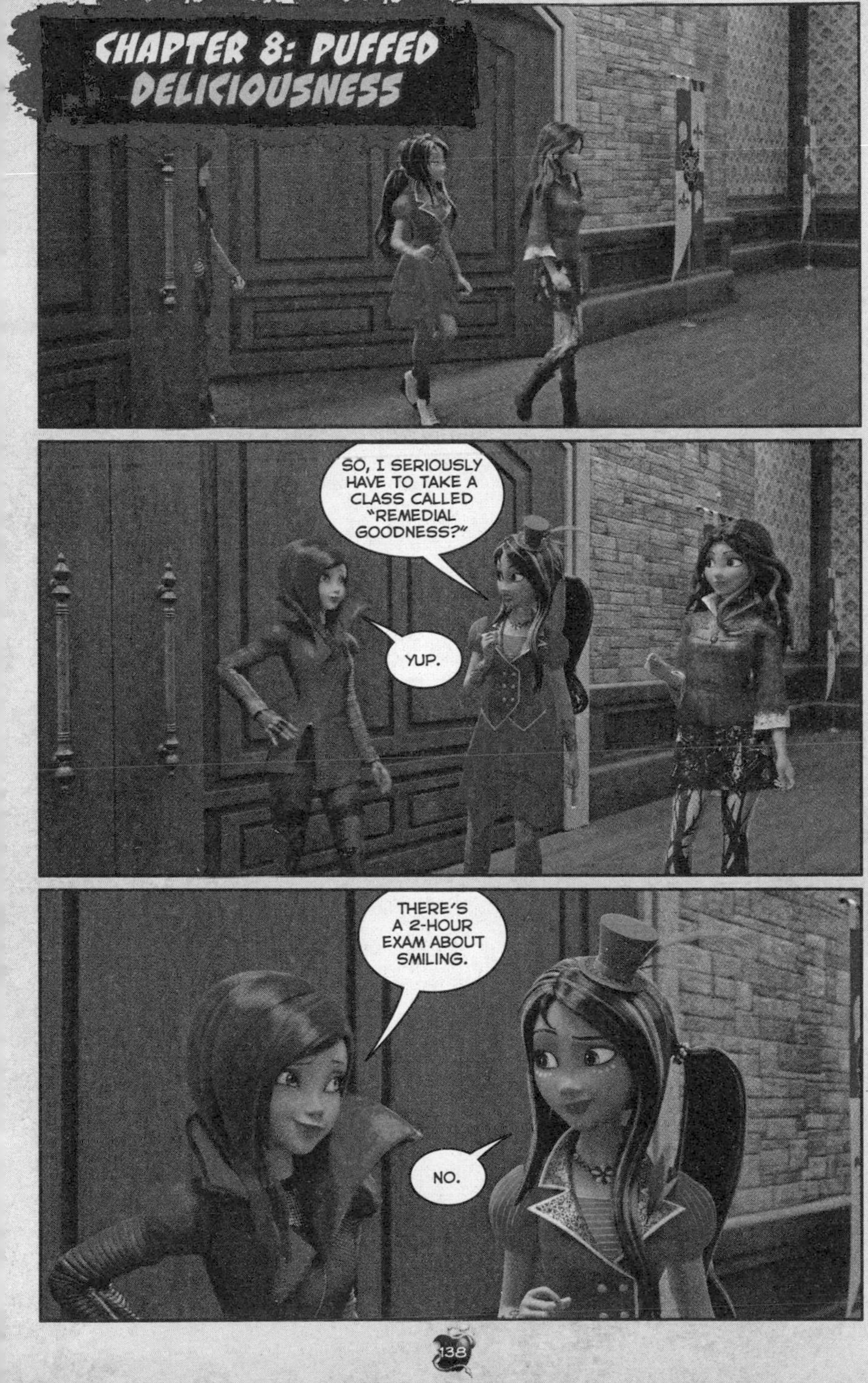
SO, I SERIOUSLY HAVE TO TAKE A CLASS CALLED "REMEDIAL GOODNESS?"
YUP.
THERE'S A 2-HOUR EXAM ABOUT SMILING.
NO.

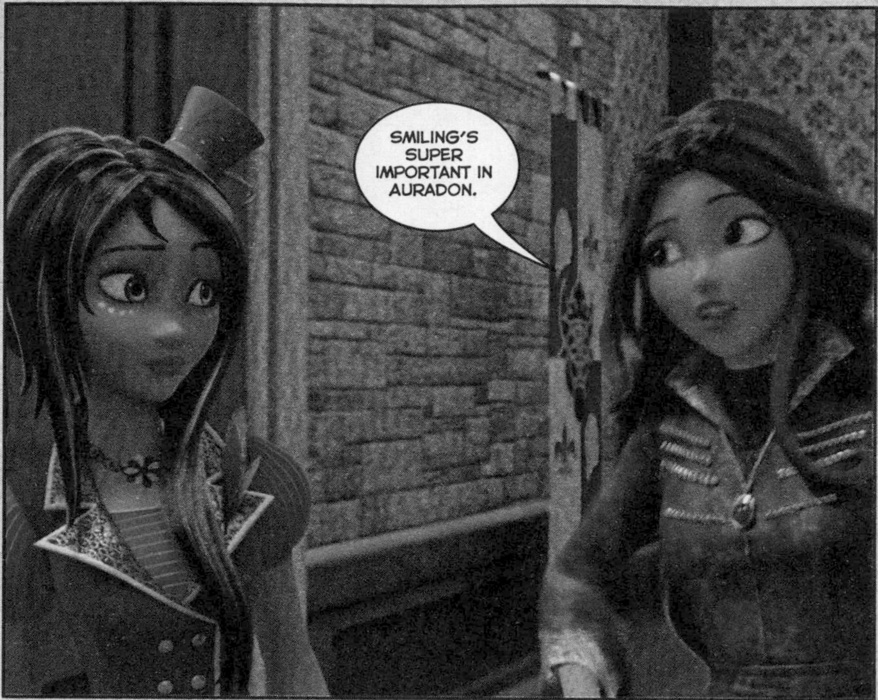
SMILING'S SUPER IMPORTANT IN AURADON.

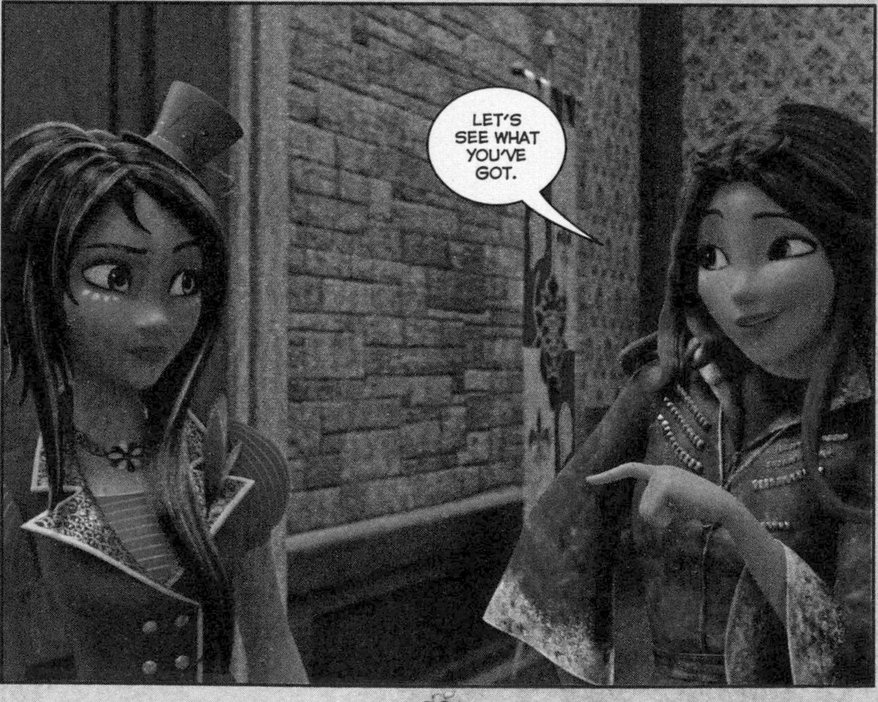
LET'S SEE WHAT YOU'VE GOT.

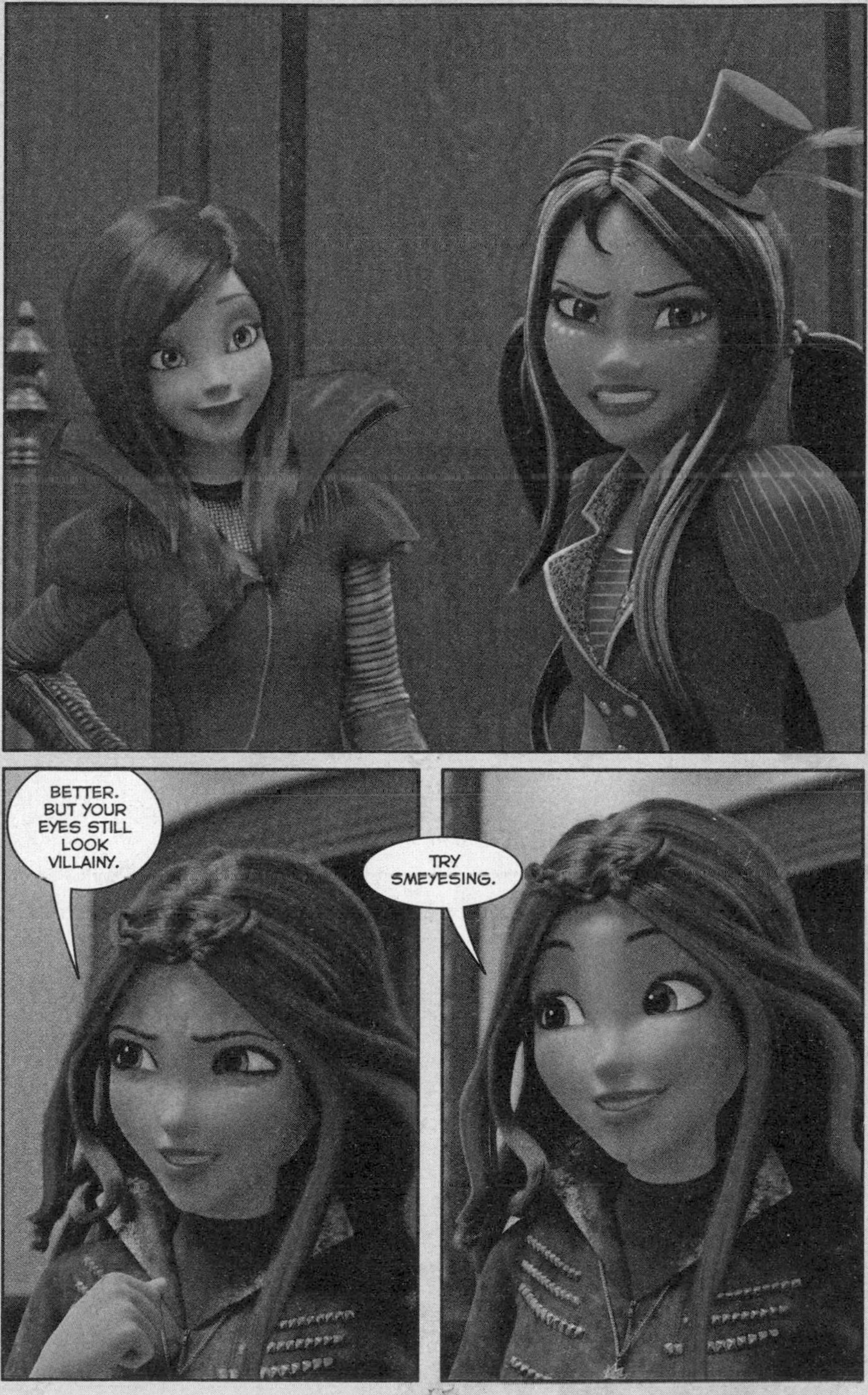
BETTER. BUT YOUR EYES STILL LOOK VILLAINY.
TRY SMEYESING.

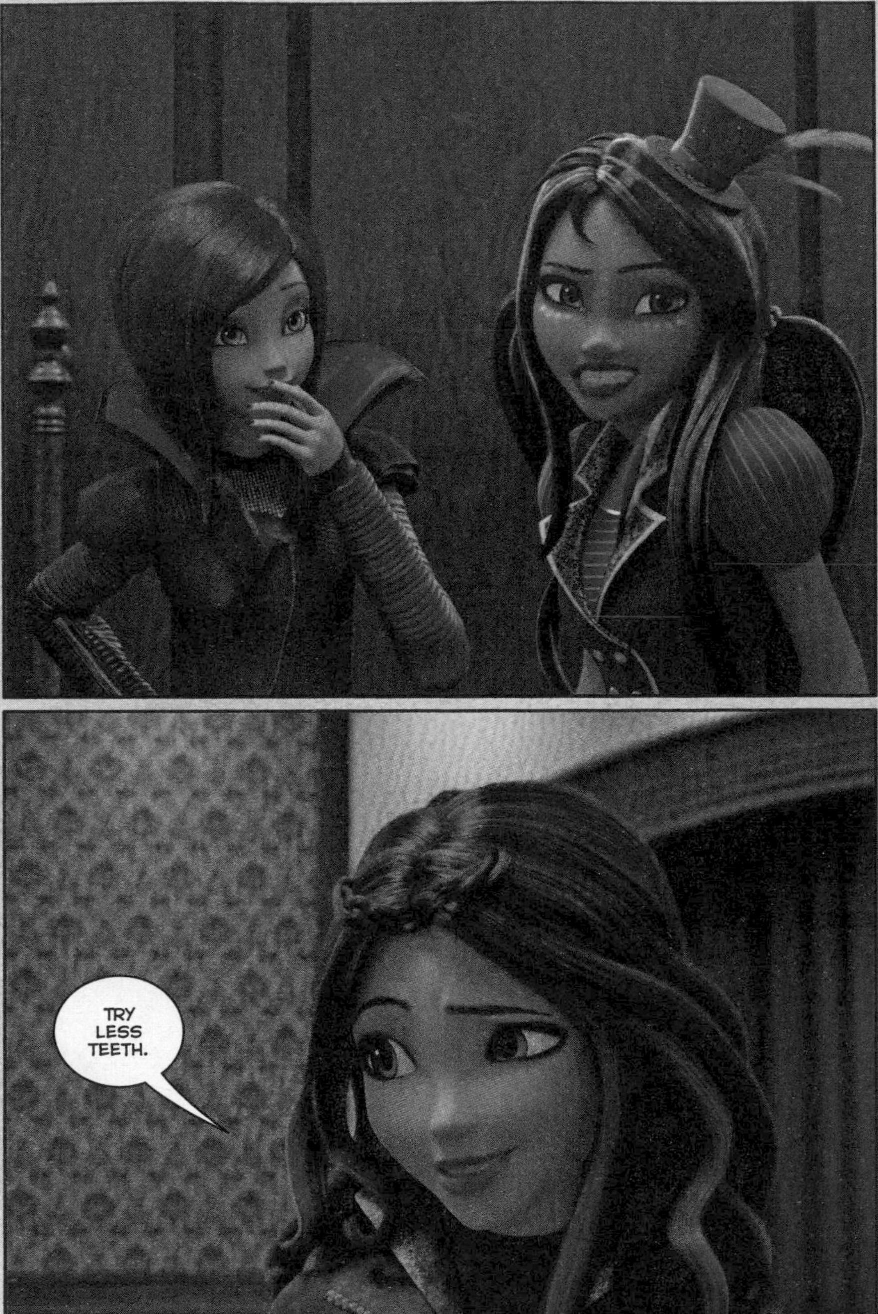
TRY LESS TEETH.

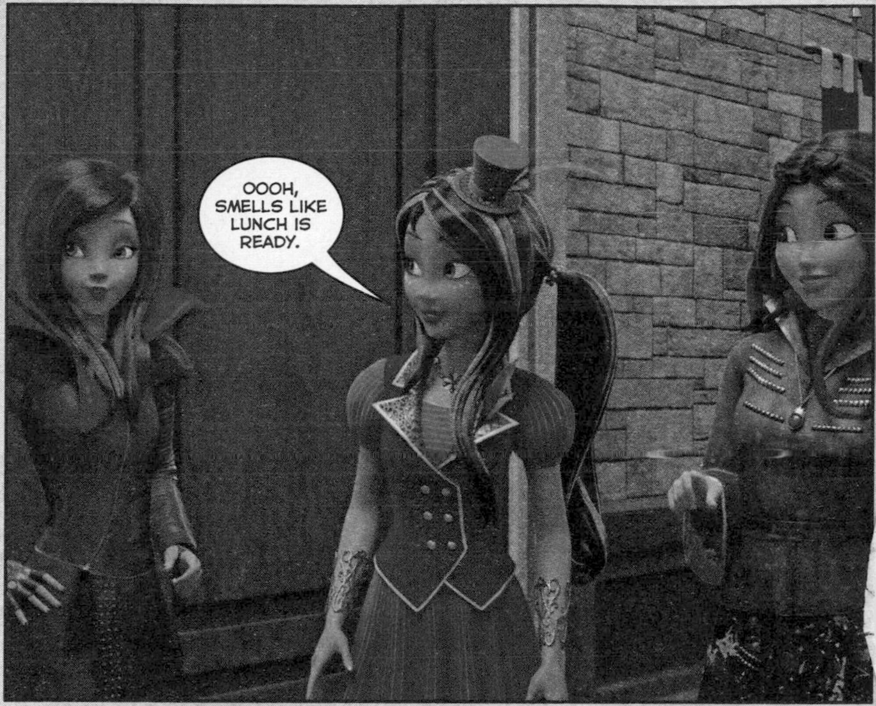
OOOH, SMELLS LIKE LUNCH IS READY.

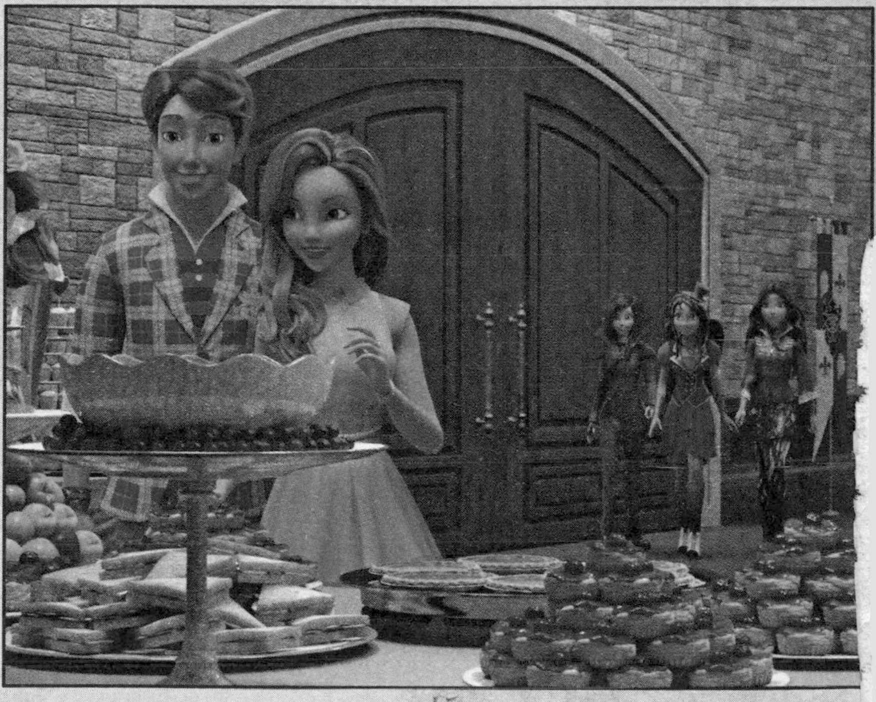

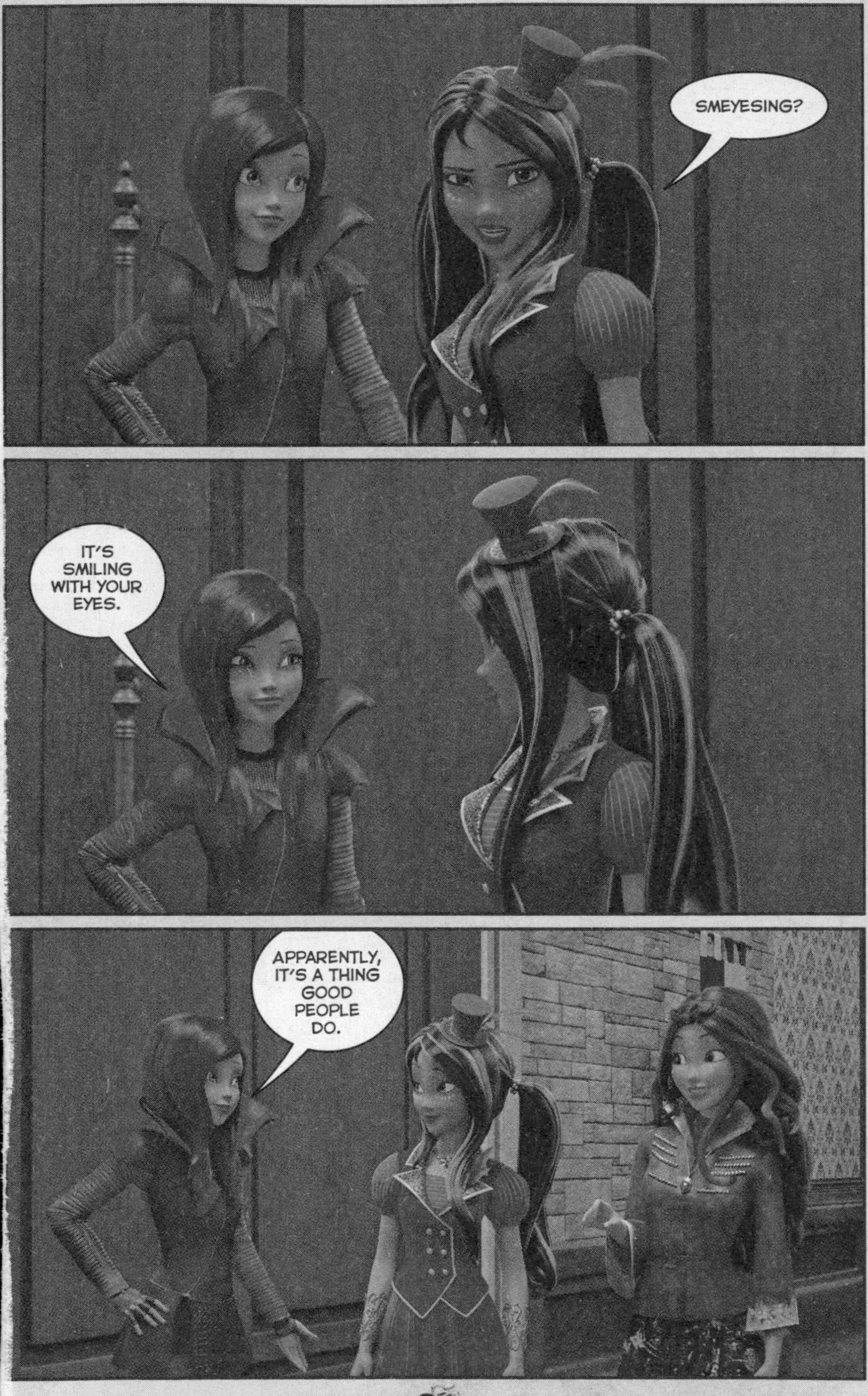
SMEYESING?
IT'S SMILING WITH YOUR EYES.
APPARENTLY, IT'S A THING GOOD PEOPLE DO.

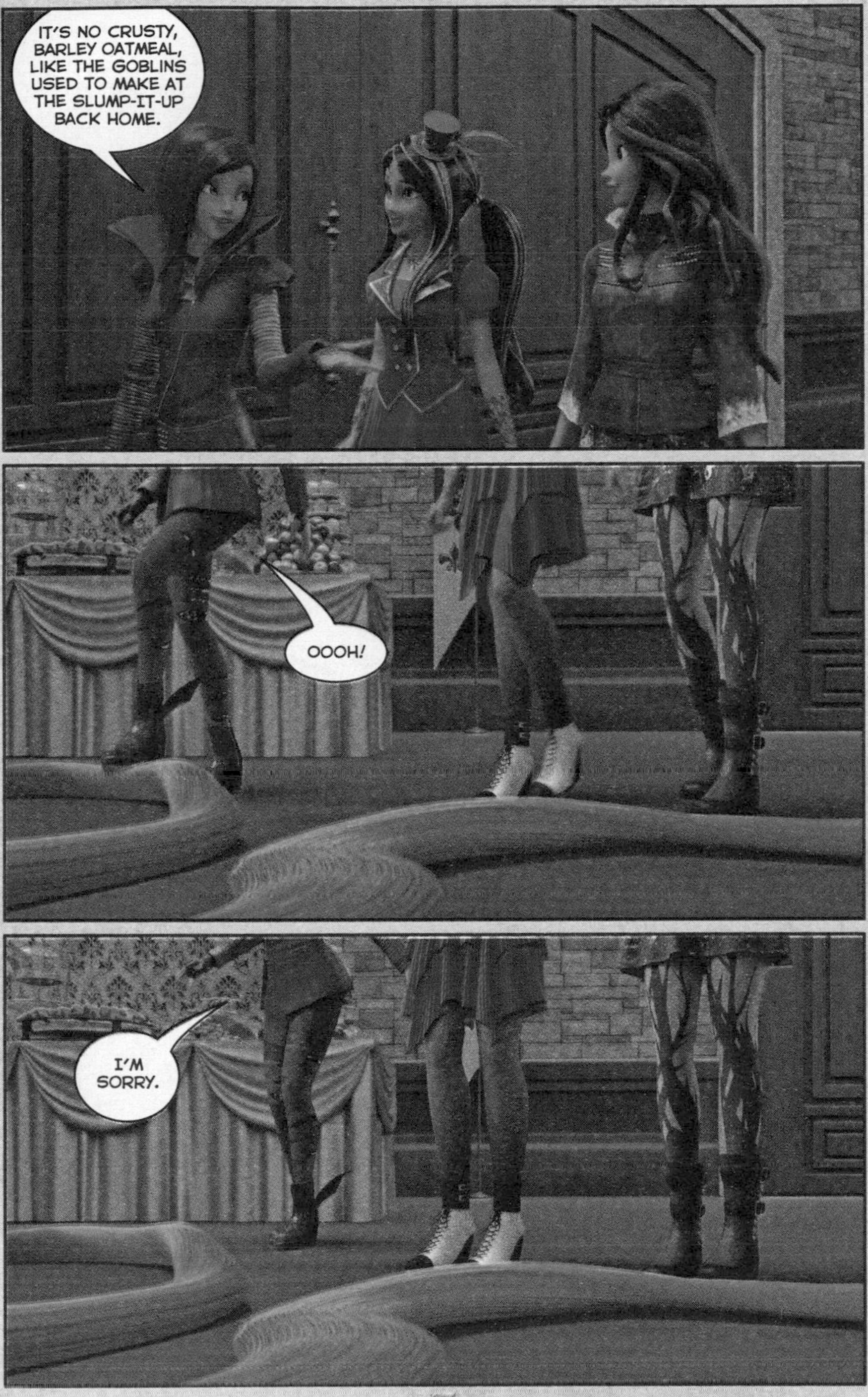
IT'S NO CRUSTY, BARLEY OATMEAL, LIKE THE GOBLINS USED TO MAKE AT THE SLUMP-IT-UP BACK HOME.
OOOH!
I'M SORRY.

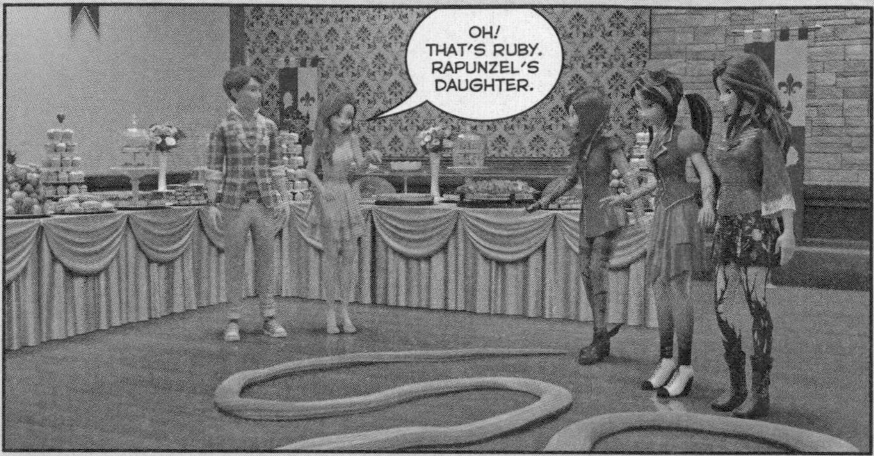
OH! THAT'S RUBY. RAPUNZEL'S DAUGHTER.

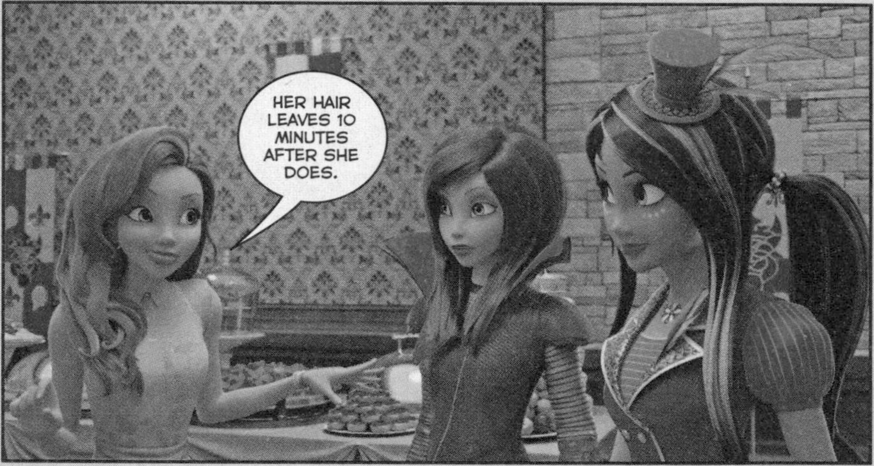
HER HAIR LEAVES 10 MINUTES AFTER SHE DOES.

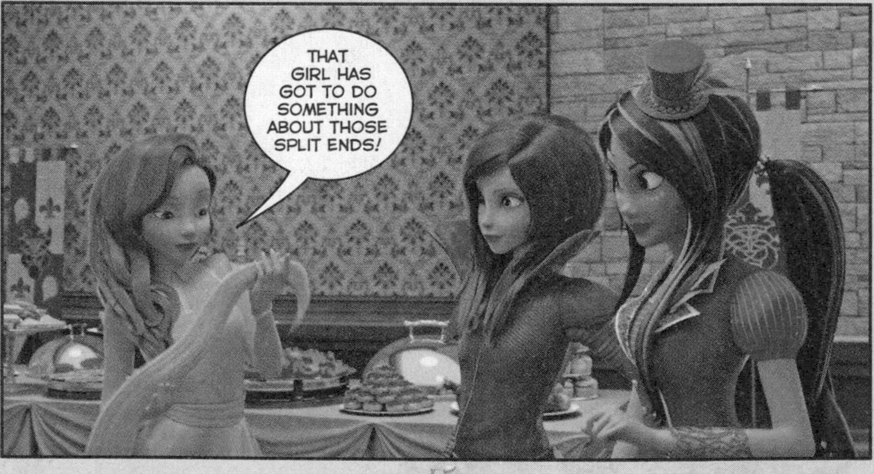
THAT GIRL HAS GOT TO DO SOMETHING ABOUT THOSE SPLIT ENDS!

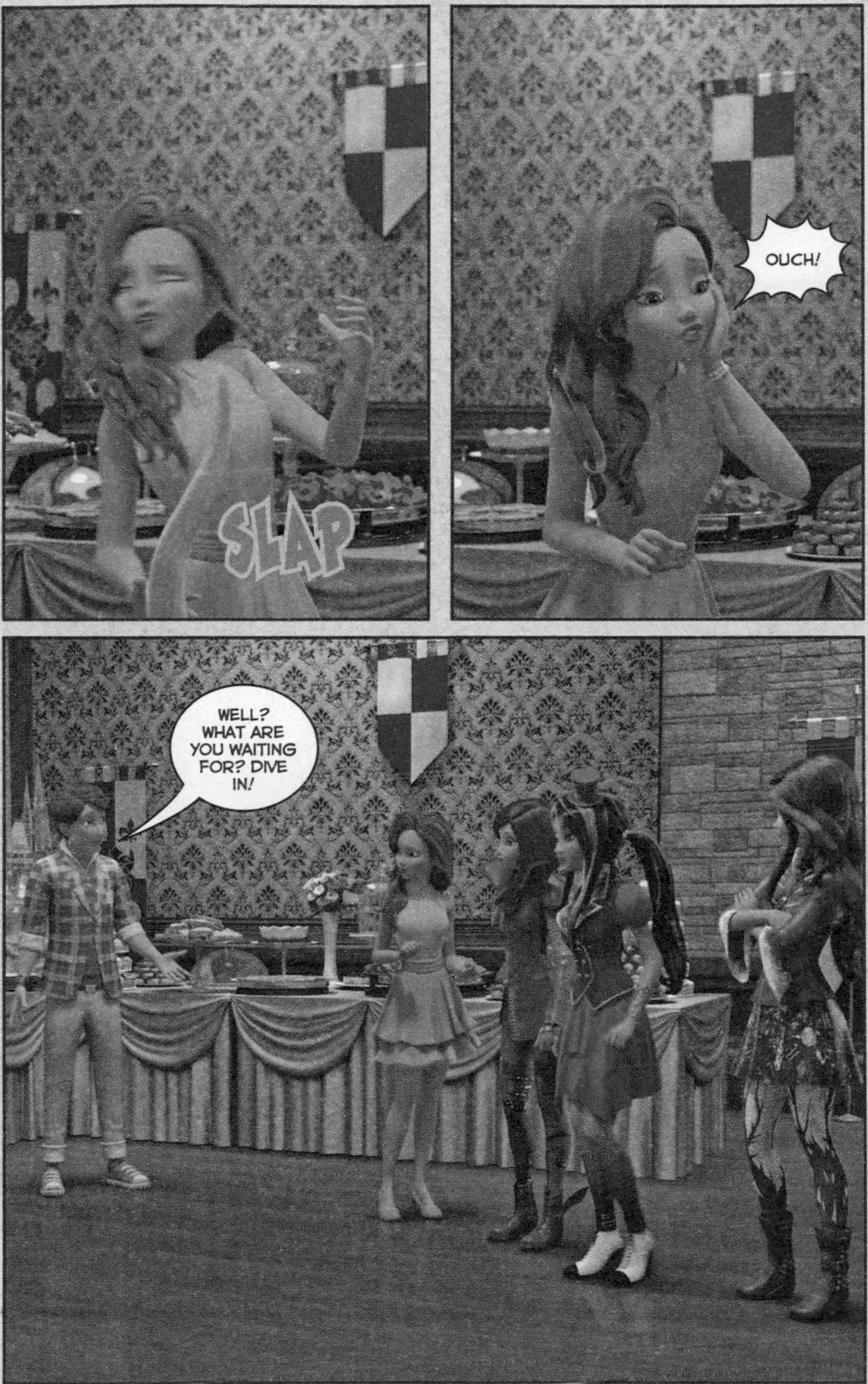
SLAP
OUCH!
WELL? WHAT ARE YOU WAITING FOR? DIVE IN!

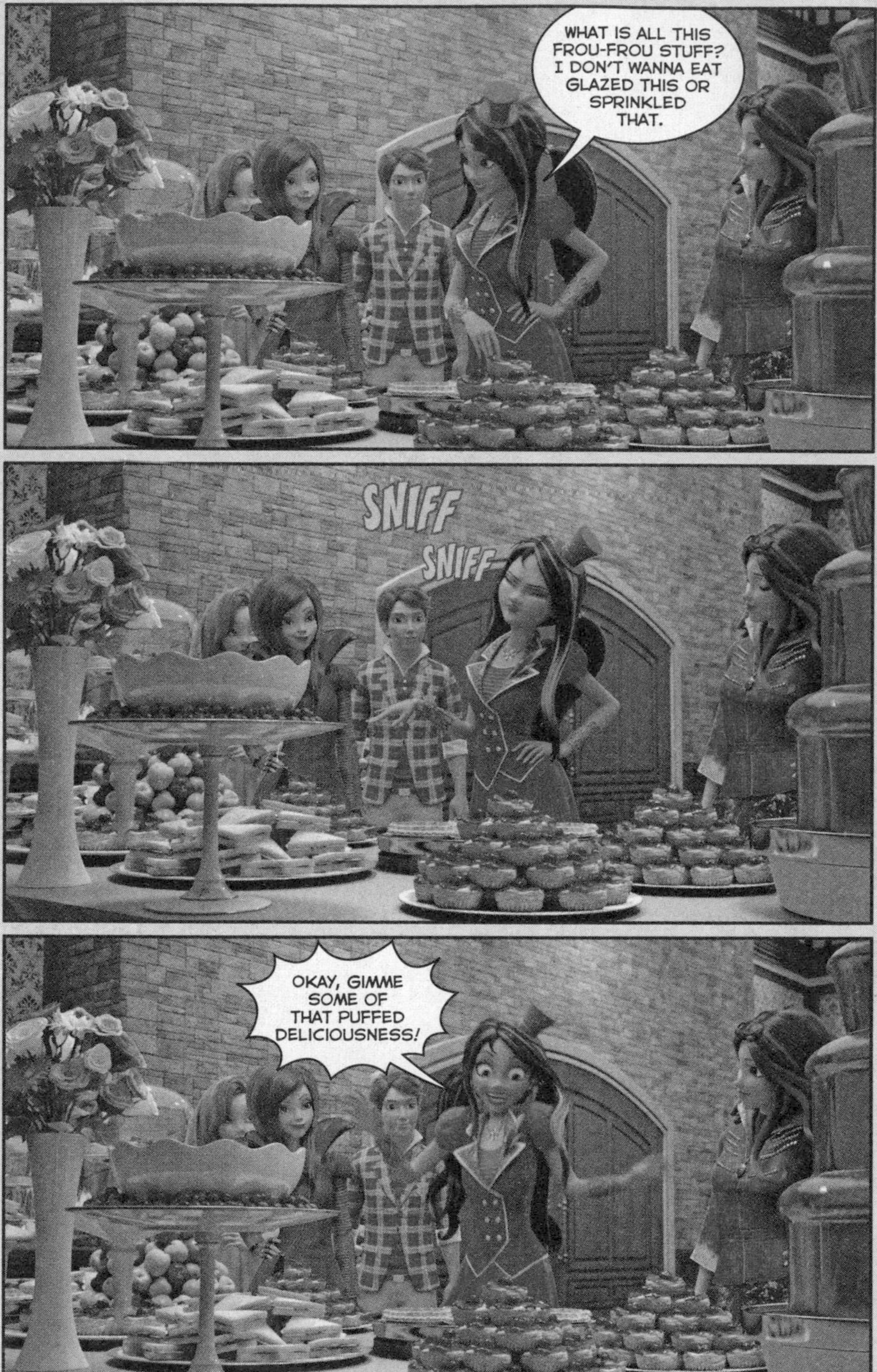
WHAT IS ALL THIS FROU-FROU STUFF? I DON'T WANNA EAT GLAZED THIS OR SPRINKLED THAT.
SNIFF
SNIFF
OKAY, GIMME SOME OF THAT PUFFED DELICIOUSNESS!

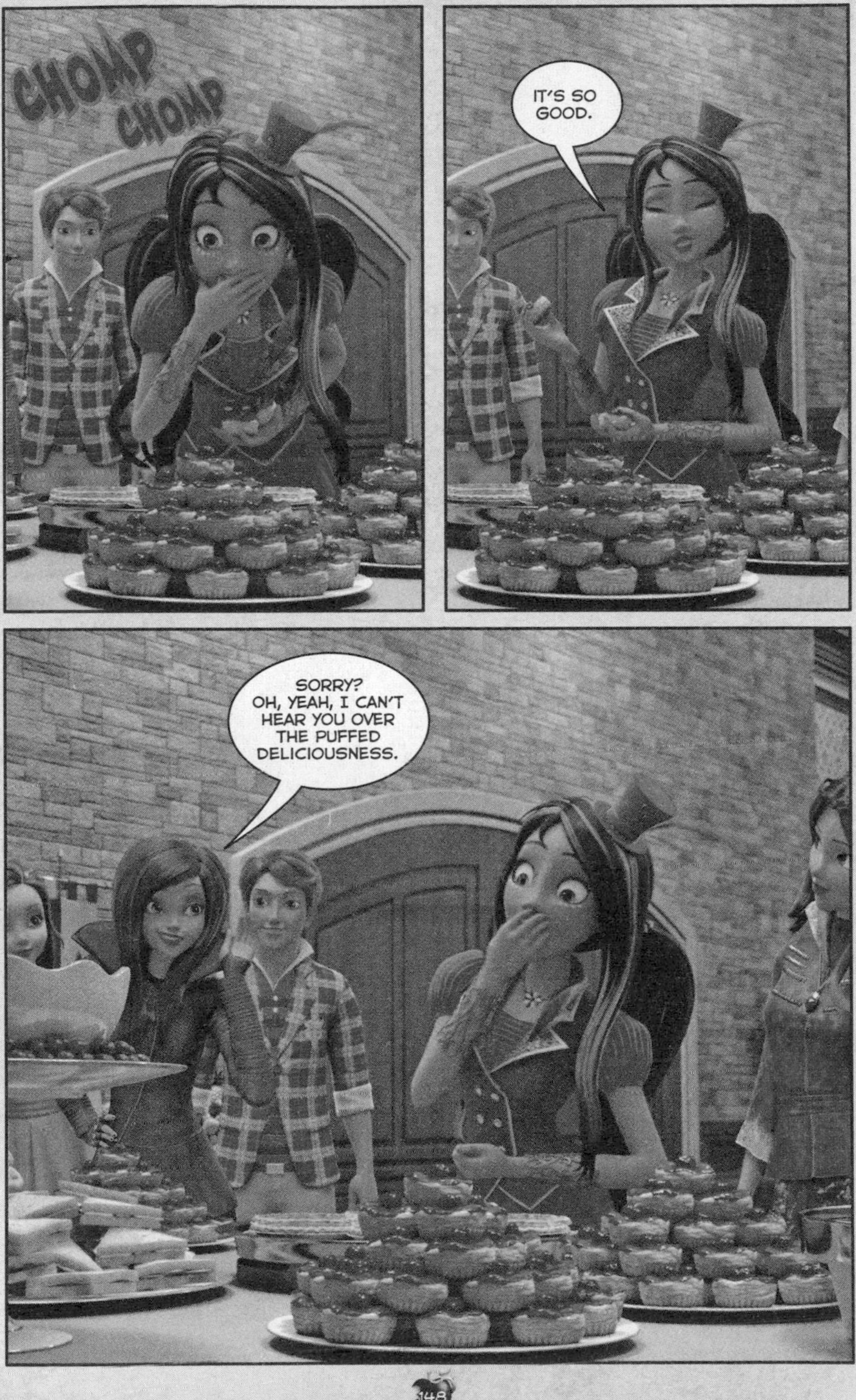

CHOMP
CHOMP
IT'S SO GOOD.
SORRY? OH, YEAH, I CAN'T HEAR YOU OVER THE PUFFED DELICIOUSNESS.

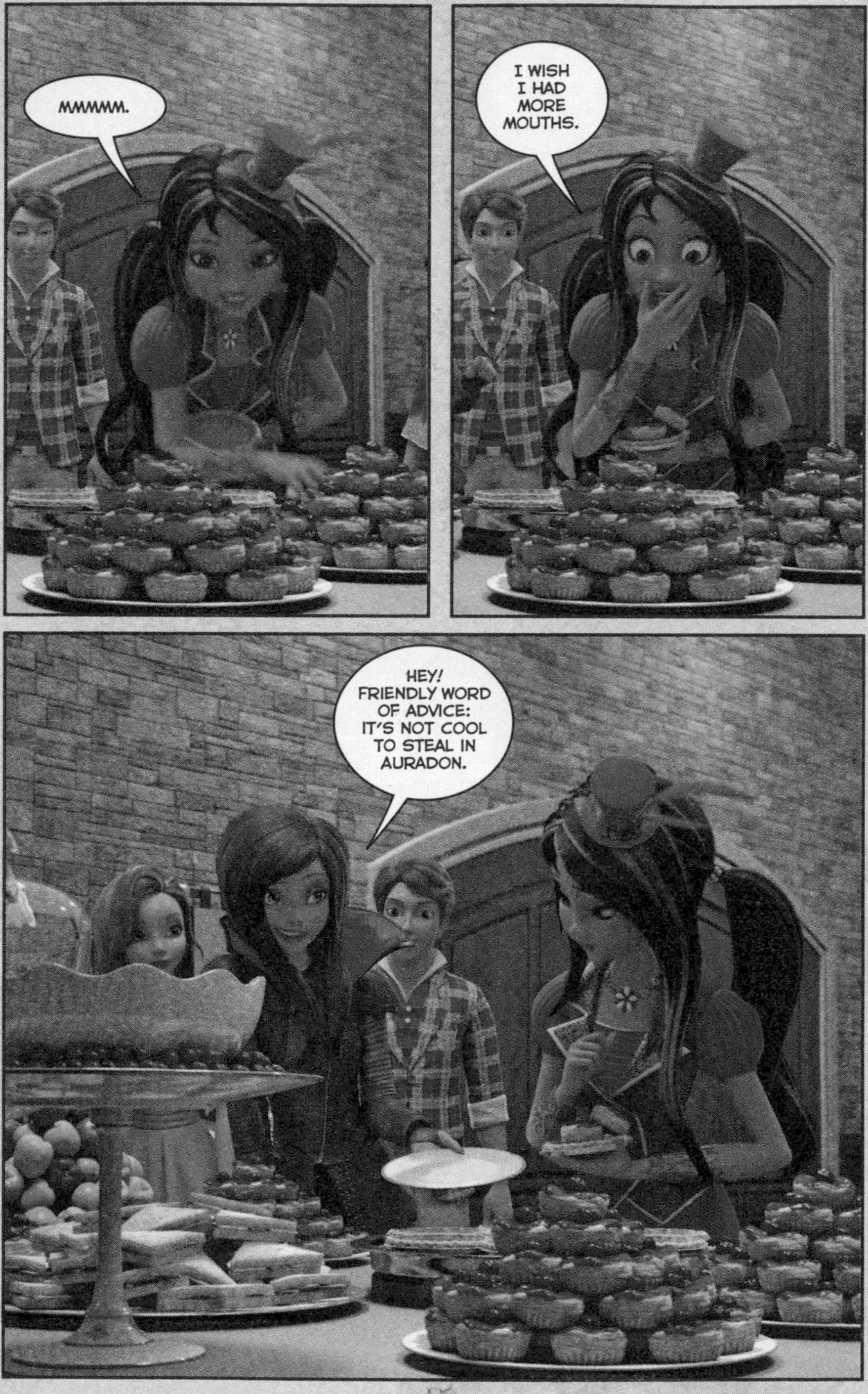
MMMMM.
I WISH I HAD MORE MOUTHS.
HEY! FRIENDLY WORD OF ADVICE: IT'S NOT COOL TO STEAL IN AURADON.

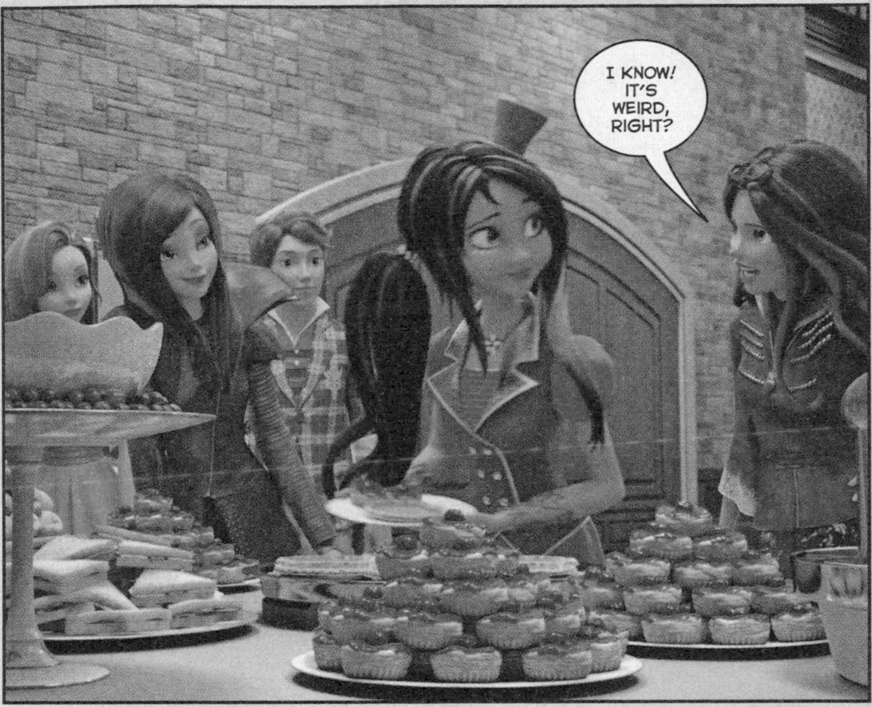
I KNOW! IT'S WEIRD, RIGHT?

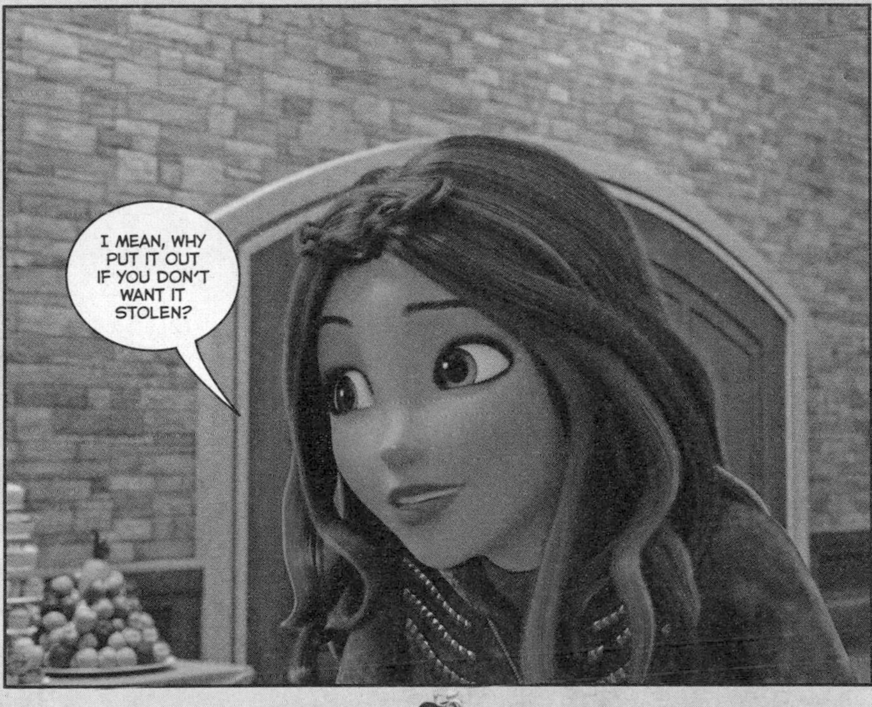
I MEAN, WHY PUT IT OUT IF YOU DON'T WANT IT STOLEN?

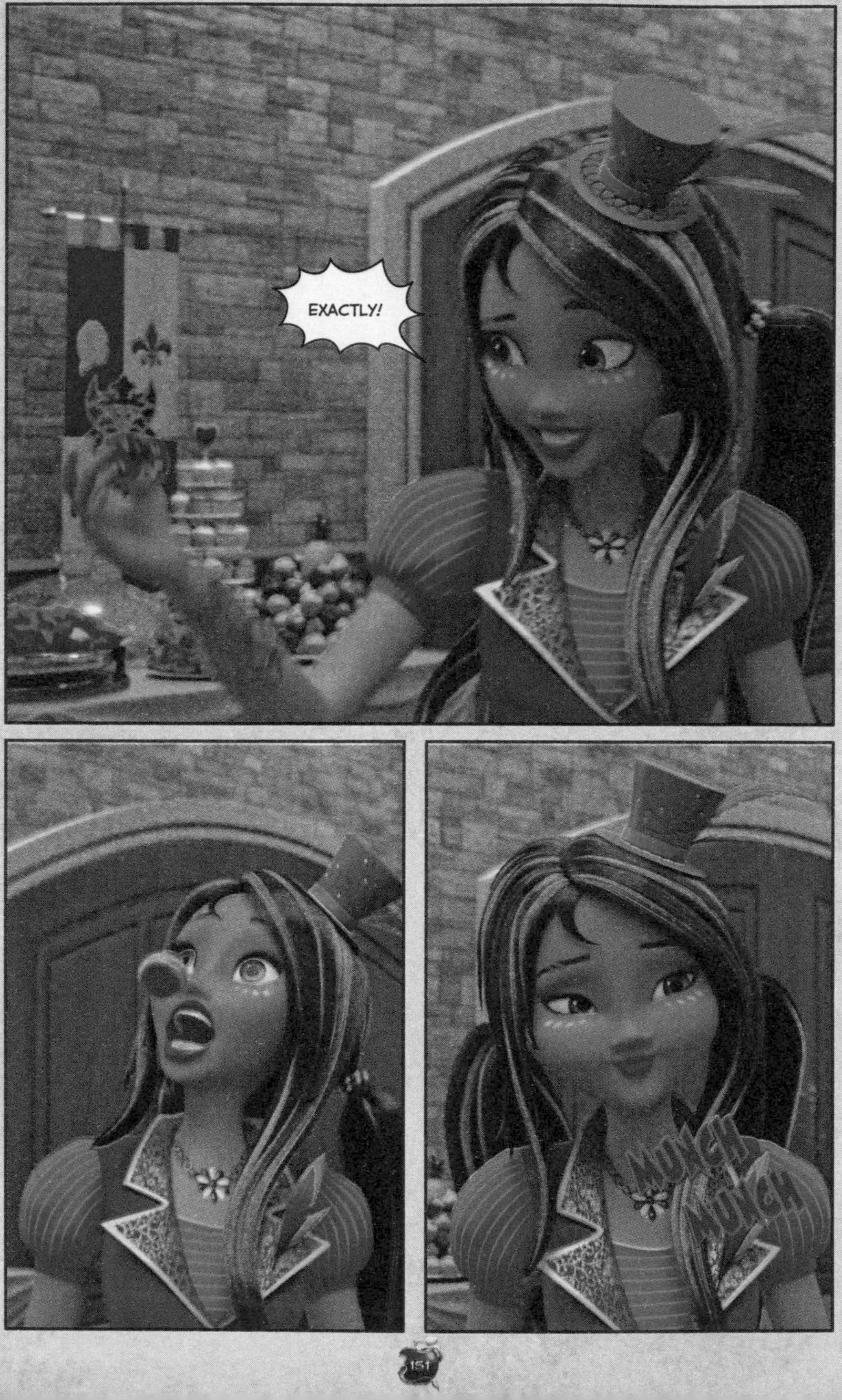
EXACTLY!
MUNCH MUNCH

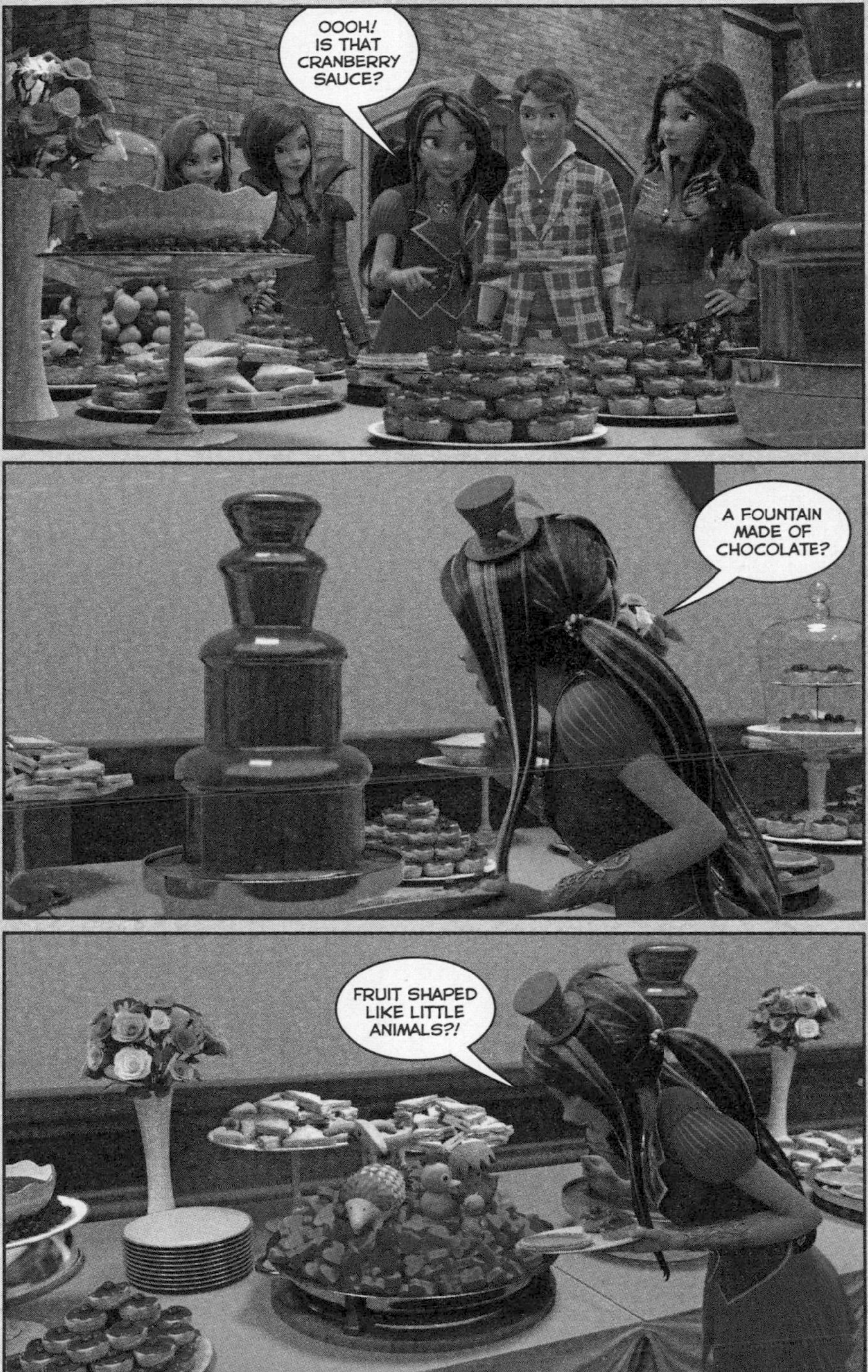
OOOH!
IS THAT
CRANBERRY
SAUCE?
A FOUNTAIN
MADE OF
CHOCOLATE?
FRUIT SHAPED
LIKE LITTLE
ANIMALS?!

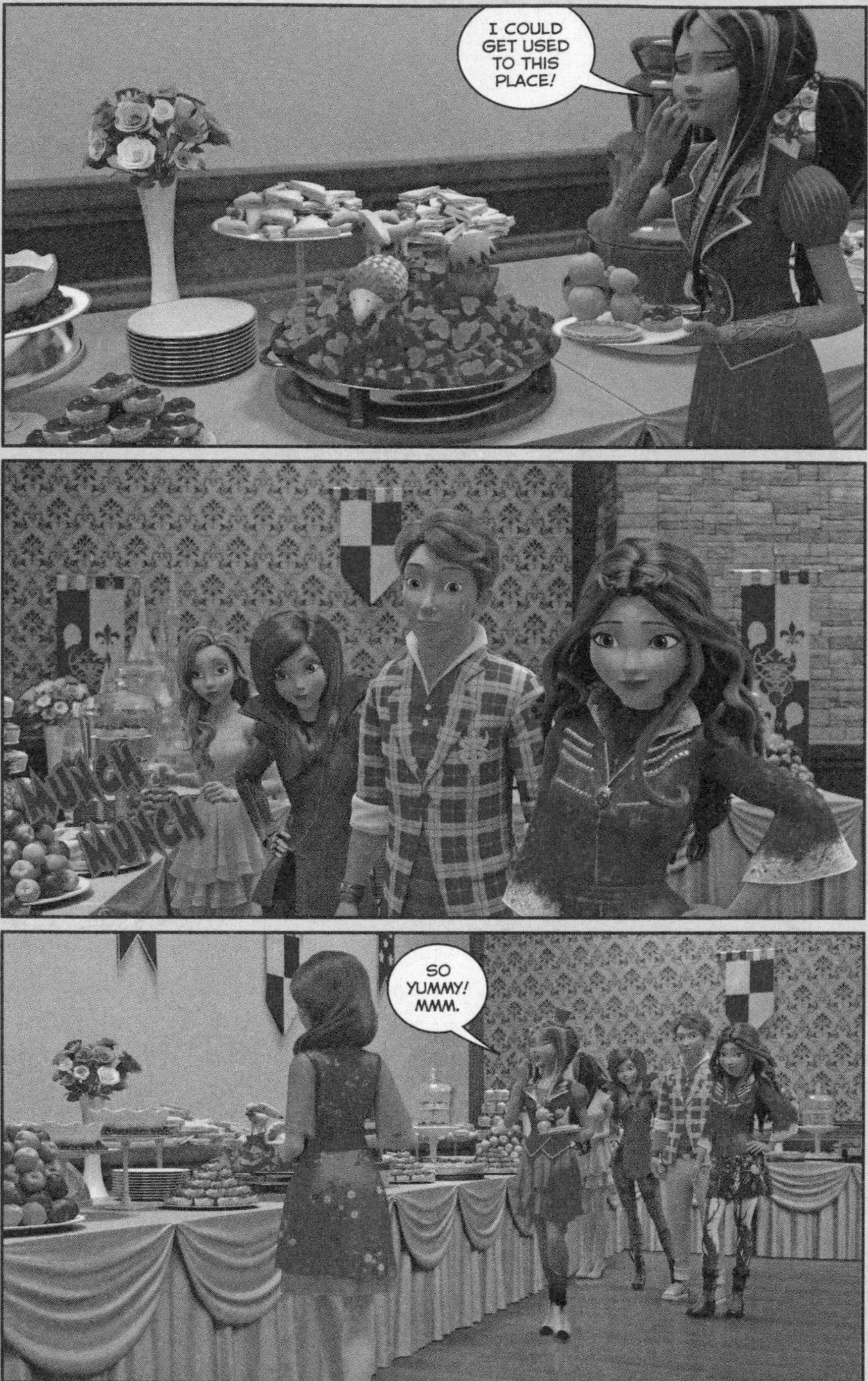
I COULD GET USED TO THIS PLACE!
MUNCH MUNCH
SO YUMMY! MMM.

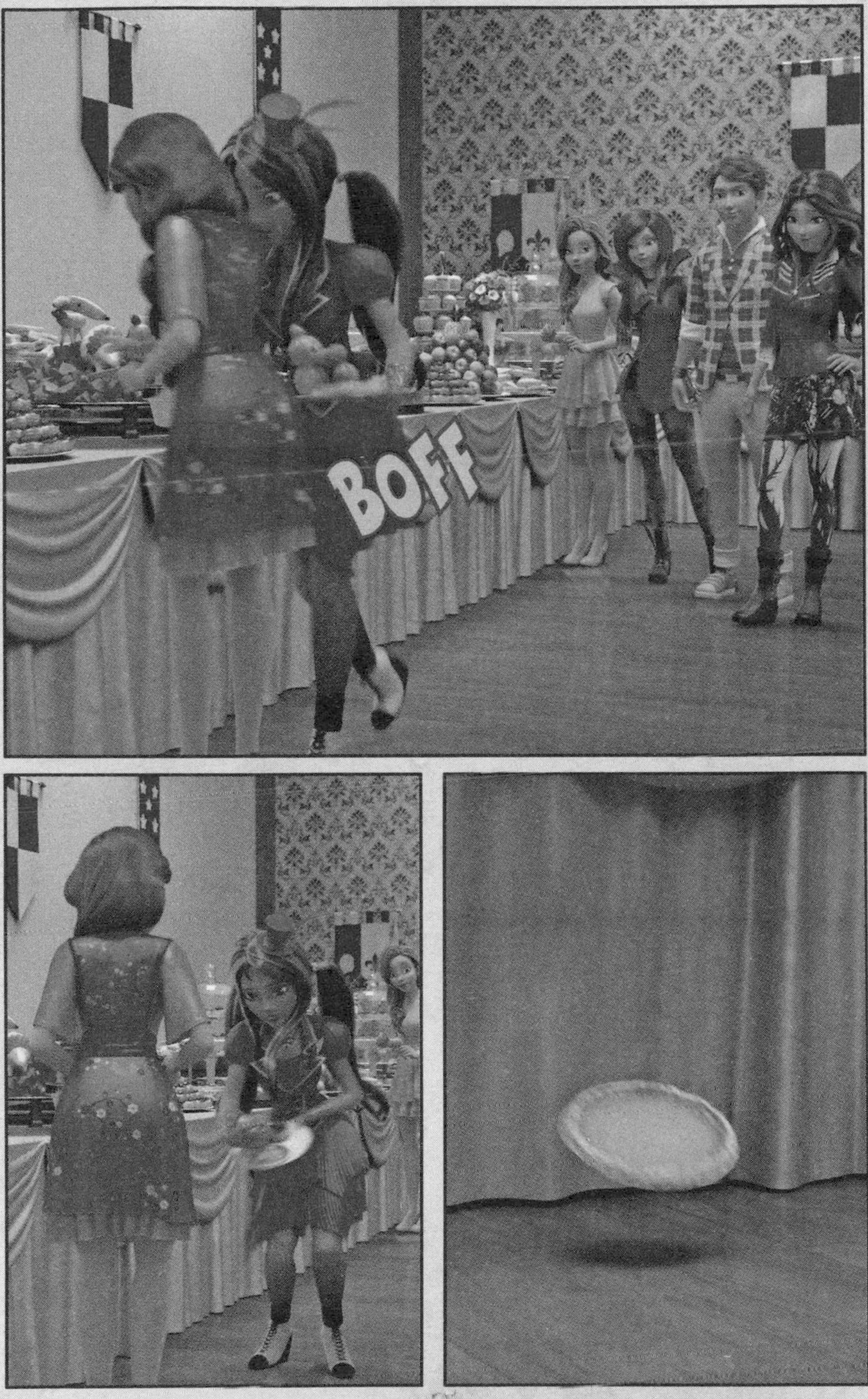
BOFF

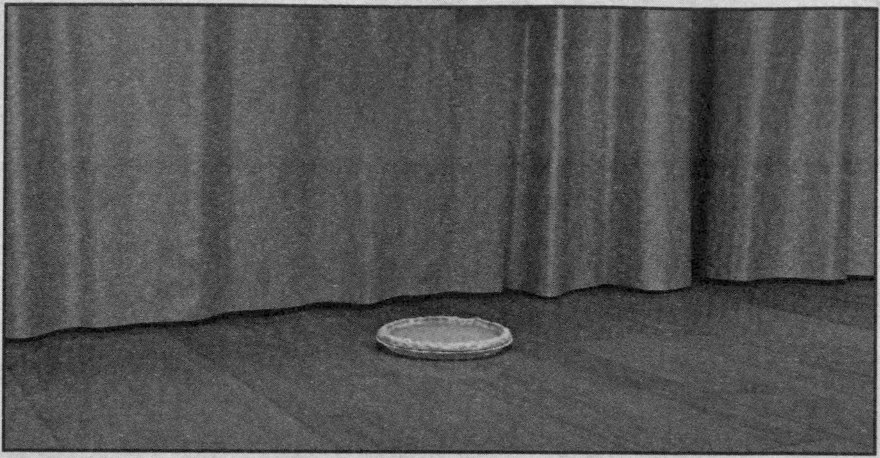

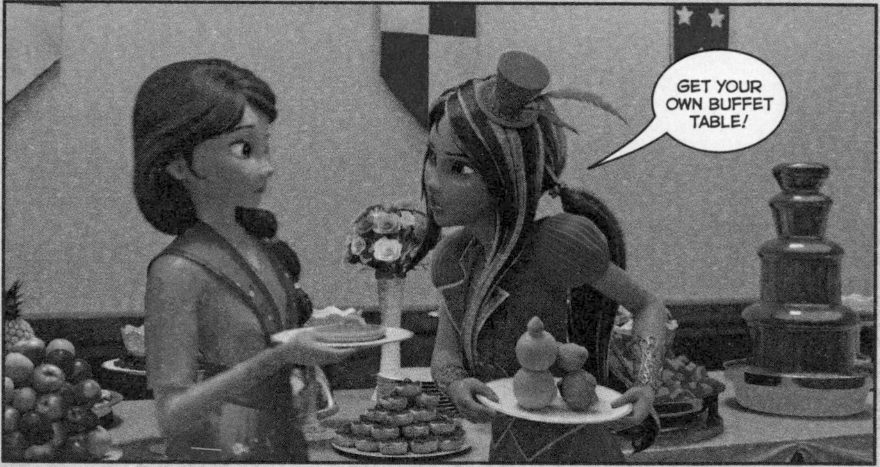
GET YOUR OWN BUFFET TABLE!

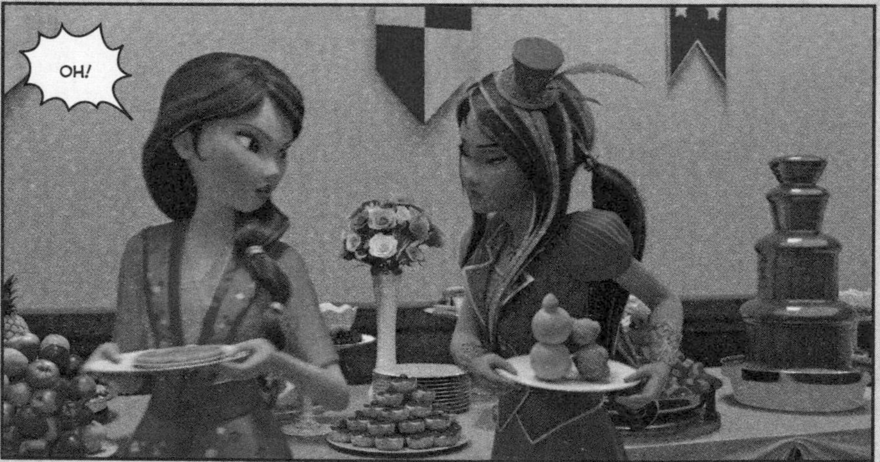
OH!

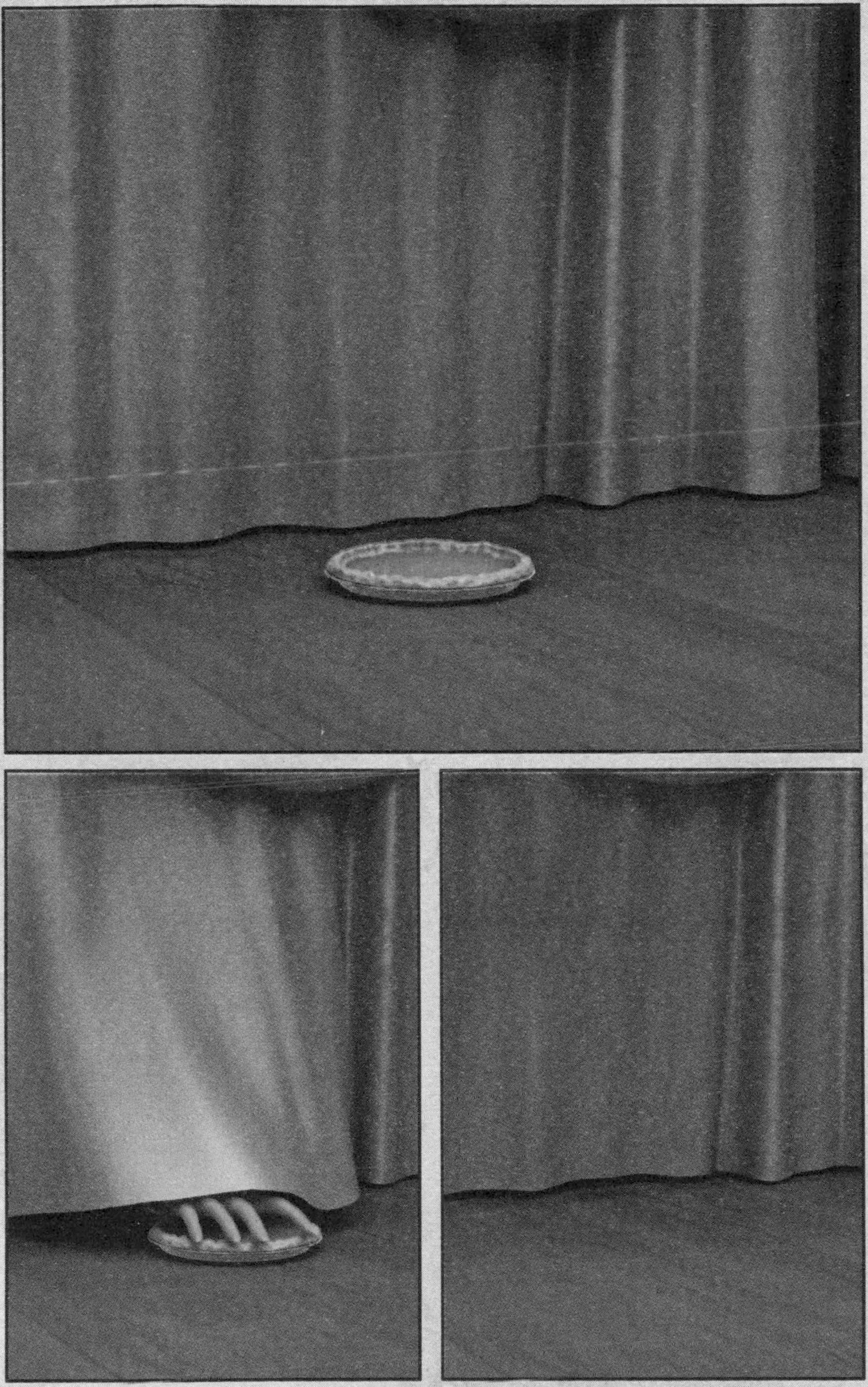

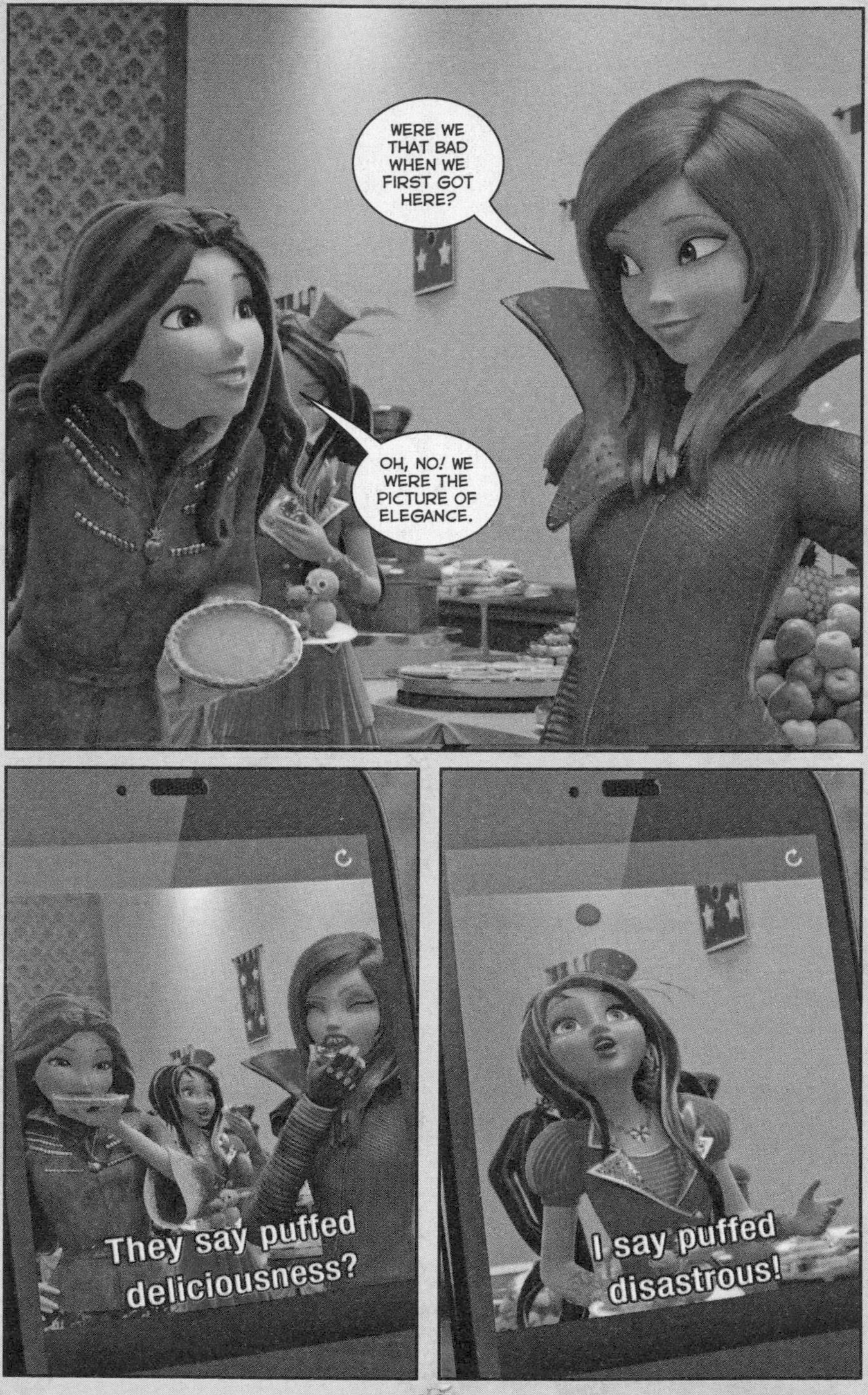
WERE WE THAT BAD WHEN WE FIRST GOT HERE?
OH, NO! WE WERE THE PICTURE OF ELEGANCE.
They say puffed deliciousness?
I say puffed disastrous!

CHAPTER 9: GOOD IS THE NEW BAD

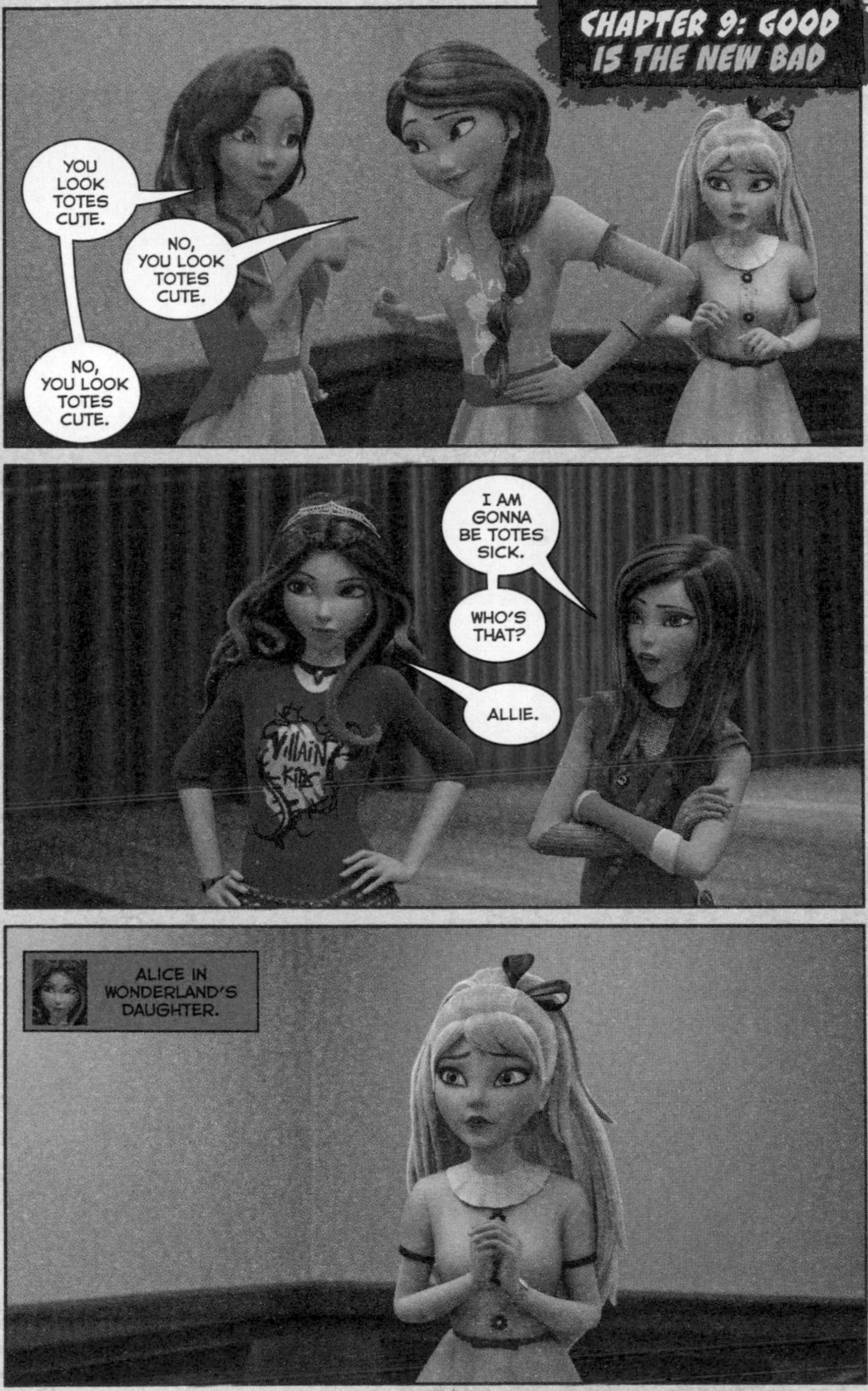
YOU LOOK TOTES CUTE.
NO, YOU LOOK TOTES CUTE.
NO, YOU LOOK TOTES CUTE.
I AM GONNA BE TOTES SICK.
WHO'S THAT?
ALLIE.
ALICE IN WONDERLAND'S DAUGHTER.

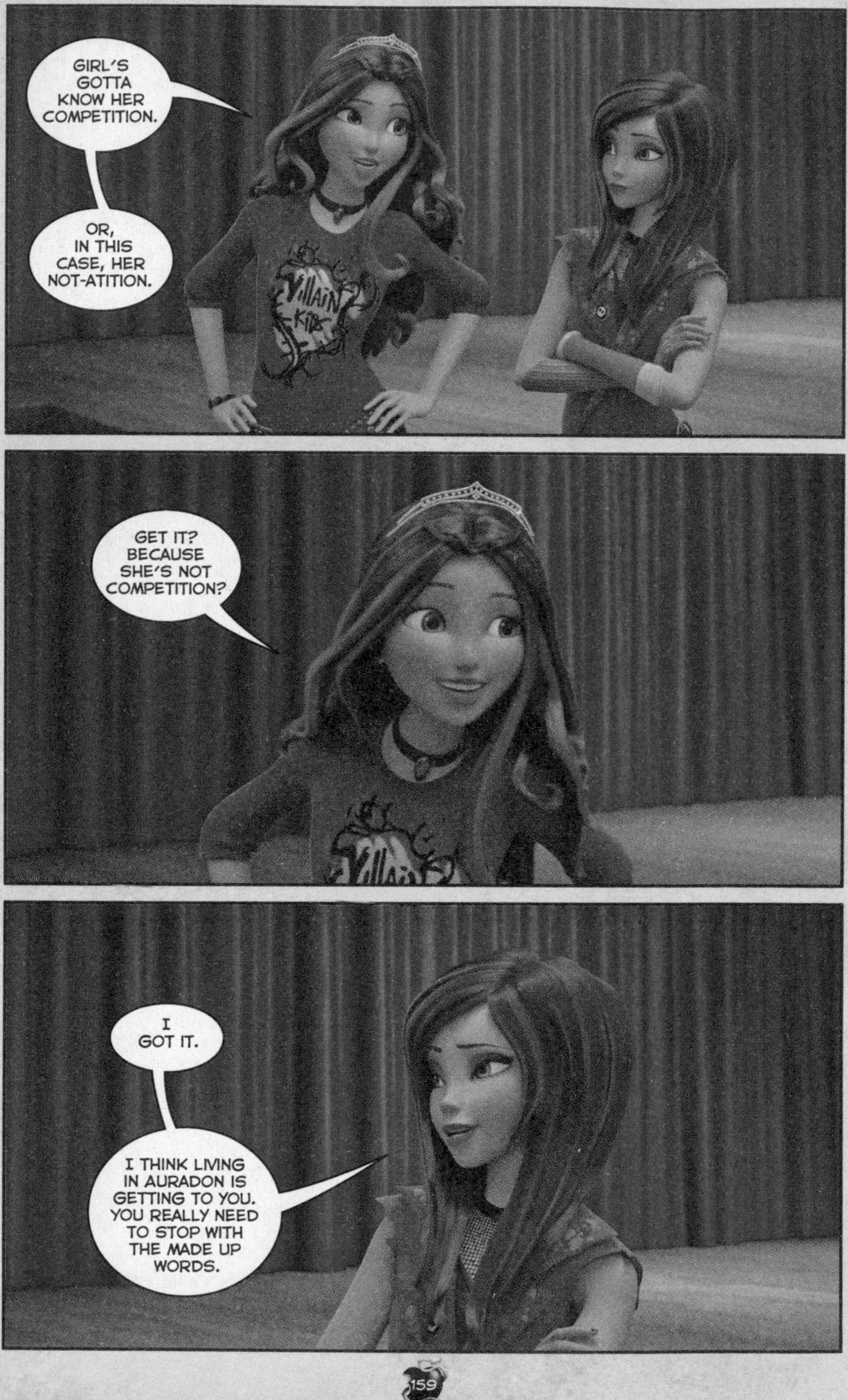
GIRL'S GOTTA KNOW HER COMPETITION.
OR, IN THIS CASE, HER NOT-ATITION.
GET IT? BECAUSE SHE'S NOT COMPETITION?
I GOT IT.
I THINK LIVING IN AURADON IS GETTING TO YOU. YOU REALLY NEED TO STOP WITH THE MADE UP WORDS.

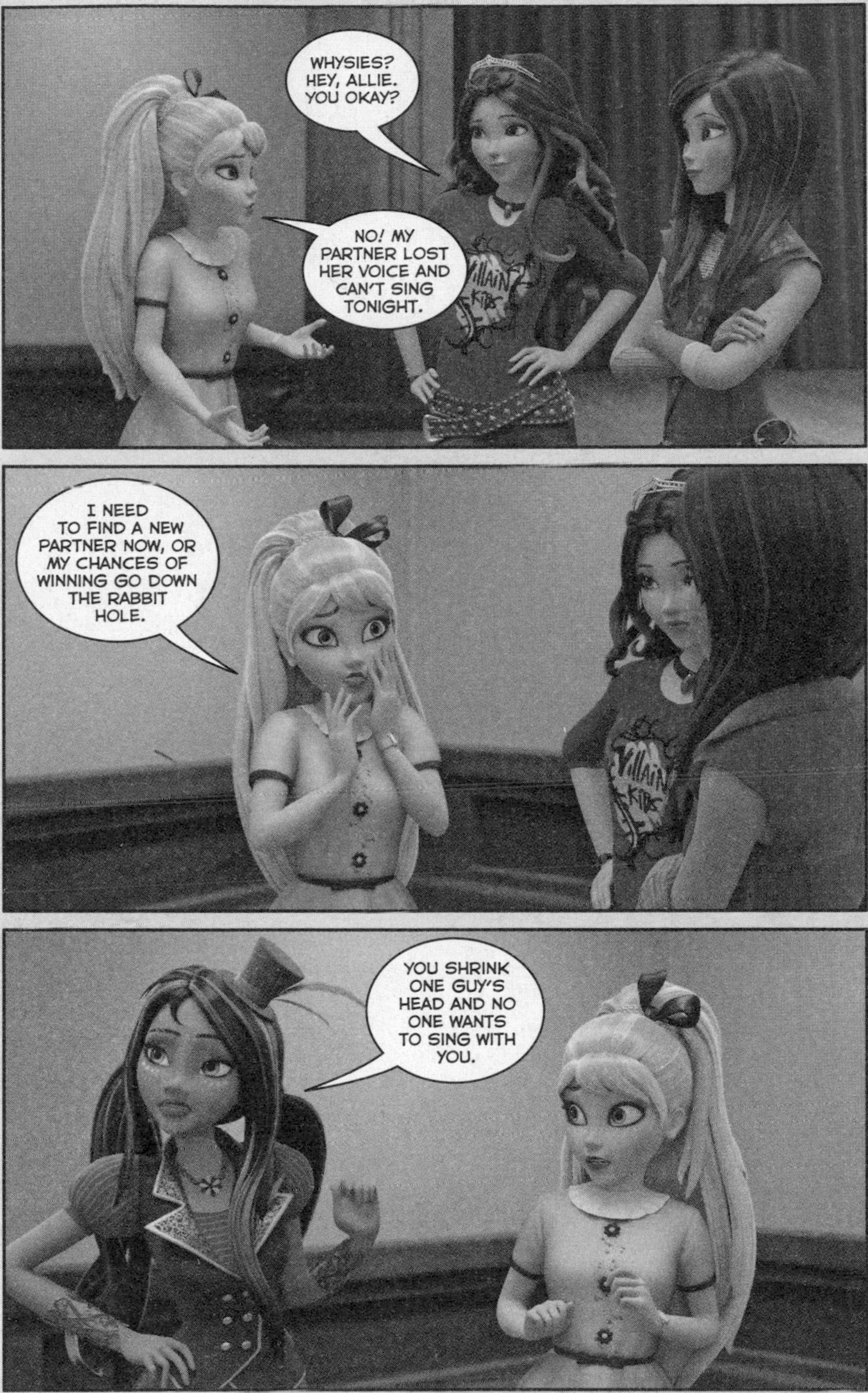
WHYSIES? HEY, ALLIE. YOU OKAY?
NO! MY PARTNER LOST HER VOICE AND CAN'T SING TONIGHT.
I NEED TO FIND A NEW PARTNER NOW, OR MY CHANCES OF WINNING GO DOWN THE RABBIT HOLE.
YOU SHRINK ONE GUY'S HEAD AND NO ONE WANTS TO SING WITH YOU.

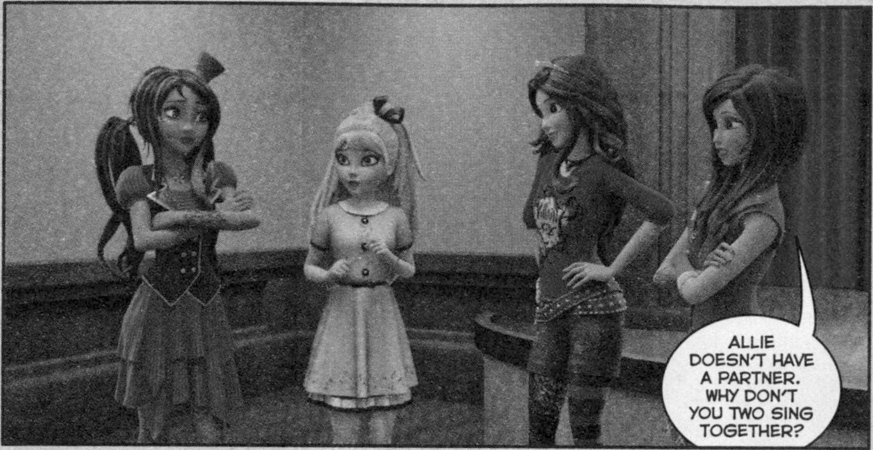
ALLIE DOESN'T HAVE A PARTNER. WHY DON'T YOU TWO SING TOGETHER?

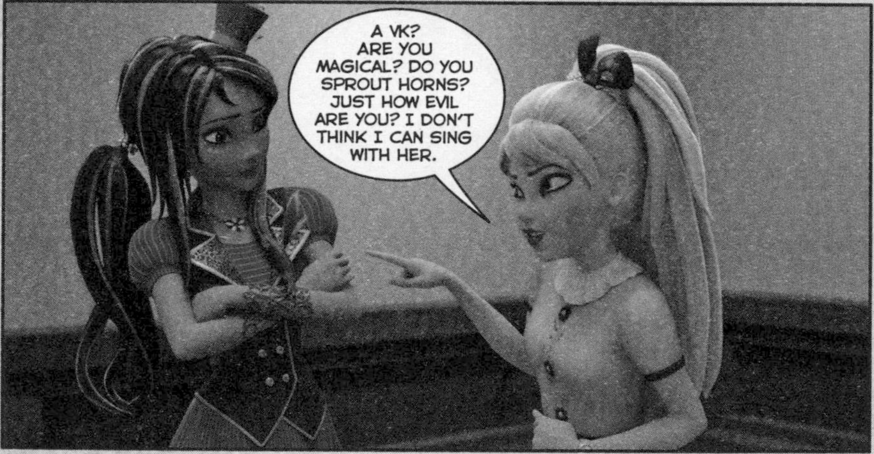
A VK? ARE YOU MAGICAL? DO YOU SPROUT HORNS? JUST HOW EVIL ARE YOU? I DON'T THINK I CAN SING WITH HER.

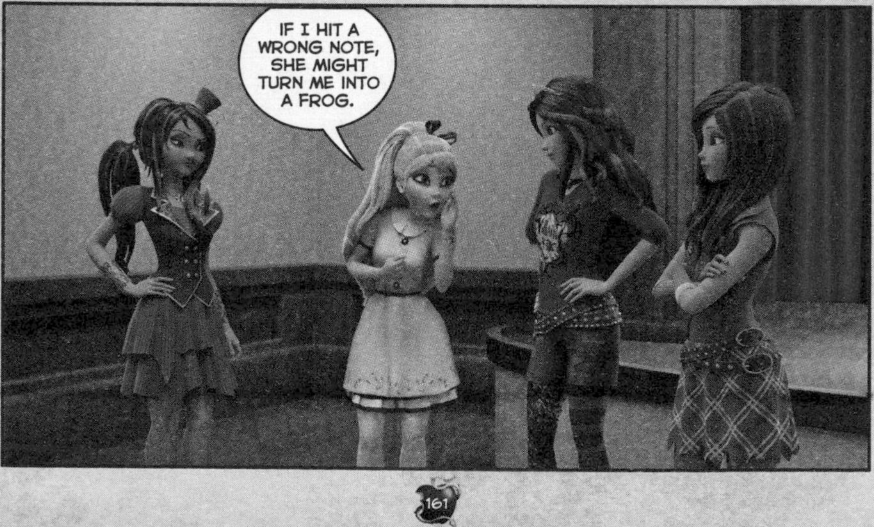
IF I HIT A WRONG NOTE, SHE MIGHT TURN ME INTO A FROG.

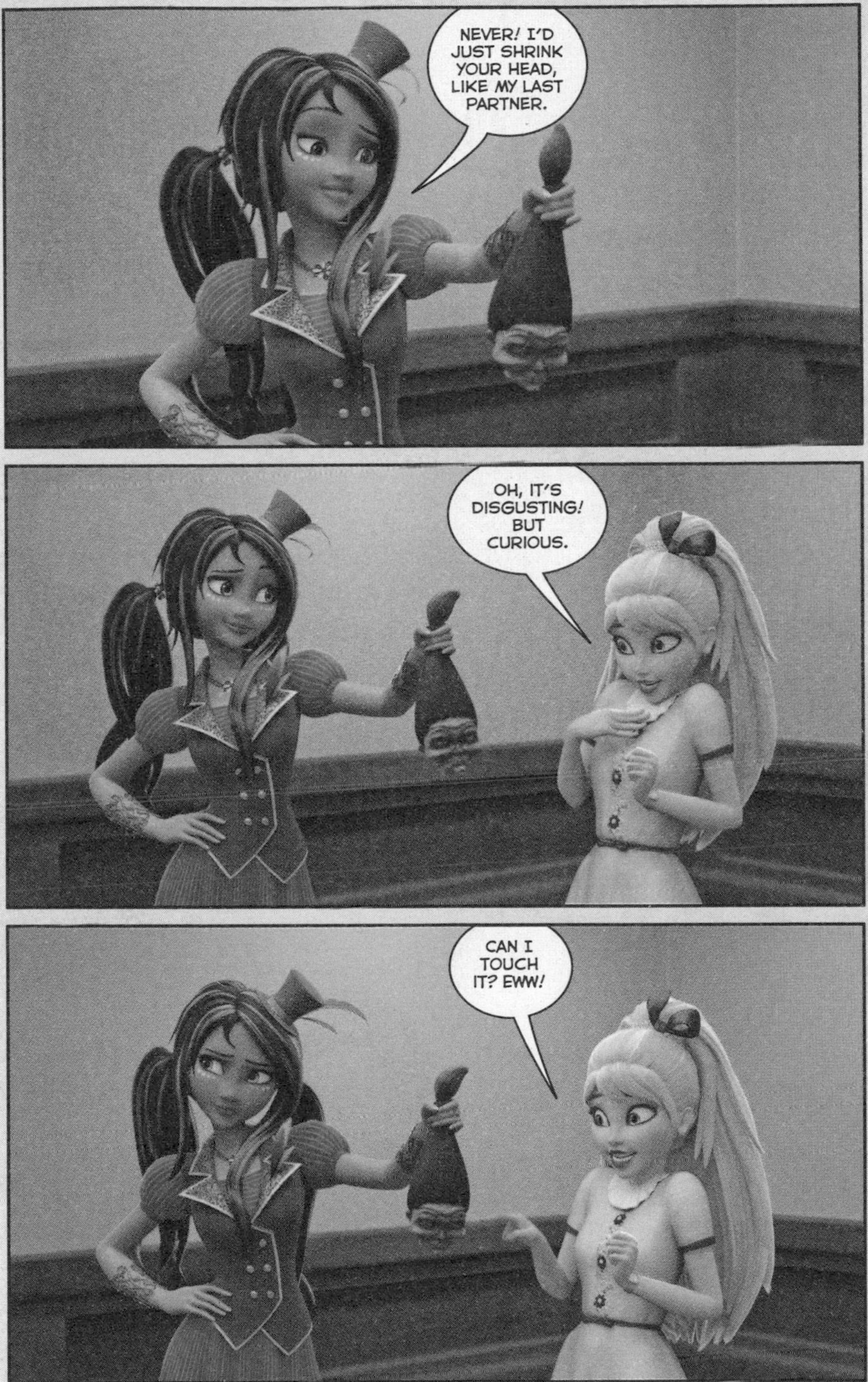
NEVER! I'D JUST SHRINK YOUR HEAD, LIKE MY LAST PARTNER.
OH, IT'S DISGUSTING! BUT CURIOUS.
CAN I TOUCH IT? EWW!

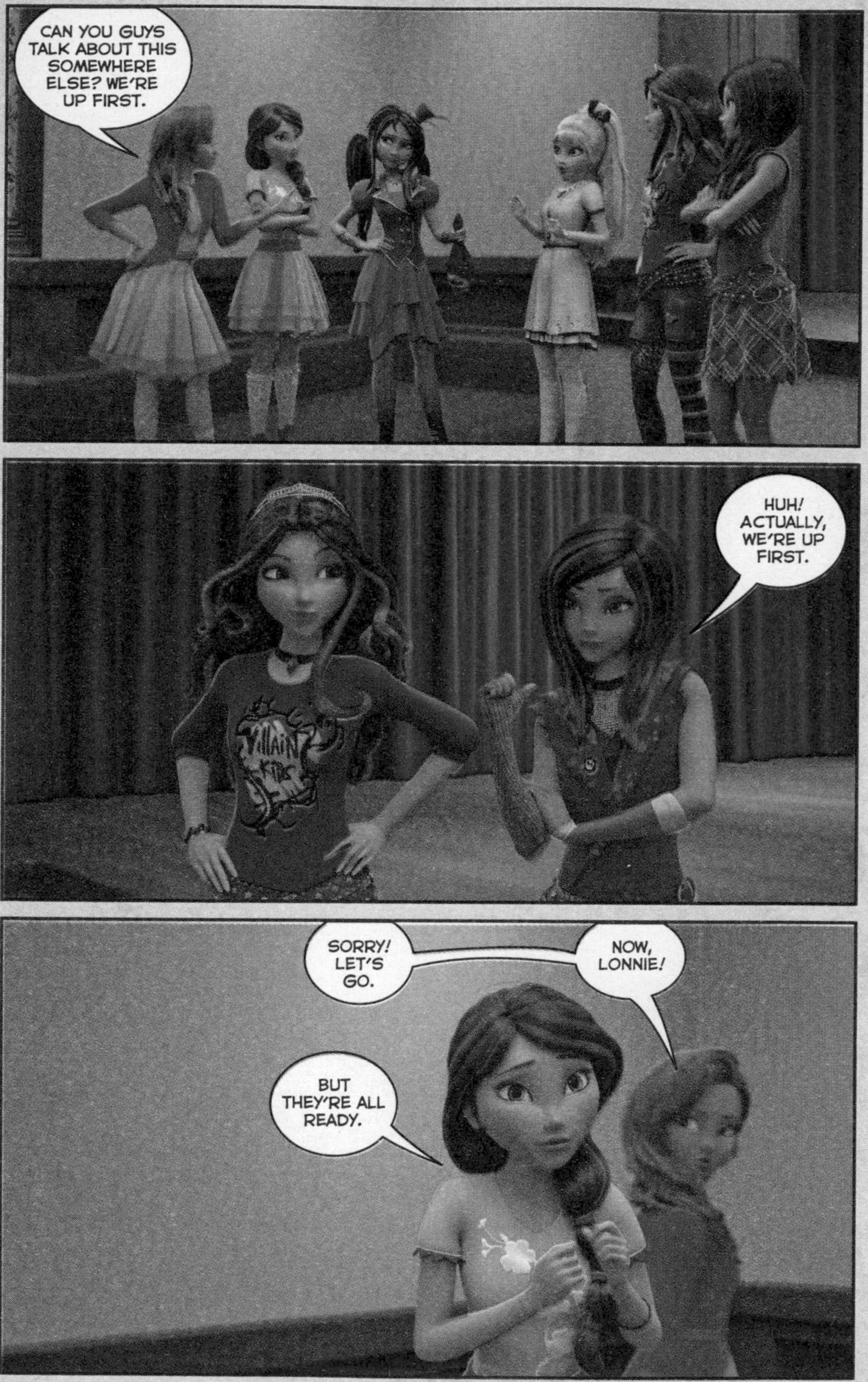
CAN YOU GUYS TALK ABOUT THIS SOMEWHERE ELSE? WE'RE UP FIRST.
HUH! ACTUALLY, WE'RE UP FIRST.
SORRY! LET'S GO.
NOW, LONNIE!
BUT THEY'RE ALL READY.

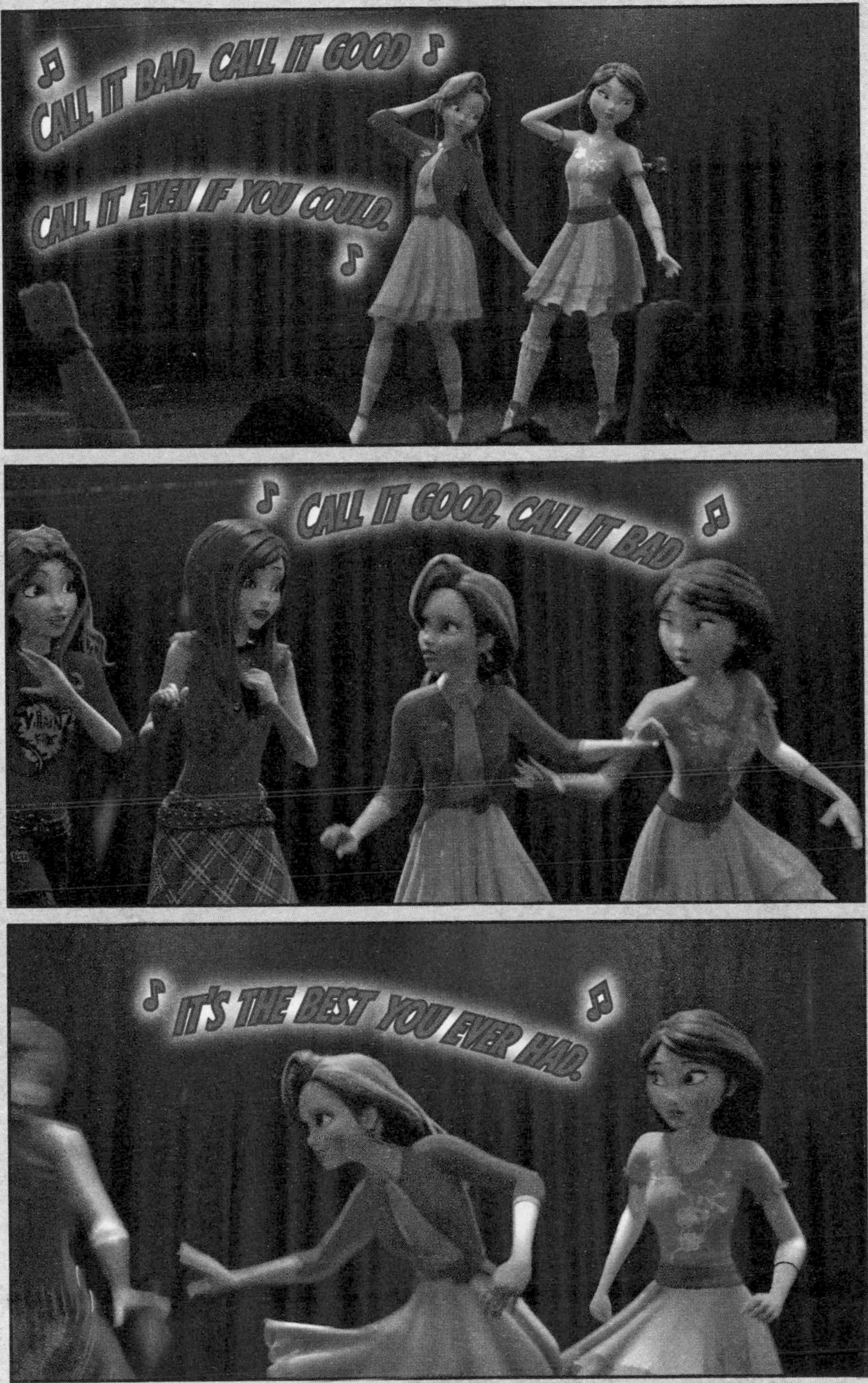
CALL IT BAD, CALL IT GOOD
CALL IT EVEN IF YOU COULD.
CALL IT GOOD, CALL IT BAD
IT'S THE BEST YOU EVER HAD.

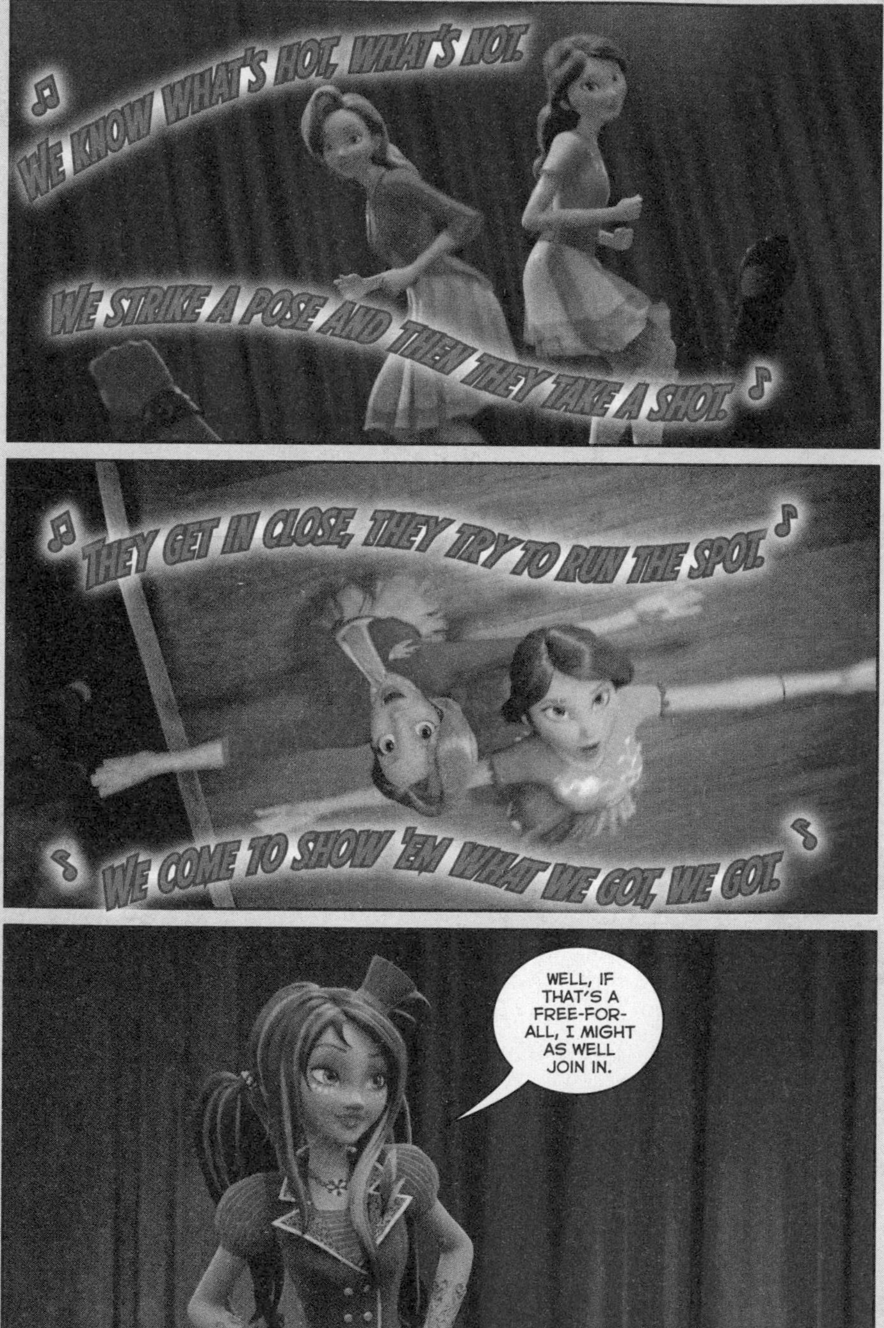
♫ WE KNOW WHAT'S HOT, WHAT'S NOT.
WE STRIKE A POSE AND THEN THEY TAKE A SHOT. ♪
♫ THEY GET IN CLOSE, THEY TRY TO RUN THE SPOT. ♪
♪ WE COME TO SHOW 'EM WHAT WE GOT, WE GOT. ♪
WELL, IF THAT'S A FREE-FOR-ALL, I MIGHT AS WELL JOIN IN.

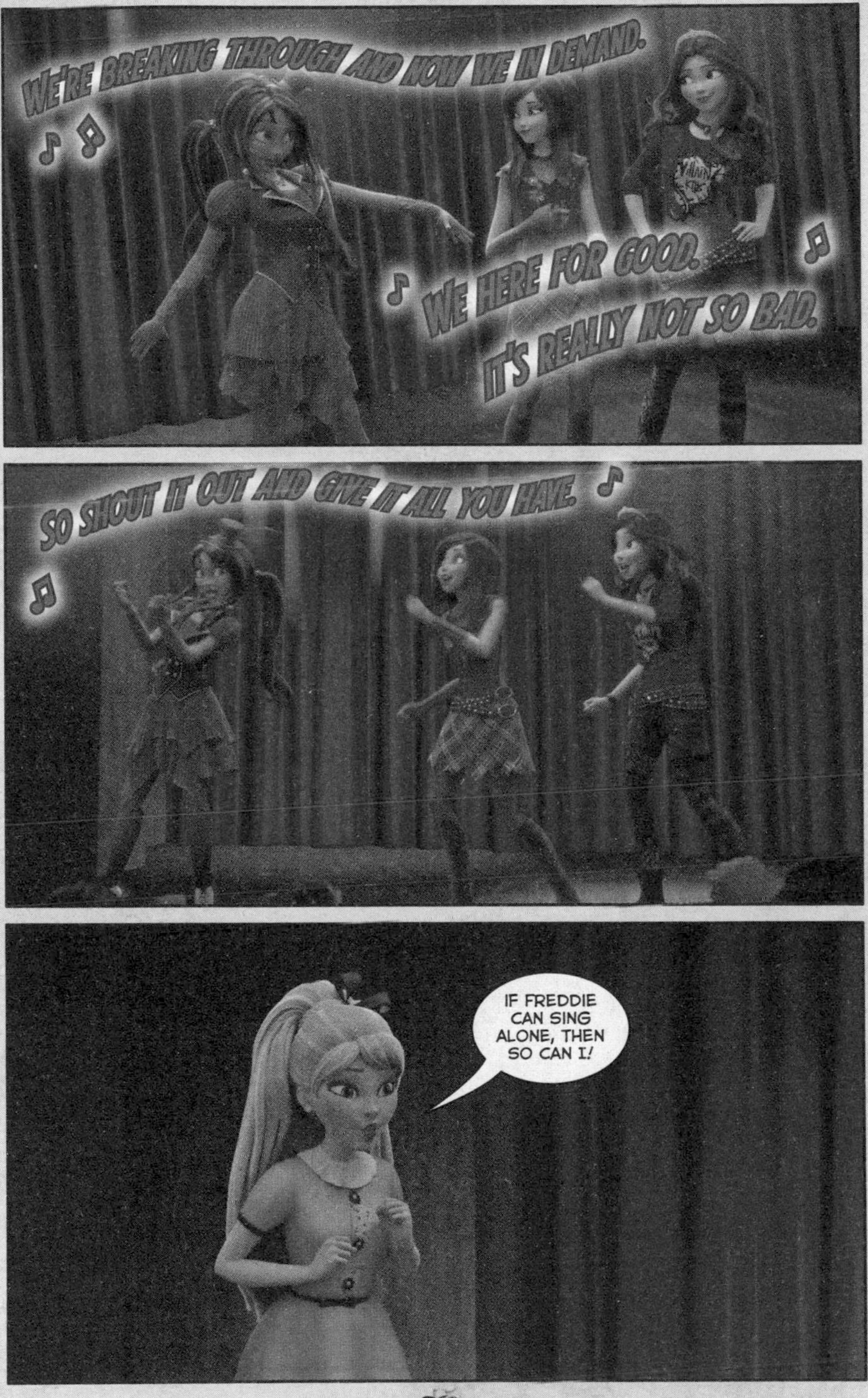
WE'RE BREAKING THROUGH AND NOW WE IN DEMAND.
WE HERE FOR GOOD.
IT'S REALLY NOT SO BAD.
SO SHOUT IT OUT AND GIVE IT ALL YOU HAVE.
IF FREDDIE CAN SING ALONE, THEN SO CAN I!

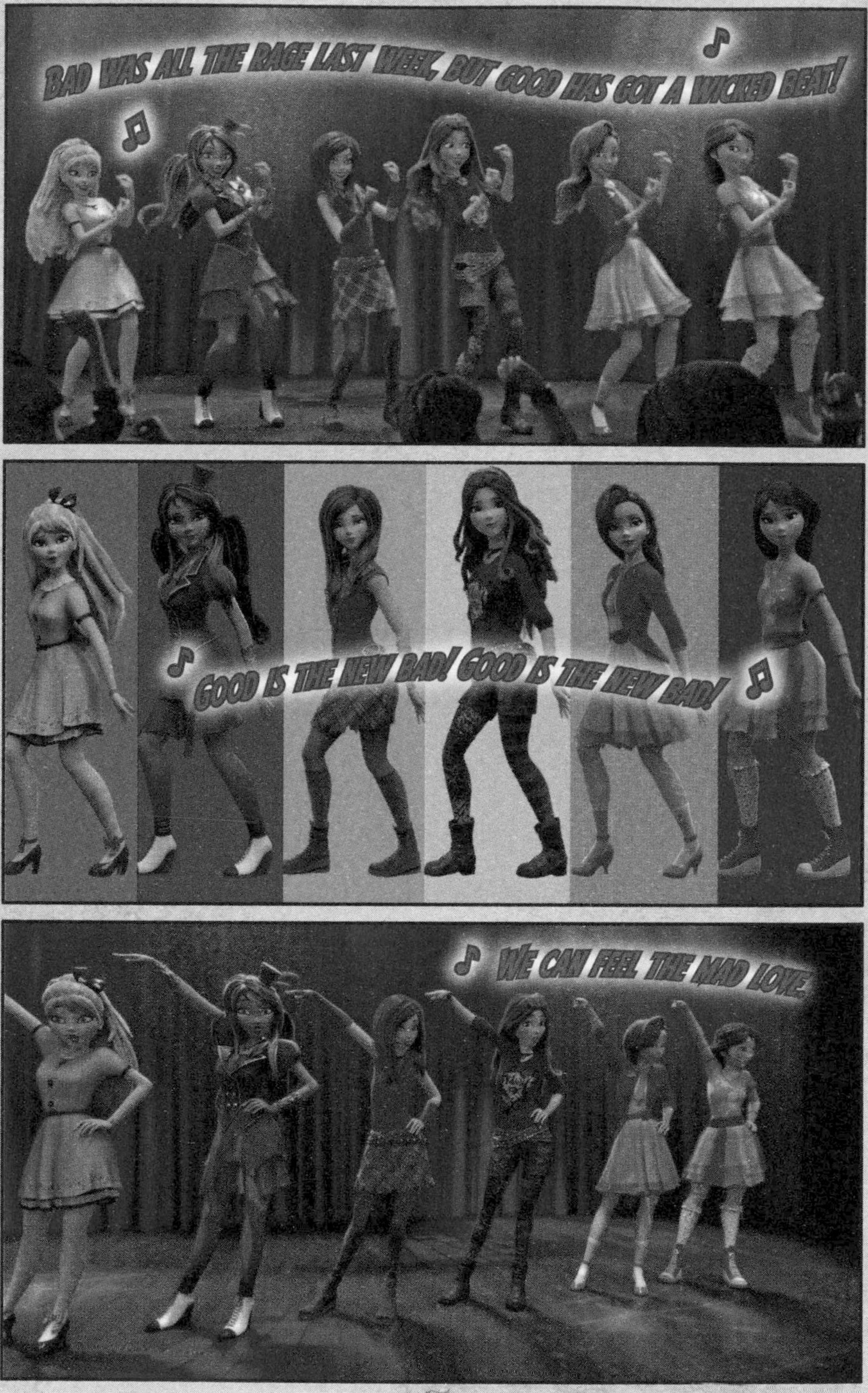
BAD WAS ALL THE RAGE LAST WEEK, BUT GOOD HAS GOT A WICKED BEAT!
GOOD IS THE NEW BAD! GOOD IS THE NEW BAD!
WE CAN FEEL THE MAD LOVE.

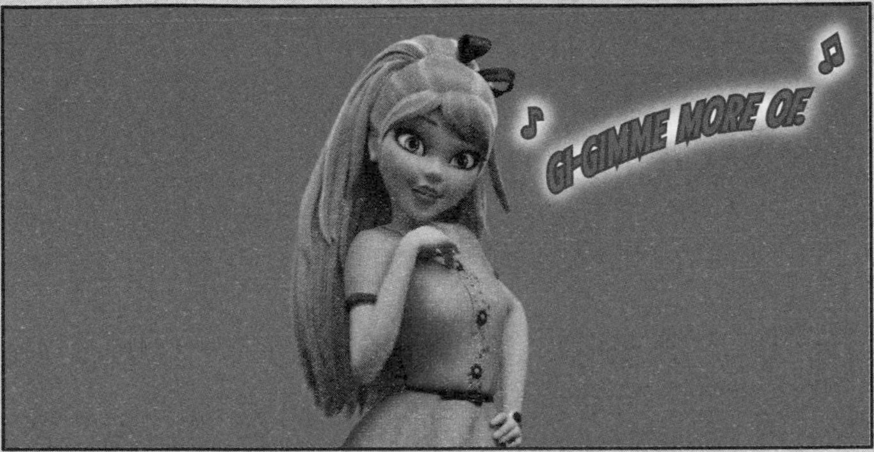
GI-GIMME MORE OF.

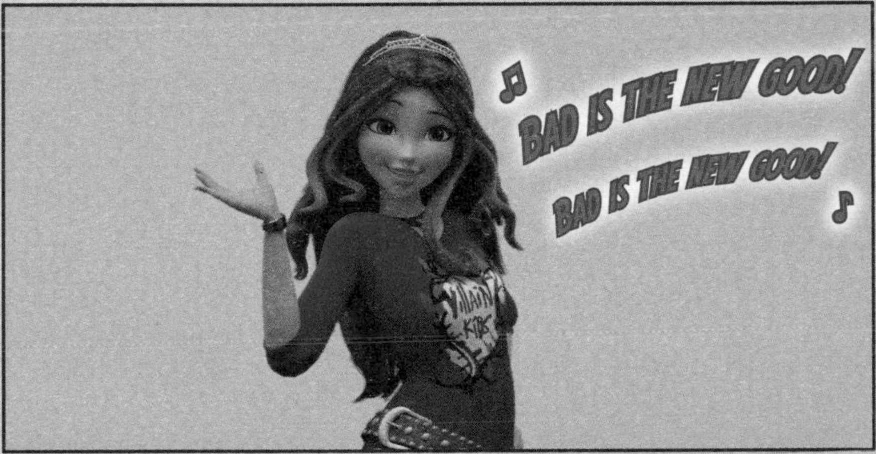
BAD IS THE NEW GOOD!
BAD IS THE NEW GOOD!

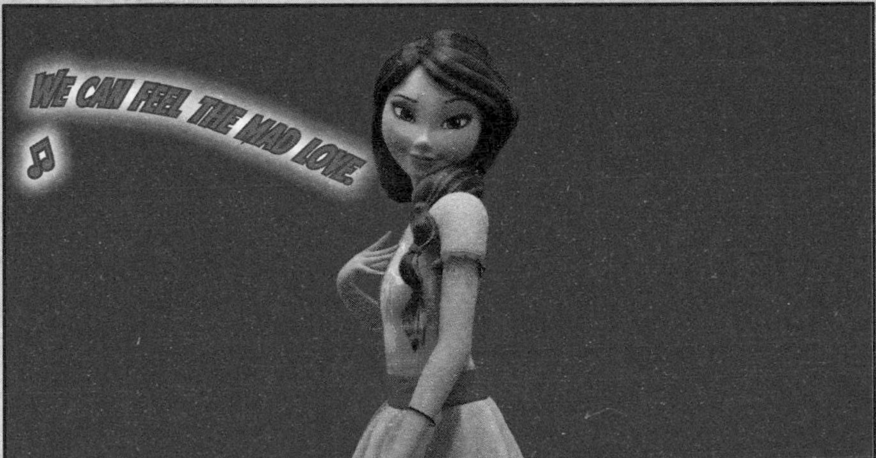
WE CAN FEEL THE MAD LOVE.

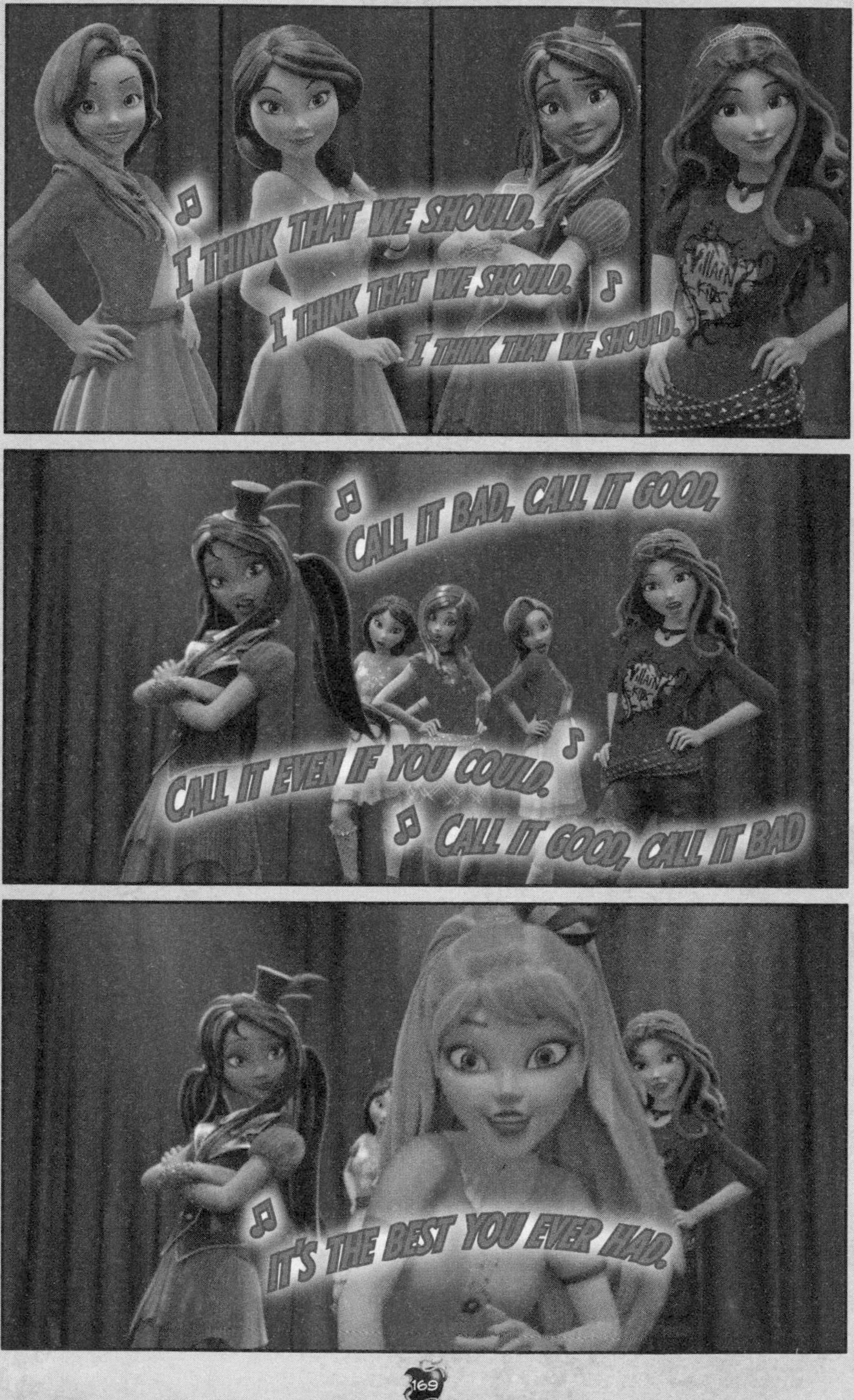
♫ I THINK THAT WE SHOULD.
I THINK THAT WE SHOULD. ♪
I THINK THAT WE SHOULD.
♫ CALL IT BAD, CALL IT GOOD,
CALL IT EVEN IF YOU COULD. ♪
♫ CALL IT GOOD, CALL IT BAD
♫ IT'S THE BEST YOU EVER HAD.

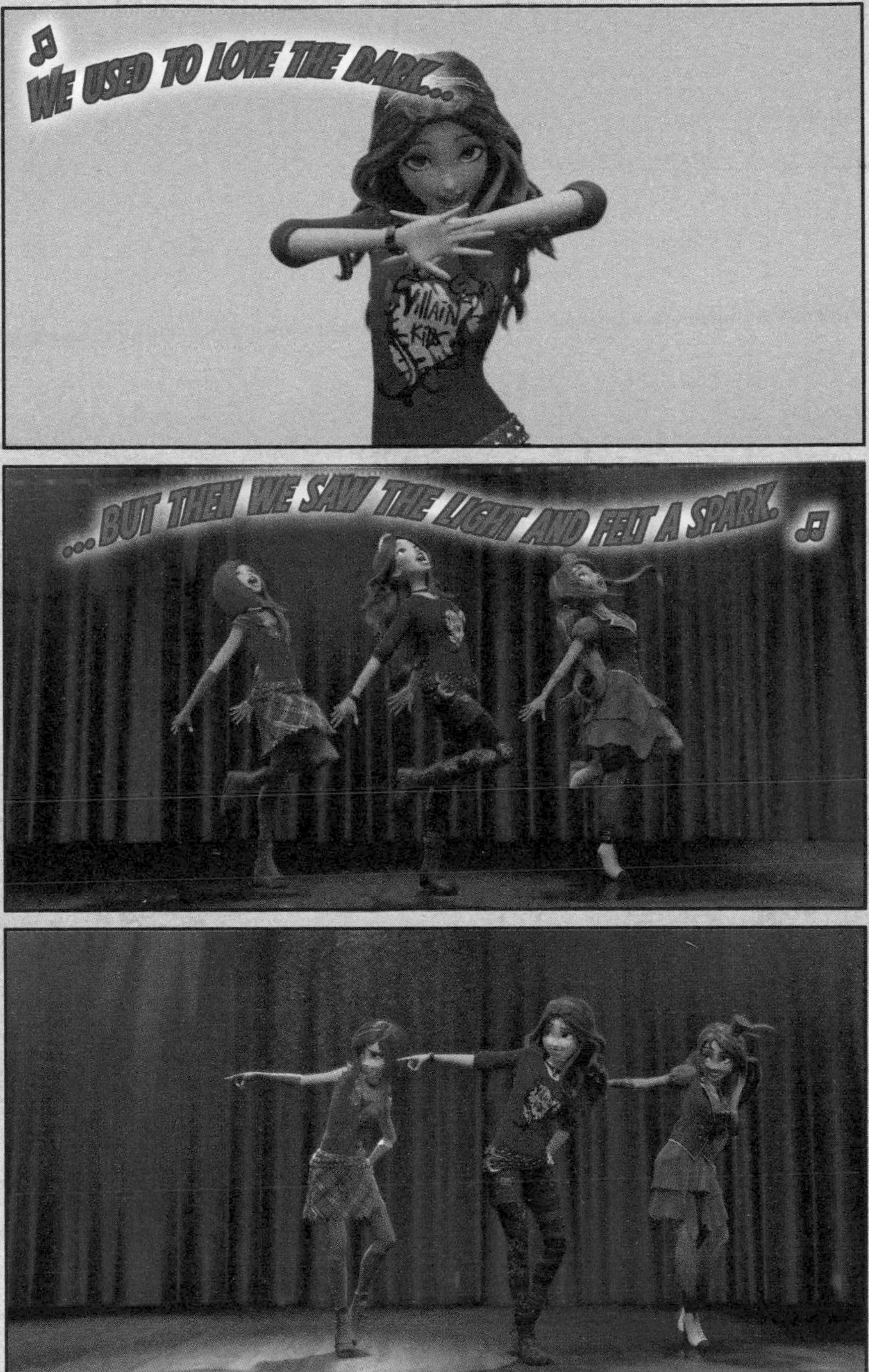
♫ WE USED TO LOVE THE DARK...
...BUT THEN WE SAW THE LIGHT AND FELT A SPARK. ♫

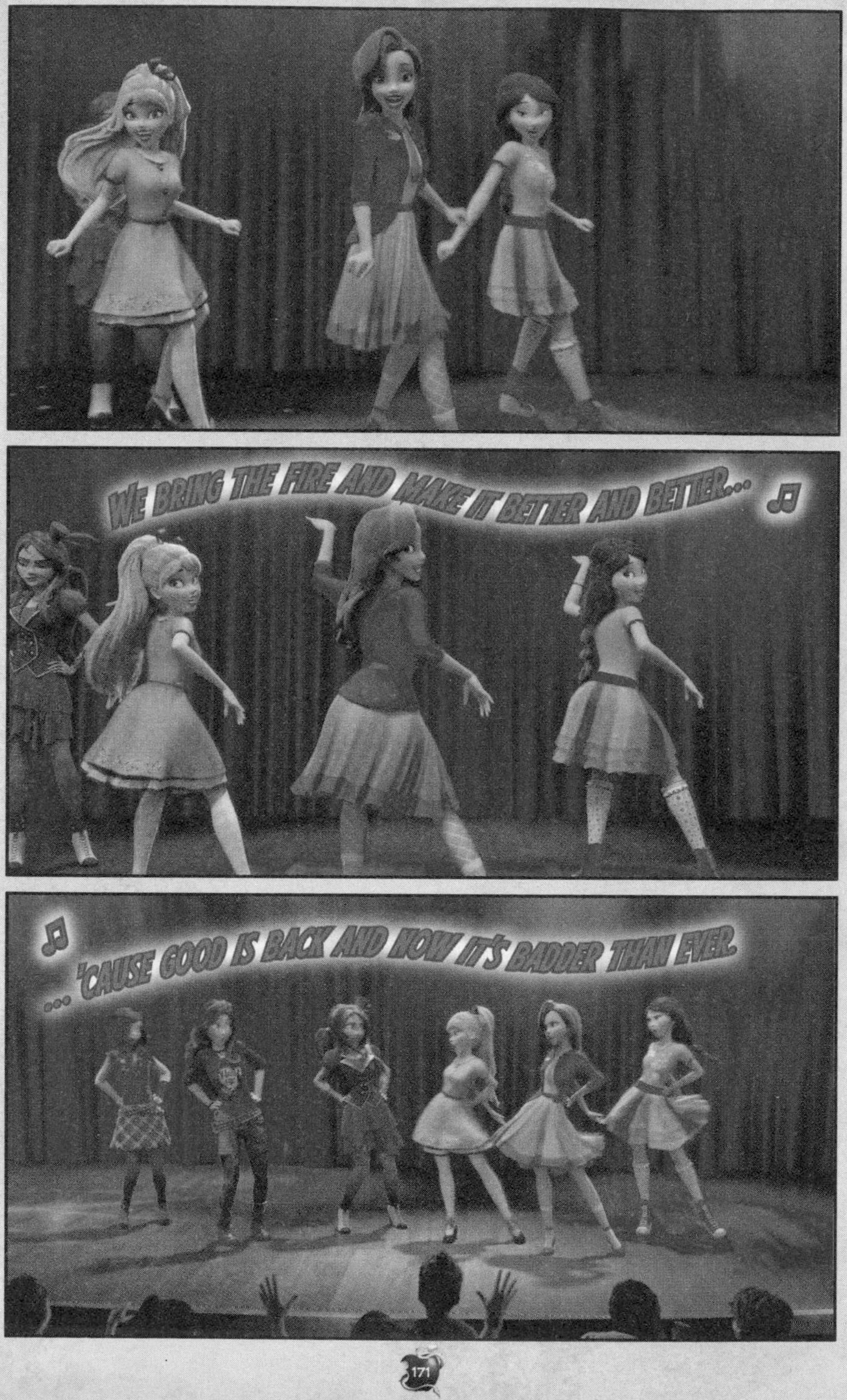
WE BRING THE FIRE AND MAKE IT BETTER AND BETTER...
...'CAUSE GOOD IS BACK AND NOW IT'S BADDER THAN EVER.

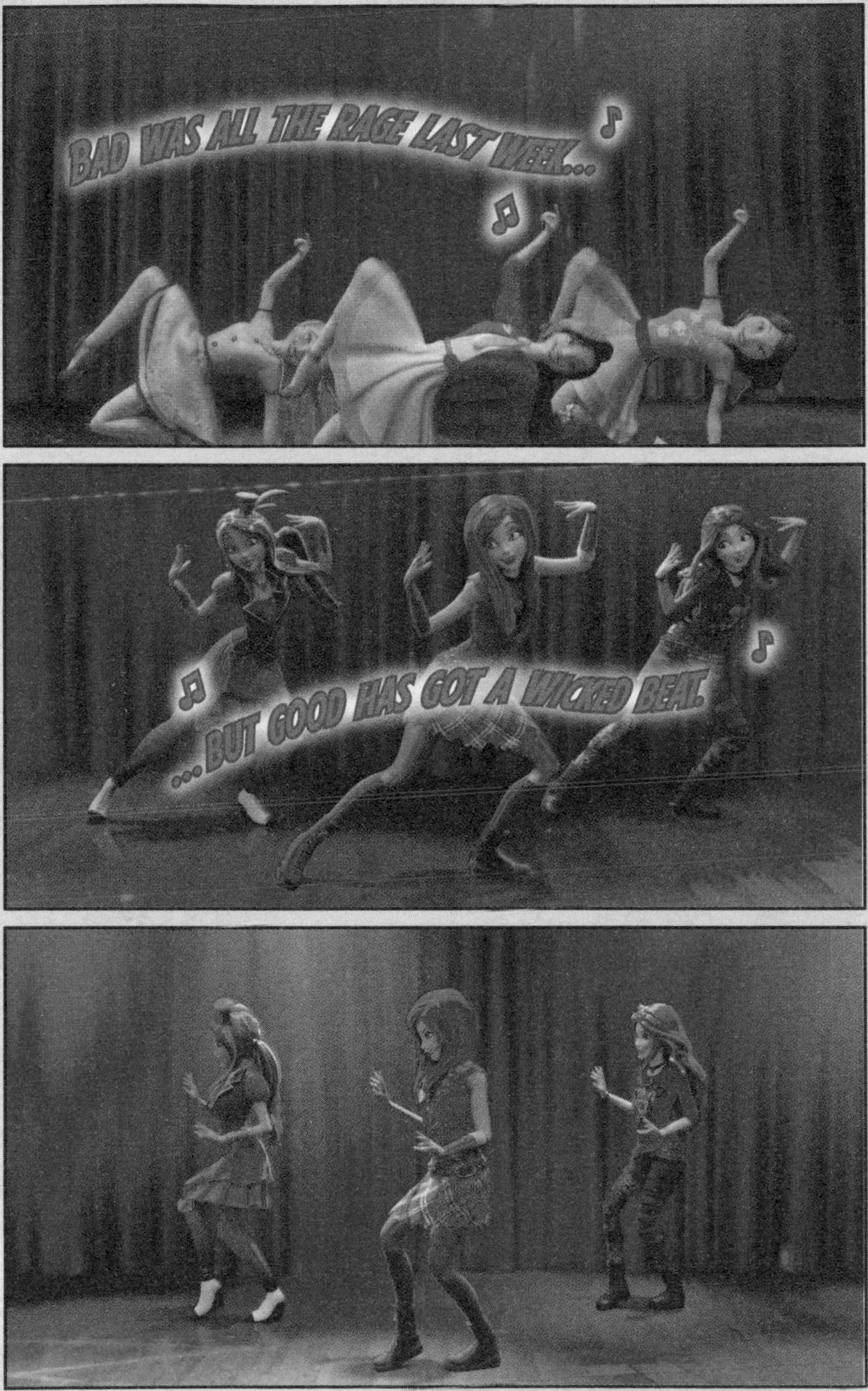
BAD WAS ALL THE RAGE LAST WEEK...
...BUT GOOD HAS GOT A WICKED BEAT.

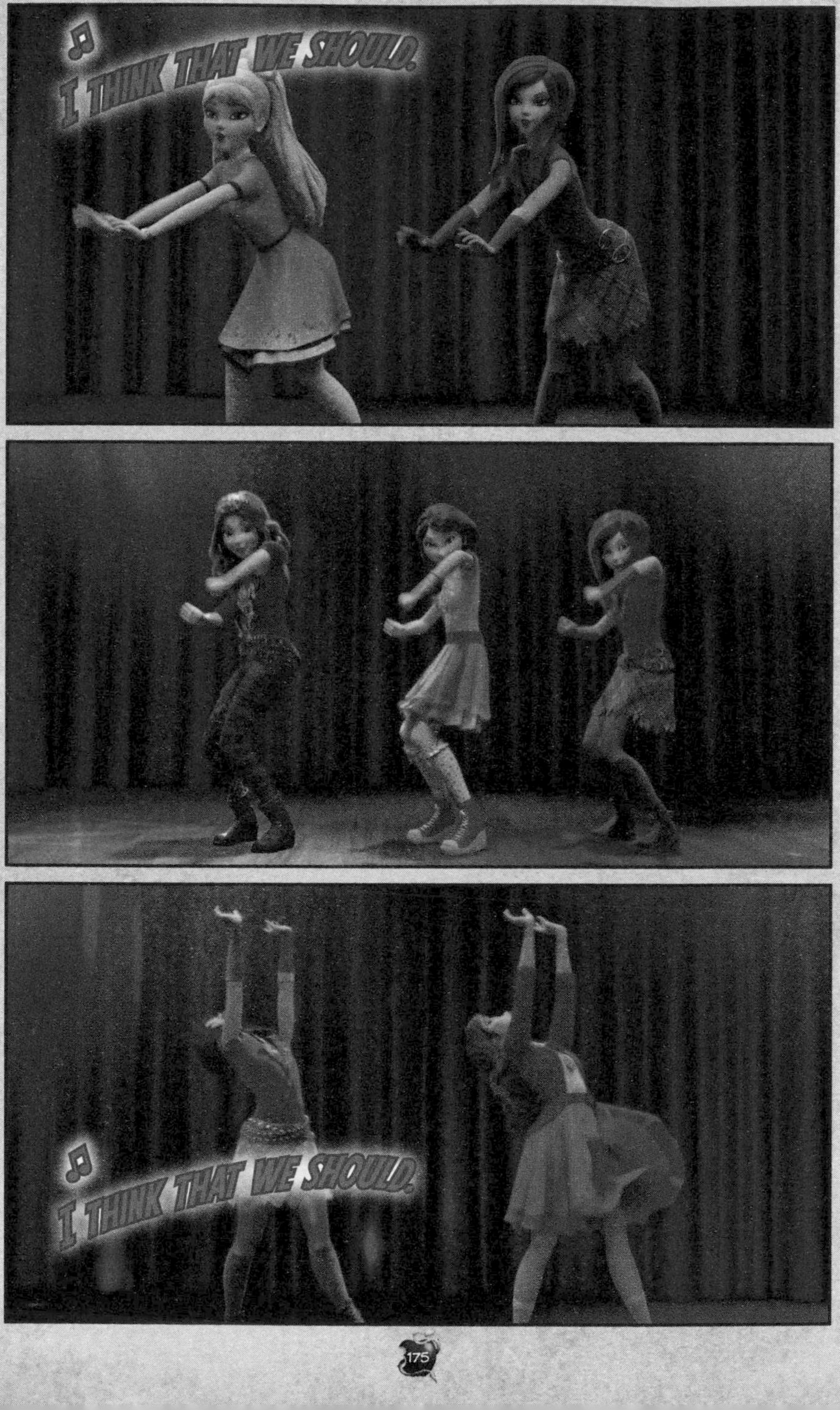
♫ I THINK THAT WE SHOULD.
♫ I THINK THAT WE SHOULD.

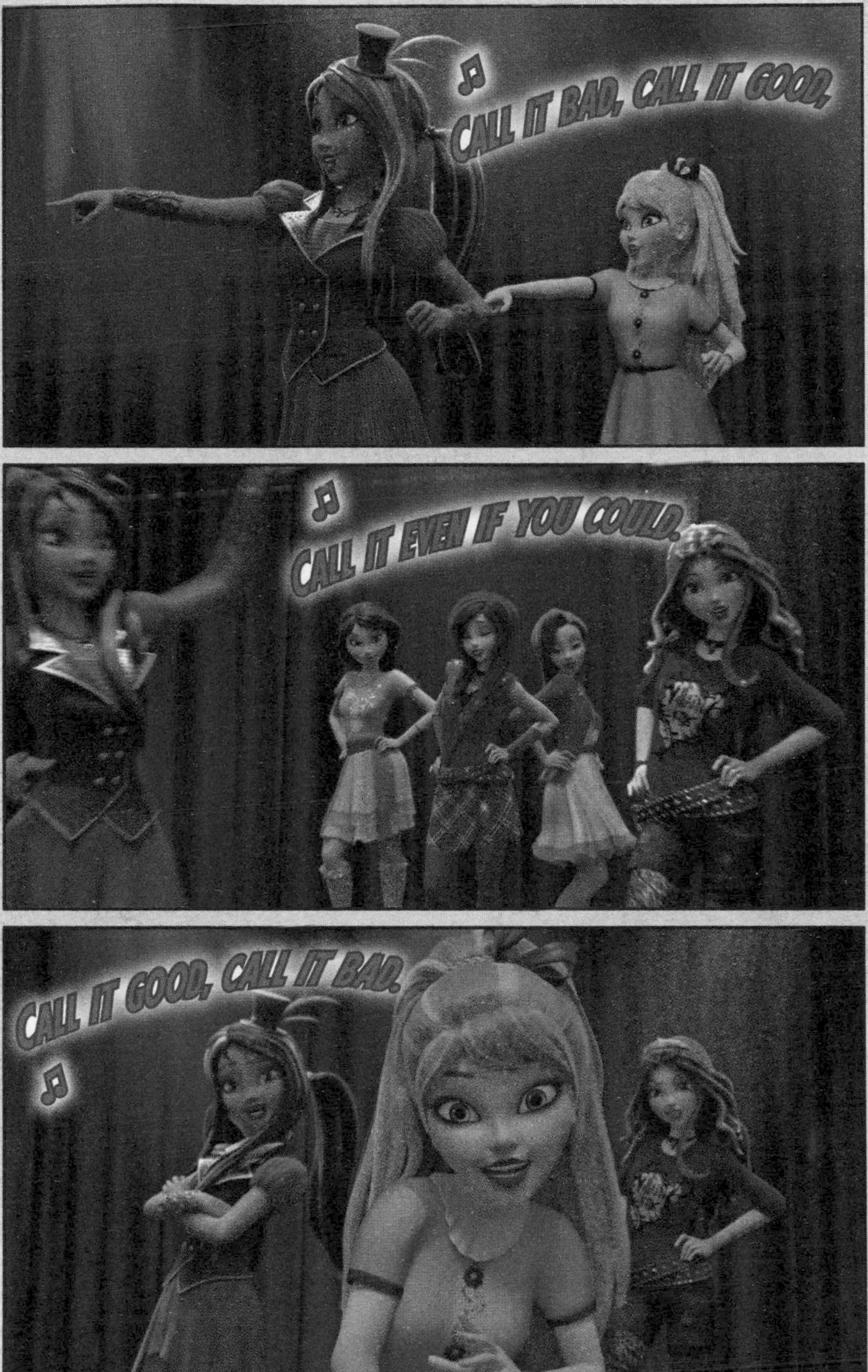
CALL IT BAD, CALL IT GOOD,
CALL IT EVEN IF YOU COULD.
CALL IT GOOD, CALL IT BAD.

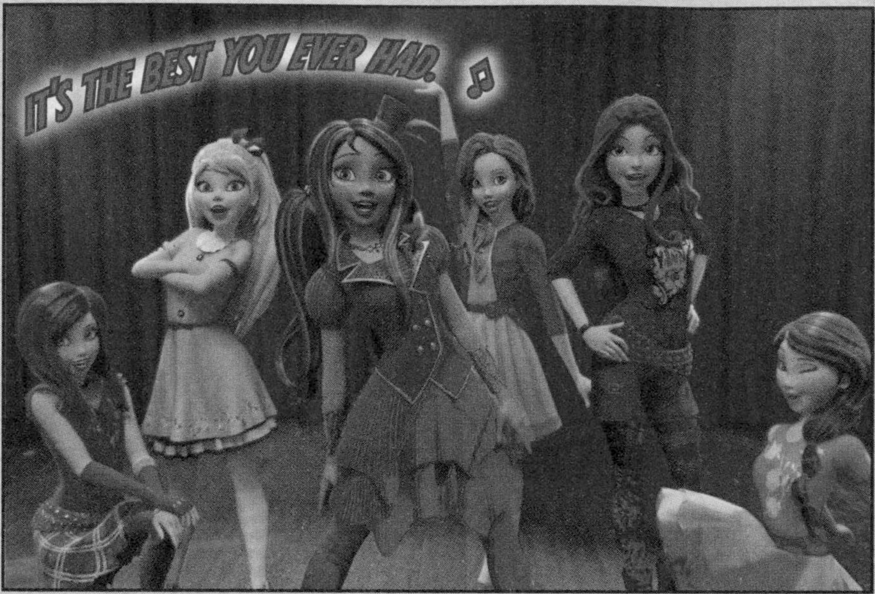
IT'S THE BEST YOU EVER HAD. ♫

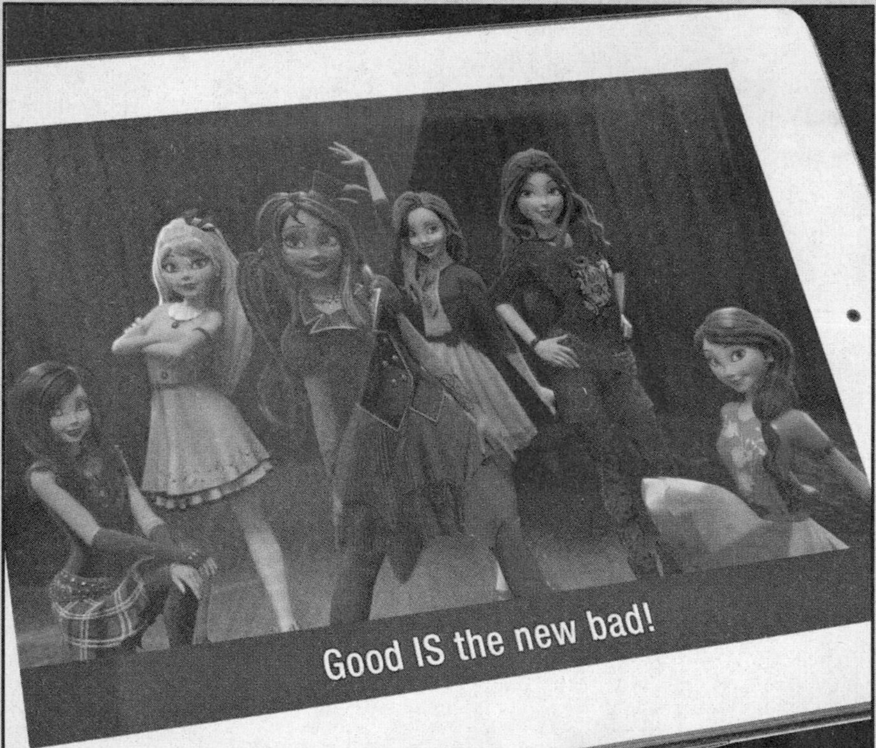
Good IS the new bad!

CHAPTER 10: SPIRIT DAY

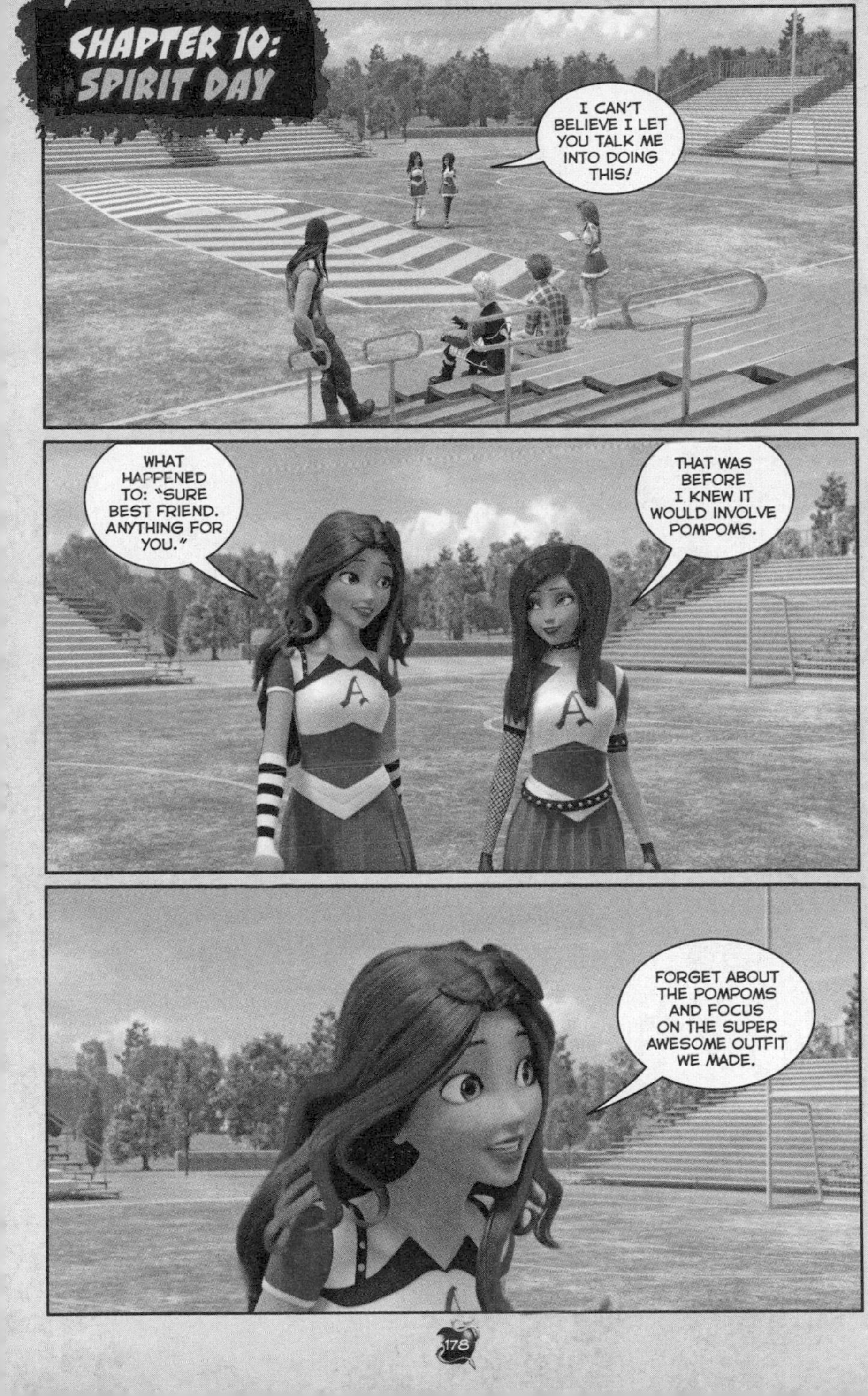
I CAN'T BELIEVE I LET YOU TALK ME INTO DOING THIS!
WHAT HAPPENED TO: "SURE BEST FRIEND. ANYTHING FOR YOU."
THAT WAS BEFORE I KNEW IT WOULD INVOLVE POMPOMS.
FORGET ABOUT THE POMPOMS AND FOCUS ON THE SUPER AWESOME OUTFIT WE MADE.

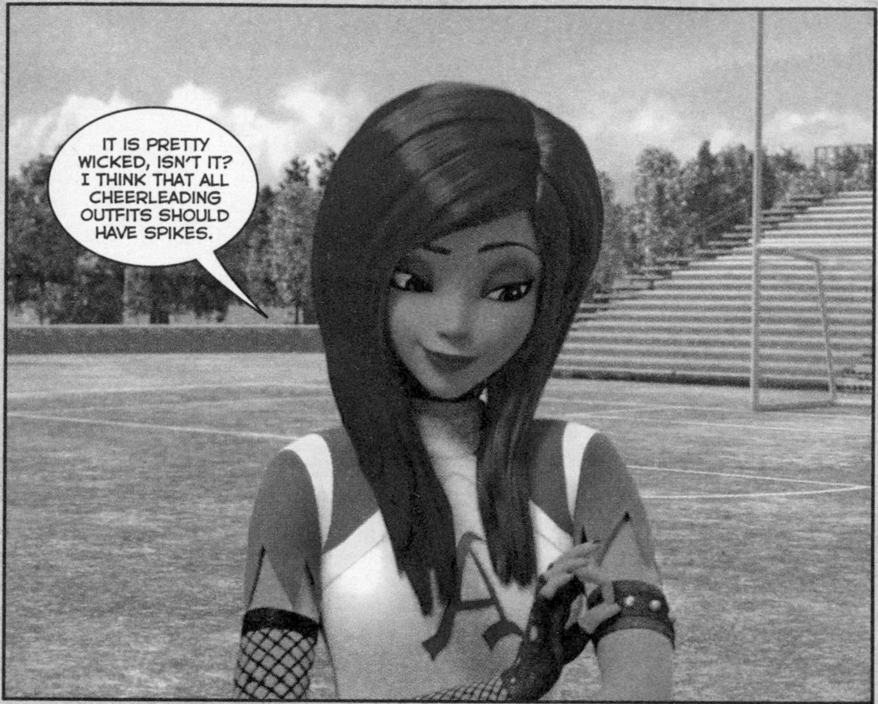
IT IS PRETTY WICKED, ISN'T IT? I THINK THAT ALL CHEERLEADING OUTFITS SHOULD HAVE SPIKES.

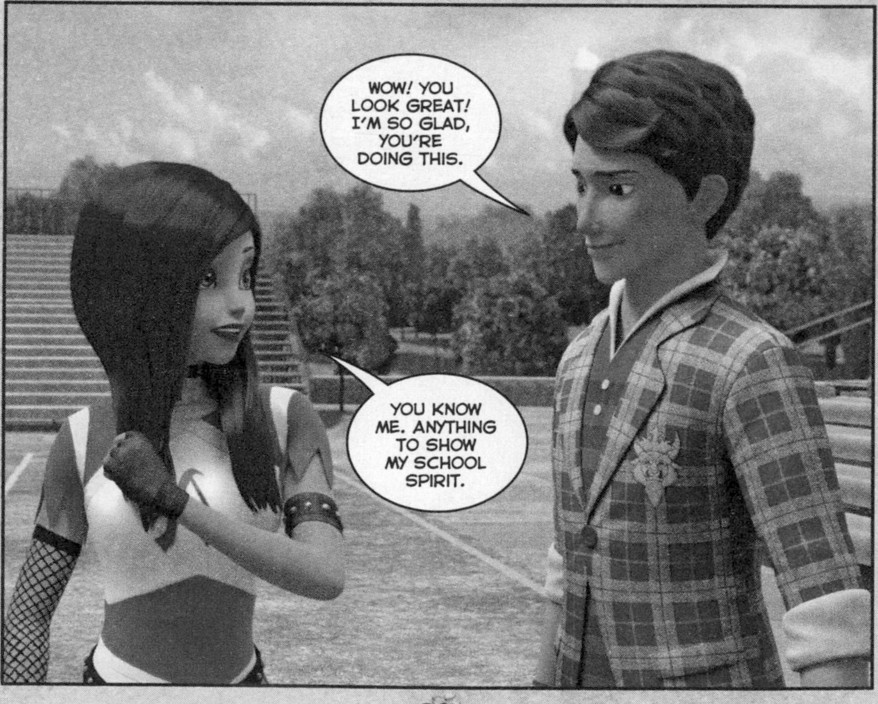
WOW! YOU LOOK GREAT! I'M SO GLAD, YOU'RE DOING THIS.
YOU KNOW ME. ANYTHING TO SHOW MY SCHOOL SPIRIT.

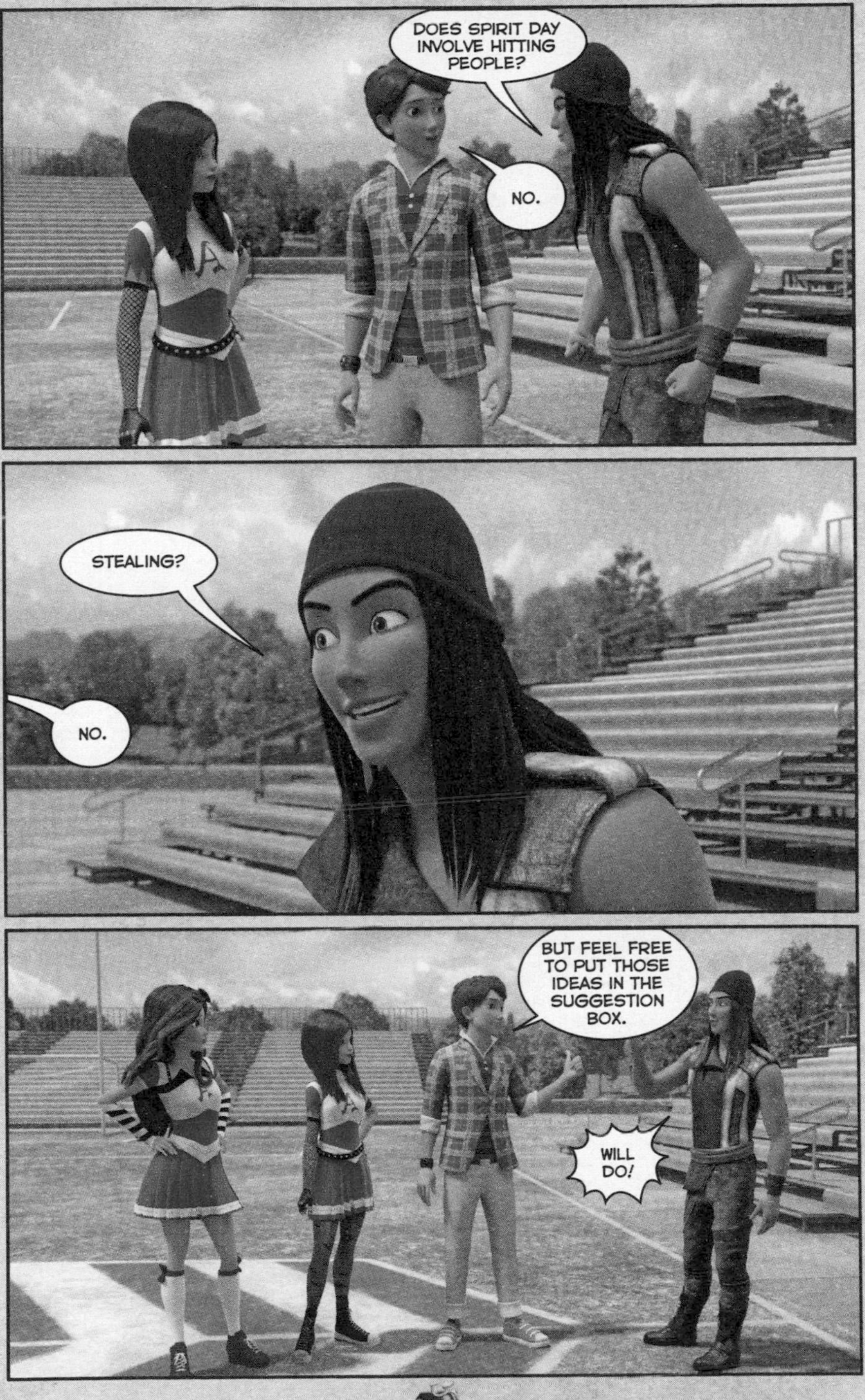
DOES SPIRIT DAY INVOLVE HITTING PEOPLE?
NO.
STEALING?
NO.
BUT FEEL FREE TO PUT THOSE IDEAS IN THE SUGGESTION BOX.
WILL DO!

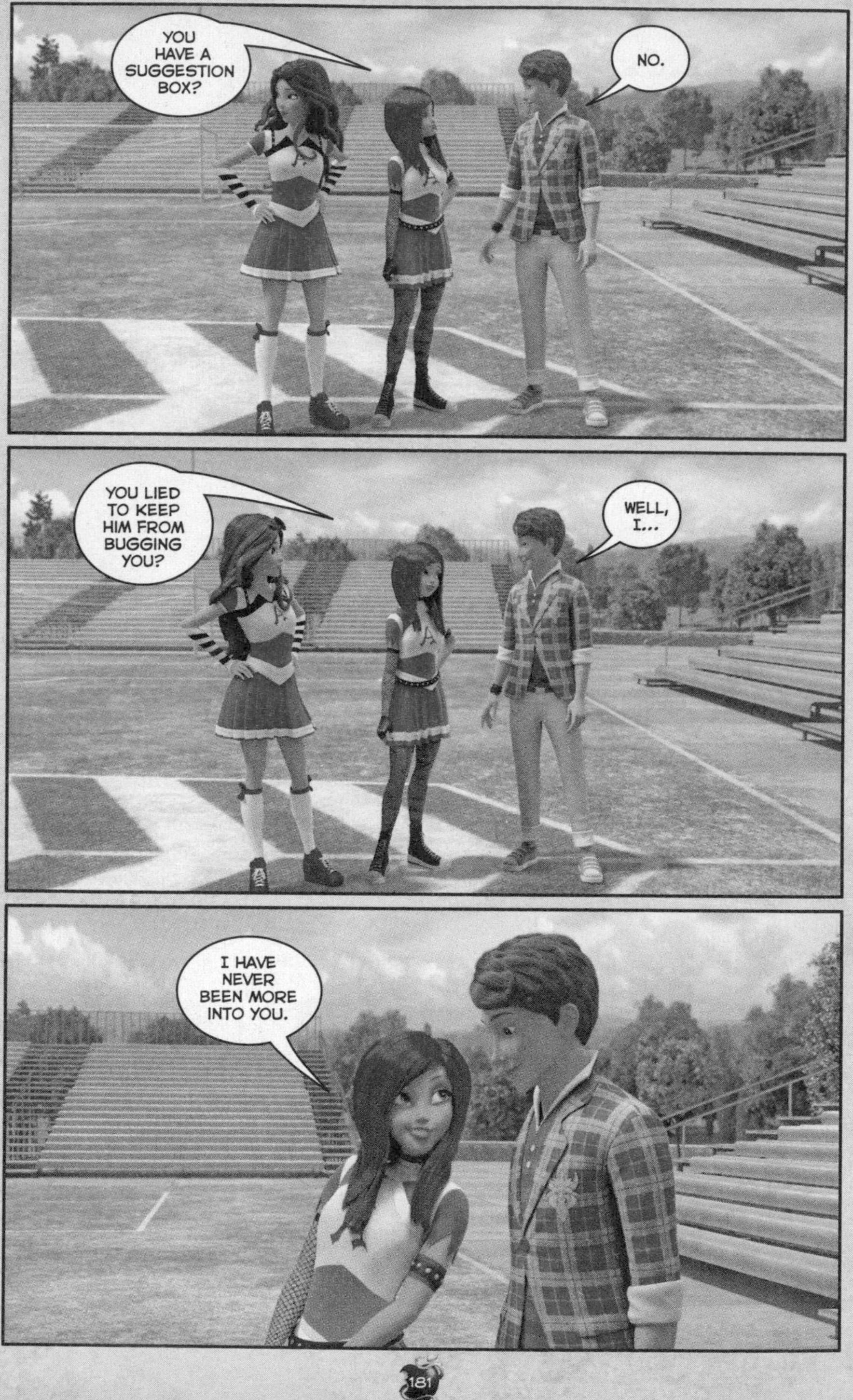
YOU HAVE A SUGGESTION BOX?
NO.
YOU LIED TO KEEP HIM FROM BUGGING YOU?
WELL, I...
I HAVE NEVER BEEN MORE INTO YOU.

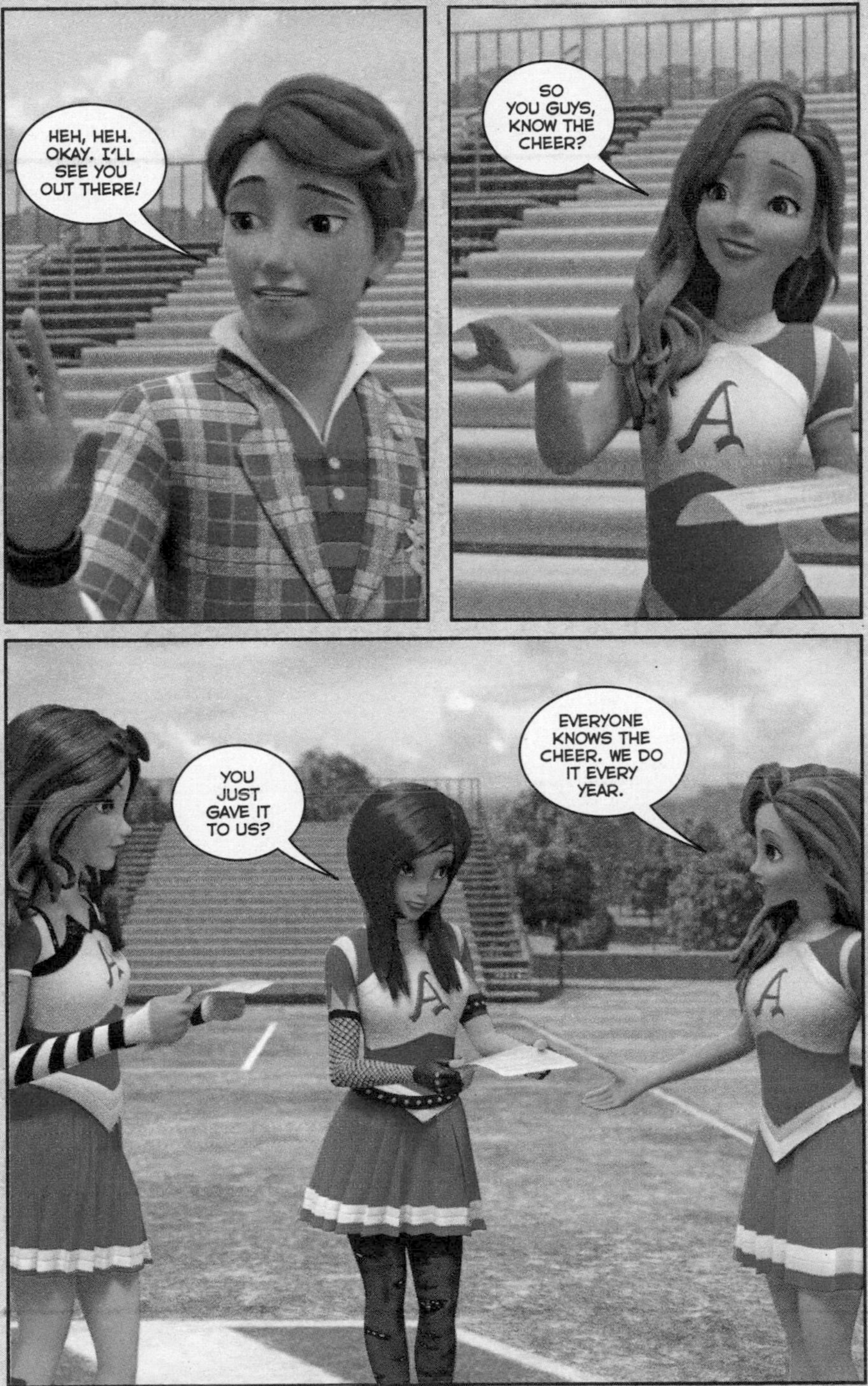
HEH, HEH. OKAY. I'LL SEE YOU OUT THERE!
SO YOU GUYS, KNOW THE CHEER?
YOU JUST GAVE IT TO US?
EVERYONE KNOWS THE CHEER. WE DO IT EVERY YEAR.

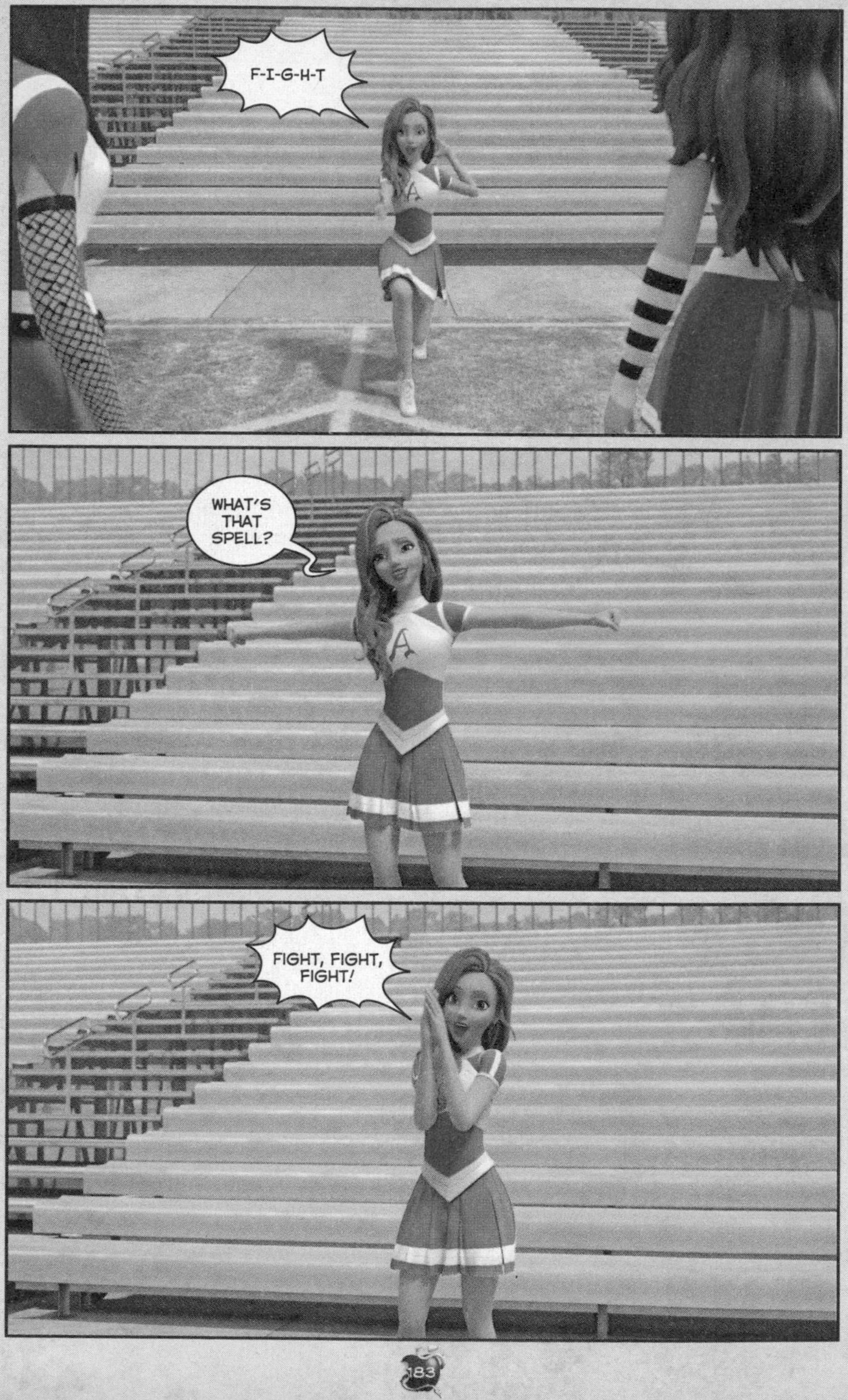
F-I-G-H-T
WHAT'S THAT SPELL?
FIGHT, FIGHT, FIGHT!

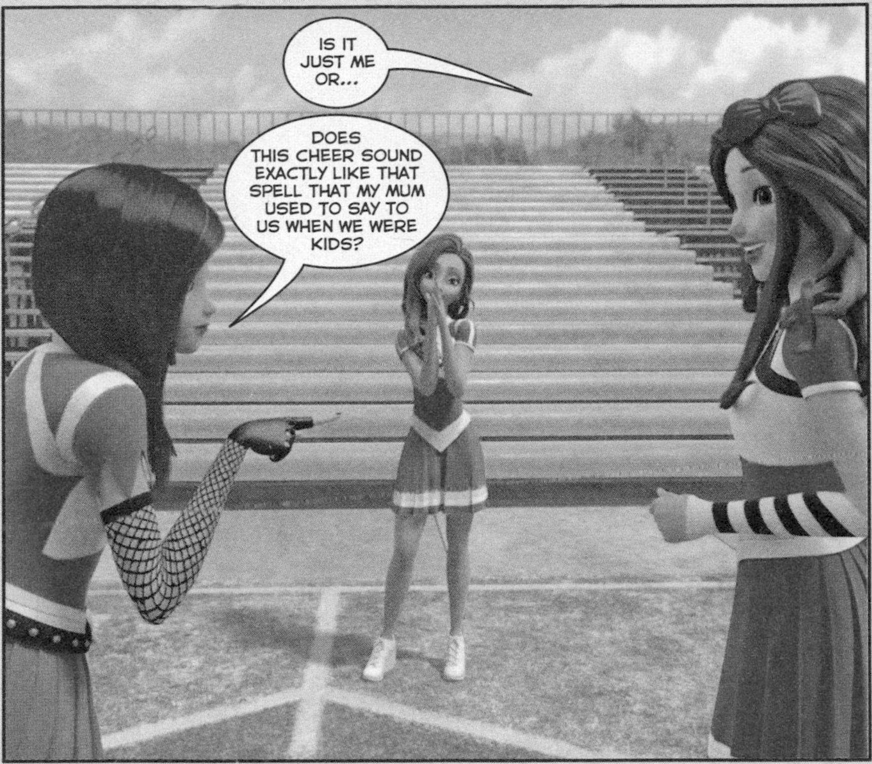
IS IT JUST ME OR...
DOES THIS CHEER SOUND EXACTLY LIKE THAT SPELL THAT MY MUM USED TO SAY TO US WHEN WE WERE KIDS?

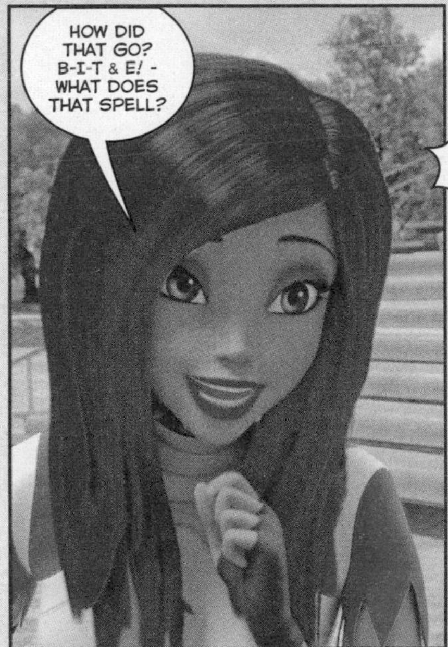
HOW DID THAT GO? B-I-T & E! - WHAT DOES THAT SPELL?

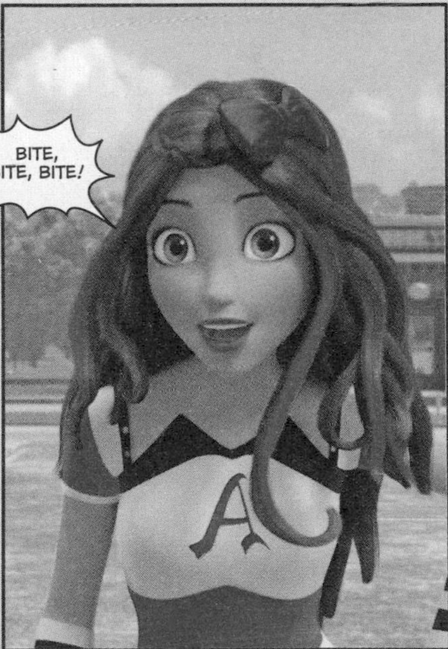
BITE, BITE, BITE!

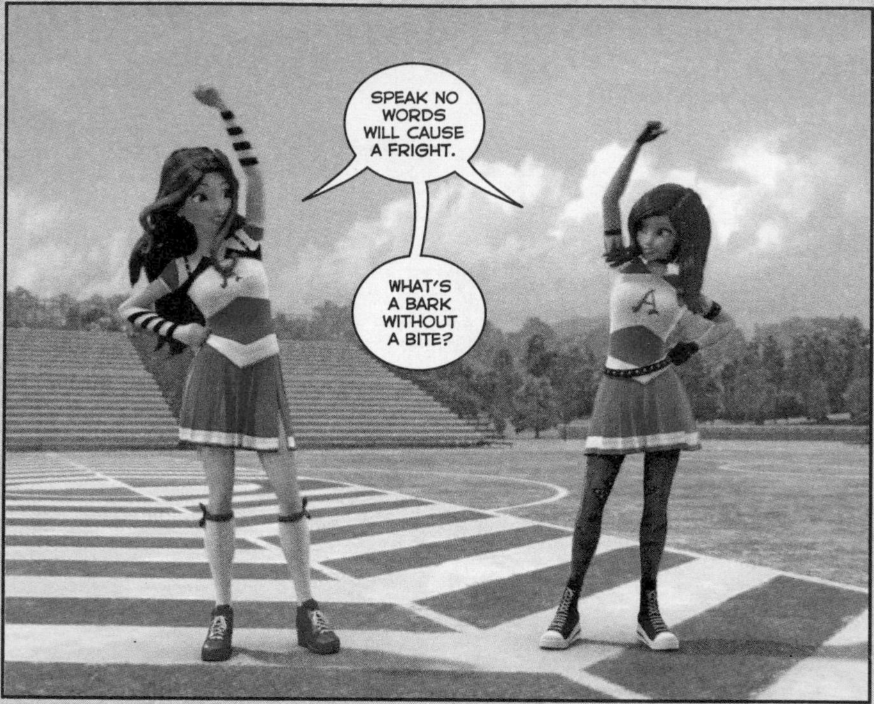
SPEAK NO WORDS WILL CAUSE A FRIGHT.
WHAT'S A BARK WITHOUT A BITE?

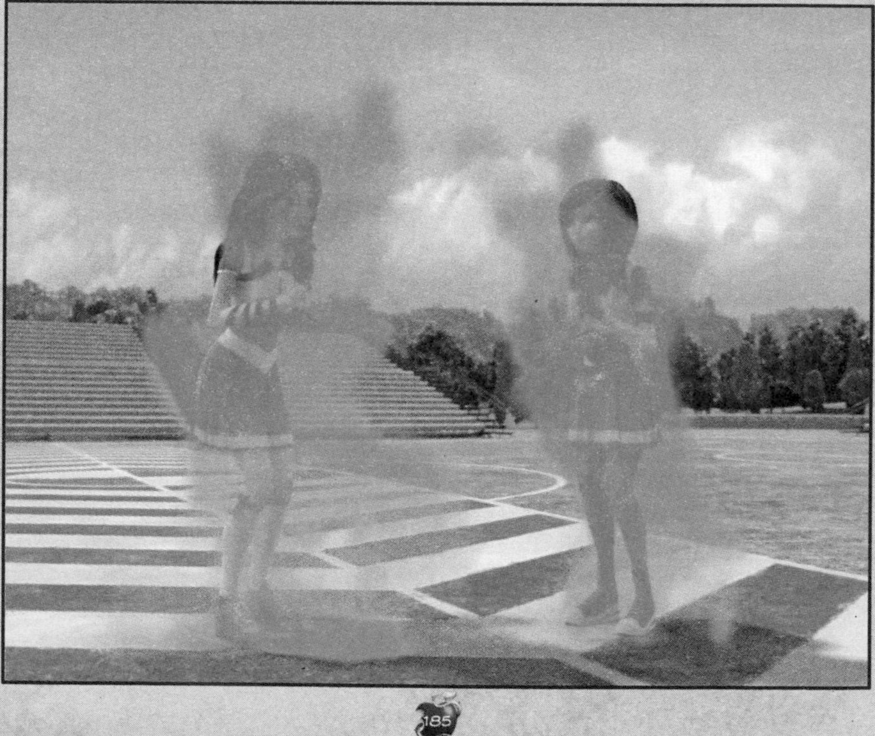

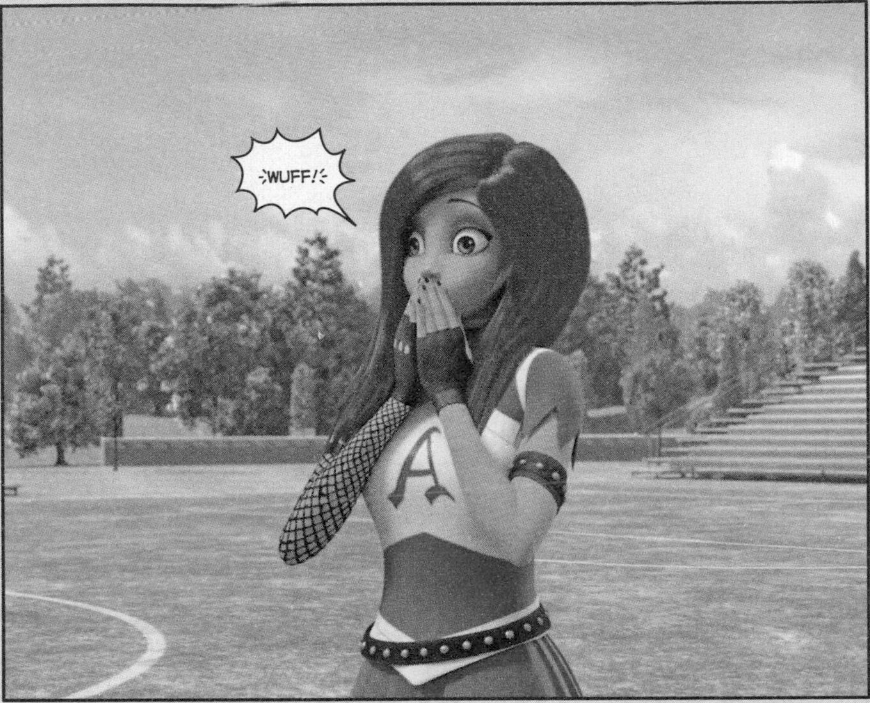
WUFF!

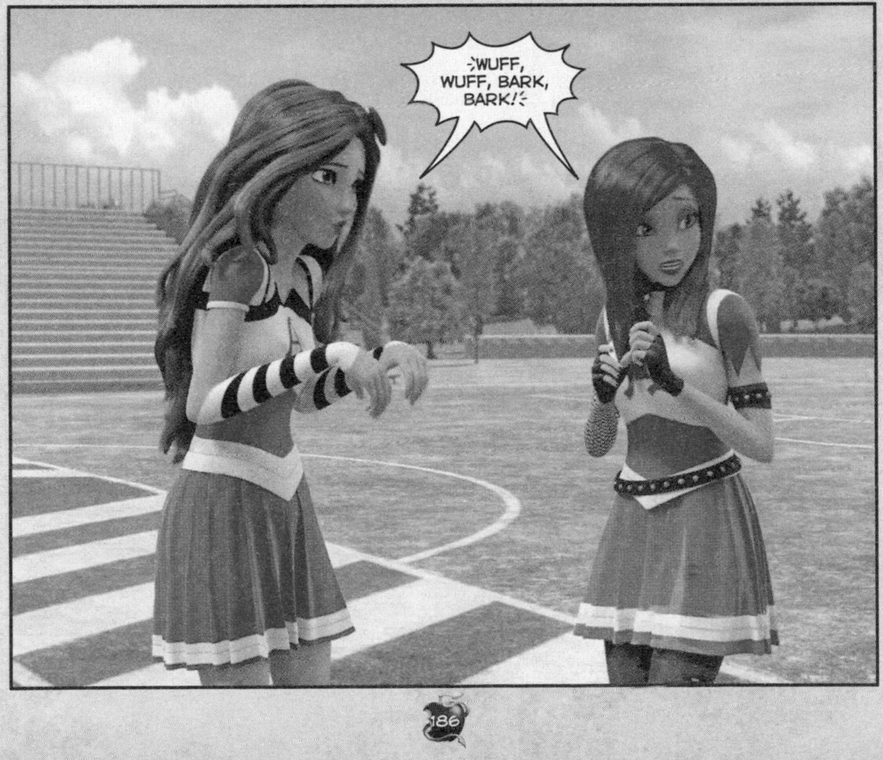
WUFF, WUFF, BARK, BARK!

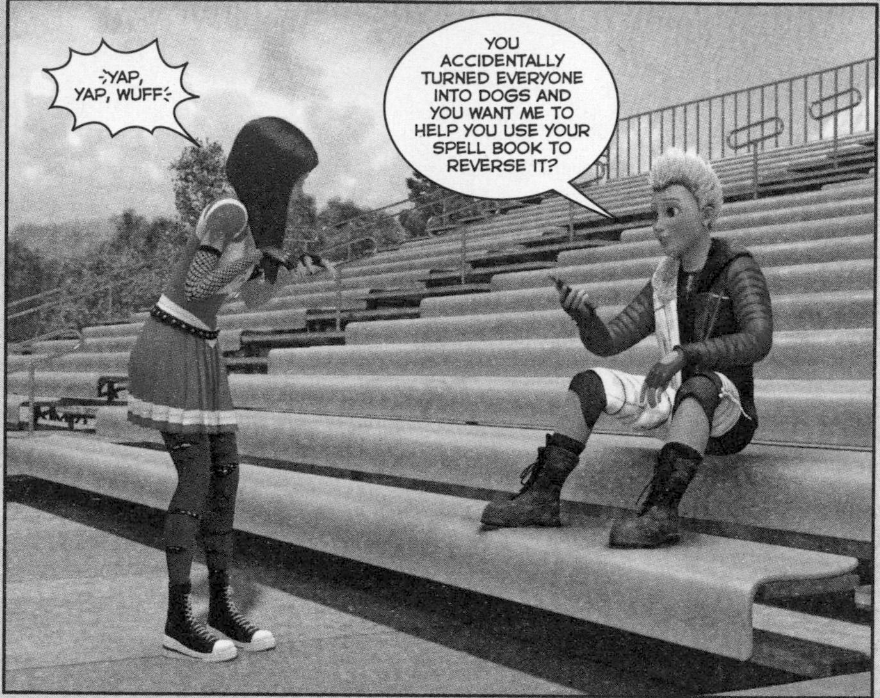
YAP, YAP, WUFF
YOU ACCIDENTALLY TURNED EVERYONE INTO DOGS AND YOU WANT ME TO HELP YOU USE YOUR SPELL BOOK TO REVERSE IT?

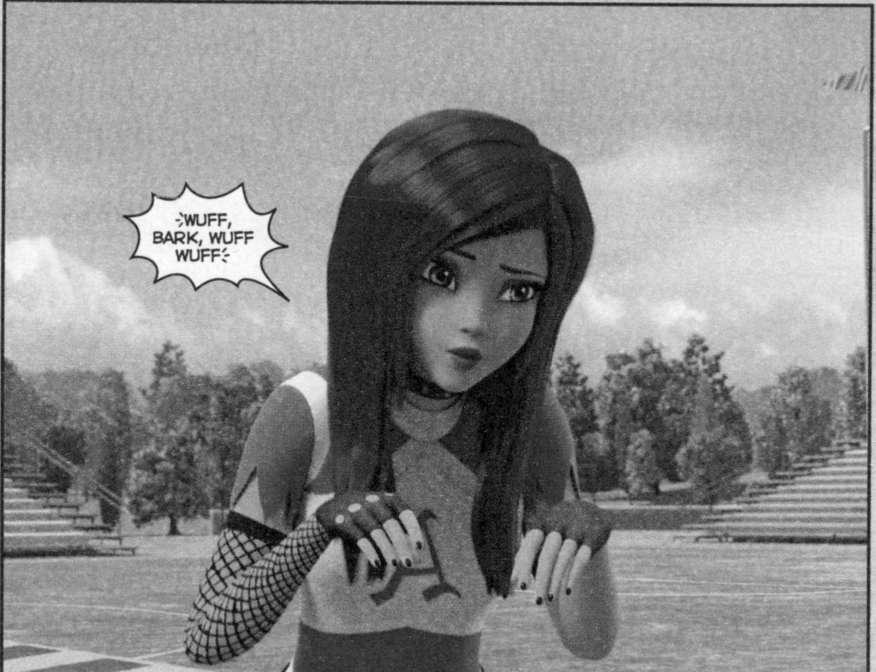
WUFF, BARK, WUFF WUFF

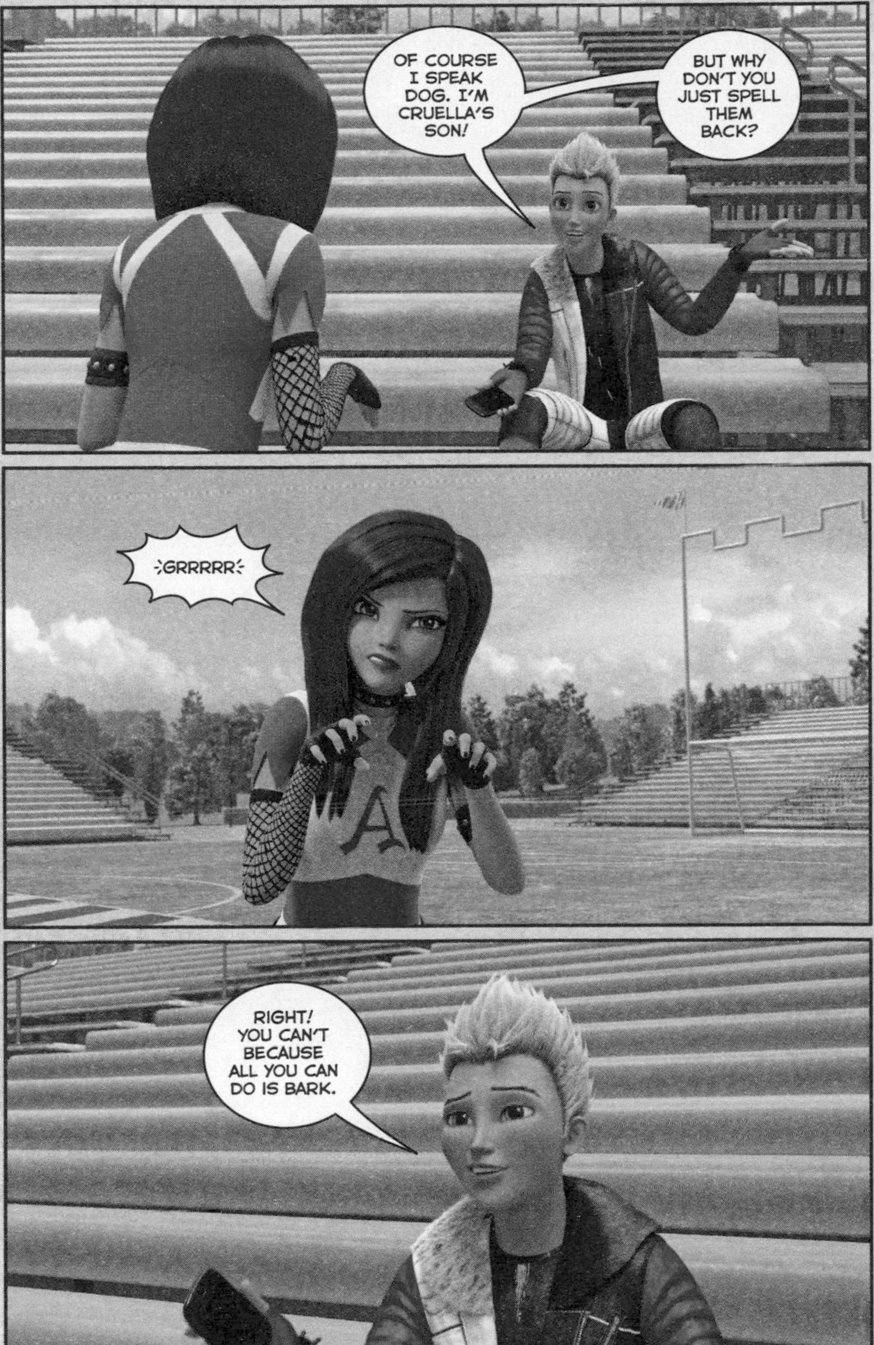
OF COURSE I SPEAK DOG. I'M CRUELLA'S SON!
BUT WHY DON'T YOU JUST SPELL THEM BACK?
GRRRRR
RIGHT! YOU CAN'T BECAUSE ALL YOU CAN DO IS BARK.

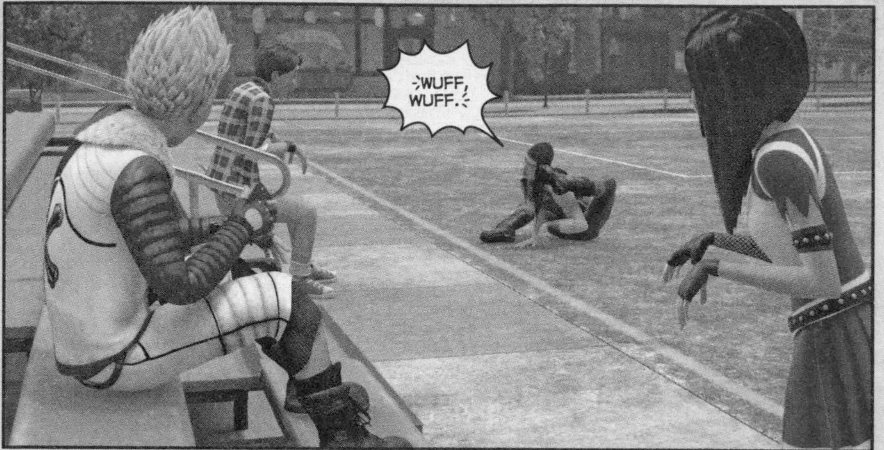
WUFF, WUFF.

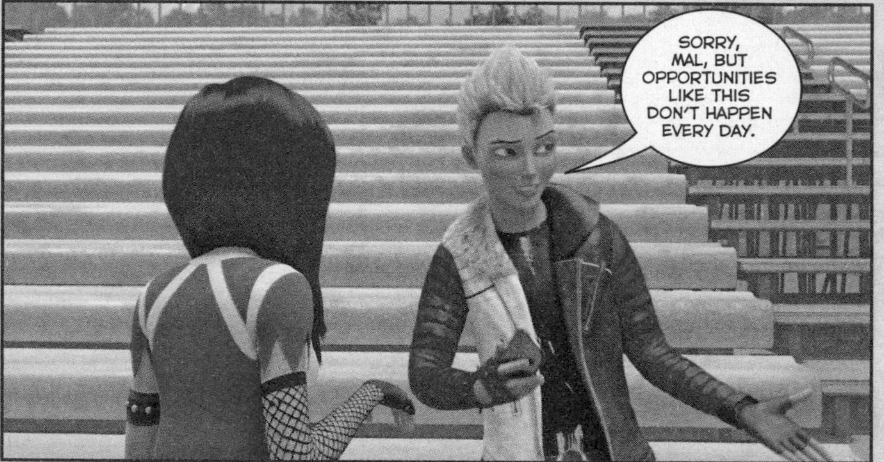
SORRY, MAL, BUT OPPORTUNITIES LIKE THIS DON'T HAPPEN EVERY DAY.

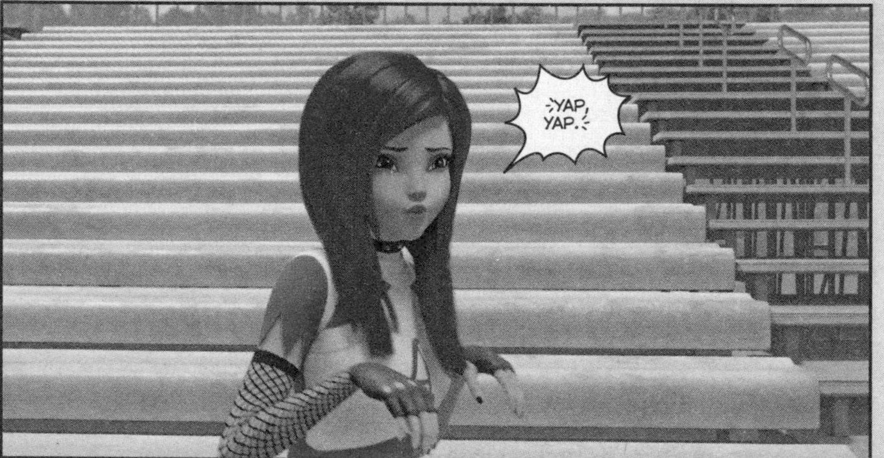
YAP, YAP.

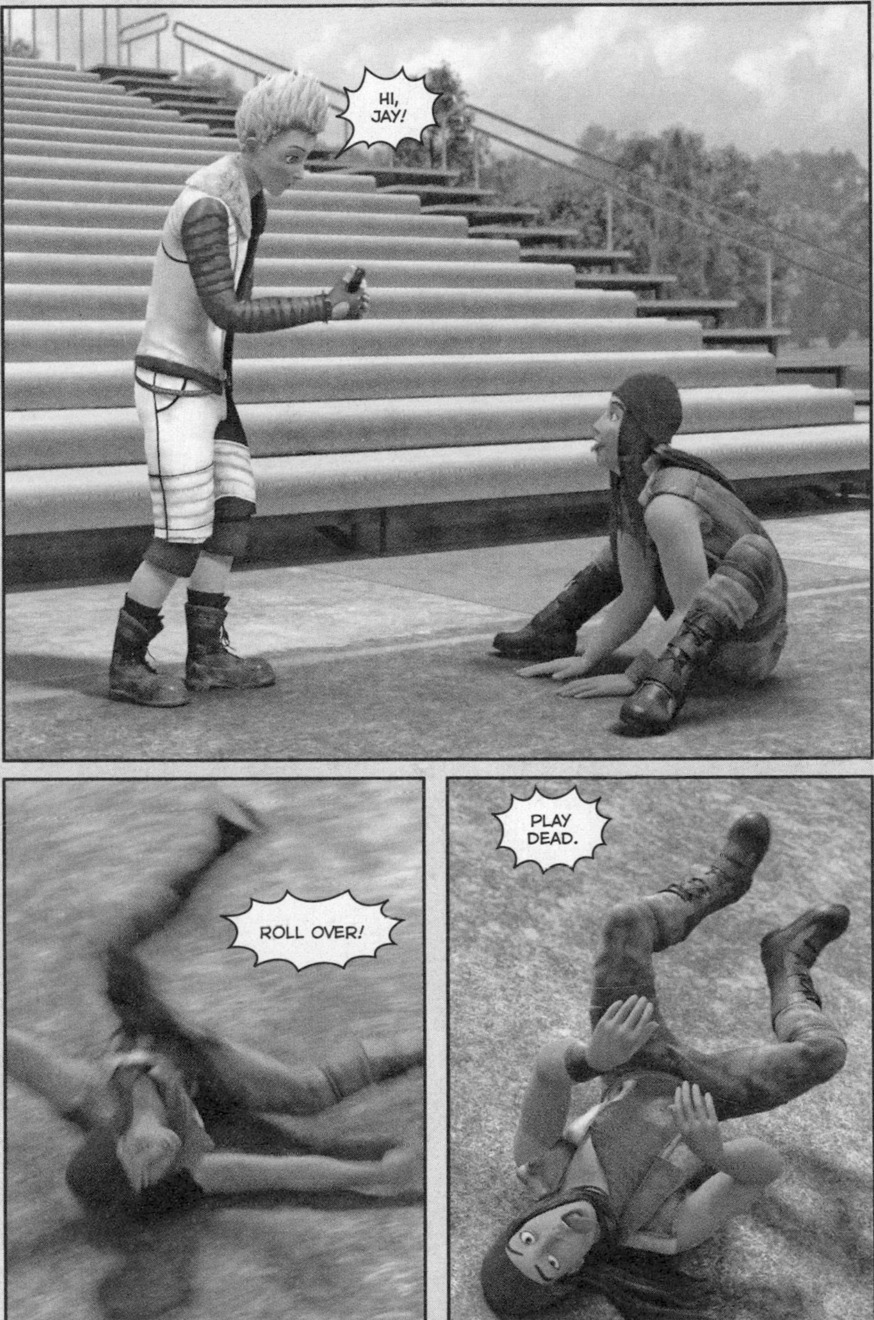
HI, JAY!
ROLL OVER!
PLAY DEAD.

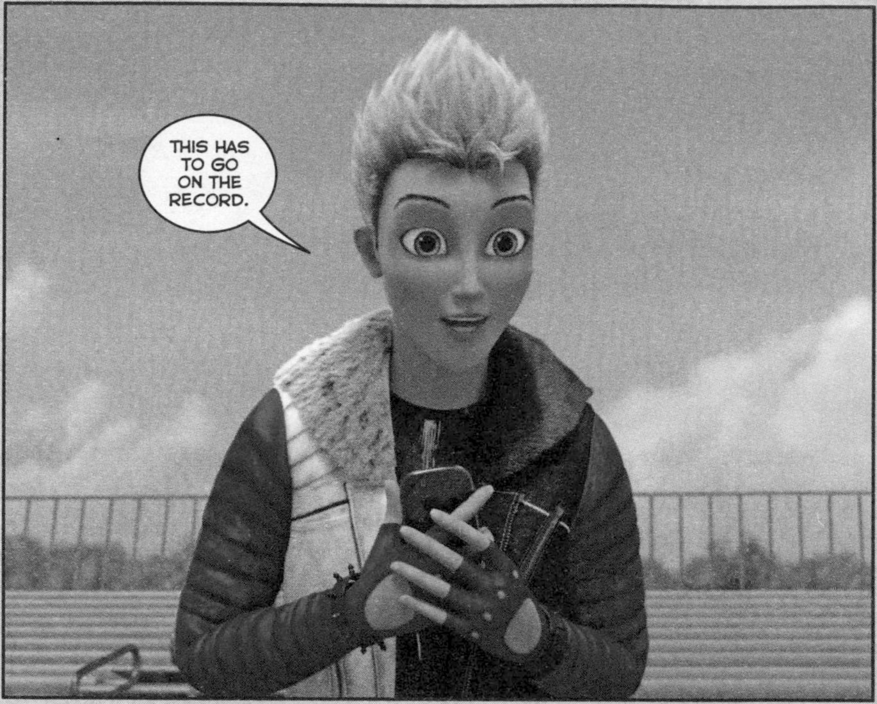
THIS HAS TO GO ON THE RECORD.

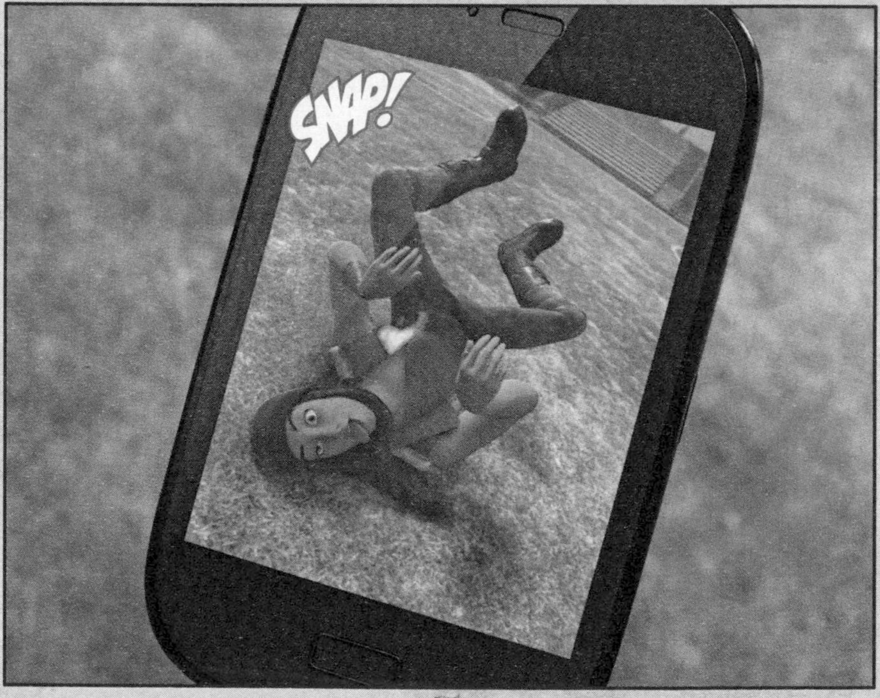
SNAP!

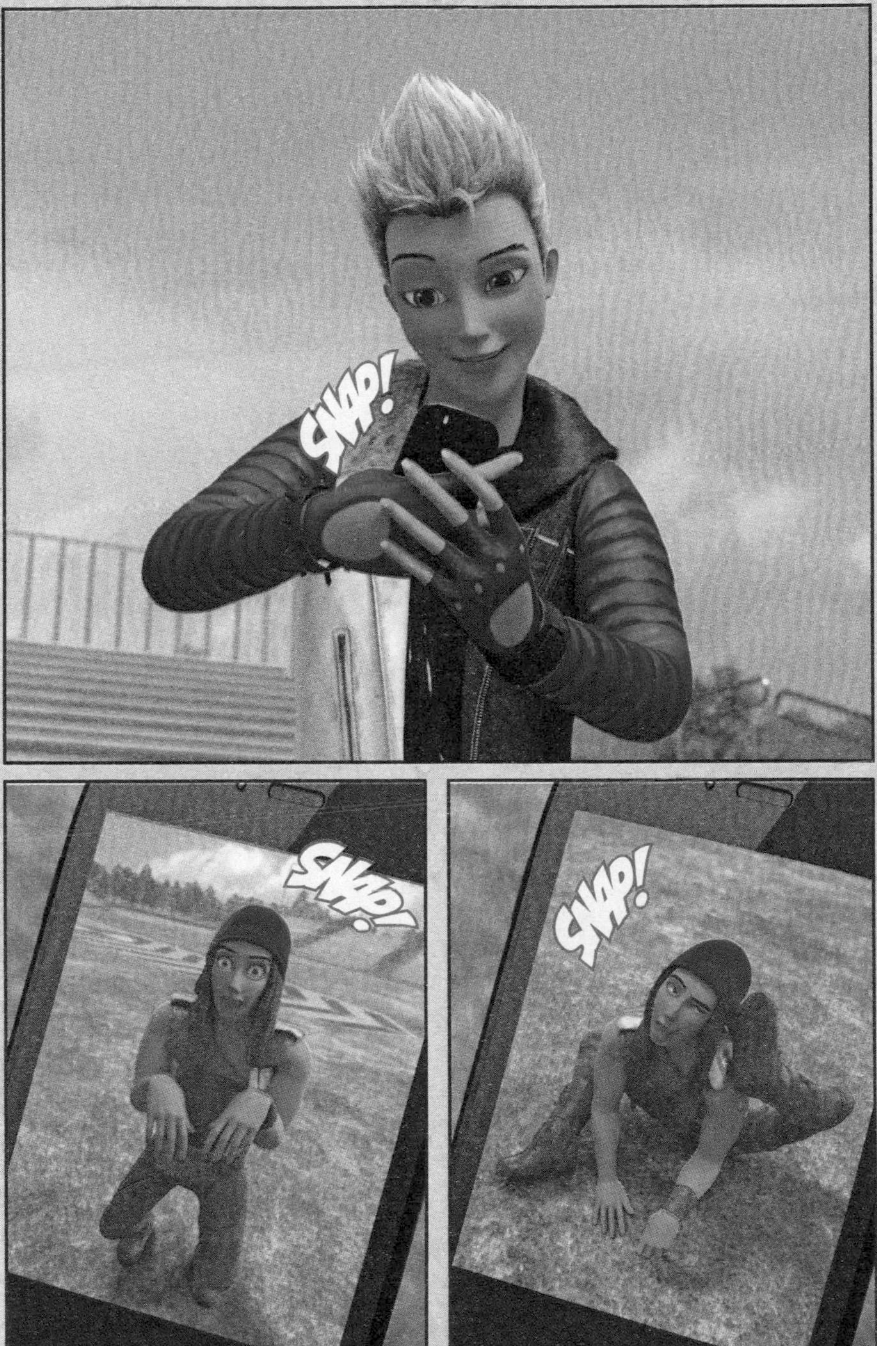
SNAP!
SNAP!
SNAP!

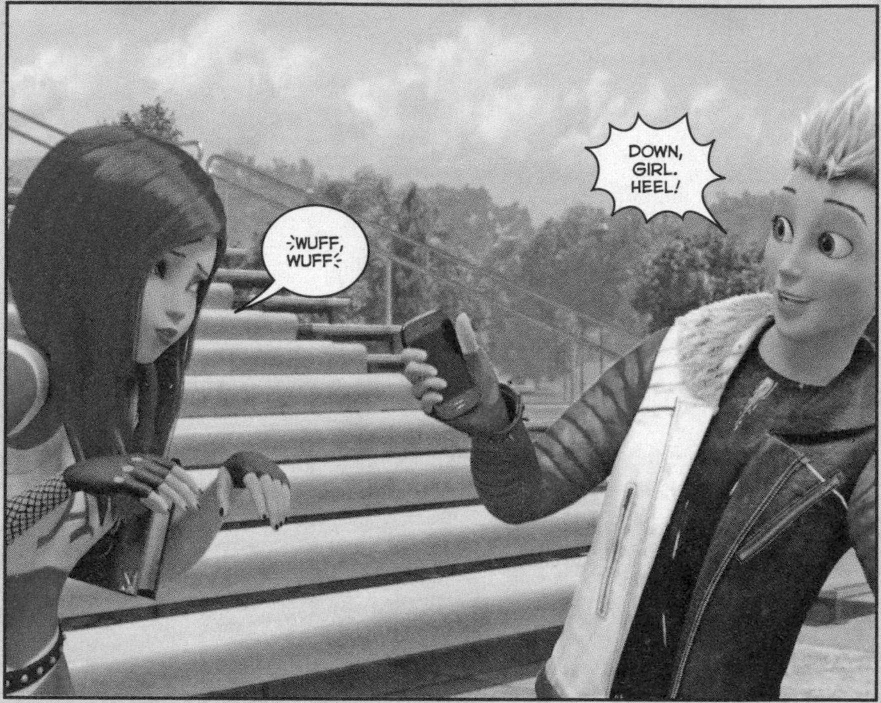
WUFF,
WUFF
DOWN,
GIRL.
HEEL!

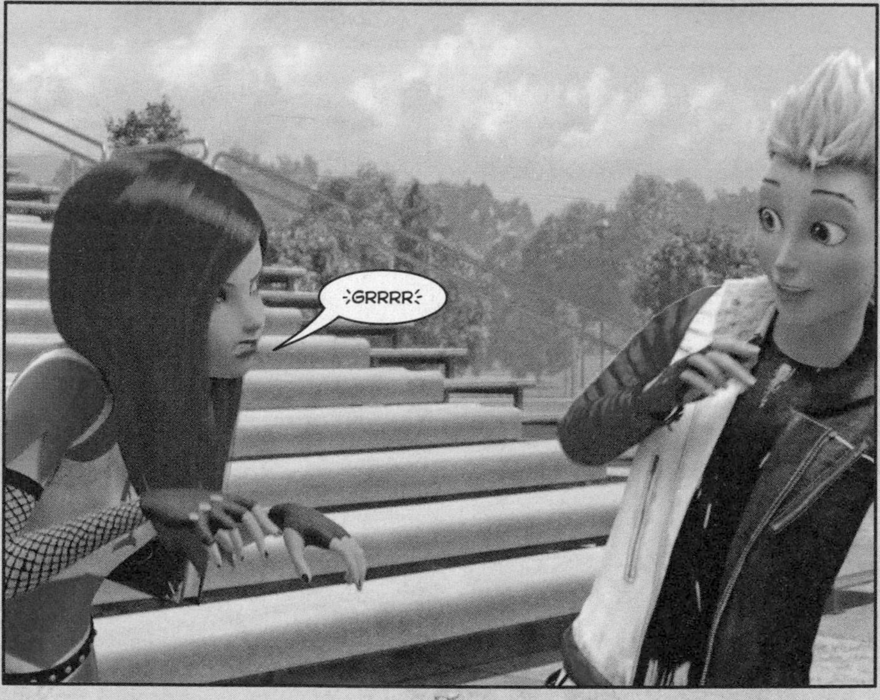
GRRRR

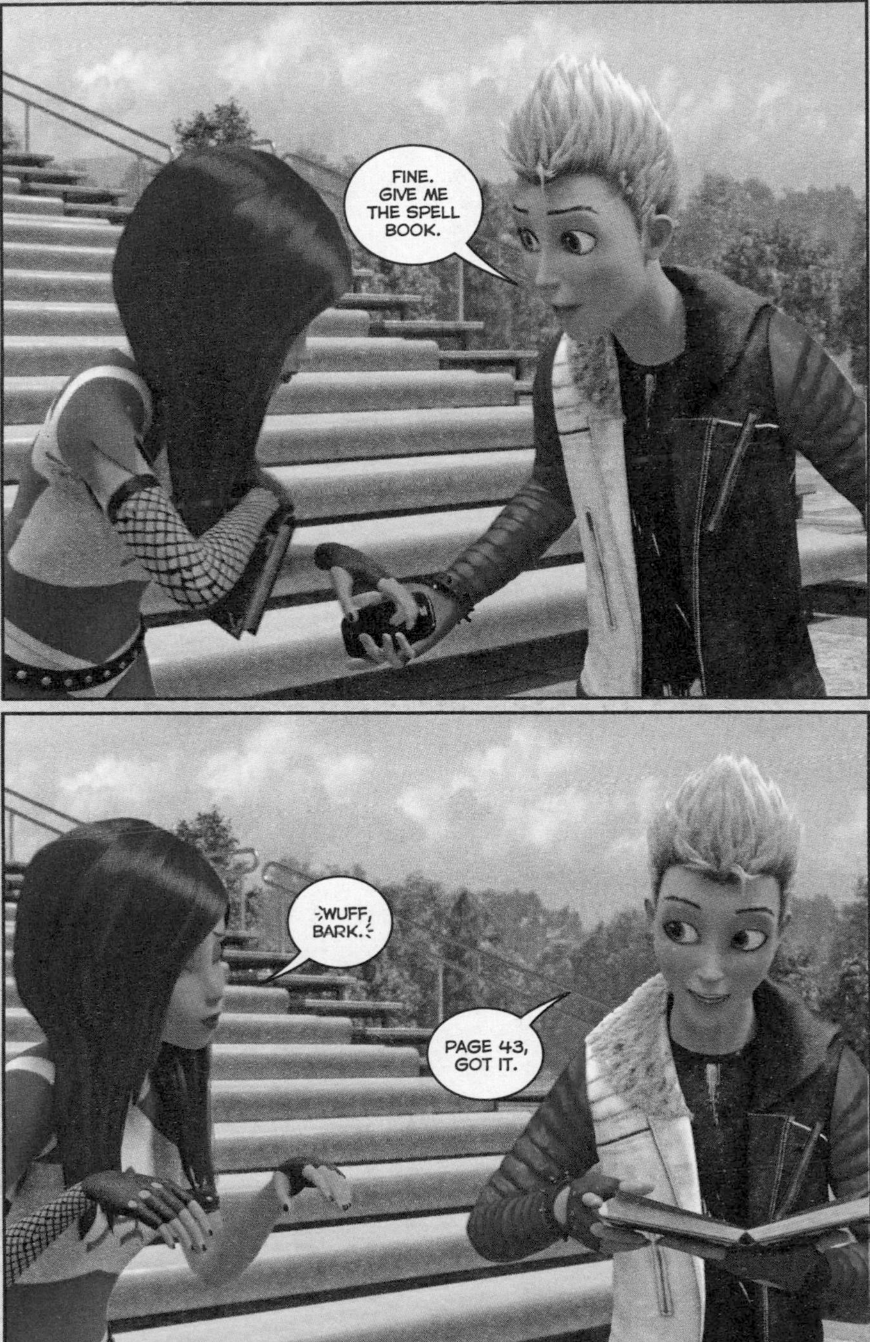
FINE. GIVE ME THE SPELL BOOK.
WUFF, BARK.
PAGE 43, GOT IT.

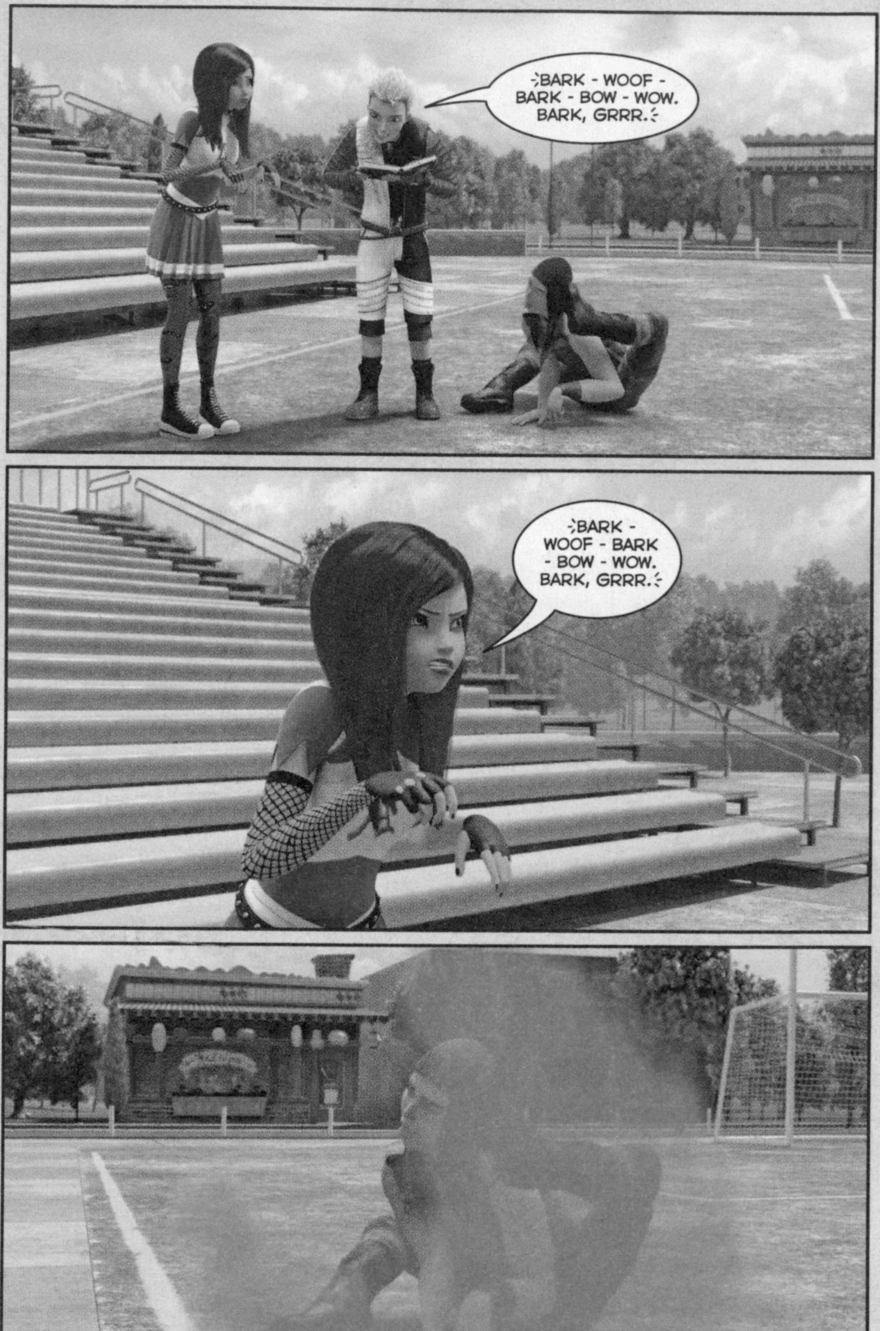
BARK - WOOF - BARK - BOW - WOW. BARK, GRRR.
BARK - WOOF - BARK - BOW - WOW. BARK, GRRR.

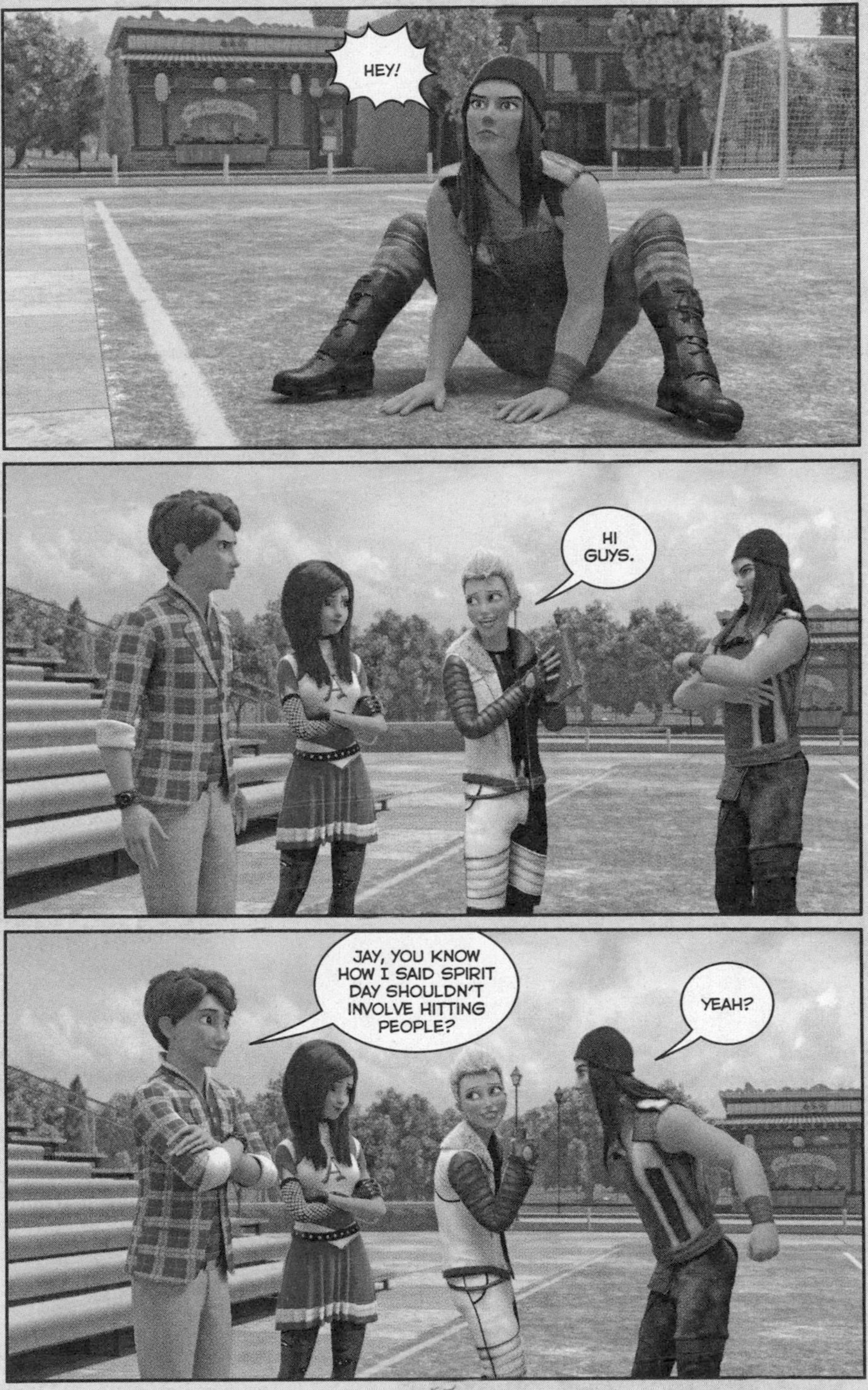
HEY!
HI GUYS.
JAY, YOU KNOW HOW I SAID SPIRIT DAY SHOULDN'T INVOLVE HITTING PEOPLE?
YEAH?

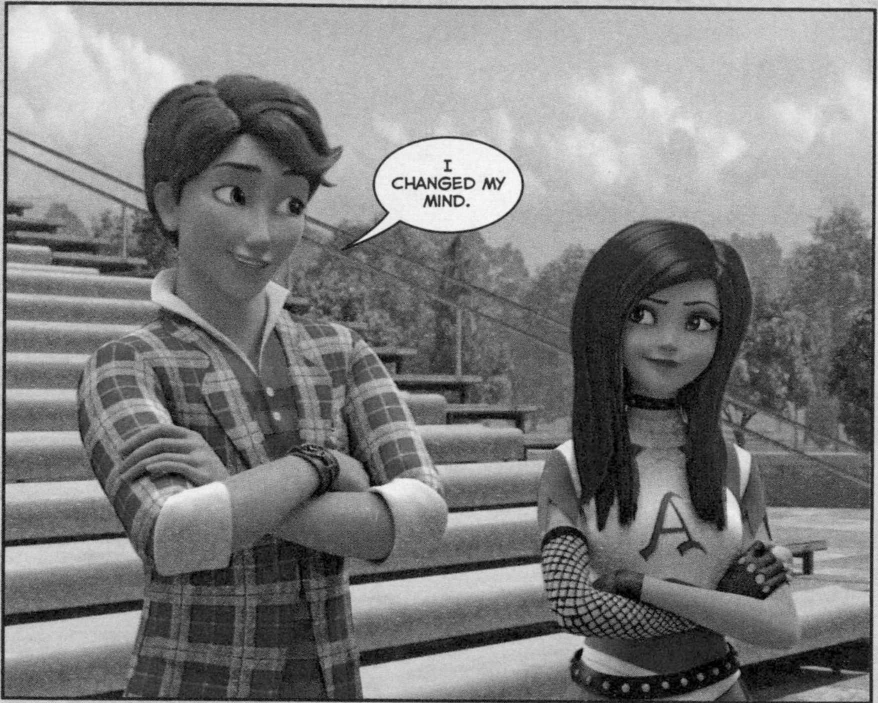
I CHANGED MY MIND.

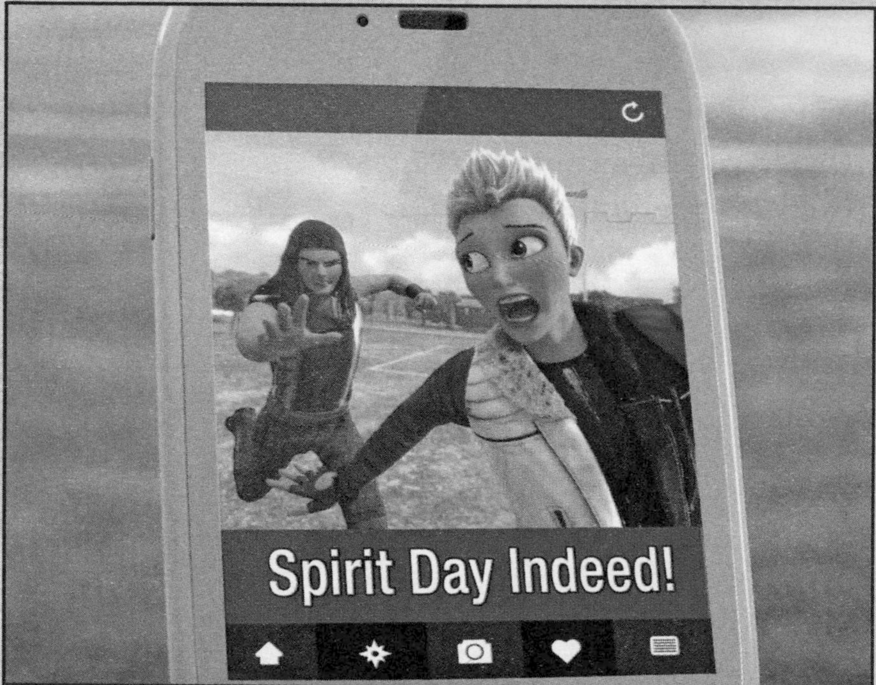
Spirit Day Indeed!

CHAPTER 11: I'M YOUR GIRL

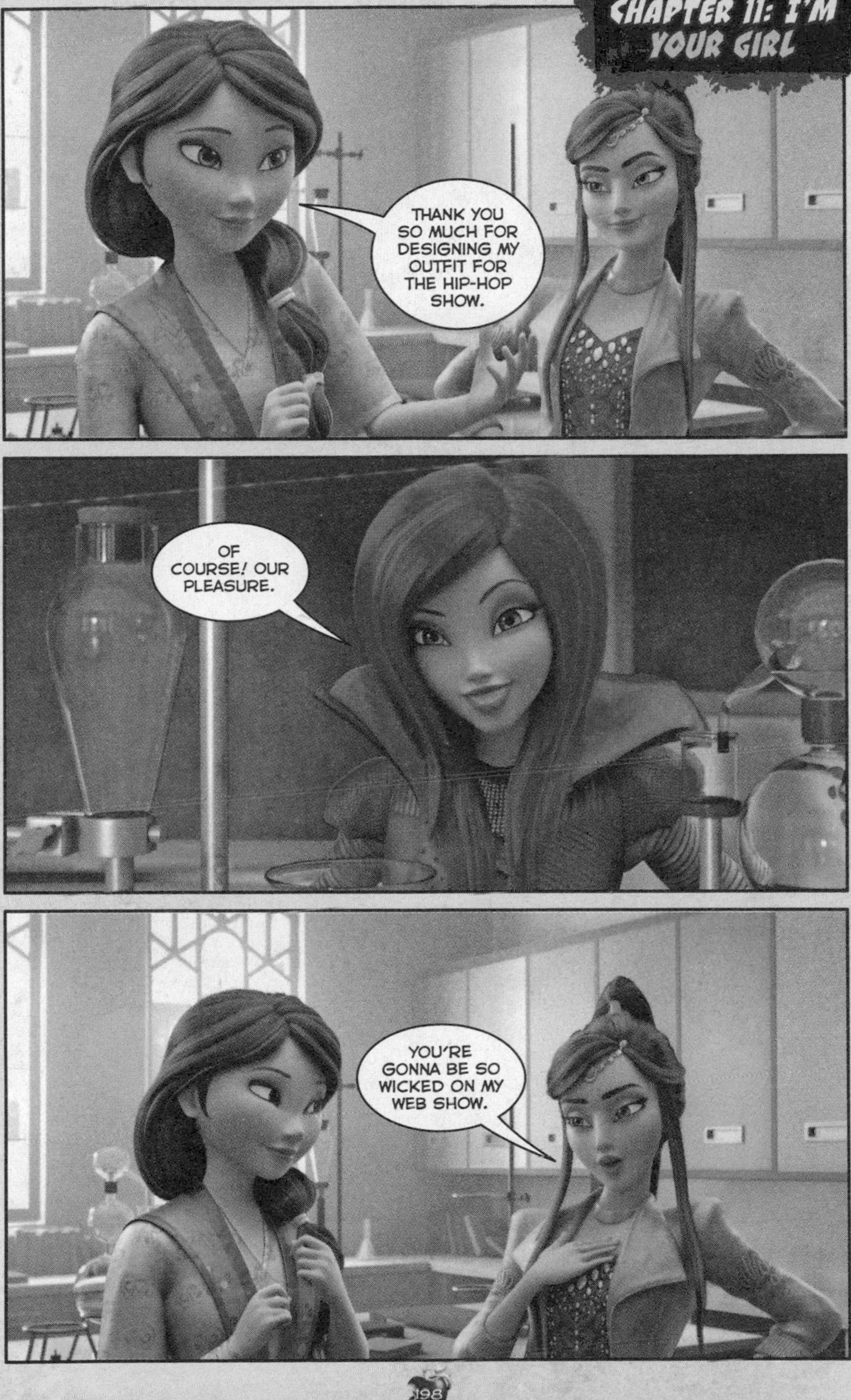
THANK YOU SO MUCH FOR DESIGNING MY OUTFIT FOR THE HIP-HOP SHOW.
OF COURSE! OUR PLEASURE.
YOU'RE GONNA BE SO WICKED ON MY WEB SHOW.

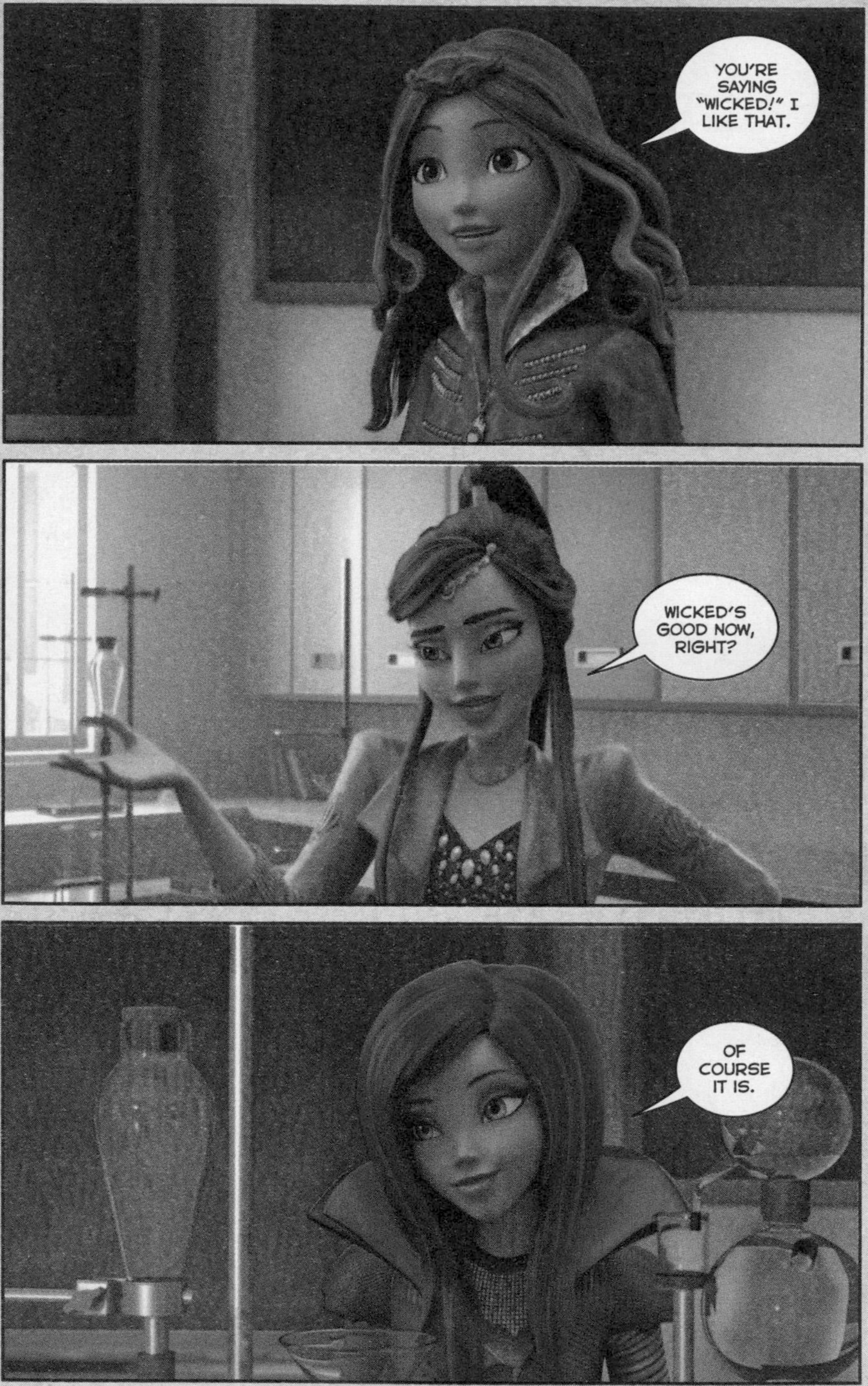
YOU'RE SAYING "WICKED!" I LIKE THAT.
WICKED'S GOOD NOW, RIGHT?
OF COURSE IT IS.

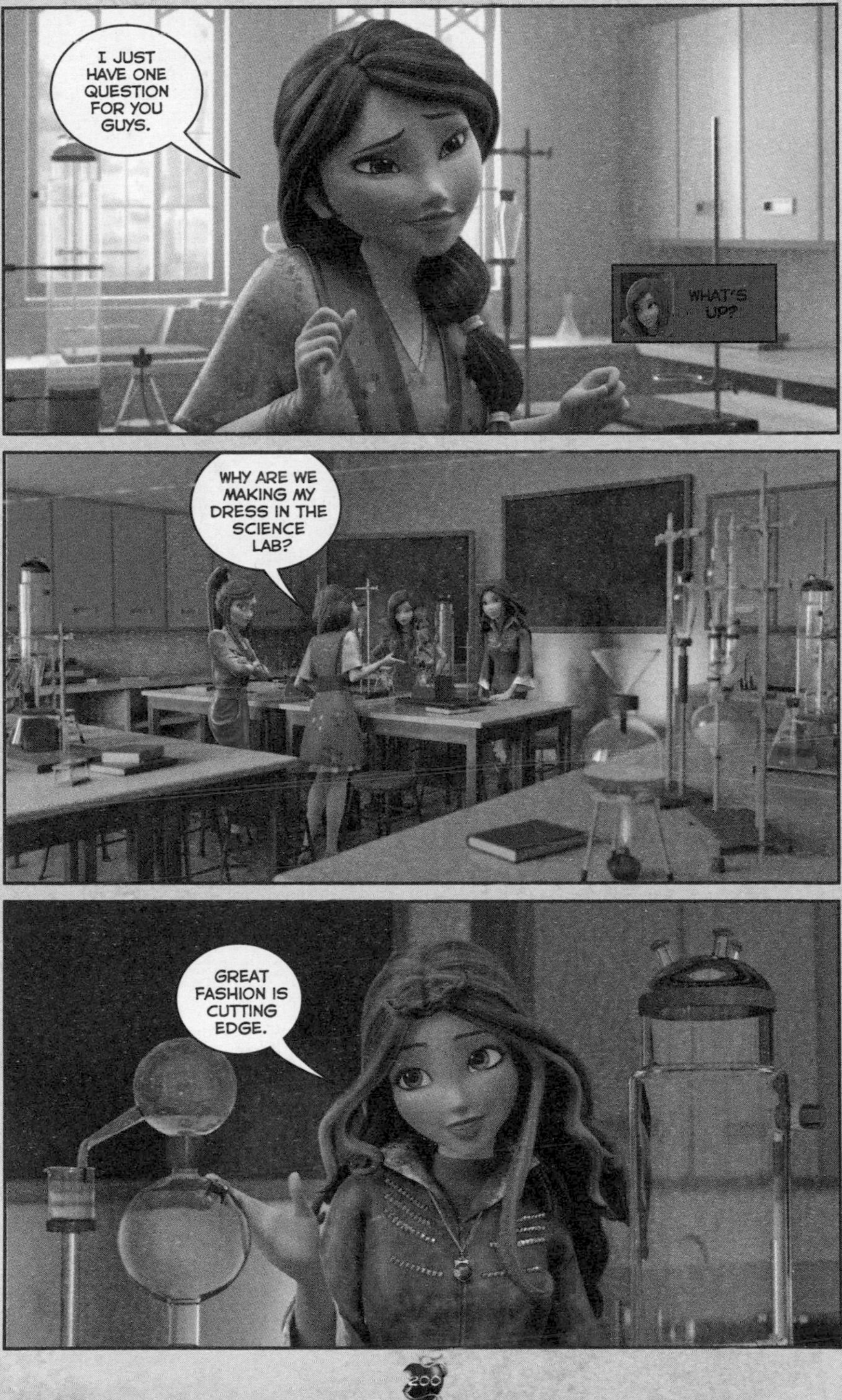
I JUST HAVE ONE QUESTION FOR YOU GUYS.
WHAT'S UP?
WHY ARE WE MAKING MY DRESS IN THE SCIENCE LAB?
GREAT FASHION IS CUTTING EDGE.

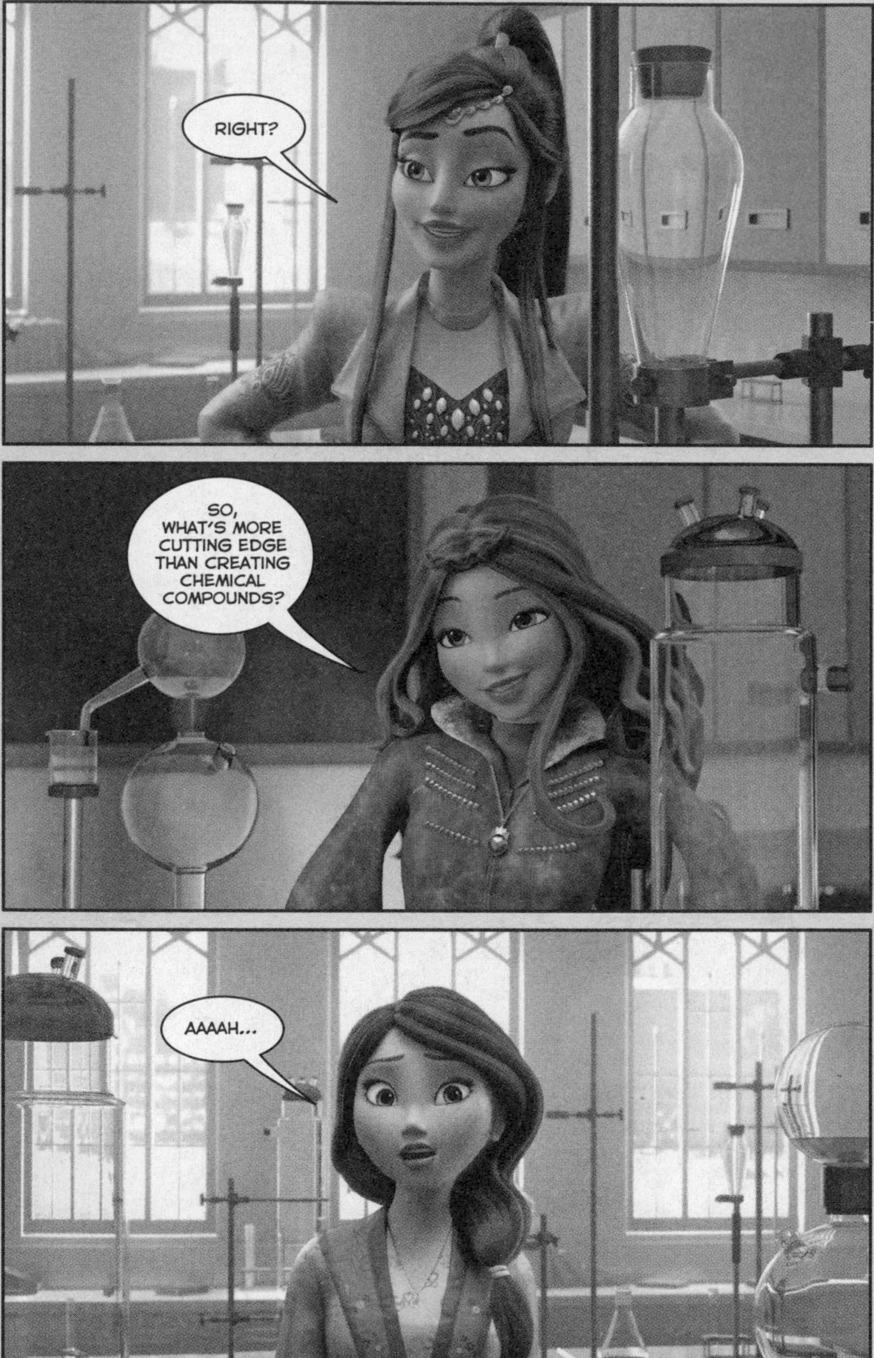
RIGHT?
SO, WHAT'S MORE CUTTING EDGE THAN CREATING CHEMICAL COMPOUNDS?
AAAAH...

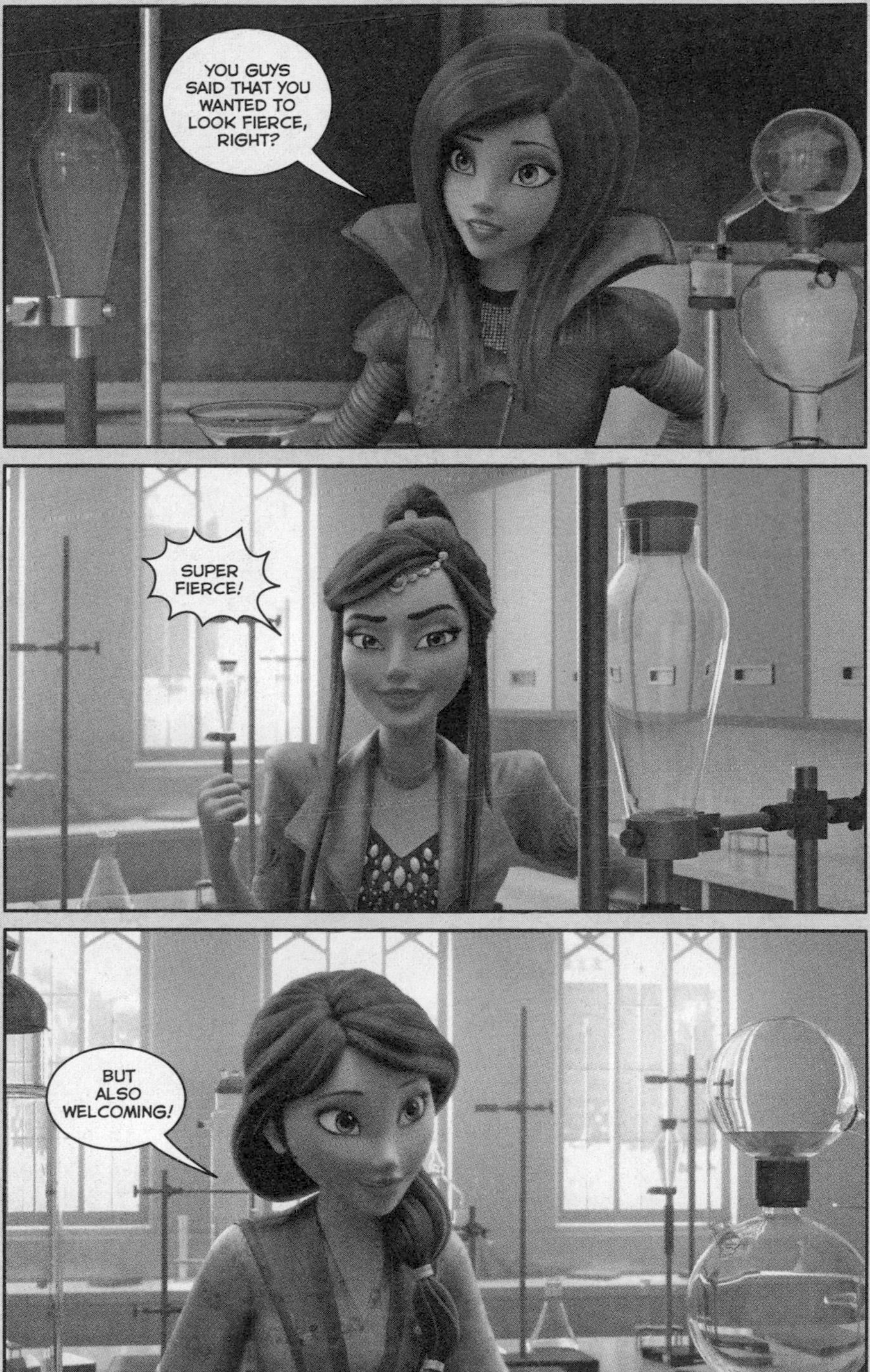
YOU GUYS SAID THAT YOU WANTED TO LOOK FIERCE, RIGHT?
SUPER FIERCE!
BUT ALSO WELCOMING!

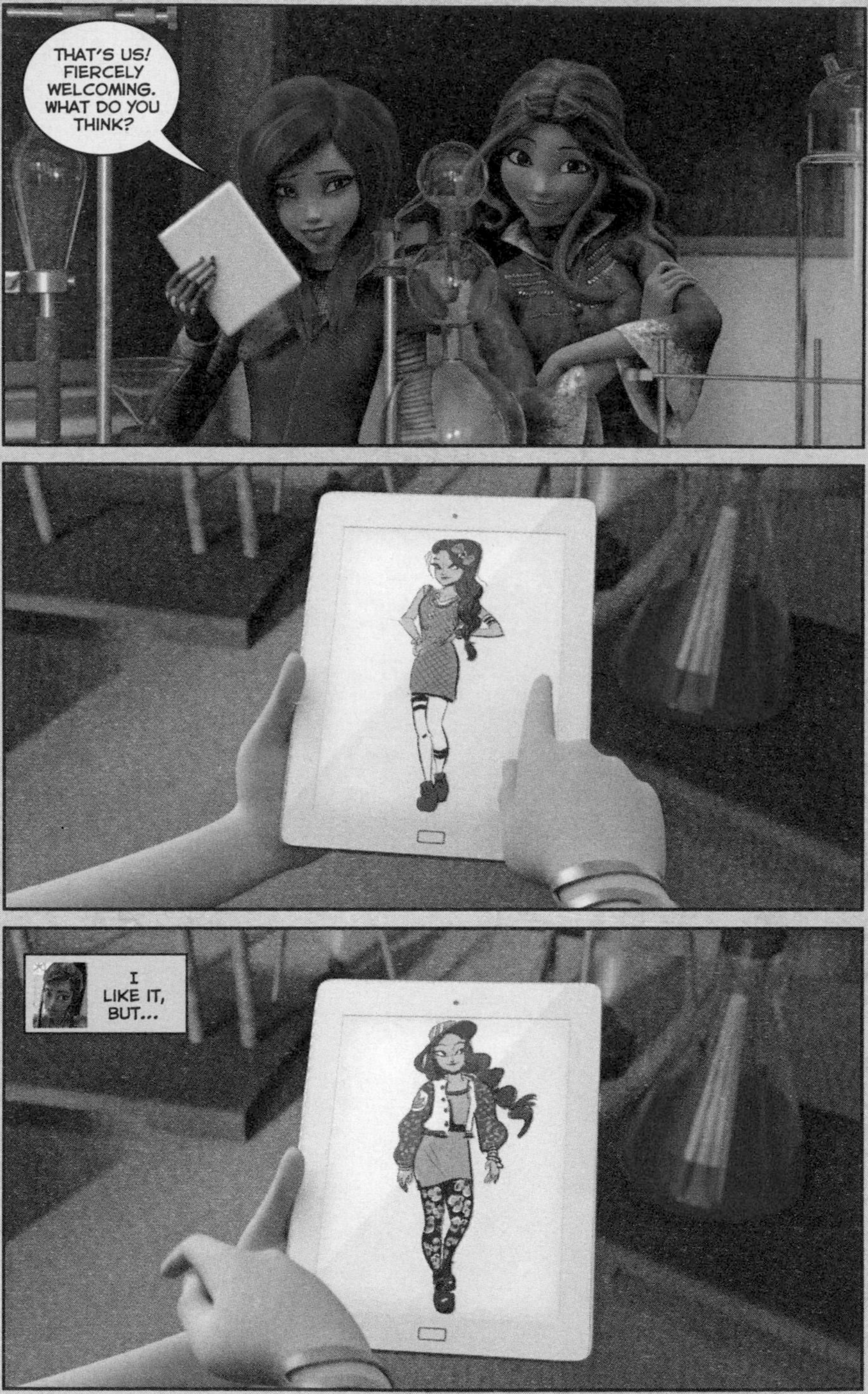
THAT'S US! FIERCELY WELCOMING. WHAT DO YOU THINK?
I LIKE IT, BUT...

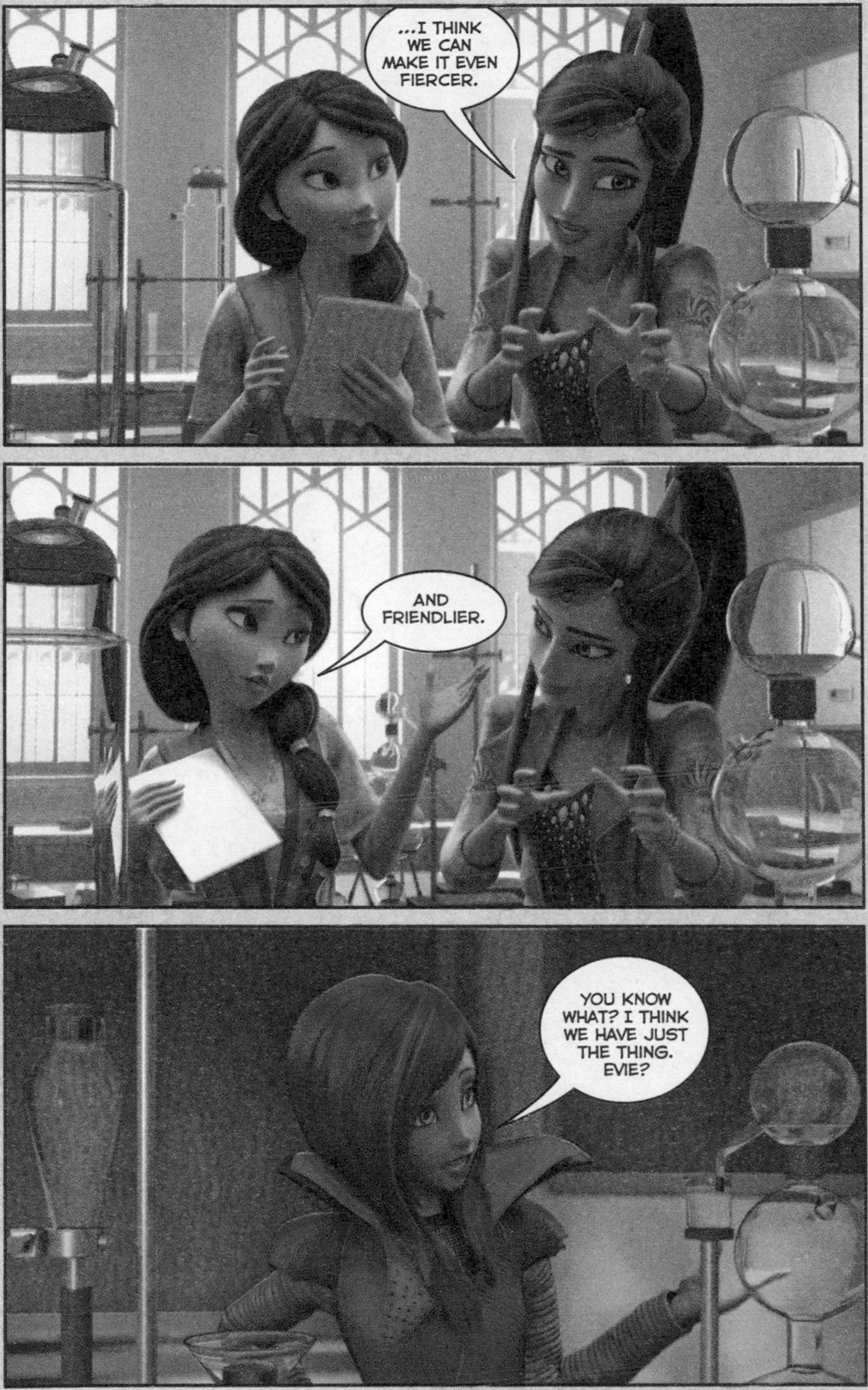
...I THINK WE CAN MAKE IT EVEN FIERCER.
AND FRIENDLIER.
YOU KNOW WHAT? I THINK WE HAVE JUST THE THING. EVIE?

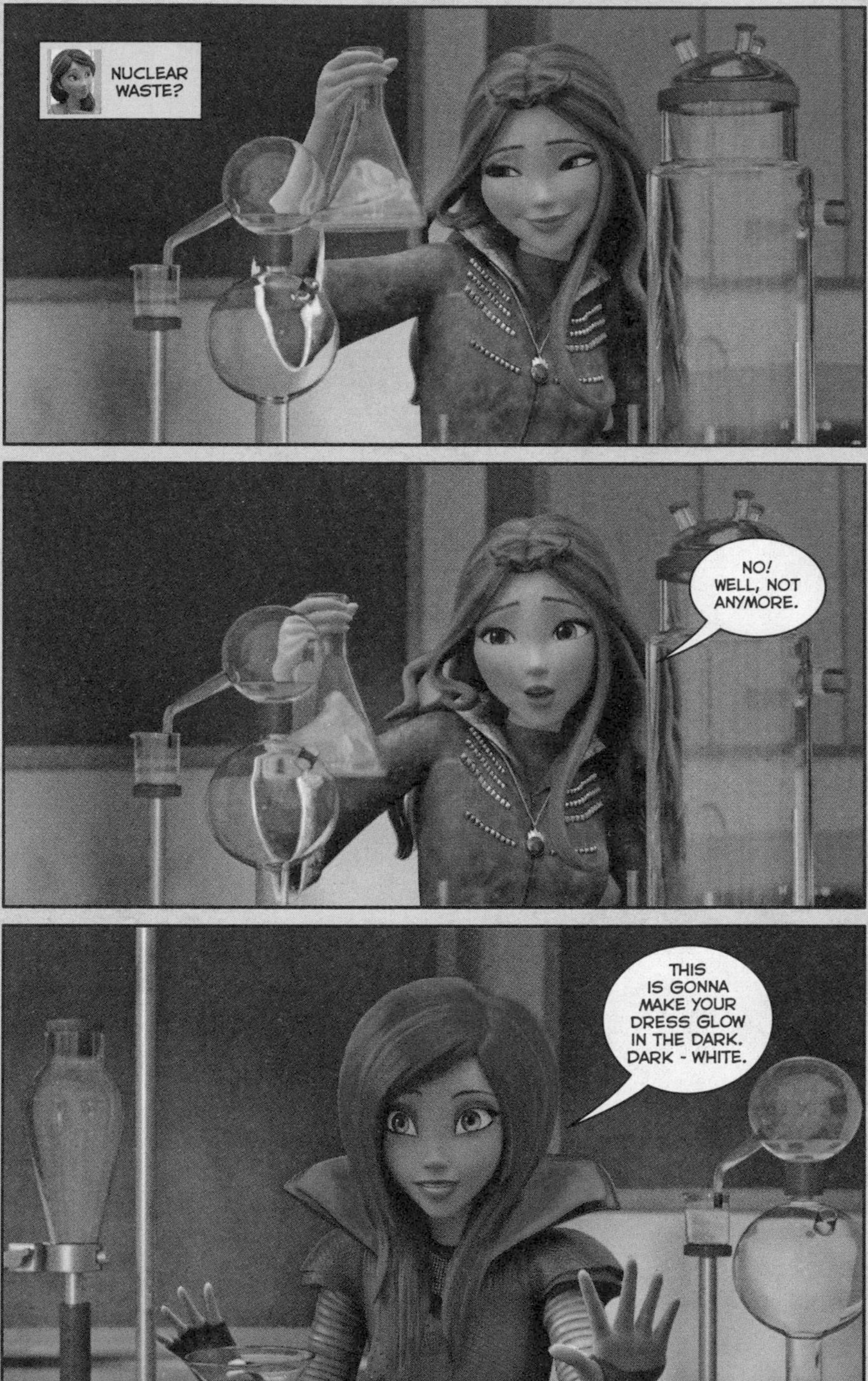
NUCLEAR WASTE?
NO! WELL, NOT ANYMORE.
THIS IS GONNA MAKE YOUR DRESS GLOW IN THE DARK. DARK - WHITE.

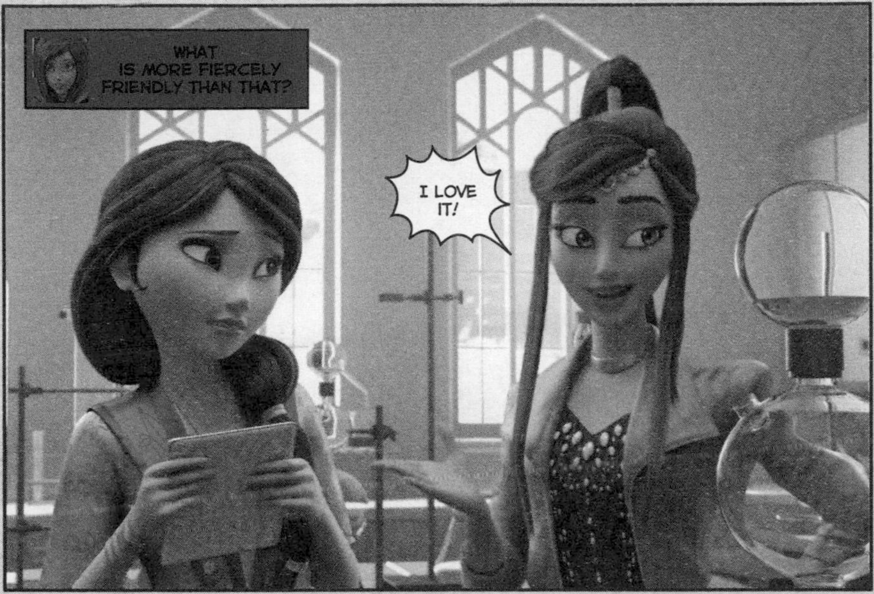
WHAT IS MORE FIERCELY FRIENDLY THAN THAT?
I LOVE IT!

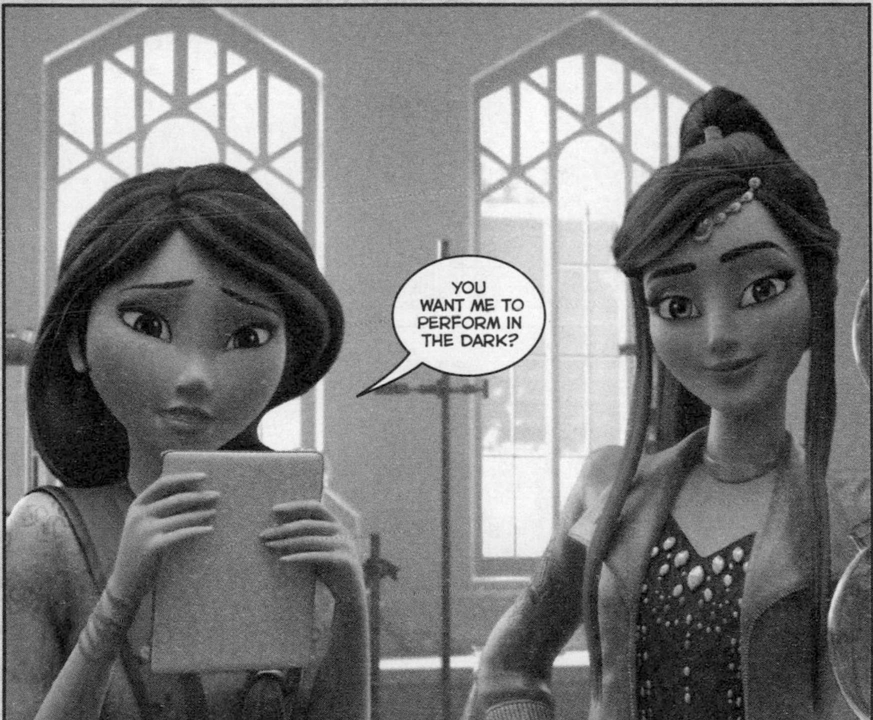
YOU WANT ME TO PERFORM IN THE DARK?

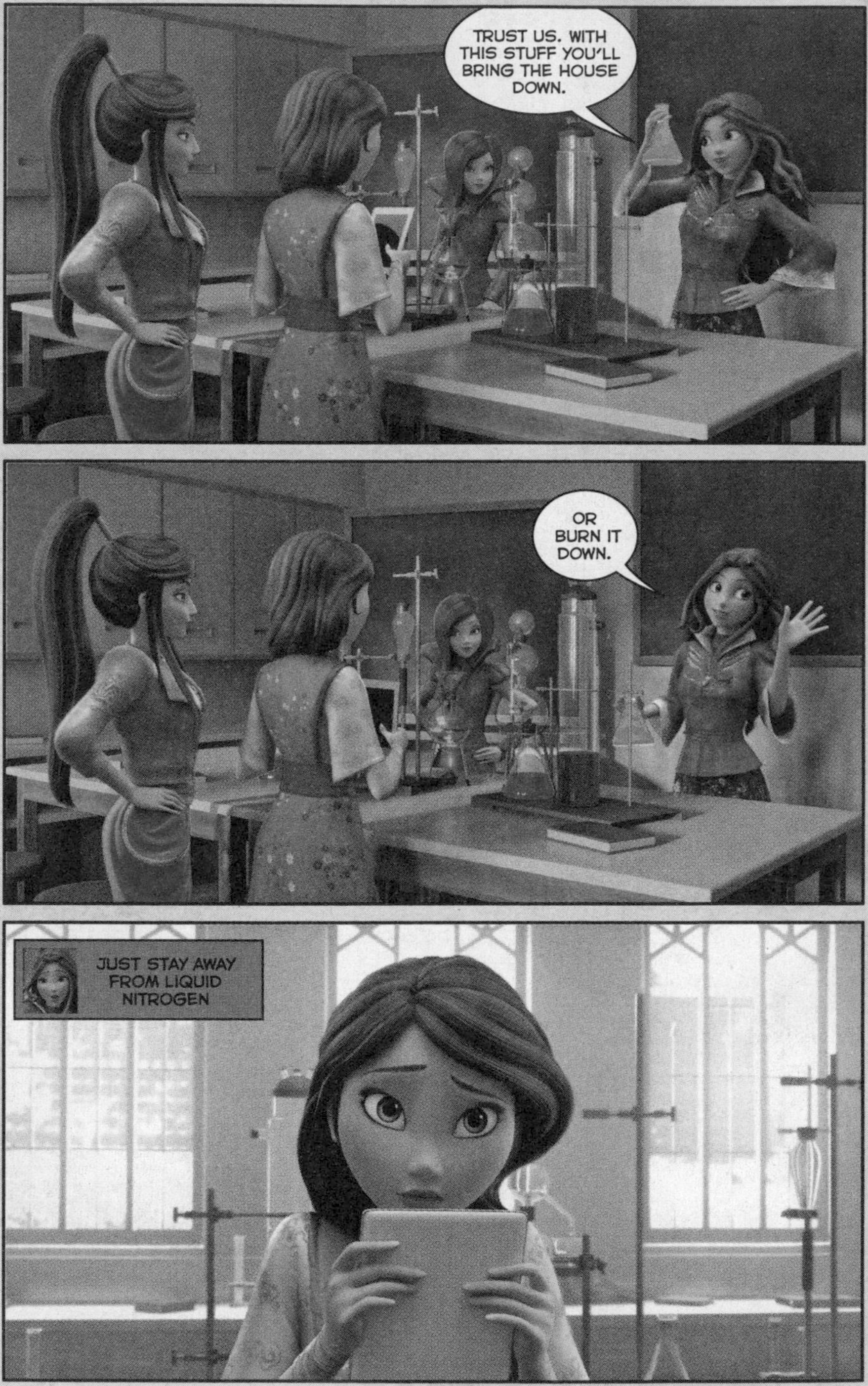
TRUST US. WITH THIS STUFF YOU'LL BRING THE HOUSE DOWN.
OR BURN IT DOWN.
JUST STAY AWAY FROM LIQUID NITROGEN

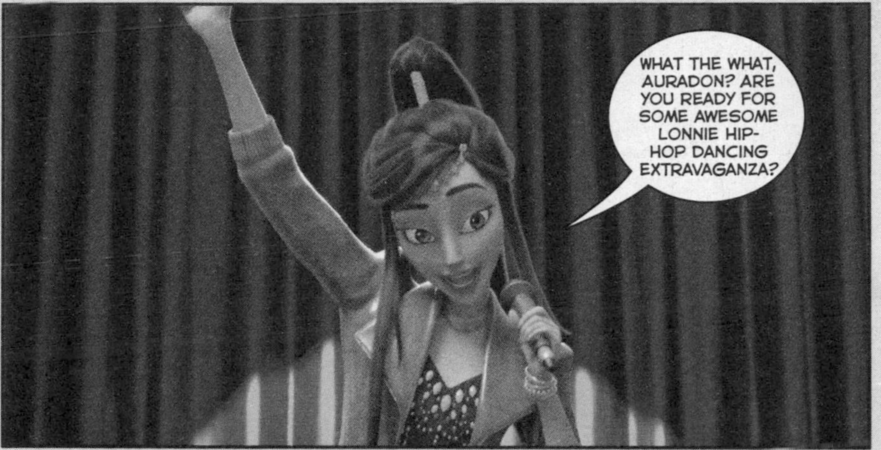
WHAT THE WHAT, AURADON? ARE YOU READY FOR SOME AWESOME LONNIE HIP-HOP DANCING EXTRAVAGANZA?

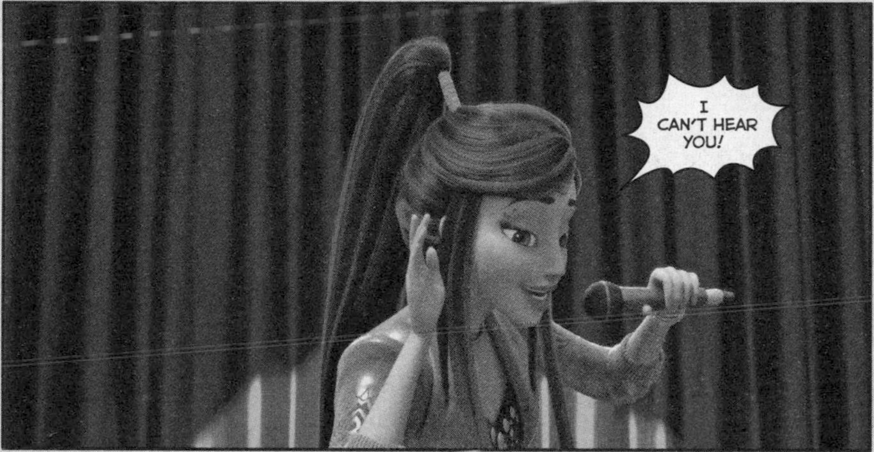
I CAN'T HEAR YOU!

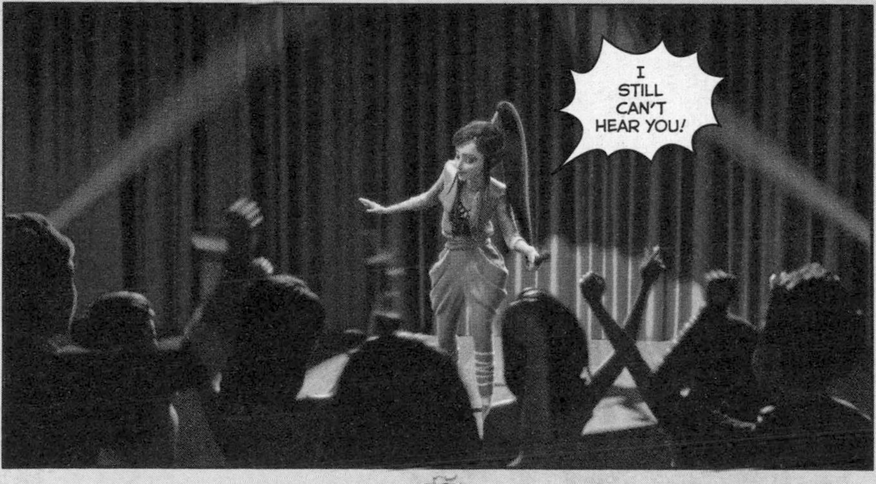
I STILL CAN'T HEAR YOU!

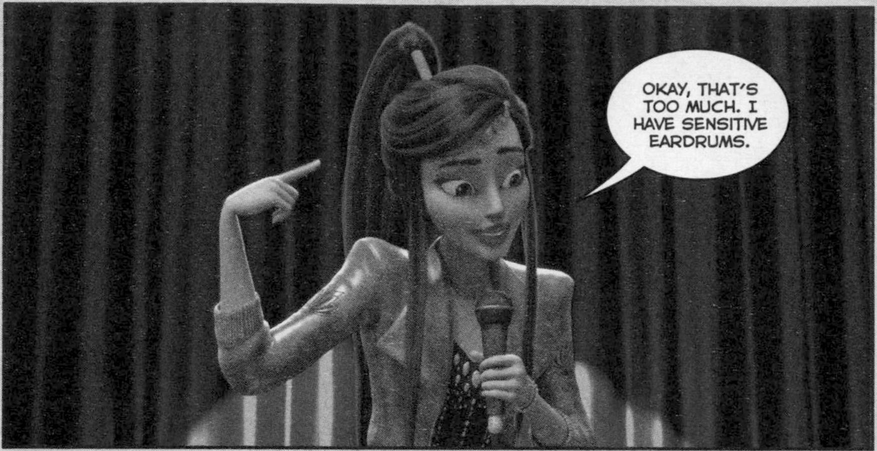
OKAY, THAT'S TOO MUCH. I HAVE SENSITIVE EARDRUMS.

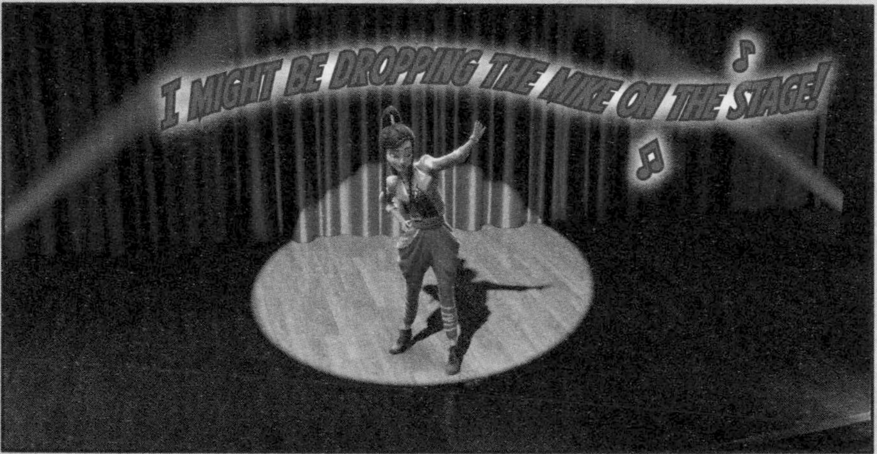
I MIGHT BE DROPPING THE MIKE ON THE STAGE!

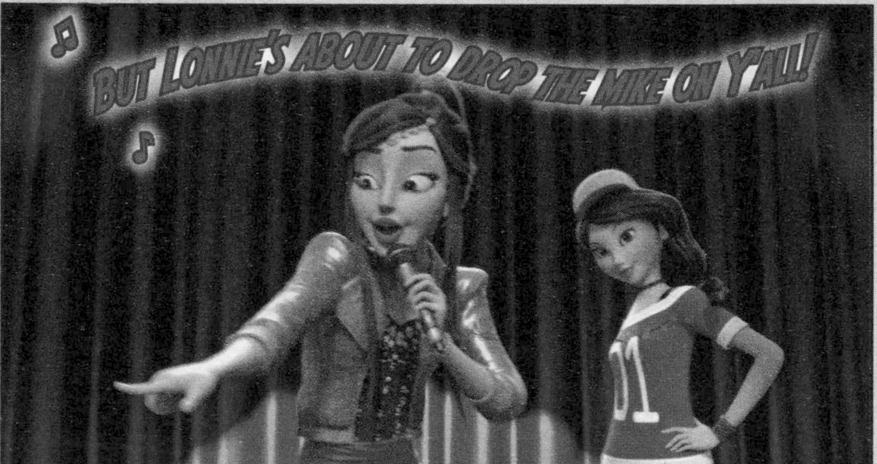
BUT LONNIE'S ABOUT TO DROP THE MIKE ON Y'ALL!

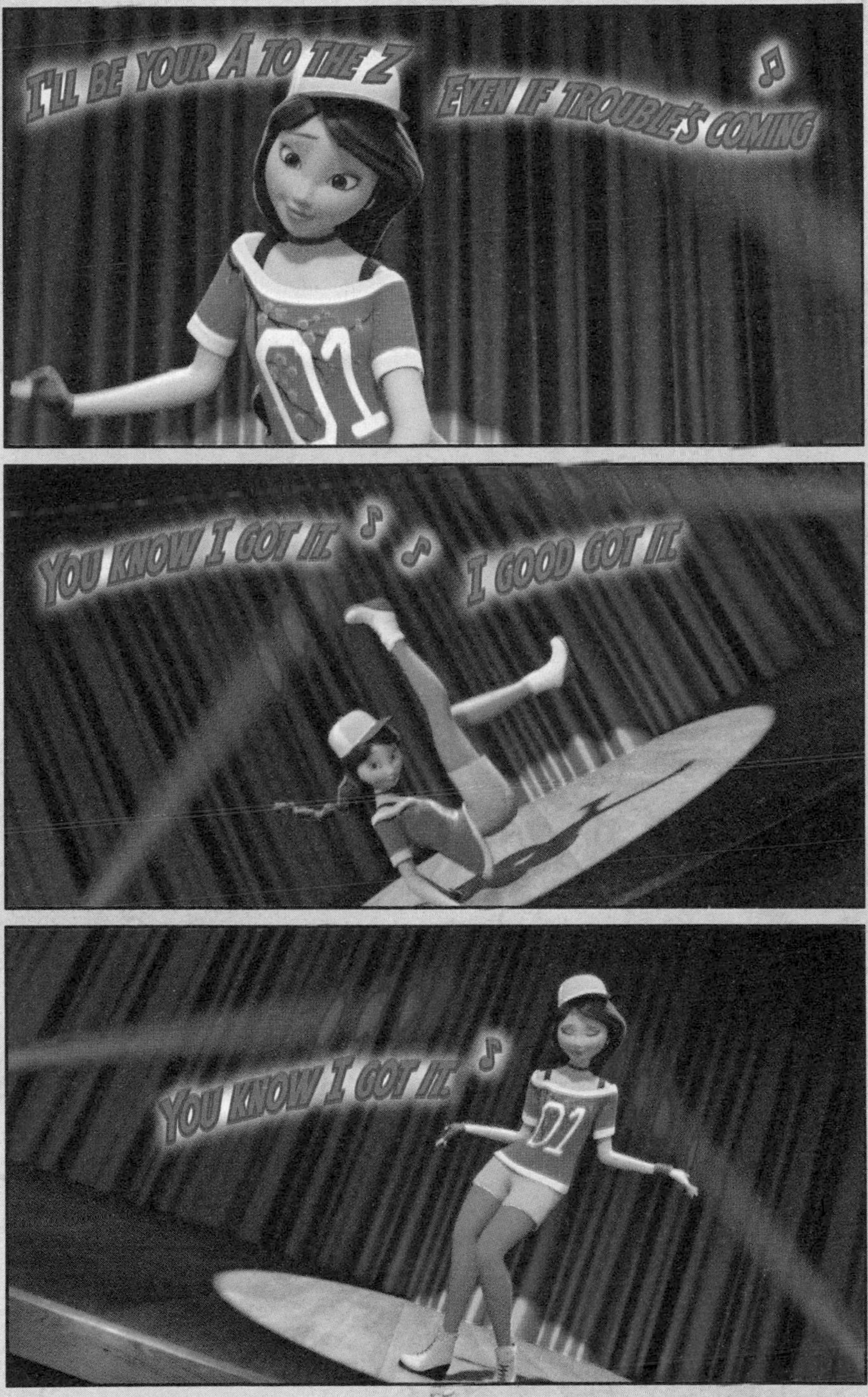
I'll be your A to the Z
Even if trouble's coming
You know I got it
I good got it
You know I got it

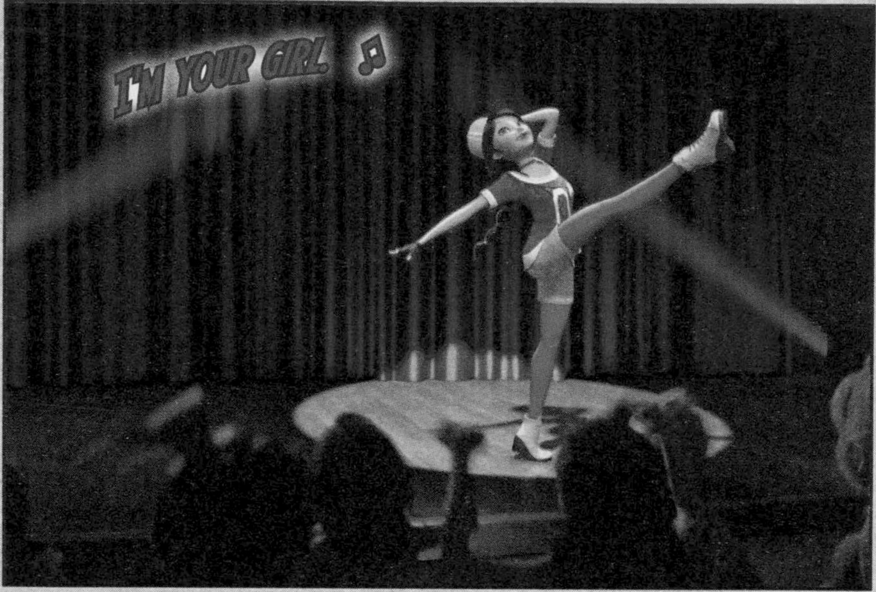
I'M YOUR GIRL ♫

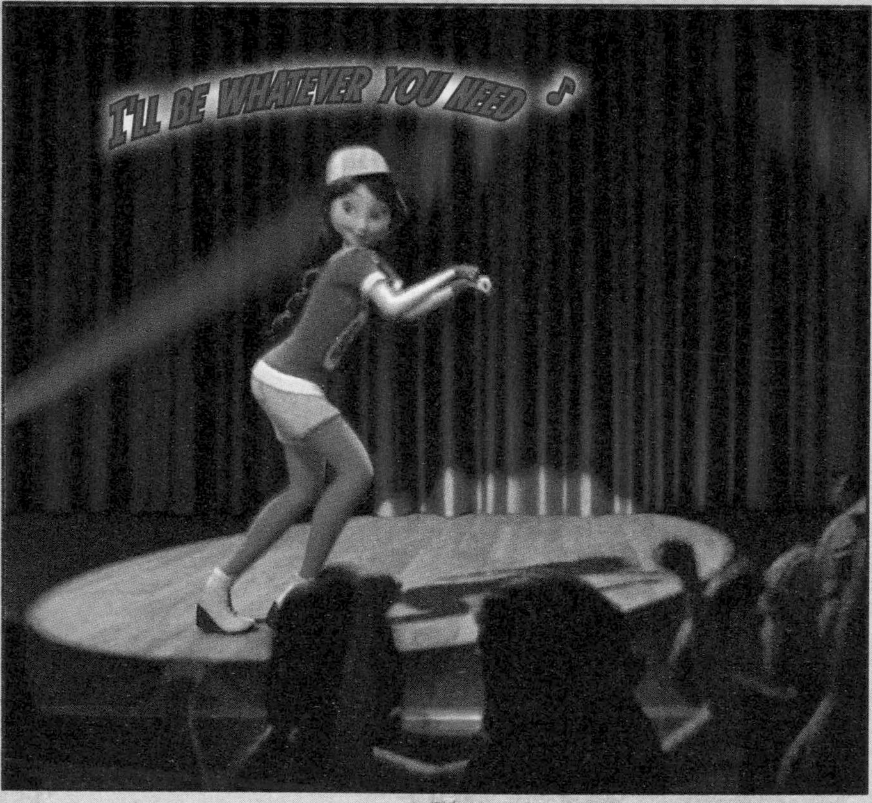
I'LL BE WHATEVER YOU NEED ♪

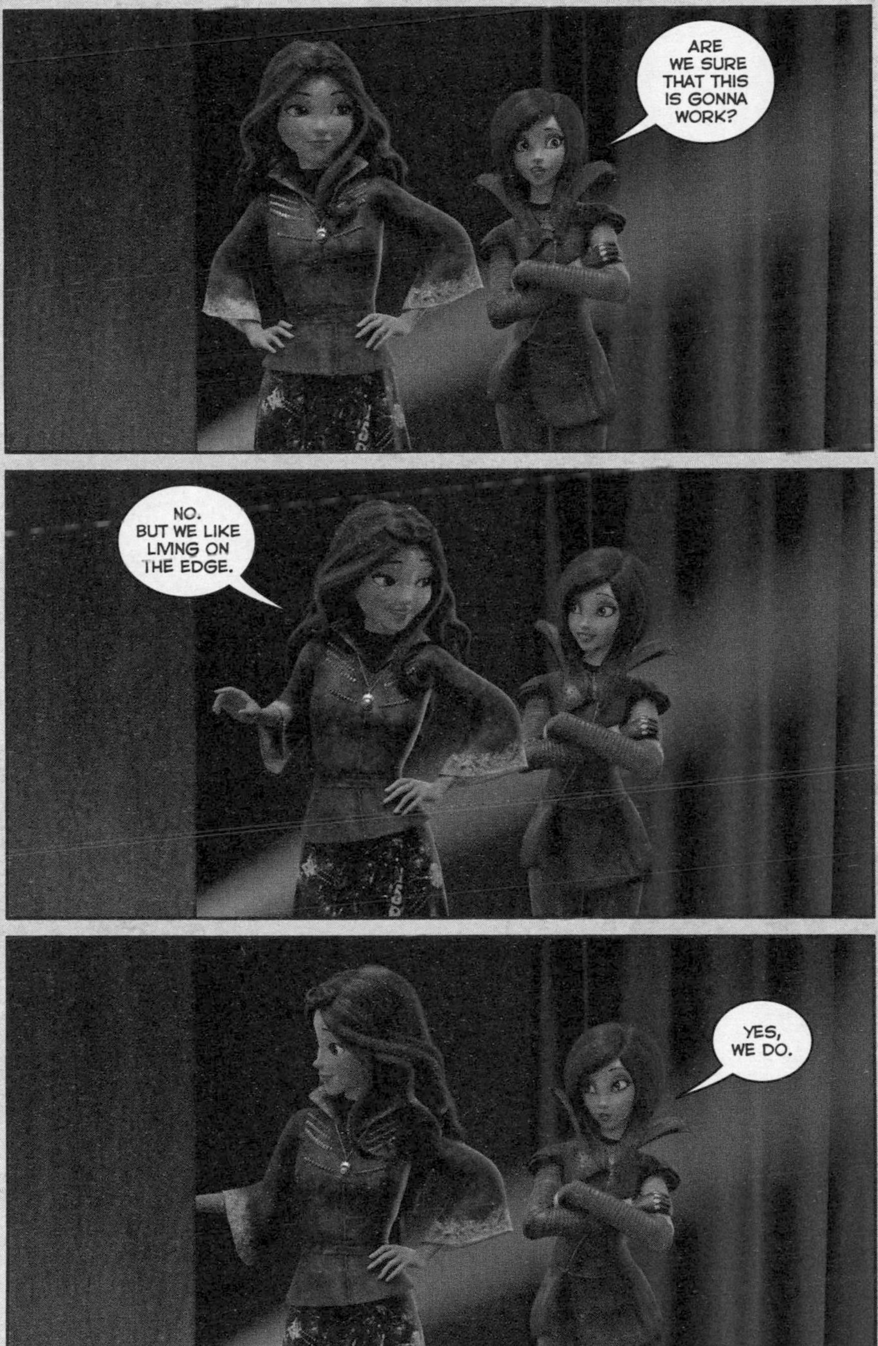
ARE WE SURE THAT THIS IS GONNA WORK?
NO. BUT WE LIKE LIVING ON THE EDGE.
YES, WE DO.

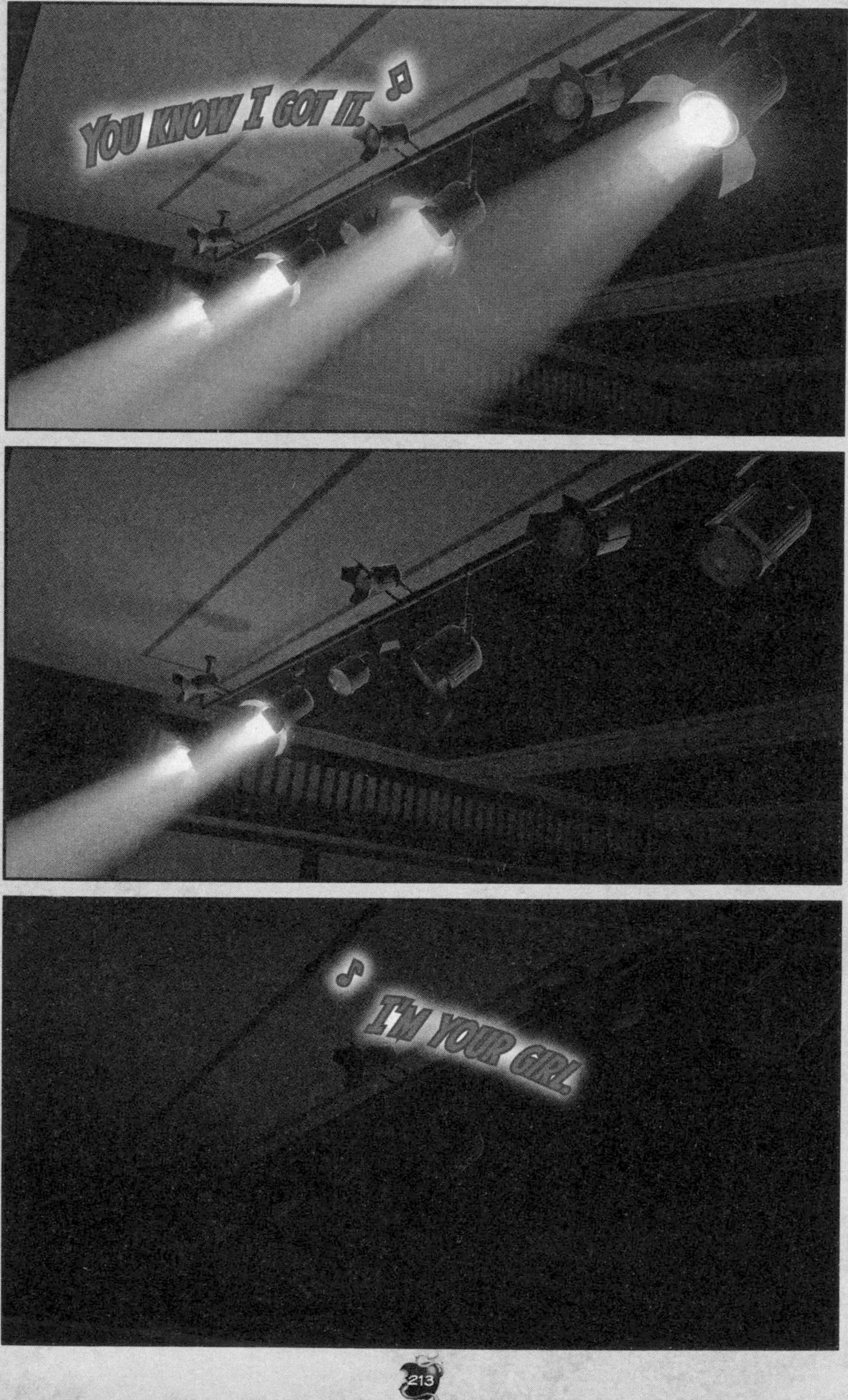
YOU KNOW I GOT IT,
I'M YOUR GIRL.

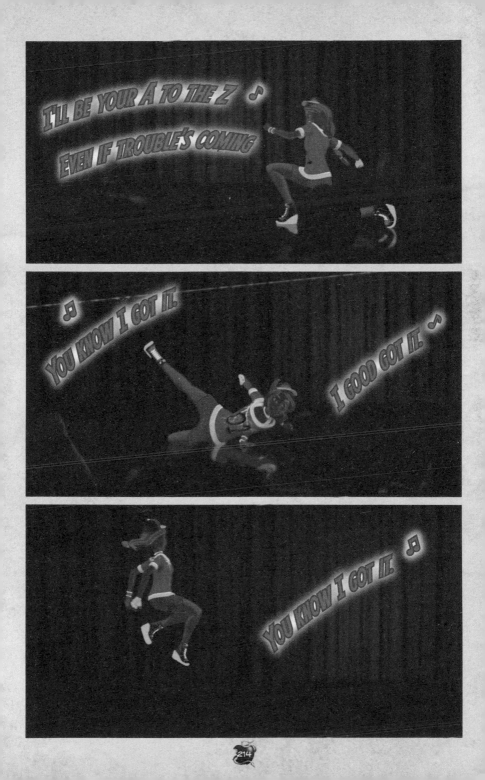

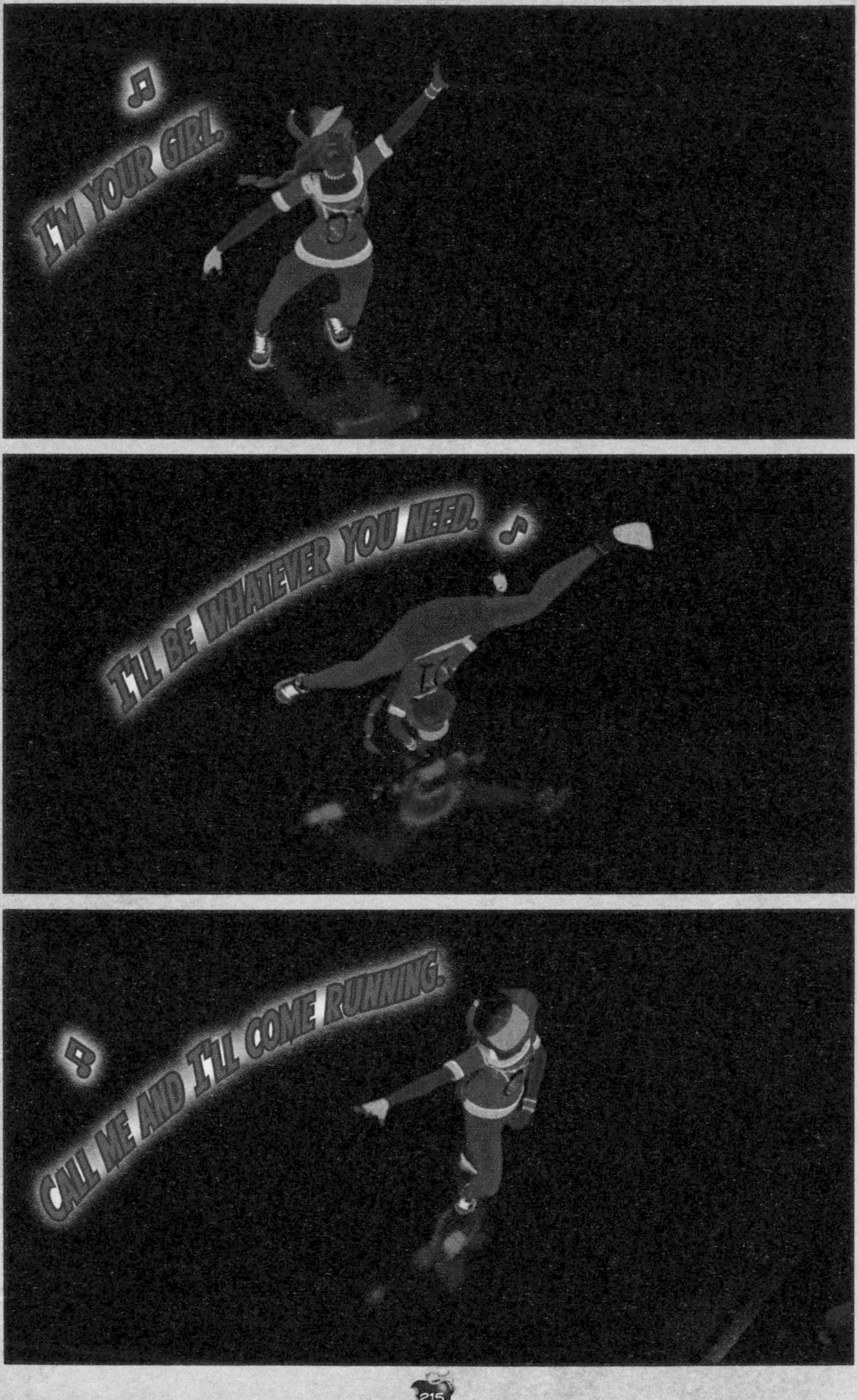
I'M YOUR GIRL.
I'LL BE WHATEVER YOU NEED.
CALL ME AND I'LL COME RUNNING.

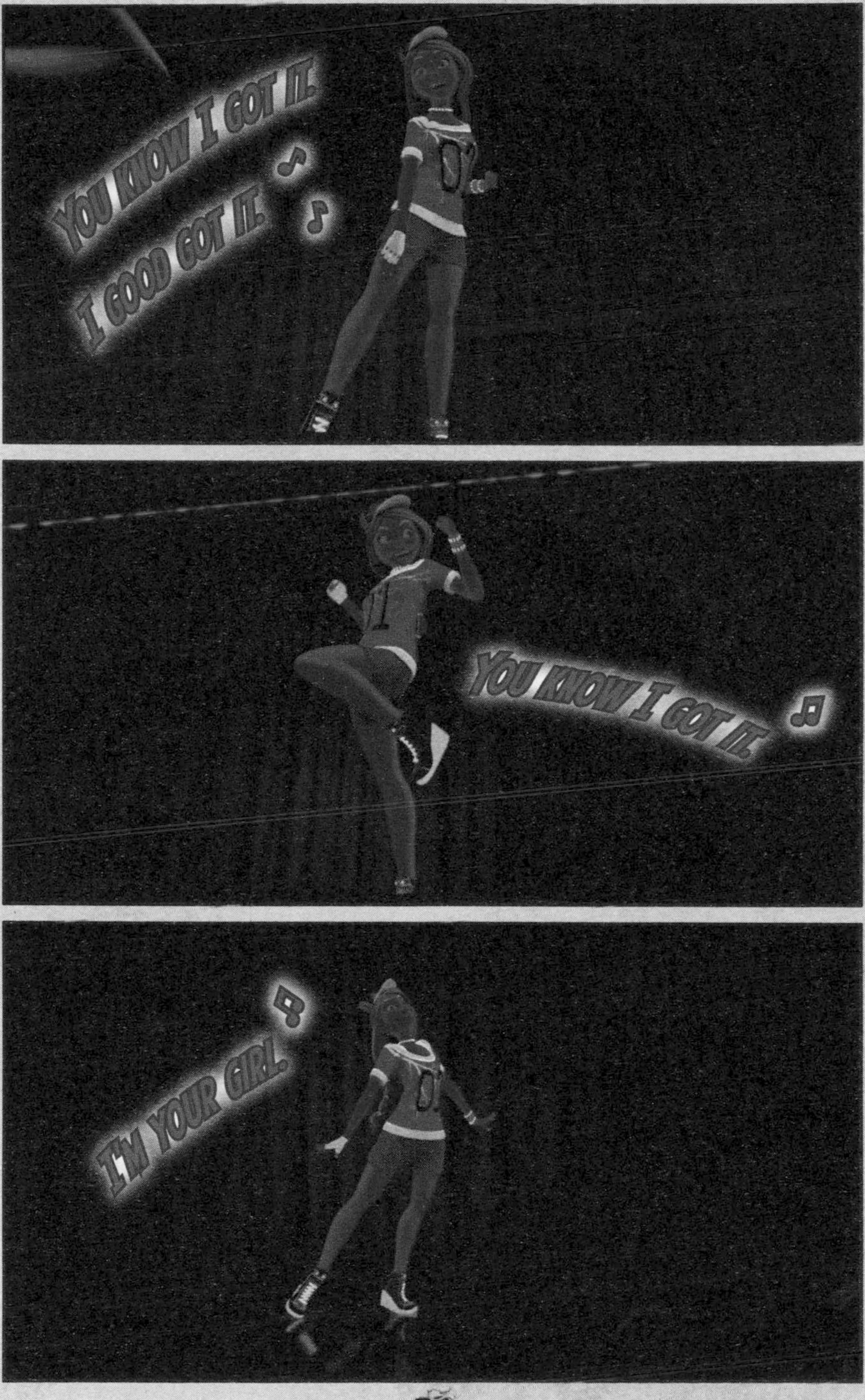
YOU KNOW I GOT IT.
I GOOD GOT IT.
YOU KNOW I GOT IT.
I'M YOUR GIRL.

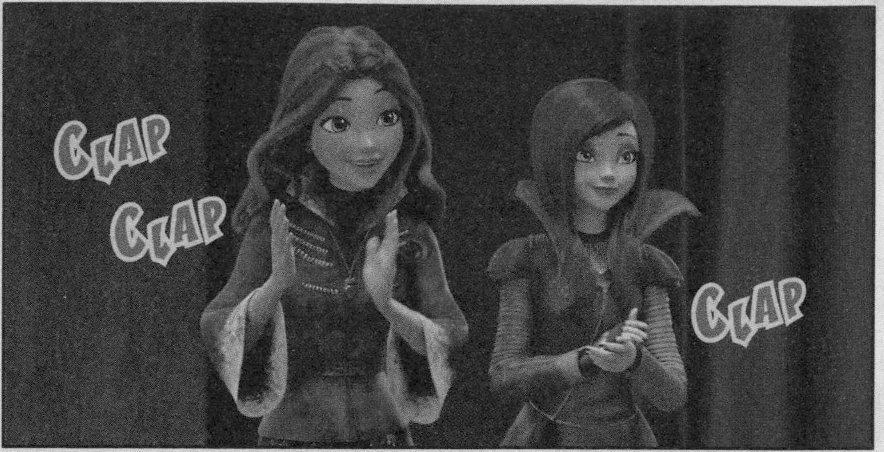
CLAP
CLAP
CLAP

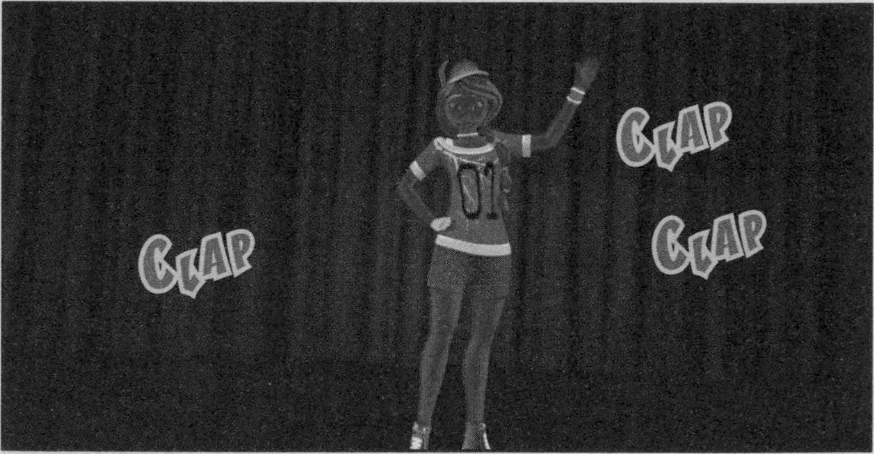
CLAP
CLAP
CLAP

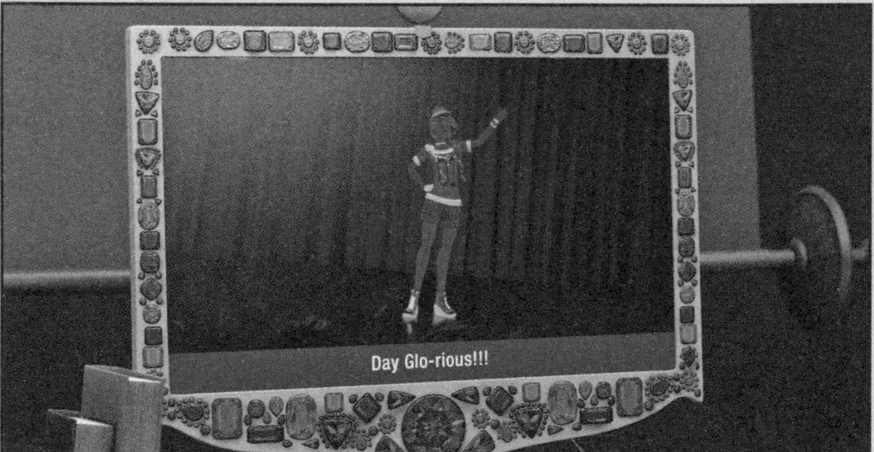
Day Glo-rious!!!

CHAPTER 12: MASH IT UP

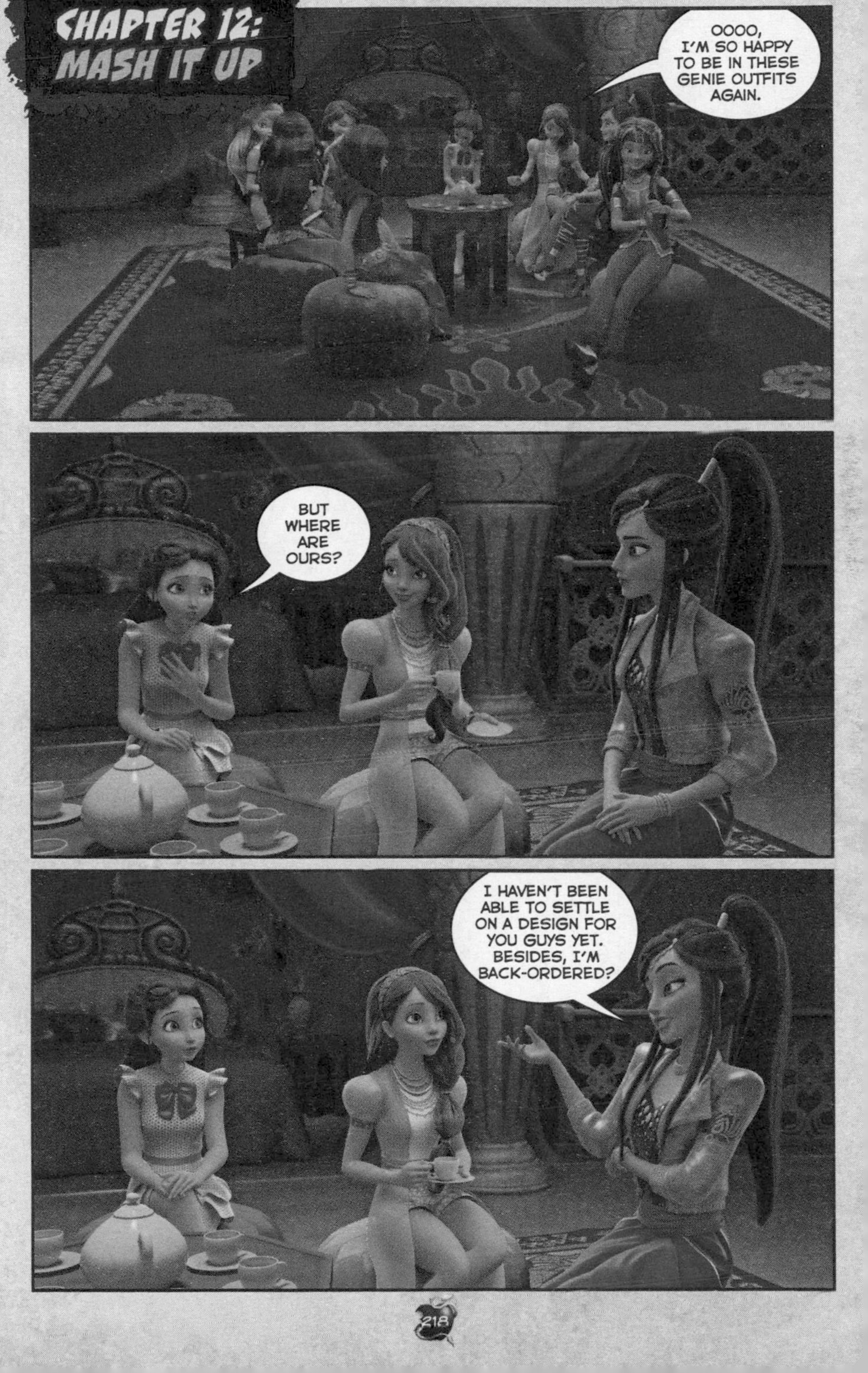
OOOO, I'M SO HAPPY TO BE IN THESE GENIE OUTFITS AGAIN.
BUT WHERE ARE OURS?
I HAVEN'T BEEN ABLE TO SETTLE ON A DESIGN FOR YOU GUYS YET. BESIDES, I'M BACK-ORDERED?

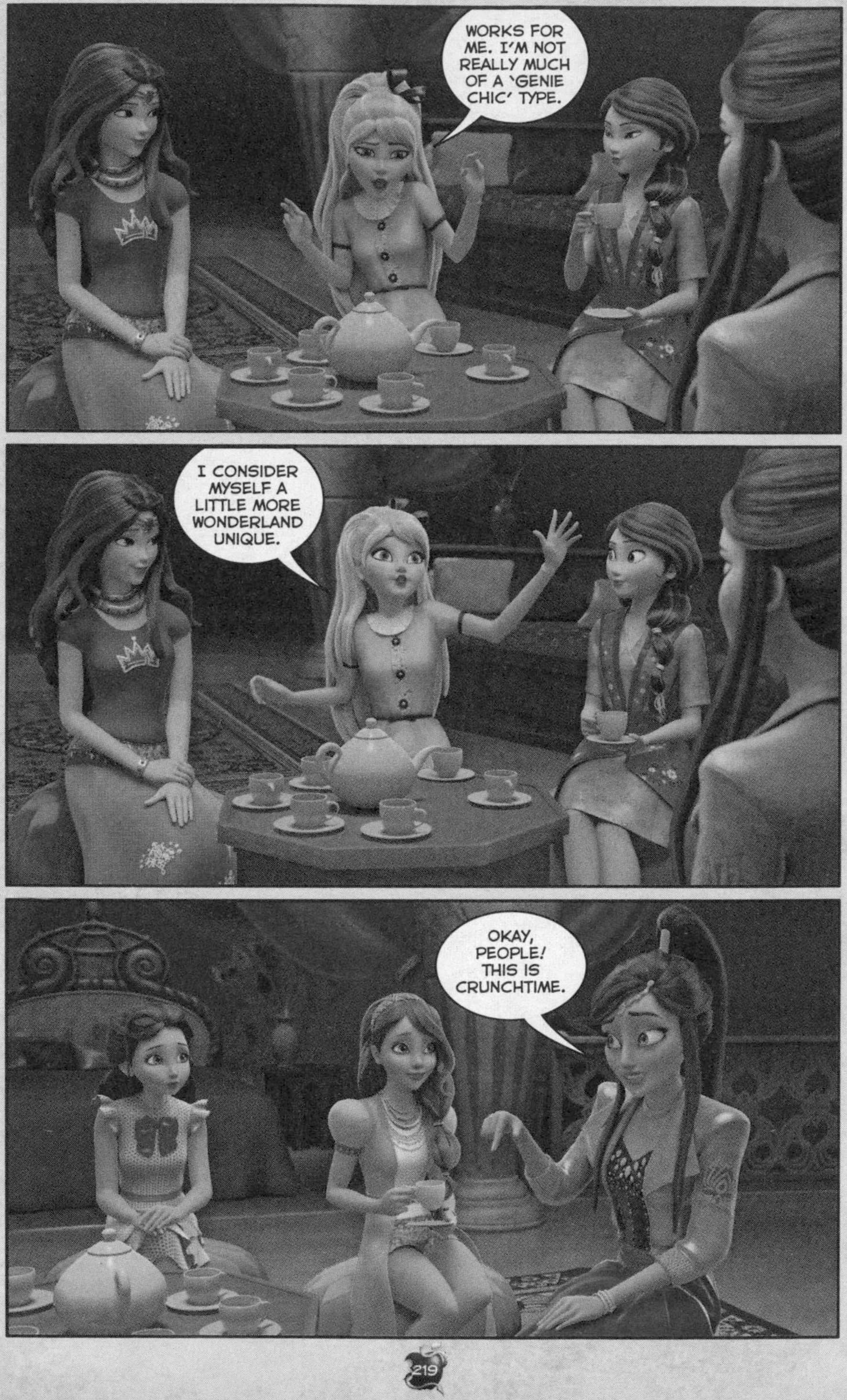
WORKS FOR ME. I'M NOT REALLY MUCH OF A 'GENIE CHIC' TYPE.
I CONSIDER MYSELF A LITTLE MORE WONDERLAND UNIQUE.
OKAY, PEOPLE! THIS IS CRUNCHTIME.

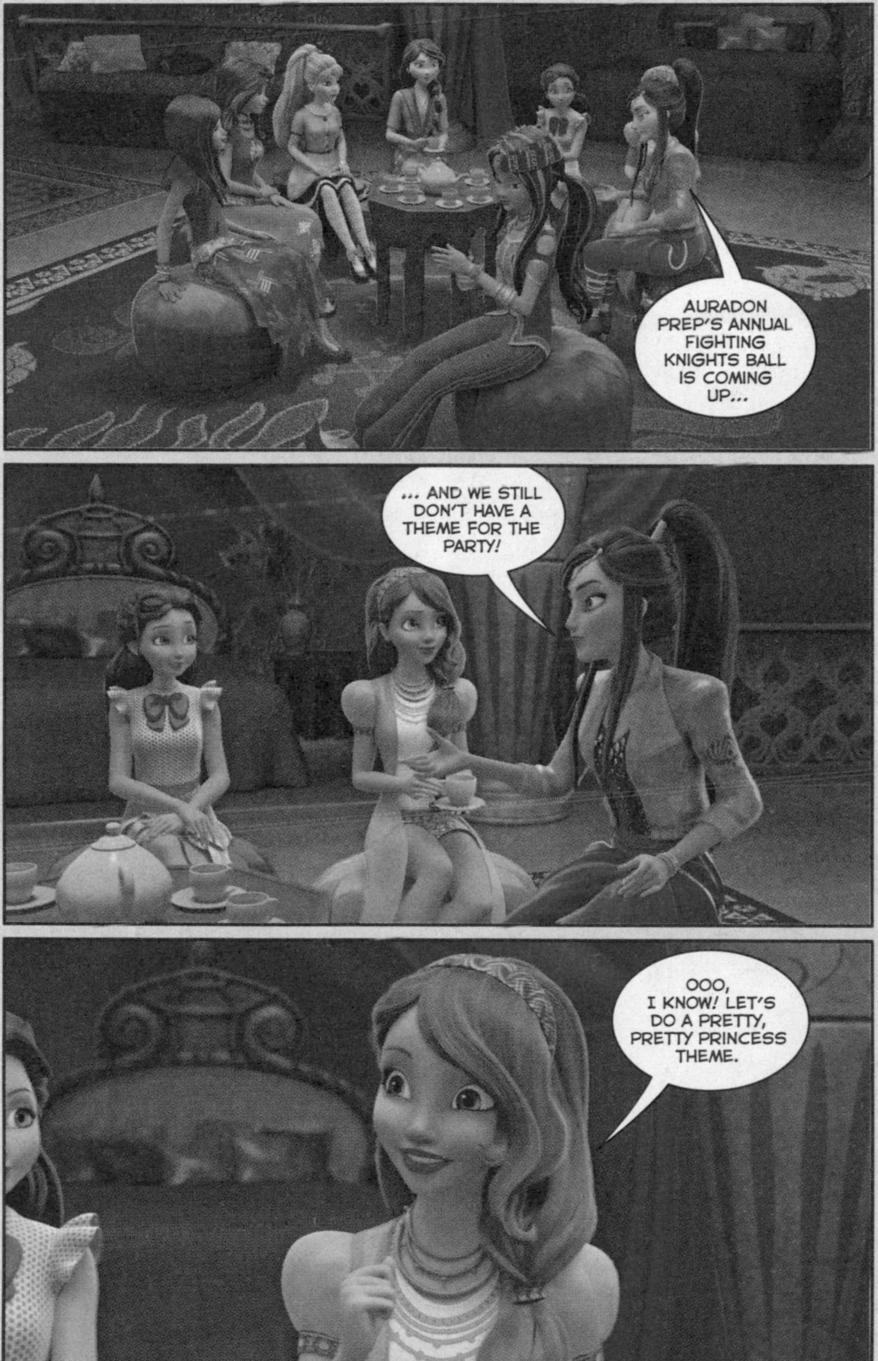
AURADON PREP'S ANNUAL FIGHTING KNIGHTS BALL IS COMING UP...
... AND WE STILL DON'T HAVE A THEME FOR THE PARTY!
OOO, I KNOW! LET'S DO A PRETTY, PRETTY PRINCESS THEME.

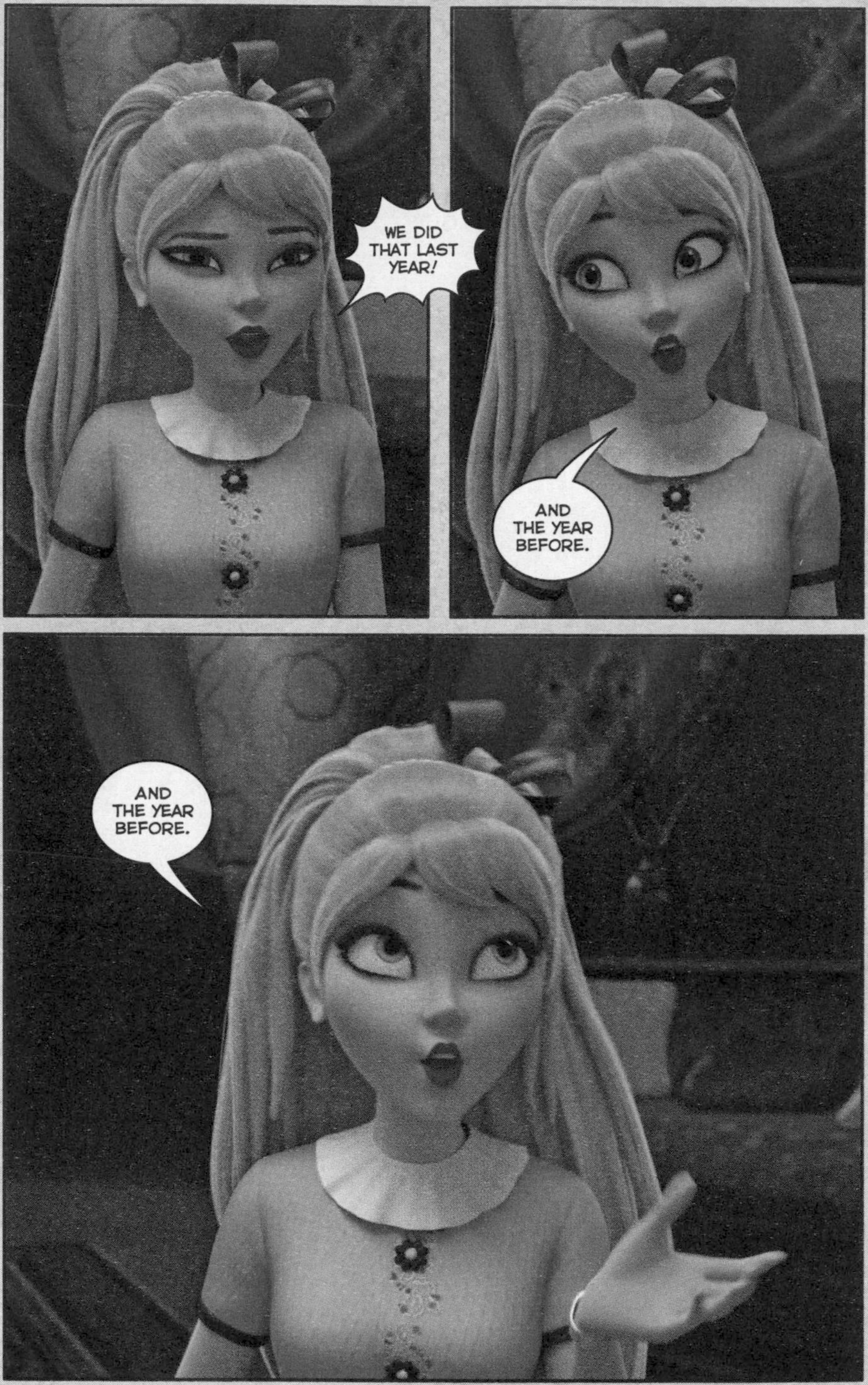
WE DID THAT LAST YEAR!
AND THE YEAR BEFORE.
AND THE YEAR BEFORE.

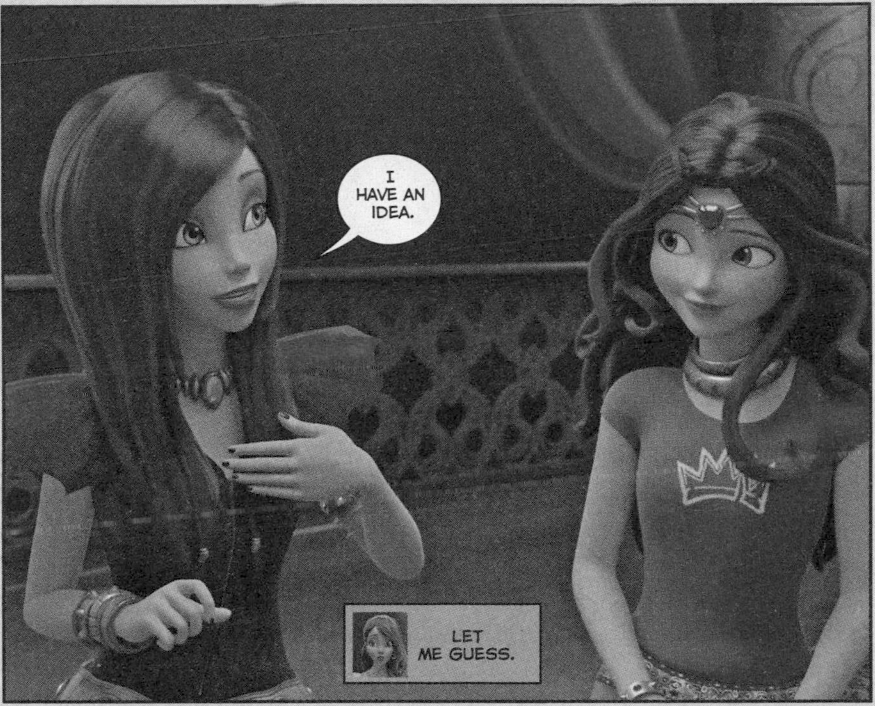
I HAVE AN IDEA.
LET ME GUESS.

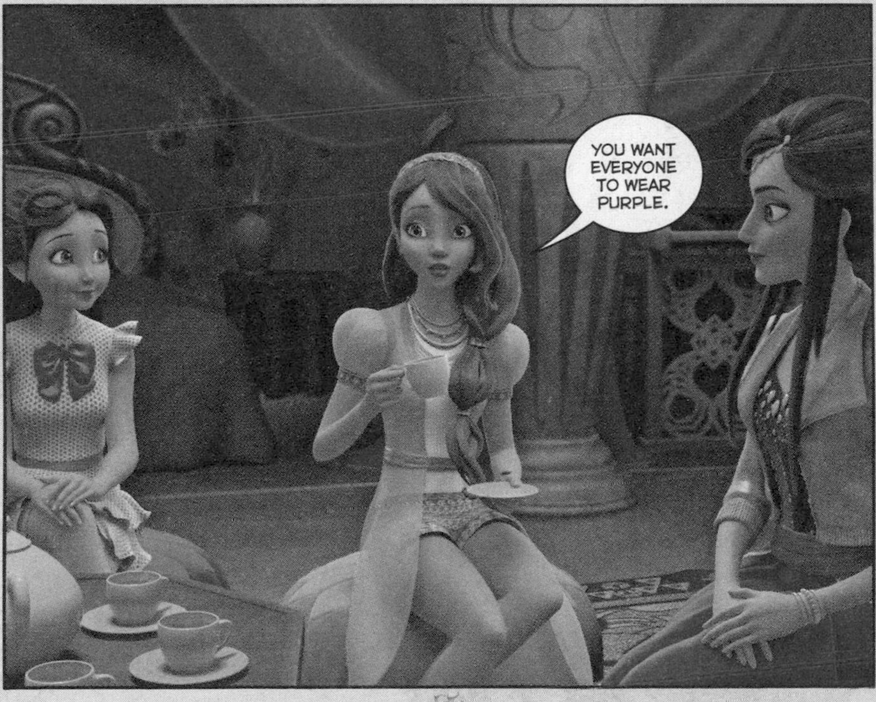
YOU WANT EVERYONE TO WEAR PURPLE.

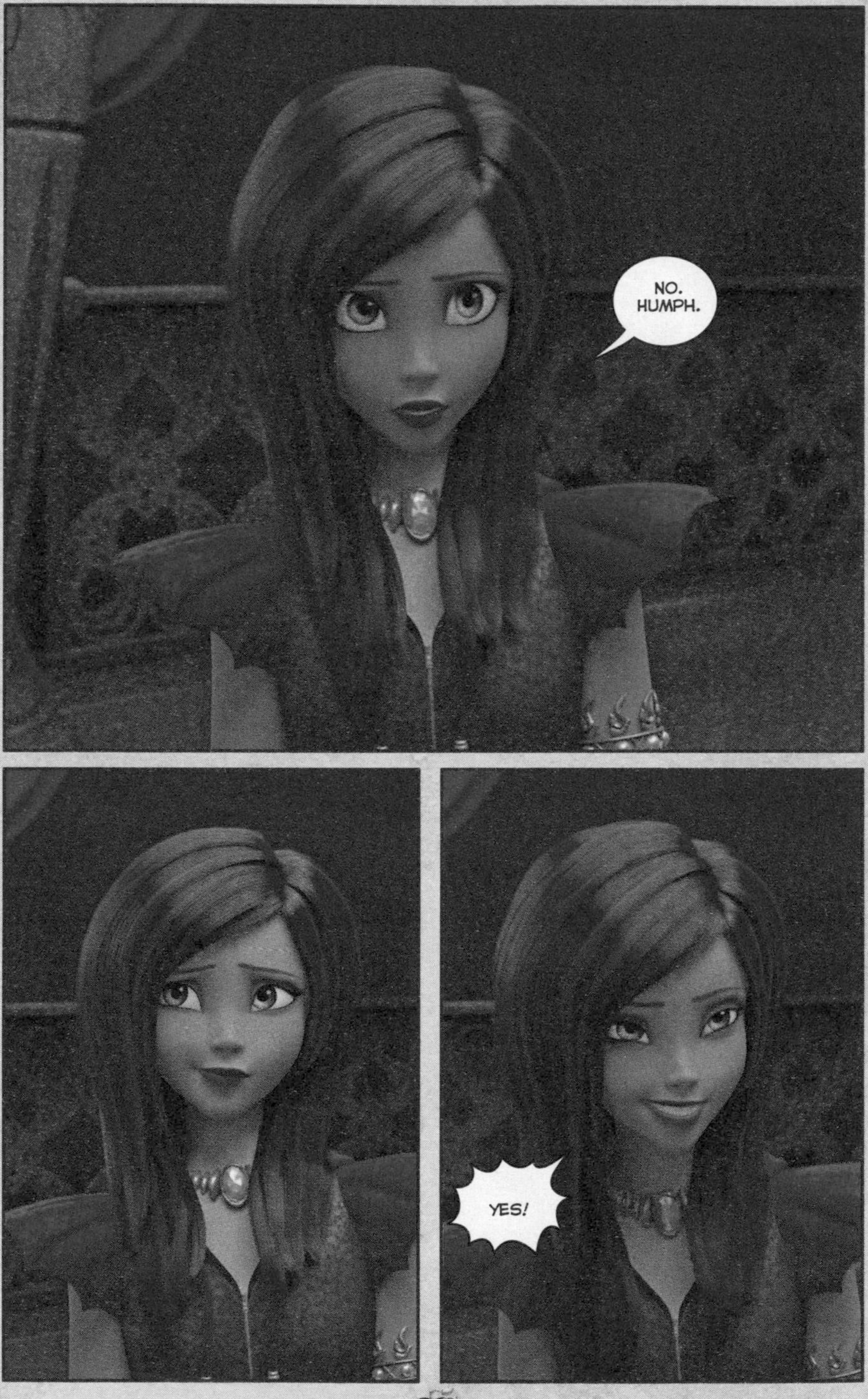
NO.
HUMPH.
YES!

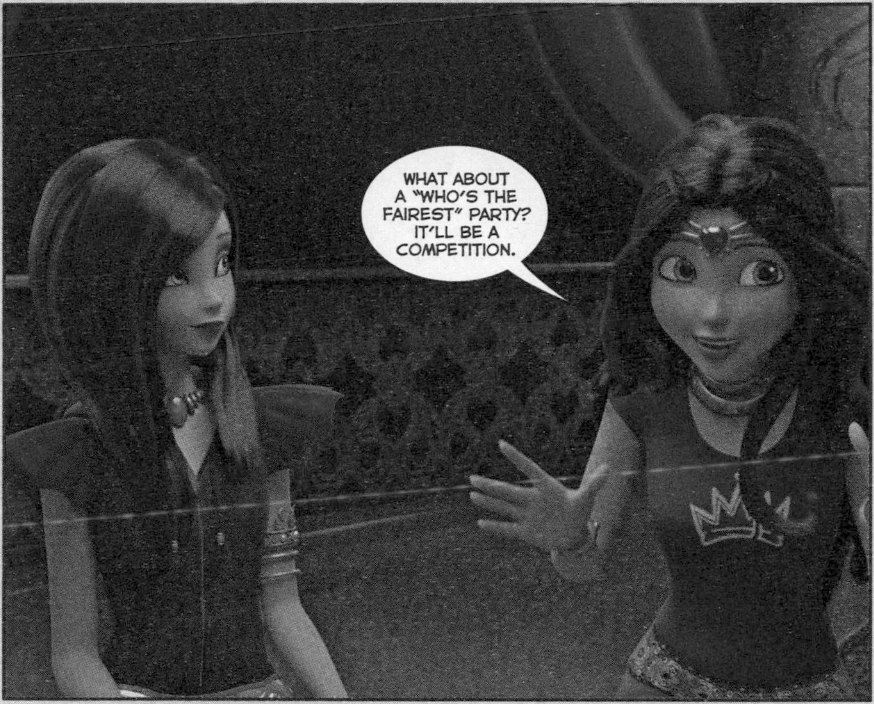
WHAT ABOUT A "WHO'S THE FAIREST" PARTY? IT'LL BE A COMPETITION.

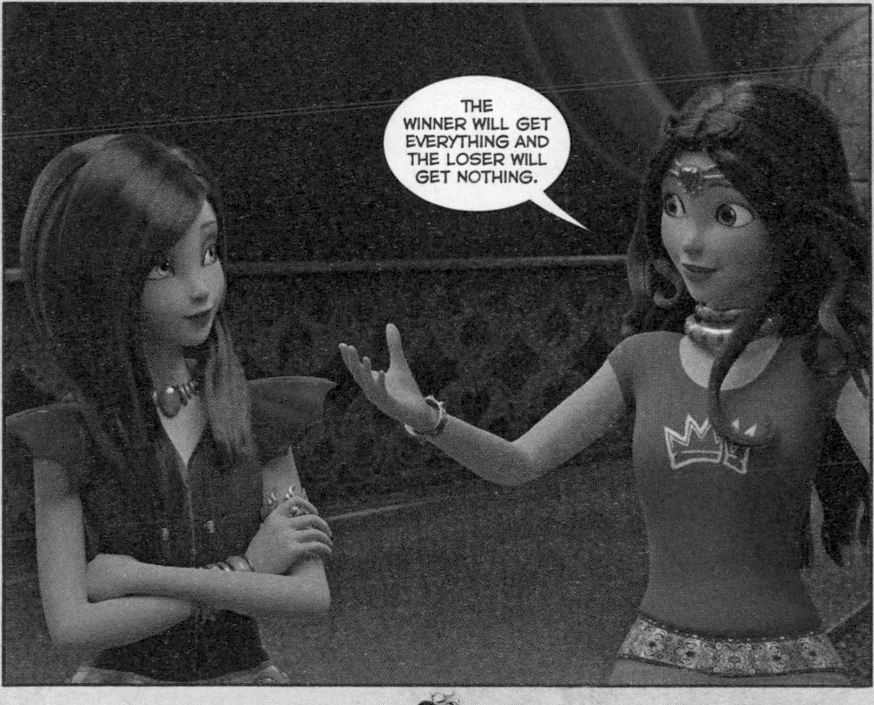
THE WINNER WILL GET EVERYTHING AND THE LOSER WILL GET NOTHING.

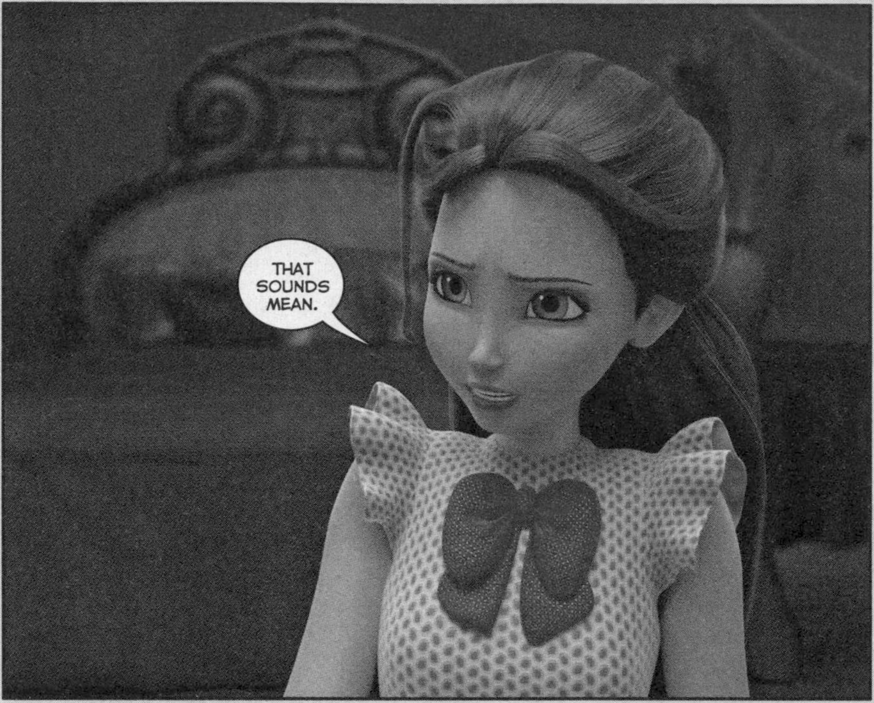
THAT SOUNDS MEAN.

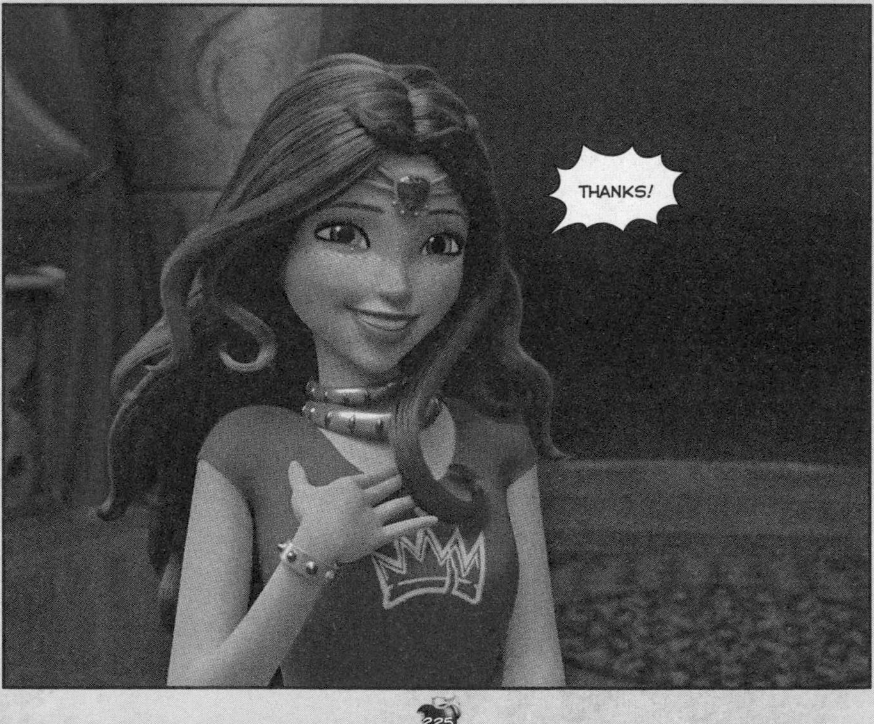
THANKS!

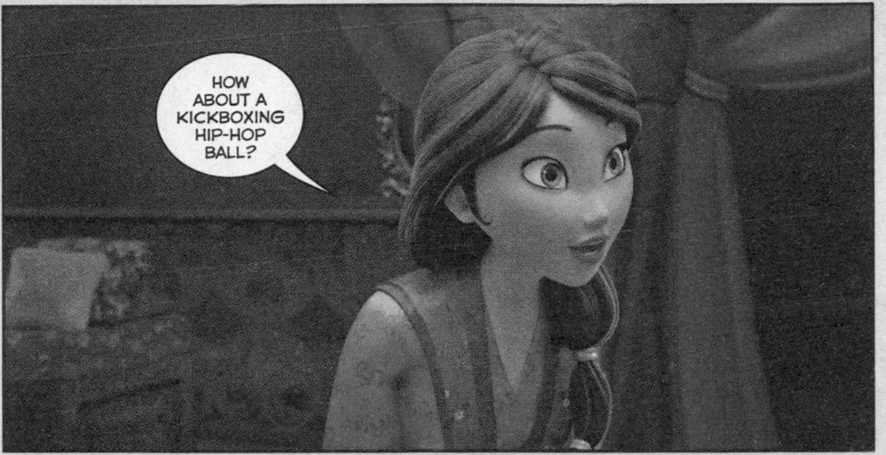
HOW ABOUT A KICKBOXING HIP-HOP BALL?

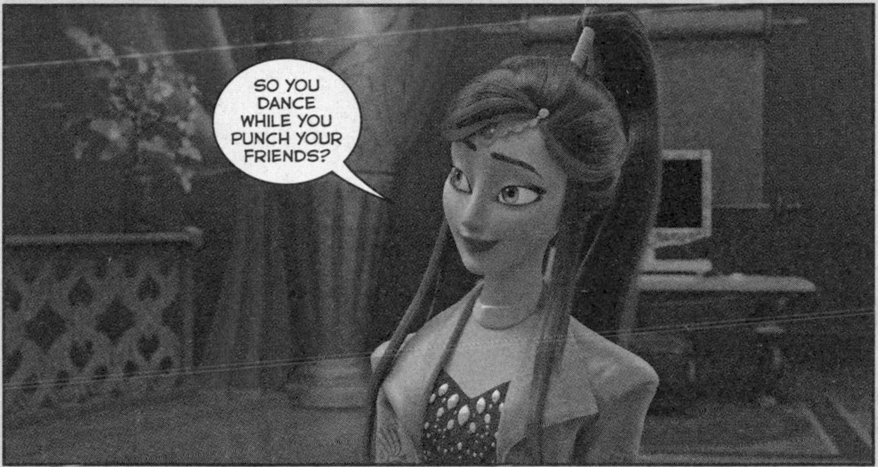
SO YOU DANCE WHILE YOU PUNCH YOUR FRIENDS?

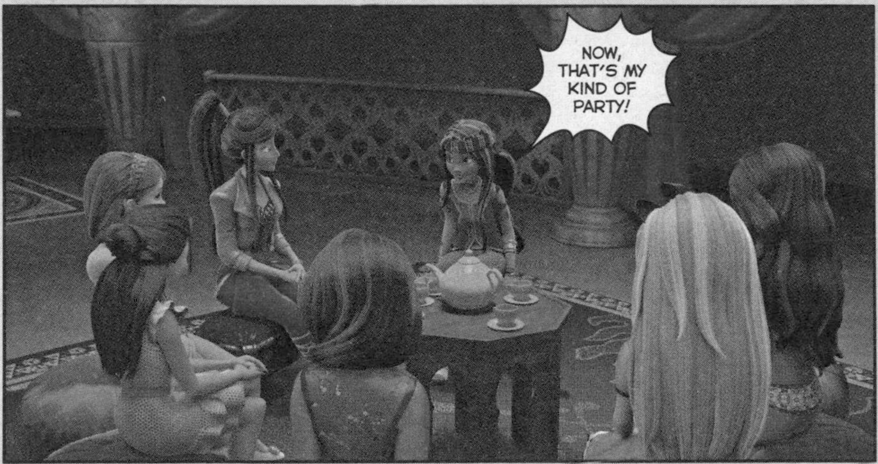
NOW, THAT'S MY KIND OF PARTY!

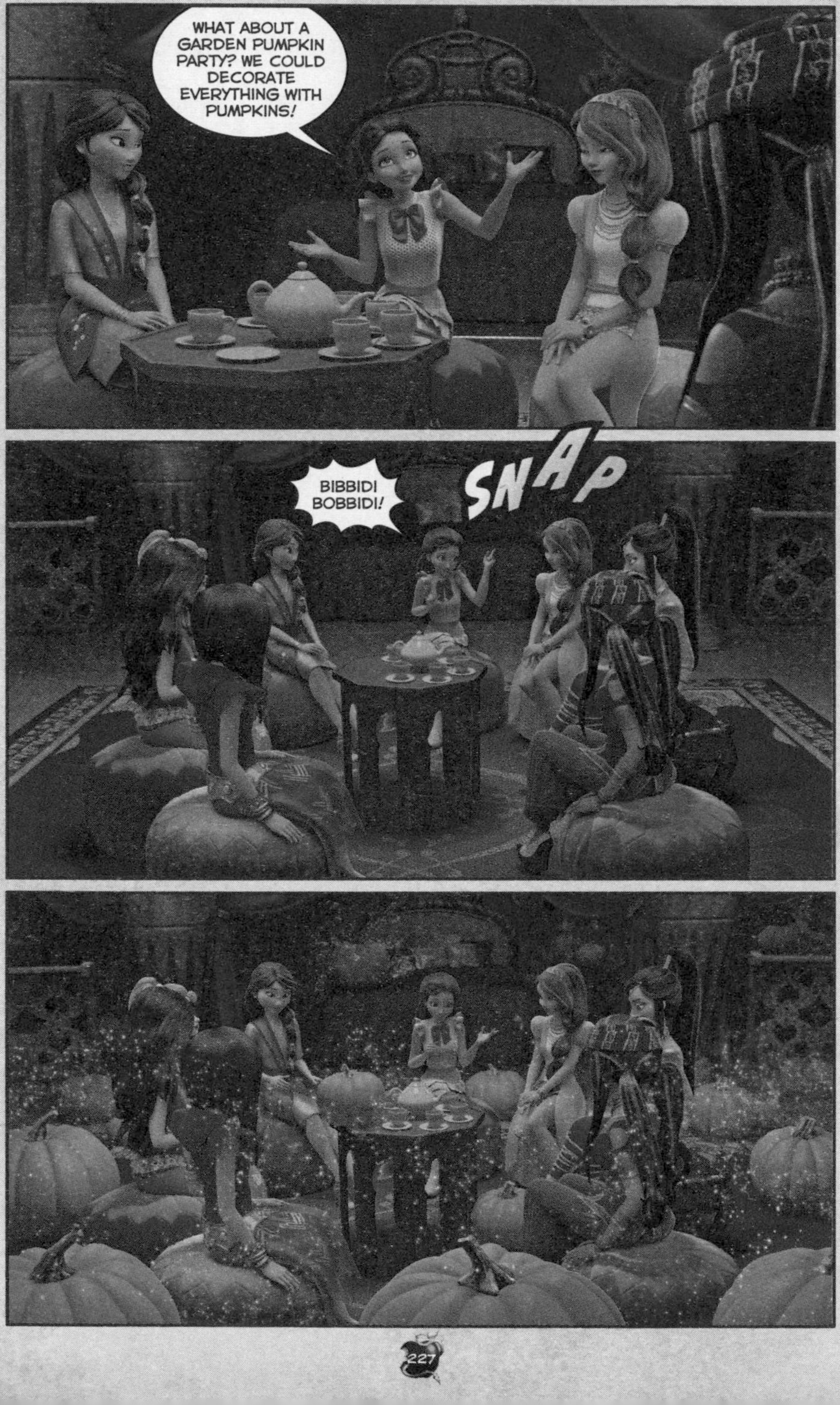
WHAT ABOUT A GARDEN PUMPKIN PARTY? WE COULD DECORATE EVERYTHING WITH PUMPKINS!
BIBBIDI BOBBIDI!
SNAP

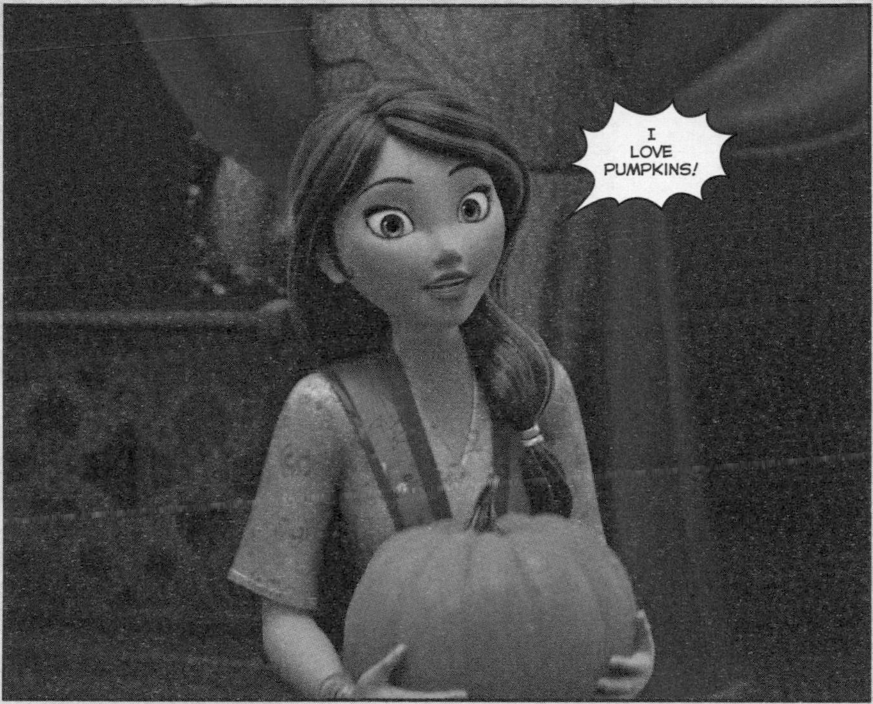
I LOVE PUMPKINS!

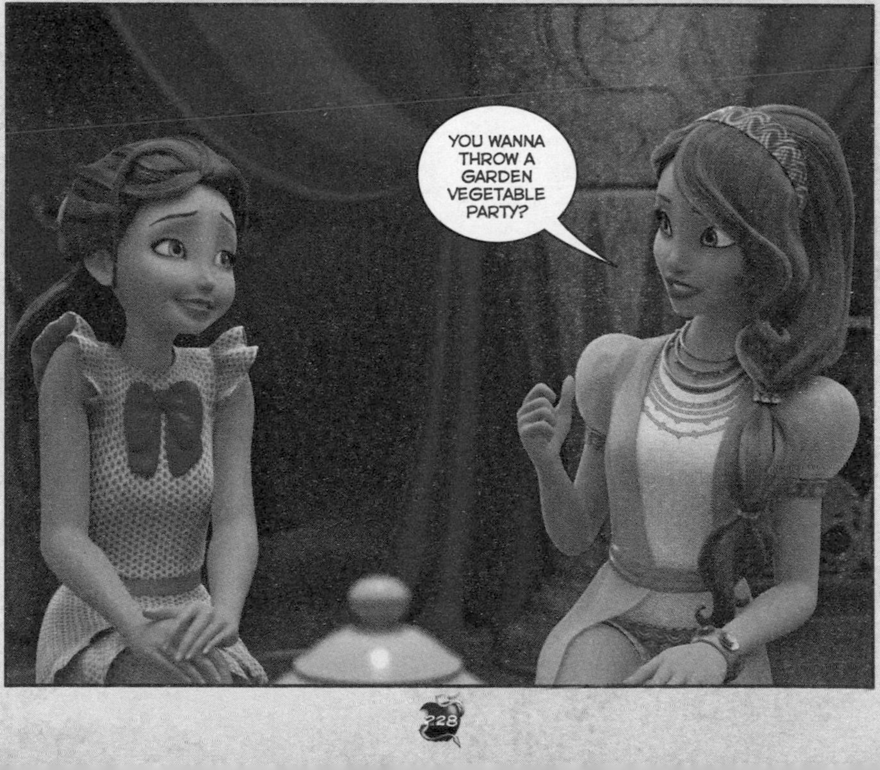
YOU WANNA THROW A GARDEN VEGETABLE PARTY?

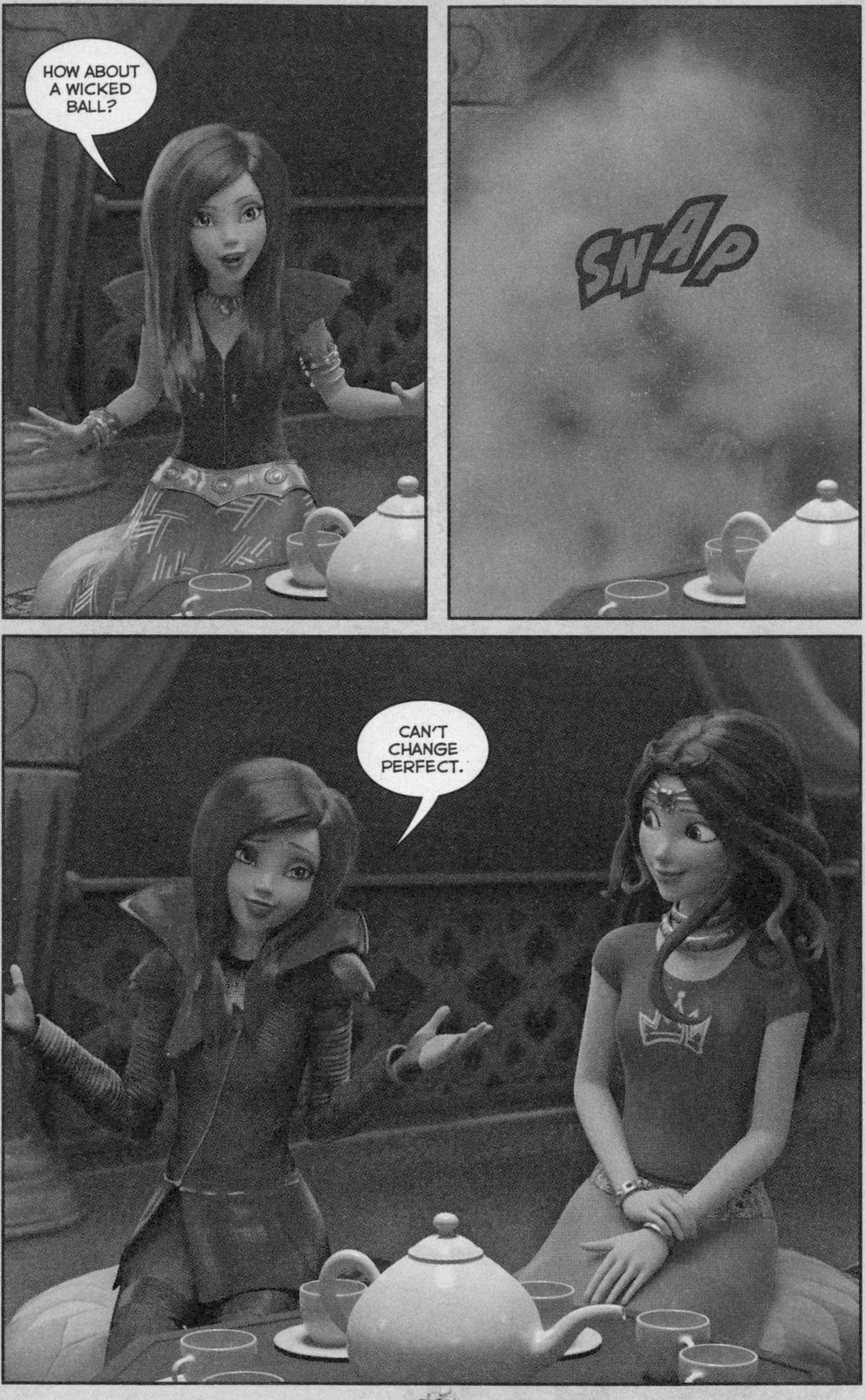
HOW ABOUT A WICKED BALL?
SNAP
CAN'T CHANGE PERFECT.

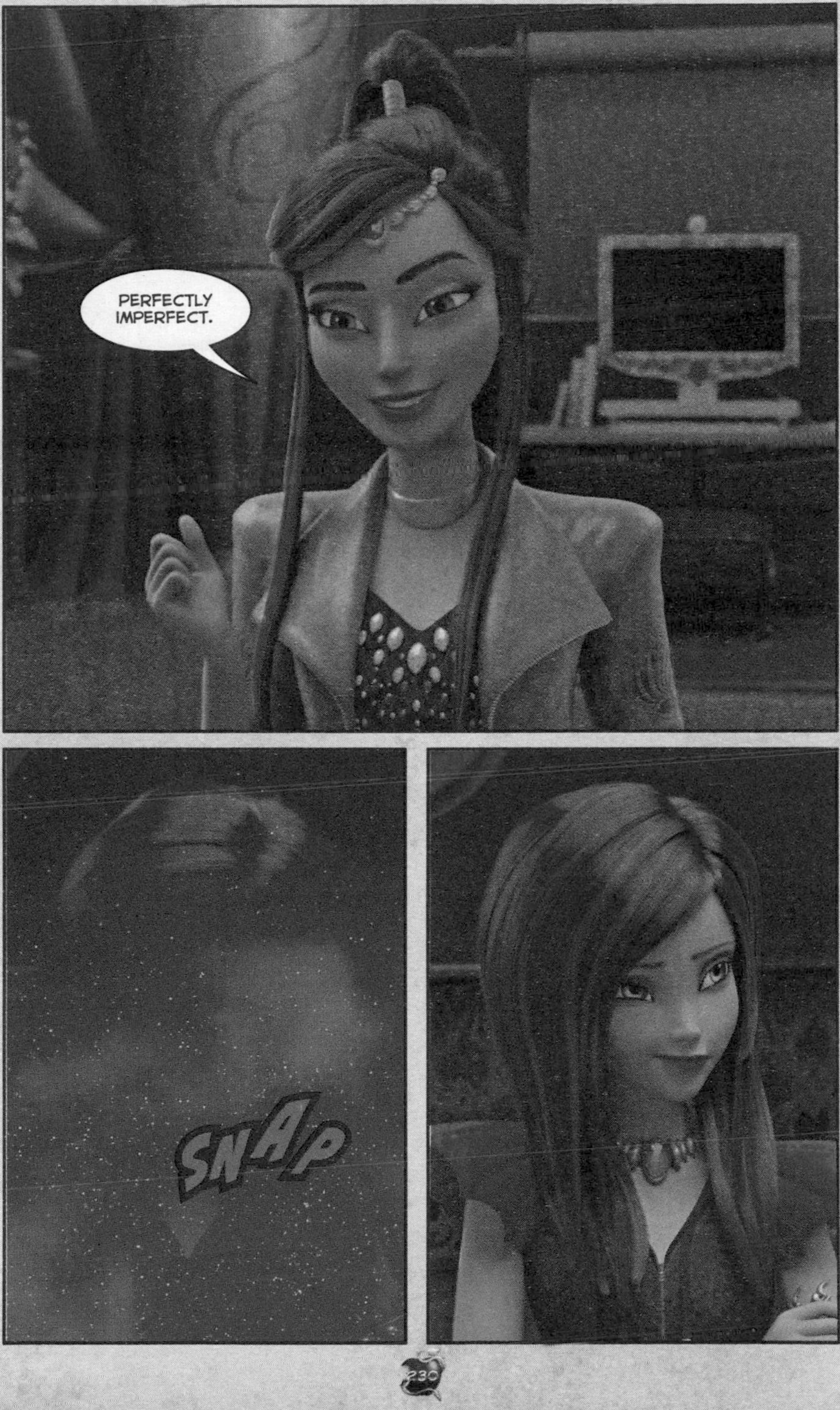
PERFECTLY IMPERFECT.
SNAP

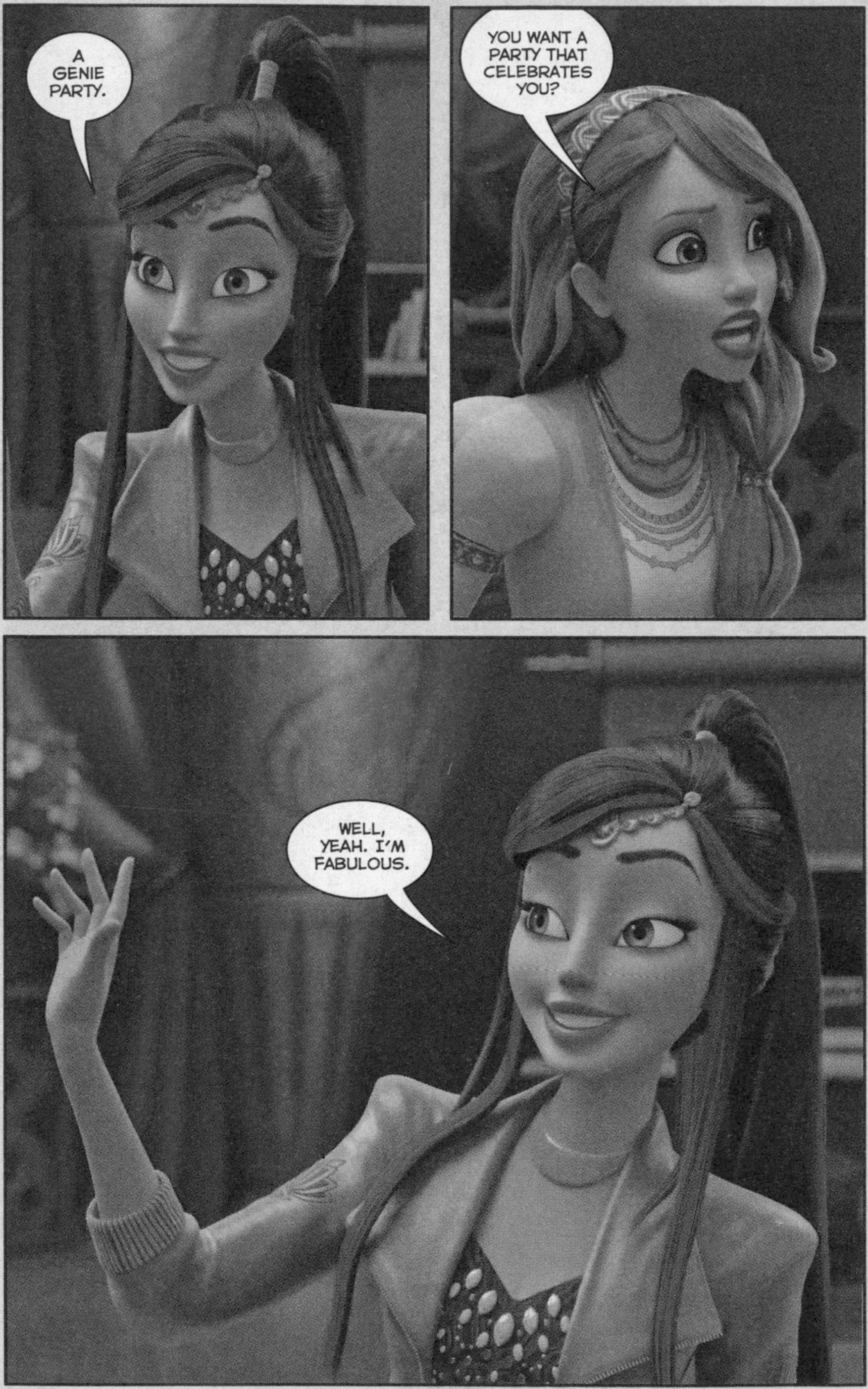
A GENIE PARTY.
YOU WANT A PARTY THAT CELEBRATES YOU?
WELL, YEAH. I'M FABULOUS.

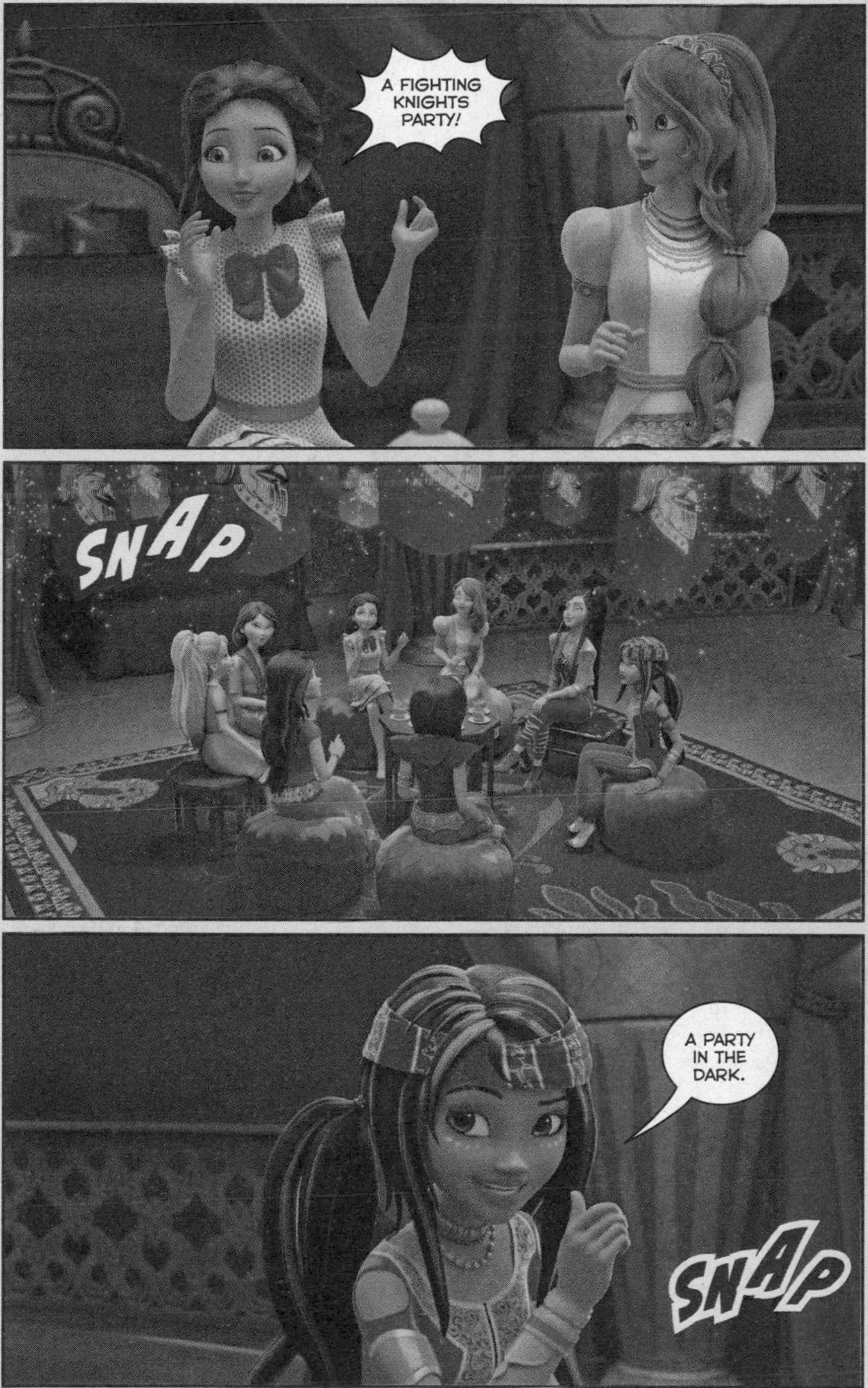
A FIGHTING KNIGHTS PARTY!
SNAP
A PARTY IN THE DARK.
SNAP

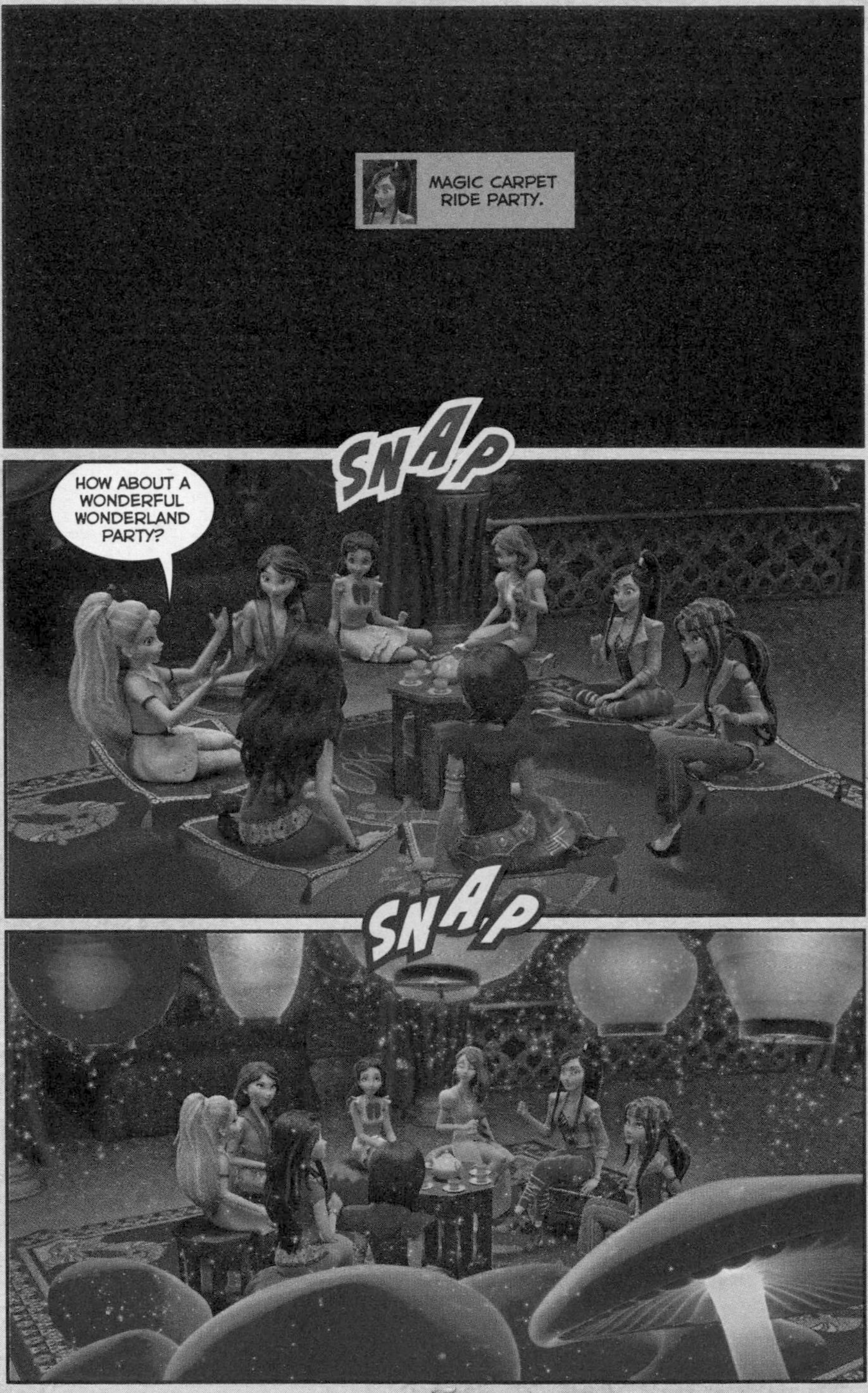
MAGIC CARPET RIDE PARTY.
SNAP
HOW ABOUT A WONDERFUL WONDERLAND PARTY?
SNAP

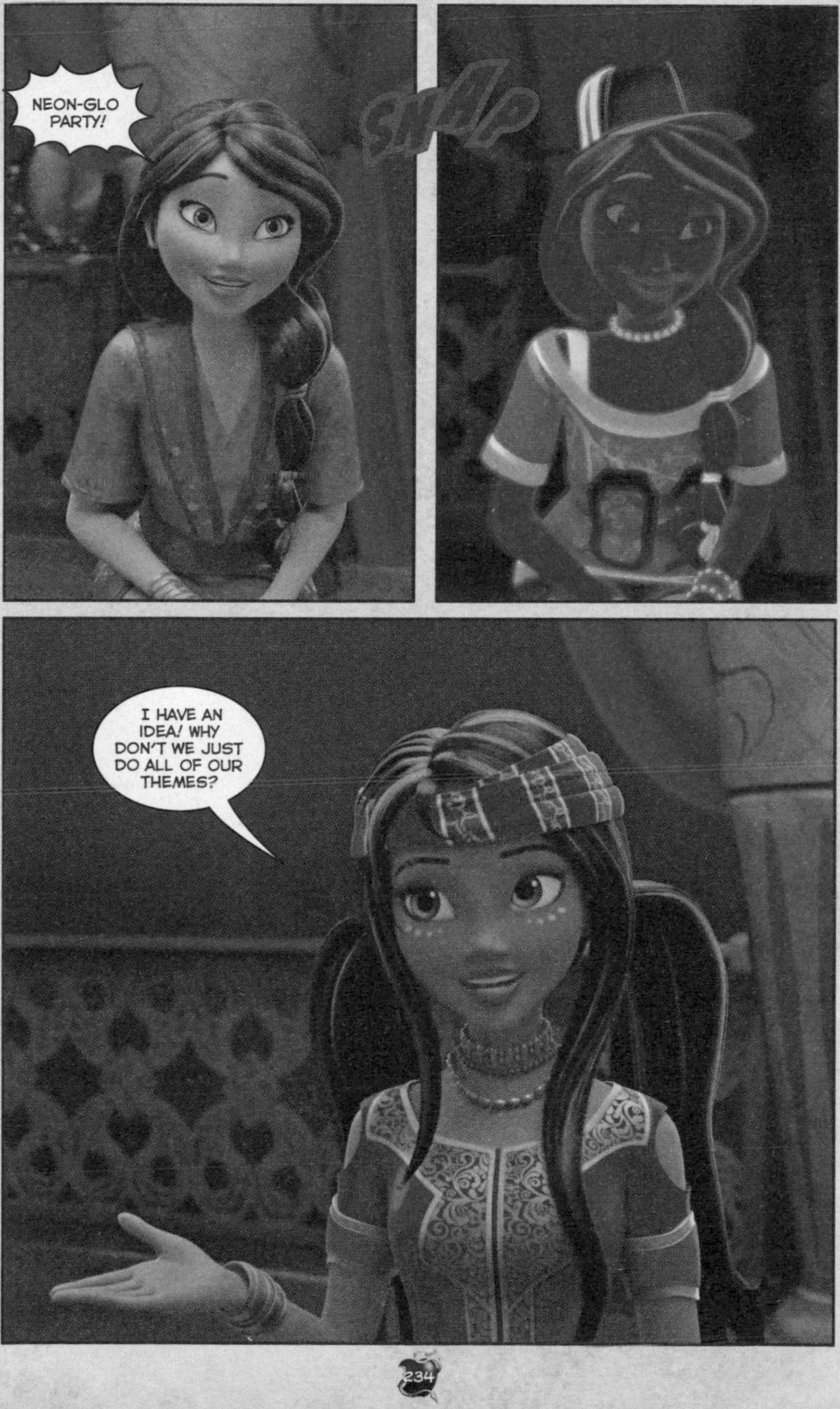
NEON-GLO PARTY!
SNAP
I HAVE AN IDEA! WHY DON'T WE JUST DO ALL OF OUR THEMES?

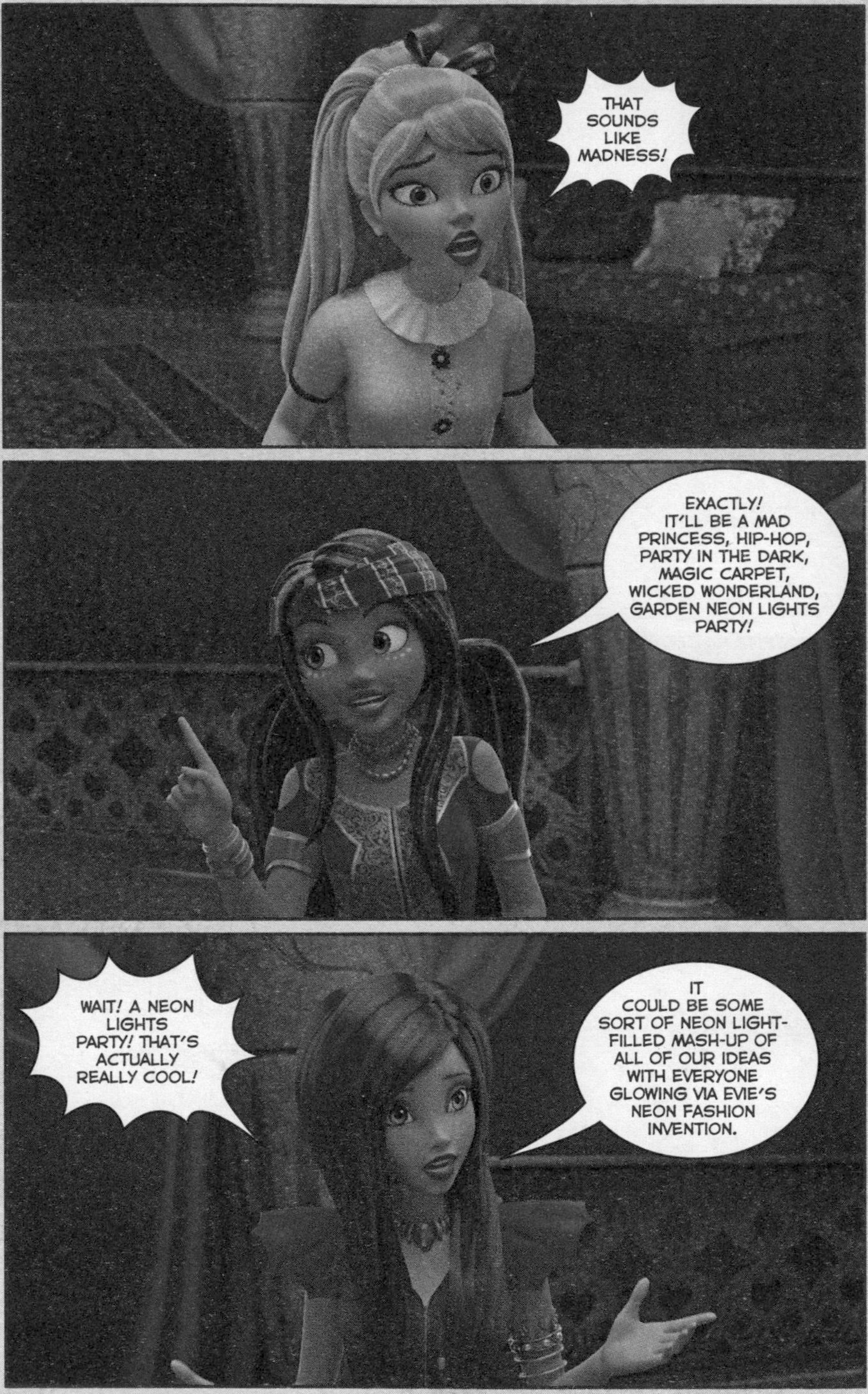
THAT SOUNDS LIKE MADNESS!
EXACTLY! IT'LL BE A MAD PRINCESS, HIP-HOP, PARTY IN THE DARK, MAGIC CARPET, WICKED WONDERLAND, GARDEN NEON LIGHTS PARTY!
WAIT! A NEON LIGHTS PARTY! THAT'S ACTUALLY REALLY COOL!
IT COULD BE SOME SORT OF NEON LIGHT-FILLED MASH-UP OF ALL OF OUR IDEAS WITH EVERYONE GLOWING VIA EVIE'S NEON FASHION INVENTION.

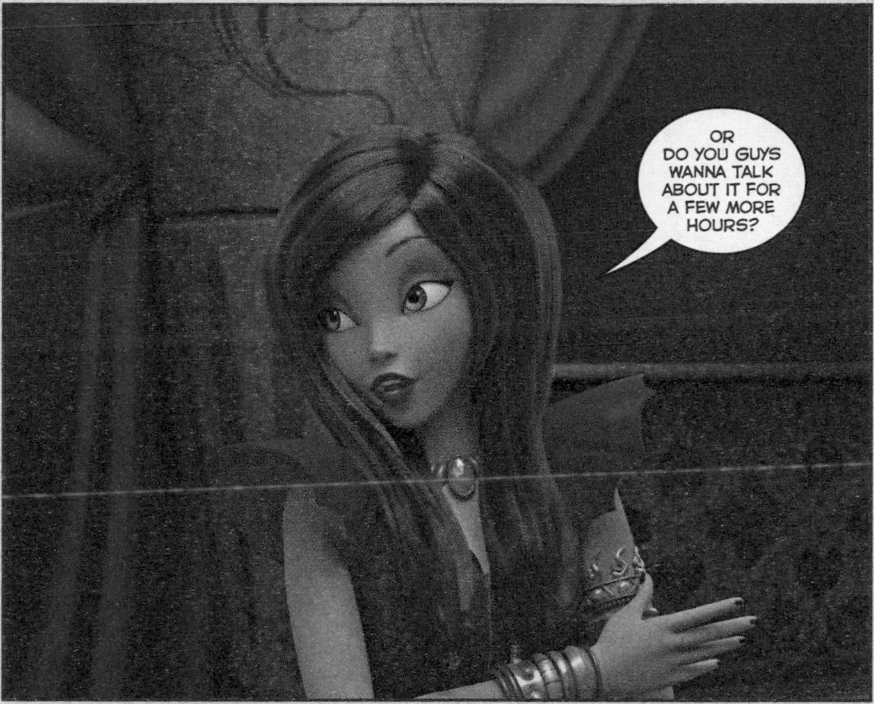
OR DO YOU GUYS WANNA TALK ABOUT IT FOR A FEW MORE HOURS?

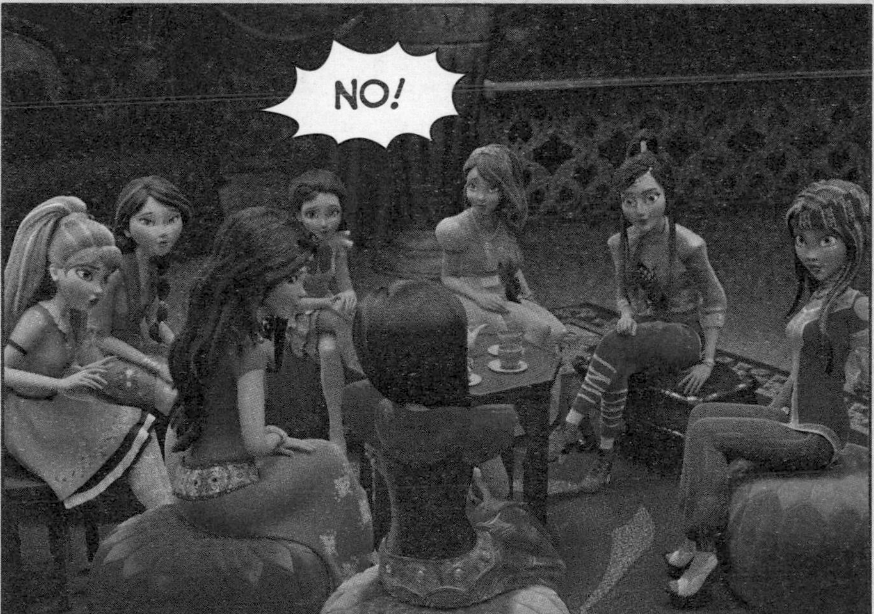
NO!

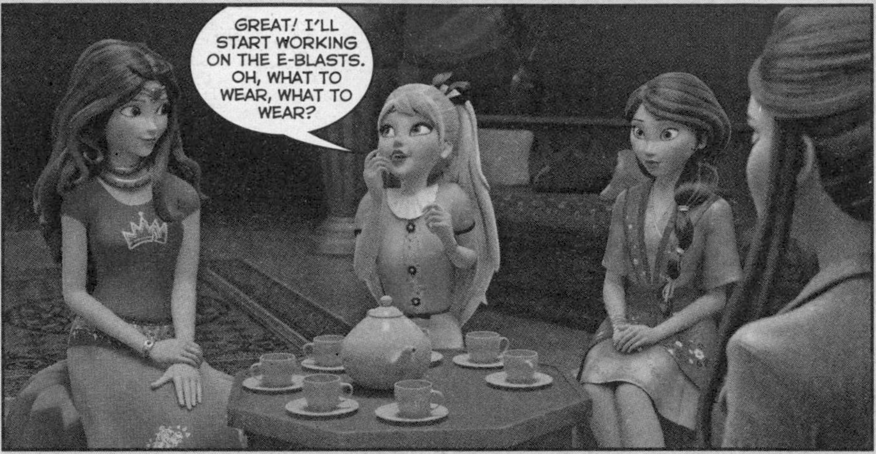
GREAT! I'LL START WORKING ON THE E-BLASTS. OH, WHAT TO WEAR, WHAT TO WEAR?

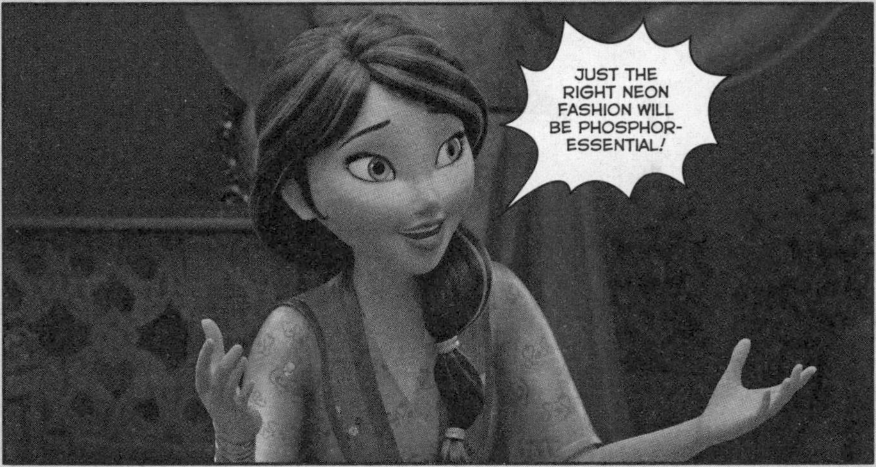
JUST THE RIGHT NEON FASHION WILL BE PHOSPHOR-ESSENTIAL!

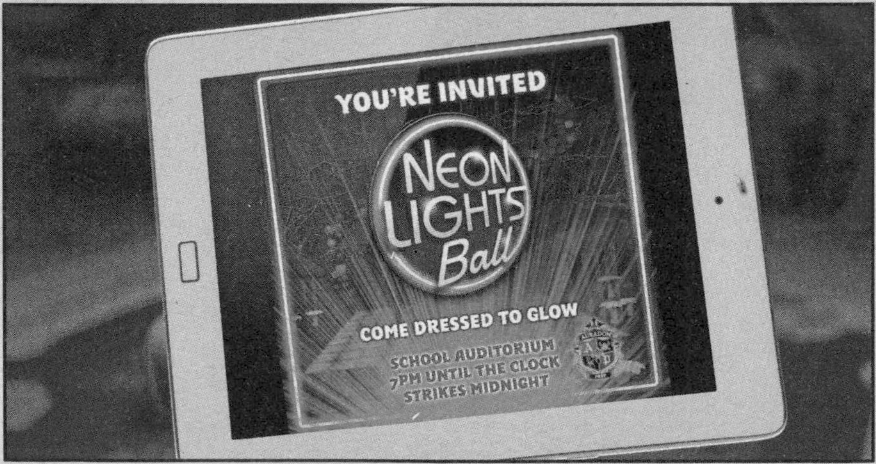
YOU'RE INVITED
NEON LIGHTS Ball
COME DRESSED TO GLOW
SCHOOL AUDITORIUM
7PM UNTIL THE CLOCK
STRIKES MIDNIGHT